To Claudia,

Congratulations & winning
a copy of Dark Legacy!

Hope you enjoy Kleko's
story as much as I
enjoyed writing it.
Wishing you the best.

With Magic

2/3/16

About the Author

DOMENICO ITALO COMPOSTO-HART was born and raised in Chicago, Illinois. He studied Archaeology and Anthropology at Boston University, and lived in Tokyo, Japan for over three years pursuing a career as a freelance musician. He currently teaches American and modern European history, geography, and economics at an international high school. He lives with his wife and son in Barcelona, Spain.

DARK LEGACY

BOOK I – TRINITY

DOMENICO ITALO
COMPOSTO-HART

DRAGON BONE BOOKS

DARK LEGACY: BOOK I — TRINITY.

Copyright © 2002, 2003, 2004, 2005, 2006, 2007, 2008, 2009, 2010 by Domenico Italo Composto-Hart.

Cover illustration copyright © 2009, 2010 by Domenico Italo Composto.

Cover illustration by Tiberius Viris.

Writers Guild of America, West

DARK LEGACY: BOOK I — TRINITY is a literary book registered under the WGAWEST Intellectual Property Registry.

Registration Number: 1453040

ISBN-13: 978-0-9850177-1-2 (hbk)
ISBN-13: 978-0-615-39869-3 (pbk)
ISBN-13: 978-0-615-55096-1 (ebook)

In Loving Memory of Chris & Adam Wyczolkowski

(espiritu)

They who planted the seeds of inspiration

DEDICATION

This book, entitled *Dark Legacy: Book I – Trinity*, is my first ambitious work of words; and it will not be my last for I have committed myself to the writing of five more books to complete this series that I have named *Dark Legacy*. This is a story now eleven years in the making and it gives me no greater pleasure than to dedicate it to a trinity of men who have always shined as a bright light for their families. Thank You: Dad (the shaper), Papa Leo (the guide), and Marc Forkins (the poet) for teaching me what it means to be a man.

ACKNOWLEDGMENTS

This book is a goodbye. It is the story of my adolescence. It is a literary work marking the milestones in the youth of my life that I now look back upon with warmth and gratitude. As a boy I had always sought what it meant to be a man. My pursuit for this understanding led me to many teachers and teachings; to many far off lands; and to many experiences both good and bad, but ultimately good, for I have learned much from the bad.

I owe the wonders of my imagination to all those who taught and inspired me when I was young.

I would like to thank the history, culture, and people of the following countries: Andorra, the Bahamas, Cambodia, Canada, the Cayman Islands, Chile, China, the Czech Republic, Denmark, England, Estonia, Finland, France, Germany, Hong Kong, Hungary, Ireland, Israel, Italy, Japan, Laos, Macau, Malaysia, Mexico, Monaco, Mongolia, Morocco, Myanmar, Norway, Peru, Poland, Portugal, Puerto Rico, the Russian Federation, Serbia, Sicily, Singapore, Slovakia, South Korea, Spain, Sweden, Switzerland, Thailand, Vatican City, and Vietnam.

I would like to thank the following friends and family: Marc & Debbie Forkins & the Forkins family, Aric Bakshy (for your love of books and fantasy), Jesse Feinkind & the Feinkind family, Oren & Jeremy Hulsh & the Hulsh family, David & Tonya Torres, Carrie Ruzicka, Alex Effgen, Stephanie Coates, Clinton Schmidt, Phil (we survived Mt. Jebel Toubkal), Jeff Stitely, Andrew Lazaro, d.o.w.n., Mr. Mortier, the Vicente family, Royce Wesley, Debbie Berlin, Timothy J.W. Honeywill, Danielle Green, and Megan Walbridge-

Nelson, Dane Nelson, & Sam Nelson.

Thomas Lee (for guiding my book), Emiko Watanabe, Kirkland (for bringing me back to music) & Mariko Hu, Mika Takemura, Phil & Suzy Annetta, Lorenzo Valentini, Ian & Tomoko Hartley, Philippe Wauquaire, Rod Coogen, Isao Ohashi, Kouichi Korenaga, Traci & the Pink Cow, Mas Hino, Kenji Hino, Nir Z (my musical brother) & Michal & Lia, Brad Holmes & The Hit Men, Tak Ikeda, Pete Mitchell, Lesley Walbridge, John Clark-Hackett (the best boss any artist could ever ask to have), Greg Clements, Frances D. Palmer (she is the secret to my success in Tokyo), Marty Feldman, Charlie Knudsen, Coleman Bayliss, Jaime Knight, Claudelle Shaw, Janusz (for being a creative genius who paints magic in a thousand directions) & Magda Migasiuk, Lune Kitakami & Malefices (for creating some of the most vibrant music), Maira Vergara, Madonna & Cam & Vida, Ivan Kozlov (for his incredible enthusiasm and help in perfecting my book), and Billy (for being a best friend and brilliant husband to my little sister), Billito, & Charles Cannon.

Antonio Bello & Catalina Jordán, Josep Jordán & Carme Carreras, Sara & Mireia Jordán, and Jeronimo Bello.

Neil Peart (an intellectual guide in my adolescent years; a master of both music and words) & RUSH, and Sting (a great lyricist and song writer who continues to influence my music and words time and time again).

The Hart & Composto Clans (both here and beyond).

And most especially to my nuclear family who celebrates me when I am victorious and cradles me when I am defeated: Keki Cannon (the flame), Lucy Composto (the earth), and Domingo Composto (the shaper); you are my sacred Trinity for I am because of you. And from three there are four and five: to my beautiful wife, María del Carmen Bello Jordán (the light), who was with me when I fell into the darkness (twice); and to my son, Leonardo Composto Bello, who is my new shining and guiding light.

CHAPTERS

THE SONG OF THE ORACLE KING
13

THE END OF THE KAI
15

CHARACTERS
17

WORDS AND TERMS
67

DARK LEGACY

BOOK I – TRINITY
77

CHARACTERS
79

PART I
85

PART II
253

PART III
471

WORDS AND TERMS
623

THE SONG OF THE ORACLE KING

It was in the last century of the Age of Virgo that a shadow had grown deep within the Atlantean underworld. The seed of this darkness was sown within the hate of a single mortal, and as it grew it overtook him and he was forever lost to the light of the world.

As his years passed and his shadow grew he conquered the many dark lords of the underworld and crowned himself king of the Atlantean dark realm. It was through him that the *Red* race slaked their addictions. It was by him that gangs and politicians were procured and swayed. And it was under him that corporations were felled and assimilated.

Time passed and rumors spread, *"What is this darkness that has gained so much power in the Atlantean Empire?"* It was not until the year thirteen of Andromeda that the darkness that had hid itself for so many decades beneath the cityscape of Atlantis appeared.

The people of the Red began to speak of the gods in the heavens. They spoke of the Great Quakes and of the final inundation that was foreseen to come by their sages and priests. The words of the Oracle King Artemis echoed in their hearts and minds:

Like the winter and the rain, darkness will fall upon the Mother. The Great Evil will bring death to the Atlantean Kai and war will fall upon the five races. The gods will stir and a flood will swallow all that is known.

Do not lose hope for in the aftermath, in an unlikely place, a child born to none will awake. This will be the beginning. This will be the Age of the Lion.

THE END OF THE KAI

CHARACTERS

THE CHILDREN OF THE LAW OF ONE

Oracle King Artemis – The Oracle King of Atlantis who ruled in the Age of Libra, the Golden Age, and who built the Royal Towers of Libra, Virgo, Leo, Cancer, Gemini, and Taurus.

Oracle Queen Andromeda – The last Oracle Queen of Atlantis who ruled before the end of the Age of Virgo. She served the High Kai Council as the High Kai Priestess of the Order of Light. She was bound platonically to Skaton-ka, the Kai Elder King.

Skaton-ka – The last Kai Elder King of the Order of the Kai Guardian guild who was bound to Oracle Queen Andromeda. He served the High Kai Council as the High Kai Guardian Elder of the Order of Light.

Arkan – The last High Kai Guardian of the Clan Order of Drakul; he was bound to Neva Yun Ra, and was one of the sixteen members of the High Kai Council.

Neva Yun Ra – The last High Kai Priestess of the Clan Order of Drakul; she was bound to Arkan, and was one of the sixteen members of the High Kai Council.

Kron – The last High Kai Guardian Elder of the Order of Taurus; he was bound to Kalia Ra, and was one of the sixteen members of the High Kai Council.

Kalia Ra – The last High Kai Priestess of the Order of Taurus; she was bound to Kron, and was one of the sixteen members of the High Kai Council.

Volan – One of the forty-nine Kai-Minor guardians; and an apprentice of Skaton-ka.

Bator-Uran – The last Kai-Minor guardian.

Kolia Ra – The youngest of the Kai-Minor priestesses.

The Children of Belial

Maniok – The being referred to by the Oracle King Artemis as the *Great Evil* of the Age of Virgo.

White Face – High Chancellor to Maniok.

The Baneful Five – The five Kai-Minor priestesses of the Clan Order of Cancer who betrayed the Oracle Queen Andromeda in her last hour.

OF GEOGRAPHY

It has been so long since we have had to recall that time. The Mother *was so much different then. Her oceans and lands were colder and icier. There were the great glaciers to the north and south. There were more of the mountainous Fathers revealing themselves—we are foolish, we do not want to confuse you. All this talk about Mother and Father will drive you mad. You see, in this world— this material world—all things are divided into light and dark; masculine and feminine; active and passive.*

But what comes before duality? Preceding two there is only one, and before one there is nothing. This nothingness prevails before all things come into being. It is the void. But there is something. And from this something all things are born. The infinite creates the finite. The shapeless takes form.

Static motion *is born from this source. It moves and separation occurs. It is still and separation combines. The emptiness is Mother. The fullness is Father. They harmoniously oppose each other like night and day. Mother is the land. Father is the sky. Mother is the sea. Father is the mountain.*

But getting back—yes, yes, yes. In that time of old your planet was referred to as Mother. Now in this age, this Aquarian age, you call her Earth. Oh yes, your sacred Earth. How her face has changed. In that time of old there were the great island continents of Atlantis—once the pride of the Atlantic Ocean. There, you see, that was how the Atlantic Ocean and the Atlas Mountains received their names, from Atlantis of course. We find it amusing that the island continents of Atlantis—actually if we were to go back further Atlantis was a single island continent, but that is for another night's discussion. Yes, getting back, we find it ironic that the once supreme Atlantean civilization is nothing now. A fantastic cosmic joke, really. Nothing remains but your myths, and of the islands themselves there is nothing except for a tiny series of islands that you call the Azores. There are no monuments to be found that bear the Atlantean name. Thus is the way of this very impermanent world; all things must pass into dust and be forgotten.

Your curiosity brings the memory of Atlantis back, and rightfully so, for it is high time that you learn of your ancient heritage. You have grown for so many thousands of years not knowing your true beginnings. You have an entire celestial family that you are totally unaware of; and like all families they have many romantic and hellish stories to share.

Oh yes, getting back, please forgive our ramblings. It is just that it has been some time since we have been asked to recall these memories, and we are getting excited as we remember them.

Yes, in the Ocean of Mu—we apologize again; we mean the Ocean of the Pacific; very confusing is it to juggle geographic names between then and now. In this ocean there were yet another great series of islands and island continents named, in that age of old, Lemuria. A lovely place it was. In our opinion it was the original Eden, although many will argue against us on that biblical interpretation.

Well, to set the stage or the scene if you will, Atlantis, at that time, was composed of three island continents. The island continent furthest east, nearest your Straits of Gibraltar, was Og; the middle island was called Aryan; and the western island continent, in the area of your Sargasso Sea, was Poseidia.

Poseidia was home to Atlas, the capital of the Atlantean Empire. In that time a city of such colossal size was defined as a city-galaxy. In its youth Atlas was a bright light, a symbol for a legacy of hope that was passed down from the Etheric races of Lemuria. Sadly it corrupted to become the center of a morally decadent empire.

In its prime Atlas had approximately fifty-five million inhabitants. It was a marvel, a monument to all the knowledge and technology achieved by your species. Atlas was spectacular with all of its sky-towers, culture, activities, people, and vehicles buzzing about. It was truly a work that has yet to be achieved again on your planet.

Now you ask, "Why did it all end?" Why did Atlantis, in all its glory, disappear from the pages of history? Time creates mountains, dissolves oceans, and wipes away great monuments leaving only faint memories. Atlantis is such a memory, an undying myth. It was felt by some that it was not worth remembering that it was best left forgotten. Although, in some respects we would agree that some things are better forgotten, we must confess that one can never *fully mature without a true understanding of one's own story, of one's former selves. We speak to you tonight to reawaken these memories. To take you back and reconnect you with a former self that had lived many thousands of years ago.*

Well, you ask again, "What was it that brought an end to it all?" This is not an easy question to answer, but if we are to begin to tell the tale we will begin in the year thirteen of Andromeda. It was in this year that the Great Evil had revealed itself as the mortal named Maniok.

CHAPTER I

The golden rays of the setting sun retreated from a wealth of ash grey clouds. Saddened by this the evening sky ignored its inevitable death by listening to the songs of doves that flew gracefully over the city-galaxy of Atlas. There, below, upon high sea cliffs and long stretching plains stood the many sky-towers of Atlas pulsating a million dots of light. Illuminated streets crossed and weaved an infinite number of webs as uncountable vehicles moved and flew over the coastal terrains of the Atlantean capital.

A dove descended into Atlas, and she found too much for her eyes to bear and for her mind to comprehend. Things that sounded high-pitched shrieks flew past her. These things had two white lights for eyes and tails that bled in bright red, but they did not bleed for she soon realized that their tails were also lights. And far down below her there were rivers of lights. Scores of stars flowed within these rivers like ten thousand leaves flowing down a glistening stream. But they were not stars. They were those birds that were not birds that flew in lines and curves. Everything was moving. There were massive images—alive and moving—covering the sides of many sky-towers. And the noise. Sound was everywhere. It was loud and long or high-pitched and short. There was too much for the dove to see, hear, and feel. She could do no more than fly in a daze of fright.

Up there, in the dusty air, was a sign of white hope, and a homeless boy stepped back to notice this beauty in the sky.

The dove took a deep breath and glided between the sky-towers before flying over a great chasm. Now in the more industrial part of the city she looked down, saw the boy, and danced for him. The boy, remembering how someone he had recently lost enjoyed watching urban birds soar, smiled at the angel in the sky; and for a brief moment he too was free. The hunger, the pain, and the scars were no longer part of his reality.

In the distance dark clouds marched toward Atlas. Lightening flashed and thunder boomed. The boy held his breath. There was a second flash of light. He waited for the grumble of thunder but heard a sharp pop instead. Frightened, he stood still. He smelled it–the burn of death–and saw that the flying dove was no more.

On days of ill will the young boy with his tribe of friends sat in back-alley streets shooting birds with rusted guns. They competed for the most kills for the winner was awarded the drug or prostitute of his choice.

He was a child of the Ideo; the sector of Atlas reserved for those who had no place in the thriving, legitimate light of Atlantean society. He had nothing to contribute to their politics, finances, and wars. He had no legitimate name, no parents, and no citizen chip embedded into his skin. He was, in all senses of the word, a ghost within the Atlantean system.

When other children his age, beyond the borders of Ideo, were in schools learning and eating candy and crying over scoops of ice cream that fell from their cones he was living deep within the tunnels of Ideo's sewers hungry, sick, and hiding from the S.K.'s.

Fornax-Serpen was what the S.K.'s were officially referred to on digital documents buried away within government and military mainframes. They were secretly approved, built, and deployed to patrol the Ideo sewer systems to prevent the flow of illegals–*Ideo ghosts*–into the citizen sectors of Atlas. But, the Fornax-Serpens did not patrol–they hunted. They were machines designed to seek and kill all things found within the dark, damp, sewer labyrinth of Ideo.

The boy had lost many from his tribe to the S.K.'s. His tribe was composed of trusted and skilled companions who knew how to survive and journey through the tunnels of the Ideo underworld. They were often utilized by one of the various competing Ideo-clans to smuggle potion-magics, weapons, sex-slaves, human and animal body parts and organs, and pirated technological goods—both software and hardware—into and out of the Ideo sector. The money they gained for their services was considerable within Ideo, but it never lasted them more than a few days for they always gambled and spent more than they could afford on women, alcohol, and drugs.

To this boy it had never meant a thing to take life. He had never contemplated the act. And why should he have? He was an unwanted child of Atlas; nothing of any moral significance was ever taught to or expected of him. He had only known abandonment, abuse, and the sweet hypnotic pleasures of the potion-magics he bought and used to pollute his veins. His tribe and he had always fed the flames of greed, lust, and wrath within the underworld of Atlas. But somehow, now, he had begun to understand the tragedy of death.

In the alley across the street from him lay the mangled dove. He stared at his wet, filthy shoes and crossed the street with little care for the vehicles that sped passed him.

Questions howled in his head: *Why was she so stupid? So, so, stupid! I told her. Stupid bitch. I'm going to fuck those S.K.'s. I'm going to fuck them. Shit! What's the fucking point? Why live in this? Why fucking deal with this when I can just put a gun to my head? Why the fuck did they have to shoot that stupid fucking bird? Why did I look up? Why did I have to see it? I should have just ignored that piece of shit. I hate this . . . I hate this!*

The boy looked up to the dark sky and screamed, "I hate this fucking city!" A man walking toward him replied, "Then fucking leave!" The boy met the man's eyes with a glare that furrowed his forehead and bent his brow. Adrenaline shot through his veins. His pores breathed anger. His muscles clenched. He wanted to reach into his tattered coat, pull out his short sword, and show the man the weapon that would end him. He wanted to see fear in the man's eyes; see his face turn into a pathetic plea for mercy; see his hands tremble; his knees give way to gravity; his bladder release urine. He wanted to see the man cry and beg for mercy.

What would he do? Yes, he would toy with him first. Kick him in the face to make his nose bleed. Grab his arm and slice it open. No, he would pull out his gun and shoot him in the kneecaps and make him kneel. He would grab his hair, pull his head back, and shoot him in the mouth—no, the eye. No, he would stab him straight in the heart and listen to him cough and choke as he twisted the blade in his chest. He would kiss his lips when he coughed up blood and spit it in his face. *Fuck him, fuck him, fuck him!*

But nothing happened. The man continued walking and disappeared around a street corner. The boy simply stood balancing between the edge of the sidewalk and the street. Vehicles continued to pass blowing up wind that caressed the back of his neck. The wind; it called to him. It whispered into his ears. He relaxed. His shoulders dropped; he unclenched his fists; he bowed his head. He took in a short breath and felt the weight that pained his heart. He inhaled again and again, each breath longer and deeper than the one before. He covered his eyes with his dirty hands; and although there was no one to hold him, to comfort him, there was something. Perhaps it was the wind.

When he had regained composure he took several steps into the dark alley and stood over the dove; the dove was lying on the broken bricks and cobblestones that lined the alley street whimpering, staring into the boy's eyes, begging for death.

"Shit, shit, shit," he said seizing his hair with his hands. He looked at his surroundings searching for any object that would end the dove's suffering. There was rotting waste along the walls of the alley and two rusted garbage dumps—a sad reminder that these streets were forgotten, no longer serviced by the sanitation department. Rats scurried into and out of crevices and thin streams flowed into the street. The smell was typical of an alley: the scent of urine, vomit, rotting food and waste.

A large muddy brick was the object the boy chose to end the dove, and as he picked it up a raindrop splashed upon his hand; *the sky had begun to weep*; and when the boy lifted the brick over his head lightening flashed and thunder boomed.

The dove looked up and saw the silhouette of her executioner. It was time, and she closed her eyes and accepted the end.

Blood flowed into the filth of the alley. The boy kneeled beside the crushed dove for a moment before leaning against the concrete wall of an abandoned building. He looked down at the beaten cobblestones of the alley street and lulled himself to sleep as the cold rains fell upon him.

OF BLACK CROWS

One could not imagine an Atlas without its black crows. Quite ugly beasts if you were to ask our opinion. They look so unmerciful, and they always steal breadcrumbs from those poor pigeons that work so hard to scavenge. You name them the dirty rodents of a city sky, but we quite like pigeons. They move their little heads back and forth as they make each and every little step. Very adorable we must say.

The barbaric black crows of Atlas were incredibly grotesque due to their unusually large size. It was for that reason that they were deemed the guardians of Atlas. Most definitely it was some war-loving group of men that knighted these black crows as such—really, what feminine creature would deem them so? Only a man could see beauty in a crow.

Getting back, you really must stop us if we talk into tangents, we won't take offense. Well, like the bats of old Kai monasteries, the black crows flew and protected the Kai palaces at night. Legend tells that the black crows of Atlas were the reincarnated beings of noble Kai warriors who promised their eternal strength to the Atlantean kings and queens. How horrible a thought to reincarnate into a black crow, quite mad really. What? Don't be foolish. We shall have you know that it's simply not done. The spirit of a crow reincarnates only into a crow.

Anyway, what we are trying to explain is that the crows were in greater number and better found near and around the historical sites that dotted the city-galaxy of Atlas. They were also in and around the gardens and forests that surrounded the Atlantean Royal Towers. It was also said that they possessed a darker quality. They were not only protectors, but also messengers of death.

It was bad luck to spot a black crow on one's wedding day. Unfortunately, we must say that upon our wedding day our cousin, Ita, spotted a black crow. Within a year of our union our husband died. He was a wonderful man. He died of an unusual disease. He was the only man we had known romantically in that lifetime. But we would rather not talk of that or of him. There we are going off topic again. Our mind is so old.

So where were we? Oh yes, of black crows, I remember. Some said that they, the black crows, could be swayed for they only served a force that was strong. For thousands of years the Kai, long allied to the Atlantean Oracle Kings and Queens, were the greatest power and symbol of truth in the western regions of the Mother—we mean Earth—but in the years of Andromeda they were small in number, and it was rumored that some among them had fallen to the dark. It was said that a few disciples of the Kai Orders had lost their faith in the Oracle Queen's ability to rule. As a result the citizens of Atlantis began to ask, "Who do the black crows serve?" Although it was unknown at the time, because of the distracting bickering between the members of the seven royal families, the black crows had found a new master. It was in the year thirteen of Andromeda that the power of the Oracle Queen came into question as senators and commoners sought a republic campaigned for by the one named Maniok . . . and deceiving was he.

CHAPTER II

The rains ceased and the young boy woke. He rubbed his eyes, curled his toes in soaked, dirty socks, and stretched out his arms. But, as his eyes focused, he saw a black crow standing near his feet picking at the spilled organs of the dead dove.

The crow paused and looked at the boy with a long strand of coiled intestine hanging from his mouth. He crooned and continued pecking.

"Get away from her!" the boy shouted; the crow feasted more. He tried to push the crow away with light kicks but the crow contested by biting at his rubber sole. Frustrated, the boy shot up to his feet to deliver a final kick, but the crow had already taken flight.

The crow, fully satisfied by his meal, ascended to meet the winds that blew foul air between the abandoned buildings of the Ideo sector. Soon he was soaring high above Atlas. Night had come and city lights both static and in motion were seen in all directions.

Although he despised the urban details of Atlas by day–its creeping decay–he loved how pleasant it could appear from high in the dark sky; the city sparkled hundreds of thousands of lights as streams of lights of all colors and shades outlined a vast shining web that stretched out to the mountainous horizon. The view was astounding, but as he looked in awe he began to despise the night for he knew that there was no real beauty in the lands below him during the light of day. The ocean was now near for instead of city stink the salty scent of the sea was filling his lungs. In the distance he could see the glorious columns of light beaming bold and strong into the night sky from the hollow of Mount Eve. There, within the heavily carved mountain that stood near high sea cliffs, was the Tower of Light encircled by the seven Atlantean Royal Towers.

The Tower of Light rose above the surrounding rock walls of Mount Eve and the seven towers. It was a white tower, an *ivory tower*, made of white marble stone. Hidden behind the Tower of Light, to the west, was the black Tower of Drakul. To the southeast of the *dark tower* was the Tower of Libra, and to the northeast stood the Tower of Taurus. Southeast of the white tower stood the Tower of Leo, and to the northeast the Tower of Cancer. The Tower of Virgo stood southwest of the Tower of Leo, and the Tower of Gemini stood northwest of the Tower of Cancer.

The towers served as the political residences of the seven Atlantean Royal Families; they each, except for the Clan Order of Drakul, held dominion over the various regions and colonies of the Empire. The Oracle King Artemis built the six zodiac towers—the white and dark towers had already been built in the ages before his time—as a monumental astrological calendar marking the coming ages. He had lived in the Age of Libra, the Golden Age: a time of balanced scales, elegance, beauty, and high art—the zenith of Atlantean peace and prosperity. It was said by him that a dark time would come in the last days of the Age of Virgo and that "a child born to none" would arise and give life to the Age of Leo; the Ages of Cancer, Gemini, and Taurus would then follow to cloak the Mother in shadow.

The crow did not rest until he reached the center of a massive, circular marble surface at the peak of the Tower of Light where stood a tall marble column with a wide base and a pointed crest he could not see. Landing in the shadow of the tall column he looked out and saw the white light of Mount Eve shooting up like a translucent wall all around the circular plane's curved edge; the winds sang a low reverberating tone that caused his bones to quiver. He heard something faint and listened; a whisper within the winds tempted him to see what was below the edge. He walked toward the edge finding shadow mixing white light into grey. Long cool moments passed. The wall of light was then before him, and just when he was about to touch it with his beak a strong draft of wind ruffled his feathers and nearly lifted his body. The wind was soon gone and he felt the full weight of his body again. He bent forward, stretched his neck over the edge, and looked down into the blinding abyss. He lost his balance but quickly managed to step back and catch his breath. It was all too much: the light, and the song of death that now howled deep within the winds. *No, it is more than I can bear; to the shadow will I return,* and the crow hobbled back to the familiar comforts of the dark.

When sight returned to his eyes he looked out beyond the wall of light and saw the vast Atlantean urban expanse. There were red, blinking dots of light outlining a forest of sky-towers. There were other lights as well, but fear gripped him when lightening flashed. He looked to the west and heard the sky growl. There was something growing there, in the distance, buzzing about in that thin line where earth meets sky. He saw what he believed to be a family of gigantic crows. *This is not possible,* he thought. He soon realized that they were not crows but things made by the dwellers of the dark city. He called out. Guardian crows soon gathered upon the Tower of Light. Disapprovingly; chaotically; they all screeched at the approaching metallic menace.

He became nervous and flew to the Tower of Drakul landing on the head of one of the many dragon statues that decorated its black marble sides. He looked back to the Tower of Light and saw his fellow crows flying frantically above it. There was a flash of light; the crow cringed, and then there was the boom of thunder. The sound was deafening, as loud as a thousand falling trees that had been cut down at their bases. Then there was fire. In all directions explosions bludgeoned the scene. The crow had never seen such anarchy. He feared for his home: the towers. His frenzied mind could only believe that Mount Eve had awoken from its dormant sleep to heave molten rock and ash into the air.

An intense wave of heat threw the crow into an uncontrolled descent. But he fought gravity and glided back into flight trying desperately to escape the exploding inferno. He wanted to return to the Tower of Drakul, but as he searched for landmarks to set his bearings he discovered that the Tower of Gemini stood no more. He cried out in horror as the metallic beasts mockingly flew by firing beams of red light through all in their path.

Filled with rage he flew between bursting flames to reach and enter the Tower of Drakul through one of its stone-slit openings. He then glided down until an explosion devoured the tower's peak unleashing a wave of fire and ash. The crow dived into the coil of an adjacent staircase, but stone fragments and clouds of dust chased after him and threw him hard against stone steps.

There was silence. There was darkness. The crow gathered himself and shook debris and dust from his body. The torches that lined the walls of the staircase were all extinguished. His eyes searched for light, but there was none. Blood trickled down his leg. He did not know where the blood was flowing from for his head ached and clouded his mind. He limped forward; a surge of pain rushed to his head. He realized that his leg was bruised and that his abdomen had been cut. Exhausted, he sat and waited for his eyes to adjust to the darkness. A moment passed and with night eyes he slowly descended the stone staircase.

Broken stones littered his path. He stepped forward trying to avoid the obstructions. The explosions were increasing in frequency causing dust to spill repeatedly down the staircase. He had only descended five steps when he heard two men call out in the distance: "Hello? Is there anyone alive up there?" He cawed in reply. The men called out again hoping to hear a human cry, but they only heard the cries of the crow again. Disappointed they shook their heads and continued, lighting the unlit torches that lined the tunnel before them. The crow listened to the men speak and whisper as they walked away hearing the fear in their hearts shiver their words. Soon their voices faded into nothing.

Afraid and desperate the crow decided to fly down the well of stairs to the flickering torchlights below. He leapt, glided, and landed safely upon the stone floor directly beneath a burning torch. He had no recollection of the tunnel he found himself in. He did not know from where it came or to where it led. He chose the corridor of burning torches the men had disappeared into. Shuffling forward he listened uneasily to the now muffled explosions that released more trapped dust from the stone-lined ceiling.

The crow stopped when he heard the voices of a man and a woman. The man's voice was angry. He looked up and saw a small vent where the wall of the tunnel met the ceiling. The voices were coming from that vent. He ascended into the air, entered the vent, and limped in search of the voices.

The male voice was growing angrier, which he did not like, but if he wanted to survive he had to go to where other living beings were located. He wobbled carefully within the dark, vent tunnel. The voices were coming from a faint shimmering light at the end of the tunnel. Ill at ease he thought: *What is that light? What is its source? Could it be a flame that I must turn away from? No, it does not burn. It does not sound. What is it then?* He reached the end of the tunnel and saw that he was standing behind the massive head of a glistening golden statue that was surrounded at its base by hundreds of lit candles.

The statue was of the Kai Goddess of the Moon; the goddess sat in a meditative position, legs crossed, hands held flat below her pelvis. The goddess was housed in a stone, high dome chamber lit by the torches that hung from the walls and by the hundreds of candles that surrounded her altar. The flames reflected off the shinning gold of the goddess, causing a fantastic glow. The crow could see that a few offerings of fruits and incense that were lined around the altar had fallen out of their place-holdings. The chamber shook again; more dust and small pieces of marble fell to the floor from the high domed ceiling. The crow called out and flew into the chamber.

Arkan shot his eyes at the black crow and thought: *It is a dark omen, yes, to see the black guardian on such a day.* His hair was wet from the beads of sweat that had gathered around his scalp. His dark robes, dirtied by dust, covered his body but revealed his boots, which ran up to the tops of his shins. He looked back to Neva Yun Ra after the crow had landed on the shoulder of the Kai goddess and cemented his grip around her thin arms. He clenched his jaw before he spoke, "You must come with me—we have to leave."

Neva Yun Ra kept her eyes down. Her elegant robes of white, light green, and blue—moist from sweat—cleverly hid her pregnancy. She stuttered, "I can-n not go with you—I can-n not leave her—I can not—"

Arkan pulled her close, "I have sworn my life to you. I will not let you be murdered in this place. I will not let my child be killed here."

"Our child!" Neva Yun Ra contested. The stone chamber echoed her words in a shrill that traveled up into the apex of the high domed ceiling; the black crow nearly flew in fright. She continued, "This child is ours, not yours. We can not leave the

Oracle. We have sworn our lives to her. How can you abandon whom you have sworn to protect?"

Arkan's hardened eyes bore into her; again she looked down. He tightened his hands around her arms, hurting her. He drew her close; his heart pulsed like a deep drum; the cold metal of his long sword bit into her waist. And as his heart thumped he began to shake: first his shoulders, then his arms, and then his chest and neck. It was a sign of his devotion to her. But his mind, his mind fought hard against his heart. *Stoic men do not tremble and never do they fear for they embrace death and honor love only from a distance.* Such was the religion of his mind.

It was nearly a year past when they had first lain together. He had not sought anything from her; he had only wanted to rest his wearied body. Before he fell to sleep she entrapped him with a passionate haste drawing her lips close to his; he began shaking as if cold air was frisking his skin. But there was no draft of wind. It was warm within her chamber; firelight danced upon stonewalls as wood burned and crackled.

He spoke: *"My body behaves so when it is filled with emotion. It does not know what to do; it trembles when my heart seeks to speak."*

She looked at him as he spoke. His eyes were closed, his face, serene. She could see that he was falling deep into his inner self. She tried to warm him, but he explained, *"I am not cold. The air is as warm as the heat I feel from your chest. My body shakes for it weeps for my heart. My mind is battling her, but soon my mind will give way and my heart shall speak, and warmth will fill me like an uborn child deep within his mother's belly."*

Then his trembling stopped as if it never were. *"This is the heart of Arkan that speaks to you."* Neva Yun Ra looked at him with intense eyes. *"I remember the first time I saw you,"* he took a deep breath and exhaled as memories filled him. *"You frightened me . . . I was in disbelief of you . . . I could not look at you. You were so beautiful . . . so, so beautiful that I could not bear it. Never had I known such sadness as when I first lay my eyes on you. I cursed our shared faith.*

"And now here we are, and I am happy for this is how it should be. My heart can not bear the silence of Kai loneliness."

A large explosion shook the chamber of the Kai Goddess of the Moon launching the black crow into a panicked flight. "I have sworn my life to protect you and only you. We don't have time for this—Yun!"

The trill echoes of the crow's cries and his thrashing wings filled the chamber. Neva Yun Ra, frightened by the crow, hugged and buried her face within Arkan's chest. Arkan pushed her away, looked into her eyes and said, "Forgive me." He jumped and kicked, striking her right temple and knocking her unconscious. He caught her before she fell to the floor and carried her into the shadow of the moon goddess.

The black crow searched for a high ledge to rest upon, but there was none and as his tired wings weakened he slowly descended to the cold floor. He was, as before, alone. He listened to the sound of his approaching death; beating drums that shook stone, freeing more dust.

CHAPTER III

The grey, serene eyes of the Oracle Queen were hidden behind her closed eyelids. Her eyebrows were thick, her lips thin, and her unadorned, straight black hair touched the seat of her throne. Large silver-loop earrings lightly caressed her exposed shoulders. Her royal robes of white, peppermint green, and light purple flowed along the lines of her petit body. Her leather belt, engraved elegantly with depictions of angelic creatures, was adorned with a crystal buckle that had seven diamonds set into it—each representing one of the Seven Stars of Pleiadia; the buckle was a gift to her royal line from the Winged Creator. Her feet were bound in white boots of soft suede with light blue silk straps that were woven and tied tightly around her shins. She sat peacefully with her legs crossed on her throne. Her right hand rested in the palm of her left, and her left hand rested in the cloth nest below her childless belly.

She was wise, but far younger than her royal appearance would confess, and even younger still in the knowledge and experience needed to play in the dangerous games of politics and government. Her allies were few for she paid no heed to the delicate balances required between her and the royal families, the corporate nobles, the politicians, the bureaucrats, the military elite, and the Ideo-clans.

In the many decades before her reign the Ideo-clans had grown strong in corporate power and political influence over the sectors, regions, and colonies of the expanding Atlantean Empire. Of the competing Ideo-clans there was one that had gained the greatest of power, controlling the ways and means of politics, economy, finance, and military conquest. Ophiuchus was the name of this clan whose leader was known to all as the corporate noble,

Maniok. Deep was Maniok's hate for the reigning light of the eight Atlantean Royal Families and its Kai guardians and priestesses. It was rumored by some that he had once been a Kai guardian apprentice of the Order of Leo many decades, perhaps centuries, ago. But this was bizarre speculation for there was no credible record describing the origins of the one named Maniok. He was, in all senses of the word, a mystery.

In her few short years as Oracle Queen, Andromeda sought to accomplish good in the name of her empire. Her heart was innocent and pure, hopeful and faithful. She strived to end the long brutal expanse of her empire; she fought to protect the natural riches of her lands, and she spoke to end the suffering of those who could not speak in political rhymes: the slaves, the poor, the children, the crippled, and the many creatures of the land, sea, and sky. But, sadly, her righteousness had failed and deceived her, and she sat on her throne in thought of what could have been now that it was all soon to end.

Her throne, the centerpiece of a massive, circular, royal throne chamber, was a flat, short, white marble column elevated by ten concentric, white marble planes. It was cut several millenniums ago from Mount Kai; considered by *the Wise* to be the birthplace of the Red race.

The Atlantean Royal Throne chamber was unlike any other of its day. It was bathed in a glorious white light whose source could not be explained; it was neither lit by the sun, nor by flames, nor by electrical means. It was said, according to myth, to have been lit by a great magic of a time long forgotten. Of course, no modern Atlantean believed in magic. There was only the truth of science, technology, and medicine to adhere to and abide by.

The true age of the royal throne chamber remained unknown; the Gods of the Seven Stars built it upon the peak of Mount Eve in the beginning days of the Red race. Over time Mount Eve was cut down and shaped to form the Tower of Light, which stood surrounded by what now remained of the seven Atlantean Royal Towers. The royal throne chamber was not only a symbol of the ancient heritage of the Red race but also the sacred link between mortal man and the Winged Creator.

The earth moved and the Oracle Queen woke from her thoughts. She stared at the towering, thick-iron chamber gates. Sitting in meditative positions in a circle around her, on the plane below her, were the High Kai Priestesses all dressed according to the traditional colors of the royal Clan Orders they represented; and standing before them, on the plane below, were their respective High Kai Guardians who were also dressed in the same colors as the High Kai Priestesses to whom they were bound. They all stood in the sequential order of the towers: Drakul, Libra, Virgo, Leo, Cancer, Gemini, and Taurus. There should have been seven guardians and seven priestesses in all but only six pairs were present. The Oracle Queen knew that Neva Yun Ra and Arkan of the Drakul Clan Order had abandoned her to save the life of their forbidden child.

Further below, sitting upon the first seven of the ten concentric planes were all forty-nine of the Oracle Queen's Kai-Minor priestesses. They were beautifully dressed in the colors of the towers they represented. The same number of Kai-Minor guardians stood in lines of seven by seven before the throne chamber gates; they were led by the Kai Elder King, Skaton-ka, who was dressed in black and grey robes that were held to his joints and waist by black leather straps. Black signified his age, superior knowledge, and skill— he was the only Kai guardian able to defeat a sword-wielding opponent with nothing more than the single whip of his unarmed hand. His shaved scalp revealed long snake like scars that wiggled when he laughed or frowned. His left wrist was adorned with a faded, yellow cotton bracelet whose long threads hung from a tight knot to his callused fingertips.

The bracelet was a gift from his mother on the day he was passed on to the Kai; he was seven years of age. His mother could not afford to feed him and his nine siblings after the death of his father. Out of desperation she decided to give him to the Kai guardians of the Girus Temple where he could be educated and fed. His time at the temple was filled with longing for the comforts of his mother's warm embraces as he cleaned, worked, and served the Kai guardians like a slave. But, he persevered in his meditations until the day came when he was granted leave to go on his three hundred day retreat into the snow-capped Mountains of Arakara. It was there that he gained the Enlightenment and trained in the art of

Kai sword under the guidance of the Sirians. *That was so long ago*, he thought.

And together they listened to the oncoming darkness beyond the chamber gates. Boom, boom, boom *was the song of its approach.*

Skaton-ka clasped his hand around the leather hilt of his double-edged long sword; the Sirian Creator had forged his sword in the volcanic fires of Maldek in the late years of the Age of Libra. It was an instrument that had the power to give and take life, and a symbol of the oppressive wars waged by the Lyrans against the Sirians. Skaton-ka was the Elder King of the Order of the Kai Guardian guild and forever bound to his Oracle Queen. He was devoted to his faith; he was a warrior-priest pure of heart, and he possessed a mind nearly devoid of any desire beyond the spiritual or ideal. Never had he loved and never would he wed for he was the holy patriarch of his guild.

He knew that his many decades on the Mother had finally come to its last hour. He had seen it in his dreams–an approaching darkness that would extinguish all that was known to him in a single night. He had trained his entire life to embrace and not fear death in the face of battle. As a Kai he was prepared to lay down his life for his Oracle Queen. He woke every morning believing that that day would be his last. He held no wants, desires, or attachments to his physical body. As a Kai warrior educated in the scriptures of reincarnation he knew that he had lived and died many hundreds, if not thousands of times. Even within a single lifetime he knew that he had died and been reborn time and time again; the Skaton-ka of age five was no longer, as was the Skaton-ka of age fifty-five. Death and rebirth were simply a part of the unending cycle that defined the material realm; all things must end, be forgotten, and be renewed. Thus were the laws of impermanence.

He stood proud and strong in the white light of the Oracle Queen's throne chamber while gazing at the metallic designs that adorned the borders of the iron gates before him. He tried to commit to memory the every detail of the hand-hammered roses and vines that crept up the outer sides of the gates for he knew that they would soon be destroyed by the force that was now upon the white tower.

He had always sought to inquire about the artisan who had fashioned such a metallic wonder; he wanted to know when he had lived, and what was known of him. Every time he had passed through those gates he reminded himself to research into the life of the artist, but always did something of greater urgency occupy his actions and thoughts. And now he stood with no time left to quench his curiosity.

What will be remembered of me? he thought. *Perhaps nothing. Perhaps my sword or a trinket of mine will be found in another age. It will be dug up from the earth that had swallowed it and placed upon an altar to be looked upon by an observer who will wonder as I wonder now about the life of this man who crafted those metallic roses. And in the place of fact there will only be imagination to answer these inquiries for nothing of my life will be remembered in a thousand years time. Only my possessions might outlive me and exist as a monument to my forgotten memory. Such is the way of things.*

He went on thinking about his life. So many years had he lived and so many disciples had he taught. Never had he kissed a woman for he had long ago succeeded in disciplining his mind to overcome the desires of his heart. The defeat of his heart was of his own design, of his own making: a sacrifice, a testament of his allegiance to the Kai. He saw the world only through the strict and narrow lense of his faith. Indifferent was he to joy, grief, pleasure, and pain. Virtue was all that he knew and lived by. He was an efficient warrior, a loyal protector of the Kai.

The Oracle Queen gazed lovingly at the back of Skaton-ka. She knew what he was thinking. She loved him dearly like a grandfather and respected his morality and high integrity, but she did not endorse the means by which he had achieved them. She only saw imbalance in his spirit; a man ruled by a mind that gave no voice to his heart. To reject the heart as Skaton-ka did was an act of cruelty, an act of inhumanity. He had gained as a warrior, yes, but he had lost his ability to feel and truly understand what he was protecting. He was cold to the women that adored him and unable to understand the free-spirited ways of children. He was an admirable man, but a sadly tragic one for he had spent all his years in emotional solitude, unattached to all those around him. But, the

Oracle Queen understood why he, High Kai Guardian Elder of the Order of Light, lived as he did. He was a warrior king: the embodiment of the Kai guardian guild's ancient ways.

Strangely now that the end was so near, Skaton-ka found his mind confused and upset. He did not understand it. He did not know what was eating at his thoughts. It caused him to feel nauseous, as if he was sailing upon a stormy sea. *This creeping feeling,* yes, *that is what it is,* was alien to him, but yet he had known of it, felt it before in his youth. It was fear; fear of the end and for the wicked things that came.

In that moment the walls around his heart began to crumble. He bowed his head and held his face with his hands. He was trembling and sad. He wanted to let out and cry the long quieted ache of his heart, but a rush of warmth overcame him, giving him strength.

"It is all right, my warrior king, to feel as you do."

"Yes, my Queen. Forgive me. I am failing you in our last hour."

"No, you are not. It is right for you to feel as you do before you fall into the Light. It is right for you to feel the heart that you have repressed for so long. Long have I loved you, learned from you, and cried for you, my Elder King. Much from your life have you sacrificed for my royal line. Now it is time for you to feel. Feel and be strong. Cry and be strong. Love and be strong. You are loved by many, my king."

"Yes, my Queen. I weep for the end of our Kai ways."

"My Elder King, both you and I know that this is how it must be. We have seen it in our dreams, this dark night. And from this darkness will a seed of light be born to awaken the Age of the Lion."

"No, my Queen! It is not right that we shall be ended!"

Skaton-ka lifted his head and fed his anger with the horrid knowledge that the entire history of his beloved Kai faith was to be wiped from the Mother. All his years of unattached focus, meditation, and prayer had now failed him. He would stand before the menace that sought to destroy all within the throne chamber and defeat it for he despised it.

Determined to fight and lead his Kai honorably he turned to face them and settled his sight upon Kron, High Kai Guardian

Elder of the Order of Taurus, and the other High Kai Guardians who stood before their respective High Kai Priestesses. The vacancy between his High Kai Guardians reminded him of his young friend, Arkan.

He believed Arkan had chosen an unwise path, but understood why he had chosen as he did. It was the duty of the Kai to swear eternal allegiance to the Oracle Queen, but Arkan had lost faith in her ability to rule. The Atlantean Empire was not what it had been for so many thousands of years for in this dark time the Empire was held sway by the strong interests of Ideo controlled corporations that sought to maintain and further their global economic hold. Bureaucrats and politicians were easily bought and manipulated by the Ideo-clans who employed poli-ki-clans and speed tribes to do their dirty work. The Empire no longer belonged to the old ways of the Kai, but to the culture of corporate greed.

He knew that to Arkan's eyes the Oracle Queen was too young to understand the need to compromise with political and corporate forces. Arkan had confessed to him his belief that she ruled by a high ideal that far distanced her from the realities and intricacies that defined the complex, modern age the Empire now found itself in.

Arkan belonged to the old and respected Kai line of Drakul. His royal ancestors were Kai kings and queens who had ruled the regions of Atlantis that now lay beneath the sea—the Second Great Quake of Ara swallowed two of the former five island continents of Atlantis. He was, unlike many of his ancestors, a radical force within the Kai. He had stirred and rebelled like an adolescent. He had always been proud and continually questioned, criticized, and even mocked the decisions of the Oracle Queen.

Skaton-ka, old and wise in the faith, was unable to quiet the young and high-spirited Arkan. He tried to teach Arkan to have faith in the Oracle Queen. He reminded him that the Kai Royal Highness was in constant communication with the Angels of the Seven Stars and that they guided her and through her the Empire. Arkan did not believe that the Pleiadians had the divine ability to guide her wisely. He felt that they had meddled in the affairs of humanity for far too long, and as a result he paid little heed to the code of the Kai; it was therefore of no surprise to Skaton-ka that

Arkan had seeded his Kai priestess, Neva Yun Ra. Their unborn child would be the first to be mothered by a High Kai Priestess and fathered by a High Kai Guardian.

The existence of the child was known of and kept secret amongst the high circles of the Kai, but it was suspected and whispered amongst the Kai apprentices and servants within the hidden halls and passageways of the royal towers. Keeping their meetings secret from Arkan and Neva Yun Ra the High Kai Council met with the Oracle Queen, they debated over what was to be done with the forbidden child. Some argued to sacrifice the child while others believed that it was the *one child* referred to in the prophecy of Artemis. The Oracle Queen was unconvinced of what action to take and decided to meditate and take council with the Pleiadians from whom she learned that the child would ultimately fall to the dark. After much hesitation she finally decided to have the child destroyed upon its birth. News of this leaked to Arkan, which caused him to begin preparations to save the life of his unborn child. It was during this time, in the months after the conception of the child, that Maniok had crushed his political and corporate rivals to then fix his attacking eye upon the Oracle Queen and her Kai, causing some of those who knew of the forbidden child's existence to see it only as an ill omen.

Never had Skaton-ka met the one named Maniok, but he had watched his power grow over a score of decades. All that was known of him was that he had emerged from Ideo and that he had aggressively led his clan into battle against those who opposed his desire to control all avenues of finance and trade within the underground. When he had gained dominion over the Ideo sector he expanded into the citizen sectors of Atlas by buying into an array of corporations, which he eventually merged into a single conglomerate known to all as the Maniok Corporation; and with this legitimate wealth he bought the support of politicians and corporate nobles to legitimize his growing economic and political power.

Skaton-ka continually advised the Oracle Queen of the dangers of Maniok's growing and overwhelming influence, but there was little that she could do. The political power she had inherited was faded, weak, and mostly symbolic.

Maniok had revealed his dark intent on the fourth day of the year thirteen of the Oracle Queen's reign. His pursuit for a republic had been false; his twisted heart had always sought to overthrow the Kai and rule Atlantean lands with an iron fist. In the years before Andromeda 13 he had gained ownership of the industries that developed military weapons and advanced CybOr-tecnologies and musca-technologies. And when finally high Atlantean generals and commanders sat firmly in the palm of his wicked hand he squeezed and ordered the deaths of all the top corporate executives and high government officials who paid no allegiance to him. All who opposed him now were the Oracle Queen and her Kai.

Skaton-ka faced his Kai-Minor guardians. He looked with pride at his young apprentice, Volan, who was standing in the front line, and noticed his camel bone necklace and silver earrings; gifts his mother had given to him on the day he was passed on to the Kai. He wished that there would have been more time to have taught Volan a better understanding of the philosophy behind Kai sword or to have shared another cup of rose tea with him. *He is a fine Kai-Minor guardian*, he thought. He then looked out and said aloud to his Kai-Minor, "This is our last hour as brothers and sisters in this world! You know what is asked of you. As Children of the Law of One we serve. As children of the Kai we protect. May your swords strike true!"

The walls of the throne chamber shivered. The small army of Kai-Minor guardians looked in disbelief as they saw cracks draw themselves down the chamber's marble walls for the first time since the Second Great Quake of Ara. Then there was silence. All stood still. The violent drums of the explosions had ceased. In unison, all the Kai priestesses woke from their meditations and looked up at the massive iron gates.

"It is time!" Skaton-ka roared with an anger that melded into the fierce explosion that tore open the gates launching thick metal fragments to the other end of the royal chamber. All Kai-Minor guardians unsheathed their long swords and held them high above their heads. They stood firm before the shattered entrance as debris fell in all directions, but not upon them for they were protected by the telekinetic will of their priestesses. The white light of the throne chamber reflected off the sheen beauty of their swords. They called out their battle cries and charged into a cloud of fire and ash.

Rapid plasma-fire flowered into the throne chamber like an unending stream of fireworks. The Oracle Queen and all her Kai priestesses immediately protected themselves from the attack by jointly creating a half-sphere, Kai-Ra energy shield that revealed itself as a dark blue hue when the unending streams of plasma-fire were absorbed by it. And although the Kai-Minor guardians fought only with swords they were each individually protected by the Kai-Ra projected around them by their respective Kai-Minor priestesses. Their swords were strong, dense alloys sharp enough to cut with ease into the heavy metal of the attacking kragita-droids whose height was four times that of a man.

Only one kragita-droid could enter the royal throne chamber at a time through the vertical crater created by the blast. Their cyclopic eyes targeted groups of Kai guardians and fired upon them from the canons that formed the whole of their forearms. For every explosive shot and blast there were two to three Kai-Minor guardians thrown into the air, but after smashing into the floor and regaining their senses they found only minor cuts and bruises upon their skin; their Kai-Ra shields did not protect them from the solid objects that struck them within it. And when the guardians rose to reengage in the fight they quickly bowed in gratitude to their Kai-Minor priestesses for shielding them.

The kragita-droids began to fill the chamber. The stomping of their immense hooved feet repeatedly shattered and shook the ground causing groups of guardians to lose their balance and fall as Kai priestesses held strong to their meditations, deaf to the loud destruction all around them.

Volan had fallen, and when he looked up he saw a kragita-droid's iron sole rise high above him. He grabbed his sword, scrambled to his knees, and rolled. There was a massive stomp. Safe, he sighed but found that the marble floor had splintered up cutting his arm. He cursed and then launched himself onto the droid's foot. The kragita-droid looked down. He wound his arm and threw his long sword straight into its single eye. Blind, the kragita-droid kicked in all directions before flinging Volan off its foot.

Kai-Minor guardians soon assailed upon the sightless droid slicing and hacking at its feet. Its legs then buckled and it fell to its knees. The guardians then overtook the droid, but it fired its last shot at the high ceiling releasing a downpour of stone and dust upon the Oracle Queen and the Kai priestesses. Volan and the men of his guild stopped and looked helplessly at the falling trail of stones and dust, but suspired when they saw it all slide along the sides of the priestesses' Kai-Ra shield.

Long swords were lost or broken as the Kai-Minor continued battling the kragita-droids, but were instantly replaced by short swords and other weapons hidden within their garments. Together the Kai-Minor took the kragita-droids down one by one in the manner revealed to them by Volan; they struck at the eye of the droids and cut them down.

As the number of kragita-droids began to dwindle a cyborg army armed with plasma assault-rifles and double-edged swords festered into the royal chamber. The cyborgs looked like men, robust in appearance, but hairless and with colorless flesh.

Skaton-ka ran at a cyborg that fired repeatedly at him; each shot rippled and illuminated his Kai-Ra in a light blue glow. The cyborg had only moments, desperately it dropped its rifle and grabbed its sword, but Skaton-ka lashed out and decapitated it.

He charged from one cyborg to the other within a battle scene filled with clanging swords, plasma-fire, and metallic limbs that bled oil upon crushed marble stone.

He moved like water flowing down a riverbed filled with jagged rocks.

Holding his long sword he ran and threw himself at the colosal kragita-droid before him, and stabbed his blade into its chest. Hanging from the sword's hilt he pulled himself up, drew out his short sword, and stabbed it into the space above his head. Hanging now from his short sword he twisted his long sword within the droid's chest before pulling it out and landing on the ground.

Fire belched from the kragita-droid's lacerated chest. It swiped its cannon arms at the flames but could not extinguish them. The droid then bent forward and targeted Skaton-ka who had already unleashed his long sword from a tight wind that sliced clean through the droid's shin. And like a mighty tree cut down at its base the droid fell; its last vision was of a Kai-Minor guardian raising his long sword over its eye.

Skaton-ka retrieved his short sword from the droid's upper chest and slid it back into its sheath. Cyborgs approached him with swords ready in attack positions. Devoid of all thought he closed his eyes, breathed the heated air deep into his lungs, and relaxed his grip on the hilt of his long sword. He squinted and smiled before lashing his sword out in a vicious whirlwind assault that defaced the humanoid opponents all around him. In eerie unison the cyborgs dropped their swords and fell into a circle of death around the Kai Elder King. He looked beyond their twitching bodies and saw his Kai-Minor guardians fighting the unrelenting storm of cyborgs and kragita-droids.

The battle consumed all within the royal throne chamber except for its sacred center, where stood the High Kai Guardians, and where sat the priestesses all around their beloved Oracle Queen. It was an unsettling sight; the constant and familiar blue glow of the Kai-Ra that protected the meditating beauty of the priestesses while giant machines, cyborgs, and men battled within smoking fumes of grey and black.

Skaton-ka looked at the High Kai Guardians. He looked at his Oracle Queen upon her marble throne, found peace in her gaze, and stood transfixed upon her enigmatic beauty and youth.

Kron interrupted Skaton-ka's thoughts and spoke to his mind, *"Let us fight."* Skaton-ka dropped his exhausted arms and shoulders. His long sword dripped with oil as sweat soaked into his garments. Cyborgs advanced upon him. He was feeling the strain of his age; his mind could only stretch the years of his body so far. The cyborgs closed in. Kron called for an answer and Skaton-ka replied, *"No, you must stand as one with the five beside you."*

He looked to the floor littered with shredded metal and blood trying to find renewed strength in his heart and suddenly, like a falcon about to take flight, he spread open his arms revealing the virility of his two crafted swords. Anger contorted his face into that of a wild boar about to strike its prey; open mouthed, fangs dripping saliva. He roared as he swung his swords decapitating the cybernetic enemy before him. Two cyborgs rushed in, but he leapt and flew high into the smoky air. A heavy array of plasma-fire came at him from below, but his Kai-Ra protected him from the shots that would have otherwise ripped him apart into globs of melted flesh. Using the force of his descent he rounded his long sword to slash in two another cyborg. He crouched before the divided cyborg and marveled at its interior circuitry.

The floor shook violently; a kragita-droid was kicking and crushing the ground. Skaton-ka raised his Sirian long sword to catch the droid's attention and then pointed the sword's tip at the droid's eye while holding his short sword perpendicular to the ground. Just as the droid approached him he ran and leapt into the ash air sheathing his swords, twisting and dodging a volley of plasma-fire, and landing onto its head. Like an agile spider he moved to the droid's shoulder while avoiding its swiping cannon arms, but its movements became more and more vicious and he slipped and fell slamming his chin hard against its metallic back before grabbing the droid's neck. As he tried to pull himself up he saw that the droid was running toward the throne chamber wall to crush him. He drew out his short sword, but before he was able to stab the mechanical beast he lost his grip and flew into the air, losing his sword. He crashed into a pile of shredded metal that cut deep into his arms and back.

There was a massive sound. Ignoring his wounds Skaton-ka saw that the kragita-droid had crashed into the chamber wall. Destruction was now everywhere. He looked and despised the desecration that now fashioned the royal throne chamber, but the mesmerizing peace of the priestesses' Kai-Ra calmed him.

The kragita-droid, now the last within the royal chamber, pushed itself out of the crater it had created in the chamber wall and charged after Skaton-ka. Skaton-ka, unable to rise to his feet, scurried away on his hands and knees. The droid was now upon him, raising its iron foot. Skaton-ka crouched and sprang away. KURAAASH!!! The droid had stomped hard into the floor creating a massive hole beside the old Kai guardian. The droid lifted its other foot for a second attempt, but Skaton-ka jumped high up, over, and behind the metallic nightmare launching his long sword straight into its armored back before falling back down to the ground. The droid collapsed.

Breathing heavily Skaton-ka looked around and realized that the first offensive line of droids and cyborgs had finally dwindled into pathetic heaps of scrap metal. His Kai-Minor guardians, who were also catching their breaths and tending to their wounds, were standing in small pockets all around the royal throne chamber counting their dead. Seven of their youngest fighters had they lost to the enemy. Tired, he shook his head severely pained by the deaths of his Kai disciples, and looked to Kron who had bent down in grief and at the Kai priestesses who continued to sit in deep meditation around their Oracle Queen. He could see sweat dripping from the priestesses' foreheads and their thin robes clinging to their moist skin. He then looked at his Oracle Queen who was also deep in meditation, but aware of him and of everything within her royal throne chamber. His eyes began to well with tears as he gazed at the vibrant blue hue of his priestesses' Kai-Ra for its beauty continued to inspire him.

The Oracle Queen spoke to him, *"You are my warrior king, Skaton-ka. You have always been faithful to the ancient ways of the Kai. You are strong in your thoughts and wise in your years. But it is not done. Awake and fight."*

"Yes, my Oracle Queen." Skaton-ka stood proud, but further aged, before his men. He pulled his long sword out from the back of the kragita-droid he had defeated and wiped it clean of the oil that oozed down its surface. The Kai-Minor guardians followed his example and wiped their swords as well. With dwindling strength he looked through the smoky air, beyond the shattered chamber gates, and saw a second offensive line of cyborgs. Looking farther ahead he saw a third and fourth offensive line; he knew that this army would ultimately overwhelm and tire his guardians.

It began; cyborgs howled like savage wolves at a full moon. These howls caused the youngest guardians to be afraid. Regardless, the guardians, together, faced the cyborgs ready to fight again.

The cyborgs charged in and Skaton-ka ran to meet them by leading his Kai back into battle. The two sides ran at each other shouting their battle cries until they crashed into one another with clanging swords and curses.

Skaton-ka slashed and hacked tearing down cyborg after cyborg as oil and blood splattered repeatedly over his face and arms. Adrenaline rushed through his veins giving him unnatural strength. His heart pounded his chest, and as it did time began to slow.

At a distance he saw Volan being besieged by seven cyborgs. He could see that his apprentice was struggling, that his defensive tactics were becoming desperate, and that there were no guardians near him to aid him. He knew that it would not be long before the cyborgs overcame him. He ran to him, and as he did he saw the failure of Volan's defense and the blow that beheaded him. He cried out capturing the attention of the seven cyborgs before ramming his Sirian sword all the way through one of the cyborg's heads. Now unarmed he stopped, turned, caught an assaulting sword between his palms, kicked it out of the attacking cyborg's hands, and drilled his thumbs into its eyes. The blind cyborg grabbed his arms and stretched them out so that a third cyborg, from behind him and armed with two swords, could slice his forearms clean off. Blood sprayed and coated his weathered face as he fell to the floor. His end had finally come.

The cyborg that had defeated Skaton-ka stood over him with hateful eyes–the other cyborgs closed in forming a circle around the two–and smiled savoring the fleeting moments of victory over the armless High Kai Elder before grabbing his left ear, pulling him up to his knees, and beheading him. It then raised the decapitated head up to his, spat on it, and threw it to the floor. The head rolled until it stopped against a mechanical limb.

Skaton-ka could still see and saw his headless body, his bloodied neck stump, and his executioner walking away. He focused his eyes on the faded yellow bracelet of his former body and found . . . his mother's warmth again.

The Kai-Minor continued fighting, but their morale was at a loss; their Kai Elder King had fallen. Fear grew stronger in them; it ate at their minds and hearts convincing them that if Skaton-ka–the most skilled of the Kai guardians–could not stand against the onslaught then they had very little chance for victory, let alone survival. Kron tried to reinvigorate them, he spoke to their minds and coordinated their defenses but it was, in the end, futile.

Despair first consumed the youngest Kai-Minor; devoid of hope they soon fell. In time what remained were only a handful of the oldest Kai-Minor guardians who stood together, back to back, within an impenetrable circle formed around them by the cyborg army. Cyborgs charged into the circle one after the other to battle the remaining Kai; and although the guardians won each engagement they were slowly worn and torn down by a collection of cuts, exhaustion, and time.

All the Kai priestesses felt helpless and frustrated as they could only sit and watch their remaining guardians be felled by enemy swords. Kron begged the Oracle Queen to command her priestesses to unleash the Spheres of Ra upon the cyborg army, but she refused; she knew it would drain too much from her priestesses; their strength was needed to maintain the Kai-Ra.

The priestesses began to weep. They watched the last Kai-Minor, Bator-Uran, hold his sword with unsteady hands. The circle of cyborgs closed in on him. He turned again and again trying to face all the enemies that surrounded him, but it was hopeless. He stopped, prohibited his Kai-Minor priestess from aiding him, and said to the minds of his Kai: *Let it be known that I shall fall with no hatred within my heart.* And with those words did he strike and fight to his death.

The cyborgs stood and marveled at their feat when all was done with the last guardian. They looked over the scores of Kai limbs, torsos, and heads that littered the throne chamber. They had fulfilled the first act of their task.

Kron, frustrated, filled with guilt, angered that such bloodshed had cursed the sacred walls of the royal throne chamber, began to yell at the young mind of the Oracle Queen begging her again to give the command to attack. The Kai priestesses followed with pleads and demands against their Queen for they had learned nothing from Bator-Uran's words and could no longer bear the horrific site that surrounded them:

We beg of you, our Queen, to let us fight!

Please, please, please let us do so.
Let us not betray them, oh the gods, no!

Please, let us finish these horrid beasts!

What have you done, but lead us to the end?

Betrayed them have you—our Kai-Minor!

And from the Clan Order of Cancer came the wicked words of five Kai-Minor priestesses:

From the Dark were you sent!

All is finished because of you!

Too young—worthless—you can not see!
The malice of our contempt shall overcome thee!

Let us unleash the Spheres of Ra upon our foe!
Or feel the heat of a heavy blow.
Vile! Vile! Vile! You are hated so!

The Oracle Queen begged them to stop their collective shrill screams that tortured her mind. Holding her hands over her ears she tried desperately to block their exhausting demands and rotten words, but it was of no use, what seemed like a hundred voices filled her mind. Never did she want to give in to their shortsightedness, but she was still young and vulnerable, and after witnessing the slaughter of so many, and having lost their respect she feared them and gave in by ordering the attack.

Simultaneously the Kai priestesses clasped their hands together above their foreheads. Small spheres of fire actualized and expanded before their hands and shot out as bright and blinding light ripping through the cyborg army. The cyborgs retreated, but the Spheres of Ra came at them unrelentingly; piercing through them; throwing them back; launching them up into balls of flame.

And when all was done of the cyborgs the Kai priestesses dropped their exhausted hands and arms, and rested.

CHAPTER IV

Arkan moved with great haste as he carried his beloved Neva Yun Ra in his arms through the dark corridors of the underground labyrinth of the Tower of Drakul until a sharp pain crossed his chest. It was done. He knew what had become of his Kai-Minor guardians. He had betrayed his Order, and in doing so he had weakened the power of his Kai enabling Maniok's forces to exploit them. He stopped dead in his tracks for it was then that he realized that what he had done would forever haunt him, but he knew that he served a higher ideal, one stronger than the wavering power of the Atlantean Kai; he stood firm in his belief that the forbidden child that grew in the stomach of his precious Neva Yun Ra was the *one child* "born to none" as described in the prophecy of Artemis. Whispering to himself there in the shadows of an unlit passageway he reaffirmed his belief that his child was worth the death of all the Kai for it would be his child that would bring the birth of a new Kai Order by overcoming the darkness of the world, bringing back the light, and awakening the Age of the Lion. Neva Yun Ra began to stir in his arms. He looked at her knowing that she had never fully accepted or shared in his creed, and that she loved him far too much to have exposed his guarded beliefs to the High Kai Council; instead she had chosen to blind herself from the now fatal consequences of his self-righteous actions.

Exiting the damp tunnels he entered a massive underground cavern and laid his priestess on the ground so that he could rest and look out in all directions. Seeing nothing of threat he relaxed and took a deep breath of the stale almost phosphorus air, but then he heard a soft familiar whimper and looked down at his priestess seeing tears flowing down her cheeks; he knew that her dreams were tormenting her. He closed his eyes and saw what she saw;

images of countless, guardian men–headless and limbless–all piled on top of each other in a lake of blood within a radiantly white chamber. Bitterness consumed his heart for he did not appreciate these horrific, telepathic images being sent from the High Kai Priestesses to his Yun as a desperate plea for her aid. He clenched his teeth in disapproval and looked ahead at the vast cavern and at the stalactites and stalagmites that surrounded him. Abruptly he felt as if a predator had just sighted him for its meal and stood still while focusing on the pool's moving surface where he heard water fizzing and something massive rising beneath its surface. His eyes widened, he knew what it was, and he bent down, lifted his priestess from the ground, and carried her into a dark crevice.

Three Aqua-Krotraks–heavy artillery transport submersibles–emerged from the water and rolled onto the cavern floor crushing hard stones and minerals while advancing toward the crevice where Arkan and his unconscious priestess were hidden. Without warning the Aqua-Krotraks stopped and released pressurized steam from their anterior–Arkan cautiously backed away from his thin view of the transports–infrared beams then shot out from the transports to scan the rough features of the cavern as hatches opened along their sides releasing small surveillance droids to hover and fly like buzzing flies. "They're looking for something . . . someone," Arkan whispered to himself with unease as he peeked at the cavern scene. Pressurized air then spat out from the transport's posterior planks which lowered to the ground allowing heavily armed, artillery droids to march out five across before breaking their formations to run out and cover the irregular walls and corners of the cavern.

CHAPTER V

A tall figure, cloaked in black robes, walked down the torch lit hall to the Atlantean Royal Throne chamber. Its pale face was eclipsed by the hood that covered its head, and as it walked it avoided the firelight by stepping in shadow; the cyborgs and artillery droids that lined the hall dropped to their left knees and bowed their heads when it passed. The figure stopped to look beyond the distant broken gates of the throne chamber, and focused its glare upon the blue, half-sphere energy shield that radiated over the Oracle Queen, her priestesses, and the High Kai Guardians.

A bald man, short in stature, dressed in black and dark grey robes, walked up to, and stood behind, the dark figure. His frail albino face had no eyebrows. His lips were black as were his twitching eyes that sat deep within their sockets.

The dark figure turned to his servant and hissed, "This night brings the end of the Kai."

"My Domek," began the albino man, "there are still forty-nine Kai-Minor priestesses, and strangely there are only six High Kai Guardians protecting six High Kai Priestesses."

"I shall thank Arkan for that. Continue the search. He is still here, deep in the beneath."

"What are we to do with the Kai priestesses, my Domek? There are too many of them, as a collective they are, perhaps, too powerful. They can destroy us if they so choose—"

"They can destroy you . . . but, not me," he sneered. "They know my mind is safe."

"How then are we to advance? We can not penetrate their Kai-Ra?"

The dark figure inched closer to his white-faced friend and whispered, "Do not be so certain that the Kai are beyond the grasp of Belial. I have felt a weakness within, a lack of hope among their young. They have seen the imminent doom of the Kai and have chosen to join me. They have betrayed the Law of One. They have consumed the spirit of the demon."

A shadow grew outlining five Kai-Minor priestesses who had awoken from their meditations with eyes that dilated into a demonic stare. Together, these baneful five, unleashed swords from within the dark of their robes and slit the necks of the Kai-Minor priestesses seated before them. They then ascended into the air and blasted Spheres of Ra from their hands at the youngest of the tiring Kai below them.

Kolia Ra, the youngest of the Kai-Minor priestesses, exploded into a ravaging wrath of flame. Her horrific screams shattered the meditative thoughts of those around her as fire delved deep into her throat and lungs; the foul scent of her burning skin filled all within the Kai-Ra.

Nearly all the young Kai-Minor priestesses scattered from Kolia Ra's blazing body of frantic arms and legs. Then another globe of fire hit and threw Kolia Ra up like a weightless doll, burning her until she moved no more. The youngest priestesses retreated from the baneful five–the Kai-Ra weakened–and one by one they were torched for none among them were able to silence the fear in their hearts and minds.

The oldest and wisest of the Kai-Minor priestesses sat calm and focused, as six of their youngest burned, easily warding off and suspending the attacking Spheres of Ra in mid-flight with their raised left arms and open hands.

Artillery droids opened fire upon the Kai-Ra; and the seated Kai priestesses replied with their right palms outstretched before them to further reinforce the Kai-Ra shield. The shield grew strong again. Together the elder priestesses looked up and arrested all motion from the five hovering traitors who they dishonored by flipping them over. The Oracle Queen then said to the wicked five, *"You are no more."* And with those words the Queen threw them spinning out of the Kai-Ra, pinning and crushing them against the high curved ceiling with the heavy strength of her mind.

Looking at what it considered a delightful sight the dark one turned to the white faced man and said, "Unfortunately, the High Kai Priestesses, and their pathetic little guardian men, are pure in both mind and spirit. We will have to be patient. Their minds are willing, but their bodies weak. As the coming days pass they will starve and meet their end. They shall die slowly, and her royal lineage shall be forever wiped from Atlantean memory.

"I will finally gain what I have sought, the pleasure of killing the last Guardians of the Kai."

The Oracle Queen felt him, the one that was a man but not. She took a deep breath and tried to break into his thoughts, but could not. He, the dark leader of this invading force, was there, but not in mind or spirit, only in flesh and synthetic parts.

Time was running out. Kron knew not what else to do other than to allow the priestesses to rest and regain their strength, but that they could not do. Kalia Ra, his High Kai Priestess bound to him, agreed that there was little else that could be done. The High Kai Council convened with their Oracle Queen as the remaining thirty-two Kai-Minor priestesses focused their fading strength upon the Kai-Ra.

Kron spoke, "Forgive me, my Oracle Queen. I was not myself when I demanded the Spheres of Ra be unleashed upon this malefic force." He bowed, and after he did each member of the High Kai Council spoke and offered their apologies as well.

"Your apologies I accept," began the Oracle Queen, "but, it is too late for such thoughts and gestures, the hour of death is nigh. You have failed me by doubting me, and I have failed myself by giving in to your demands. Nevertheless, I am the Oracle. I am your Queen.

"Long has my line been in communion with the Pleiadians and Sirians. They have always guided our people. But events occur, as they should. And here we are at an end. You all know the words of Artemis. You can all feel that this is how things must be. Two from our Council have we lost. One will escape. And from his seed that has yet to be conceived will our Legacy of Light begin.

"Do not fear. Come near and welcome my Light for soon it shall consume all."

A black raven flew through the corridor that led to the throne chamber and eyed his master, the one he called White Face. He glided and landed upon the extended arm of his master and projected his thoughts to him.

White Face petted his bird, "My Domek, there are two in the cavern beneath."

"It is Arkan and his priestess. Ensure that they do not escape. I will face them."

"Yes, my Domek."

The raven understood the instructions of the one he called Dark and took flight back down the corridor to deliver the directive.

CHAPTER VI

Arkan was trapped behind the crevice. There were too many heavy artillery droids, and although they hadn't already, they would soon detect his movements, or body heat, and with his Kai priestess unconscious he was unshielded and thus unable to fight through to an escape. Turning around he kneeled, held the arms of his Kai priestess, and lightly shook her.

"They know we're here," he whispered, "Yun wake up." There was no response; he continued shaking her, "Yun . . . Yun."

Neva Yun Ra emerged from her fitful slumber and murmured, "We must go back—my sisters will soon pass into the Light."

"Yun, please, we can not, we must save the child that grows within you."

She hesitated, "No, we must kill this child. Maniok," her eyes widened, "He is coming—He is near."

"What?"

"Arkan you must kill me."

"What?" he repeated shocked and angered.

"Arkan please . . . you must understand . . . kill me and leave me."

"Never."

"You must. Within me grows a forbidden Kai child . . . If Maniok succeeds in killing off the Kai . . . then all that will remain is this child . . . Maniok will seize the child—bend him—twist him into the shadow—He—No! It is here . . . it is here . . ."

Heavy artillery droids advanced upon the hiding place of Arkan and his priestess. Arkan stood up with clenched fists and a furrowed brow ready to face the one named Maniok. He exited the crevice. The droids responded by parting a path to reveal a figure silhouetted by a backdrop of transport floodlights.

The figure spoke, "Is that you, Arkan? So happy to see me? I must confess I can not contain my twisted self. It is a pleasure to see you again . . . Step closer–more into the light so that I may see you. No? Pity–Let's be done with it fool! Unsheathe your sword. Face me!"

Arkan stepped back into the crevice to look a final time at his Neva Yun Ra.

"Face me!"

He kneeled before her and said, "Yun, I love you with all that is good within my heart."

"Come out and face me!"

He kissed her gently upon her lips and said, "Give me the Light. I will face Maniok."

Arkan stepped out of the crevice; the space around him filled with the blue light of his Kai-Ra.

"How you've grown," slurred Maniok. The droids widened the path between the one they served and Arkan. It then disrobed exposing its eyeless, earless, white bony face that had two slits for a nose, black lips, pearly white teeth, and a tongue the color of blood. The black, raw silk garments hanging loose from its body swelled from a draft of wind like the dark sails of a ship over a moonless sea. It eyed Arkan with a contorted smile and exploded into a run, gaining speed with each step that kicked up dirt, and unsheathed two double-edged long swords before leaping into an attack aimed for Arkan's heart.

Arkan unsheathed his double-edged long sword, charged, and leapt high into the air. Bright, lightening-like flashes erupted from the clash of his sword against Maniok's swords sending shrill echoes in all directions. Gravity then reclaimed them.

Back on the ground and crouched like a wild cat Arkan heard the clanging echoes of the swords continue into the far reaches of the cavern and noticed blood from a thin cut on his right thigh. He placed his hand over his wound feeling the blood ooze between his fingers and saw Maniok clench its teeth, tighten its grip on its swords, and leap into the illuminated air. He jumped after his enemy who slashed with both swords at him. He was not fast enough to counter the strikes; his right arm was cut; and he fell in an uncontrolled descent crushing a coarse stone with his back when he hit the ground. He shouted out in pain and grabbed his bleeding arm before rolling off the crushed stone that had stabbed several stone splints into his bruised back. He sat up and tried to lift his forearm, but could not; his muscle had been cut clean through.

"I've waited too long for this!" Maniok bawled. "Already you have been cut twice by my sword! There is no hope for you. Soon your Yun shall lie with me."

"Never!" Arkan grabbed his sword with his left hand, bolted up from the ground, and ran at Maniok.

Maniok easily jumped high over Arkan, but Arkan threw himself onto his back and hurled his sword up in a deadly spin.

A horrific scream filled the underground cavern. The entire length of Arkan's sword was sticking out through Maniok's left arm. Maniok crashed into the cavern wall and tumbled down to the ground; its left arm was mangled, its flesh broken and streaming with blood and black oil. It stumbled up to its feet shaking its head, realigning its neck, and looked down at its wrecked left arm before gripping the hilt of the long sword that stuck out from it and yanked the sword down ripping the arm out of its socket. It waved the sword throwing the battered arm off it and held it out proudly. "I know this sword, and you will die by it! This is the sword of your grandfather and now it is mine. I will take more pleasure in killing you with it for this sword will end you and your seed forever!"

"Then come and finish it!" Arkan shouted.

Maniok lifted its right arm, sword in hand, and pointed three fingers at Arkan. The heavy artillery droids began firing. The shots were all absorbed by Arkan's Kai-Ra, but the collective force of the assault threw him hard against the cavern wall, knocking him unconscious.

Maniok, satisfied, pointed to the resting place of Neva Yun Ra. The droids altered their stream of fire to the dark crevice, but Neva Yun Ra's Kai-Ra, which had begun to fade in strength, consumed it all; the Kai-Ra's blue hue was no more, it was now a cloud white.

The firing ceased and Maniok approached Arkan's motionless body and stood over him, eclipsing him in its shadow. It raised and aimed the Kai sword over Arkan's heart, but paused when Arkan's eyes fluttered opened. Maniok was delighted to have Arkan look at it one last time, "It is finished—"

Blinding white light filled all within the underground cavern; Maniok dropped Arkan's sword to cover its face from the brilliance. The sword fell on Arkan's chest; he grabbed it and covered his eyes. The floor shook as cavern waters splashed. A terrible wind howled paralyzing all of Arkan's senses and thoughts with disbelief and shock.

Time stopped. There was no sound, no pain. There was nothing that Arkan could see or feel. He believed that he had died, that he had somehow failed and been struck down by the sword of his ancestors. But, there began a murmur that grew rapidly into a thunderous blare that disabled all machines and devices within the cavern. The wind, now as fierce and as strong as a hurricane, lifted Aqua-Krotraks, threw crippled droids, and cast Arkan across a great distance.

He crashed into the cold waters of the underground cavern. All his pain flooded back. The sea salt stabbed at his open wounds like a thousand daggers. *I have fallen into the liquid of hell*, he thought. He looked up seeing a great fire blazing like a red wind over the surface of the waters before a current pulled his body down pressing the air out of him. His body cringed; he realized that he was still holding his long sword. The current pulled him down deeper and deeper, carrying him away from the fires. Soon there was only darkness and the cold airlessness of water.

He could not fight against the deep ocean currents and surrendered to his dark watery doom. And although the hands of death were upon him he held firm to his sword. He was fading away but rising, flowing up to a surface of crashing waves. There was lightening and the boom of thunder. He gasped and swallowed in great gulps the rainy air. Life breathed back into his torn body as hard rains pelted his face. The constant rise and fall of the stormy ocean waves began to nauseate him. He looked out and saw only the dark unending ocean. He splashed his hands and arms against the violent waters to turn his body. He then saw sharp, jagged mountain walls. He looked up and saw the Tower of Light broken by fires that burned in flames of blue and white.

A black crow flew low over the waters of Ida, circled above Arkan, and abandoned him. Flying against the rains the crow ascended to the broken Tower of Light and rested upon one of the many burnt angelic statues that decorated its sides. He looked down at the watery place Arkan had been, but was unable to find him in the crashing waves. He then flew up and over the flames that cursed what had once been the Tower of Light. He wept for his home, the Tower of Taurus, scarred red by the flames that consumed it. The fires burned in the night, unaffected by the black rains of the malicious sky.

Beyond the mountainous boundaries of the Atlantean Royal Towers there was nothing. The entire city-galaxy of Atlas was unlit; fooling the black crow to believe that the city had somehow vanished by some dark magical means, but lightening struck the Sea of Ida and in a flash Atlas reappeared and was gone again from the eyes of the crow. And as the towers crumbled the storm clouds rolled beating the crow with unrelenting winds and rains.

And it was into this darkness that the black crow flew, forever lost.

OF ENDINGS AND BEGINNINGS

Oh, dear. We do not mean to sadden you with such a disheartening tale. It ends dark. Yes, this we know. But all things begin in the dark. Always before the light there is darkness, in this realm the material.

Do not fear for here we all are, many thousands of years after these events. It is said by some that history has taught us nothing. Hmmm . . . yes, we may understand this point of view, but we do not agree. The legacy of your kind has been smeared with acts of war and hate and greed, all expressions—all acts of fear. Long has your kindred feared—and for good reason. But, yes, this we know, you are not ready yet to hear of these reasons. In time the answers you seek will come.

And here we are, happy, yes. We must admit that we were not looking forward to the telling of the tale we have just told. Too many sad and dark memories does it bring. But, we are quite pleased to begin to tell the tale of the one named Kieko. His story is long, but still when it ends you will find that we are still at a beginning. So far is it to the end—although there are, before we find that end, many endings and beginnings.

This is a beginning. We are getting excited: yes, yes, yes. Its setting is far to the East of Atlantean lands. It is in the region of Kadek, on the Island of Kadek, in the Kingdom of Lemuria that this story . . . trinity . . . will begin and end.

Words and Terms

A

The Age of Virgo – The last Age of the reign of the *Atlantean Oracle Kings and Queens*.

> See also: *the last days of the Age of Virgo*.

Amilius the Wise: The most ancient and revered prophet of *Atlantis* who reigned during *the Golden Age*; founder of *the Law of One*.

Angels of the Seven Stars – Refer to the list of defined words and terms in *Book V: Time* of the *Dark Legacy* books.

Aqua-Krotrak – A heavy artillery transport submersible.

The Ara Mountains – Also referred to as the *Moutains of Ara*. It is a chain of mountains surrounding *Atlas*.

The Arakara Mountains – Also referred to as the *Mountains of Arakara*. It is a chain of mountains on the island continent of *Og*.

> Of Note: It was where *Skaton-ka* (refer to the list of characters in *The End of the Kai* of the *Dark Legacy* books) went on his three hundred day retreat and gained the *Enlightenment*.

Aryan – The island continent of *Atlantis* between *Poseidia* and *Og*.

> See also: *the Second Great Quake of Ara*.

The Atlantean Empire – The territories, regions, colonies, and kingdoms under the supreme rule of *Atlantis*.

The Atlantean Ocean – One of the five great bodies of salt water on planet Earth. It is located in the *West*.

The Atlantean Oracle King, Queen – The sacred and traditional ruler of the *Atlantean Empire*. Only one Oracle King or Queen can be elected to rule *Atlantis* at any one time.

> Of Note: The Oracle King has the power to oversee the *High Kai Guardian Elder*, the *Kai guardians*, and the *Kai*

priestesses. The Oracle Queen only has the power to oversee the *Kai priestesses.*

See also: *The High Kai Guardian Elder.*

The Atlantean Royal Families – There are seven platonic Royal Families: Drakul, Libra, Virgo, Leo, Cancer, Gemini, and Taurus. Each Royal Family is composed of a *High Kai Guardian,* a *High Kai Priestess* and the *Kai Order* bound to them. Each family governs (with the aid of regional governments) one or more regions of the *Atlantean Empire.*

See also: *Kai Order.*

The Atlantean Royal Throne – The royal seat of the *Atlantean Oracle King, Queen.*

The Atlantean Royal Towers – The eight royal towers of the *Atlantean Empire* that are the official residences of the *Atlantean Oracle King, Queen,* and the seven *Atlantean Royal Families.*

Atlantis – The most powerful civilization in the *West.*

Atlas – The largest *city-galaxy* of *Atlantis,* and the capital of the *Atlantean Empire.* It is located on the island continent of *Poseidia.*

B

The Blood race – Also referred to as the *Red race.* It is a term used to describe the human populations of *Atlantis.*

C

The Children of Belial – Any and all disciples who oppose the *Kai.*

See also: *The Children of the Law of One.*

The Children of the Law of One – Any and all disciples of the *Kai.*

See also: *the Law of One.*

City-galaxy – A city with a population of more than twenty-five million people.

Clan Order(s) – Refer to *Kai Order(s)*.

Corporate noble – An individual of significant wealth and political power possessing hereditary rank in a corporate conglomerate.

CybOr-technology – Referring to any technology that synthesizes a living organism with mechanical or electronic devices.

Cyborg – A cybernetic organism.

D

Domek – A citizen in *Atlantis* who has authority, power, or control over others.

E

The East – The portion of the world influenced or ruled by the *Lemurian Kingdom*.

The Enlightenment – The blessed state achieved by a *Kai* or *Ki* disciple who transcends all attachments and desires.

The Etheric races of Lemuria – Refer to the list of defined words and terms in *Book V: Time* of the *Dark Legacy* books.

F

Fornax-Serpens – Also referred to as *Seeker Killers* or *S.K.'s*. In *the last days of the Age of Virgo* they were the machines built by the Atlantean military at the request of the Atlantean government to patrol the *Ideo* sewer systems to prevent the flow of *Ideo ghosts* from illegally entering into and out of the citizen sectors of *Atlas*.

G

The Girus Temple – A *Kai* temple of *Atlantis* located on the island continent of *Og*.

> Of Note: It was the temple where *Skaton-ka* (refer to the list of characters in *The End of the Kai* of the *Dark Legacy* books) was raised and trained.

The Golden Age – The spiritual apex of *Atlantis* under the enlightened reign of *Amilius the Wise*.

Guardians of the Kai – A general term used to refer to both the *High Kai Guardians* and the *Kai-Minor guardians*.

H

The High Kai Chancellor – The position held only by the *High Kai Guardian Elder* who serves the *Oracle King, Queen* as secretary and chief confidant.

The High Kai Council – A council composed of the *Oracle King, Queen*, the *High Kai Guardian Elder*, the *High Kai Guardians*, and the *High Kai Priestesses*. Upon the death of the *Oracle King, Queen* they are vested with the power to appoint a new *Oracle King, Queen* to the *Atlantean Royal Throne*.

The High Kai Elder – Refer to the *High Kai Guardian Elder*.

The High Kai Guardians – There are seven High Kai Guardians, and each is bound to a *High Kai Priestess*. They each lead and protect, with their *High Kai Priestess*, the *Kai Order* to which they are bound.

> See also: *The Atlantean Royal Families*.

The High Kai Guardian Elder – Also referred to as the High Kai Guardian Elder of the Order of Light; the Kai Elder King of the Order of the Kai Guardian guild; the *High Kai Elder*; and the *Kai Elder King*. He serves the *Oracle King, Queen* (who he is bound to) as *High Kai Chancellor*. He also serves the *High Kai Council* (who he is a member of) as its sole protector.

> Of Note: If the High Kai Guardian Elder is in service to an *Oracle Queen* he is first in command of all *Kai guardians*. If the High Kai Guardian Elder is in service to an *Oracle King* he is second-in-command of all *Kai guardians*.

The High Kai Priestesses – There are seven High Kai Priestesses, and each is bound to a *High Kai Guardian*. They each lead and protect, with their *High Kai Guardian*, the *Kai Order* to which they are bound.

> See also: *The Atlantean Royal Families*.

I

Ida – Refer to *The Sea of Ida*.

Ideo-clan(s) – A secret, criminal organization(s) based within the *Ideo sector*.

Ideo ghosts – The non-Atlantean citizens of the *Ideo sector*.

The Ideo sector – The economically decaying, industrial sector of *Atlas* where all non-Atlantean citizens in *Atlas* must reside.

K

Kai – 1. The *life force*: the vital force of nature and of all living things. 2. The religious faith and practices of the *Atlantean Oracle King, Queen* and the *Atlantean Royal Families*. 3. Any and all laymen disciples of the religious faith and practices of the *Atlantean Oracle King, Queen* and the *Atlantean Royal Families*.

Of Note: The word was derived from the *Lemurian* term *Ki*.

See also: *the Law of One*.

The Kai Elder King – Refer to the *High Kai Guardian Elder*.

Kai guardian – A general term used to refer to either a *High Kai Guardian* or a *Kai-Minor guardian*, or both.

Kai line(s) – Referring to one or all eight of the ancestral lines of the *Kai Orders* that a *Kai guardian* or a *Kai priestess* is derived from or adopted into.

The Kai-Minor guardians – There are a total of forty-nine Kai-Minor guardians. They are divided into one of the seven *Kai Orders*, and thus there are seven Kai-Minor guardians for each *Kai Order*. They are each bound to a *Kai-Minor priestess*.

The Kai-Minor priestesses – There are a total of forty-nine Kai-Minor priestesses. They are divided into one of the seven *Kai Orders*, and thus there are seven Kai-Minor priestesses for each *Kai Order*. They are each bound to a *Kai-Minor guardian*.

Kai Order(s) – Also referred to as Order, or *Clan Order*. There are eight Kai Orders: Light, Drakul, Libra, Virgo, Leo, Cancer, Gemini, and Taurus.

Of Note: The Kai Orders of Drakul, Libra, Virgo, Leo, Cancer, Gemini, and Taurus are composed of both *High Kai* and *Kai-Minor* guardians and *High Kai* and *Kai-Minor* priestesses. The *Order of Light* is simply composed of the *Oracle King, Queen* and the *High Kai Guardian Elder*.

See also: *The Atlantean Royal Families*.

Kai priestess – A general term used to refer to either a *High Kai Priestess* or a *Kai-Minor priestess*, or both.

Kai-Ra – Energy shield that only a *Kai priestess* can create while in an intense meditative state.

Kai Royal Highness – Refer to the *Atlantean Oracle Queen*.

Ki – Refer to the list of defined words and terms in *Book I: Trinity* of the *Dark Legacy* books.

The Kingdom of Lemuria – Refer to the list of defined words and terms in *Book I: Trinity* of the *Dark Legacy* books.

Kragita-droid – A colossal, heavy artillery droid.

L

The last days of the Age of Virgo – The last decades of the *Age of Virgo*.

The Law of One – The holy doctrine of the *Kai* faith established by *Amilius the Wise* during the *Golden Age* of *Atlantis*.

The Lemurian Kingdom – Refer to as the *Kingdom of Lemuria*.

The life force – Refer to the list of defined words and terms in *Book I: Trinity* of the *Dark Legacy* books.

M

Maldek – Refer to the list of defined words and terms in *Book V: Time* of the *Dark Legacy* books.

Mount Eve – The hollowed mountain enclosing the *Atlantean Royal Towers*.

Mount Kai – Mountain on the island continent of *Poseidia* that *the Wise* considered to be the birthplace of the *Red race*.

>Of Note: The *Atlantean Royal Throne* was cut and made from this mountain.

The Mountains of Ara – Also referred to as the *Ara Mountains*. It is a chain of mountains surrounding *Atlas*.

The Mountains of Arakara – Also referred to as the *Arakara Mountains*. It is a chain of mountains on the island continent of *Og*.

>Of Note: It was where *Skaton-ka* (refer to the list of characters in *The End of the Kai* of the *Dark Legacy* books) went on his three hundred day retreat and gained the *Enlightenment*.

Musca-technology – Referring to the science and technology of constructing electronic circuits and devices from atomic and subatomic particles.

□

The Ocean of Mu – One of the five great bodies of salt water on planet Earth. It is located in the *East*.

Og – The eastern-most island continent of the three island continents of *Atlantis*.

>See also: *the Second Great Quake of Ara*.

Ophiuchus – The most powerful of the *Ideo-clans* in the Age of Virgo.

The Oracle King, Queen – Refer to *the Atlantean Oracle King, Queen*.

The Order of the Kai Guardian guild – The fellowship to which all Kai guardians belong to, which is led by the *High Kai Guardian Elder*.

The Order of the Kai Priestess guild – The fellowsip to which all Kai priestesses belong to, which is led by the *Atlantean Oracle King, Queen*.

The Order of Light – The fellowship composed of only the *Oracle King, Queen* and the *High Kai Guardian Elder*.

P

Plasma-fire – The discharge of highly ionized gas from a fast-action firearm.

Pleiadia – Refer to the list of defined words and terms in *Book V: Time* of the *Dark Legacy* books.

Pleiadians – Refer to the list of defined words and terms in *Book V: Time* of the *Dark Legacy* books.

Poli-ki-clan(s) – A radical right-wing political group(s) of *Atlantis*.

Poseidia – The western-most island continent of the three island continents of *Atlantis*.

> See also: *the Second Great Quake of Ara.*

Potion-magics – Any of the illegal substances in *Atlantis* that caused addiction, habituation, or drastic changes in consciousness.

R

The Red race – Also referred to as the *Blood race*. It is a term used to describe the human populations of *Atlantis*.

S

The Sea of Ida – Sea in the *Atlantean Ocean* that *Atlas* faces.

The Second Great Quake of Ara – The horrific series of earthquakes that swallowed two of the once five island continents of *Atlantis*.

Seeker Killers – Also referred to as *S.K.'s*. Refer to *Fornax Serpens*.

The Seven Stars of Pleiadia – Refer to the list of defined words and terms in *Book V: Time* of the *Dark Legacy* books.

The Sirian Creator – Refer to the list of defined words and terms in *Book V: Time* of the *Dark Legacy* books.

Sirians – Refer to the list of defined words and terms in *Book V: Time* of the *Dark Legacy* books.

S.K.'s – Also referred to as *Seeker Killers*. Refer to *Fornax Serpens*.

Sky-towers – The tall buildings and towers of the cities of *Atlantis* defined as having more than 150 floors or levels.

Speed tribe(s) – A gang(s) of adolescents within the *Ideo sector* who are often hired by or in league with one or more *Ideo-clans*.

Spheres of Ra – Compact orbs of highly volatile ionized gas that a *Kai priestess* can create instantaneously while in an intense meditative state.

T

The Tower of Light – The *Atlantean Royal Tower* where resides the *Atlantean Oracle King, Queen* and the *High Kai Guardian Elder*.

W

The West – The portion of the world influenced or ruled by the *Atlantean Empire*.

The Winged Creator – Refer to the list of defined words and terms in *Book V: Time* of the *Dark Legacy* books.

The Wise – Refer to *Amilius the Wise*.

DARK LEGACY

BOOK I – TRINITY

CHARACTERS

THE ROYAL CLAN OF UMINOTE

Queen Aikoke – The woman sovereign of the Lemurian Kingdom.

THE IKISHI PRIEST

Shinsei – The village priest of Ikishi who resides in the Kadek Temple.

THE IKISHI ELDERS

Elder Subo – The Chief, and the oldest, of the seven Elders of Ikishi; and a wealthy landowner.

Elder Haru – One of the seven Elders of Ikishi; and a wealthy landowner. Shitsu (see: *Ikishi Villagers*) and Tonono (see: *Ikishi Villagers*) have debts to pay off to him.

Elder Rinton – One of the seven Elders of Ikishi; and a wealthy landowner.

> See also: Rinton-no and Koko-maki under *Ikishi Villagers*.

Elder Sobu-Ta – One of the seven Elders of Ikishi; and a wealthy landowner.

Elder Jime-Ro – One of the seven Elders of Ikishi; and a landowner.

Elder Tobu-Jo – The second youngest of the seven Elders of Ikishi; and a landowner.

Elder Muraka – The youngest of the seven Elders of Ikishi; and a landowner.

THE HOUSE OF KONO

Tomo-Katsu – The deceased father of Kono and Buko.

> See also: *Deceased Ikishi Villagers*.

Kono – A wealthy landowner in Ikishi, and father of Aiko.

Kania – The deceased wife of Kono, and the deceased mother of Aiko. Atlantean soldiers killed her and her brother, Nam (see: *Deceased Ikishi Villagers*).

> See also: *Deceased Ikishi Villagers*.

Aiko – He is the only son of Kono and Kania.

> See also: Niko (see: *The House of Tsuwata*) and Taka (see: *Ikishi Villagers*).

Buko – The younger brother of Kono.

> See also: Shitsu and Tonono under *Ikishi Villagers*.

The House of Tsuwata

Tsuwata – A wealthy landowner; and the elder brother of Rakima (see: *The House of Rakima*).

Niko – The son of Tsuwata. He is one of Aiko's (see: *The House of Kono*) friends.

> See also: Taka under *Ikishi Villagers*.

The House of Rakima

Rakima – A well respected fisherman and farmer in Ikishi.

> See also: *The House of Tsuwata*.

Ruka – The wife of Rakima.

> See also: Mamoto under *Ikishi Villagers*.

Kira – She is the only daughter of Rakima and Ruka. She is Kieko's (see: *The House of Nishiaka*) closest friend.

> See also: Isao under *Ikishi Villagers*.

THE HOUSE OF REON

Reon – A poor farmer; he left Ikishi, with his wife Rika, before his daughter, Madonai, married Nishiaka.

> See also: *The House of Nishiaka.*

Rika – The wife of Reon and the mother of Madonai. She forced her husband, Reon, to leave Ikishi with her before their daughter, Madonai, married Nishiaka.

> See also: *The House of Nishiaka.*

Reon-no – The deceased son of Reon and Rika, and the deceased brother of Madonai.

> See also: *The House of Nishiaka* and *Deceased Ikishi Villagers.*

THE HOUSE OF NISHIAKA

Nishiaka – The only man of the Red race to have lived in Ikishi. He married Madonai and is Kieko's father. He is believed to be dead.

Madonai – The mother of Kieko. She married Nishiaka without the approval of her mother, Rika (see: *The House of Reon*).

Kieko – He is the only son of Nishiaka and Madonai.

IKISHI VILLAGERS

Old farmer Toasu – The only man of Ikishi who, in his youth, had traveled far beyond the western borders of Lemuria.

Jomana – The dog of old farmer Toasu.

Sekihi –The blacksmith of Ikishi.

Rinton-no – He is the eldest son of Elder Rinton (see: *The Ikishi Elders*) and father of Koko-maki. He is also a friend of Kono (see: *The House of Kono*).

Koko-maki – She is the only daughter of Rinton-no.

Kesake – He is the owner of a popular tavern in Ikishi.

Kesake-no – He is the married son of Kesake.

Hirotake – A shy fisherman, farmer, and hired laborer of Ikishi. He has a close friendship with Watanoro (see: *Ikishi Villagers*) and Raki-ka (see: *Ikishi Villagers*). He is married to Tomoko.

Tomoko – The wife of Hirotake.

Watanoro – A modest fisherman, farmer, and hired laborer of Ikishi. He has a close friendship with Hirotake (see: *Ikishi Villagers*) and Raki-ka (see: *Ikishi Villagers*).

Raki-ka – A humorous fisherman, farmer, and hired laborer of Ikishi. He has a reputation for flirting with women. He has a close friendship with Hirotake (see: *Ikishi Villagers*) and Watanoro (see: *Ikishi Villagers*).

Shitsu – A troubled fisherman, farmer, and hired laborer of Ikishi. He has a friendship with Buko (see: *The House of Kono*) and Tonono (see: *Ikishi Villagers*).

Tonono – A simple-minded fisherman, farmer, and hired laborer of Ikishi. He has a friendship with Buko (see: *The House of Kono*) and Shitsu (see: *Ikishi Villagers*).

Mamoto – He was the young man that Ruka (see: *The House of Rakima*) had loved in her adolescence before marrying Rakima (see: *The House of Rakima*).

Isao – The three-year-old cousin of Kira (see: *The House of Rakima*).

Taka – A friend of Aiko (see: *The House of Kono*) and Niko (see: *The House of Tsuwata*). He is slightly overweight.

Deceased Ikishi Villagers

Tomo-Katsu – The deceased father of Kono and Buko.

> See also: *The House of Kono*.

Kania – The deceased wife of Kono, and the deceased mother of Aiko. Atlantean soldiers killed her and her brother, Nam (see: *Deceased Ikishi Villagers*).

> See also: *The House of Kono*.

Nam – The brother of Kania. Atlantean soldiers killed him and his sister, Kania (see: *Deceased Ikishi Villagers*).

> See also: *The House of Kono*.

Reon-no – The deceased younger brother of Madonai.

> See also: *The House of Reon*.

Historical Characters

King Kanda – The Lemurian king whom Kurai IV corrupted.

> See also: Kurai IV under *Historical Characters*.

Kurai IV – The dark warlord who violently tried to unite the northern islands of Lemuria.

Quin-Zu – Founder of the Lemurian faith.

Please note: The Houses and characters are presented and organized according to the traditional rules of Lemurian social hierarchy.

PART I

CHAPTER I

It was a beautiful spring morning. The ocean winds blew gently against the leaves of an old tree that stood near a high ocean cliff. A seagull, flying away from the rising sun, flew right over the old tree. She, the seagull, was searching for something. There was a strong gust of wind and she glided until a long stretch of beach appeared far down below her; she had just flown past the sharp edge of a towering mountain wall. Beside the sea she could see scores of thatched huts cluttered around a circular plain, and from the western and northern edges of this village she saw flooded rice fields and newly plowed vegetable fields, both irrigated and not irrigated, leading up to a forested valley. And at the far end of the beach she saw a second mountain wall. She was relieved. She had finally arrived. She descended searching for someone.

A man emerged from his thatched hut and sniffed the air; he could smell the lingering scent of the night rains. He looked at the sky and felt the faint chill of winter saying its last goodbye. He clapped his hands three times, kneeled, placed his hands on the ground, and bowed his head until it touched the ground. He prayed to the goddesses of the sea for he was a fisherman of Ikishi. When he was done he grabbed the spear that he had stabbed into the earth the night before and walked to the beach. Along the way he saw the pink buds of the cherry trees beginning to bloom. *Hmmm*, he thought, *they are blooming a bit early this year.*

When he arrived at the beach he stopped and looked out to where the sea met the sky before clapping his hands, kneeling, and bowing his head to the ground again. He prayed to the gods of the winds. When he was done he stood up and saw his small sailboat at the end of a long pier made of wooden planks and bamboo stems. He walked to the pier, and he smiled when he saw a familiar seagull circling above him. "There you are, old friend. Come looking for food to feed your young?" He stepped up onto the pier, walked to his boat, stood before his boat with his hands held together before his heart and whispered a few words. He then stepped into his boat, untied the rope that held it to the pier, and shoved off.

He set his sail, which was heavily marked by long curving lines of his own poor stitch work, and relaxed as he looked back and saw his young son dart across the beach waving at him. He waved back and smiled and thought of how proud he was of his little friend. When he had sailed safely past a reef of jagged rocks he prepared his traps and threw them into the ocean. He then lay in his boat and waited as the morning sun began to shine upon him.

When the sun had risen high into the morning sky he awoke and found the seagull that he had seen earlier sitting patiently within his boat. He rubbed his eyes and said, "Let's see if I have something for you." He sat up and pulled in one of his traps. "Looks like I've got nothing. But, anyway, you wouldn't like a crab now would you? Let's see what I can do." He grabbed one of his nets and threw it out into the sea. "I have yet to wake," he yawned. He yanked the rope that was attached to the net and pulled it back in. The net lay in his boat and both he and the seagull were pleased to find a few lively fish squiggling within it. "Now I have something for you," he said with pride. "The gods are looking favorably on me today, now wouldn't you say?" The seagull agreed by flapping her wings. He picked out a fish from the net and asked, "Are you ready?" to the seagull. She replied again with flapping wings. He threw the fish high into the sky and the seagull flew up and caught it with her beak. "There you go," he commended as he watched the bird fly away to feed her young.

By midafternoon the seagull had returned to Ikishi. She stood on a high tree branch watching the rush of activity among the villagers who were preparing for the spring festival. Women ran to and from the marketplace trading and bargaining for the ingredients they needed to bake their cakes while old men debated over whose cows were to be sacrificed; children could be heard in the distance singing with glee: *One cow to feed the gods, a second to feed our forebears, and a third to be eaten by the adulty-dult men . . .*

The air was cool and the sky bright blue. The Ikishi villagers savored days like these because they were so few in the year. It was the seventeenth day of the third month of the year forty-three, of the reign of Aikoke, in the island region of Kadek, on the Island of Kadek, in the Kingdom of Lemuria.

The villagers of Ikishi pursued their doings and undoings with rarely a word from the outside world. They revered their Queen, although none had ever seen or been affected by her royal decisions. Nonetheless they all adored her, their land, and their ancient ways.

It was said by those in the West that the people of Lemuria were a primitive race whose technology and beliefs had not advanced for millennia upon millennia. Of course, such opinions of the *Yellow* race–the *Sun* race–were based not upon understandings but upon ignorance, propaganda, and fear. It served the *Blood* race– the *Red* race–to diffuse such misunderstandings of the Yellow for the more primitive they made them appear the easier it became for their minds and hearts to conquer them in the name of their Atlantean Empire.

Regardless of the thoughts and opinions of the West the people of Kadek carried out their ways and lives. They were a people dedicated to the sea for it was their "breadbasket," although they had never called it that for none among them, except for one, had ever seen or tasted a loaf.

Nishiaka, the western man of the Red race that had come to them some twenty odd years ago, had named their sea their "breadbasket." He attempted to bake them a loaf, but failed continuously, and in defeat he explained that bread was to his people as fish was to the people of Lemuria. Old farmer Toasu, the only man of the village who, in his youth, had traveled far beyond the borders of Lemuria, later corrected this explanation. The old farmer explained that bread was to the people of the West as rice was to the people of the East. No villager paid any heed to the old farmer unfortunately. And so the old man kept to himself by plowing his fields and rarely visiting the sea or those who took bounty from it.

The sea bore nearly all that was to be eaten by the villagers. Fish was eaten raw, baked, or dried, and with rice or in soup. After fish came squid, crab, and the many seaweed plants. They also ate vegetables, fruits, and berries from their gardens and from the wild of their lands and mountains.

For the many holidays that they celebrated they slew and ate poultry and swine, and for the days that marked the birth of a new season three cows were sacrificed. It was a great honor for the farmer whose cows were chosen to be slaughtered for the gods would grant him many good fortunes, and in Kadek there was no greater a cow farmer than Kono; his cows were rich in soft and sweet fat. Season after season Kono's cows were chosen, and in return he received many riches from the Elders and the villagers of Ikishi. Kono had the favor of many men for he satisfied their lust for cow's meat. Had it not been for the rules of Lemurian men so many centuries ago that forbade the consumption of meat, except on the days that marked the seasons, Kono would not have enjoyed the wealth he possessed and used to spoil his only son, Aiko.

Aiko had no memory of his mother, Kania, who had been raped and killed by Atlantean soldiers when he was an infant. She was on a four-day journey to Erima, her home village, to pay her last respects to her dying father when Atlantean men seized her and her older brother, Nam. Weeks later their bodies, severely mutilated, were found by Kono and his search party; Kono's hate was deep for the Red race, and deep had he sown it into the heart of his son.

Aiko was a very masculine and handsome boy. Many girls adored him from a distance. He was a natural athlete in the sport of Teshi-do, and he was clever in devising traps for small creatures. His closest friends were the plump but strong Taka, and the skinny but quick-mouth Niko. The three of them would spend their spare time torturing Kieko, the boy of mixed blood.

Kieko was the only boy, for several days in all directions, mothered by a Lemurian and fathered by an Atlantean. And although his mother, Madonai, along with the young girls of his village delighted in his exotic features, he found little comfort in his physical differences. He was a constant reminder to the elder people of his village of the past abuses waged against them by the Atlanteans, and for that he was treated like an unwanted disease.

It was late afternoon. The seagull, thinking of her young ones, took off with the blowing winds and flew up the valley that cradled Ikishi. In the distance she saw a boy running through a farm field. She flapped her wings more and flew straight over the boy.

Running as fast as he could through old farmer Toasu's vegetable farm Kieko looked up and saw the seagull. *I wish I were like her*, he wished. Fast behind him were Aiko, Niko, and Taka.

"I'm going to get you, Akai!" Aiko shouted as he ran, reached, grabbed Kieko's long black hair, "Got you!" and pulled. Kieko tumbled to the ground. Aiko dropped to his knees and slammed his fist into Kieko's face. Niko kicked Kieko in the head. "Did I say you could cross through here?" Aiko demanded as he pounded Kieko. "I can't hear you, Akai!"

"To hell with you!" Kieko shouted trying to fight back, but both Niko and Taka began kicking him in the ribs and legs.

"What did you say, Akai?" Aiko threw a hard punch into Kieko's jaw releasing streams of blood from his lips. "What did you say?" he continued punching until blood splashed up onto his own fists and arms. He stopped and looked at his hands, "I am stained by Akai blood!" He spat on Kieko. "Worthless Akai! Be gone from here!" he threw another fist into Kieko's jaw launching a spray of blood onto Taka's face.

Taka jumped back, "That's enough—leave the Akai alone."

Aiko shot his hateful eyes at Taka; "It'll be enough when he leaves Ikishi!"

Kieko reached and grabbed a handful of loose topsoil and slammed it into Aiko's face, rubbing it hard into his nose and mouth. Aiko coughed violently trying to spit out the dirt. Kieko kicked him in the groin.

Aiko rolled onto ground cupping his bruised manhood moaning, "Get him, you fat cow!" Taka advanced, but his heavy momentum betrayed him when Kieko sprang up from the ground and tripped him into a small pile of rotten cabbages.

"Come on, filthy Akai! Fight me!" Aiko, now standing, roared. "You're nothing like your Kai father." He threw a punch, but Kieko blocked it. The next thing he knew Kieko had grabbed his head and shoved him down to the ground.

"What did you say about my father?" Kieko demanded before being knocked to the ground by Niko who had struck him across the back of his head with a thick tree branch.

Aiko got up and wiped his lips. "Your father was a coward. Run, run he did to the far corners of the Mother," he pinned Kieko down by sitting over him and began pummeling his fists into his face. Kieko, slightly unconscious, could not fight back. Aiko finally stopped, stood up, and jumped onto Kieko's stomach causing him to heave an airless cough.

"Stop it before you kill him!" Taka demanded.

Niko turned to Taka and sneered, "What's the matter, Taka? Can't kill an Akai?"

Aiko reasoned, "If the Akai can kill my mother then I can kill the Akai!"

"Wicked devils!" Niko cursed. Aiko looked up and saw Shinsei, the village priest, approaching. Niko sprang into a run, as did Aiko and Taka.

Shinsei, quickening his steps to reach Kieko, laughed lightly to himself when he saw Taka, who was trailing far behind Aiko and Niko, bobbing up and down as he ran like an apple in the sea. When he reached Kieko he kneeled before him and took his right wrist into his coarse hand, "Another fight, my young friend?"

The wind blew causing the priest's dark brown, raw silk robes to flap gently against Kieko who mouthed the word, "Shinsei."

"Quiet, my young friend. Do not try to speak, just rest." Shinsei placed his index and middle fingers over Kieko's wrist and closed his eyes; his eyes moved rapidly beneath his eyelids like dogs wrestling beneath a wrinkled blanket. He opened his eyes, "Young Kieko?"

Kieko was fighting back his welling tears. Shinsei wanted to comfort him by placing his hand over his forehead, but Kieko rejected the gesture by shoving the old hand away, "Leave me alone."

"You are always alone, young friend. You are no different than your father."

Kieko stifled his tears; he did not want to appear weak before the spirit of his father.

"I see I have your attention."

Kieko waited.

The priest continued, "I also know that the beautiful Kira can hold your attention as well"–Kieko gave a confused look–"She is quite unique, wouldn't you say? She possesses a rare and simple beauty. She reminds me much of your mother."

Kieko was angry; he did not appreciate what Shinsei had done to get his attention. Bitterly he said, "Don't talk to me about her."

Shinsei was silent for a moment. He then tried to apologize, "I am your friend–"

"I'll consider you a friend when you begin teaching me how to fight against three. I hate Aiko and his stupid friends."

"I'll never teach you if that is your attitude toward him and them."

"What? Do you expect me to love him like a brother?"

"Yes," Shinsei stated as if the answer was quite obvious. He then stood up and began walking toward the sea while running his fingers through his long white beard. He stopped to look back, and asked, "Young Kieko, are you coming?"

Kieko ignored his throbbing pain, gathered his remaining strength, stood up, and limped over to Shinsei.

As they walked Kieko thought of his father, Nishiaka. He had very little memory of him; he had left Ikishi when he was two years old. His mother had explained that his father's journey back to his homeland in the West was prompted by the news of a death in his family. Many in the village speculated that a journey to the far lands in the West would take years to reach by foot; and after ten years of waiting for his return Madonai and Kieko finally took council with Shinsei.

Madonai asked Shinsei to visit the spirit world, and it was there that the priest discovered that Nishiaka was dead. When Madonai asked how he had died Shinsei said nothing more than that his spirit was at peace and watching over Kieko.

Kieko did not want to accept Shinsei's words; he did not want to end his hope that his father would one day return. But, gradually, his dreams of the day when his father and he would sail the open sea faded into the endless nights of his mother's cries.

In the distance Shinsei saw smoke rising from the thatched homes of Ikishi. He could smell the faint scent of grilled fish and looked over to Kieko who was keeping pace and said, "You take after your father. You heal quickly."

Kieko said nothing, but he wanted to ask a question.

"I can see that you would like to ask something, young Kieko."

Kieko was not surprised to hear the priest's keen observation; he was a holy man, a man devoted to the spirit, and as a result he was very perceptive of the feelings and thoughts of those around him. He looked up and asked, "Was my father a Kai guardian?"

"What causes you to ask such a question?"

"There are rumors that I hear, whispers in the forbidden dark, when I sleep—"

"Enough! Do not mock me with your renditions in the high tongue. No time for mystic foolishness. Who told you?"

"Aiko. He says it's true. He says that my father left because he was being hunted."

"When did he tell you this?"

"A day ago."

"Aiko is always a thorn in my side. His father especially . . ."

"Is it true?"

Shinsei looked at Kieko choosing his words carefully, "In another land very far from here he was."

"Atlantis," Kieko said with a disapproving hiss as his thoughts bent around the stories he had heard of the western empire from the elder men of his village.

"When I was your age Atlantis was not what you now understand it to be."

"I hate Atlantis."

"Quick to anger, young Kieko. It can be your ally, or so you may think. It may win your wars, but it will never defeat your fears. And fear is what cradles your unhappiness."

"What do you expect from me? I have no friends here. I'm hated here because I'm Red. You want me to be happy? You want me to pretend that I'm happy?"

"No. That is good that you acknowledge that you are unhappy, but do not use your anger to hide your unhappiness. Be angry, be unhappy, be who you are. Don't hide it. Those feelings, like everything in this world, come and go. Be angry now, and let it go when it is done.

"All of your emotions are beautiful, powerful, just like the winds, the rains, the sun, and the mighty oceans. When the Sky is happy he shines a light upon the face of the Mother. When the Sky is angry he becomes a rage that feeds the Mother strong rains. Both the light of the sun and the rage of a storm feed and nourish the soul of the Mother, neither is good nor bad. It simply is, just as you are. Do not use one emotion to hide another. Do not hide, that is simply what I ask of you."

"I don't want to hide," Kieko acknowledged. "I want to face my enemy. Teach me Ki sword."

Disappointed with Kieko's request the priest said, "If you can answer this koan—your koan—with a clear mind, I will begin teaching you. Name the face of your enemy."

"Aiko," Kieko responded sarcastically.

"Come and find me when you have found an answer that is closer to your heart." He turned away and continued toward the village leaving Kieko behind to contemplate the koan.

It was a cool night and Kieko, with a face washed clean by fresh waters, approached his hut that sat along a white path made from countless crushed seashells. When he entered his home he stared at the dirt floor and his sandaled feet with exhausted eyes. His mother was asleep, but she had left his dinner ready in a ceramic pot near the hearth. He walked over to the hearth and warmed his hands before lifting the lid to peer into the pot.

"Kieko?" Madonai said with a sleepy voice.

Surprised, Kieko dropped the lid back onto the pot, "You scared me, mom."

"Why should you be scared?"

"I don't know. You should go back to sleep, you look tired. We'll speak in the morning."

Madonai, too tired to see the cuts on her son's face or the markings of blood on his clothes, fell back to sleep. Kieko walked to her futon and placed a thick wool blanket over her; his grandmother, Rika, had made the blanket when his mother was young. It was an old and ragged thing now.

Rika had never trusted outsiders and as a result she had forbidden her daughter from marrying Nishiaka, but young love knows no boundaries, it knows no scars; nothing could have stopped Madonai from marrying the man she loved. Angered that her only daughter had refused to obey her words Rika decided to leave Ikishi with her frail husband, Reon.

On the night of their departure Reon snuck away from his wife and gave to his daughter the wool blanket. He was a broken man, crippled in a war he had fought when he was young, and saddened by the death of his only son, Reon-no.

The blanket was the only possession Madonai had to warmly remind herself of her father, but it also reminded her of her mother's cruelness. The blanket brought up mixed emotions; the mother she despised had made the blanket, but the father she loved gave it to her as a wedding gift.

Kieko knew that she wanted to rid herself of the blanket by burning it, to, in some symbolic way destroy her mother's fiendishness. But, destroying the blanket would cut her only link to her father. A frustrating emotional mess the blanket was: a blanket of coarse wool to prick the skin and ignite a rash, but a refuge of warmth during cold winter nights. The blanket did not remind Kieko of his grandmother or grandfather. But it was a reminder. It reminded him of the sharp and delicate line between love and hate.

He had seen too many repeated examples of lovers in his village soon at each other's throats. His grandmother had raised his mother adoringly, but despised her when she fell in love with his father. He did not understand how love could turn so fast against itself. He often wondered if all forms of love decayed into hate. He did not want to hurt others as his grandmother had hurt his mother, as his father had hurt her in his disappearance, in his death. He loved his mother, but he was afraid. Would he one day betray her or would his love always remain constant and true? He did not know.

He walked over to a small wooden chair by the hearth and sat down to stare at the reds and yellows of the firelight dancing with shadows on his mother's face. Deep in his admiration for his mother he forgot about his hunger and soon fell asleep in the chair that his father had built long ago.

The next morning Madonai shook Kieko's body yelling, "Kieko! Kieko! What happened? Damn the heavenly stars! Are you all right?"

"I'm all right!" Kieko barked back.

"Don't speak to me with that voice."

"What would you like? You were screaming and shaking me in my sleep."

"Aiko! I'm going to burn his skin. Look at your clothes! Why did he do this to you?" Her voice was trembling with eyes on the brink of tears.

"I'm a man, mom. Leave Aiko alone. He's my problem, not yours."

"I'm going to talk to Kono about this!"

"No, you're not! You're just going to make it worse for me if you do that."

"Then what in the name of the gods am I supposed to do?"

"Nothing! Don't you understand? You can't protect me anymore."

"You are so ungrateful for all that I have done for you."

"I never asked you to do anything for me!"

"How dare you say such a thing!" she raised her hand as if about to slap him.

He stepped away from his mother. He bowed his head, clenched his teeth, and guarded his heart with his arms. Madonai's body depressed. She now regretted screaming at him. She did not want to become enemies with him, she needed him; he was all she had.

"I'm sorry . . . I'm sorry," she apologized approaching him, but he stepped back trying to appear strong by fighting off his sadness. He was suffering. She could see that he wanted to cry, but that he did not want to do so before her or the spirit of his father. She knew that he wanted a man in their home, a father to look up to. He was pushing his hurt deep into his heart, into a dark place that he would try to forget. She wanted to hold him to allow his tears to flow, but he did not want to be touched by her. She began to cry, "Please . . . come here."

He stepped back again as she approached. He knew that she wanted to hug him and cry with him, but he had had enough. He was a man, or at least trying to be. He did not want to tear like a child anymore.

"Please . . . Kieko . . . come here." She stepped closer and closer until he was trapped against the thatched wall of their hut. He covered his face with his hands. She closed in and tried to hug her son, but he resisted, "Leave me alone . . . leave me alone," until his voice faded into his body that had begun to shake. He collapsed to the floor defeated by his heart and wept.

She held her son and whispered a sweet melody. Moments passed and she eased him with her words, "You're my baby. You will always be my little baby. I held your little body in my arms, your little fingernails and toes . . . my poor baby." She continued holding her son. He wept less and less and soon took deep breaths to calm himself.

"I love you, my little monkey."

"I love you too, mom."

They continued to hold each other. Kieko knew that his mother was finding it difficult to adjust to him as a son who was no longer a boy but a young man seeking to solve his own affairs. Soon thoughts of his father and what Shinsei had said the day before filled him. He opened his mouth to speak, but stopped. He gently pushed his mother away to look into her eyes, "Why did father leave us?"

"You know why he left."

"I know the reason you gave me as to why he left. Now I want the truth."

"Your father was a good man . . . He left to protect us."

"Protect us from what?"

"From his people."

"I know that. I've gathered that, but why?"

"Your father feared that . . . that one day his people would find him. He was afraid that they would find you and hurt you."

"So my father was a Kai guardian."

"Who in the name of Mount Kadek told you that?"

"Aiko."

Madonai, unable to look into her son's eyes, said, "He's a liar."

"Shinsei told me as well. My father was a Kai guardian, a guardian of the Kai, an Atlantean Kai guardian."

Madonai did not speak. She only bowed her head and allowed the silence to fill the space between her and her son.

"Why did my father come to Lemuria? He was a guardian of the Kai. He was a guardian of the Kai in Lemuria? Why was my father here in Ikishi? Why lie to me about him? Am I going to learn everything about my father from Shinsei and Aiko?"

Madonai looked at her son confused. She wanted to stand firm, but she wanted to cry as well. Tears began to well in her eyes, but she held them back when she saw how agitated he was becoming with her. She knew that if she began to cry he would not hold her, but, instead, walk out into the cold spring morning. He was too similar to his father in that way. She could see his anger begin to swirl and mix with his intense desire for knowledge. He wanted answers and would not accept anything less from her until she spoke the truth. She held herself together and said with a faint voice, "You're right . . . I've kept this from you for far too long. Shinsei knows more than I do, he knows more than I can ever tell you about the ways of the Kai. One day, soon, he will give you your koan and you will answer it . . . and you will begin training with him," she paused. Kieko thought to tell her that Shinsei had already given him his koan, but said nothing. She continued, "When the time is right you will learn of your father's past through Shinsei. He will teach you. He will answer your questions."

"I don't understand why you can't tell me?"

"Because I don't know of your father's past. Your father was a good man. He ran from a past that haunted him, and he never shared it with me . . . I remember him waking up in pools of sweat from nightmares. He would wake shaking and I would beg him to open up to me . . . he wouldn't let me help him. He only sought help and council from Shinsei.

"Shinsei was a good friend to your father. Shinsei is the one who knows more than I do about your father . . . your father, the Kai guardian."

"Yes, I know, but Shinsei tells me very little about my father the Kai guardian. He only has stories to tell about my father the fisherman or my father the farmer."

"In time Shinsei will tell you all you want to know about your father."

Kieko was tired of waiting for the day when all would be revealed to him of his father's past. He muttered, "My father was an Akai coward."

She slapped her son across the face and with a finger aimed at his eye she shouted, "Don't you ever speak down to the spirit of your father! I never want to hear that word come from your mouth again!"

Kieko could not speak; he was in shock as he held his hand to his stinging cheek. Blood began to seep through his fingers from his dry scabs.

She looked at her son who refused to look at her and felt guilt and shame wash over her.

Kieko, head bowed, fought the tears that threatened to drown his eyes again and hurried out of his hut.

The sun was beginning to set, and Kieko watched it as he leaned against his mighty Thinking Tree; the tree stood near the edge of a sharp cliff that overlooked the Ocean of Mu. He then recalled his first memory. His mother had insisted that at the age of a year-and-a-half it was not possible for him to remember the time when both his father and her took him to the noble tree. But he remembered the cloudy images of his father and mother, and the grand light that shined upon his Thinking Tree.

His Thinking Tree was wise from the score of years that he had lived, and he was bold. He was bold enough to be the only one of his kind to stand at the edge of a retreating cliff. The thousands of trees that lined the borders of the Great Forest of Ikishi stood far back for they feared the rocky edge that was being eaten away by the majestic ocean waves.

This matter of an approaching death did not concern the Thinking Tree for in return he had the most magnificent view of the setting sun and of the Ocean of Mu. The Thinking Tree saw no grander death than that of falling into union with the deep ocean blue.

Kieko had learned from his mother that his father had spent much time meditating under his Thinking Tree by facing the sun that rose in the far beyond of the eastern horizon. Although he rarely enjoyed or saw any point in zazen–sitting meditation–he would, from time to time, engage in the practice beneath the long branches of the tree in the hope of capturing some essence of his father.

"You must meditate, in silence, by sitting like the Buddha," were the words that repeated in his mind. Shinsei had insisted that he, as a young man that sought to study under him, adopt the regular practice of zazen, but he only pursued the practice in times of convenience, never as a disciplined routine. He remembered one of the old priest's lectures on zazen and how it cleared the mind and relaxed the body, but all that he had gathered from that speech was that zazen was no different than being filled by the peace and quiet of a beautiful ocean view or a dreamless sleep.

On this particular evening he sat under his Thinking Tree, dwarfed by its massive size, and thought about his father as he often did. He dreamed of the grandfathers he had never known and dwelled in the sadness of never having learned the wisdom that came from sitting on the lap of a wise old kin. He had grown envious of the village children who took for granted the teachings passed down to them from their grandfathers. This was not to say that he did not learn the many ways of the world from an ancient heart for before he counted Shinsei a mentor he learned much from his Thinking Tree.

The Thinking Tree had taught him that all rivers run into the oceans, and from the oceans the clouds gathered water, and when it was deemed right the clouds shed rain upon the Mother, and so continued the cycle. He learned of the many great cycles of the world, and discovered that not all cycles were good, and that some cycles had to be changed. He learned that after every storm the sun would shine, and he learned that fire had the power to both destroy and bring new life. He learned that death and life were forever a part of one another and that even in one lifetime he would die a thousand times. The Thinking Tree explained that his former self, of the age six, for example, was forever dead, just as who he was today would be dead and forgotten in even one day's time. From this Kieko understood the lessons Shinsei had taught him regarding impermanence.

Kieko knew that as long as he lived in this world all things would be divided from their oneness into two, and from two into many. He knew that all things were torn apart into far and opposing ends; where there was light there would be shadow, where there was heat there would be cold, where there was love there would be hate; and where there was life there would be death. From this he discovered that the beauty of the world was not in its ability to appear static, but in its ability to flow from one condition into another.

So there before Kieko was the magnificent view that his Thinking Tree had bravely chosen to stand before so many centuries ago. The bright orange horizon had cast itself across the clouds. Seagulls danced across the splendid evening canvas and the ocean winds sang through the leaves and branches of their old friend, the Thinking Tree.

The long grasses bent and moved with the winds and caressed the outstretched hands of a beautifully young, Lemurian girl. She approached Kieko and his courageous tree on a cliff. She walked barefoot over the soft grasses for it pleased her. The sea winds touched and massaged her, and blew her long hair from her face.

Kieko's tree knew her, as did the setting sun. They understood her desire to surprise Kieko and assisted as best they could in her attempt. Unfortunately an abandoned broken branch did not agree with her plan and cracked loudly beneath her foot. Kieko heard the branch, but he did not look back for he knew who was approaching him.

"I've been looking for you," were her soft words.

"I wanted to be left alone today," he said without breaking his gaze from the setting sun.

"You've had the whole day to be alone. I think that's enough." Uninvited, she sat beside Kieko to enjoy the evening scene. "It's beautiful," she whispered so as not to disturb him. He did not respond. She rubbed her arms trying to warm them but shivered. She then moved closer to him to gain some of his warmth.

Alarmed, he moved away; his mind began its talk. It cautioned him to not give in to his heart's innocent want to touch her. He began to shake as his mind battled his heart, giving her, the girl, the impression that he was shaking from the cold winds.

She moved closer; he blushed as his body quivered more. Concerned, she placed her arm around him to ease his trembling body, and as she warmed him she noticed that he did not break his stare of the setting sun.

"Why do you hide?" she asked.

He did not reply.

"Why do you keep everything to yourself? I want to know you, Kieko, but you make it nearly impossible for me."

He continued his silence.

"Speak to me."

Breaking his silence he said, "I'm sorry, Kira."

"Why are you sorry?"

He became nervous and his body began to shake more than it had before. She now knew that he did not shake from the cool winds, but from his uneasiness in being touched by her.

She had grown up with Kieko as if she was his sister in some sense; but they were no longer children, they were young adolescents. During her infant years she watched Madonai's loving hands raise and try to protect Kieko. When she was five-years-old she realized that Kieko did not have any cousins or brothers or sisters and approached him as a playmate; well, at least that is what her mother, Ruka, explained. As the years passed she felt tremendous sympathy for Kieko; he was often treated like an outsider in their village, causing him to be, more often than not, alone. As for the elders in the village they saw little more than his father in him; his father the Red who belonged to an empire that ate away at the peaceful lands and islands of Lemuria. What saddened her most was that Kieko had grown used to the hushing sounds of adults who silenced their foul whispers of him when he passed.

In the years before Kieko befriended Shinsei and old farmer Toasu he had only his mother and Kira to look to for comfort and laughter.

And as he thought of his mother and Kira while staring at the setting sun he felt shame cross his heart for the times he had taken his anger out on them. He needed a father, someone strong who would teach him how to fight and hunt and release the rage that burned beneath his flesh. It was not until the autumn of two years past that he had acquired Shinsei and old farmer Toasu as trusted friends, but they were old men, too old to keep up with him, or so he thought, and all they really offered him were warm cups of tea and story upon story both fiction and not.

Kira's arm rested warmly around Kieko, but he was torn, his heart was content but his mind was in a state of unease. His mind beckoned him to feed the hate he held for his face and eyes, but his heart reminded him of how much his mother adored those aspects of him. *My mother is the only one who loves the differences that sets me apart.* Nothing brought him greater happiness than his mother's love. *How like an angel she is; so beautiful, so much like a rose; and more loving than anyone I have ever known.* He remembered how she would hold him in the night, of how she would pray with him before their modest shrine, of how she comforted him and confided in him. He had only known love through her.

He wished for his mother a better life than what she had known. He wished that justice be served harshly against his grandmother who had shunned and abandoned his mother for loving his father. He wanted so much to wish away the sadness he saw deep in his mother's eyes for he knew that she was alone in the world, and that all she had was him, but he had only brought her pain. He knew that the villagers spoke in dark tones behind her back, that they mocked her; and that he was the source of their malice against her for he was a constant reminder that the Red could one day come and destroy their way of life.

The more he went over these dark thoughts the more he wanted to live his life away, alone. He did not want Kira to experience what his mother went through. *No, that must never be—I will never be the deliverer of suffering to her,* his mind had declared not too long ago. And from that was born the seed of his distrust for his heart. He swore to never reveal his feelings for her in the light of day; he would bury them deep within, *yes.*

Only in the night, when all was still, would he allow his heart to reign over him. He would dream of her and of a place where they could be with no fear of hatred or judgment passed onto them. He would dream of their children-to-be and of becoming a father and a grandfather, but with the light of dawn he would always be reminded that his dream was only that.

In an attempt to convince her, and even himself, he began, "It's hard for me to be open to you Kira. I've always been alone. I'm content to be anywhere by myself. I don't feel a need to be open to anyone."

"What about your mother?"

He paused, "She is the only one. She knows when I'm sad . . . when I'm content. She knows me . . . she knows me, but still there are things that I do not tell her."

"Kieko, I want to know you. I . . ." she wanted to say more, express more, but her thoughts coupled with the way he looked into her eyes caused her to blush with rosy cheeks of embarrassment. She looked down, "I saw your mother today. She worries so much about you. She told me that Aiko hurt you again."

"I can't wait until Shinsei begins teaching me Ki sword so that I can beat him to dust!"

"If that is your attitude I doubt that Shinsei will ever begin training you. What is the big point, anyway? All you boys ever do is dream about training with Shinsei."

"And all you girls ever do is talk about how beautiful you'll look when it's time for your Hakunus."

She smiled and said with a hint of sarcasm, "You know that the Elders have chosen Kono's fat cows again."

"Great! I'm so happy for him," Kieko replied. "I hope they all choke on his meat."

"No, you don't," she said. "Are you planning to stay up here all night?"

"No, I've just got to think about some things."

"You think too much. What is so important that you had to spend the whole day thinking about it? I'm sure that you've been thinking so much that you haven't eaten a thing today."

She was right. He hadn't eaten anything. His stomach then growled.

From within her garments she produced a small leather satchel. Kieko recognized it; it was a gift given to her from her grandmother. It was a little bag, worn down by years of use and the natural elements, such as rain and the salt waters of the sea, but ardently did it protect its contents from all the muddle of the outside world. Her soft white hand reached into the satchel, and his eyes filled with curiosity. She pulled out a small cotton bag made of a fabric with a loose open weave. She reached into the bag and revealed what appeared to be a small ball wrapped in moist plant leaves, "This is for you."

He recognized the gift as a rice ball; it was the loving habit of Kira's mother to bestow her daughter with treats of food both bitter and sweet. He bowed his head, gently took the rice ball from her delicate hand, untied the coarse cotton strings that held the leaves to the rice ball, peeled the leaves away, and smiled when he noticed the hardened edges of the rice ball.

She felt a wave of heat brush over her like a warm summer wind; she was lifted by Kieko's smile, a small sign of his gratitude.

To not taint the rice ball with his dirty fingers he used the leaves to hold it and then broke it in two. He offered Kira the larger half.

"No, that is too big. You take it, please."

Kieko did not withdraw the half that he was offering her. He insisted that she take it, "Here, it's yours."

"I'm fine. I'm not that hungry, really."

Growing impatient he said, "If you don't take it I won't talk to you anymore."

Kira took the piece of rice half-smiling.

"I knew that would work," he said with a hint of laughter.

She teasingly punched his arm with a bright smile.

"There it is!" he said with joy.

"What?" she asked confused.

"Your smile. I love that smile."

Blushing she said, "You really are a mysterious one, Kieko. One moment you try to be as cold as ice, then the next moment you melt it all away with words so sweet."

He blushed and tried to hide his flushed face by turning his head from left to right before finally bowing his head to eat his food.

Kira's smile faded. She knew that she could uncover no more of Kieko's sentiments. He was guarding them now; to pry a bit would only anger him, like poking a stick into a beehive. So she settled and did as Kieko did, she ate her small meal while listening to the sound of his tongue softening his food with the wet of his mouth.

When they had finished she asked, "So, what thoughts were so important that you almost gave up food to sit up here all day?"

Kieko was caught off guard by her question. He was still in the midst of trying to savor the remaining bits of rice in his mouth. He repeated the question in his mind and thought for a moment.

"I'm just like my father."

"What?"

He looked down to the blades of grass all around him. He placed his hands over them; he often likened grass to fur, or at least thought of grass as the fur of the Mother. The winds blew and the sun couched into the now rose horizon.

"My father kept secrets from my mother. He hid part of himself from her—I wish I knew him. All I know of him are the stories I hear."

"One day, Kieko, you will be a father, and one day you will be a grandfather. Your children will adore you. You will give them what you never had as a child."

"You know that Shinsei will begin training me soon, as soon as I answer his koan."

Kira was taken aback by Kieko's sudden change of topic. She felt hurt, even insulted that Kieko had not been listening to her, but as she repeated his words in her mind she realized that he was putting up his defenses again; she was getting too close. Swift of mind she asked with a joyful curiosity, "What is the koan?"

"I must name the face of my enemy."

"Let me guess . . . Aiko," the two began to tickle with laughter.

He smiled at her, a sign of his praise, and she accepted with the wink of an eye.

As Kira had known Kieko to do from time to time, he began reciting one of the many legends that he had learned from Shinsei:

"There was a monk who sought the great enlightenment on the Kadek Mountain many centuries ago. He bathed in cold stream waters and ate pine needles for 100 days. He sat in zazen during the peak hours of the night and focused his gaze on a star.

"One night great demons and hellish fires danced around him, but he was not afraid. He only gazed at his star. There was only his mind and the star. And he saw his reflection in the star and the star saw its reflection in him. It was then that the monk had become Buddha. The Buddha returned to his village and shared his light. He saw his reflection in the face of everything around him. The Buddha is the dirt, the grass, the tree, the rock, the ocean, the sun, the sky, the birds, the stars, the gods, you, and me.

"There is no dirt there is no grass, no tree, no rock, no ocean, no sun, no sky, no birds, no stars, no gods, no you, and no me. There is no ally. There is no enemy. I am you and you are me. I am not you and you are not me. I am you and you are me. I am not you and you are not me. Ra di ra di ka gi di . . . These are only words. This is only a story."

Kira had heard this story recited on several occasions by Kieko, but to hide her boredom she entertained him by appearing as if she was genuinely interested in what he was saying. She watched him adoringly as he spoke and focused her gaze from his crooked nose to all the small imperfections of his face. When he was done she took his hand, drew him close, and whispered, "You think too much."

He nervously replied, "Not really."

The sun had set leaving the two young souls to listen to the songs of the winds and ocean waves crashing into sharp cliffs. Stars began to appear and all was as at peace.

CHAPTER 11

It had begun to rain in the night. Kira said goodbye to Kieko at the fork in their path, and as she walked away avoiding the collecting pools of raindrops she felt the urge to follow him with her eyes. She could hear his footsteps fading away upon the crushed seashells that lined his path back home. They had not embraced in their goodbye, but she had felt his desire to reach out and hold her, as she so wanted to reach out and hold him. She began to see him in her mind's eye as she walked. His eyes were dark and brown, deep and mysterious like the eyes of a stag that protects an ancient moon forest.

Kira often likened Kieko to a deer; she never spoke of these thoughts to anyone but her mother. She began to dwell on the tale of the deer spirit who protected the hallowed grounds of the Ikishi forest, as told to her by her grandfather and her great uncles when she sat on their laps as a child before a warm hearth.

It was said in the fables of the old tongue that deep within the forest there was an enchanted center, a sacred ground forbidden to mortal man. No one of flesh could ever see or penetrate this center for it was the center of all things, of all life, in the lands of Kadek. It was to where the souls of animals and trees traveled to in the wake of their death to become one with the *Great Spirit* before returning to the Mother through the womb of all things.

It was said that if ever the Ikishi forest was destroyed its sacred center would be lost and all life would cease in the lands of Kadek for the spirits of the animals and the trees would travel far and away in search of new lands of pasture.

In the age before the birth of the Ikishi forest the lands of Kadek had been a terrible wasteland. *Black soot filled the air from the fume column breaths that arose from the mouth of Mount Kadek.* The spirit beast of the mountain had been a seven-headed dragon whose eyes bore red flame into all things.

The dragon had come from the land of the setting sun with a mind bent to destroy the guardian doe of the then lush Kadek land for it despised her and all her precious makings:

> *Cleverly did the dragon beast seduce the guardian spirit with its lies, and swiftly did it slay her in her sleep. And for an age did it, the dragon, live in the heart of Mount Kadek, blackening it with its eyes, spitting fire and scorching the earth into a horrible dark of stone, ash, and smoke.*

Centuries had turned into millenniums and the lands of Kadek were avoided by all life.

Then there came the day when a young boy clad in an armor that shined in a bright, divine light, and armed with the sword of his father's line, entered the black lands of Kadek to challenge the beast of the mountain.

> *The dragon lashed fire and ash upon the boy, but he did not burn.*
>
> *The boy attacked! And easily did he cut the seven heads of the dragon from their long slithering necks, spilling thick streams of blood into the land as if from the cracks of a river dam.*

The sword . . .

> *The boy then poured his water drink from his flacon upon the ground and life returned.*

. . . had given life.

The winds blew the foul air to the west, and the sun shined in a heavenly sky that beckoned the grass to grow and creep up through the charcoal of stone and volcanic ash.

The boy then sheathed his father's sword and gave it to a wandering Ki priest who had followed after his light.

The priest had been the first mortal, in an Age, to enter the once lifeless land. The boy said unto him:

"This sword wields the power of life, but it is an instrument of death. It is the sword of my fathers. It is now the sword of your people. It is a divine instrument forged by the hands of the Gods in the Heavens above. You are now its guardian, its keeper.

"In time a vision will appear to you, and you will find the sacred place where a temple devoted to this sword will be built. Within the walls of this temple will this sword be kept, until it is forgotten."

The boy turned away from the Ki priest and leapt high and far falling straight into the sea. The priest lowered his hand—no longer did he need to shield his eyes from the magnificent light of the boy—and lifted the long sword to marvel at it.

And from the waters that the boy had leapt into a doe emerged approaching the newborn Kadek land eager to graze upon its grasses. *Seeds of life rested in her belly*, but she collapsed and passed on into the light. And as her body faded and decayed her precious seeds grew, *growing into trees they did*, into a new forest. The forest soon called to the animals and birds, and they heeded and nested within her.

The Ki priest befriended the forest and kept hidden from her his sword for the forest feared iron and the means by which it is made. Then, one night, a stag of the forest, glowing in a wonderfully bright, white light, appeared before the priest and led him away from the campfire he had just built. *Deep into the forest did they go, and deep into Mount Kadek did they travel.* When the stag stopped he turned to the priest and gave him a bewitching stare. *Within the dark eyes of the stag the priest saw the sacred sword and its place within the cavern walls of Mount Kadek.*

When the priest awoke from the enchantment he found himself at rest on soft grasses with vines wrapped around his limbs. He asked the winds: *Have I slept for two full moons?* He noticed a handful of white daisies poking through his dirty beard, and when he sat up he looked at his worn garments and found that they were spotted with more daisies. He stood up and strangely recognized his surroundings: *These trees, yes, I know them. No longer are they saplings. Tall, old oak trees are they.* He wandered through the wise trees and walked through fields and fields of daisies until he came upon a small pond. He kneeled at its banks and drank, but stopped when he saw his reflection in its rippling waters. His long hair was as white as snow and his eyes looked as if they had seen all the years of a century. His appearance frightened him, he did not know this aged man that stared back at him through the pond's twinkling surface.

But as the seasons passed into winter the priest grew proud and strong of the wisdom that came with his many years, and he set to work at building the temple for the sacred sword of Kadek.

Decades passed, and as they did mortals began to enter Kadek for *the land was plentiful in rich soil for tilling, fish from the sea, delicious meats from the forest, and sweet fruits and berries from the slopes of Mount Kadek.*

A village was soon raised and named after the forest of Ikishi.

The villagers abided by the holy laws of the Ki priest and paid homage to the forest, the giver of all life, with sacrifices and prayers . . . And often did they sight the mystical stag that strolled along the borders of the forest.

The priest explained to them: "The stag protects the forest, and he leads all those away from her center for it is forbidden that any mortal of flesh and bone may enter it."

Time passed and stories were told to sow reverence into the hearts of the young for their beloved forest. But there came a day when a boy, in an act of defiance, sought the womb of the forest and ventured far into her with the threat of fire and metal. The forest grew angry and called upon the guardian stag to find the boy and lead him astray. The boy saw the stag and followed after him while night approached; he soon panicked for he could not find a way out of the organic labyrinth. In fear the boy cursed the forest and began burning and hacking down at its trees with his torch and iron axe. The earth moved in retort, throwing him to the ground. In anger the boy rose and continued pillaging life from the forest. The land then sounded a roar through the mouth of Mount Kadek. *Red plush stained the clouds that hovered above the lake of flame at the peak of Mount Kadek. Villagers ran and screamed in fright.* An earthquake tore open the lands of Kadek raising towering cliff walls that cleft the sky. When all was done the villagers found that they were within a sharp valley, which would serve as a reminder of the Mother's awesome power over them. And so it was from that day forth that the villagers of Ikishi kept a distance away from the forest, approaching her only to sacrifice and pray.

As for the boy, he lost his torch and axe in the turbulent movements of the earth. He wandered aimlessly for days through the never-ending columns of Ikishi trees to finally starve to his ill-fated end.

Kira, terribly wet from the now pouring rain, neared her home thinking of the dream she had had some nights before. In the dream the stag of the Ikishi forest had approached her.

She was facing the eastern sea near the cliff where Kieko's Thinking Tree stood; and although Kieko was nowhere in sight she felt him, his spirit. The stag emerged from the forest to graze upon the tall grasses that swayed with the winds. He moved cautiously toward her, and as he did she watched him, admiring his strength, his beauty, his silent movements. His brown fur looked so soft to her eyes. She wanted to caress his back with the palm of her hand, to feel his fur beneath her fingers.

The stag was now just within her reach. His head was bowed to the ground. She made two small steps toward him. She extended her arm; her hand was shaking. Her eyes widened as her fingers drew near his head. She could feel his body heat. She could see his snout and his moist tongue soften his black lips. She was afraid, but so eager to touch him.

His head shot up. Startled, she retreated from the deer with her arms crossed over her chest. He did not run. She sighed in relief. He looked at her. She looked at his horns and followed their curves down to his eye. His eye was black and forever deep. Suddenly she was within the eye, somehow falling within it. It was frightful, painful, but peaceful? There was no wind anymore, no sky, no earth, no flame, and no sea. There was only silence.

Abruptly she felt the heavy clay of her body again and the wind pressing against her skin. Her eyes focused. The stag had run away, retreating back into the forest.

Ruka waited eagerly for her daughter to return; she was worried that she might catch a cold from the wet outside. She was pacing around her hut waiting for the water in an iron kettle that was hanging over the hearth to boil while checking to see if the wool blankets she had set by the hearth were warm. She then began to bite her lip as she thought about what her husband had said the night before on their futon.

His words had not been many for he did not care to discuss or wallow in her spiraling afterthoughts. He had said what he had to say and then rolled onto his side leaving his broad back to her. She looked sadly at his back before staring up into the darkness. She heard Kira, asleep, breathing at the other end of their small hut and thought fearfully of how things would change between them when she told her of what her father had explained. She then prayed that they could continue their secret talks of the joys and excitements of young love.

She knew she would have to talk to Kira tonight about her husband's words, but she didn't know how she would begin. *It seemed like only yesterday that my mother had to have this talk with me*, she thought. *How time turns child into parent and parent into grandparent—*

There was a rapid knock at the short door. Ruka jumped in fright. "It's me, mom," Kira said as she entered her home soaked from the cold rains.

Grabbing the warm blankets Ruka immediately placed them around her daughter and began rubbing her arms. "Look at you."

"Yes, mom," Kira said rolling her eyes.

"You're going to catch a cold—or worse!"

"I'll be fine, mom."

"Take off those clothes and sit by the fire."

Kira began untying the knots of her thick cotton dress as her mother went to peer into a pot that was hanging over the hearth.

"How is Kieko?"

"He's fine," she answered with a sigh.

Ruka approached her daughter, held her by the arms, and admired her youth and beauty. She smiled, but it was a sad smile. She could see that her daughter was in love. *It shouldn't be like this. She shouldn't be kept from loving who she pleases.*

"What's wrong, mom?"

"Nothing sweety . . . nothing . . . You are so beautiful," she said with pride.

Kira shied away from her mother's words.

"Youth is so wonderful," she sighed. "I'm beginning to think of Mamoto again."

Kira had heard more than enough of her mother's adolescent stories over the past couple of years. She already knew every fine detail of how her mother had fallen in love with Mamoto, and the hardship of their forced breakup.

Ruka waited for Kira to ask about Mamoto, but she didn't. *That would have been a proper way to begin what I need to tell her*, she thought.

Kira put on her nightgown and collapsed onto the fur rug that was covered with pillows.

"Mom."

"Yes, sweety."

"What do you think about Kieko?"

Ruka's heart sank.

"Mom. Mom, what's wrong?" she asked reading the sudden change in her mother's facial expression.

"Nothing . . . nothing dear."

"Come here and sit," she said patting a pillow.

Ruka sat down beside her daughter.

Kira, unable to hide her excitement, smiled and began, "There is something so unique about him." Ruka nodded. "But he is like a wall. I can see that he wants to reach out, that he wants to hold me, but there is something keeping him from doing so. Do you remember my dream?"

Ruka nodded again with sincere eyes.

"The moment I try to touch him he runs away—will father be home soon?" she asked afraid that he would learn of their love-talk.

Ruka shook her head, "You know your father. He is out feasting and drinking—I'm not looking forward to his farts in the night."

They giggled.

"Men can be so foul," Kira began. "They scratch themselves and dirty themselves, and sweat and bleed, and have rough skin. Sometimes I do not understand why we are attracted to them."

"Men are different . . . they are not women. They are men. They have their own ways as we have our own. That is why you will be celebrating Hakunus, and that is why boys celebrate their fights, or their time with Shinsei, or their hunting retreats into the mountains with their fathers."

"They are nearly impossible to understand. Do you still love father?" Kira asked.

Ruka paused before she answered, "Sometimes, I find it difficult to be with him. Sometimes, he pulls away from me when something is troubling him. Sometimes, he doesn't want to talk when I do. Sometimes, he leaves me with no choices." She looked at Kira and saw that these were not the words that she wanted to hear. She continued with a clever smile, "Sometimes, I feel that he doesn't know how to love me on our futon–"

"Mom!" Kira cried, "I don't want to hear that."

Ruka laughed as Kira shook her head. "To marry a man is to love him, and the art of love," she explained. "That is why we celebrate Hakunus." Kira listened intently. "In the eyes of the villagers you will be seen as a woman, not as a girl, after Hakunus. A woman brings life into the world–just like the Ikishi forest. Men sacrifice and pray before the altars of the forest in respect, admiration, and appreciation of all that the forest has given us. Women," she whispered, "are as sacred as the ocean and the stars. I remember when I was your age. I remember my desire to learn more about the divine art of lovemaking," she said teasingly. "Now that you bleed you are ready to be initiated into this world of womanhood. You are no longer a girl, you are a woman."

"I'm afraid," she confessed.

"Do not be, sweety. There is nothing to fear. In the arms of your husband you will not fear," she instantly regretted what she had just said.

"Mom."

"Your aunts and I have been preparing."

"Mom. Do you think–"

"The full moon is only three nights away," she said over her daughter's words.

"Mom?"

"Soon you will be a woman in the eyes of all the villagers–"

"Mom!"

"Yes, yes. I'm sorry. What is it?"

"Do you think Kieko will ever ask me to be his wife?"

Ruka was silent.

"Mom. What's wrong? What is it?"

"It's too early for you to think of such things."

"But, you just said that I am a woman."

"Yes, yes, I know, but there is simply no reason to be thinking of marriage. You are still young. You will look so beautiful for Hakunus."

Kira looked at the hearth watching the red embers float up toward the small opening in the roof of their hut and said with faint words, "I have no say as to who I am to marry . . ."

"You do not need to worry of such things," Ruka tried to assure her daughter.

"What does that mean?"

"Hakunus—that is all you need to worry about for now."

"I've heard my uncles talk!" she shouted abruptly. "They are already talking about who I should marry."

"They are only looking out for you."

"I have no say. Why!" she cried out.

"Because you would be the first in our family if you did!" Ruka quickly covered her mouth with her hand.

Kira looked down and crossed her arms over her chest. Tears began to well in her eyes.

"Kira," she pleaded, "listen to me. It was the same for me as it was for all the women in our family." She reached out and held her daughter's arms. "We have all gone through what you are going through. We were all in love with someone other than who we were to marry." Kira began to weep. "I didn't want to marry your father. He didn't want to marry me. But it happened. And here we are. And I love your father, and he loves me. Please, trust us. Trust our judgment."

"No! I will n-not," she stuttered trying to fight off the tears.

"Kira, I know how you feel about Kieko," she said as she rubbed her daughter's arms. "You have always been a kind friend to him. It's only natural that you find yourself attracted to him. You are changing. Your body is changing. He is changing. But love is blind. You can not see why he is not right for you."

"Do you believe that?" she spat out. "Do you think he is n-not right for me?"

Ruka took her daughter into her arms. "Kira, your father and I love you and worry about you."

"You ha-ave spoken to father about Kieko?" she asked resisting her mother's hold.

"He spoke to me about him," she corrected. Kira was not convinced. "He knows you. He knows that your feelings for Kieko have grown."

"He kn-nows . . . he kn-nows . . ." she cried feeling embarrassed.

Ruka hugged her daughter. "We don't want you to suffer. There are those in our village who will not tolerate any hugging or kissing between you and Kieko."

"That's not fair!" Kira contested in her mother's arms. "I hate them. Why are they so cruel? Mado-n-nai is a good woman, and Kieko is k-kind."

"It doesn't matter. Too many here have lost loved ones to the Red. You know your father lost his father to them."

"But he does not hate the Red race."

"Your father does not trust them. He did not care for Kieko's father. But he is wise to see that Kieko was raised as a Lemurian.

"Kira, your father and I do not want you to suffer. Soon— I'm sure—Kieko will be with Shinsei. You will not see him for a time. Please, be open to the possibility that you may find another."

"I don't want another. I love Kieko," she said as she trailed off into tears again. "Why then . . . why did you encourage my feelings for him? Why . . . why are you n-now telling me to find another?"

Ruka held her daughter tightly, rocking her like an infant. "I'm so sorry, Kira. I love you so much. I love you so, so much. I want to be your friend–"

"You are not my friend! You d-didn't fight against what father had to say."

"I'm so sorry. Please, I'm so sorry. Your father and I love you. He worries about you. He knows what is best for you."

Kira wanted to openly curse her father, but she didn't have the strength for another argument. She decided to stay quiet and lay in her mother's arms as she wept.

The two sat together listening to the crackles of the burning wood. Time passed, and as it did Ruka hushed and hummed sweet melodies into her daughter's ears calming her into the quiet of the night.

Kira was beginning to drift away into her dreams, but Ruka woke her with warm words, "Are you hungry, sweety?" Kira nodded; her eyes, drowsy, were red from the exhaustion of tears. Ruka hugged her daughter and stood up to finish preparing her soup and tea. The patter of rain against their thatched roof and the collecting puddles outside soothed Kira as she sat alone on the rug. She watched her mother sip the hot watery contents of the pot from a ladle. She then reached and pulled a wool blanket over her head, and snuggled into it to soon fall asleep.

When Ruka had finished cooking she knelt beside her daughter with a cup of tea and whispered, "Kira, wake up." Kira awoke and sniffed the air scented with mint tea leaves. She looked sadly at the ceramic cup. She sat up and lifted the cup from her mother's hands and sipped the hot tea.

"Be careful," Ruka warned. "Drink it slow. It's unusually cold outside. It feels as if the cold breath of autumn is upon us."

"The heart of winter is not so far behind us," Kira said correcting her mother's observations of the night air.

"Drink your tea. I'm going to get your soup," Ruka said when her husband, Rakima, stumbled into their hut. She looked at her husband who was drenched from the wet outside and commented, "You're a mess."

"Well, of course. It's raining, is it not?"

Ruka greeted her husband who smelled of garlic and beer by kissing him on the scar that traversed his left blind eye and said with distaste, "You're drunk."

"Leave me be, woman. I'm a man, am I not? I do as I please." He then slapped his wife on her behind with a wide grin. Ruka looked at her daughter with a face that read: *Do you believe that I am married to this beast?* Kira let out a short laugh.

"What are you laughing at?" Rakima demanded as he scratched his thick beard. Kira bowed her head, she was now too angry to look at her father. "Women," Rakima shook his head, "I do not understand the lot of you." He started to undress himself in clumsy, drunken motions.

Shocked, Ruka hollered, "What are you doing?"

"What?" he asked confused.

"Your daughter!" she exclaimed with waving arms.

"Tell her not to look then. This is my house!" Rakima continued to strip until he was naked. Kira turned away in disgust. She then heard a thump, turned her head, and saw that her father had collapsed to the ground.

"Don't worry," Ruka assured her daughter. "Your father is drunk." Kira gave a look of complete apathy to her mother. "He passed out. First time I've seen him fall straight on his face in fifteen years." Rakima abruptly mumbled and flipped himself over revealing his manhood. Kira cringed, shutting her eyes, covering them with her hands. Ruka grabbed a blanket and threw it over her husband. "Oh, the joys of marriage," she said with a sigh. "Never marry, Kira, unless you want to care for a man-sized child."

Kira did not reply.

"Have some soup. It's getting late. You need to rest."

Kira sat closer to the hearth. Ruka poured soup into a ceramic bowl and served it to her daughter. She then poured herself a bowl and the two drank their evening meal in silence.

After finishing their soup Ruka took her daughter's bowl and cup and cleaned them. Kira began getting ready to go to sleep. When Ruka was done she looked and found her daughter already asleep. One by one she blew out the candles of their home and kissed her daughter on her forehead before whispering a short prayer in the old tongue, "May the three gods guide you. And may you be so lucky as to pass into the light in the arms of the man you love."

The crickets sounded and the night winds blew. The moon shined her silver light upon the sea and land and enchanted a stag that looked up to her crescent shape from a high sea Ikishi cliff.

CHAPTER III

The spring festival took place on the twenty-first day of the third month of the year forty-three, of the reign of Aikoke. Kieko did not care for such festivals; men drank to be drunk, children stuffed their faces with sweets and berries, and women gossiped their talk. But, there was one event he did care for, the Teshi-do tournament held to honor the masculine spirit of the young men of Ikishi.

It was in the summer festival of last year when both Kieko and Aiko competed in the tournament for the first time. They were the youngest two boys of the sixteen that competed. Although Kieko did display some promise in the combative art he was thrown out of the tournament ring in the first round. Aiko, on the other hand, surprisingly defeated all of his opponents and won the title of Teshi-do Ko-Tenso. In the weeks that followed Aiko, Niko, and Taka, along with a few other Ikishi children, taunted Kieko about his embarrassing defeat. Kieko then promised himself, *I will make Aiko eat his words—I will face him and beat him in the autumn tournament.* He began training every night beneath his Thinking Tree. The autumn festival arrived and he advanced to the second round, but was defeated again. Aiko ultimately won the tournament, and soon after he launched a new wave of ridicule against Kieko. Kieko trained more; and when the winter tournament came he fought and advanced to the final round finally proving his strength and valor to all, but Aiko—the reigning Ko-Tenso—defeated him with a brutal punch to the nose.

Women, young and old, disliked the tournament—especially mothers—for they could not bear to see their young men—their sons, cousins, brothers, or young lovers—viciously bruised and cut. At times there was a broken bone, which was mended by Shinsei's hands.

Regardless of the danger Kieko loved the sport. He did not mind the hard punches and kicks for it was the means he thought necessary to toughen the skin; he often looked at his bruises imagining battle scars. And as he thought of the tournament he cracked a smile for today, before all, he would face Aiko and bring him down to his knees.

Madonai noticed the smirk on her son's face as he drank his afternoon soup. She knew exactly what he was thinking, "You are not entering the tournament."

"Yes, I am!" he said in defiance.

"No—you are not! I am your mother and that is the end of it."

"I'm not a baby. I'm a man. Do you not see the hair that grows on my face?"

"Yes, it looks hideous."

"Good! Better that than pretty like a girl!"

"Am I disturbing?" Shinsei, plainly dressed, asked kneeling at the low entrance of the hut. He was holding his staff and placed a wrapped item by his foot.

Kieko calmed himself, as did his mother, and replied, "No, Shinsei. You are not disturbing us. You are always welcome here."

"Good," Shinsei said with a warm smile as he entered into the dark of the hut. "I have come to say hello to you, Madonai. It is not often that I see you. Is all well?"

"Yes, Shinsei, all is well. It is good to see you too."

"Good, good. And you, young Kieko, how are you today?"

"I'm fine, Shinsei," he said as he stood to then bow his head in respect. "I was just telling my mother of my decision to participate again in the tournament."

Madonai glared, "You are not partaking in that." She turned to the priest and said, "Shinsei, please explain to my son that he can not fight today."

"I am afraid, Madonai, that I am in no position to make decisions for your son."

Upset with Shinsei's response she retorted, "Thank you so much, Shinsei."

"Madonai, your son will be fine."

"Last time his nose was broken!" she protested.

"Your son is skilled in his defenses. He has much potential in the art. Today is a day of celebration, a day to play the sport of Teshi-do. All the men of this village have youthful memories of the tournament, as have all their ancestors for as long as time can remember."

"It's a stupid tradition. It only encourages hate and anger."

"The sacred ring where the tournament is held is where this hate and anger is quelled. Within that ring young boys who believe in the glory of warfare discover only pain and hurt. They discover that there is no honor in fighting, that true men use their wits to settle conflicts, not brute force."

"You speak of the ideals of the game, Shinsei. For some boys that ring may dry their lust for blood, but for most it does not teach the wrong in stabbing pain and hurt into others."

"I will not disagree with you, Madonai. Your opinion, I respect. But, you must also respect the wishes of your son. He is no longer a boy and can no longer be protected by the care of your nest."

Shinsei's words hurt Madonai. She stood silent, nearly frozen in sorrow. She did not want to be reminded that she was losing her son to the ways of men. Gone were the days when she would bounce his small body on her knee and feed his lips with a wooden spoon. Soon he would leave her and the gap between them would grow. He would think less and less of her as she thought ever more of him. She knew that there would come a day when she would prepare his favorite dish to find that his taste of things had changed. He would move brightly into the future as she was left behind savoring fading memories.

"You are free to do as you please," she said in defeat.

Kieko saw his mother's body deflate and approached her to hug her, but she pushed him away.

"Go," she said bitterly.

"Mom, I'm sorry."

"I said go! You don't need me anymore."

"That's not true. I'm sorry. If you don't want me to fight I won't."

"Damn it! Make up your stupid little mind."

Kieko was taken aback by his mother's words. Shinsei motioned for Kieko to leave, which he did.

Shinsei paced around the hut running his fingers through his beard. He noticed when he bowed his head to avoid the low arch of the thatched roof that Kieko had not finished his meal. He kneeled to pick up the bowl Kieko had carelessly left on the ground and placed it on a table. He stood up and said, "I know that you wish that I had not confirmed Kieko's suspicion that his father was a Kai Guardian."

"Yes, that's right, Shinsei!" Madonai barked. "You had no right. Some things are better left secret–forgotten."

"Although I would like to agree with you, I'm afraid that sooner or later his father's past will find him whether he is prepared for it or not."

"He is still too young to know of his father's past–" Madonai shot her eyes at the door; she knew her son was eavesdropping.

Shinsei whispered, "He is no longer a boy. He is a young man and as a young man he has a right to know of his father's past, of his ancestors, of the color that separates him from all those he has ever known."

"You know my son does not belong here. You know that his desire to travel west beyond the borders of Kadek is growing stronger. You know more than I about his father's Kai line and what curses it bears upon him." She stopped and bowed her head, "I've been dreaming, Shinsei. I've been dreaming of things that no mother should dream. They are visions. Perhaps the gods speak to me a warning. Perhaps they are guiding me. I don't know–"

"What? What are these visions that you speak of?"

"There is a shadow in the West. It is growing and spreading like a disease into the East. I see the face of a man that is not a man—he has no face. I see a city beyond imagination, beyond understanding. And I see my son—" Madonai collapsed to the ground.

Shinsei rushed to her and held her, calming her with hushes and asked, "What was it that you saw of your son?"

"My son . . ." she said staring blankly at the ground, "my son . . . will see this dark city . . . He will roam in its belly . . . and he will be lost within it."

Shinsei knew that the gods had spoken to her. They were trying to warn her. "Did you see or feel an animal spirit in these visions?"

Madonai thought for a moment and replied, "I heard a hiss. I felt the spirit of the snake."

"Sirians," Shinsei whispered to himself.

"What?"

"Nothing . . . you should rest."

"What does it mean?"

"It is simply a nightmare," he tried to assure her. "It simply means that you are tired. You need to rest."

"I don't plan on enjoying the festival today. I will eat a mid-day meal and nap for a time."

"I will watch over Kieko for you."

"Thank you, Shinsei. You were a good friend to my husband."

"He was a good friend to me," he smiled and left.

As the priest expected he found Kieko waiting outside sitting against the thatched wall of his neighbor's hut and said, "Do not think you are clever in trying to hide the fact that you were eavesdropping."

"I was not," he said dropping his eyes.

"It does not matter."

"What did you two talk about?"

"It is none of your concern. What was said was between your mother and me, not you." Changing topics he asked, "Have you an answer for your koan?"

"It's some kind of riddle, so—"

"No, it is not. It is your meditation. I know you think that zazen is a foolish practice but it will become something that you will develop a great respect for. You will begin and end your tiring days in zazen. There is no way around it. If you seek to train under me you must pursue the regular habit of meditation. You will not discover the answer to your koan without it. The koan is the door and zazen the key."

"Yes, Shinsei."

"Are you ready for the tournament?"

"Yes, I 'm ready."

"Did you stretch?"

"Not yet. I thought that I would do so when we arrive at the ring."

"It is only mid-day. Everyone is feasting and drinking now. You still have several hours before Hakunus," he smiled. "I suggest that you stretch and meditate in the mean time."

"Yes, Shinsei," he turned and walked away.

"Where are you going?"

He stopped and looked back, "To the beach to stretch and meditate. I like the sound of the ocean waves."

Shinsei laughed under his breath and began walking. He had to prepare for the spring rites he was to perform in the evening.

Kieko loved the ocean. It was vast and soothing to his eyes, a dark blue ocean parted by a light blue sky. Kira once expressed that she feared the vast horizon of the sea. She liked things to be tangible, filled with borders of the known. She did not like the infinite and the unseen. When she had confessed this to him he knew that they were two entirely different creatures; he would never be able to compromise his desire to travel and explore the unknown lands of the world with Kira's want to settle within the small confines of Ikishi.

When he arrived at the beach he found that it was deserted. It was a rare moment. All the fishermen's boats were flipped over so that their sea moss covered keels faced the mid-day sun. Nets were laid over large rocks and spears stood with their heads buried in the sand. He was grateful that everyone was within the village celebrating; he had the entire beach to himself. He sat down for a moment and took in a deep breath as the sea winds caressed him and ran through his hair. He looked out over the sea with squinting eyes trying to see any far off islands. He only saw flying seagulls.

He took a moment to listen to the hymns of the sea and the ocean winds rustling tree leaves. He stood up and began stretching his arms and legs; he enjoyed the sore sensations from his muscles. When his routine was done he sat down and assumed the zazen position that Shinsei had taught him a year ago. He folded his legs and rested his hands below his navel. He closed his eyes and took a deep breath. The air was cool, fresh, and scented with sea salt. His mind and body began to relax.

The *clank-kli, clank-kli, clank* of copper mallets hitting bronze bowls broke the silent air with rhythmic patterns that aligned against the polyrhythms of high-pitched and low-pitched drums. The festival music had begun and sang in the distance disturbing Kieko. He brushed off the sounds with a passive thought and returned to his inner world of dark. The winds blew and he felt a chill run down his spine. The dark was growing in his mind causing the presence of all things to become faint. In the darkness he saw a light as small as a grain of sand that was warm and bright. He wanted to touch the light, but it was as unattainable as a star in the night's sky.

Abruptly he shot his hand out and caught the downward blow of Aiko's fist.

Aiko, shocked, had never seen such speed and accuracy in Kieko's defense.

Kieko opened his eyes and was surprised, and confused, by what he had done. He released Aiko's hand and sprang to his feet to stand before him and his two friends, Niko and Taka.

"Look what we have here," Aiko said as he regained composure.

Niko sneered, "Think you're a priest you red faced freak?"

"He wasn't meditating," Aiko commented. "He was praying. There is no god in these lands, Akai, that can save you tonight."

"There is nothing that can save you from me, Aiko," Kieko declared. "That is why you come to me in a pack of three. If you want to face me then face me one to one."

"I can break you, Akai, as I did in the last tournament."

"Prove it!" Kieko demanded.

"I'll do it," Niko said. "Let me feast," he threw a heavy punch.

Kieko deflected Niko's strike, tripped him to the ground, and pushed his right hand up behind his back. Niko struggled as he screamed in pain. Kieko pressed his lips to Niko's ear, "You're a stupid—" but before he could finish Aiko kicked him off Niko. Taka then jumped on Kieko and pinned him to the ground. Kieko could do nothing except watch Aiko spring a kick that launched sand into his eyes. Blinded by the sand he heard Niko shuffle his feet.

"Wicked curses!" Niko screamed after he had kicked the side of Kieko's head. He limped around holding his foot, trying to massage it of the throbbing pain as he continued to curse, and heard Kieko chuckle with glee. Furious, Niko jumped down onto his knees, bent down to Kieko's head and said, "What the hell are you laughing at, Akai?" and spat in his face. He rose to his feet and commanded Taka, "Get off him, you fat cow!"

Aiko slapped Niko across the back of his head and reminded him, "He's one of us." Niko clenched his teeth and tensed his brow.

Kieko felt Taka roll off him; his labored breath eased. But Niko jumped and banged his knee into Kieko's stomach knocking the wind out of him. Kieko began clawing at the sand as he panted for air, but Niko unleashed a fury of punches at his head and chest. He could barely fight back and every time he tried to Aiko would kick him in the head. He felt his nose pop and warm blood pour down onto his lips and chin splashing up onto Niko's arms and fists.

When Niko had had enough he stopped, stood up, and spat again on Kieko who was curling his legs into his chest, and saw from the corner of his eye Taka taking a fearful step away from him.

Aiko, satisfied, declared the end of their fun by kicking Kieko in the groin, "See you at the tournament, Akai." He then walked away with Niko and Taka following right behind him.

Kieko felt the grains of sand continue to roll and scratch his eyes. Pain pounded throughout his body; and when he opened his tearing eyes to look at the light of the sun he saw blood spill from his lips, splatter, and sink into the white sand.

He got up and sat on his knees to look at the tumbled sand that marked the violent movements of his opponents against him. He spat on the ground and stared at his bloody saliva. The cool air blew into his face and hair. He breathed and grew angry. Raging against his pain he stood up and punched and kicked in all directions until he collapsed into the soft ocean waves exhausted.

Floating on his back he looked at the blue sky and watched the white clouds move and the seagulls fly. He thought about the tournament and of his determination to finally defeat Aiko while ignoring the stinging pain of the salt water that was biting into his bloody wounds. His strength gradually returned, and with renewed vigor he rose from the froth of the washing waters and walked back onto the white sands. He touched his nose and was relieved to find that it had stopped bleeding.

Jomana, old farmer Toasu's dog, ran at Kieko kicking trails of sand up behind her. Kieko darted his eyes to the scene behind her tracks trying to spot the old farmer. Old farmer Toasu was standing at the line where the white sands stopped and tall grasses grew. Jomana arrived at Kieko's feet and sprang all around him in a wild display of happiness. Her short tail wiggled with such ferocity that Kieko could not help but laugh. She jumped and barked around him until he finally kneeled down to pet her, but she pushed him down to the ground kissing his lips before finding his wounds and cleaning them with her tongue. Kieko delighted himself in the attention Jomana gave him and praised her, "That's a good dog . . . that's a good dog."

"She has always taken a liking to you, boy," old farmer Toasu said casting a shadow over him.

Kieko looked up and saw the old farmer's silhouette. He then looked at the old farmer's legs and saw that he was dressed plainly and holding his staff. "You aren't going to the festival?"

"What makes you say that?"

"You're not dressed."

"Since when have you known me to where robes of extravagance? I'm too old to be bothered by such nonsense."

It was true, Kieko had never known the old farmer to dress and perform in the traditions of his people; and his hesitation to stand and bow before him was another example of the old farmer's disregard for tradition.

It was Lemurian custom that all boys, when greeted by the elder men of their village, stand and bow; but the old farmer had pounded into Kieko's head that he should never do so before him. The old farmer had always explained: "I am an old fool who knows very little of the ways of the world. Do not stand before me and pretend that I do."

"Don't even think about it," the old farmer ordered Kieko.

Kieko relaxed.

"That's it. No standing or bowing."

"Yes, old farmer Toasu," he then noticed that Jomana had settled down by sitting by her master's side; her light brown tail was whipping at the white sands.

"You were in my fields again," the old farmer said with a wry grin as he scratched his short, dark grey beard.

"Yes—I was—but I won't do it again."

"Yes, yes. I rather wish I were there. I would have had Jomana charge after those boys–Aiko and whoever else. Speaking of which, what may I ask happened to you?"

"I got into a fight with 'those boys.' "

Old farmer Toasu let out a distasteful sigh. "Why is it that all boys fight?" he asked shaking his head. "I remember the fights I was in when I was your age."

"Who used to pick on you?" Kieko asked.

"No, no, boy. I was not picked on. I picked the fights. I was the aggressor. I guess that you could say that in many ways I was once much like Aiko. I assume that is the reason why I dislike him so. I see too much of my former self in him."

"Why did you pick fights?"

"That is a good question. Perhaps, it was important for me, then, to appear strong to others. For some reason I despised those who I thought were weak and I fought them. Then, as you know, my parents died and I left this place for the lands in the West." There was then a lull between the old farmer and Kieko. Jomana, uncomfortable with the silence, sniffed the air and sneezed when a gust of wind blew into her nose. "Well, I best return to my fields. Come now, Jomana."

"You're leaving?" Kieko asked with a quizzical look.

"Of course. What? Do you think I am in a mood to celebrate?"

"That is not what I meant—"

"What will people think if they see me having fun? I must maintain my oddity, Kieko," he said with a wink. He turned and made in the direction of his farm. Jomana barked a goodbye and followed after her master.

In the few hours left before the tournament Kieko trained. He ran along the beach and went through a series of exercises to strengthen and loosen his muscles. He punched and kicked as if fighting an invisible foe and ended his training by resting on the beach while gazing at the wonderful scene before him: a canvas of dark blue ocean waters and a light pink evening sky.

The sun was setting; the horizon shone in gently fading hues of blue, pink, orange, and red. Men drank their rice wines and wheat beers as they shouted and debated. Children ran and played their games: games of hiding, games of chance, and games of athletic skill.

A group of women prepared for the dances that they were to perform. They busily dabbed white powder on their cheeks and foreheads and brushed a vibrant red cream on their lips. Their colorful gowns were made of dyed silk and embroidered with depictions of cranes, tigers, and flowers against a background of mountains and the sea. Their hair was done up in a wavy fashion meant to reveal the sensuality of their necks and fixed with crafted hairpins that were shaped like the full bloom of exotic flowers. And they wore white socks and stood on platform sandals made of wood.

A bell rang seven times. Men quieted their voices and children stopped and ran to sit and gather around a large white ring—near the entrance of the Council Hut—that had been chalked into the circular plain of the village. A woman who was old, but nonetheless beautifully dressed in her festival robe, plucked the first note from her three-stringed guitar with a large T-shaped plectrum that she had carved years ago from dense driftwood. She plucked the second note and then the next series of notes in a gradual increase in tempo and volume until her melodic line peaked at its musical climax. The song soon slowed until it had faded back into a soft whisper.

The audience patiently waited in silence, and in a lined formation of seven by seven the dancers entered the ring. When they reached their places within the ring they stepped away from each other to create a square within the ring. The music began again but with the accompaniment of four more women who plucked their instruments with solemn grace, mixing soft melodies and harmonies. The spring dance had begun.

The dancers moved together with subtle hand and arm movements that mimicked the bloom of flowers. They looked at their hands, then up into the evening sky, and then out into the audience before shying away. All the men who watched sat in awe of the beautiful women before them; a few men gazed with open jaws.

Buko watched the dancers with a covetous eye as he coughed out his stinking beer breath. He wiped his mouth of its drool and took another sip from his mug as the dancers pulled out fans from their garments and spread them open to hide everything below the almond shape of their eyes. He became frustrated–he had been denied view of the dancer's wet lips–and turned and stumbled out of the crowd. A few of the dancers closed their eyes relieved that Buko had left.

Raki-ka, a humorous man with a reputation for his love of women, could not bear the sight of the dancers who had closed their eyes. *That is too much*, he thought. *I must have them. Oh, the gods how I love this dance.*

Three of the dancers noticed and watched several children giggle at their fathers and older brothers who could not look away from their dance. They, the dancers, then waved their hands calling to the men, tantalizing them, before removing the fans from their faces. The men leaned forward in rapt attention when what they sought to see was once again revealed to them. The dance continued in a rhythmic fashion that tempted and forbade. Children looked on and enjoyed but did not see or understand the hidden meanings layered within the dance. The dance progressed into dusk.

When the dancers withdrew from the ring to the sound of applauding hands adolescent boys began lighting the fire staves that stood all around the ring. Kieko had arrived just in time to see Kira and her peers celebrate Hakunus, their rite into womanhood. One by one the nine girls who had bled in winter stepped up to the outer edge of the sacred circle. They were all wonderfully dressed in their spring robes but flowery hairpins did not adorn their hair.

Kieko, slightly hidden within shadows, watched Kira who was the last of the young women to walk up to the ring, and admired her beauty. Her thick black hair flowed over the back of her neck. Her face was powdered white, her lips were painted red, and the upper rims of her eyes and the fullness of her brows were painted black. Her light pink gown was decorated with designs of grey mountains and embroidered with exotic flowers of red, yellow, and green. She held in her hands a small wooden box, as did all the girls who were partaking in the Hakunus. Kieko knew that the white gown she had stained with her first blood was within the box. He looked at her fan that was tucked into the upper folds of her robe, just below her breasts, and looked at her face again. Never had he seen her so beautiful and so pure in both heart and spirit. He then realized that his lips were frozen into a wide smile. At that moment Kira looked at him and smiled revealing her snow-white teeth. Kieko blushed, which for Kira was a wonderful gift.

The nine girls formed a curved line along the edge of the circle and stood before all in silence; only the crackles of the flames could be heard. Soon the mothers of the nine girls appeared and entered into the circle one by one. They stood before their daughters and bowed to them acknowledging their coming passage into womanhood. They unburdened their daughter's hands of the wooden boxes, bowed again, and turned to face the large iron cauldron that sat before the entrance of the Council Hut. The cauldron, covered by an intricately designed bronze roof, was filled with ash that was littered by scores of lit incense sticks that sent thin columns of smoke into the night sky. Before the cauldron there was a large altar made of stones and sticks. The mothers of the nine girls walked up to the altar and placed the boxes upon it. Ruka, the last of the nine mothers to approach the altar, set the altar on fire with a torch to burn into the air the blood-offerings of the Hakunus girls.

Kieko looked and saw Kira's aunts wiping tears from their eyes. Rakima stood behind them with his large arms folded over his chest. His thick beard, and the scar that ran over his left eye, gave him a dark and hardened look. He was robed in ceremonial warrior garments. His top gi, which covered his chest and arms, was a sea blue with yellow and white ink designs depicting ocean waves. His brown, dress-like trousers hung down to his ankles. His short and long swords were sheathed and tied to his thick, blue cotton belt.

Rakima, feeling Kieko's stare, turned to him, and nodded. Kieko nodded back, and looked back to Kira and her mother. The altar was burning.

Shinsei appeared from the crowd and entered into the ring. He was wearing his ceremonial garments. His body was covered with a thick, black, wide-sleeved cotton robe that folded over a succession of thin, white cotton gowns that were all tied to his waist with a royal blue sash. His white gowns neatly crossed over his chest in the same fashion as his robe, but could only be seen as thin white lines in the shape of a V just at the base of his neck where hung his wooden prayer beads. His arms and his hands were wrapped with a tight white cloth that was covered by the wide-open sleeves of his robe. On his robe, at the two sides of his upper chest, was an embroidered white flower. He wore baggy white trousers that stopped at his knees. Long, dark leather gaiters protected his shins. His feet were bare but fastened to rope sandals. He held in his right hand his tall ceremonial staff; its tip was adorned with a bronze ornamental eye that was wreathed in leaves with two rings that hung from it; the rings rang a high-pitched note every time they clanked against the staff. The light of the fire staves glistened off his bald scalp. His white beard flowed with the winds.

Shinsei pulled out a scroll from within his robe and bowed his head. Accordingly all the villagers bowed their heads as a few mothers hushed their children. Shinsei unrolled the scroll and began his chant of an ancient song singing from memory with no real need to read from the ancient text of his faith.

Kieko thought of Kira during the hypnotic hymn. He went over her beauty in his mind. He saw her brown eyes, her long eyelashes that were the envy of all the girls, and her nose that held the shape of a raindrop, her wet red lips, and the tongue that moistened them. He wanted to touch her lips with his and then kiss her nose and eyes and forehead. He became aware of a warm throbbing between his legs and tried to fight off his romantic thoughts by picturing Aiko and the offensive moves he would use against him.

When Shinsei was done chanting in the old tongue he spoke aloud and said, "You, sisters of the Hakunus, are welcomed into this sacred ring. Like the seasons of the year, and the days and nights, your bodies will be in rhythm with the waxing and waning of the moon. And like the great forest of our lands, giver of all life, you shall bear children so that we, as a people, never die. We honor you as children of the Goddess of the Wood. We honor you as Children of the Moon. We honor you as Angels of the Mother.

"Step now into this circle that turns and moves, and be recognized by all no longer as children, but as women."

The nine girls, now reborn, entered into the circle and stood before their families, friends, and villagers. In honor of their divine ability to give life, everyone, including Shinsei, kneeled and bowed their heads to them.

Festive music began. Husbands took their wives into the ring and began dancing with them. Kira along with the other Hakunus girls stepped back and stood just outside the ring waiting for someone to ask them to dance. Kira looked for Kieko but could not find him in the crowds, instead she saw Aiko approaching her. She tensed trying not to look at him, but she could not help from feeling attracted to the confidence that he exuded in his walk.

"Kira, may I have the honor of dancing with you?"

"T-thank you, Aiko, but no."

"Is there hesitation in your voice?"

"No, no, I'm just exci–," she blushed, "I mean, I'm a little excited after Hakunus." Regaining herself she went on, "I'm sure it's the same feeling you get after picking on Kieko or any of the other boys you deem below you."

"What?" Aiko asked defensively.

"I think you should go. Ask someone else to dance with you."

"I don't see Kieko anywhere. Don't expect him to come and ask you to dance, Kira. I know you are waiting for him."

"Aiko, please go. I don't want to hear anything more from you."

"Fine then–well, I hope you have fun just standing here watching everyone else dance." He looked over to Yumi, a girl that Kira did not like, and asked her to dance. Yumi gladly accepted and the two danced and laughed and danced.

Kira tried not to look at Aiko and Yumi, but she did. And she watched the other boys who had mustered the courage to ask each of the Hakunus girls for a dance. After rejecting another two invitations to dance she stood alone waiting for Kieko. She could see Elder Subo talking his *important* talks with the other Elders as she overheard mothers and grandmothers chat about their own long ago Hakunus celebrations. She soon grew bored and watched children play hoping to ignore those who danced.

Kieko was hiding from the laughter and dances of his people. He knew his mother was within their hut alone, probably eating her meal in silent protest against his decision to fight again in the tournament. He wanted to be with her, but he also wanted to stay near Kira in the hope of sharing one dance with her, although he was much too shy to approach her. In his mind he imagined himself dancing with Kira, and winning her heart when he defeated Aiko before all in the tournament.

He found a spot next to a hut hidden from the light of the moon that was not too far from the activities of his people. He sat and watched the smoke from the festival fires billow into the air spreading the scent of delicious meats that sizzled and burned in fat. His mouth watered. He was not a man in the eyes of the village men and, as a result, was prohibited from eating their meats. His stomach hungered for food and grumbled a rude reminder. He thought it foolish to hide and decided to partake in the feasting of his people. He stood up and dusted the dirt from his legs but felt a dark presence. The motions were quick; Niko had snuck up behind him and kicked him down to the ground.

"Shouldn't you be at the beach, Akai?"

Kieko felt the bruises along his face and chest sting as he gathered himself. He swiped his hand across his lips and spat on the ground where Niko stood.

"Not wise, Akai." Niko pulled his right fist back to strike a blow at Kieko but it was caught. He turned and saw that his uncle Rakima had grabbed his wrist.

"Look what I caught today," Rakima said as he applied pressure to Niko's wrist paining him in such a way that it brought him down to his knees.

Fast to insult his uncle's famous appetite Niko called out, "The gods! Don't eat me!"

Rakima applied more pressure.

Niko's voice faded to a panting whisper, "I'm sorry, I'm sorry, I'm sorry . . . uncle Rakima."

"What business have you here?" Rakima demanded.

"I was fetching Kieko for the tournament."

"Do not take me for a fool! Be gone. I do not wish to see you until tomorrow."

"Yes, uncle Rakima." Niko walked away, but with his back to his uncle he glared at Kieko and shouldered past him.

When his nephew was gone Rakima advised Kieko, "You should be eating. You shouldn't fight on an empty stomach."

"I was just resting here," Kieko replied nervously with his head bowed.

Rakima shook his head and walked away.

Kieko let out a sigh and relaxed. The fading clank of Rakima's swords against the buckle of his belt echoed into the night. He stared down at his dirty toes and agreed that he should eat before the fight.

He went to the tables near the Council Hut, which were blanketed with mats of dried grass and surrounded by men, women, and a few children, and picked at the cooked vegetables and sea foods with the shi sticks he always carried in his cotton belt. He placed all his pickings on a large, fresh leaf he had plucked. He returned to the shadows of the huts and found a quiet spot to sit and eat. When he was nearly finished with his meal he heard soft footsteps.

"There you are," Kira said in a sweet and innocent manner. "What are you doing here?"

Kieko looked at her small feet that were clothed in white socks. Her ceremonial sandals were simple in design, but elegant nonetheless. He did not look up to her face.

Kira kneeled and asked again, "What are you doing here? Everyone is celebrating and here you are–what happened to your face?"

Kieko kept silent.

"Aiko! That wicked—" she stopped and tried to calm herself. "What happened?"

"Nothing. Don't worry. I'm fine."

"Of course I worry."

"Don't!" he barked.

Kira was silent.

Kieko continued eating.

"I was hoping you would dance with me tonight. I was looking for you, but I couldn't find you."

He kept his head down.

"Aren't you going to look at me?" She wanted Kieko to admire her beauty and comment on her robes and makeup. She had waited and dreamt of her Hakunus for so long, and had rehearsed in her mind time and time again of how beautiful she would look, and how in love Kieko would be when he saw her. But here he was, feasting upon his food with no apparent regard for her womanhood.

Kieko's eyes darkened with worry as Kira began to frown. He did not know what to do or say. Worried, he clenched his teeth, breathed, and said, "I'm sorry Kira . . . It's just that . . . you look so lovely," he held his breath, "so beautiful. I only have rags to wear . . . I didn't want to dirty your dress. And I can't dance."

She let out a short laugh and said, "You're wonderful." She then leaned over, grabbed his shirt, and kissed his greasy lips.

Kieko was frozen with joy, but embarrassed by the sudden warmth between his legs. He did not breathe as he stared wide-eyed at Kira's eyebrows that were delightfully arched.

Kira, lost in a realm of bliss and imagination, soon lost her balance and fell over Kieko. Together they giggled like children. It was their first kiss.

Kira raised herself, looked at Kieko, and let out a laugh that she cut short with her hand.

Kieko gave a confused look and asked, "What?"

"You've got makeup all over your lips and chin."

Kieko rubbed at his lips with his forearm. "Is it gone?"

"Yes," Kira answered. She kissed him again and again losing herself in her affection. A great drum was then struck. Its sound was deep and penetrated their hearts.

Kieko faced the sound and said, "It is the call of the tournament."

Kira wanted him to look back at her, but she could see that his heart was now devoted to the upcoming fight.

"I–I need to get ready . . . uhh–you should go."

"We can go back together," she said cheerfully.

"No! I mean . . . you need to fix your makeup and I need to stretch so," Kieko frowned, "go ahead."

Kira's face fell. She did not understand Kieko's odd behavior, but she thought it was best to leave him and kissed him before walking away with a radiant smile.

When Kieko was sure that Kira had gone he got up and adjusted his desire appropriately in his pants. He cleaned his shi sticks, tucked them into his belt, and decided to run through the maze of huts to warm up and relieve his mind of all romantic fantasies. When his desire had finally left him he began stretching his legs and arms and then proceeded to the tournament ring.

The first person he saw after he had shouldered past the crowd to reach the tournament ring was Aiko; he was with his father who was helping him go through a series of punching drills. Kieko took a good look at the crowd. All the men were speaking with excitement in anticipation of the tournament. A few barked and called in drunken slurs as they lined up along the tournament ring trying to get the best view. Women, both young and old, stood away while children peeked between the legs of their fathers to view the upcoming fight.

Kieko was getting nervous. He looked at the other contestants and knew that he could defeat them. His only worry was with Aiko.

Traditionally the art of Teshi-do was passed down from father to son, but in Kieko's case he learned what he could from

Shinsei and old farmer Toasu, although they did not teach him much. The majority of his understanding came from simple observations and mimicry. From a distance he would watch fathers teach their sons at the beach or near the Ikishi forest. He would then rehearse in his mind what he had seen and then practice alone, usually at night under the light of the moon by his Thinking Tree. He knew that the art was based on animal and insect movements and as a result he studied how the praying mantis defeated its opponent or how the crane moved through tall grasses. His style of Teshi-do was unique; it was very fluid compared to the hard linear movements of the traditional style that was taught in the village.

Kieko jumped in place as he studied Aiko's footwork and punches against the drilling attacks of his father. Aiko's style was both hard and soft; Kono had taught his son an unsurpassed understanding of the art for in his youth he had been the best tournament fighter. Aiko was wearing a sleeveless, dark blue top gi, which revealed his muscled arms. A light blue belt was wrapped around his waist. His baggy pants hid his feet; Kieko knew that without being able to see Aiko's stances it was going to be difficult to read his advances and retreats.

Shinsei walked into the ring. He stopped and stood in its center. "Now that it is night, and near the end of this day of spring, we celebrate the skills of men to defend our homes, our women, and our children. Women give life and men guard life with their hearts and minds. Brutal and harsh is the way of the warrior. Thus is the path of man. We honor you young fighters. Please step forth the sixteen."

Kieko moved past the crowd and entered the circle as did twenty other young men and boys. As was done every year Shinsei eliminated the youngest contestants from the tournament until sixteen were left.

"Stand before me in four lines of four," Shinsei requested.

The sixteen young men did as asked; Aiko stood proud and full of confidence in the first line; Niko stood in the second line with a dirty look and Kieko stood in the last line seeking no attention at all.

"The first line will fight."

The second, third, and fourth line of boys and young men left the ring while the first line broke into pairs.

"Stand at your places."

The pairs: Aiko and Tanai, Tsuita and Naka faced each other by standing behind the white markers that had been chalked into the ground at the ring's center. Aiko smiled at Tanai. Tanai's face tensed. Shinsei stepped back until he stood outside the ring.

"Bow," Shinsei commanded.

Aiko did not bow.

"Bow!"

Aiko smirked and did as asked.

"Take your stances."

The four took their stances.

"Begin!"

The crowd of men burst into an explosion of roars and yells. Aiko advanced punching with swift arms. Tanai, a novice, retreated to the circle's edge where Aiko simply tripped him out to be eliminated.

Tsuita, dressed in yellow and black, bounced on his feet with his hands up guarding his face. He watched Naka carefully but looked at Tania when he was tripped out of the ring. Naka seized the opportunity and rushed Tsuita and kicked him in the stomach. Tsuita fell to the floor doubling up in pain.

Aiko leapt and swept at Naka's leg. Naka, caught by surprise, fell hard on his back. Aiko then jumped on Naka's stomach knocking the wind out of him and threw his fist into his face.

Shinsei could see that Naka could not breathe or fight back. "Naka is eliminated," he called out. Two boys sprang into the circle and dragged Naka out.

Tsuita rose to his feet while holding his stomach and saw that Aiko held the center of the ring. He began circling around Aiko waiting for him to attack, but he did not. Aiko simply watched Tsuita. Tsuita kept circling. Aiko then dropped his hands to his sides openly inviting Tsuita to attack him, but Tsuita was not tempted, he kept circling. The crowd was growing impatient, they shouted for the fight to begin again.

Aiko looked at his father and saw him place his hand over his fist; it was a signal. He nodded to his father and dropped to his knees, closed his eyes, and placed his hands behind his head.

Tsuita gave a confused look at Aiko. *What in the name of the gods is he doing?* He ran in to kick Aiko in the face, but Aiko sprang his hand at his foot, grabbed it, spun around on his knees, and backhanded his fist into his groin. Tsuita cupped his sex and fell to the ground defeated. Aiko stood up, straightened his gi, bowed to Tsuita, then to Shinsei, and walked out of the tournament ring. Men and young boys cheered in approval of Aiko's clever tactic.

Shinsei named Aiko winner of the first line of fighters and called in the second line. The fighters lined up, bowed, and began when they heard Shinsei's call.

Niko was ruthless in his attacks. He never defended; he took the blows to his head and chest. His face, red with hate, frothed at the mouth like a wild dog as he pummeled his opponents with his fists. He threw one opponent out of the circle; beat down another after spitting blood into his eyes; and broke the wrist of his last opponent, Tonodo. He walked out of the ring with blood dripping from his head and lips onto his cream colored gi. Children frightened away from him, *the beast*, as men and women quieted their cheers after Tonodo's injury.

Shinsei quickly named Niko winner of the second line and rushed to Tonodo with two splints. He kneeled before the boy and placed the splints by his side. He closed his eyes, raised his arms to the night sky, and inhaled Ki from the air. He then filled Tonodo with the Ki he had gathered into himself by expelling it from his fingertips over the boy's head, chest, and arms. Tonodo shook uncontrollably while his eyes fluttered. Shinsei placed his hands over Tonodo's broken wrist and held it tight. Tonodo moaned and whispered, "It burns." Shinsei opened his eyes and looked to Tonodo's father, Hakini, and asked him to hold the two splints along the sides of his son's wrist. The splints were placed appropriately and Shinsei began wrapping a long white cloth around them.

When Shinsei was done he assured Hakini that all would be right and prescribed a tea to help his son sleep and heal during the night; he also explained that he would come in the morning to tend to him with an assortment of remedies from his temple's kitchen and gardens.

When the priest was ready he called the third line to fight. The fight was clean between the four contestants. There was no biting, spitting, or breaking of bones. Tarori defeated his three opponents by wrestling and grappling them out of the circle in the traditional monkey-style of Teshi-do.

Kieko's heart was pounding. Shinsei called the fourth line and he walked into the tournament circle stretching and rolling his neck, lifting and dropping his shoulders, and wiggling his arms and hands. He took his place before the white line and faced Toru, an opponent two years his senior. Standing next to him was Bouto, and facing Bouto was his cousin, Natana.

Kieko took a neutral stance by placing his hands at his sides leaving himself completely open. Toru stood in a defensive stance while Bouto and Natana stood in offensive stances. Kieko knew each of his opponents's fighting styles for he had learned and mastered them through secret observations of their training. Natana trained with Bouto under the guidance of their uncle, Mitana. They always trained at the beach in the late afternoons and began and ended their sessions with a long run along the beach; Mitana had explained to his two nephews that running on sand was the same effort as running twice the distance on hard earth. Mitana was a conservative and taught a very rigid and tight style of Teshi-do. Toru on the other hand was very fluid in his fighting style. He loved the sea and the rivers of Kadek. He believed water to be the superior of the five elements for water could wear away rock and flow past all jagged obstacles.

Kieko knew that Bouto and Natana would work as a team to defeat him and Toru, and because their style was aggressive he also knew that they would first try to take out Toru before focusing their attacks on him.

The fight began. Natana threw his arm at Toru's head. Toru, not expecting the blow, took the hit. Bouto then tried to kick Kieko, but Kieko stepped back. Bouto advanced launching a vast array of kicks, but Kieko simply leaned away from the strikes. Bouto felt like a fool when none of his kicks connected with Kieko's body. A few men in the audience, as well as several children, laughed. Bouto, red-faced and infuriated, charged at Kieko. Kieko swiftly rolled onto his back, planted his foot into Bouto's solar plexus, and sent him flying out into the audience. Men and women quickly moved and Bouto crashed hard onto the ground outside the ring.

Kieko sprang up onto his feet and faced Natana who had defeated Toru by knocking him down with a strong kick to the head. Both Natana and Kieko held their fists above their heads. Natana held the center of the ring and bounced toward and away from Kieko. Kieko was calm as he circled around Natana, but he could see that a rush of excitement was growing within his opponent. He stopped circling and dropped his guard. Natana stopped and stared trying to discern Kieko's next move. Kieko turned his back on Natana and squatted on the ground and waited. Natana stepped toward Kieko to strike him down with a hammer punch but Kieko jumped up, over, and behind Natana, and kicked him in the back sending him out of the tournament circle.

The crowd was split between insults and praise for Kieko's achievement.

Kieko saw Elder Subo clapping for him as he walked out of the ring and he heard Kira's sweet cheers. He smiled to himself.

Shinsei announced the next level of the tournament by declaring, "Odd faces odd and even faces even. Aiko, winner of the first line, will face Tarori, winner of the third line. And Niko, winner of the second line, will face Kieko, winner of the fourth line."

First was the fight of the odds. Aiko and Tarori entered the ring; their clothes were dirty from spit and blood. They faced each other, bowed, and awaited Shinsei's call. The fight began. Aiko was on the defensive; he knew that Tarori was skilled in tackling and grappling and he kept his distance by forfeiting the ring's center to him ready to kick him if he tried to attack.

Tarori knew that he would have trouble blocking Aiko's rapid kicks and punches. He held his open hands above his head in the neutral stance of the monkey-style.

Aiko kept his fists near his face as he bounced on his feet circling Tarori. Tarori then tried to tempt Aiko by repeatedly jumping toward him, but Aiko never took the bait, he just kept circling.

Someone in the crowd shouted for Aiko to make a move.

Aiko paid no attention to the comment. He kept his eyes on Tarori looking for a break in his concentration. Soon enough a loud insulting call distracted Tarori and he went in for the attack. He ran, jumped, and kicked Tarori in the face. Tarori fell to the ground but rolled back up to his feet again and raised his hands to guard his face while moving and keeping his center of gravity low to the ground; his motions parodied that of an excited monkey. He tried to read Aiko's eyes but could not because Aiko kept his head tilted down. He decided to move in so that he could grab one of Aiko's wrists. He somersaulted and threw himself at Aiko. Aiko jumped and flipped himself over Tarori landing behind him like an agile cat. Tarori turned and dived at Aiko. They were now wrestling on the ground. Tarori pinned Aiko's arms to the ground and kneed him in the groin. Aiko let out a yell and spat at Tarori's eyes. Tarori, blinded, released Aiko. At that moment the fight was over. Aiko threw his fist into Tarori's chin and kicked him across the face. Tarori collapsed defeated.

Men clapped and cheered for Aiko. They soon quieted in anticipation for Kieko's fight against Niko. Shinsei called Kieko and Niko forth into the ring and had them face and bow to each other. Niko kept his bow slightly above Kieko's in a clear sign of disrespect. Kieko noticed the gesture but was not bothered by it; and from the corner of his eye he saw Kira in the crowd covering her nose and mouth with her hands with her mother and aunts at her sides and her father, Rakima, standing behind her.

Rakima placed his solid hand on Kira's shoulder to comfort her. He had seen his daughter cringe at every fist or kick that connected with flesh or bone, and he had seen her cover her eyes and suffer during most of Kieko's first fight. He knew her feelings for Kieko had grown beyond childhood friendship. This concerned him greatly for his elder brother, Tsuwata, was wary of the relationship between his niece, Kira, and Kieko, and now that she was a woman in the eyes of the villagers suitors would soon begin approaching her. *Impossible to believe that she is a woman,* he thought, *she is but a girl, my girl.* A list of potential suitors filled his head, but he knew that she would not accept any of them; she only wanted to marry Kieko. Whether or not Kieko would ever summon the courage to ask him for his blessing remained to be seen, but somehow he knew that he never would.

He watched Kieko and Niko enter the ring and banished all thoughts of suitors and courtships from his mind.

The fight began. Niko dove at Kieko and held him down with his knee as he punched wildly at his head. Kieko's wounds broke open. Blood streamed from his nose and splashed all over Niko's fist. "You bastard!" Kieko shouted; he had had enough of Niko. He grabbed the skin of Niko's lower stomach and twisted it. Niko shouted out in pain. He then wrapped his arms around Niko's head and squeezed it against his chest. They rolled on the ground until Kieko let out a yell; Niko had bit hard and deep into his chest, freeing flesh, drawing blood. Adrenaline now ran rampant throughout Kieko's body; he released a fury of uncontrolled punches. The two fought like rabid dogs wrestling on the ground.

Shinsei hung his head in shame, but he knew that it was necessary for both Kieko and Niko to release the hatred they had for each other than to let it grow and fester like a poisonous disease. Men shouted and cheered for Niko who appeared to be winning. Then Niko began choking Kieko. Kieko's face turned red and then purple as he clawed at Niko's neck and mouth. No one in the audience could believe what they were seeing. They all stopped cheering waiting for Shinsei to stop the fight.

Shinsei raised his staff and called out, "Niko!"

The air moved filling with a tense electrical static. Niko's eyes widened. Kieko roared a terrible cry. Then it happened. A burst of light launched Niko into the air. The crowd looked in disbelief. Niko's limp body landed near the ring's edge. Kieko scrambled to his feet, ran at Niko, and kicked him clear out of the tournament ring. He then collapsed at the ring's edge.

Tsuwata, Niko's father, fell to his knees at his son's side and slapped him across the face to rouse him. Niko's eyes fluttered as he moaned and coughed. Tsuwata was relieved.

The crowd stood in awe. They had never seen anyone other than Shinsei summon the *life force* for only a Ki priest could harness the power of the Ki after decades of uninterrupted meditation and martial training. Yet Kieko had been able to channel it in a fit of rage.

Shinsei was astonished. He could not believe that Kieko could channel the Ki at such a young age. But the fact that Kieko achieved the feat through anger greatly concerned him.

"He is a demon child!" Tsuwata declared as his kin, who all stood behind him, called out in agreement. Rakima did not speak. He slowly distanced himself from his elder brother and family.

Kieko looked at the crowds. He did not know what he had done. He was tired and only wanted to rest before his final fight. He looked down at his wounds and touched the blood that soiled his garments. He coughed up spittle and more blood.

Kono stepped forward, "This child is cursed! It is an ill omen that he can channel. He should be sent away from these lands!"

The majority of men in the crowd agreed with what Kono had said. They nodded their heads and pumped their fists into the air as women stood silent and children watched.

Kieko searched the crowds for those who did not agree and saw Raki-ka and his friends, Hirotake and Watanoro.

Watanoro whispered, "Perhaps we should speak up for the boy."

"Are you mad," Hirotake replied. "I now have a wife to care for. And one day I will have children. No. I will say nothing."

"He's, right," Raki-ka agreed. "I will not speak up for the boy at the cost of losing work." He looked at Kieko. "Besides, he has the priest on his side."

Shinsei approached Kieko as Kono and Tsuwata kept working the crowd up into a craze and stood behind him.

Kieko turned his head and looked up, "Shinsei, I don't understand what they are yelling about?"

"Quiet. It is best that you do not speak."

Elder Subo walked into the ring, "Silence you fools! What is this superstitious talk? You speak like masses of idiots!"

Raki-ka shook his head at the Elder and said to himself, "The bastard. Can he, for once, not talk down to us?"

Watanoro commented, "He thinks that everyone here is a peasant."

"He thinks Nishiaka is watching him. That is the only reason he speaks up for the boy."

Watanoro agreed, "He makes me sick."

Elder Subo pointed at Kieko, "He is no different than any of us. I will not tolerate any more foul talk of him—"

"And why should any of us trust you?" Kono interrupted the Elder. "You have more respect for his Akai father than for your own people. For all we know you are allied to the Empire of the West."

"That is right, Subo!" Raki-ka called out. "Why should any of us trust you?"

Elder Subo heard the slander against him but dismissed it from his mind as baseless. "I will be respected! I am Chief Elder in these lands!"

"You all shame me!" Shinsei shouted. "Never have I seen such talk against an Elder. Never! You have all lost yourselves. All of you! If there was ever an ill-omen it is this—villagers speaking up against their own Chief Elder."

Kono, Tsuwata, and the crowds all quieted down.

Shinsei continued, "Let us forget this senseless talk and finish the night with the final fight between Kieko and Aiko."

Kieko stood up when he saw Aiko enter the ring to take his place at the white marker.

"Yes, let it be done," Aiko declared. "I will fight and slay this demon child!"

Kieko still did not know why he being referred to as a "demon child." He looked at Aiko and at Tsuwata perplexed.

"Don't give me that look," Tsuwata pointed at Kieko. "You know what you are. You are a demon—a curse to the people of these lands."

"Enough!" Kono said silencing all those around him. "My son will fight. And he will win in a testament of the strength of our people over the wicked ways of the Red."

A great many men and women cheered and clapped at Kono's words.

Shinsei shook his head disappointed that so many of his people would side with Kono, not because they agreed with him, but because they wanted to gain something from him. But, he saw that Raki-ka, Watanoro, and Hirotake were not cheering with the others. They stood silent and still.

Kieko looked at the crowds and felt the weight of their ridicule begin to pierce him. Shinsei stormed into the air, spinning his staff, and crashed his sandaled feet into the center of the ring; the earth moved beneath him. "Quiet! I say!" His voice thundered and echoed throughout the valleys of Kadek causing birds to fly into the night air in panic. Animals, both within and near the Ikishi forest, recoiled and trembled.

Shinsei pointed at Kieko and said, "This is a child known to all as Kieko. He is no demon. He is neither Red nor Yellow but a creature of the Mother. There is no separation in mind, spirit, and body between all of you and him. You all shame me!" Men, women, and children bowed their heads to avoid the priest's glare. "Let us be done with the night with this final fight," he then exited the tournament ring while Kieko approached its center.

Kieko felt even more pressure to win this fight against Aiko. *It must be done. I must win. I can not afford to lose again to him. I will not be bullied anymore.*

Kono called his son. Aiko left the ring to heed his father.

"Yes, father?" Aiko asked.

"You listen to me," he grabbed his son's arms and held them tightly. "I will not have you lose to an Akai. You know what this fight now means. It is no longer about you and him. It is about Lemuria and Atlantis. Everyone needs to see you punish him. Beat him to dust. Beat him till he can neither speak nor move. Is that understood?"

"Yes, father."

"If you do not win—if you do not—then I am done with you for no son of mine will lose to an Akai."

Aiko's eyes dropped, "Yes, father."

"You look at me!" he gripped his son's arms tighter.

He looked up, "Yes, father."

"Now finish it."

"Yes, father."

Aiko walked back into the ring flexing his arms, grinding and clenching his teeth. He rolled his neck cracking it in several places. He tensed his fingers and stretched his arms. He began bouncing around Kieko waiting for the fight to begin.

Kieko snorted and spat on the ground.

"Let it begin, Akai," Aiko hissed.

"Let it begin," Kieko said with a confident breath.

The two bowed to each other. The crowds began to cheer and chant for Aiko. Kieko looked at the crowd. He saw Rakima holding his daughter to comfort her from the sights and sounds that she could not bear. Her hands were shaking over her face. Shinsei's voice then boomed and the match began.

Aiko circled Kieko and blocked his view of Kira, casting her from his mind. He waited for Kieko to make the first move, but he did not, instead he swiftly ran through the first twelve movements of his crane-style kata and finished by standing before him with his hand over his fist. Aiko smiled and gracefully went through the first twelve movements of his tiger-style kata and finished with his hand also over his fist. They bowed again—Aiko kept his bow slightly above Kieko's bow—and sprung into their stances.

Aiko shaped his hands into claws. Kieko left his hands open. Aiko advanced, grabbed Kieko's right wrist, pulled, and threw him to the floor, but Kieko sprang back up to his feet. He launched a swift kick at Kieko's head, which Kieko blocked with his forearm, and received a hard punch to his knee. He then blocked the kick that was aimed for his groin by grabbing Kieko's foot and twisting it, spinning him into the air. Kieko landed and rolled on the ground. Aiko jumped and slammed his right knee into Kieko's stomach. The crowd winced in unison as Kieko folded his body in agony. He then grabbed Kieko's leg and dragged him to the center of the tournament ring. The crowd called out exhilarated when Aiko raised his arms in victory.

A vehement storm surged through Kieko's veins. The zeal of hate consumed his spirit. Darkness shrouded his mind. All of time moved like a sluggish snail. There was no pain. There were no voices. There was only the sound of his breath and the sight of Aiko standing before him. He launched himself to his feet, swung his arms at the back of Aiko's head, and kicked him in the legs and waist. Aiko turned. He then punched Aiko in the face—breaking open the flesh above his eye—and punched him in the chest before swinging his arm at his head and kicking him back all the way to the edge of the ring, but his unbalanced stance betrayed him. All of time returned when Aiko drove his fist up into Kieko's chin. Kieko flew up and landed on his back dazed. Aiko, bleeding from his brow, stumbled toward Kieko, and before Shinsei could stop him, he lifted Kieko's left arm and snapped it in two over his knee.

CHAPTER IV

Kieko woke up gasping for air. *No, it was a dream, a dream*; he had dreamt that he was drowning in a sea near high volcanic cliffs that spat fire into the night sky. His eyes focused; he saw Shinsei looking over him; he collapsed his head back to the ground.

"Do not move," Shinsei said before patting Kieko's brow with a cloth.

He tensed his abdomen to sit up but pain surged through his left arm.

"Do not move!" the priest commanded.

He saw that the priest's robe and garments were wrinkled, spoiled by sweat, and stained by dirt. "Where's Kira?"

"She fainted after your fight. She is resting now with her family."

"Oh." He looked around searching for things that would remind him of how he had been knocked unconscious. The tables were still decorated with bouquets of flowers but were cleared of food and drink. Colorful flags flapped and sounded with the blowing winds. The dying fires crackled. He then recalled his fight against Aiko, "Did I win?"

Shinsei let out a laugh while shaking his head.

"Aiko won? How?" he asked angered.

"That is not important," he took a moment to knot a bandage. "Your arm is broken, Kieko."

"What? Mother is going to kill me."

Shinsei frowned; a rush of cold air had slithered down his back.

"What's wrong?"

"We must see your mother," he said with urgency.

Kieko felt that something was wrong. He tried again to sit up but Shinsei held him down, "I am not done yet."

"Hurry up!"

"I am almost finished wrapping your arm. Just wait–"

"Damn the gods. Hurry up! Something's wro–"

Shinsei slapped Kieko hard across the face. With a finger pointed like a knife at his eye he said, "Do not speak to me with such a curse!"

He lay still holding his breath.

"Speaking against the gods," the priest said shaking his head as he finished mending Kieko's arm by securing it in a cloth sling that he had tied around his neck. "There, it is done." He helped Kieko up and took up his staff.

The two made out in hasty steps.

Kieko's heart sank when he saw two drunken men, Shitsu and Tonono, standing outside his hut. He knew what they were doing, keeping watch, deterring all. He ran at them marking them for death with a charging scream.

Shitsu stepped forward ready to strike Kieko with his staff but it was knocked out of his hands with a rock that Shinsei had thrown. Tonono dropped his staff and ran away when he saw the priest charging at him.

Kieko jumped and kicked Shitsu in the face knocking him down to his knees. He began kicking him in the stomach until Shinsei stopped him by holding him back.

"Let go of me, old man!" Kieko demanded as he tried to wrestle out of Shinsei's hold.

Shitsu scrambled away.

"He's getting away!" Kieko exclaimed.

"Let him go—"

"What?"

"Let him go—we'll deal with him soon enough. We need to take care of your mother first."

He realized that the priest was right. Just then the leather sheet that covered the entrance door of his hut flew open revealing a man cloaked in shadow and armed with a sword.

"You should go, old man," the shadow said to the priest as he wavered in his stance.

Shinsei struck the dark figure down with his staff. Kieko ran into his hut and found his mother beaten, bloodied, and violated. He crashed onto his knees and cradled her head into his lap. He looked at her; her hair had been ripped and cut by a short sword; blood streamed from her lips, nose, and cheeks; bruises spoiled her skin into hardened purples and blacks. He looked at her naked body pumped with drunken lust and covered her with her wool blanket. He lowered his head to hers and cried.

Madonai spoke with a faint voice, "Kieko, it's all right . . . it's all right. You're here." She smiled as she felt his tears drip upon her cheeks.

"I'm sorry, mom," was all he could say before rocking his body and beating his fist into the dirt. *Be strong, you must be strong for her*, his mind reminded, but he began to pant and choke between his words, "I'm sorry . . . I'm sorry I left you . . ."

Shinsei entered the hut and comforted Kieko by placing his hand on his back and said, "Kieko, let me heal her."

Kieko nodded and placed his mother's head between his knees. From near the hearth Shinsei took two buckets that were half-filled with water and placed them by his side. He then ripped strips of cloth from a sheet, sat before Madonai, and chanted a short prayer. He washed his hands in one of the buckets and soaked a strip of cloth in the other bucket before removing the blanket that covered Madonai. Kieko closed his eyes.

The priest began wiping the blood and semen from her skin. Cuts made by clawing fingernails and bites marked her breasts, stomach, and inner thighs. They were not deep cuts; he knew that they would heal in time. He asked Kieko to feed the fire and to boil water. When he had finished washing her body he covered her with a fresh blanket and explained to Kieko that he had to leave and gather the herbs, roots, and plant leaves needed for the medicinal potions he had to prepare. Kieko said goodbye and watched the old priest leave.

Shinsei stepped out of the hut ready to deal with Buko, the man responsible for the crime against Madonai, but he was not lying on the ground in a drunken sleep as he had expected. He bent down, read the tracks on the ground, and saw that Buko had not been aided by anyone, he simply woke up and stumbled away. *He is likely on his way to Kono's home seeking refuge.* He then made his way to the Kadek Temple.

Madonai slept. Every so often her body would jerk or move, but Kieko could see that her mind was at ease. He thought that perhaps she was dreaming of his father or that he was with them, watching them, caring for them, guarding them. He began to long for his father. He needed him, but he had abandoned them so long ago for the West. And here he was with a broken arm and a broken mother with no one to look to for help or protection. "I curse you, father," he said openly. "You are nowhere and no one to me." His right hand and forearm tightened and he began punching the dirt floor until his knuckles bled.

Hours passed. The night drew on. The fire grew faint. His eyes began to weigh heavy until he fell asleep.

Shinsei returned with the morning sun. He woke Kieko up and asked him to start a new fire and to boil more water. Kieko, drowsy, asked where he had gone. The priest explained that he had returned to his temple to fetch a few obscure herbs and roots. He then sat down and began his medicinal work while Madonai continued to sleep. From a leather pouch he poured the contents he had collected onto a wooden cutting board. Kieko looked and saw an unfamiliar root.

"What is that odd looking thing?"

"This is for you," the priest explained. "It is a rare root from a land far to the southwest. In its native land it is called Ashwagandalaha. It will help to heal your broken bone."

"What are those twigs and leaves?"

"These leaves I will use on your mother. It has been kept secret within my gardens. It is also very rare. It was a gift to my ancient Ki line many centuries ago. It grows in an eastern land far beyond the great ocean and it goes by many names. One name, the one I find the most amusing, translates into our tongue as 'devil's fuge.'"

" 'Devil's fuge'?" Kieko said with a quizzical look. "What will it do?"

"You have many questions, Kieko. Once you answer your koan I can begin teaching you all that you seek to know."

"The art of Ki sword," he whispered.

"Is that all you think I have to offer you? Fighting is foolish."

"Then why do you host the tournament every season?"

"It is the traditional way to teach young men that fighting is foolish. Look at you, Kieko. You have a broken arm—"

"So! If I had someone who would teach me how to fight it would be Aiko with the broken arm."

Shinsei shook his head, "Ki priests pursue the art of Teshido and Ki sword as only that, an art. It is a means to discipline the heart, mind, and spirit. Through the art we slay the darkness so deep within us that we become true men: men of compassion, men of integrity, men of the heart, and of the mind, and of the spirit. The true master is meditative in his thoughts, actions, and words. The true master heals. He does not slay with a sword or a fist. He defeats by becoming so clear that he is a mirror to all those around him."

"I don't understand."

"Of course, you do not. You have not experienced enough. The longer you live the more you will experience. Many years from now you will understand.

"Look at your broken arm. Aiko does not hate you because of your Red blood. There will come a day when you will empathize with him. He is much like you. No mother does he have. No father do you have. He envies the love that you receive in your home for he is only greeted by the fighting fists of his father."

Kieko looked down in animosity.

"You have too much anger."

His body tensed.

Shinsei read Kieko's thoughts and decided it best to begin teaching him of herbs and medicines, "To answer your question. These leaves will end any seed within your mother's belly," he immediately regretted what he had just said. He continued, "When you come to study with me I will teach you a thousand remedies. Anyone can maim. A true artisan heals."

But Kieko began to shut out the priest's words. His mind spoke: *Do not think of the evil done against her, only think of the evildoers and what you will do to them. Be patient and quiet the cries of your heart. Be strong and stoic for such are the ways of men.*

"We will begin with your drink," the priest continued. "It is simple to brew. We only need about this much root," he cut a piece the length of his thumb. He then stood up and went to where Madonai kept her cooking pots and plates and found a pot of an appropriate size. He filled it with water and sat down again. Placing the root into the pot he looked at Kieko and said, "Here, take this, and place it over the flame. Let it boil until this," from his satchel he produced a small hour glass, "has turned once, and then pour yourself a cup, but do not drink it until it has cooled enough for your tongue."

Time passed, and as it did Kieko observed Shinsei cut, boil, and even chew at the herbs and roots he used to make his medicines, assisting whenever he could. When the priest had finished making a medicinal cream he gently smeared it upon Madonai's cuts. He then woke her to drink from a warm cup of devil's fuge tea. The sun rose turning morning into early afternoon and when all was done Kieko, his mother, and Shinsei rested and slept.

There were towers tall and black reaching for the sky as storm clouds rolled with unnatural speed above a vast urban expanse. In all directions there were pillars of concrete and steel and things that darted across the vast city. And there were crows, guardians of the night swooping, gliding, hovering above all; serving the one they called *the ancient black*.

To the woman that saw and did not understand, the sight was horrific. With a sharp eye she could see that the city did not know of pasture greens and horizons blues. There were no trees, lakes, and streams. But there was a vast ocean. Its waves were wild and traitorous. They broke hard upon high sea cliffs. And the winds of the storm howled and thundered and spat down heavy rain.

She heard an old song echo through an infinite number of alleys and streets, and a voice that said to all in their sleep: *Be afraid for I paint in vast colors of greed, hate, and sick.*

People consumed; buying and selling, adhering to the chant: *I need this and I need that, and I will not settle until all that is material is beneath my bed.*

She looked into the shadows of the city and saw the suffering of many: veins pierced by needles filled with a poisonous liquid; diseased women bought and sold to be raped and torn; deformed babies wanted for their limbs and parts; eyeless men who roamed the dark.

She heard a thundering roar and searched with her eyes to find its source. On a black path rode seven upon seven horse-machines. They were swift and loyal, but cruel and vengeful. Tears welled in her eyes when she recognized the carved face of her son.

She screamed and jolted up from her futon waking Shinsei and Kieko who had instinctively grabbed their weapons; Shinsei held his staff and Kieko held a kitchen knife.

"What is it?" Shinsei asked. Kieko rubbed his forearm against his exhausted eyes relieved to find no intruder.

"I had a dream. I had a dream of that place," she looked at Shinsei, "that I told you . . . that place . . . so dark."

"What did you see?" the priest questioned.

"I don't know. I don't know how to describe it. There were towers everywhere, dark towers. And the sky was black. Columns of smoke rose into the air. There were no trees–no grass–there was an ocean. There were people deformed and twisted. I could not stand it. And machines, and there were seven . . . seven . . . seven."

Shinsei thought for a moment, "It was just a dream. You are safe. You are with us."

Madonai shook as she felt the muscles around her pelvis tighten. Her shoulders collapsed, she covered her face with her hands and began to cry. Kieko and Shinsei huddled around her to hold her. She squeezed her son. She wanted to feel his warmth, his love, and his beating heart. Shinsei's beard tickled her cheeks reminding her of her father's kisses when she was young. She looked at Kieko's bandaged arm, and with a trembling voice she asked, "My monkey, what happened?"

Kieko hesitated to tell her.

"What happened?" she asked again.

"I . . . I . . . broke it."

She gripped his fingers and squeezed as she shook her head with disappointment. "You see–you see, Shinsei."

"What is done is done," the priest said with authority. "There is no point in getting upset on what cannot be changed."

Madonai shook her head again and relaxed her grip on her son.

Kieko held her tightly, "I'm sorry . . . I'm sorry. I should have been with–"

"Enough!" the priest exclaimed. "What is done is done."

Kieko looked down trying not to acknowledge what the priest had just said. He filled with guilt and repeated in his mind: *I should have been with her. I should have listened and stayed by her side.* He began rocking his mother as if cradling a baby.

"Everything will be all right," the priest said to both. "Do not worry. Rest."

Madonai's eyes bulged, "Buko, what will you do to Buko?"

"Rest, Madonai. You must rest."

"What will you do to Buko?" she asked again.

The priest took in a deep breath, "Was he the only one?"

She did not answer.

He ran his fingers through his beard and twisted a few strands of hair between his thumb and index finger before whispering into her ear, "It was not your fault, Madonai. You have nothing to fear. I am with you as is your son. We are here by your side and we will protect you, but you must tell me if the others did as Buko did."

"I will not speak. If I do they will come again," she then quieted her voice; she did not want her son to hear her words. "I do not wish to bring this upon the Council. What's done is done–as you said–let us leave it at that and be grateful that I am here with my son . . . and you, my husband's old friend."

"That is not good enough, Madonai."

"Do not speak to me of what is good!" she coughed.

The priest leaned back so that he could read her eyes. He had seen this before, *so long ago*. He knew that she feared what Buko and his men would do if she were to bring any word of the crime to the Elders, but more than that he knew that she feared the embarrassment and humiliation of having all within the village know what had been done to her.

"You are a stupid old man if you think the Elders will place judgment against Buko," she began. "Have you forgotten that he is Kono's brother? That I am hated here? Have you? Have you?" She then covered her distressed face with her hands.

Kieko could not stand to see his mother ridden with so much shame, guilt, and fear.

"Kieko," the priest said.

"Yes, Shinsei."

"Leave me with your mother."

He was relieved. He hugged his mother and looked at her. She nodded that it was all right for him to leave. He stood up and exited his hut, but when the light of the sun hit him he felt ashamed for abandoning her. Defeated, he sat within a cool shadow behind his hut and imagined that he could hear in the wind the songs of those lost at sea.

Shinsei looked at Madonai, held her hands in his, and said, "He is a strong boy. He is growing stronger everyday. His father is proud of him. He is watching."

"I miss him so much."

"I do too. He was a good friend."

"Yes . . ."

"Madonai, you know that Kieko will need to hear from me of his father's past. Things are moving swiftly. There is a shadow growing in the West. I can feel it. It is coming. You are having visions—your dreams—Kieko living far beyond the borders of Kadek, beyond the Kingdom of Lemuria. What will become of him I do not know, but we must prepare him, we must continue to show him that we are not victims of our circumstances, that we are strong."

"Strong?"

"Strong and able to fight."

" 'Fighting is foolish,' are these not your words, Shinsei? Fighting is a wicked way. It has stolen from me my husband."

"But it gave you your son."

"What do you mean by that?" she asked defensively.

"For what other reason did Nishiaka leave Ikishi? To face what hunted him, to fight and protect his family and the people of these lands. I do not believe in fighting for political or territorial gain, but I do believe as Nishiaka did—to fight and protect what is sacred . . . our families."

"And what will become of my son when he travels into the West? My dreams are nightmares. He will grow dark and devoid of hope. He will live in the belly of this beast that breathes flame to the East."

"That is why we must show him that it is the good fight that he is to fight."

"Fighting will steal my son."

"Your son will leave because he seeks the West. Nothing can ever break the bond that binds him to you–you are his mother. He will always be with you. He is your life."

"Then my life is a sad one, Shinsei. My father I will never see again, my mother a witch, my husband dead, my son soon to be gone from me."

"Do not speak like this. Life is life; it is as it is and suffering defines all our lives, it is everywhere, in all things, in all directions. We are born into this world screaming, but always do we have the choice to live as either victims or as individuals of intent. Choose victimhood and live your life in hell, but there are those, like your husband, who have chosen to own their losses and rise above them. You are a fighter, Madonai. That is why Kieko chose you to be his mother before he came into this world, to learn from your strength and kindness. You have made him into who he is, but you fear what he will become. Teach him his final lesson. Stand and fight against your fear for if he sees you cower now, then surely he will fall when he arrives in the West."

"Then what is it that you want of me?"

He paused and then asked, "Was it only Buko?"

She did not want to think of him and what he had done; she wanted to pretend that nothing had happened and to simply go on with her life, but Shinsei was right, she had to be strong for Kieko, she had to make a stand. Thoughts of her son filled her heart and mind, and through him she found strength. "Yes . . . they all beat me . . . but only Buko . . ." she left her words at that.

"Do not worry," he whispered as he held her. "I am here with you as is your son."

She opened her heart and cried.

"He should be killed!" Kieko demanded grinding and clenching his teeth as he stood within his hut again.

The old priest looked at him. "I will find him, Kieko. You have my word. And I will find Shitsu and Tonono; they will all face the judgment of the Elders."

Jomana pranced into the hut and cut the tense air with her wagging tail and panting tongue. She sniffed and snorted and sneezed as she looked into the pots scattered around the hearth searching for food. And although she found tasty scraps she did not eat them, instead, she turned to Shinsei and barked a hello. The priest smiled. She then approached Kieko and licked his hand.

"Hi Jomana," Kieko said with a small grin.

Madonai was happy to see Jomana. Jomana sniffed Madonai's face and wounds and licked and kissed. Madonai giggled. Jomana's tail wagged. Madonai petted Jomana's fur and for a moment forgot her sorrows.

Old farmer Toasu entered, "Jomana!" he called out.

"It's all right," Madonai assured him.

Jomana sat obediently by Madonai's side; her wagging tail swept at the dirt floor.

"Are you all right?" the old farmer asked.

Shinsei approached his old friend and silently explained what had happened to Madonai the night before. When Shinsei was done the old farmer looked down with his hand over his mouth. When the silence between all became too great Jomana barked.

"Quiet!" old farmer Toasu requested. He approached Madonai and kneeled before her. "When I was young my father always said to me, 'Treat women like princesses because that is what they are.' " He smiled as memories of his father's comedic ways filled his thoughts. "There is nothing that I can say to heal your heart, Madonai." He paused for a moment, and continued, "Jomana brings me much happiness. She licks at my old scars. She is a good dog. She protects me in the night. She will stay with you for awhile."

"Thank you, Toasu."

"It is my pleasure and for Jomana an honor."

Jomana barked in agreement, bringing smiles to all, and licked Madonai's hand.

"Now that that is settled I can see that Kieko broke his arm," the old farmer said jokingly.

Kieko bowed his head in shame.

Defending him Shinsei said, "He heals with speed." He then directed his words to Kieko, "Since you can not train in the art of Teshi-do as much as you would like you now have no other choice than to mind-train, meditate. Remember, I can only begin training you when you have answered your koan."

"Yes, Shinsei."

"Toasu, please stay with them. I must attend to Tonodo–"

"Let me guess, he has a broken body part as well."

"You are quick, old friend."

"I am quick because I am a fool. Do not forget."

"Yes, yes, I must go."

"Will you speak to the Elders when you are done with Tonodo?"

"Yes, old friend."

"I want to go with you," Kieko said to Shinsei.

"I need you to stay with your mother and prepare the teas and medicinal tablets that you and she must take."

"He knows how to make such medicine?" the old farmer asked.

"Yes," the priest answered, "I taught him last night."

"Well, Kieko, it seems that the priest has already begun training you."

"Yes . . ." was all that he could say.

CHAPTER V

Word of the crime committed against Madonai spread throughout the village. Women and men talked their foul gossip and speculated on what had really happened that spring festival night. It was agreed by many that Madonai had put a spell on Buko and seduced him into her wicked net like a witch, or that she had sought to poison him like the black widow spider of their tales and fables.

Ruka did not pay any attention to the ridiculousness of the stories that floated through the air. When she had first heard the news she, shocked, rushed to Madonai's hut with Kira to begin caring for her. And when they had returned home they found Rakima sitting by the hearth warming up his tea as he smoked a bitter weed from his pipe.

"We have returned, sweety," Ruka greeted her husband. "I will begin cooking your meal. I'm sorry that I didn't have a chance to get started on it earlier. We were with Madonai caring for her."

"Yes, this I know."

Kira stood behind her mother; she did not want to look at or speak to her father.

"I know what you had said," Ruka continued, "but, you must understand that Madonai needs us . . . as does Kieko."

"Yes, I know."

"And I needed Kira's help so I brought her with me, but only for today—only for today, sweety. I will care for Madonai and Kira will stay here to cook your meals—"

"No." He took a puff from his pipe, exhaled the scented smoke, and looked at his daughter with hardened eyes. "You will do no such thing."

"What do you mean 'no'?" Kira shouted ready to fight her father's words.

"Do not talk to me in such a way, girl!" he barked silencing her. "I gave you life and I can as easily take it from you. You pay your respects to me as long as you live under my roof," he said pointing up.

"Rakima," Ruka pleaded.

"I am not finished. Let me speak woman . . ." he took another puff from his pipe and thought for a moment. "Kira, my daughter," he began, "I know that you do not understand why I say what I do and why I forbid you from doing what you desire to do. I don't expect you to understand me. I did not understand my father, or my mother. Regardless of that you should know that I say what I say because I know the realities of this Ikishi world. I am trying to protect you." Ruka held her daughter as her husband spoke. "But, I can not keep you under my wing forever, and that . . . saddens me. You are becoming a woman, and I fear that. I am uncomfortable with it. I do not like speaking to my brothers of suitors and such. I do not enjoy it. You are my child and your mother has raised you wonderfully." A warm feeling flourished in Ruka's heart. "And I am grateful to her." Ruka smiled. "Kieko is a good boy. If I could have things my way I would keep him away from you, not because he is mixed in blood, but because I can see that he will hurt you. He is not right for you. He has too much anger–too much. You think that you will be able to help him, change him, but I am telling you that he will not change. Not for many years. I can see it. I was much like him when I was young. Much like him I was.

"But, I realize that I can not cage you. I will not keep you from seeing him. My brothers will not agree with me but they are my problem, not yours. But, know this. Kieko can never be a suitor for you. That simply can not be."

"Why!" Kira cried. "Why, can he n-not be?"

"Because I will not bless such a union and neither will any of your uncles. And that is the end of it. Do you understand?"

Kira fell to her knees with her hands over her tearful eyes. Ruka continued holding her trying to comfort her.

"I will not keep you from seeing Kieko. Under these circumstances Madonai and Kieko need you both."

Ruka nodded. She was grateful that her husband would support her and her daughter's care of Madonai.

"Now, I must leave. There are some things that I must discuss with our kin." He walked out without drinking a single sip of his tea.

CHAPTER VI

Kieko was waiting outside the Council Hut; he was thinking about his mother who was at home under the care of Ruka, Kira, and Jomana. He looked at the armed men who were guarding the only entrance into the hut and cursed the laws of Kadek that forbade all women and boys from ever entering the hut. He kicked the ground and looked up at the hut's thatched roof that shot up in a sharp arc from its oblong circular base and saw the red flag at its peak; a sign that a meeting had been called. He took a step back to stand next to the ash filled cauldron that sat before two rows of fire staves, which lit a short path to the hut's entrance.

Old farmer Toasu walked into the circular plain of the Ikishi village and saw Kieko. He approached him, and when he stood beside him he inhaled the strong scent of the incense sticks that burned within the cauldron.

"It's not fair that I can not enter. It is my mother who's the victim of this crime."

The old farmer looked at Kieko, "There are too many things in this world that are not fair: it is not fair that my parents died when they did; it is not fair that you lost the tournament; it is not fair that the Atlanteans pillage whatever lands they point their wicked fingers at. But, in all my long years, from all that I have seen in this world, I have discovered one thing." Kieko waited for the answer. "Justice is served to each and every one of us, in this life or the next. What we reap is what we sow. This you know, Kieko. There are no victims in this world. We choose what ails and benefits us."

"I don't believe in reincarnation and karma and all of that."

"We both know that that is a lie. I know what beliefs you hold dear to your heart. And even if that were true then how or why would you want to train with Shinsei? You cannot be a Ki disciple if you reject these truths. Regardless, things are as they are whether you believe in them or not. And you speak with little knowledge or experience of the world. There will come a day when you will understand things because you have seen them with your own eyes, felt them with your own heart."

"That is all I hear from you and Shinsei." He then mimicked Shinsei's voice, " 'You will know when you experience, you will know when you experience, you will know when you experience.' Do not tell me such things."

"You are a stupid little boy! You will respect the Ki priest." Kieko shook his head and kicked the ground again. "I've had enough of your words, *boy*. I'm going in to speak with *men*," he then walked toward the Council Hut through the path set by the fire staves.

Kieko continued kicking the ground and whispered, "Stupid old fool."

The old farmer stopped before the guards, turned around, and said, "I heard that. I may be old but I have ears to rival yours. And yes, I am a fool," he then disappeared into the dark of the hut.

Rakima was speaking to his brothers and cousins within the Council Hut as he drank his tea; they were arguing over who would serve as a proper suitor for his daughter. Although he did not enjoy the topic he engaged in it because it was expected of him, and as he listened he heard Aiko's name and the arguments for the wealth and prestige that would be gained from Kono in return for his daughter's hand. Angered by their matchmaking talks he excused himself, noticed the old farmer entering the hut, and went to greet him.

"Strange to see you here, old man."

"Yes, it is strange. I find it odd too that I am here." The two laughed. "Although I am old, as you have been so kind to remind me, I am not wise but a fool, and because I am a fool I am wise to know that you have chosen to speak to me because you do not wish to continue your talks with your kin over there. Am I right, old father of a beautiful daughter?"

"You're too quick, old man, and too odd for most here. How are things on your farm?"

"Trying to change the topic are you?"

"Yes, I do not wish to speak of my daughter. I've had enough."

"In denial are you? Your daughter is a woman. Everyone in the village sees her as a woman. Perhaps, you should begin to see her as a woman too."

"Listen, friend, I do not wish to speak more of her. Is that understood?"

"Yes, yes. Well, how goes these talks of the three offenders over there?" he said nodding in the direction to where Buko, Shitsu, and Tonono were standing between several guards.

"There is no question that Shitsu and Tonono will receive a punishment appropriate for their involvement in the crime, but Kono will protect his brother, he has much sway with the Elders. I do not know how severe Buko's punishment will be?"

"Why is it so easy to punish Shitsu and Tonono? They are allied to Kono, are they not?"

"Yes, that is true, but there is not much Kono can do about the debts they owe to Elder Haru."

"How he became an Elder I will never know," the old farmer said shaking his head. "Well, it is good to hear that justice is in good order here. No different than in Atlantis, I say."

"You should watch your tongue in this place, old man."

"You are right, Rakima. I am old, and because I am I have nothing to lose. My years are spent. No one's favor do I need." The old farmer then shouldered past Rakima, but Rakima grabbed his arm and asked, "What did you mean by that?"

"I know it must be difficult for you, Rakima. I am not a fool—yes I am," he smiled. "You are protecting the interests of your kin in this place. Your older brother, Tsuwata, has many debts to be paid to Kono, does he not? His gambles have afforded him nothing but a rotten child."

"Shut your mouth, old man. You do not know of my brother's circumstances."

"And what of the circumstances of Kieko and his mother? They are honest and good, but in this place it will gain them nothing. I am here in their favor. I can not be swayed or bought."

"You watch yourself," he warned again with anger deep in his voice.

The old farmer paid no attention to Rakima's final words and walked away.

The seven Elders were sitting on their wooden thrones, which were collectively positioned in an arc that was centered before the long thatched wall farthest from the entrance. Chief Elder Subo, who was seated at the center of the arc of thrones, stood up and said aloud, "Let us begin. Quiet your talks and take your seats Ikishi men."

The crowd of men began hushing at each other, sitting down on the ground, and waiting until all was silent.

"It has been brought to our attention," the Chief Elder began, "that a crime has been committed against a woman in our village. Shinsei, who came upon the crime, has already explained to us—the Elders—that both Shitsu and Tonono stood guard before the house of Nishiaka while Buko abused and raped Madonai within it. Whether or not Shitsu and Tonono beat or had the intention to abuse and rape Madonai can not be discerned, but they were accomplices to the acts committed by Buko. As a result we, the Elder men, have decided that both Shitsu and Tonono will be punished by sowing and reaping the fields of Haru's lands for no less than seven years—"

"Are you mad!" old farmer Toasu contested.

"Who speaks? Stand before all!" Elder Subo commanded as the crowd of men began to whisper. The old farmer took his time to stand and when Elder Subo saw the old farmer's weathered face near one of the hut's four wooden pillars he said with ridicule, "Well, if it is not the hermit of Kadek."

Everyone laughed.

The old farmer waited for the laughter to die down, "Yes, it is. Good to see you too, Elder Subo. I see you have aged a great many days since I last saw you, but you have grown no wiser."

Rakima shook his head at the old farmer's words.

Elder Subo replied, "You risk, old hermit, being thrown from this Council. Watch your tongue."

"I am immune to such nonsense. Is it not Lemurian tradition to respect the thoughts and words of elder men who prove themselves still competent and sane?"

"Yes, it is old hermit. Whether or not you are sane remains to be seen." Short bursts of laughter erupted from the crowd. He continued, regretting what he had to ask, "What is it that you wish to say?"

"I find it funny, old friend, that the punishment fitted Shitsu and Tonono appears appropriate not for the crime against Madonai but for their debts owed to Haru—"

Elder Haru shot up from his seat, "You know nothing, old hermit! Do not question the decisions of the Council!"

"I am not questioning. I am reminding," old farmer Toasu retorted.

"What are you reminding us of?" Chief Elder Subo asked as he signaled Elder Haru to calm himself and sit down.

"I am reminding you of the appropriate punishment placed against those who desecrate our women."

Kono spoke out, "Those are old ways, old man. Punishment by death is no longer heeded here."

"Funny that you should say such a thing Kono since it is you who curses death upon the Atlantean men responsible for—"

"Be silent, old fool!" Kono shouted nearly choking on the tealeaves he accidentally swallowed from his cup. "Atlantean men," he coughed, "deserve death not because of what they have stolen from me and my son, but for what they have always stolen from Lemurian lands. They are a race bent on greed and hate–"

"Are you describing yourself or Atlanteans?"

Tsuwata shot up and shouted with a threatening fist, "You watch your tongue, you old disease!"

Rakima's face paled into severe unease.

"Oh, Tsuwata," the old farmer said. "What a surprise to see you rising to attack my words against Kono."

"Shut your tongue!" Tsuwata shouted back before looking down at his younger bother, Rakima, with angered eyes.

"Why do you look to your bro–?"

"Be gone, you old fool!" Kono hollered. "We are all tired of your aimless talk." Many within the crowd agreed with nods and malicious shouts.

"Kono," the old farmer stated, "you are a lost and pathetic, drunken cause!"

"You are gone from here, old farmer Toasu!" Elder Subo declared as angry shouts against the old farmer continued to fill the air.

Two armed guards approached the old farmer–the old farmer did not resist them–and escorted him out of the hut as cups and splashes of drink were thrown at him.

Outside the old farmer wiped himself off. He then walked over to the cauldron and cupped his hands to waft the smoke of the burning incense over his head; a symbolic means to purify his body of evil spirits and diseases.

"Why is there so much yelling?" Kieko asked.

Startled, old farmer Toasu exclaimed, "You nearly frightened me."

"What happened to you? Why are there tea leaves hanging from your robes?"

"I spoke like a disobedient child in there. As you can see it did not do me well. A bit embarrassing it is to be thrown out of a council meeting. I am too much of a radical fool. I best be going, Kieko. All things happen as they should, remember that."

"What do you mean? My mother . . . was she meant to be hurt as she was? Is that what you're saying?"

He thought for a moment, "It is late . . . I should go."

"Then go. I don't need you."

The old farmer looked at Kieko with gentle eyes, "Kieko, do not blame yourself for what happened to your mother. It is not your fault. Remember, we are the sum of our decisions. Buko did what he did and he will pay in this lifetime or the next. Justice will be served. In that you must trust."

"If that is true–if I am to believe that–then it means that my mother is paying for some kind of karmic debt. That the violence enacted against her is the result of some kind of justice. Is that what you're saying?"

"Kieko, I will not convince you to believe anything. Believe in what you would like. Good night."

The sound of insects silenced the steps of the old farmer as he walked into the night. Kieko watched him, thinking of what he had said, until he disappeared. He decided that the old farmer's talk of cosmic justice was worth no more than fly dung. Hunger began to pain his stomach. He looked at the red flag that flapped from the summit of the Council Hut and sat down near the cauldron waiting for the Elders to announce their decisions and call an end to their meeting.

After everyone had calmed down Chief Elder Subo asked if any man had any objection to the punishment given to Shitsu and Tonono. No one raised a hand or spoke against the decision. Shitsu and Tonono were then escorted out of the hut by three guards while two guards moved Buko to stand alone before the seven Elders and the priest.

The Chief Elder raised his voice to the crowd, "As for you, Buko. Your crime cannot be disputed for it is based upon the holy words of Shinsei who struck you down when you exited the house of Nishiaka. And as Toasu so kindly reminded us your crime was once punishable by death. But, this punishment we no longer honor for Shinsei forbade it many decades ago. As a result we, the Elders, have given Shinsei the power, and responsibility, of assigning you an appropriate punishment since it was he who came across the doings of your criminal act. May he show mercy on you."

Whispers filled the air.

"Silence!" Elder Subo demanded.

Shinsei approached Buko and looked him in the eye, "Marked will your skin be; a warning to all. You are banished from Kadek—"

"What is this?" Kono contested as he stood up and rushed toward the Chief Elder. "What is this? Is it not the duty of the Elders to assign the appropriate punishment? Why is a priest meddling in the affairs of justice?"

"Silence!" Elder Subo commanded. "I am Chief Elder here and it was my decision to appoint Shinsei as the one to assign Buko his punishment. I know you and your ways Kono—don't give me that face!" Kono, who now stood before the Chief Elder, continued raveling his face with hate. "You know of what I speak. I will not allow you to meddle in the affairs of justice so be gone and accept the punishment befitting your brother's crime. He has three days. This meeting of men has ended."

"Curse you!" Kono shouted, and before he could launch his hands at the Chief Elder several guards took him and held him back. Frightened, the Chief Elder exited the hut, followed by Shinsei and the other Elders, while the crowd began to argue and shout.

CHAPTER VII

Out on the northeastern edge of the village near the towering jagged wall of Mount Kurohi and the border of the Ikishi forest was the prison chamber; it was the only prison chamber in the village, and hardly was it ever occupied, which, naturally, resulted in its constant disrepair. The prison, a deep hole dug into the earth and roofed by a strong bamboo gate, could comfortably hold three men and as many as fifteen if they all stood shoulder to shoulder. Buko stood alone within it.

It was night. He was watching the clouds roll across the moonlit sky as he waited. He then heard footsteps.

"Hello down there," Raki-ka greeted. Buko looked at Raki-ka but did not reply. "It's time to lower your bucket of yummy slop."

"Leave me be, idiot."

"Listen—I'm just here to lower your food—"

"Where is the other idiot guard, the one from this morning?"

"He's gone. The Elders want a rotation. They don't trust anyone. Guess they know that your brother would try to bribe one of us—*idiot* guards—to look the other way if he tried to bring you something—you know . . . something to escape with."

"Curse you."

"Yes, curse me. I have to raise and take away your waste bucket."

"Leave the bucket!"

"Fine; spend the night with your bucket of filth."

"Don't mock me, peasant."

"No food for you then, and don't bother me tonight. Don't call on me for anything."

"My brother will come."

"He is here."

"Then leave and send my brother to me!"

Raki-ka shook his head, whispered, "Cursed devil," and walked away.

Buko kicked the prison wall and shouted, "Curse you, Raki-ka! I will find you—in this life or the next—and stab you to death!" He accidentally kicked his waste bucket spilling its foul contents all over the floor.

"Not wise, my brother."

"Kono," Buko replied looking up.

Kono crouched down and turned his head to look at Raki-ka from the corner of his eye.

Raki-ka placed his hands before the campfire to warm them but felt very uncomfortable. He looked to where Kono was and saw that he had just looked away from him. His brow furrowed with concern; his eyes focused. He could see that Kono was now speaking, whispering, to his brother. He tried to hear a hint of what was being said between them but he could not hear a word. He waited patiently keeping a firm grip on the hilt of the short sword that was tucked into his thick cotton belt.

When Kono finished speaking to his brother he looked and sneered at Raki-ka, stood up, and walked back toward the village.

Raki-ka took his spear and stood up. And when he saw Kono disappear into the darkness of the night he sat back down in relief and tried to warm his hands before the campfire again. A gentle wind rustled the branches of the trees. He relaxed and looked up at the stars, and began to whistle. "Quiet, you!" Buko shouted. Raki-ka ignored the request and continued whistling with a smile.

CHAPTER VIII

Out of concern for the safety of Madonai and Kieko, Shinsei had decided to spend the three nights that Buko was imprisoned in their home. His routine with them was simple: he woke up every morning at dawn to meditate, prepare breakfast, and tend to Madonai while telling old Ki fables and tales to Kieko. Ruka and Kira would arrive by late morning bringing the foods and spices they needed to prepare a midday meal for them all. After eating, Shinsei would meditate again, and by late afternoon he, accompanied by Kieko, would travel to the circular plain of the village to teach history, philosophy, and poetry to the young men and boys who could attend. After his lessons he dismissed Kieko and the young boys and took the remaining young men to the border of the Ikishi forest to teach them intoductory skills in Teshido and Ki sword while also testing their knowledge of the medicinal properties of various plants. And in the hour before sunset he took those who desired to read the ancient scrolls of the old tongue to the beach where he drew into the wet sand with his staff the characters of their writing system.

Jomana began barking while her tail wagged feverishly. She went to the door of the thatched hut of Madonai and waited as she continued to bark and scratch at the door.

"Someone is coming," Madonai said nervously to Kira.

There was a knock at the door. Jomana began whimpering as she looked to Madonai to open the door.

"Who is it?" Madonai asked.

"Not to worry. It is Toasu." Madonai and Kira let out a sigh of relief. "May I come in?"

"Yes, yes, of course, old farmer Toasu," Madonai went to the door and opened it. "Welcome, come. Come in."

Jomana danced around her master as he entered.

"Thank you, Madonai," the old farmer greeted. "And good evening to you, Kira."

"Good evening, old farmer Toasu," Kira answered as she bowed her head in respect.

"No need to bow. I am no different than you." He took a few steps not paying much attention to Jomana who was moving frantically in front of him. "I apologize for the intrusion, but I wanted to make sure that Jomana was behaving herself here, in your home."

"She is a joy, a great source of joy, Toasu," Madonai replied. "Every night she sleeps by my side, warming me with her fur. And in the morning she wakes me with her pleasant yawns, stretches, and licks. I would love to keep her if I could. Please, please do not worry. I assure you that she has been a true and helpful friend here."

"That is good, that is good," he smiled, but he glared at his furry friend and called her to his knee. Jomana approaced her master with her head bowed, tail pointed down wagging only slightly, and eyes looking up to his. When she was at his feet she sniffed and licked his ankles. "Jomana!" he called out as Madonai and Kira looked in fear for their beloved friend. She looked up to her master, but he cracked a smile and crouched down to pet her. Relieved, she jumped around her master with her tail wagging. He then took Jomana by the head and kissed her above the eyes, "That's a good girl." She barked at her master and rolled onto her back so that he could pet and massage her stomach. "Where are the priest and Kieko?"

"The priest is still away teaching, and Kieko is away trying to meditate on his koan," answered Madonai.

"I see. Will they be back soon?"

"Yes, they should. Perhaps, any moment," Madonai answered.

"That is good." The old farmer then continued to pet and praise his dog with child talk.

"May I prepare a cup of tea for you, old farmer Toasu?" Kira asked.

The old farmer stood up and said, "No, no, but thank you. Well, I should be off. I have made more visits to Ikishi in these past few days than I have in some years. People will begin to think that I am losing my old hermit ways. I must return to doing what I do best . . . maintaining my oddity and mysteriousness," he laughed.

"You are always welcome here, old farmer Toasu," Madonai said.

"Thank you. You do not mind then if Jomana stays a few more days with you?"

"No, no, no, we would love to adopt her if we could. She brings Kira and I much joy."

"Yes, yes she does," the old farmer agreed. "She brings me much laughter. She is a saint. At times a fool and dumb, but a saint nonetheless. Isn't that right, old friend?"

Jomana barked and licked her nose.

"All right, I am off," the old farmer bowed and left.

Jomana waited by the exit, and when she knew her master was gone she returned to Madonai and Kira, who were sitting by the hearth, to give them company during their talk about the old farmer.

"He is so gentle. Why doesn't he have a wife to care for him?" Kira asked.

"It is not his way," Madonai explained. "He lives alone so that he can dream of the past."

"Do you know of his past?"

"Only a little. What I know I learned from my husband–the old farmer shared many talks of the West with him . . . My husband did not believe in gossip so he kept most of the old farmer's secrets to himself."

"What did he tell you?"

"Only that Toasu misses someone he had loved long ago."

"A bride he had in the West?"

"I do not know. My husband only said that there was someone who he had loved in his travels long ago, and that she is forever gone."

"There is much sadness in his eyes."

"Yes . . . he is a good man. He does not deserve to live out his days alone, but that is what he has chosen for himself."

"He is cruel for choosing so."

"Such are the ways of men," Madonai whispered to herself.

Kira caught her words and asked, "What do you mean?"

"Nothing . . . nothing . . ."

"Please tell me. What—what did you mean by that?"

Madonai thought for a moment before she began, "Men . . . men love pain. They pride themselves on it. They find strength in their scars. They seek danger and dragons and wars. Their lives are as coarse and as rough as their bearded, chiseled faces. They are very different from us. They seek what we do not." Kira was silent. She thought of Kieko's broken arm and of all of her father's scars. "It is late Kira. It is time for you to be with your family."

Kira realized that she was right. "Will you be all right?"

"Yes, yes. Thank you. Shinsei and Kieko will be home soon. Please, take some soup with you for your parents."

Kira stopped Madonai from getting up and said, "No, please, you should rest."

"No, Kira let me do this. Your mother and you have been so kind to me. Please, let me give you both thanks in this way."

Kira nodded and helped Madonai stand up.

With a ladle Madonai scooped the warm soup from the metal pot that hung above the hearth and poured it into a clay bowl.

She then placed a lid on the bowl and with a small blanket wrapped it. "Here you are," she said passing the wrapped bowl into Kira's hands.

"Thank you, Madonai," she carefully gave her a hug. "Please give Kieko a warm hug for me."

"I will, sweety."

"See you tomorrow . . . good night."

"Good night," Madonai smiled and waved.

Kira opened the door and walked out into the cold, dark night.

The cloudy sky blocked the light of the moon, but Shinsei could still see the old farmer making his way home. Kieko walked up to where the priest had stopped with his lantern and saw the old farmer as well. He asked, "Is that Toasu?"

"Yes, it is. Come, let us go down and greet the old fool." Kieko nodded. The priest gripped his staff, and together they walked down the slope of a hill.

"Who goes there in the night?" the old farmer asked aloud in the old tongue.

Shinsei answered, "It is I old fool, the priest, Shinsei."

"And at your side? Is that Kieko, old friend?"

"Yes, it is."

"The two of you should make fast steps back to the home of Nishiaka. Madonai and Kira are waiting for you both with warm food to fill your empty stomachs. Good night," he finished and continued on his path back home.

"Old friend, wait. There are matters that I would like to discuss with you." Shinsei hurried down the hill with Kieko following right behind him.

"Hurry then. It is cold," he replied annoyed. He waited cupping his hands and warming them with his breath. When they were close enough he bowed and said, "Good to see you, old priest."

"It is good to see you too, old friend," Shinsei said and bowed.

"It is good to see you too," Kieko said and bowed.

"What are you doing?" the old farmer asked.

"What did I do?" Kieko asked confused.

"I keep telling you to never bow to me."

"I'm sorry, Toasu," he apologized.

"Why do you teach him such things?" Shinsei asked. "He is a respectful boy. Don't teach him to be otherwise."

"Yes, yes, yes. I forget that you are bound to the codes of priesthood: rites, ceremony, conduct, and such nonsense."

"Do not mock my faith and my way," Shinsei said with a half smile.

"What are the two of you doing so late at night?"

"I found Kieko on my way back to the home of Nishiaka—"

"Let me guess. Near his tree?" the old farmer said looking at Kieko.

"Yes," Kieko answered.

"Kieko, you should find a new place to hide," the old farmer teased. Kieko nodded not appreciating the old farmer's comment. "So, what do you want of me, old priest? It is cold."

"Yes," Shinsei paused and looked at Kieko. "I must speak in private with the old farmer. Go and comfort your mother. I will be at your home shortly."

"Yes," Kieko said relieved that he was excused to go home and escape the frigid air.

When Shinsei was sure that Kieko was far enough to not hear his words he began, "Old friend, it has been long since you have visited Ikishi so often. Is something troubling you?"

"No, no, no. Do not worry, old friend. I am fine." The old farmer could see that something was eating at Shinsei's thoughts.

"All is fine?"

"Yes, yes."

"Then what brings you to Ikishi so often?"

"What? Am I not allowed to visit the sea?"

"Is that it? That is why you have been visiting Ikishi?"

"Old friend, you know that at the beginning of every season, when everyone is celebrating within the village during their festivals, I go to the beach with Jomana. And you know that I care deeply for Kieko and his mother so end your game and tell me what troubles you."

"Yes, you are right. I was hoping you would say something first."

"Say something about Kieko you mean?"

"Yes."

"You have been worried about him, haven't you?"

"Yes, of course."

"As have I, but I keep such thoughts to myself."

"Then you know."

"Old friend, come out and say what it is you mean to say before I cease to feel my toes and fingers in this cold."

"You're right, old friend. Kieko . . . he can channel Ki."

"Yes, I know."

"You know?" Shinsei asked abruptly.

"Don't be foolish. Of course I do. It is in everyone's whispers; everyone is gossiping about Kieko and his ability to channel the Ki."

"What are they saying?"

"They are scared of him. Never has a child so young channeled Ki in these lands. They are afraid of what it means—of what it means for them. They see it as an ill omen, a sign of dark things to come. They fear Kieko, and some wish him dead." Shinsei shook his head. "Friend," the old farmer continued, "do not worry, people talk and talk, rarely do they pursue their thoughts. Nothing will happen to Kieko. Just make sure that he begins studying with you within your temple soon. When he is out of sight they will all forget about him and what he is able to do."

"No, I'm afraid that is not true. I fear that the villagers will grow more fearful of him when they know he is learning of the Ki and how to channel it within my temple walls–"

"They *will* fear him if they know that there is no one disciplining him in the ways of the Ki. They are afraid that his anger will grow and he will use his talents against them. If they know that he is away, within your walls, they will be assured that he is being tamed."

"Perhaps you're right, old friend, but I fear that I have lost the trust and respect of many for banishing Buko."

"You know better than to speak such nonsense. Do not plague me with your doubts, old friend. You are wise and able to *see* farther into the future than I. No one's trust and respect have you lost. You have only lost the favor of Kono and his clan–and thank the gods for that," he said with a witty voice. "Everyone admires you priest. You are a good man who has banished a bad seed. Remember, many here simply can not show their support of your decision against Buko because they are protecting the interests of their families."

"I hope you are right, old friend."

"I am because I am a fool. Good night. I am off to a warm home," he finished and left.

Shinsei entered the home of Nishiaka and discovered that Madonai and Kieko were both asleep. He fed more wood into the fire and hung a kettle filled with water and tea leaves over it. He waited, and when the water began to boil he lifted the kettle with a thick leather glove, poured himself a cup, and sat down. He carefully sipped his tea as he looked at Kieko and thought of what the old farmer had said. When he was done he placed the cup on a table and ran his fingers through his beard as he watched the dancing flames of the hearth. He then straightened his back, inhaled the warm air, and exhaled expelling all doubts and thoughts from his mind and body. Over and over he breathed until he was lost within the abyss of his mind and heart.

There was darkness, and within the darkness there was silence. But, there was light. It was faint, but it was there; it was as small as a grain of sand set far into the horizon sky. It beckoned him to come and he flew to it over a dark sea and sky. Slowly the light grew until everything around him was bathed within its brilliance. But there was a shadow within it. It was cold, and it called to him. He was not afraid. He went to it, and met the angel of death.

The priest asked: *"What news do you have from the dark realm?"*

The shadow hissed before it spoke: *"Trouble my friend, trouble from the West."*

"Yes, this I know."

"Then also know this. There is trouble within. Two conspire against one, but strike do they not. A youth do they send to end he from the West."

"The boy of the Kai is the one who has been marked?"

"Yes . . . and now I must return to the dark."

Shinsei awoke in a cold sweat from his meditation. He looked at Kieko; he was still asleep. Relieved, he sighed and wiped his brow with his forearm. "A youth do they send to end he from the West," he whispered to himself. He was afraid of what the words could mean for Kieko. He picked up his cup and drank all that was left of his now cold tea, and prepared to go to sleep.

CHAPTER IX

The day had come for Buko to be exiled into the lands beyond the borders of the village. Guards armed with family swords and spears stood near the prison chamber while an afternoon campfire burned. Chief Elder Subo and the Elders stood before the guards, and near the Elders stood Shinsei and Kieko. In the front line of the crowd that had gathered Rakima stood with his elder brother, Tsuwata, and Kono stood behind his son, Aiko.

The air, tense, filled Kieko's lungs. He did not want to be there. When he could he stood behind Shinsei trying to hide from the glares of the men around him; he felt, and believed, that few of the villagers were satisfied with the priest's decision to banish Buko.

More villagers gathered to watch and gossip.

Elder Subo approached the prison, looked down into it, and saw Buko staring back at him.

"You will pay, Elder," Buko said under his breath.

The Chief Elder did not reply. He pitied Buko. The voices of the villagers began to rise behind him. He turned to face them, "Below me is a savage. And for his crime he is cast from these lands into what lies beyond Kadek."

"He is no savage!" a villager shouted. "He is a man who was lured into a trap set by a witch—a sorceress."

"You are a fool to believe such a thing," the Chief Elder began. "What of Shitsu and Tonono? If Buko was seduced, why then did they not rescue him?"

"A spell was placed upon them!" another villager exclaimed.

"Beliefs in spells, witches, demons, and goblin-men are for the weak-minded. Truth is truth. Buko raped. How many of you would blame a ghost if your mother, daughter, or sister were fouled—raped? Would you hunt down and bring to court an apparition? I think not! Brutal crimes are made not by figments, but by men of flesh and bone. I am Chief Elder and the punishment will stand and be honored." The Chief Elder's words penetrated the hearts of the villagers silencing their wicked thoughts. He then signaled a guard to open the prison gate.

After the gate was opened another guard slid a bamboo ladder into the prison chamber. Buko climbed out and when he stood before all his ankles were shackled. Streaks of dirt and dried mud stained his face, hands, feet, and clothes. His hair was oily and his beard filthy.

Kono dug his fingers deep into Aiko's shoulders when he saw his brother.

"You're hurting me, father."

"Shut your mouth and take the pain."

Kieko was keeping his head down, but he could see from the corner of his eye Kono squeezing anger into his son's shoulders.

"Don't look," Shinsei said.

Kieko lowered his eyes.

"Go home, Kieko. You can no longer hide behind me."

"I am not hiding."

"Do not argue. Do as I say. Be gone."

Kieko kicked the ground and walked away.

"Shinsei!" Elder Subo called. "Come, it is time to mark the prisoner before our trek."

Kieko looked back when he heard the priest's name and saw the priest staring back at him with angry eyes motioning with his head for him to return to the village immediately. He turned and continued down to the village.

Relieved that Kieko was on his way home, Shinsei approached the Chief Elder and stood by his side. Elder Subo signaled to Kono to approach him, and when Kono stood before him he said: "You may have a final word with your brother before he is marked and taken to the borders of Kadek."

Kono spat at the Chief Elder's feet—surprisingly, the Chief Elder was not offended and gestured to Shinsei to let the offensive act go unpunished—turned to his brother, and led him to a group of pine trees where they could talk in secret. Elder Subo and Shinsei watched but could not hear Kono's words.

"I wonder what he conspires to do, old friend," Elder Subo confessed.

"As do many here," Shinsei commented.

"What do your *eyes* see?"

"There is danger, yes."

"Do you think Buko will return?"

"I do not believe so. He will not risk it. But, he has a wish and Kono will strive to achieve it.

"And that wish?"

"He is hateful. He wishes death."

"For me?" Elder Subo asked with fear.

"I do not know. My thoughts are not clear. Time will tell."

"Your words do not comfort me, old friend."

"Do you regret giving me the power to decide his punishment?" Shinsei asked looking into the Elder's eyes.

"No, I do not. Elder Haru and the others shame me. Easy is it for Kono to corrupt them. It would have been to my advantage to side with Kono, but I am old, and like you I seek only peace of mind. And I am in need of a good, long walk," he smiled.

Shinsei laughed lightly while thinking of the longtime rivalry between the Chief Elder and Kono.

Kono returned with his brother following behind him and said with bitter words to the Chief Elder, "Guide him well to the ends of Kadek." He gave a last strong hug to his brother and took his son back home.

Elder Subo looked to the crowd of villagers and said aloud, "Banished are you, Buko, from these lands." His words shot into Kono's heart like a poisoned arrow as he walked away. "Never are you to return for death will you find for all here know to end your life upon sight."

Buko ground his teeth and said, "Let's be done with it, old man." Two guards approached him to hold him down. "I do not need them!" he shouted. "Just do it." He kneeled and held out the palms of his hands. Elder Subo nodded to Sekihi, the village blacksmith, who lifted an iron bar out of the campfire with a thick leather glove revealing its burning, pointed end. Sekihi walked over to Buko with the hot bar, bowed his head, and, under his breath, asked for forgiveness.

Buko, impatient, ignored the blacksmith's faint words and grabbed the hot iron tip with his right hand and screamed as he heard his flesh sizzle and foul the air before letting go and crouching down in agony.

"Your left!" Elder Subo shouted. "Now your left. Let us be quick."

Buko raised his left hand. Sekihi grabbed it and burned it as swiftly as he could. He screamed and cursed the gods as he rocked his body back and forth trying to ease himself of the pain. Shinsei kneeled before Buko to mend his charred palms, but he spat in his face. Elder Subo commanded a guard to strike Buko down, but Shinsei waved the guard away as he wiped his face with the sleeve of his robe.

"Leave me be, priest," Buko said.

"Let me heal you," Shinsei said.

"Do not touch me, priest. I would rather have my wounds infect with a wasting disease than to allow them to be treated by you."

"So be it," he said and stood up.

The guards shackled Buko's wrists. The Chief Elder announced in the high tongue, "It is time. Into the west do we go until the borders of Kadek do we meet." He picked up his leather satchel, and began his walk into the sharp valley of Ikishi with his staff. Three guards—Hirotake, Watanoro, and Raki-ka—attempted to lift Buko to his feet, but he shrugged them away and stood up on his own and followed after the Chief Elder. The three guards then followed carrying their spears and packed bags. Shinsei lifted the strap of his bag over his head, put on his conical-shaped hat made of dry grasses, and followed after the guards with his staff.

The villagers watched the small caravan begin their trek into the western wild of Kadek before returning, one by one, to their homes and work as the ocean winds cooled the air and blew the pink pedals of the cherry trees across the sky.

Chapter X

It was late when Aiko heard his father enter their home with stumbling steps. He could hear the sound of his father's rope sandals dragging mud onto the wooden floor. He grew nervous as the steps neared his room. The door slid open. He kept his eyes shut pretending to be asleep while his father looked in. He could hear him breathing heavily and slobbering at the mouth.

"Boy, wake up."

He kept still, praying that his father would walk away.

"Boy, I know you're awake. Get up!"

His body stiffened.

"Stupid boy," he said and walked away.

Relieved, he sighed and opened his eyes. He could see the living area through his room's open door; the hearth's fading fires warmed the iron kettle that was hanging above it. He knew he had to clean the muddy mess his father had made before morning–he did not want to be blamed again. He decided to wait until he was absolutely sure that his father had fallen asleep before getting up to clean the mess.

His home was not a thatched hut with a dirt floor. It was a temple devoted to the worship of his family's ancestors. His ancestors believed that purity of mind and spirit was of grave importance and as a result they built the temple on stilts an-arms-length above ground. It was forbidden to wear sandals or any other type of footwear within the temple; to bring dirt into the temple was sacrilegious.

Kono became guardian of his family's home after the death of his father; he was the eldest son and had inherited all of his family's possessions. As the years passed Buko grew resentful of his brother's wealth, and for a time the two did not speak to each other. But, when Kania's body was found raped and mutilated their troubled bond was mended and the two grew close over bouts of drinking and malicious rants of the Red race.

Nearly every night since the burial of his wife did Kono drink and return home too drunk to remember the following morning that he had fouled his home with dirt or mud. He always blamed and beat Aiko for the mess.

There was a loud noise. Aiko sat up. It sounded like his father was in the kitchen. He heard cups and bowls clang and fall to the floor.

"Father, are you all right?" he called out.

"Come here, stupid boy. I want to drink. It is too dark."

"Yes, father." He stood up and walked barefoot to the kitchen with only the fading light from the hearth to guide his steps. The kitchen's sliding door was open revealing nothing but darkness. He stepped cautiously into the kitchen and whispered, "Father?"

Kono's hands bolted out of the darkness and grabbed him.

"Aaaggghhh!"

"Shut your worthless mouth!"

Aiko went silent. His father then dug his fingers into him. "Father–you're hurting me."

"Stupid boy," Kono looked at his son with disgust, punched him in the face, and threw him to the floor. "Get up. Get up, I said. Get up and fight."

"No," Aiko said tasting blood.

"I said get up, Akai!" Kono kicked his son in the stomach.

He coughed, spat blood, and crawled away from his father.

"What are you doing–stupid boy. Stand up and fight!"

"No–please–father–you are not yourself."

"Fight me!"

"No."

Kono grabbed his son by the hair and repeatedly pounded his fist into his face. Aiko fought back with punches and kicks but his father's strength and anger overwhelmed him.

"You are weak and worthless!" Kono roared with his dirty, beer breath as he threw his son against a wooden pillar. "Burn you Akai, burn you."

"Father, don't . . . please."

"What did you call me?"

"Please."

"No son of mine is so pathetic. Burn you, Akai."

"Father, it's me. I'm not . . . Akai!"

"Men do not cry!" He grabbed his son, threw him near the hearth, and beat him until blood streamed from his nose and lips. When his son could no longer struggle against his heavy weight he lifted the iron kettle that hung above the hearth and said, "You listen, Akai. From this pot will boiling water pour and burn away your worthless skin."

Aiko's eyes widened with terror, "No! Father, No!"

Kono silenced his son with his hand and poured, but only a half cups worth of water fell and burned his chest. "Bastard!" he shouted.

Aiko was relieved.

Frustrated, he shouted, "Bastard!" again and slammed the kettle into Aiko's stomach.

Aiko screamed. A rush of steam sprang up and with it the horrid smell of burning flesh. Neighbors heard his horrific cry, but they ignored it for they had become used to his wails in the night.

Kono threw the kettle at the wall and collapsed into a drunken sleep an arm's length away from Aiko.

Aiko panted for air. His fingers and toes coiled and tightened. His arms tensed. He looked at his stomach and saw that the kettle had torn off bits of flesh. He could not move. He lay on the floor stiff trying desperately to endure the searing pain.

His father began to snore.

Fresh tears dripped down his cheeks. He was afraid and alone. He knew that his father would not permit him to go down into the village until his face had healed from the bruises and cuts that now marked it. Taka and Niko would probably come and visit in a few days, but it did not matter, his father would send them away.

When the pain began to subside he slowly stood up and limped to the kitchen to light a candle. He saw that his cotton shirt was charred over the bottom left portion of his stomach and that it was sticking to his skin. He tried to lift his shirt but could not. He panicked. He then calmed himself and decided to try again. He gently pulled the shirt off and removed it. There were blisters forming. He took a cup from the kitchen counter, dunked it into a bucket of lukewarm water, and poured it over the wound. He breathed in short gasps as the water trickled down his stomach. He ripped a clean white towel into long strips and began dressing the scarred skin. When he was done he went to his room to rest before spending the rest of the night cleaning up after the muddy mess his father had made.

The sun began to rise. He was ready to go to sleep. He looked at his home and saw that all was clean and as it should be. His father was still asleep and sprawled upon the floor underneath the blanket he had covered him with. He stepped into his room; and before he slid his door closed he met the sun with his eyes, listened to the birds that had begun to chirp, and thought of Kira. She was so beautiful, and in need of a suitor. Perhaps, his father would speak with Rakima. His eyes brightened. But, he was still not a man. He had yet to be sent off into the mountains for his meditation retreat by his father or by Shinsei, and it had been a few years since Shinsei had had an apprentice study under him within the Kadek Temple. It was his father's desire that Shinsei elect him to be his next Ki disciple, but he did not want this honor and did not care to solve the koan the priest had given him less than a year ago. He wanted to learn more about the sea, and how to sail a boat and navigate by the stars. He had had enough of plowing, sowing, and reaping the fields of his father's farm while caring for his stupid cows.

The sea. To him it was grand and eternal, never ending, stretching far beyond the horizon. He had heard stories of sailors who had left their homeland on magnificent ships to never return. There were pirates, storms, malicious sea gods, and lands beyond Lemurian imagination. Far into the East would he like to sail for it was said that there was a continent of grand mountains, jungle, and exotic riches.

In his dreams he would take Kira on his travels leaving Ikishi and his father forever, but he knew that Kira would never agree to go for she was not one for adventure and not one to fall in love with him. This saddened him for he knew she fancied Kieko. He cursed Kieko. Why she was so taken with him he did not know. He was filthy, an Akai, and worthless; he had nothing to offer her, nothing at all.

And with those bitter thoughts he went to his futon and slept.

CHAPTER XI

Three days had passed. Elder Subo was leading his caravan along a rocky, narrow path lined with tall grasses. Behind the Elder was Buko who limped as he walked for the iron shackles rubbed and cut into his ankles leaving small trails of blood on the ground. Buko stopped to look at his swelling hands; he still refused to allow Shinsei to treat them. Behind Buko were Watanoro, Hirotake, and Raki-ka. Watanoro called out, "Keep moving." Buko sneered before limping forward again. Shinsei was at the end of the caravan keeping a worrisome eye on Buko.

The trees swayed with the winds. The Mountains of Shinohi, with their peaks covered in snow, were now before the caravan; the mountains marked the end of the Kadek region and the beginning of the Shinohi region. Beyond the long rugged cross through the Shinohi Mountains was a fertile plain that stretched all the way to the East Sea; the sea, with its few uninhabited islands, marked the western end of the Lemurian Kingdom and the beginning of what was once called the Middle Kingdom.

The East Sea was named long ago by the Middle Kingdom; a kingdom that was now fragmented and fading from the pages of Lemurian history. Many aspects of Lemurian culture—their religious practices, philosophies, writing styles, art, medicinal methods, and techniques of war—were derived from the Middle Kingdom over the scores of long-ago centuries that the two kingdoms had traded in goods, ideas, exotic plants and animals, and raw materials.

Shinsei, as he looked in awe at the Mountains of Shinohi, thought about the founder of his Lemurian faith, Quin-Zu.

Quin-Zu arrived in Lemuria from his native Middle Kingdom land near the end of the Age of the Tiger. He was a Ki priest and a traveler spreading the word of his faith to all those in need. It was said that in the months after his arrival to Lemuria he came across a small and impoverished farming village near the Shinohi Mountains. He discovered that the village was at the mercy of a gang of gambling bandits that raided the village every harvest moon for their food and women. He decided to live with the villagers to help them plant their seeds, hunt their meats, and heal their sick. He taught them the words and actions of his faith and trained them in the meditative ways of his kingdom's philosophies and martial arts.

The villagers found peace with the Ki priest for never again did they see the gang that had haunted them for so many years. It was believed that the Ki priest, in the night, had tracked and found the gang of bandits and warned them to never again return to the village. It was said that the gang laughed at his words and attacked him, but they were all defeated by his will and might.

Buko collapsed. Shinsei ended his thoughts and ran to him.

"Are you all right?" the priest asked.

"Leave me be, priest."

"You must let me heal your wounds. If you do not you may die from what ails you."

"Leave me be!" he barked.

Elder Subo, now standing behind the priest, placed his hand upon the priest's shoulder and asked, "How is he, old friend?" Shinsei stood up and whispered, "He is not well. I'm afraid that if I do not begin healing him soon he may fall fatally ill." Elder Subo massaged his brow with his fingers, "Buko, you must allow the priest to heal you. If you do not you risk death."

"Why should that matter? I am banished from my homeland with marks upon my hands to warn all those who find me to never come near me. I am already dead." He stood up with clenched teeth and carried on.

Elder Subo whispered to Shinsei, "Tonight we will bind him and heal him." Shinsei nodded. The Elder then passed Buko to take the lead again. Shinsei went to the three guards and explained what they were to do in the night to heal Buko.

The sun began to set behind the Shinohi Mountains casting a pink hue across the evening sky. Shinsei walked and admired the beauty of both the sky and the cherry trees. *So early are they blooming this year*, he thought as he heard the clanking sound of the pots that hung from Watanoro's bag. A strong wind blew causing a thousand pink pedals to clutter the scene before him. He took a deep breath from his long pipe, savoring its bitter taste, before airing it out of his lungs and mouth. His scalp was beginning to chill from the cool evening air. He stopped, reached into his leather bag, and pulled out a black wool cap. He removed his grass hat and fitted the cap on his head. *Yes, that is better.* He placed his hat back on his head and carried on with the aid of his staff.

Little by little the sun eased into the distant horizon until it was gone from sight. Shinsei looked at the mountains and thought: *We are only one more day away.* It had been many years since he had seen the Mountains of Shinohi so close. He began to think of his childhood and of the dark mountains that surrounded his homeland with jagged peaks that bit the sky.

His homeland had been a harsh one. It was not green and lush like the lands of Kadek. No, the toils of industry had ruined his land. It was a black land of cursed stone and broken shale. In his mind's eye he saw the wretched castle he had once called home. There was only one light lit within it. The light glimmered from a long and thin window high up in the castle's central tower. It came from his father's chamber, *yes*. His father was always awake in that dark place. Never did he sleep. Always at work was he, looking over scores of maps and battle strategies.

Shinsei shook his head to cast the memories from his troubled mind. He looked down with tired eyes at his sandals and callused feet that were covered in dirt and mud. He then looked at his dry, cold hands and saw that the skin above his knuckles was beginning to crack open and bleed. The cold winds blew stronger. He began to worry about Buko's wounds and how painful they must be, but he put his mind at ease for he knew that in the night, with the help of Elder Subo and the three guards, he would begin healing him. *For that is what I do*, he assured himself. *I heal . . . I heal. Not like my father . . . no, I am not like him.*

He heard Hirotake and Watanoro laughing at one of Raki-ka's foul jokes; he did not hear the joke but guessed that it had something to do with women or sex or both. Looking past the three guards he saw Elder Subo shaking his head; he knew that the Elder had heard the joke and disapproved of it.

He had noticed during their journey that Elder Subo did not engage in any talks with the three guards beyond what was required of him. He thought that it was hypocritical of the Elder. He had always heard the Elder encouraging the people of Ikishi to not look down upon Kieko, but yet here he was looking down upon these three guards. He knew that Elder Subo admired Kieko's strength, but, really, beneath that, he knew that the Elder saw the flesh and blood of a man he respected, Nishiaka. He knew that Nishiaka, in Elder Subo's eyes, was a man of integrity, an artisan, a warrior knowledgeable of a score of topics ranging from history to engineering to philosophy and poetry. He then realized that that was why the Elder did not like the three guards. He feared them. Of course, Subo would laugh at such an accusation, but he knew that it was true. Elder Subo feared those three guards for they cared little for what he upheld as the "fine Lemurian arts."

Elder Subo was feeling terribly alone as he walked along the path toward the Mountains of Shinohi. It had been years since he had had a good long intellectual talk; he had hoped that he could speak candidly with Shinsei during their journey, but Shinsei chose to stay at the back of the caravan while he led it. He went over his memories of Nishiaka and the roundtable talks he had had with him and Shinsei years ago. But, after Nishiaka had left for the lands in the West everything had changed. Shinsei began spending more and more time with old farmer Toasu and less and less time with him.

Elder Subo did not care for the old farmer. To him Toasu was a senile, old man who hid from his village and from the codes of conduct expected of an aging Lemurian man. Why Shinsei chose to spend his hours with that old fool was beyond his understanding for he knew he offered the priest more. He felt hurt and insulted, and perhaps betrayed that the priest had sided with an ignorant old man than with him. He then noticed that the dark of night was fast approaching. He stopped and called out, "Time to set up camp with what remains of the fading light." The three guards dropped their bags, stabbed their spears into the ground, stretched, and began work at setting up a campfire that would cook their evening meal.

Buko, shivering, dropped to the ground. Shinsei approached Buko and covered him with a blanket he had pulled out of his bag. Surprisingly Buko accepted the blanket and pulled it tightly around his body. The priest looked at Buko's feet seeing that they were bleeding profusely, walked over to Elder Subo who was about to scout the land, and said, "We need to be quick. Buko will not last another night if I do not begin treating him soon."

"Soon enough, my friend," the Chief Elder assured him. "Once the fire has started and I have cooked and fed their mouths," he said pointing condescendingly at the three guards, "will we do what needs to be done."

"Be swift," the priest asked.

"I will," the Elder replied before walking into the dark of the surrounding trees.

Shinsei assisted Watanoro in collecting enough dry tree branches to last them the night as Raki-ka placed rocks around the campfire that Hirotake was working on.

When Elder Subo returned he found a strong campfire, the three guards unpacking dried meat and salted fish parts from their bags, and the priest taking another close look at Buko's feet.

"Elder Subo, please come," the priest said. The Elder went to the priest. "I need the key to unlock his shackles."

Buko's eyes widened.

The Elder looked at Buko's torn feet and ankles and determined that he would not be able to travel far if he tried to escape. He handed the key to Shinsei. Buko stared at the key. Shinsei unlocked the shackles and removed them from Buko's feet. He then placed the key into a leather pouch that hung from his belt and said, "Here," he pulled out his flask of water, "use it to clean your feet."

Buko swatted the flask out of Shinsei's hand.

Frustrated, Shinsei said, "Fine then," and walked away.

Buko massaged his feet and ankles with his dirty infected hands while watching Hirotake and Watanoro build a tripod from three long branches. When they had completed the tripod they placed it over the fire and hung an iron pot from it. Elder Subo went to work at preparing the ingredients for the meal he was about to cook.

A thick soup of rice, fish, and vegetables boiled within the iron pot filling the air with a salty fragrance. The three guards waited eagerly with their bowls and wooden spoons in their hands as Elder Subo sipped the soup from the ladle he had been using to stir the pot's contents. Taking a pinch of salt from a small wooden box the Elder sprinkled it into the soup and looked at four other small boxes he had placed on an unrolled leather sheet trying to decide which herb or spice, and how much of it, he should put into the soup.

"Chief Elder Subo, is it ready?" Raki-ka asked.

"Do not rush me," the Elder barked as he kept his eyes on his boxes of salts, herbs, and spices. "Cooking is my art. I am striving for perfection here."

Raki-ka gave a comical look at the Elder's back–bubbling giggles escaped from Hirotake and Watanoro's lips–and said, "Chief Elder Subo, I do not think any of our mouths, or bellies for that matter, will recognize whether another pinch of salt or some herb was needed or not. All we care about is easing the hunger that pains our tummies."

Hirotake and Watanoro broke out in laughter. Elder Subo frowned, "Tummy? Tummy? What kind of childish word is that?" He shook his head and continued, "I am an artisan cook and you are obviously a fisherman who knows nothing of the finer things in life."

Insulted, Raki-ka asked, "And what would those finer things be?"

Elder Subo threw down the ladle, "Art for one. Poetry second, philosophy, books, and the like. Should I go on? I can write them down for you since your small mind is so fast to forget–Oh, that's right. You can not read. Pity–"

"Elder Subo!" Shinsei called out embarrassed that the Chief Elder was speaking out with such cruel demeanor.

"How dare you belittle me!" Raki-ka retaliated.

"Belittle you?" the Elder said. "Put you down? You put yourself down with the manner in which you choose to live your filthy, ignorant life!"

"Elder Subo," Shinsei called out again.

"Shut your mouth, Elder, before I leap at your throat!"

"Elder Subo," Shinsei called out for the third time.

"Threaten me? Threaten me? I'll have you banished fisher—"

"Elder Subo!" Shinsei roared silencing all with the boom of his voice.

"What?" the Elder asked annoyed that the priest had interrupted him.

"You will speak with me."

"Can it not wait, priest? I am cooking. Isn't that plain to your eyes?"

"Your soup is done! Serve them now and get up!"

"They can serve themselves," the Elder stood up and followed Shinsei to the trees.

"What is wrong with you?" Shinsei asked. "You are Chief Elder. Never have I seen such behavior."

"They were disturbing me while I was pursuing my art. They should know better than to pressure an artisan to finish his work."

"Have you lost your mind?" Elder Subo was shocked by Shinsei's words. The priest continued, "You are cooking a meal in a forest! That is it. What rubbish are you talking of?"

Mortified that Shinsei had spoken so rudely to him in plain view of the three guards he shouted back, "How dare you speak to me in such a manner!"

Shinsei knew he had publicly shamed the Elder. He bowed making sure that the three guards could see him doing so and murmured, "There, your image and authority has been saved."

"Why do you embarrass me?"

"Embarrass you? You embarrass yourself."

"You disappoint me, priest."

"Don't call me that."

"You are a priest. Are you not?"

"I am your friend."

"No friend of mine can be so willing to side with those fools and hermits."

"Is that what this is about?" Shinsei asked. "My friendship with Toasu?"

"I do not know what you are talking about," the Elder replied shaking his head.

"I think you do. You shun people like him or like them," he pointed at the guards, "detest them, reject them, and trash them. Why? Why do you loathe them?" Elder Subo continued shaking his head. Shinsei continued, "What? Are they not as sophisticated and knowledgeable as you? Do they sicken you with their disregard for your codes, or their gossip talks and profane jokes? That is not their problem, old friend. It is yours—yours and yours alone."

"You shame me. Never have you understood me." The Elder tried to walk away but Shinsei grabbed him by the arm and pulled him back. "Let go of me priest before I strike!"

"You speak and act like a child! You will calm yourself or you will face the wizardry of my staff," the priest threatened with hardened fingers that dug into the Elder's arm. Elder Subo looked from the corner of his eye at the three guards with a face flushed red in embarrassment. The priest continued, "Enough of this— maintaining face. You will not block my words with the defenses you have built around your heart. I will say what I need to say and you will listen!" He looked hard into the Elder's eyes. "You will listen to my every word for your very life depends on it like a prey that is under the knife. Do you understand?"

Elder Subo nodded under Shinsei's spell.

Shinsei began, "How long have I known you?"

"For many years," he answered.

"And long have I trusted you, and long have we talked of honorable matters, but this ridiculousness that coats your heart sickens me." Elder Subo began fighting Shinsei's grip. "Hold still! It is time that you hear this." Elder Subo cowered. "Those men over there are good men. They care for their families. They did not have the good fortunes you had growing up. They worked their parents' fields and sailed the seas to hunt the fish that fed your mouth. Your education came at their expense. Was it not your family who once owned their lands and made them till it to pay off their debts? Do not forget that, friend. Do not forget that. Respect them as true men." Elder Subo continued trying to break free. "Why do you fear them?"

Elder Subo's eyes twitched. He did not want to answer. His face boiled red, "Let go of me! Release me of your spell–I demand it!"

The three guards, not having touched their soup, stared at Shinsei and Elder Subo who were both covered more in the night's darkness than in the light of the campfire.

"Is everything all right, Shinsei?" Watanoro asked with squinting eyes trying to see Shinsei and Elder Subo.

"Yes, all is all right," Shinsei answered and released Elder Subo.

"Why are you afraid, Elder?" Buko cried out. "Why are you afraid of the priest's words and questions?"

"Damn you and your brother!" Elder Subo retaliated.

"We are already damned. Tell me Elder, does it bother you that my brother thinks that you are lower than an Akai?"

"Silence!" Elder Subo snapped. Shinsei grabbed his arm.

"Why should I? What will you do? Banish me?" he laughed.

"Silence that mouth of yours or I will silence it for you," the Elder warned.

"Come and do it then, you pathetic old man. Come here and do it," spittle sprayed from his mouth. "Come here coward. Come here you spineless little fish." Elder Subo's entire body began to shake from an explosive mix of resentment, hatred, and rupturing bitterness. "Come you ignorant fool," he coughed. "Come and face me—"

Elder Subo broke away from Shinsei and charged at Buko screaming a vicious war cry. The three guards stared in shock.

Buko did not move; he simply sat on the ground feeding the Elder's run with more curses. Then, just before the Chief Elder was upon him, he lashed his leg out and tripped him. Elder Subo fell hard to the ground and Buko leapt on him, wrapping the iron chains of his shackled hands around his neck. "Don't move!" Buko ordered. "I'll kill him I swear!" Watanoro adjusted his feet. "I said don't move!" Buko stood up and pulled the Elder up by the neck to his feet. He began strangling the Elder and whispered into his ear, "See, it is I who will silence you." Elder Subo began clawing at the chains around his neck, and Buko pulled him back dragging him into the dark of the surrounding forest.

"Let the Elder go!" Shinsei demanded taking a step toward Buko.

"Stay where you are, priest."

Hirotake moved his hand toward his spear.

"Don't even think it," Buko said between coughs.

"Buko, what do you plan to do?" Shinsei asked.

"Quiet, priest!" he moved back dragging the Elder toward the trees.

Shinsei continued, "Kill him and we will be upon you."

"I said quiet, priest!" Buko coughed again.

"You do not have the strength to kidnap him."

"Shut your mouth, priest, before I—"

Shinsei shot his right hand up. His fingers, tense and stiff, pointed at Buko's neck. Buko released the Elder and fell to his knees; the Elder fell to his knees as well and grabbed his neck as he panted and coughed. Shinsei walked toward Buko with furrowed eyebrows. The three guards watched in awe of Shinsei's power.

Buko spat out, "Let . . . go—off . . . me . . ."

"It is Ki," Watanoro whispered to himself. Hirotake nodded, as did Raki-ka.

"Wicked, wicked are you, Buko," Shinsei said as he stepped closer and closer to Buko who was now squirming like a cut snake on the ground.

"It burns . . ." Buko called out.

Shinsei flicked his wrists expelling a stronger unseen beam of Ki from his fingertips into Buko. Buko's body jolted.

"Hold still I say for this will heal you," the priest informed with a straining voice.

"Why are you going to do that?" Raki-ka asked. Elder Subo nodded and coughed, "Why?"

"I am a priest, that is what I do," Shinsei explained exhausted. He inhaled the cool air into his lungs and expelled more Ki into Buko. "Hirotake and Watanoro, tie Buko down."

"Yes, Shinsei," the two answered in unison.

"Raki-ka, attend to Elder Subo."

"Yes, Shinsei."

When Hirotake and Watanoro had finished tying Buko against a tree Shinsei lowered his hand and collapsed his shoulders. Raki-ka darted to Shinsei and asked, "Are you all right, Shinsei?"

"Rest, rest is all I need," he wheezed. "Help me sit by the fire."

"Yes, Shinsei." Raki-ka walked Shinsei to the campfire and helped him sit down on the ground.

"It is not good, you see," the priest began. "It is not good to draw in the Ki at night."

"I do not understand your magic, Shinsei, but we are all impressed by it."

"Do not be . . . do not be," the priest puffed. "Buko will fall to sleep, but before he does feed him some of the Elder's soup."

"As you wish, Shinsei," Raki-ka said as he stood up.

Shinsei grabbed Raki-ka by the arm, "I must apologize . . . I must apologize for the Elder."

"Do not. It is all right."

"No, no . . . please listen."

"It is all right," he said looking into the priest's eyes. "You need not say more. Rest."

"You are a good man, Raki-ka. Remember that. You are a good man."

"Thank you. But, do not forget that you are also a good man."

The priest was silent.

There was only the sound of the crackling fire and the rhythmic calls of the insects in the night. A million stars shined in the dark sky; the moon was hidden behind the tall pine trees. Shinsei was asleep as were Elder Subo and Buko. Hirotake, Watanoro, and Raki-ka were all huddled around the campfire chewing dried deer meat.

"I could drink a wheat brew now," Watanoro commented.

"As could I," Raki-ka agreed.

Hirotake nodded as he chewed.

"How do things be with Tomoko?" Watanoro asked Hirotake.

Hirotake finished chewing his deer meat and said, "Yes, things are well."

"She is a sweet one," Watanoro complimented. "Quiet and sweet."

"Yes, she is—and long have you eyed her," Raki-ka laughed. Hirotake laughed as well.

Embarrassed, Watanoro asked, "What do you mean?"

"Long have we been friends and long has it been obvious that you have always fancied Tomoko," Raki-ka answered.

"I do not," Watanoro objected.

"How you," Raki-ka began referring to Hirotake, "the shyest man I have ever met, beat Wata as a suitor to her I will never know."

"Hiro, please, I mean you no envy," Watanoro apologized.

"Don't worry," Hirotake assured Watanoro. "We are all having a bit of a laugh." He then asked Raki-ka, "So, when are you going to settle with a woman?"

"I do not know. I have yet to find my perfect wives," he smiled.

"That is you," Watanoro said shaking his head with disapproval. "You're always on the hunt. Always polluting the only thing a woman has before marriage–her reputation."

"What can I say," Raki-ka replied. "I am a gift to all women. It is my duty to show them my light before the shackles of their arranged marriages."

Hirotake and Watanoro both spat chewed deer meat at Raki-ka, and together they all laughed.

"Quiet–quiet," Hirotake said silencing them. "We do not want to wake them."

"So, master seducer of women, what secrets have you to share?" Watanoro asked Raki-ka; Hirotake moved forward to hear what he had to say.

"Secrets? Me, holding secrets? I have no secrets," he paused. Hirotake and Watanoro looked impatiently at Raki-ka.

"Come now, we don't have all night," Watanoro pleaded.

"But, you heard me, old friend. I have no secrets."

"You know what I'm talking about."

"No," he shook his head, "I'm afraid I don't."

"You know–*secrets*."

"Sex," Hirotake declared and blushed.

"Ahh, yes, *secrets*," Raki-ka smirked.

"Well, do tell," Watanoro asked.

"So, you acknowledge that I am a gift to all women."

"Shut your stupid talk," Watanoro shot back.

"All right, all right," Raki-ka said with his hands waving at his two companions. "Women, my inexperienced friends–"

"I'm not inexperienced," Hirotake said defensively.

"We don't care. Just be quiet and let the man speak," Watanoro uttered.

"As I was saying, before I was so rudely interrupted. Women, my inexperienced friends, are not like men."

"Thank you for the wonderful insight," Watanoro remarked.

Raki-ka looked at Watanoro, "Can I speak? Can I talk?"

"Yes, yes. Go on."

"As I was saying before I was so *rudely* interrupted." Hirotake and Watanoro both rolled their eyes. "Women are not like men. They are women and must be understood as so. To compare them in anyway to men is an act of stupidity. We do not say that apples are like oranges and vice versa. An apple is an apple, and is understood as an apple, just like an orange is an orange, and is understood as an orange. Is that clear?"

Hirotake and Watanoro nodded annoyed that Raki-ka was lecturing them like children.

"Men are rough and toughed skinned. Big boned, hairy and brutish you could say. We like things fast and unforgiving. No foreplay do we need. When we are ready, we are ready.

"Now, it has often plagued my mind why this is so. Why are men quick when women like it slow? I thought it would be to the advantage of both the man and the woman to be the same in their design, either designed by the gods to be quick or designed by the gods to be slow. But, then, I realized something when I was hunting on Mount Kadek. I accidentally came across a white, male tiger laying his seed within a female tiger–"

"You're sick," Watanoro joked.

Ignoring the comment Raki-ka continued, "The male tiger had just deposited his seed and then roared at me, and then guarded the future mother of his cubs. I slowly backed away and left unharmed. But, I realized that the gods designed the male of all species to be quick so that they could protect the female of their species from all danger as soon as their deed was done. It would not be to the advantage of the male tiger to take too much time in intercourse when other predators lurked and could take advantage of his vulnerable position.

"So, knowing this I realized that women are far different in what they seek from sex. Men seek an immediate release. Women do not."

"Really?" Hirotake asked.

"Yes, please do listen closely since you are the only one of us who is married."

Hirotake blushed again.

"Wait, but that observation didn't answer your original question as to why the gods had not designed men and women to be the same," Watanoro commented. "If it is a fear of predators then women should also be inclined to want sex to be done quickly."

"Yes, well, that does not matter anymore now does it? What is important is that men have to be quick and women do not. Men are stronger, and naturally the guardian, and so it does not matter if the woman would like it slow or fast. In the end the man must be quick so that he can protect."

"Your theory is flawed, my friend," Watanoro noted.

"Fine then. It is obvious that I do not know what I am talking about."

"Will you shut your mouth and allow him to talk," Hirotake said to Watanoro.

"Thank you," Raki-ka said to Hirotake.

"Sorry, old friend," Watanoro apologized. "Please, continue."

"Yes, well. As I was saying before I was so *rudely* interrupted . . . hmmm . . . oh yes . . . Women are beautiful in their design. They are voluptuous, just the sight of them causes our mouths to water. They are soft and smooth and hairless. They are gentle and sweet. They love flowers and dance. And they love to be pampered. Indulge them with poetic words of how beautiful they are, of how lovely they are, of how you love to feel their warms curves tight against your skin. Always remind them of how much you love them with small gifts of sweet foods and flowers–this I can not emphasize enough. Women love to receive flowers. Give them flowers when they wake, before they sleep, on a random day. Do this and they will melt into you, giving you their precious little heart."

"Is that when you break their hearts, old friend?" Watanoro asked with a grin.

"These are your tricks?" Hirotake asked. "Flowers and sweet foods, and whispered nothings of your so called love?"

"It is not my fault that women can not resist me," Raki-ka answered. "Always in the beginning, I can honestly tell you, am I truly in love with the woman I eventually share myself with–"

"So, what happens?" Watanoro asked. "Every time we hear the same story. You are in love, but then, suddenly–soon after you penetrate the poor victim of your lust–you are done with her and on to your next prey."

"Yes, well. I am not proud of that."

Hirotake shook his head in disbelief.

"All that I am saying is that I am thankful to the gods that my sister is happily married and untouched and unscarred by your sexual conquests," Watanoro finished.

"Well, thank you very much. I will end sharing my secrets then. I wish you much luck in ensuring that the woman of your life achieves her sexual bliss."

"No, no, no. Please don't stop," Hirotake pleaded.

"You especially need to hear of my secrets," Raki-ka advised Hirotake.

"What do you mean by that?"

"You have been married for a few months and I can tell that Tomoko has yet to experience the ecstasy of sex."

"How would you know?"

"Because I can tell. When you give her what she has already given you she will beam."

Hirotake looked down with perplexed eyes.

Watanoro apologized, "I'm sorry, old friend. Please, go on."

"Thank you. Remember, I am telling you this for your benefit, not mine. So, do not continue with your envious insults Wata."

"Yes, old friend," he agreed.

"As I was saying before I was so *rudely* interrupted." Hirotake and Watanoro rolled their eyes again. "Women are soft and gentle. So, approach them as such. They are not a lamb to be slaughtered by warrior hands. They are cute little kittens that you need to pet for an infinite number of hours–"

"Sounds terribly boring," Watanoro commented. Raki-ka stopped speaking. "Sorry," he apologized again.

"Yes, as I was saying. The secret to loving a woman is time. Do not rush. There is no need to rush. No reason in the world to rush. Take your time. If you truly love her then explore her every part. Kiss her gently everywhere. Kiss her feet, her toes, her ankles, her long thin legs, her waist, her chest–but do not kiss her breasts–wait. Leave the best parts for last," he smiled. "Kiss her neck–and take all your time doing so–and kiss her behind the ear, kiss her shoulders, her arms, her hands, and her fingers. Imagine that you are blind and that you must kiss her every part to paint a portrait of her in your mind."

"And then what?" Watanoro asked.

"Yes, and then what?" Hirotake asked.

"What? Do you want to ram her then?"

"No! That is not what I was thinking," Watanoro said in defense.

"Good. Of course, women may like it as rough as we like it, but, do as I have told you and she will feel as if you completely understand her, her body, her every wish, her every desire."

"I see," Hirotake nodded.

"Now, after you have spent ample time kissing her every part, you can spiral your tongue around her breasts. Begin at the base of her breast and spiral in," he said with his finger in the air as if tracing a coil. "But, do not touch her nipple when you have arrived at the peak of her breast. Let her burn for you to touch her there, and begin again on her other breast. Take a lot of time, my friends. Take all your time. Then repeat again, but, this time, tease her by swiftly touching her nipples as if you have done so by mistake."

Hirotake listened with growing excitement.

"What in the name of all the wicked demons of Mount Kurohi is the point of all that?" Watanoro asked.

"You are easing her into you. Women are not simply ready to go as men are. They have to be taken by the hand and gradually introduced into their hot spring bath."

"That doesn't make any sense," Watanoro reflected.

"Then don't try it if you think—"

"No, I mean your analogy—"

"Now you are concerned with my analogies?"

"Sorry, please continue."

"I forgot what I was talking about!"

"Be quiet. You will wake them."

"You were talking about their nipples," Hirotake reminded.

"Oh, yes," Raki-ka smiled. "Well, if you have done everything I have said then she is nearly ready, and you may do as you please. I leave everything else to your imagination. Just remember, treat her as if she is the most fragile creature you have ever known. Soft touches and warm words will travel far into her heart—and even farther still into her body."

Watanoro applauded Raki-ka by lightly clapping his hands. Hirotake raised his ceramic cup to salute Raki-ka. Raki-ka responded by standing and bowing in a comical fashion.

When their fun had ended Watanoro whispered to Hirotake, "If you ask me, Raki-ka will be the next of us to wed."

"You speak nonsense," Raki-ka remarked.

"No, no, I speak truth—I have felt it, seen it in my dreams."

"Seen what?"

"Yes, seen what?" Hirotake asked.

"I don't know. I can't put it into words. But, put simply I have a strange feeling that you will fall in love and wed soon."

"Well, don't expect me to wager on that," Hirotake commented.

"Yes, you are definitely not a priest endowed with the gift of the all-seeing-eye," Raki-ka commented.

"Fine then," Watanoro concluded. "Only time will tell if I am wrong or right."

Raki-ka began thinking of what Shinsei had told him; a curious look grew on his face.

"What are you thinking about?" Watanoro asked.

"Something Shinsei had said to me some months ago."

"What did he say?" Hirotake asked.

"I'm not sure, actually. His words were a bit of a riddle. I was in his kitchen. I had just finished repairing one of the banisters in the Kadek Temple. We were eating and then suddenly he uttered a few words that made no apparent sense. It was very peculiar. I asked him what it meant, but he simply shook his head and carried on as if nothing had happened."

"I have heard of this before," Hirotake said.

Raki-ka waited, as did Watanoro, for Hirotake to enlighten them, but Hirotake simply began drinking the warm tea he had prepared for himself.

"Well," Raki-ka asked anxiously, "go on then."

Hirotake placed his cup on the ground, "I've heard from my uncles that a Ki priest may have visions and that he will utter what he sees."

"The all-seeing-eye," Raki-ka murmured.

"Do you think that was what it was?" Watanoro asked.

"Perhaps . . . I don't know?" Raki-ka answered.

"Well, do tell us what he said," Hirotake said.

"He simply said: 'You will find the one–and long has she been before you. And you will join as one . . . in a dark place. And the dark will come.' "

"What in the name of the wicked gods did he mean?" Watanoro asked.

"I don't know. What do you think it means?" Raki-ka asked his two friends.

"I will not try to decipher it. I will rest instead," Watanoro replied. He then lay on his side and looked into the campfire.

"I think you will soon realize who you are to marry," Hirotake said as he massaged his chin.

"What does Shinsei mean then about the 'dark'?" Raki-ka asked.

"I think you will marry her in secret–"

"And a tree will grow out of my ass," Watanoro burped.

"I've heard enough. I am going to sleep." Raki-ka stood up, spread out his blanket on the ground, lay on it, and stared up at the stars. "Good night, my friends," he said before releasing a loud and foul gas from his ass.

Watanoro gave a disgusted look, sniffed, and exclaimed, "Curse the gods! What did you eat?"

Hirotake and Raki-ka both burst into laughter. The winds began to blow causing the branches of all the pine trees to sway as an owl sounded into the night.

Chapter XII

Thin strips of smoke rose up into the cold, morning air from the dying campfire. Raki-ka, sitting on the ground with his arm wrapped around his knee, took a few stabs at the burnt wood before him with a long stick; he was trying to chip off bits of charred bark. He then stopped and yawned, and watched as the fog retreated from the surrounding pine trees seeing that the land was a sad grey coupled to a cloudy sky. But he could see that a few trees had buds that were beginning to bloom. He was relieved, and he prayed that the sun would soon appear for he did not like the morning gloom.

He looked at the tree that Buko was tied to and noticed that all of its bare twisting stems and branches pointed accusingly at all the other trees; it was an angry tree, and Buko continued to sleep beneath it. It did not comfort Raki-ka during his watch at night that Buko had not stirred once. He could not wait until they had sent him off into the lands west of Kadek so that they could return home. He looked at Buko's pale face, and at his ankles seeing that the blood around them had dried and crusted, and felt no sympathy. High above birds began to squawk. He looked up and saw seven, agitated black crows flying from treetop to treetop. They were hungry. He looked for a stone, found one, and threw it at them. "Get out of here!"

Watanoro's hand bolted to his spear. "What? What is it?" he said with a frantic strain in his voice.

"Nothing . . . just some birds. Sorry I woke you."

Watanoro collapsed to the ground, "You scared the hell out of me."

"What's wrong?" Hirotake asked as he emerged from his sleep.

"You're worthless," Watanoro complained to Hirotake. "I was up ready to fight in the blink of an eye, and you are now just getting up? Thank the gods we were not under attack."

"There, there, all is well," the priest said as he rose from his wool blankets. "No need to start off our day with a fight."

"I'm sorry to have woken you, Shinsei," Watanoro apologized.

"Do not worry. It is time for us all to begin our day." Shinsei brushed his robes clean of all the dirt and dried leaves that had clung to it during his sleep. He stretched out his arms and yawned; the three guards yawned as well. He stood up and walked over to Elder Subo, kneeled, and shook his body, "Elder Subo . . . Elder Subo it is time to wake."

"Yes, yes, leave me be. I can hear you," he rubbed his eyes.

"How are you feeling?"

"Fine, I say. Fine," he cracked his neck.

"How is your neck?"

"My neck . . . yes," he massaged his neck. "It's a little stiff. I can feel that it is bruised. But, it is fine. It is fine." He looked into Shinsei's eyes, "Thank you, old friend. Thank you." He took Shinsei's hand and held it tightly in gratitude. "I apologize for how I behaved."

"That is all right, but I believe it is not I who you must apologize to."

Elder Subo became tense; he released the priest's hand and rubbed his temples.

"It would be nice if you apologized to them in your own way."

Elder Subo hesitated, "And what does that mean?"

"You could cook the best breakfast you have ever cooked for them," he recommended with a smile.

Elder Subo laughed lightly as he shook his head. "All right, all right, everyone is hungry. I will cook."

"Thank you, old friend."

"How is Buko?"

"I do not know. I will check on him."

Shinsei walked over to Buko, sat on the heels of his feet, and took a long look at Buko's face, hands, and ankles. He had improved. The Ki had done its work in the night. He placed his fingers over Buko's wrist and closed his eyes; his eyelids began to flutter. He opened his eyes and looked once again at Buko's face, hands, and ankles. He scratched his beard, stood up, and inhaled the cool air deep into his lungs as he held his arms out with his palms facing the trees; he was drawing in Ki from the surrounding trees. Slowly he moved his left hand so that it was over Buko's head and began expelling the Ki into him; Buko began to moan and move, but he did not wake. The three guards stared at the priest in awe.

"Have you ever been healed by the Ki?" Watanoro asked.

Hirotake and Raki-ka shook their heads.

"My uncles told me that a Ki priest only draws upon the Ki when someone is in dire need of it," Hirotake explained.

"Do you learn everything from your uncles?" Watanoro asked.

"No."

"Get on with your work," Elder Subo reminded the three guards. "We all have things to do."

"Yes, Elder Subo," Watanoro replied.

"Yes, Chief Elder," Hirotake replied.

Raki-ka did not say a word. He packed his bag and ignored the Elder.

Elder Subo was not offended by Raki-ka. He carried on by placing more wood over the ash of what had burned during the night and set to work at starting a morning campfire.

When the flame of the campfire had grown strong the Elder unrolled a short leather sheet on the ground and placed his wooden boxes of herbs and spices on it. He then poured water from a clay jug into an iron pot, hung it over the campfire, and began cutting and stripping off the skin of the two rabbits Raki-ka had caught the previous day.

The air soon began to fill with the scent of a tasty broth causing the mouths of the three guards to water. The Elder finally finished and called everyone to feast upon the rabbit soup he had prepared. He took the bowls from the three guards, poured their soup, and gave it back to them leaving the priest who preferred to pour his own bowl. Together they all ate around the campfire trying to keep warm from the chilly morning air.

When they had finished Shinsei took a bowl of soup to Buko, who was awake but slightly delirious, and spoonfed the soup to his lips; Buko drank the soup slowly.

"Do you think he will make it to Shinohi?" Elder Subo asked the priest as he walked toward him.

Shinsei stopped feeding Buko. He placed the wooden spoon into the bowl and said, "Yes, he has the strength in him to make it that far. After that I do not know. Winter is not that far behind us. The cold may get to him. I do not know how long he will last on his own."

"We should move soon, then."

"Yes, we should."

It was midafternoon. Elder Subo was leading the caravan of men, but their pace was not as quick as it had been during the past three days for Buko was weak and appeared bewildered, and spoke nonsense and drooled from his lips.

"Elder Subo," Watanoro called out.

"What? What is it?" Elder Subo asked as he continued walking with his staff determined to make it to the base of the Shinohi Mountains by late afternoon.

"It is afternoon. It is time for a midday meal."

"We will not stop. We are nearly there."

"Yes, Elder Subo," Watanoro said disappointed.

"Do you think it's an act?" Hirotake asked his two friends as they walked.

"What?" Watanoro asked annoyed.

"Do you think it's an act?"

"What's an act?"

"Buko. Do you think Buko is pretending to be mentally lost?"

"I don't care," Raki-ka answered. "I can't wait to get to those mountains and leave him there."

"Yes, but what if Buko tries a trick again? Like last night?" Hirotake asked.

"Then we'll put him out of his misery," Raki-ka answered. "It's five to one. He has no chance. If he is pretending then let him."

Hirotake nodded, but he continued to think of what Buko may try to do.

The number of trees began to thin as the caravan continued along an inclining path. Hirotake was having difficulty keeping up with Watanoro and Raki-ka. "Aren't we nearly there?" he puffed.

"What? What did you say?" Raki-ka asked giving a jocular look to Watanoro.

"I said, aren't we nearly there?"

"I'm sorry—I can't hear you from back there. You're going to have to catch up."

Hirotake hurried his step, and when he caught up to both Watanoro and Raki-ka he asked, "How much longer?"

"I don't know," Raki-ka answered. "Why don't you run up to Elder Subo and find out."

"Never mind."

"We have arrived!" Elder Subo called out causing everyone, except for Buko, to look up ahead. "I can see the mountain gate."

"Thank the gods," Hirotake sighed.

Elder Subo led the caravan up to a massive red and black tori gate that was seven times the height of a man; it stood in an open clearing of rocks and stones devoid of any trees against an incredible view of the snowcapped Mountains of Shinohi, which stretched endlessly from north to south. The gate's two red pillars held up a black-pitched roof; Raki-ka could just see the score of rafters that supported the roof, causing his jaw to hang open.

"It's beautiful," Watanoro whispered.

Hirotake nodded.

Shinsei walked past the three guards to stand directly before the gate. He clapped three times and then held his hands, which were now clasped together, to this forehead. "We, a caravan of six, summon the Kami of Shinohi. We honor you and stand in awe of you. Please let us pass." The winds blew causing the priest's robes to flap and sound. He gave three deep bows and passed through the gate. He turned around and said, "Come now, one by one."

Elder Subo did as Shinsei did. He clapped his hands three times and bowed three times before passing through the gate. Hirotake followed. Watanoro pushed Buko through the gate. Raki-ka was the last to pass.

"Kneel, Buko," Elder Subo commanded.

Buko did not move; he stood as if he was deaf to all sounds. Raki-ka punched Buko in the stomach with the end of his spear. Shinsei grabbed Raki-ka's hand preventing him from delivering another blow, "Enough, he has had enough." Raki-ka stood back.

"Kneel, Buko," the Elder commanded again.

Buko looked at the ground as the winds hissed and blew through his hair.

Elder Subo nodded to Hirotake and Watanoro; together they forced Buko to kneel by pushing him down to his knees.

Shinsei, Elder Subo, Hirotake, Watanoro, and Raki-ka all stood before Buko. The winds grew stronger, harsher, and colder.

Shinsei stepped forward and said, "Unforgiving is this current mountain wind. Pray that it may be merciful in the days ahead for you are now cast into the wilderness and forever banished from the lands of Kadek. Have you anything to say for your crime before the gods of Shinohi?"

Buko mumbled beneath his tattered breath.

"Speak up."

"Come here priest . . . hear what I speak."

Shinsei took a step toward Buko, but Hirotake grabbed the priest's arm. Shinsei turned and looked at Hirotake and saw that he was shaking his head while mouthing the words, "no, no, no."

Then it happened. Buko launched himself at Shinsei's throat with a sharp and jagged stone he had kept hidden within his clothes. But, Shinsei had been long aware of Buko's ill thoughts and intentions. He swiftly turned and faced Buko throwing him far back and away with the light touch of his finger that sounded a deep boom.

"Did you see that?" Watanoro exclaimed as he and his two friends looked in disbelief of what Shinsei had done.

Bright beams of light broke through the clouds and shined upon the mountain land as Shinsei walked up to Buko who lay sprawled upon the rocks and stones. The priest stood over him and looked down at him. Buko looked up but could not see the priest's eyes for the light of the sun was shining too bright behind him. He tried to sit up and shield his eyes from the light with his hand but a terrible pain crossed his chest causing him to hack and cough. There was a metallic taste in his mouth. He touched his lips and saw that his fingers were covered in blood. He tried again to sit up, but the pain was too much. He cried out, "You bastard! What have you done?"

"I have done to you what you wished you could have done to me," the priest replied.

Buko collapsed to the ground and traced the lines of his ribs with his fingers and discovered that a few were broken. "You can not leave me like this," he pleaded. "You can not leave me here broken."

"I am not leaving you like this. It is by your design, your wish that you are to be left here like this. You chose to attack. Neither I nor anyone else is responsible for you for all the choices you have made in your life were made by you, and you alone. Now you must face the consequences of those choices . . . alone. I bid you farewell. I bid you farewell."

It was the first time Buko had heard Shinsei speak so coldly. "No!" he shouted as Shinsei walked away. "Come back! Come back you bas–!" he hacked up more blood. "Come–" he coughed and coughed.

"Are we to just leave him there like that?" Hirotake asked Shinsei.

"Yes, we are. Come, it is time to go."

"But, Shinsei, he is broken. He will not last the night on this mountain."

"Do you think that I do not know that!" he shouted. Hirotake cowered. "Do you think I am proud that he will surely die this night? I am finished with him. His heart is bent and cruel. I have watched him and tried to aid him these past days, but all I have found in his heart was his unrelenting desire to hurt us–kill us if he could. It is by his choice, and his choice alone, that he tried to take my life. What he threw at me is exactly what I threw back at him. His life is spent. Perhaps, in his next life he may grow beyond his wickedness. He is ended. Let us go." He clapped three times and bowed three times before passing through the gate again. The three guards all looked at each other silently; they were too afraid to speak.

"Come, it is time to go," Elder Subo said as he patted Raki-ka on the back to then follow after the priest. Raki-ka stepped toward the gate, clapped and bowed three times, and walked through it. Watanoro was next. Hirotake was left. He looked at Buko who continued to cry, plead, and curse. He felt sorry for him. He prayed that the gods would look after him and bring him a fast death. He then faced the great gate before him, clapped and bowed in the same manner as those before him, and stepped through. He thought of his wife, Tomoko. He missed her and could not wait to fall asleep holding her in his arms.

CHAPTER XIII

A few days after returning to Ikishi Raki-ka decided to go out for a drink. He left his humble home and headed first to Watanoro's hut. Along the way he passed several thatched dwellings and listened to the variety of conversations within them: husbands and wives arguing; fathers dictating to their children; mothers laughing with their daughters; brothers and sisters giggling.

He tried to peer into a few of the huts as he walked passed them, but thick leather sheets had already been pulled down to cover their open doors. *So private we are*, he thought. It was then that he began to feel alone and shivered. He rubbed his arms.

His mother died giving birth to him; he was her first child. His father died when he was six years old from a terrible fever. From then on he was passed from uncle to uncle; they each had many children, and thus many mouths to feed. When his uncles were unable to continue caring for him they decided to build him a home so that he could care for himself; he was only twelve years old. And so that was how he came to be, a solitary man.

He was thinking about what Watanoro had said to him a few weeks ago. *Perhaps, that is why I love women as much as I do. Perhaps, Wata is right; I seek the attention of women because I starve for the affection I never received as a motherless child.* He took a deep breath and marched on for Watanoro's home.

When he arrived he parted the leather sheet that hung over the door and knocked. The door cracked opened and Watanoro's mother peered out, "Oh, it's you."

"Good evenin–"

"He's not here," she interrupted. "He's sowing nets by the beach. If you have the sense you'll let him be—let him work."

"Yes—"

She shut the door.

"Okusen," he finished. He looked down, shrugged his shoulders, and decided to go to Hirotake's home hoping to steal him from his wife.

He arrived, parted the leather sheet, and knocked on the door.

"Agh . . . who is it?" Hirotake asked out of breath.

"Don't worry, Hiro," Raki-ka said realizing what he was interrupting. "It's me. I can hear that you're busy," he smiled. "I'm just going for a drink. If you want, you can join me later."

"Ahhh . . ."

"Goodbye, my mountain tiger," he joked.

"Ahhh . . . yes . . . ahhh . . . goodbye."

He turned away happy; he was pleased to find his friend in love, and loving his wonderful wife. And so he went, alone, to Kesake's hut for a brew or two, or three.

He heard Kesake's hut before he saw it; loud bellowing laughs sounding into the night air; hard aggressive coughs; bitter arguments; disagreements; foul jokes and curses. He did not frequent the place. He only went when he felt he was thinking a bit too much about his past.

He parted the leather sheet and walked in through the open door. The cloudy tobacco air hit him. It seemed that everyone was smoking from their pipes between sips of their brews.

"Raki-ka!" Kesake called out from behind his kitchen stone counter.

Raki-ka smiled and bowed.

Kono, seated behind a worn table in the darkest corner of Kesake's hut, stared at Raki-ka. Tsuwata, seated next to Kono, turned and also stared. Rakima, seated across from Tsuwata, kept his eyes down to his drink. There were other men seated at Kono's table, and they were all looking at Raki-ka.

Raki-ka felt uncomfortable. His body became tense, and then he saw Kono and his table of men. He wanted to leave, but Kesake had already crossed the room and threw his arm around him.

"Been a few weeks, eh?"

"Yes, it has, old friend."

"Come, come and sit. A brew for you," he said leading Raki-ka to a small table near the kitchen counter. "Have a seat. I need to take care of some fish on the grill. I'll be back." And just like that he left.

Raki-ka looked again at Kono's table. *They're still looking.* He turned away. Little by little he began to look around. He saw fishermen sitting around their tables talking of their morning catches. He looked up and saw that the thatched roof was still in need of repair. *Everything is the same*, he thought.

The cloudy haze within the hut swirled around Kesake as he moved with plates of sizzling grilled fish. Raki-ka smiled. He could see that Kesake loved to serve and entertain his guests. He watched him as he placed the plates down on a table where three fishermen were sitting before flapping his hands and arms in the air as he began to talk. He then saw him slap one of the fishermen on the back and knew that he had just made his point. *Funny old man*, he thought. He watched him help himself to a beer before wiping his dark grey beard and spitting out a few words that he concluded with a boisterous laugh. He then thought about the events that led Kesake to open his own tavern.

Kesake, for all of his life until the loss of his wife, knew not how to cook a single meal. He knew nothing of spices and sauces or pots and pans. He knew only how to fish, skin a rabbit, trap crabs, grow vegetables, and ferment wheat into a potent brew.

In the days after burying his wife he found himself eating only raw fish and vegetable plants. Soon his hut fell into disarray for he knew not how to care for it. Weeks passed.

One day, his son, Kesake-no, came to visit from the far away village he now lived in with his wife. His son was shocked to find that he had lost so much weight and that his home had become a habitat for mice and small critters. He listened as his son explained that he needed to take better care of himself; he realized that he had only two options: either rise above his circumstances or continue falling victim to them. At that moment he decided to begin learning how to cook, and as his mind revolved around how he would gain the skill he had a vision. He shared his vision with his son and the two became excited. Not only did Kesake want to learn how to cook, but he also wanted to do so for the other widowed men of Ikishi. He wanted to rearrange his home so that many could come and eat, drink, and talk.

He worked with his son on his home. They built small tables and chairs and arranged them around the hearth. But, they both realized that he would not be able to use the hearth to cook with crowds of men sitting at tables all around him. So they expanded the rear of his home to make room for a stone kitchen counter of grills, open flames to heat cauldrons of soup, and the copper apparatuses he needed to brew his beers. And during the night, after their hard work on the hut, his son—who had learned how to prepare fish and soups from his mother-in-law in the early years of his marriage—taught him as much as he could of cooking. He was delighted to learn how to prepare and cook fish and special sauces. He was even more delighted to discover how easy the whole process was and wished that he had taken up the culinary arts in his earlier days.

The night before he was ready to open his home to his peers he prepared dinner and celebrated with his son. They spent the whole night feasting and getting drunk, and when they quieted down they spoke of her, she the blessed wife and mother, and how much they missed her laughter, and into those thoughts did they fall asleep.

When the morning sun rose Kesake embraced and said goodbye to his son who had to begin his journey back to his wife and home. With loving eyes he watched him walk away thinking of how he could not wait until they were together again.

"I apologize, young friend. As promised, here is your drink," Kesake said standing happy and proud.

"Thank you, okusan," Raki-ka replied. "Tomorrow, I'll bring you fresh fish."

"Oh, do not worry or speak of such payments. Drink and enjoy, drink and enjoy. That is all I want and ask. And besides, with all these friends, I already receive too much. Do not worry," he looked up and smelled something burning. "The blessed gods! I must tend to my kitchen," he ran off.

"Thank you," Raki-ka blurted, but Kesake did not hear him. He drank his beer; it was warm and heavy, just how he liked it. He put the cup down, wiped the froth from his lips, and let out a satisfied, "Ahhh." Sitting quietly he watched the activity in the room, and looked down at his drink. He began feeling uncomfortable again.

"Well, hello, Raki-ka," Kono greeted him with a hard slap on the shoulder. Before Raki-ka could respond Rinton-no and Tsuwata sat down at his table. "Do you mind?"

"No, no, not at all," Raki-ka answered shaking his head as he stood up to bow while smelling the strong scent of alcohol in their breaths.

Kono did not bow; he simply sat down. "What's wrong?" he asked with a sly smile. "Are you not happy to see us?"

"No, no, no. It is good to see you all," Raki-ka replied avoiding Rinton-no's eyes. "How go things?" He then saw Rinton-no's hands turn into fists.

"Not so well," Kono answered.

Beads of sweat began forming around Raki-ka's forehead.

"I've had enough!" Rinton-no shouted as he stood up and banged his fists on the table. Everyone in the room stopped and looked. "I can not stand to be seated before this bastard!"

"I'm sorry," Raki-ka cowered.

"What? What? You're sorry? What does sorry give me? What does it give back to my daughter? You disgraced her!"

"Okusan–"

"Shut up! You! Shut up! I am sick of you! Sick, sick, sick! A lesson I will teach to you. Never–ever–shall you touch and foul another woman–Never!"

Raki-ka nodded fearfully.

"That is enough for now," Kono said to Rinton-no. "You will have your way. Sit. For now sit."

Rinton-no, breathing heavily, shook his head and said with a sharp and deadly finger aimed straight at Raki-ka, "I'll be waiting for you outside." He threw his seat against the table and walked out.

"Oh, the gods," Raki-ka whispered as he sat back in his seat.

"Ah, the gods," Kono began. "You wish them to help you, no? What foolishness!" he said aloud looking at everyone. "The gods do not care. They are not watching. They have done nothing!"

Tsuwata took Kono's arm and whispered, "Watch what you say about the gods here–you've had a bit too much to drink–"

"Shut up, shut up–shut up! Do not tell me what to do. I am tired of you! And I am tired of all of our prayers for the cursed gods. Don't speak to me, Tsuwata. Don't speak to me of what I can say. Don't–I have prayed. I have prayed. And what? My life. My wife–Don't you speak to me of what I can say!" he turned to Raki-ka. "And you! Tell me what happened to my brother! Tell me you illiterate fool!"

"What?" Raki-ka, now angered by his comment, asked. "What is it that you want to know?" Kono was quiet; he was caught off guard by the sudden strength in Raki-ka's voice. Raki-ka stood up.

"Where in the name of Mount Kadek do you think you're going?" Kono snapped.

"Out, you literate drunk!" he bowed, headed to the door, and exited. Tsuwata stood up and followed after Raki-ka.

Kono looked at Kesake realizing that he appeared like a drunken fool in his establishment. He did not care. He grabbed the table before him and threw it up spilling beer all over the floor, "To hell with all of you!" He turned and left.

Outside Kono found Rinton-no and Tsuwata arguing with Raki-ka; it was obvious that they were trying to provoke a fight. He called out, "Rinton-no." Rinton-no looked at him. "If you want to beat him then beat him!"

Tsuwata lunged at Raki-ka. Raki-ka, swift and sober, stepped aside and tripped him to the ground. He then saw Rinton-no swing his arm at him; he took the hit and fell to the ground. Rinton-no began kicking him. Kono gladly joined in. Tsuwata stood up and began releasing a fury of kicks as well.

Kesake and the patrons of his tavern soon gathered around to watch. Raki-ka saw Kesake's foot—another kick slammed into his chest—he called out, "Help—" another kick hit his face breaking his nose releasing a flood of blood, "Hel—"

Kesake could see that the kicks were becoming more and more brutal. He thought of his son and shouted, "Stop! Stop it!"

Tsuwata paused and looked around slightly shocked as if he had suddenly awoken from a terrible dream. Rakima grabbed Tsuwata and pulled him away.

"Stop it!" Kesake continued to call out. "Stop it, I say!"

Tsuwata, now standing beside his brother, looked at Kesake and at Kono whose mouth was full of spit and eyes so full of hate. "Kono!" he called out.

Kono and Rinton-no kept kicking, but then Rinton-no stopped and stepped away as if he too had awoken from a nightmare.

"Kono!" Kesake shouted again. "Stop!"

Tsuwata stepped toward Kono, as did Rinton-no, and together they grabbed Kono by the arms and pulled him away from Raki-ka.

"Get the priest," Kesake said to the young man beside him. The young man did not move. Kesake grabbed the young man by the shoulders and shouted, "Get the priest!" The young man shook his head to rouse his mind and ran in the direction of the Kadek Temple. Kesake looked at Raki-ka, as did everyone in the crowd. Raki-ka gurgled and spat out thick blots of blood; his entire body ached and screamed of pain; his arms and legs moved back and forth; his fingers curled and stretched; his ankles moved in small circles. He could see only from one eye.

Kono broke out of Tsuwata's and Rinton-no's hold, ran, and crashed on his knees before Raki-ka's broken body, grabbed his head, and said, "I know my brother is dead, and that cursed Akai will pay for it."

Raki-ka looked at Kono, "Curse," he coughed, "you." And before Kono could slam a last punch into Raki-ka's face Tsuwata and Rinton-no had grabbed him again and pulled him away.

CHAPTER XIV

Several weeks had passed for Raki-ka who, with three broken ribs and a broken nose, was unable to fish or plow fields as a hired hand; he could only lie on his futon waiting for his body to heal. He passed the days and nights thinking, and what he found in the dark recesses of his mind he did not like. *What causes you to move from one female to the next?* This was the question that ate away at him in the night.

The day had its few distractions. He could hear children playing outside both near and far from his home, but he would worry when he heard one, or all, of the children being scolded by some old woman or man who disapproved of their harmless games, tricks, or acts. On one occasion he heard a child cry from his mother's harsh words because he had muddied his freshly cleaned shirt. *Poor child*, he had thought. Then there was Shinsei who would come and sit by his side so that they could talk about the sea, and those that had been successful from fishing that day. And he would ask about Kieko for it seemed that he was always on the priest's mind.

"You worry too much about the boy," he observed of the priest.

"Yes, yes I do . . . his arm is nearly mended."

The two were quiet.

"So, all he does now is sit beneath his father's old tree, look out to the sea, and meditate."

"Yes, that, while also caring for his mother."

"I'm surprised that he is so committed to zazen now. I remember your lectures and how bored I became every time I tried to meditate."

"You were always difficult to teach."

Raki-ka smiled.

"Well," the priest cleared his throat, "since he broke his arm, and his will so strong to train in Teshi-do, he has had no other choice but to practice zazen."

"I see," he said. "So, how much longer must I sit in my futon like this? If I didn't have Hirotake, Watanoro, and you to bring me food I'd starve. I need to begin working again."

"Do not think of that. The more you worry about when you will be ready to work the longer it will take for you to heal. So do not worry. Just rest and enjoy the comforts of your home and futon."

"That I don't like, Shinsei. I'm here on my futon weak and defenseless. I'm surprised that Rinton-no has not yet come to finish me."

"That would not, and will not, happen. You are under my protection. You have nothing to fear. Just rest and relax."

"There is only so much I can take of spending all the hours of the day alone. Your visits are one of the only highlights of my day, Shinsei."

"What of Hirotake and Watanoro?"

"Hiro's wife is becoming stricter with him. He comes to leave food, we chat for only a moment, and then he is off; usually, back to her."

"And Watanoro?"

"You know how his mother is and of what she thinks of me. So, it's a bit of the same. Wata comes to drop off some food, we chat, and then he is off to fish with his father."

"What of your uncles?"

"All of them have come to visit me, but only once. They are all too busy with their own children and wives."

"That I understand."

Raki-ka nodded with a sad face.

The priest ran his fingers through his beard.

"Do you get lonely living alone in that temple, Shinsei?"

The priest thought for a moment, "Yes . . . yes, I do."

"Do you miss your family?"

"Family?" he asked. "Family," he said to himself.

"Yes, your family—like your mother. What do you remember of her?"

"I did not know my mother."

Raki-ka looked at the priest, "Why? What happened?"

"She died when I was very young."

"I'm sorry, Shinsei," he bowed his head. "Do you . . . do you have any memory of her?"

"No," the priest said as he began scratching his beard, "I have no memory of her."

"You were raised by your father then."

"In a sense you can say that."

"What do you mean?"

"My father," he said with discomfort. "My father was always busy. He had very little time for my brother and I."

"I didn't know you had a brother."

"Yes . . . yes, I did," he said as he continued scratching his beard with greater unease.

"Where is your brother now?"

The priest stood up, "I should be going."

"I . . . I didn't mean to pry into your past, Shinsei."

"I know. Do not worry. I should go . . . I should go." He shook his head ridding his mind of uneasy thoughts. "Do you want me to bring you anything tomorrow?"

"No, Shinsei. I'm all right. Thank you. So, I'll see you tomorrow."

"Yes, until then." He picked up his staff and left.

On a dark, cloudy evening Raki-ka received a new guest. He was frightened when she rushed into his home for she was covered from head to toe by a hooded crimson robe.

"Who are you?" he demanded as he urgently searched for the short sword he had placed by his futon.

She turned to him slowly, raised her hands to her hood, and revealed herself.

"Koko-maki!" he exclaimed. It was Rinton-no's daughter. With a sharp whisper, "What are you doing here? You must leave."

"Shhh, I'm staying."

"Maki–please–"

"Shhh," she hushed as she approached him with a finger pressed to her lips. She sat down beside him, and stopped him from sitting up by pushing him down.

"You must go. Look at me. If your father finds us I'm finished."

"You know I should be mad at you."

"Maki–look–I'm–"

"But, I'm not."

He stopped; his mouth hung open from a word he hadn't the chance to utter.

"Look at you," she laughed. "You're like a little boy."

He frowned, "Is that what you came here to tell me?"

"No, I came because I wanted to talk . . ."

He waited for her to continue.

"When I heard what had happened to you, I didn't know what to think. Perhaps I should have felt good–that is what I thought. But, I didn't. I didn't think anything. I simply felt horrible.

I didn't like knowing that you had been hurt, especially this severely, and by my father. I felt ashamed that something private between us had become public, and violent–a public, violent spectacle . . ."

Raki-ka looked away from her for a moment.

She continued, "I love my father. He worries about me. He only wants the best for me. But, I know that what happened between us was what I wanted . . . what I hope you wanted . . . I don't blame you–I don't regret anything. I loved that night," she smiled. "You were so sweet and kind and gentle. I am only sad that it ended." She then waited for Raki-ka to say something. But, he did not say a word; he simply stared at her with a blank, confused face. "Well, I should go," she stood up abruptly, placed her hood over her head, and rushed out.

He didn't know what to think. He hadn't expected such words from her. He heard mother's calling their children home for dinner and listened as they giggled and ran past his thatched home. Then there was silence, and within the silence he thought of her. He regretted not having said a word to her after she had finished what she had said to him. He hoped that he had not hurt her in his inability to think of something to say. He felt ashamed and guilty as he remembered her face while she waited for him to say something, anything. "How could I be so stupid," he cursed. "I'm such an idiot!" He heard a dog bark outside as if agreeing with what he had just said. "Shut up!" he shouted to the dog. He shook his head and banged his fist into his futon. His stomach growled, but he did not feel like eating. He calmed himself slowly by listening to the growing collective sound of the insects as the sun dipped into the west.

Night soon came and he lay on his futon staring up at the shadowy, thatched ceiling with no desire to light a candle. He felt alone and guilty. And within the shadows of his home he saw her again and all that he had done to the women in his past. Thoughts of his mother then entered his mind, and sadly he wished that he had had some memory of her. He prayed to the gods of the winds that he would not continue to live alone, and that he would not die alone as well.

Later that night the winds howled and shook his humble home. A storm was coming and he welcomed it for he liked the sound of hard rains drumming down on his roof, but before the first raindrop had struck the lands of Kadek he had fallen deep into a dark, restless sleep.

CHAPTER XV

It was a hot summer's day and Kieko walked through a field of tall grasses. His right hand glided above the grasses. His left arm was still bound in a sling. He could hear the river. It was flowing, singing its liquid hum. He shivered feeling something slither down his neck and back. *Was it the wind?* He did not know. He breathed the warm air deep into his lungs and arrived at the river.

The river was thin and shallow. He could see pebbles and stones tumble and turn beneath its shiny surface. He took off his sandals and sat down along the bank of the river. He stretched out his right leg and dipped his foot into the moving waters. It was cold, very cold. Another chill slithered down his back. He withdrew his foot from the river and crossed his legs. The grasses moved with the winds touching and tickling his neck. He enjoyed the sensation. He wetted his upper lip with his tongue and felt a few thick hairs that were growing just above it. *Soon I will have the look of a man,* he thought.

The river continued singing. He closed his eyes, and his mind retreated into emptiness; his thoughts vanished; all things vanished, but then he heard the song of the stream again. He opened his eyes, leaned forward, and stared into the stream. In its glimmering surface he saw his reflection, but when he smiled he saw his face distort and turn into the face of Aiko. He was frightened. The face—Aiko's face—twisted and turned becoming the face of a hellish horned beast with flaring red eyes. He could not move. His eyes widened. He watched as the beast vomited poison into the waters turning it into a putrid black. A shadow then spread across the sky casting it into an unbearable dark. The grasses burned and crumbled into ash.

The horned beast rose out of the polluted waters and stood over Kieko. It bent its back and fixed its eyes into Kieko's eyes causing him to tremble with fear. The horned beast roared. Fire ignited in the palms of Kieko's hands. He could not move to shake his hands free of the flames. He wanted to scream, but could not. Sweat poured down from his scalp as droplets of melted flesh fell to the ground from his hands. The burning droplets rolled into the polluted waters and ignited it causing it to become a moving stream of fire and lava.

Thousands of demons began breaking through the ruined earth. Covered in dirt and ooze they limped toward Kieko and began stabbing their long, black nails and bent claws into him. Terrified, he screamed. The demons and fires backed away, but then advanced clawing at him, ripping flesh from his sides. They soon stopped and parted a short path for the horned beast.

The beast growled and spoke, "I have found you, and I have found your mother. And I shall slay her!"

Kieko screamed again and fainted.

A column of light appeared from the dark sky and shined over Shinsei who was arising from the scorched earth with his staff. The demons ran away from his light. But, the horned beast did not. Shinsei approached Kieko's body. The horned beast growled again. "You shall not have him!" Shinsei declared. "Be gone!" The beast, towering over the priest, roared and began circling around him and Kieko.

Shinsei kneeled and placed his right hand over Kieko's forehead, "Stay with me, my young friend." He glided his hand over Kieko's body mending his ripped flesh and broken bones.

"Leave him, priest," the beast demanded. "He is mine. I will take him!"

The priest stood up with his staff and faced the monster. "You will not!"

The beast stepped forward and swiped its claws at the priest, but the priest spun his staff and slammed it into one of the beast's palms piercing it open. The beast roared in pain and stepped back cradling its injured claw.

"Step back!" the priest commanded. "Step back and be gone from this place!"

The beast roared causing the cursed land to shake.

The priest stabbed his staff into the ground. The land shook violently.

The beast nearly fell.

"Be gone!" the priest commanded again.

The beast roared another horrible cry and charged at the priest.

The priest dropped his staff and threw his hands up pointing his palms at the beast. He breathed in, and exhaled. A beam of light shot out from his hands hitting and throwing the beast back. The beast crashed into the broken earth. "Be gone, I say!" the priest demanded. The beast shook its head and stood up. The priest exhaled again and shot out another beam of light at the beast throwing it back to the ground. "Be gone foul creature! Be gone from this place. This boy you will not take for he is a child of the Light!" The beast howled and crawled back, retreating, taking with it the darkness of the bitter land.

The stream flowed again in a clear blue; the warmth of the sun returned and the grasses grew. Shinsei's light was now gone. He was no more than a simple priest in old robes.

Kieko was sweating and shaking uncontrollably. His eyes fluttered as he moaned. Shinsei held him down and shouted his name. He began shaking less and less. He opened his eyes and stared blindly at the sky. Shinsei waved his hand over his eyes. His eyes did not respond. "He is still lost in a world of nightmares," the priest said to himself. He lifted and carried his young friend back to his thatched home.

The priest placed Kieko down on his futon, took off his sweat-drenched shirt, and saw that he was still staring blankly as he mumbled and shook. Immediately Madonai sat by her son, held his hands, and cried, "I trusted you, Shinsei! I trusted you."

"Your son will not be consumed by the beast," he tried to assure her. "His spirit is too strong–"

"Damn you!" she said shaking her head.

"Madonai, you must leave me alone with him if you want me to help him."

"No, I will not!" she puffed.

Impatient, Shinsei commanded, "You must if I am to bring him back! Kira!"

Kira, who had been waiting nervously outside, entered the hut, "Yes, Shinsei?"

"Take Madonai with you."

"Yes, Shinsei," she nodded, approached Madonai, whispered into her ear, and hugged her. Madonai took a deep breath, looked at Kira, and stood up. Kira led Madonai out of the hut to meet her mother who had been waiting outside.

Shinsei took Kieko into his arms, carried him to the hearth, and placed him on the ground again near a few lit candles. He sat down, crossed his legs, placed his left hand above Kieko's forehead, and began chanting as smoke rose up from the hearth to escape through the small opening in the roof. Outside Ruka, Madonai, and Kira waited and prayed in the old tongue that the gods would heal Kieko and bring him back from the world of spirits.

The morning sun rose into a sky filled with seagulls that sang and played. Madonai was awake. Kira was still asleep, but Ruka was beginning to wake up from the light of the sun that was now shining on her.

Shinsei had not moved during the night; his left hand was still hovering above Kieko's forehead while his right palm pointed up. He ended the last verse of his chant, opened his eyes, dropped his hands to the ground, and whispered, "Kieko."

Kieko murmured, "Shin . . . Shinsei."

"Kieko listen to my voice . . . relax . . . feel the Mother pull you toward her . . . Focus your heart on your breathing–"

"Where is my mother?" he asked as his eyes fluttered open.

"She is outside."

"Bring her to me."

Before Shinsei could call her Madonai had already entered the hut and ran to her son to embrace him.

"Mom!" Kieko cried when she grabbed him and held him tightly. "I'm sorry . . . I'm sorry–"

"I know, I know, I know . . ." was all she could say as she held him with tears running down her cheeks. She looked at him and saw that the light of the candles was glistening off his sweaty forehead. She brushed the sweat off his brow and noticed the stubble that grew above his upper lip. He was no longer her boy, but a young man.

A few days had passed. The sky was gold. Shinsei was meditating on a cliff that overlooked the sea near Kieko's Thinking Tree. He felt the warmth of the summer sun begin to fade. He welcomed the cool night for he had had enough of the summer heat; the sweat and constant need to bath in cool waters, no, he did not like that; he preferred the cold months of the year.

During cold winter night's he, as a child, used to sit looking into his fireplace watching a line of ants along the edge of it move from one stonewall to the other before staring into the moving flames as the burning branches crackled. *What did he see?* He saw himself as a warrior clad in black armor waging wars against the separatists in the name of his father's kingdom. He fought alongside his elder brother. He fought bravely and destroyed his enemies with single blows. Arrows deflected off him and peasants were crushed beneath his bloodstained boots. He then felt Kieko approaching and awoke from his thoughts.

"I am here to begin my training," Kieko said standing before the priest.

The priest smiled and looked at him, "Well, the day is near its end. You best answer your koan before the sunset. Name the face of your enemy."

Kieko sat down and stared into the black of the priest's eyes seeing his own reflection.

"Good," Shinsei complimented. "Now, answer this, what is your greatest fear?"

"Attachment."

"Good, but it is an answer that I feel you do not yet understand. When you see the beauty in all that surrounds you your fear will simply cease to exist within you. You will have faith in all that you have chosen for your life, and all that life has chosen for you. You will simply be . . . like the tree that welcomes the rain; like the blade of grass that bends with the harsh winds; like a flower that reaches for the light of the sun."

"I do not understand what you mean. How could I have chosen my life?"

"I cannot explain that to you, young Kieko. I am afraid that the understanding you seek will only come when you experience the truth. That is why you must meditate. I cannot explain the truth. I cannot show it to you with words. If you seek the truth through zazen you will experience it."

"I did not choose to be born in this place," he said with a hint of resentment. "I did not choose this life. I did not choose to be born different or to lose my father or for my mother to suffer. I do not understand this truth. I think this philosophy is flawed."

"Do not think, and do not question me!" the priest shouted. "Listen and respect my words!" He calmed himself. "You have much to learn, much to learn. You know much, and in your heart you know the truth, but it is your mind that bends your heart, twisting it . . . Why did you answer attachment as your greatest fear?"

"Because attachment is the source of all suffering."

"Just words. Those are just words, Kieko. Why is attachment the source of all suffering? Attachment is a desire to hold and control. People do so to feel secure over their insecurities. By controlling others they feel secure over their own self-hate. Attachment, it keeps us in our past, it does not let go of the ghosts that haunt and ail us.

"Never answer me with words that hold no meaning for you, Kieko. Do not tell me what I want to hear. You either know or do not, but I sense that you do recognize that you are your own enemy. The demons you wish to slay are not an outside other. They are deep within you. You must draw them out and slay them if you are to become a man in your own eyes."

"And if I fail to slay these . . . inner demons?"

"Then you will deliver much pain, hatred, and malice to the world. You will become a betrayer to the order that you are now seeking to serve."

"I will not betray."

"Nothing is promised in this life, Kieko. We do not know what the future may bring. Events will come that you may feel you are not prepared for, but you will learn that all things happen for a reason. You will see that there is a divine order to all things."

"Yes, I will seek to know and understand."

The Thinking Tree stood proud that he had just witnessed Kieko's first step into manhood. The Tree waved to the priest and Kieko with the aid of the cool, ocean winds, but they did not wave back. The Tree waved again, but Kieko did not notice. This saddened the Tree. *Did he forget about me, the Thinking Tree?* the Tree thought. The Thinking Tree felt like a mother bird whose chick had left her nest for the open sky. The Tree went over his memories of Kieko, having so much faith in him, the young boy, or rather the young man. And although there was still much anger within him there was still some inner air that was peaceful, strong, and wise. It was the Tree's hope that Kieko would always remain true. The Tree then noticed Shinsei and Kieko standing up and making their way back to the village. They had not waved a goodbye or even looked at him. Soon they were gone and the Tree stood alone again on his cliff looking out to the horizon watching the day soon come to its glorious end.

PART II

CHAPTER 1

It was the last day of the ninth month of the year. Madonai, within her warm hut, had just finished cooking a modest feast. There was a knock at the door. *They're early*, she thought. She went to the door and opened it feeling the cool autumn air.

"Good afternoon, Madonai," Elder Subo greeted.

"Good afternoon to you, Elder Subo," she said and bowed.

Elder Subo bowed. "I hope I have not arrived too early."

"No, no. I just finished cooking. Please, come in."

"Thank you. It smells good," he complimented as he looked at the mess of pots and pans.

"Oh–oh, please forgive the mess, Elder Subo," she blushed. "Would you like some tea?"

"Yes, that would be nice."

She sat on her knees near the burning hearth and piled several pots on top of each other in a hurried effort to clean.

"It is a big day for Kieko, isn't it," he smiled looking for a place to sit.

"Yes, it is. Just like his father he is," she lifted the kettle she had hanging over the hearth with a thick cotton rag and began pouring a cup of tea.

"How I miss him."

Madonai stopped pouring, "Yes . . . how I miss him too." The two were silent for a moment. She then finished pouring the cup of tea and placed it on a short-legged table before standing up to take off her apron.

"That is a beautiful dress, Madonai," the Elder said of the dress she was wearing.

She looked down shyly. "Thank you. It was my wedding dress." She thought of her son, "Will he . . . will he be, all right?"

"What do you mean?" the Elder asked taking the cup she offered him.

"Will he be all right in Shinsei's temple?"

"Of course, he will," he laughed. "You have nothing to worry about—nothing to worry about at all."

"I'm losing him, aren't I? I'm losing him to the Ki . . . just like I lost my husband to the Kai."

"You shouldn't say such things, Madonai. You did not lose your husband, and you will not lose your son. They will always be with you. Always."

"Yes, but . . ." she wiped her eyes, "it is so difficult. It is so difficult to know that I will not see him everyday. I will not wake up and find him sleeping. I will not wake up and begin preparing his morning meal. My life is dedicated to him . . . and now he is leaving me."

Elder Subo placed his hands on her arms and looked at her, "It is all right, Madonai. It is all right. I know how difficult it must be for you to lose him in this way. But, today is his day. Be proud of him. Show him that you are strong. Show him that you will be all right when he is gone."

"Yes, yes," she wiped her eyes again. "I will."

"Good then, good," he smiled. "Do you need any help taking this wonderful feast outside?"

"Oh, it is not much of a feast. I wish I could make more food for everyone. I do hope that many people will come and support him."

"It does not matter how many people will come. His father is here with us in spirit. That, I think, is really all that Kieko wants."

"I hope you are right."

"I am . . . for that I am an Elder, am I not?" he joked.

She cracked a smile.

"Hello, Madonai," Ruka greeted from the door. "Am I disturbing?"

"No, no, don't be silly."

"Hello, Madonai," Kira greeted from behind her mother.

"Hello, Kira. You look beautiful!" Kira blushed and looked down. "I didn't see you standing behind your mother. Please, please come in."

"Thank you," Ruka and Kira said together as they stepped into the hut and bowed to Elder Subo.

The Elder bowed back.

"Do you need any help carrying anything outside?" Ruka asked.

"No, no I'm all right," replied Madonai. "Do you want something to drink?"

"No, I'm fine thank you."

"I'm fine," Kira said. "Where is Kieko?"

"He isn't outside?"

"We didn't see him."

"He's probably with Shinsei then. I'm sure they'll return soon." She lifted several plates of food.

"Let me help you," Ruka insisted.

"Yes, let us help," the Elder said.

"Ah . . ."

"Don't be foolish, Madonai. We are all here to help. Let us help," Ruka said lifting a few plates of food.

"Ah . . . yes . . . thank you—"

"Don't be silly, Madonai. You don't need to thank us for anything. Kira, take those plates over there."

"Yes, mother."

Elder Subo picked up a few ceramic cups and the teakettle.

"Thank you," Madonai said again.

"It is a pleasure," Elder Subo replied.

Ruka looked at Madonai annoyed, "Don't worry, and don't be silly.

"I'm sorry."

"Enough!" Ruka shook her head and exited the hut.

The rest followed.

Outside they placed the plates on tables that Madonai had already decorated with flowers and leaves.

"Please help yourselves and eat," Madonai said to the Elder, Ruka, and Kira.

The Elder took a piece of dried fish and popped it into his mouth.

"There's Kieko!" Kira said with excitement.

Madonai saw her son walking proud and strong with Shinsei. She smiled and waved, as did Kira and her mother. Kieko waved back.

When he arrived he bowed to Elder Subo and shyly greeted Kira and her mother. Shinsei greeted everyone as well.

"Kieko, please eat," Madonai asked of her son.

"Mom, I'm fine."

"Please, eat."

"Mom—"

"I have fruits and berries."

Kieko looked at the tables and saw the effort his mother had put into the feast; he could see that she had made enough food for fifteen people. But, sadly, he knew that no one else from the village would come to celebrate his Cutting ceremony. He watched his mother as she offered more food to Ruka and Kira, and noticed her looking out hoping to see if more people would arrive, but there was no one.

Madonai looked at her son and forced a smile as she thought of the dream she had had: *The storm, the storm rained upon this land and destroyed . . . no, no, do not think of such things; it was just a dream, a nightmare with no meaning.*

A dog barked. Everyone looked and saw that Jomana and old farmer Toasu were coming. Kieko smiled. Elder Subo rolled his eyes.

"Please, let us begin," Shinsei said. Everyone placed their food and drinks on the tables and gathered around Kieko. The priest instructed Kieko to kneel before his mother, to touch the ground with his forehead and forearms, and to point the palms of his hands up to the sky. He began chanting in the old tongue asking the gods to protect Kieko and his mother. Kieko thought of Kira as he listened to the priest; he was grateful that she would take care of his mother while he was gone. The priest finished the short chant and instructed Kieko to rise and bow twice, and asked him to remove his top-gi and to sit down with his legs crossed. He then took out a pair of scissors from his leather satchel and began cutting Kieko's thick, long, black hair.

Kieko watched his hair fall in clumps on his legs and on the ground. Everyone was looking at him causing him to feel uncomfortable.

After some time Shinsei stopped cutting and looked carefully at Kieko's head. Satisfied, he picked up a jug of water, poured the water over the scissors, wrapped the scissors in a cloth, and placed them back in his satchel. From his belt pouch he pulled out a razor and sharpened it with a whetstone. When he was done he washed Kieko's head with soapy water and began shaving it.

Kieko was worried that the priest would cut his scalp accidentally, but the priest was very cautious as he ran the razor over his scalp. Time passed and Kieko relaxed into his thoughts of Kira, and dreams of mastering Ki sword.

"It is finished," the priest declared.

Kieko placed his hands on his head and felt something thick and wet. He looked at his right hand and saw blood.

"You were thinking, Kieko," the priest said. "If you were *present* you would have felt the cut." He dabbed oil over the cut and nodded to Madonai.

Madonai held her hands together, bowed, and picked up a bowl of water that she poured over her son's head. When she placed the bowl back on the ground she gave three half-bows to her son by kneeling and touching the ground with her forehead three times. Shinsei nodded to the others to do the same.

Elder Subo, old farmer Toasu, Ruka, and Kira all gave three half-bows to Kieko. Kieko watched finding it odd to see old farmer Toasu bowing down to him. *What do I know*, he thought. *Toasu has seen more of the world than I will ever see, and here he is bowing down to me.*

Everyone, now smiling, stood up and clapped with pride. Kieko blushed. Madonai began offering sweets to her guests. The priest asked Kieko to go into his hut to change out of his wet bottom-gi.

"I should be going," Elder Subo said to Madonai.

"And why is that?" the old farmer interrupted.

"I was not speaking to you."

"Yes, I know. You never want to speak to me," the old farmer smirked.

Elder Subo ignored the old farmer's words and said to Madonai, "I should go. The food was delicious. You are a wonderful cook."

"Thank you, Elder Subo—"

"Yes, thank you, Elder Subo," the old farmer interrupted again.

Madonai gave the old farmer an angry glare.

"Oh, sorry—off I go," he said and left to eat.

"I'm sorry," Madonai apologized to the Elder.

"There is nothing to apologize for. The food was delicious, Madonai."

"Perhaps—perhaps you would like to come and eat with me in my home," she felt a heat begin to rise within her.

The Elder stared hard at the ground. He forced a cough, "Uh, well . . . yes, sometime we will do that. But, I do not feel now is the best time to—I should go. Thank you," he finished, bowed, and walked away.

Madonai watched the Elder feeling a wave of embarrassment wash over her. *What was I thinking?* she thought. She shook her head, walked to a table, and picked up a plate of thinly sliced pieces of raw fish, which were placed over clamshells and decorated with slices of ginger and dried seaweed.

"Those look wonderful," Ruka complimented to Madonai.

"Agh . . . thank you," she said still irritated with her imprudent invtation to Elder Subo. "My father showed me how to prepare these. Would you like one?"

"Yes, of course." She picked up a clamshell, held it to her mouth, and sucked the raw fish into her mouth. "Delicious."

"Try the soup."

"What kind of soup is it?"

"It's a vegetable noodle soup; the broth is made from pork bones."

"Yes, I will try it as well. Kira!" she shouted, "Have some of these fish dishes."

"Yes, Mom," Kira replied.

Madonai saw that Kira was busy speaking to Shinsei, the old farmer, and Kieko. "You have a beautiful daughter."

Ruka looked and saw that her daughter was now feeding a handful of berries and nuts to Jomana. "Yes, she is beautiful—Kira! Don't feed Toasu's dog!"

"It's all right!" the old farmer assured her. "It is quite all right."

Madonai could see that her son was nervous around Kira by the way he avoided eye contact with her, and by how he fidgeted with the knot of his cotton belt. She knew her son had deep romantic feelings for her, and that he had been surpressing them for the past year. *It is best that he does not share his heart with her, just yet,* she thought.

"Madonai, are you all right?" Ruka asked.

"Yes, yes, I'm sorry. I was just thinking about my son."

"It must be difficult for you. The Cutting ceremony is never an easy time for a mother."

"Yes, it is difficult, but the time he will have with Shinsei in his temple is something that he needs. I can see that he is getting restless in not having a father, or a male figure, around to teach him, guide him in what it means to be a man.

"Please, have some more food," she said eager to change the subject.

"Oh, thank you," Ruka took another clamshell.

"And how are things with Kira now that she has gone through Hakunus?" Madonai asked.

"What a question," she sighed. "It is difficult to be honest. Now I understand what my mother went through when I was her age."

"As do I," Madonai agreed.

"She is in love," she paused to choose her next words carefully. "Or I should say she thinks she is in love. What does any child . . . or young woman, know of love at that age."

"Not much, but that is the beauty of that age; the purity and the intensity of the love that they feel," Madonai added.

"Yes, you are right. It is the way of things. They should feel as they do about those that they love, or perceive to love."

"But tradition dictates otherwise."

"Yes, yes exactly what I was thinking. That is the difficulty that I have with Kira. Explaining to her . . . trying to make her see the realities of our ways, of our traditions, and arranged marriages are not a topic that any girl . . . young woman, wants to hear."

"Yes, you are right."

"So for now I will let her be," she said looking at her daughter as she laughed with the old farmer and Shinsei while Kieko smiled. "And I will let time pass."

"With time she will see things as you would like for her to see them . . . or not. Time will tell."

"Yes, time will tell."

When all was said and done it was time for Kieko to gather his belongings and say goodbye to everyone. Shinsei had already left, but he had explained to Kieko that he would be waiting for him in the hills not too far from the village. Kieko went into his hut. He checked his packed bag and looked around his home searching for anything that he might have forgotten to pack. He paused. He knew that this would be the last time he would call this place home. Shaking his head of his thoughts he threw his bag over his shoulder, looked around for the last time, and left.

Outside he placed his bag on the ground. Everyone was looking at him. He looked at his mother and could see tears welling in her eyes. He went to her and hugged her.

"I love you, so much," she whispered into his ear. "I am so proud of you. You should be proud of everything you have accomplished. Your father is so proud of you. He is watching us now. I can feel him."

Kieko held his mother tightly, "I'm sorry that I have to go. I don't want to go," he said trembling.

"You don't have to go. You can stay here with me."

"I . . . I have to do this. I don't know why, but I have to do this."

"Don't worry about me then, I'll be here. Don't worry. I'll be fine and so will you. We will always be together. You are my son. I have Kira." Kieko looked at Kira and Ruka. "We will look after each other. Do not worry about us."

"I'll be fine too, mom. Don't worry. I will work hard to finish what I have set out to do and return back to you."

"You must go. It's getting late." Madonai held her son one last time and released him. He was no longer hers.

Kieko picked up his bag, took a few steps back, bowed to his mother and then to the old farmer, Ruka, and Kira. Jomana barked. "Sorry, Jomana," he apologized. He bowed to her as well and began walking away.

Kira watched him leave; she was upset that he had not said goodbye to her by hugging her. Kieko then stopped and turned to wave to his mother, but he was looking directly at Kira. She quickly waved back as did Madonai. Kieko smiled, bowed again, and continued on.

The priest greeted Kieko when he had reached him on the path in the hills and explained to him that he had to shave his head every three days as a disciple of the Ki. Kieko heeded the priest's words, and together they walked to the Kadek Temple in silence.

Kieko used the long walk to go over memories of his mother and Kira while also wondering what he would learn from Shinsei concerning the Ki and his father.

"We will be there shortly, Kieko."

"Yes, I know, Shinsei."

"I am Master Shinsei!" he corrected. "I am no longer your friend. I am your master. You will always address me as Master Shinsei. Is that understood?"

"Yes, I–I understand . . . Master Shinsei." Kieko did not like this drastic change in their relationship; he assumed that they would continue treating each other as friends. He was now beginning to have doubts about his decision to pursue the Ki arts, but he realized that this was probably how it was for his father and all the Ki, including Master Shinsei.

It was dusk when they reached the Kadek Temple. Kieko had never seen the temple at night. Its sharp roof edges, tall towers, and chimneystacks frightened him. It looked like a castle from the stories he had heard as a child, a castle plagued by wicked creatures. Chills ran up his spine. He then saw what he thought were birds hovering and diving over the temple feasting on some prey that he imagined them tearing apart.

"Those are the temple bats that you see, young Kieko," the priest explained. "They are the guardians. When I am away they protect these grounds. They nest in the high ceiling of the main hall. As you begin training you will learn to appreciate and respect them. You will train in the midnight hour. You will meditate to the sound of their flapping wings. Just be warned of their droppings, which we will clean in the mornings after breakfast.

"Yes, Master Shinsei."

They arrived at the temple's tori gate, which was composed of two towering red pillars supporting a grand, black-pitched roof. The priest bowed and passed through. Kieko did the same. The priest led Kieko to a large, stone water basin that was covered by a wooden roof and picked up a wooden ladle that was resting along one of the basin's sides. He dunked the ladle into the water filling it and drank from it. He motioned for Kieko to do the same, which he did. They then walked through the temple's garden before walking up several granite steps to the temple's main entrance door. The priest slid the dense wooden door open and stepped into an antechamber. Kieko followed. The priest placed his staff against one of the corners of the antechamber and removed his rope sandals while motioning for Kieko to do the same, "Point your sandals away from the temple."

"Yes, Master Shinsei." He removed his sandals and pointed them as instructed.

"Come with me."

The priest slid another door open and walked into another antechamber. Kieko followed and saw three calligraphy paintings hanging on the wooden wall before him and potted plants by the windows to his right. *Nothing has changed*, he thought to himself. The priest slid another door open and walked into the reception hall. Kieko followed and started counting all the calligraphy paintings he saw hanging on the walls. "Place your bag over there," he said pointing to a corner of the room. Kieko did as asked. The priest then walked to another door; it was the door to the main hall. "Now you may see what is behind this door."

"Yes, Master Shinsei," he said eager to see what was within the main hall.

"You must always bow when you step into this room. Do as I do."

"Yes, Master Shinsei."

The priest slid the broad, oak door open.

Kieko saw a bright golden glow. He squinted and realized that the glow was emanating from a massive golden statue of a Buddha sitting on a large altar at the opposite end of the hall. His jaw dropped. It was a glorious sight.

Master Shinsei held his hands together before his chest, gave a deep bow, and walked into the main hall. Kieko bowed in the same manner as his master and walked in.

Kieko first looked at the altar that was covered with hundreds of lit candles and the offerings of peaches and apples on silver plates placed before the Buddha. He then looked at the dark surroundings to his left and right and was amazed to see how clean the hall was kept. And along the old wooden walls of the main hall he saw neatly stacked columns of zabutons and long vertical calligraphy paintings.

"Stand here," the priest ordered.

Kieko stood still, but he heard something hit the floor. He looked down and saw bat droppings. He grimaced, and then noticed that the grains of the wooden floorboards were all pointing toward the Buddha. *Strange,* he thought.

Master Shinsei bowed and took three steps toward the shrine and bowed again. He lifted the shrine bell, rang it three times, and opened a finely carved box filled with incense sticks. He took three sticks from the box and lit them with a candle before placing them upright in a small bowl filled with white ash. He bowed again and lifted a bekuru and wooden mallet from the altar. Kieko had seen Master Shinsei chant and pray before with the bekuru, which to him looked like a wooden ball with a handle that had been hollowed out. Master Shinsei held the bekuru and mallet to his chest and bowed again before taking three steps back.

"Do as I will do, young Kieko."

"Yes, Master Shinsei."

The priest placed the bekuru and wooden mallet beside his left foot and gave three full bows. Kieko followed by kneeling, placing his hands on the ground, and lowering his forehead to the wooden floor. He then turned his hands over so that his palms were pointing up to the ceiling and flipped them back before sitting up to kneel again and stood up. He repeated the full bow two more times.

"Good. Those are good, full bows. Now, wait here."

"Yes, Master Shinsei."

Master Shinsei turned to his left, walked to a stack of zabutons, picked up two zabutons, and returned. He gave one zabuton to Kieko and placed the other on the floor before him; Kieko placed his zabuton on the floor as well. The priest stepped over his zabuton and sat on it. Kieko did the same. He then picked up his bekuru and mallet, bowed, and waited. Kieko bowed. The priest closed his eyes. Kieko closed his eyes.

Time passed, and as it did Kieko grew bored and peeked at his master to see if he had moved. The priest had not. He took a deep breath filling his lungs with the scent of the burning incense sticks and closed his eyes again. His mind wandered from one thought to the other. His posture began to slouch, as he grew tired. And at the very moment he was about to fall asleep he heard a loud wooden smack. Master Shinsei had hit his bekuru with his mallet. Their meditation session had finally ended. Kieko was relieved. Master Shinsei began chanting with a beautifully low and strong voice. Kieko did not understand any of the words that his master was reciting, he was chanting in the old tongue, so he simply sat and listened to the rhythmic pulse of his master's voice.

Master Shinsei ended his long chant by hitting his bekuru from a rapid to slow decrescendo. He bowed–as did Kieko–stood, bowed again, and took three steps toward the altar. After placing the bekuru on the altar he bowed again and took three steps back.

"You will learn this chant," he said to Kieko. "It will be your chant. It will clear everything that is troubling your heart and mind. From this chant will the universe be revealed to you; all the answers that you seek; all the riddles that poison your mind will be remedied by the rhythm of those word-sounds."

"Yes, Master Shinsei."

"Come, let us eat. It has been a long day for the both of us. Come, I will show you the kitchen chamber, your bowl, your cup, and your new shi sticks."

"Yes, Master Shinsei."

The priest took a bronze lamp he had lit from the altar and led Kieko to a door at the far left side of the altar. He slid the door open, the door creaked, and a cool draft of wind blew out. He walked into the darkness; Kieko followed.

"Put those on," Master Shinsei said pointing to several pairs of wooden sandals that lined one of the cobblestone walls within the dark chamber. Kieko slipped his feet into a pair. The priest put on a pair as well and lit a torch that was hanging on the wall. Kieko could now see old cobwebs flapping with the cool draft that was blowing up from a spiraling stone staircase in the floor.

"Come," the priest said as he walked down the staircase lighting the torches that lined its spiraling walls.

Their sandals echoed as they made each step down the staircase. When they reached the bottom Kieko saw a tunnel ahead of them lined with cavern chambers; he could see lights flickering from within a few of the chambers. He had never seen a dungeon before but he considered this dark place beneath the main hall an excellent example of what he thought one would look like. He saw more cobwebs and spiders nesting their eggs along the tunnel walls of the temple underground. They began walking down the tunnel. He looked into the chambers as he passed them and saw statues of Lemurian gods and goddesses carved from out of the bedrock and lit candles on stone altars before them; the flickering candlelight animated many of the stone faces; a few looked as if they were laughing in an evil delight.

"The Kadek Temple was built over these chambers," the priest explained. "This has been a place of worship for at least two thousand years. In an age long ago the people of these lands worshipped many gods. They worshipped the gods of the trees, the winds, the goddesses of the seas, the gods of the mountains, the goddesses of the underworld, and . . . well–you understand. In these depths they worshipped both light and dark forces."

"Don't these statues frighten you, Master Shinsei?"

"I remember the first time I saw them. Yes, I was frightened, but you will learn to appreciate them–even like them. And you should know that there are spirits residing here. They will come to you in the night, in you dreams, guide you, and at times torment you," he smiled. "But, do not mind them. They have a wonderful sense of humor."

"Yes, Master Shinsei," he said with fear.

"Here we are–the kitchen chamber. Please mind your head," the priest said pointing to a low wooden beam at the entrance to the kitchen chamber. He walked in and pointed to a shelf within a cupboard filled with bowls, "Over here is where we keep our bowls and utensils. These will be yours, over here." He gave Kieko a steel bowl. Kieko looked at it and saw that within the bowl there was a steel soup bowl with a lid over it. The priest also gave him a ceramic cup, metal shi sticks, and a cotton napkin. "You must take care of these instruments. Without them you can not eat. You must always keep them safe and in there proper place, and you must always wash them after each meal and dry them with your napkin." He walked to a cauldron that sat on a metal grill by the wall between two granite counters and lifted the lid that covered it with a thick cotton rag. He placed the lid on one of the counters and struck a fire in the open fireplace below the cauldron; above the cauldron there was a metal pot hanging from a long iron bar. "It will take some time for my broth to warm. Take a seat at the kitchen table, young Kieko."

"Yes, Master Shinsei." He sat down and looked around the chamber noticing a long curved groove in the bedrock walls that was covered with pillows.

"Do you know how to cook?"

"I can cook simple things, Master Shinsei. I'm not a picky eater so I don't cook a very pleasant meal. As long as the food finishes my hunger and treats my body well, I am content."

"I see . . . well, I will have to teach you how to cook a more pleasant meal than what you are used to? If you want to live you must learn how to cook. In any case you will impress your future wife if you can cook a delicious meal." He began sharpening a knife.

"Yes, Master Shinsei," he said rubbing his hands together nervously.

The priest continued sharpening his knife, but he noticed Kieko's behavior and asked, "What are you thinking of?"

Kieko looked up; he was still rubbing his hands together, "Is it all right if I ask you a question, Master Shinsei?"

"Yes, of course."

"Have you . . . have you ever loved someone, Master Shinsei?" he looked down.

Master Shinsei put the knife down. "An odd question you ask. But, I know why you ask it. Yes, you could say that I was in love once, but that was a long time ago."

"What was it like? What did it feel like, Master Shinsei?"

"I can assure you that the feelings I had for her were the same as the one's you have for Kira."

"How do you know that?"

"Master Shinsei!" he hollered.

"I'm sorry . . . Master Shinsei."

"That is better." He returned to sharpening his knife. "Well, to answer your question. The look you have on your face when you are with her is the same look I had when I was in love."

"What happened?" he asked with great curiosity.

"What did I just tell you?" he said pointing the blade at Kieko.

"Master Shinsei—I'm sorry—I won't forget again."

"I'm afraid that the story is a long one, and it is not one that I care to tell tonight. I am too old and tired to think of my younger days," he said bitterly. "Although, I will tell you this. If you love someone you see nothing but the beauty within her, and sometimes you will see a beauty that even she can not see. It is a wonderful thing to fall in love. Never lose it when you find it. There is nothing greater in this world than that."

"Yes, Master Shinsei."

"Well, I think it is time to celebrate don't you, young Kieko?" the priest said to change the subject.

"What do you mean, Master Shinsei?"

"Let us drink to your new life. I have several bottles of a vintage rice wine. Give me a moment to retrieve a bottle or two."

"Yes, Master Shinsei."

The priest left the kitchen chamber with a skip in his step; his behavior now reminded him of Kira's three-year-old cousin, Isao. He soon returned with a couple of old and dusty rice wine bottles. He placed them on the table, pulled out the cork lid of the bottle with a red silk label, and poured Kieko a cup. Kieko reciprocated by pouring a full cup for his master.

"To a long and wonderful life, young Kieko."

"To a long and wonderful life, Master Shinsei."

They drank, but Kieko put down his cup and began coughing; his face was cringing with disgust.

"Not used to a strong old wine?"

Kieko shook his head as he continued coughing.

Empty bowls sat on the kitchen table. Not a scrape of food was left. Kieko's belly was full of soup, rice, and dried fish.

"Drink more, young Kieko."

"Yes, Master Shinsei," he said with great hesitation. He did not like the taste of the rice wine, and he didn't like what it was doing to him either; he felt lightheaded, dizzy; he wasn't even sure if he could stand, but he wanted to please his master and so he slowly sipped from his refilled cup.

"You do not like to drink?" the priest joked.

"No, no, I do, Master Shinsei. It's just that . . . I don't like to lose control of myself."

"You don't like to lose control? A noble quality, my young friend . . . It is good to maintain control, in that way, you will not hurt anyone–only yourself."

"What do you mean, Master Shinsei?" he said not appreciating the comment.

"Who are you afraid of hurting?"

"No one, Master Shinsei."

"Oh, let me guess . . . your mother and Kira."

"And what of it!" Kieko barked.

The priest shot up from his seat and slammed his fist against the table. "Don't you ever use that voice with me!" Kieko cowered. "You have to learn to control your anger first," he sat down. "Afraid of losing control–it is a joke. Don't you ever break out at me. I am your master! I will provide you with food and shelter. I will educate you in the Ki. Respect me or I will throw you out."

"I'm sorry, Master Shinsei, but you had no right to say what you did."

"I had every right. I am your master. Now you must ask yourself why did my words upset you? Does the truth hurt you? Does it offend you?"

"I did not like how you said it, Master Shinsei."

"I am testing you, Kieko. Remember that. I am testing you. I have much work to do with you. And as for your mother and Kira, it is plain to see that you do not want to hurt them. I know that is why you have distanced yourself from Kira, and nothing is wrong with that, but don't fool yourself into believing that hiding from her will protect her. There is no greater tragedy than to not reveal your feelings to those you love."

"Yes, Master Shinsei," he murmured.

"Well, I think it is time for you to go to sleep. Clean your bowls, put them away, and you may go."

"What about you, Master Shinsei?"

"I have to train."

"But, it's late."

"Yes, I know. What is your point?"

"Nothing, Master Shinsei," he stood up and took his bowls to the sink to clean them.

"I will train in the dharma hall and forbidden are you to enter while I train. I have trained every night for all my days as a Ki priest. Whether I am drunk, tired, or sick, I train." He stood up and began wiping down the kitchen counters. "You may go. There is a staircase in the room that is next to where we used to have our tea. Follow it up. There is only one door. It is open. It is the door to your room."

Kieko's face lit up, "Yes, Master Shinsei." He wiped his bowl dry and placed it on the shelf.

"Remember, the dharma room is forbidden to you while I train."

"Yes, Master Shinsei."

"Don't forget to bow in the main hall. You may take a candle from the altar to light your way, but you must bow before and after taking the candle. Is that understood?"

"Yes, Master Shinsei."

"You may go. Good night, young Kieko."

"Good night, Master Shinsei."

Kieko took a last look at the priest; he was washing his soup bowl with a soapy sponge and then burped. He smiled, but there was something in his master that he had never seen before, it was something deep, something somber. He turned and walked as fast as he could to the staircase.

He ascended the steps that led to his room. He was delighted to have his own room, but he realized that he had nothing to decorate it for all he had brought were a few rags of clothing. He arrived at the top of the stairs and slid the door open. It was dark. He walked in and could not see much, but he could tell that it was a large room. He bumped into a desk, found some candles on it, and began lighting the candles with the one he had brought from the altar to illuminate the room. He looked around and loved what he saw: there was a fireplace to his left, an old table and chair, temple shoes by the door, and a narrow staircase at the end of the room leading up to a lofted futon. The room had a high oak ceiling with a small window, and the floor was covered with rugs of various shapes and sizes. He was happy; his room was comfortable and warm. He then got ready to sleep on his futon.

After lighting a fire in the fireplace and unpacking his bag he went up the steps that led to his lofted futon and crawled under the blankets of his futon. He found the futon to be uneven and thus uncomfortable; he reasoned that whoever had slept in it before had slept on only one side of it. He got up, lit one of the candles his mother had given him, and placed it on a short table by his futon. He began punching the futon trying to force the cotton that had accumulated on one side of it to the other. He eventually gave up and lay down.

Staring into the flame of the candle he began thinking about his mother. His thoughts soon drifted to the dinner he had had with his master. He was disappointed. He did not like seeing the priest slightly drunk. He had always seen him as perfect and ideal, flawless. And he had noticed something deep within his master's eyes. It was sadness. *Yes, that is what it was.* He wondered if his father had ever seen this side of the priest. *Maybe he drinks to forget the sadness,* he thought. *No, that is not so. He drinks to touch it. He hides it by day and drinks with it by night.* He wondered what the story was about, the love story he did not want to tell before dinner. *Did he tell it to my father? The gods only know.*

Lightening struck and called out with terrible thunder. "The dragons," he whispered, "are stirring." Rain began to patter down on the window. He looked at the window hoping to see the lightening. Lightening struck again and he listened to the grumble of the thunder. He rested his hands over his chest and thought about Kira and how he would protect her with the aid of the dragon spirits. He then rose out of his futon, kneeled beside it, and bowed his head to pray to the winged gods of the *drakul.* "I call upon the dragon spirits to protect Madonai and Kira. I know, Nishiaka, that you are listening, and I ask that you protect them when I can not." He leaned forward and touched the floor with his forehead. He took a deep breath, exhaled, and relaxed feeling proud that he was on the path of the Ki. He uncurled his body, rolled back onto his futon, and stared at the ceiling while listening to the hard rains.

The rains lulled him into the dark of his dreams.

He was somewhere deep within the Great Forest of Ikishi. It was night, but there was a misty light. He did not now how or why he was within the forest. He walked and listened to the crinkling leaves beneath his feet. He heard a voice. His body froze. "Who's there?" he asked. There was no reply. The hairs on his arms and neck rose. He looked to his sides and saw nothing. He took a step forward, but there it was again, a voice whispering. "Who's there?" he demanded. There was no reply again. He became angry.

A sweet voice then spoke through the winds, "Kieko, we are with you, we are here. We are one."

"I don't understand? Where are you?" he looked in all directions.

"You will not find us. We speak to you only in your dreams. We guide you through your heart. Your mind will never find or understand us."

"I don't understand?"

"You will one day see that you are never alone. You will one day find that there are forces in this world, unseen forces, guiding you."

"Are you an evil force?"

"We see . . . You wonder if we can lead you to an ill-fated end. You want to know if we have a vengeful mind."

"Yes, I do," he said feeling very uncomfortable that he was conversing with something that held no form.

"Well, that is for you to decide."

"What do you mean?"

"You hold the answer. You have the key. Your heart will guide you and your mind will take you there. If you trust in your instincts you will know what is real and not. You will know what is good and what is not."

"Why are you speaking to me?"

"We wanted to remind you."

"Remind me of what?"

"That you are good."

"What?"

"We have read your thoughts. We know that you seek the answer to a riddle."

"What riddle?"

"Aiko . . . Is he good or not in your eyes?"

"Not, I would say."

"Ahhh . . . that is your mind speaking. What do you feel in your heart?"

"Why do I feel that you already know what I feel in my heart? Why should I speak what you already know?"

"Because words are powerful when given a voice, and you have yet to say what you believe. That is why we are here."

"So, you want me to say it, although, I don't know it to be true."

"Yes, you do. Do you believe Aiko to be good? Or do you believe that he is devoid of what is good?"

"Yes, he is devoid of what is good. Why else does he harm me?"

"You will find that we are all mirrors for one another. You will find that your enemy is your greatest teacher and that you are in fact your own worst enemy. You will see that in this way your enemy has served you lovingly."

"Are you mad? How can I accept such foolishness?"

"You already know this to be true in your heart, but your mind—your mind is too full of anger to let the will of your heart speak."

"My mind is there to protect my heart. My heart is too weak to stand on its own. My mind is its shield, it protects my heart."

"Why do you hate Aiko?"

"Are you blind to his rage against me?"

"Why does he rage against you, Kieko?"

"Because I am Akai."

"Why would that matter to him?"

"Because his mother was killed by Atlanteans."

"Do you not feel compassion for the young Aiko? Aiko has never known his mother just as you have never known your father. And his father misses his mother so terribly that he can only express it by lashing out and beating Aiko down. Do you not feel compassion for Aiko?"

"Why don't you ask Aiko if he feels compassion for me?"

"You believe that Aiko is not compassionate towards you?"

"Yes, I do."

"Aiko is teaching you in his own way."

"What the hell am I supposed to learn from him?"

"You are learning how not to be."

"What?"

"You are learning how not to be to others."

"I know that already. Do you see me going around spreading my hate with punches and kicks?"

"That is what we fear, Kieko. We fear that you are not learning from Aiko's ways. We fear that when you do step out and walk to the West you will spread your hate to all those around you."

"That will never happen. I will never do such a thing."

"Do not be so sure. We are only here to remind you that Aiko is teaching you in his own way."

"Well, then, what is the answer to my riddle?"

"You know the answer. It is simply up to you to voice it, and with this do we bid you farewell."

Kieko woke up. The room was dark. He knew that he had had a dream but could not remember what he had dreamt about. *There was a misty forest.* He tried to remember more, but could not, and fell back to sleep.

OF TEMPLE CLEANING

Well, you couldn't have inquired into a more uninteresting aspect of Lemurian culture than what you have asked us to discuss. We are sorry; we don't mean to be rude. We should probably congratulate you on your curiosity into this aspect of Lemurian Ki temple culture. Most unfortunate that you are not . . . How do you call them? Oh yes, an anthropologist. You are young, so there is still time for you to become such a thing.

Well, if we must begin, let us begin with the temple kitchen. Usually, temple cleaning would begin there. After dinner one of the Ki monks would begin his cleaning practice by sweeping the kitchen floor. Once all the dust and crumbs were swept up, the Ki monk would then fill a bucket with warm water and soap. He would then soak a rag—we do hope to imply the unisex form of the word "he."

When we say "he" we do not mean that only men were Ki monks. Oh no, no, no. Do not be so silly to think like that. What we mean to say is that both men and women were Ki monks. Is that clear? Most unfortunate that your language does not have a term that implies both male and female.

So, yes, getting back . . . Where were we? Oh, yes, silly us. The Ki monk would soak the rag in warm water, squeeze it before using it on the kitchen floor, and—

Dear us, we find it quite rude that you want to interrupt us. Let us remind you that we are answering your question.

You want to ask another question? Well, make up your mind then. You want to know of the importance of temple cleaning? Oh, we are sorry, you want to know what the importance of temple cleaning is, not the, um . . . process.

Well, let us see . . . the importance of temple cleaning? Yes, yes, yes. Well, temple cleaning was extremely important for the Ki monks. It was a meditation, you could say. You see, for the Ki, everything was meditation. The Ki believed that . . . well, actually we should say that the Ki knew that every single moment was an opportunity to be in the present, to bring the mind into the present, completely.

You see, most of us go through our days never fully in the moment. Our minds are attached to thoughts of the past, or concerns for the future. When we do this we lose touch with all that is before and around us, here and now. The martial arts for the Ki was not a practice in offensive or defensive tactics, it was a practice to bring their being into the here and now. Chanting served the same purpose for the Ki monks, as did cleaning.

Of course, not every master Ki monk pursued the practice of cleaning whole-heartedly. Many master Ki priests, diseased by their self-fed egos, left the entire task to their Ki learners. Most unfortunate we must say. You may wonder how to tell a wise master Ki monk from one filled with self-pride and well . . . how do you people say? Shit. Yes, that is the word. Excuse us—negative words attract negative thoughts. Well, the way to tell is to simply see if the master Ki monk practices the good habit of temple cleaning everyday.

Temple cleaning taught a Ki monk of his relationship with his fellow monks, his environment, and with himself. If a Ki monk failed to clean thoroughly it would create conflict, resentment, and distractions between that Ki monk and his fellow Ki monks. Of course, this conflict would be a test for all the monks. If a monk could cut through the conflict and voice his anger at the monk who was upsetting him then that monk was clear and true. If a monk kept his anger to himself then he was failing to remain clear, and dark thoughts would fill and poison his mind.

All Ki monks had to pursue their tasks and practices with sensitivity and integrity. If harmony was to be achieved everyone had to be clear in their actions.

You must also consider the psychological affects of temple cleaning. Cleaning your environment brings order and a sense of control. It gives you a sense of intention and clarity, you could say.

Well, we hope that answers your question. We must say that we are happy that you chose to inquire about the importance of temple cleaning as opposed to the actual process of it.

CHAPTER 11

"This is how it is done," the priest explained, sitting on his knees, holding a rag. He dunked the rag into a bucket of soapy water, pulled it out, and twisted it before folding it. "This is the desired shape and size," he placed the folded rag on the wooden floor of the dharma hall. "If it is larger than this then dust and dirt will escape. You want to place your hands over the cloth," he stretched his hands over the length of the cloth, "like this. And place your weight on the cloth as you move up and down the floor. Now watch." He leaned forward, his legs pushed against his hands, and he moved forward gathering dirt and dust into the cloth. When he reached the end of the hall he turned around and repeated the floor cleaning exercise. "Now, you try," he said when he had returned.

Kieko took his rag, dunked it into the bucket, lifted and squeezed it, folded it, and placed it on the floor. He got on all fours and pushed the rag against the floor. When he reached the end of the hall he turned around and returned to his master.

"Good," the priest complimented. "That is exactly how it is done. Do that and only that. Do not stray, do not rush, and do not find some other means to perform this task. Remember, cleaning clears out your mind if you clean and clean only. Is that understood?"

"Yes, Master Shinsei."

"Good, clean the entire dharma hall floor. Do not let the rag collect with too much dirt. As soon as the rag is dirty rinse it and start where you left off. When you are done come and get me. I will be in my study," he stood up and left the dharma hall.

Kieko began cleaning the floor as thoroughly as he could. It took about half-an-hour to clean the dharma hall, which he thought made for good time. He dropped the rag into the bucket and went to his master's study.

The door of the study was closed. He knocked and waited wondering what his master's study looked like. The door slid open. The priest stepped out and closed it; Kieko saw nothing more of his master's study than its dark interior and a few lit candles.

"Are you done?"

He nodded.

"Speak!"

"Yes, Master Shinsei. I'm finished."

"Half-an-hour it took you. Soon you will be able to perform the task in half that time."

"Yes, Master Shinsei," he said disappointed.

"Follow me."

He followed.

The priest entered the dharma hall and bent down to check the floor. "Yes . . . this is good . . . very good cleaning indeed. Now the bucket," he said standing up, "pick it up and come with me."

Kieko picked up the bucket and followed his master to an antechamber in the rear of the temple. In the antechamber the priest slipped his socked feet into a pair of wooden sandals, slid open the heavy exit door, and stepped out into the cold. Kieko shivered when he felt the cool autumn breeze. He placed the bucket down, put on a pair of sandals, picked the bucket up, and followed his master.

"Come here, Kieko!"

"Yes, Master Shinsei."

"There," Master Shinsei pointed. "Over there, pour the bucket."

Kieko walked past his master to a pit and poured the dirty water into it.

"And that is that. Now, refill the bucket at the well, soap it, and clean the floor of the Great Hall of the Buddha. Come and get me when you are done."

"Yes, Master Shinsei."

Kieko stood at the entrance of the main hall and bowed. Picking up the bucket he entered the hall and decided to start cleaning the floor from the corner farthest from the altar and the entrance. He put the bucket down, looked at the golden statue of the Buddha, kneeled, and dunked the rag into the bucket. He pulled the rag out, squeezed it, folded it, and began cleaning.

The main hall was three times larger than the dharma hall, and when Kieko was nearly half way done he felt his neck begin to stiffen and his legs begin to tire. He thought that cleaning the temple floor on all four limbs was an unnatural and inefficient method. He believed it was better to use a broom so that he could at least stand up straight while he cleaned. The rag began to fill with hair, dirt, dried bat droppings, and dust. He cleaned a bit more and then stood up to stretch his legs before walking back to the bucket. After rinsing the rag he stood up again and wiped the collecting beads of sweat from his brow. He assessed his progress and sighed before returning to the spot where he had stopped and continued cleaning.

To pass the time as he cleaned he daydreamed about how impressive he was going to look once he began training with a sword. He saw himself performing sword forms near the cliff where his Thinking Tree stood, and Kira sneaking up on him, watching him, and being so impressed by his mastery of the Ki art.

It took him over an hour to finish cleaning the floor in the main hall. Exhausted, he walked to the bucket, dropped the rag in it, and went to his master's study.

Standing before the door he knocked; he heard the priest get up and walk to the door. The door slid open.

"You are finished?"

"Yes, Master Shinsei."

"Good," the priest exited his study and slid the door closed.

The priest bowed and entered the main hall. Looking carefully at the floor he walked to the center of the hall, kneeled, wiped his finger across the floor, and examined the grime on his fingers. "Did you begin from that corner?" he asked pointing to the corner farthest from the altar and entrance.

"Yes, Master Shinsei."

"Yes, I can see that. You used only one bucket of water to clean this hall. This part of the hall is not as clean as that end because the water you used had accumulated with too much filth. Clean a third of the hall and then dump the water out and refill it and re-soap it before cleaning another third. Do it all again."

"Just the last two-thirds of the hall, Master Shinsei?"

"No, everything again. From start to finish it must be done correctly."

"Yes, Master Shinsei," his shoulders collapsed.

"And be quick this time. I am getting hungry and tonight you are the cook."

"Yes, Master Shinsei."

"I will be in my study."

"Yes, Master Shinsei."

The priest left. The hall was growing dark as the sun began to set. "Curse the gods!" Kieko cussed when he was sure that his master was far enough not to hear him. "Wicked! Bloody wicked beasts and demons!" He kicked the floor. "This is ridiculous!" He bowed his head in defeat and ground his teeth. "This is such utter nonsense," he groaned.

He picked up the bucket and walked to the rear of the temple. He exited the temple to pour the water into the pit outside and refilled the bucket with fresh water from the temple's well. He soaped the water, cleaned the rag, and returned to the main hall.

He cleaned, and he was angry. He thought of how much he hated Aiko. He wanted to beat him and break his bones, and he wanted all the villagers to fear him so that they would never say or do anything to harm his mother. Another hour passed. He finished cleaning the floor.

He knocked on the door of his master's study. The door slid open.

"You are finished?"

"Yes, Master Shinsei."

"Good."

The priest exited his dark study and slid the door shut. He led Kieko to the Great Hall of the Buddha and for the second time examined his work.

"Yes, this is good, Kieko," the priest said standing up from the floor. "Now, it is time to cook. Come with me."

"Yes, Master Shinsei."

In the kitchen the priest poured water into the cauldron that sat on a metal grill over the open but unlit fireplace; and when the cauldron was a third full he then lit a fire. After that he pointed to a large basket beneath the cupboard and said, "Over there, in that basket, you will find rice. Inside are two cups. Fill the cups and bring them over here."

"Yes, Master Shinsei." Kieko did as asked.

"Grab that pot and fill it with the rice."

Kieko took the pot that was hanging over the sink and poured the two cups of rice into it.

"Fill the pot with water and rinse the rice with your hands."

"Yes, Master Shinsei."

Kieko knew how to clean and prepare rice for he had performed the task many times for his mother. He poured water until the pot was half-full and ran his hands through the rice. The water was cold and fogged into a cloudy white. He then poured the water into the sink, refilled the pot again, and continued cleaning the rice; he did this three more times. When he was done he filled the pot one last time, but only with enough water to rise just above the rice, and placed it on the grill beside the cauldron.

The priest walked over to the baskets beneath the cupboard and explained, "This basket has onions, this basket has carrots, that basket has cabbage, that basket over there has white radishes, and that one has broccoli." He then opened the pantry doors revealing many drawers. "In here you will find burdock roots, kabura—"

"I'm sorry, Master Shinsei. What is kabura?"

"Turnips . . . What else?" he asked himself as he looked at the labels on the drawers of the pantry. "Ginger, of course, horse radish, acorns, bamboo—do not cook with bamboo if you have not done so before. You will find an assortment of beans, peppers, and nuts in these jars over here and—well, I will leave it up to you to find what you need."

"Yes, Master Shinsei."

"I will be back in about half-an-hour for dinner."

"Yes, Master Shinsei."

The priest looked at the kitchen memorizing where everything was placed and left.

Kieko heard his master's wooden sandals echo down the tunnel. He looked around at the jars and baskets filled with dried goods and at the steam that was rising from the boiling water. In the pantry he found a few jars of sugar, salt, ginger, and a bottle of cider vinegar; he took what he needed and placed the items on a cutting board. He then lifted a saucepan that was hanging on a hook over the kitchen sink and placed it on a counter. With a wooden mortar he crushed stones of salt into fine grains of sand and brushed the crushed salt into the saucepan with his fingers; he then crushed stones of sugar into grains as well before brushing it into the same saucepan. He poured a small amount of cider vinegar into the saucepan and heated it over the fireplace. He stirred the contents until the sugar and salt had dissolved. After, he placed the hot pan on the cutting board and waited until the simmering, vinegar sauce cooled.

Under the cupboard he pulled out a basket filled with onions and pushed it back. He pulled out another basket and found the cabbages; he took out one head of cabbage and walked back to the cutting board where he pealed off several leaves, cut them into small pieces, and threw them into a large sieve, which he placed into the cauldron of boiling water. After whistling a short tune he lifted the sieve, placed it in the sink, and poured cold water over it. He then cut the ginger into thin slices and placed them and the cabbage leaves into a large bowl before pouring the vinegar sauce he had made into it.

He dipped his finger into the vinegar sauce and tasted it, "The gods–this tastes like cow's dung." He scratched his head. *What did I do wrong?*

The pot of rice began to shake violently. "Curses!" he lifted the pot with his hands, but threw it to the floor, "Demons!" He looked at the tips of his fingers and saw that he had burned them, "Cursed damn!" He took a thick rag, lifted the pot, and placed it on the counter. He then grabbed a wooden spoon and poked it into the cooked rice and found that the rice at the bottom of the pot had burned. "Damn it! How the hell am I to scrub that off?" He spooned as much of the rice as he could out of the pot and into a wooden bowl. With no space left on the counter he decided to place the bowl of rice on the kitchen table.

Master Shinsei walked in and looked at the mess Kieko had created, "What are you doing?"

Kieko turned to his master, "I'm sorry, Master Shinsei. I'm not finished cooking."

"Yes, that I can see. I heard your foul mouth upstairs. What are you doing?"

"I'm cooking, Master Shinsei."

"Cooking what?"

"I've made," he hesitated. "I've made a kind of mustard cabbage relish and–"

"Let me see." The priest walked to Kieko and saw the bowl. "This is not mustard relish. First of all you have to keep this in a cool place for four days before you can eat it. Where were you planning to keep it cool?"

"I . . . I don't know, Master Shinsei," he answered.

"Yes, I can see that. And what the hell is this?" the priest asked pointing to the pot of burnt rice. "After dinner you are going to scrub that for as long as it takes."

"I'm sorry, Master Shinsei."

"I thought you were joking or being modest when you said you didn't know much about cooking. Did your mother teach you nothing?"

"I–I just help my mother cook."

"Really? Do you just stand next to her, looking, not picking up on the art of it all?"

"I just do what she asks me to do, Master Shinsei."

Shaking his head the priest said, "That is ridiculous, Kieko. If you were fully aware during your cooking sessions with your mother–between what your mother was doing and what you were doing–you would have seen how all the pieces fit together to create a meal. All that time you spent with your mother helping her cook was a waste for you learned nothing. Instead you were probably dreaming and fantasizing about things of no relevance to what you were doing to help your mother cook. When you cook you cook only. No thoughts other than what you are cooking."

"Yes, Master Shinsei," he said defeated.

"Do not give me that! When you speak to me you speak with confidence!"

"Yes, Master Shinsei," he tried to say with intention.

"Aghh–you are frustrating me, Kieko. Clean this entire mess. All the scraps of food go into that basket in the sink. I will be back soon. Clean and only clean. No thoughts outside of cleaning this kitchen!"

"Yes, Master Shinsei," he said again as he watched his master leave.

He looked at the sink and its clutter of pots, and the cutting board and its scraps of ginger and cabbage. He mumbled to himself before putting the pot of burnt rice into the sink and released water from the faucet. A hissing cloud of steam rose from the sink. He waved his hands at the cloud until it faded. The water was ice cold and his fingers went numb as he scraped clean the bowls, mortar, and sieve. When all was done he dried the bowls and pots with a cloth and placed them where he had found them around the kitchen.

The priest returned, "Now that I am to teach you how to cook you must first remember that nothing is ever wasted in the kitchen of a Ki. Food is life. Without food there can be no life. Every grain of rice from your bowl must be eaten. Leave nothing to waste. Food is that precious. Is that understood?"

"Yes, Master Shinsei. I understand."

"Water is life. Do not waste a drop. I heard the water running when I was upstairs. Simply fill a bowl with water and turn the faucet off. Clean the bowl with the water that is within it, pour it into the next bowl, and clean with that water. If the water becomes too oily pour it into the sink and pour more water from the faucet and continue. Is that understood?"

"Yes, Master Shinsei."

"You do not understand. After I show you how to cook properly and clean you will perform, and then you will know."

"Yes, Master Shinsei."

"Let us begin." The priest sat on his heels and pulled several baskets from beneath the cupboard. He grabbed a ball of onion, two sticks of carrots, a head of broccoli from a smaller basket, and asked, "Is the mortar you used dry?"

Kieko checked, "No, Master Shinsei, it's damp inside."

"It will take a few hours for the wood to dry completely. You crushed sugar and salt in that mortar?"

"Yes, Master Shinsei."

"Why does that not surprise me? Use your head, Kieko," the priest shook his head. "Do not mix powders in a mortar. I have several mortars and pestles. Use one mortar to crush sugar and another to crush salt."

"Yes, Master Shinsei."

The priest placed the onion, carrots, and broccoli on the cutting board. "Watch how I cut the onion."

"Yes, Master Shinsei."

He cut the onion at its top and bottom and threw the scalped pieces into the basket that was in the sink. He stripped a couple of layers off the onion, cut it in half, and began slicing it. Grabbing the sieve that Kieko had washed he threw the slices into it and placed it on the heavily worn granite counter on the other side of the sink. He picked up a knife and began scraping the carrots before slicing them and placing them into the sieve. Next he cut the broccoli and placed its sliced pieces into the sieve as well. "That is how you cut an onion, carrots, and broccoli."

"Yes, Master Shinsei."

"Tomorrow you will cook what I am now preparing."

"Yes, Master Shinsei."

"You will enjoy cooking, Kieko. It is a meditative art."

"Yes, Master Shinsei."

"Simply nod from now on. This constant, 'yes, Master Shinsei' will drive me mad."

"Yes–" Kieko stopped and nodded.

The priest placed the sieve under the faucet and washed the sliced pieces of onions, carrots, and broccoli. When he was done he bent down, slid open a door beneath the sink, pulled out a large metal ring with a hook and long chains that hung from its sides, and attached the hook to the iron bar that was hanging over the fireplace. He then lifted a metal pan that was shaped like the shell of a turtle off the wall and placed it on the kitchen counter. He took a bottle of oil from the pantry, poured the oil into the pan, and moved the pan with his hands so that the oil swirled within it. When he was done he fitted the pan into the metal ring so that it sat suspended beside the cauldron and over the grill and the flames of the fireplace. He then took the wooden bowl of rice that was sitting on the kitchen table, placed it on the granite counter, and poured the chopped vegetables from the sieve into it. With a long wooden spoon he mashed the rice, onions, carrots, and broccoli together. After that he spooned the mixed rice into the suspended pan. The pan hissed and sizzled as the hot oil stung the clumps of rice. He stirred the rice to ensure that it did not burn.

When the rice was ready the priest lifted the pan carefully off the metal ring with a thick cotton mitten, spooned the rice back into the wooden bowl, and placed it on kitchen table. Steam from the hot fried rice rose into the air. The priest then picked up the bowl of the mustard relish that Kieko had made and poured it into a ceramic jar. "I have some kimu ki. Follow me." He placed a lid over the jar and walked out of the kitchen chamber with a lantern. Kieko followed his master into a corridor that branched off from the tunnel. As they walked and descended into the earth he heard the chattery whispers of running water.

"There is a small spring—a stream down here," the priest explained. "It carries cold water from the mountains. It is cold enough to keep cool some things such as your relish."

When they arrived Kieko could see that the spring was only a thin stream within a small bedrock chamber. The priest placed the jar of mustard relish into the cold stream, picked up another ceramic jar, took off its lid, and showed it to Kieko.

"Kimu ki," Kieko said with a mouth that began to water.

"Yes, cool and fresh it is. In a few days we shall try your mustard relish."

Kieko looked at the other jars in the water below and saw a porous basket made from twisting metal wires full of eggs. "I didn't know you had chickens, Master Shinsei."

"I do not. The old farmer visits every so often to chat. He usually brings eggs or lettuce or something else from his farm as gifts."

"Am I allowed to cook with these eggs?"

"If I am supervising your efforts, yes. Otherwise, no. Come. It is time to eat."

Back in the kitchen the priest and Kieko got their bowls and cups and sat down at the kitchen table. Kieko served his master fried rice, kimu ki, and poured hot water into his cup of dried tealeaves. He then served himself and ate.

The meal was delicious. Kieko, hungry from all the work he had done that day, shoveled spoonful after spoonful of food into his mouth. A few grains of rice fell from his lips onto the kitchen table.

The priest slammed his hand against the table. "Do not eat like a pig. You are making a mess. Look," he pointed to the rice on the table, "at that. When you eat enjoy your food. We are at the table. There is nowhere you need to run to. Take your time. Focus on eating and eating only. Eat those grains of rice."

"Yes, Master Shinsei," he picked up the grains with his shi sticks, ate them, and continued eating.

"That was good, Master Shinsei. Thank you," he said after finishing his food.

"You are not finished."

"I'm full, Master Shinsei."

"What about this rice?"

"What about this rice?" he remarked.

"Do not speak to me so! I am your master!" The volume and power of his words stabbed like javelins into Kieko's heart. The priest calmed himself, "What did I tell you? Do you not listen when I speak? We do not waste food. There are still grains of rice left in your bowl."

"Yes, Master Shinsei," he said obediently. He began picking and eating the rice.

"Every grain must be eaten."

Kieko nodded.

When Kieko finished the priest stood up, walked to the pantry, and pulled out a jar of pickled garlic. He sat back down at the table and took out two cloves for himself and two for Kieko. "Eat them," he requested.

"Raw, Master Shinsei?"

"Yes, of course. They are more potent that way," he popped a clove into his mouth. Kieko took a clove and ate it. His face cringed. The priest laughed.

"Drink more tea to settle your food and to quell the garlic."

"Yes, Master Shinsei," Kieko grabbed his cup and drank his tea.

"Now we must clean the kitchen." The priest stood up with his bowls and cup and placed them in the sink. Kieko did the same.

The priest released cold water from the faucet. The water poured into the top bowl of his pile. He turned the water off and soaped the top bowl before scrubbing it. When he was done he poured the soapy, oily water into the next bowl and cleaned it. He moved to his right toward the worn granite counter to dry his bowls with a cloth and nodded for Kieko to begin cleaning his bowls and cup.

When Kieko had finished cleaning both he and the priest left their bowls and cups to dry on the granite counter.

"Now it is time for you to wash the bowls and pans we used to cook. After that, sweep the kitchen floor." The priest pulled out a broom and dustpan from the kitchen closet. "Sweep all corners of the kitchen and beneath the kitchen table. Wipe down the kitchen table, cutting board, and all the counters. Put all the dust and grime into the garbage bucket over there by the sink. When you are done bring the bucket of garbage and the basket of food scraps that is in the sink upstairs and leave them by the main entrance door. Then come and get me. The basket of food scraps will drip so place it in this bowl here," he pointed to a ceramic bowl by the pantry door and left.

Kieko swung his fist into the air, "I'm not a Ki. I'm a servant." Acting out like the priest he said, "You must clean this, you must wash that, you must eat this, and you must bend over and take a kick up the ass—curses!" He then sighed, looked at the kitchen, and began cleaning. He twisted the faucet knob, filled the empty rice bowl with water, and scrubbed it. When he was finished washing the bowls and pans he placed all the scraps of foods into the basket that was in the sink, wiped down the cutting board, hung all the pots where they were supposed to be hung, and with a thick brush swished the remaining pools of water within the large sink into the drain. Everything was left clean and clear.

He swept the kitchen floor with a broom collecting all the dust into small piles at each corner of the chamber. He lifted the kitchen chairs, flipped them over, and placed them on the kitchen table before sweeping under it. When all his sweeping was done he gathered all the dust piles into a dustbin and emptied it into the garbage bucket. With a wet rag he wiped down the kitchen table and counters.

When he had finished he realized that he actually enjoyed cleaning the kitchen. He felt his mind become clear and peaceful as he worked. He took a moment to look at the kitchen and smiled proudly. He then placed the broom and dustbin in the closet, picked up the ceramic bowl that his master had pointed out to him before, and placed the basket of food scraps within it. Holding the bowl in his left hand he lifted the garbage bucket by its rope handle with his right hand and left the kitchen.

Ascending the spiral staircase to the ground floor he flicked off his wood sandals and slipped on his temple shoes. Sliding the door open with his elbow he entered the main hall and bowed to the Buddha; he could hear the bats swooping far above him. Only a few candles on the altar were lit. A shiver ran up his spine. He slid the door closed, walked hastily across the main hall, and turned to bow to the Buddha before exiting.

He stopped before the temple entrance door and placed the garbage bucket and ceramic bowl on the floor. All was silent within the temple; he did not hear the howl of the winds, the clank of underground pipes, or the creek of settling walls. He enjoyed the silence and breathed easily. He closed his eyes and relaxed for a moment enjoying the empty sound.

Slap!

He screamed, jumped, and fell to the floor; the priest had snuck up and struck him lightly from behind.

"Did I scare you?" the priest asked with a grin.

Kieko, panting, nodded and then collapsed to the floor relieved. "You almost . . . ended me . . . Master Shinsei."

"The element of surprise is a powerful tactic. It is a maneuver that a true Ki will never use, and one that a Ki can sense and avoid from his opponent." Kieko listened. "Stealth and deception are too tricky for your eyes and mind to perceive. That is why you must put away the mind–but you believe in mind, Kieko. The mind is blind, and is blinding you."

"I . . . I see, Master Shinsei," he said not fully understanding what his master was explaining to him.

"You do not see, Kieko. You will see when you know of what I speak."

"Yes, Master Shinsei."

"Get up. I will show you where we throw our food waste away."

"Yes, Master Shinsei."

Kieko rose to his feet and picked up the bowl and bucket. They traded their temple shoes for their outdoor sandals and went outside. The priest led Kieko to a large deep hole just past the temple garden and said, "Throw the waste in there."

Kieko placed the ceramic bowl on the ground and dumped the bucket's dust and dirt into the hole.

The priest then led Kieko back to the temple garden to another hole that was not as deep; the smell rising from it was not pleasant. "This is the compost hole. I use this mixture of dirt and organic waste to enhance my crops. Just as is done in our village and in Toasu's fields. Go ahead and throw the food waste in there."

Kieko did as asked. The two then returned to the temple in silence.

CHAPTER III

Kieko shot up from his futon with his eyes wide open. Frightened, he looked around unable to see anything except for the faint moonlight shinning in from his bedroom window. He rubbed his eyes, listened to the percussive noise that had awoken him, and waited for his eyes to adjust to the darkness. "Stupid bekuru," he said as he heard the percussive knocks getting louder. *He's coming to my room*, he realized. It was early, very early.

The knocking sound began to fade; then it stopped. He knew that the priest had returned to his chamber. He waited. The knocking sounds began again and aligned with the chants of his master. He crawled out of his futon, searched with his feet for the staircase, and carefully descended it. He picked up the towel that he had left to dry on the chair by the table and looked into a large tin box next to the fireplace seeing that it was empty. "I need to get more wood," he reminded himself. He took off his sleeveless shirt and cotton pants and wrapped the towel tightly around his waist before sliding open his bedroom door, closing it behind him, and descending the staircase.

From the foot of the staircase he walked across an empty room, slid open the door to the tearoom, and continued from one room to the next until he finally arrived at the door to the main hall. Sliding the door open he bowed to the Buddha, closed the door behind him, and walked across the hall noticing the fresh fruit offerings on the altar. When he arrived at the other side of the hall he bowed again and slid open the door to the antechamber with the staircase that led down into the temple underground. The antechamber was dark. With his feet he searched for a pair of wooden sandals and put them on. He slid the door closed and felt his way to the staircase by touching the walls and followed it down.

He arrived at the tunnel that led to the kitchen chamber and saw that the torches that lined the tunnel had already been lit. Slightly frightened he walked with quick steps down the tunnel not daring to look at the shrines in the chambers to his right and left. Just before the kitchen he turned right and walked down another tunnel that was lined with torches that had also been lit. *Master Shinsei has already taken a bath*, he noted. *When does he sleep?*

The air became warm and moist as he continued down the tunnel. He reached the end of the tunnel and entered an antechamber of cobblestone walls and a floor of wooden planks. He took off his towel, hung it on the wooden hook on the wall, and removed his sandals before sliding open the only door before him. Steam flew out causing him to cover his eyes. He walked carefully into the bath cavern waving the steam from his face until he found a small wooden box that was near the edge of a hot spring. He sat down on the box and began scrubbing his body with a small pumice stone. When he was done he stepped slowly into the hot spring, sat down so that the waters were up to his neck, and relaxed allowing the warm water to soothe his mind and muscles.

He woke up after a half-hour surprised and worried that he had fallen asleep. He stood up feeling the full weight of his body again while enjoying how his muscles felt soft and relieved of the previous day's temple cleaning hardships. He stepped out of the bath, slid open the door to the antechamber, took his towel, dried himself, and put on his sandals before walking back to the spiraling staircase. He ascended the staircase and touched the walls feeling his way again through the dark antechamber until he found the door and slid it open.

"You take too much time!" the priest hollered.

Kieko shouted back in fright and collapsed to the floor of the dark antechamber. Embarrassed, he looked up at the priest and agreed, "Yes . . . yes, Master Shinsei."

The priest bowed, turned, and walked across the main hall.

Kieko wiped his brow, and when the priest had exited the hall he stood up and entered it; he bowed to the Buddha, closed the door behind him, and walked as fast as he could back to his room.

Kieko prepared breakfast dressed in the white cotton pants and white top-gi that the priest had given to him his first morning at the temple. There was a small cauldron of boiling seaweed soup sitting on the metal grill over the fireplace and a pot of steaming rice sitting on the granite counter.

"Good morning," the priest greeted Kieko.

"Good morning, Master Shinsei," he replied as he turned to his master to give him one full bow before going back to the fireplace, putting on a thick mitten, and hanging an iron teakettle over it.

The priest took his bowls and ceramic cup from the shelf and sat down at the kitchen table. Kieko placed the pot of rice on the table and served his master before attending to his soup. When the soup was ready he took his master's soup bowl and poured the seaweed soup into it with a ladle. The teakettle began to whistle. He took the kettle and poured his master a cup before setting it down on a coaster. He then sat down and served himself some rice.

"You forgot your soup," the priest said as he ate.

Kieko stood up with his soup bowl, poured himself some soup, and sat down again. The priest stood up, "I am finished," and took his bowls and cup to the kitchen sink to begin cleaning them. Kieko began to eat his rice as fast as he could.

"Do not eat so fast," the priest advised.

"Yes, Master Shinsei."

The priest looked at Kieko as he dried his cup with his napkin, "When you wake up tomorrow do not forget to shave your head before taking a bath."

"Yes, Master Shinsei," he replied remembering again that he had to shave his head every three days.

The priest finished drying his bowls and cup and placed them on the shelf. "I will be waiting," he said and left.

"Yes, Master Shinsei." He finished eating and cleaned his bowls and cup as fast as possible. He then ran around the kitchen cleaning it before running up to meet his master in the Great Hall of the Buddha.

He slid the door open, bowed, and entered the main hall seeing that his master was already seated on his zabuton facing the Buddha. He ran to grab a zabuton.

"Walk!" the priest commanded.

He did as asked and picked up a zabuton. He approached his master, placed the zabuton on the floor beside him, bowed, and sat down.

Master Shinsei bowed and smacked the back of Kieko's head, "Bow!"

"Yes, Master Shinsei," he replied upset that he had been hit.

The priest bowed again. Kieko bowed attentively. The priest picked up his bekuru and mallet, bowed again, as did Kieko, and began chanting.

Kieko listened to the chant in the old tongue of the Middle Kingdom not understanding a word, and bowed as soon as he saw his master do so while trying to become familiar with the repetitive rhythm of the chant.

When the chant was done the two bowed together. The priest then stood up, approached the altar, and bowed several times before placing the bekuru and mallet back on the altar. He bowed again and returned to his zabuton.

Kieko stood up and bowed with his master. The two then picked up their zabutons, bowed again, and approached the wall of the Great Hall to place their zabutons on one of the several columns of stacked zabutons.

The priest said, "Follow me," and Kieko followed.

In the tearoom Kieko, sitting on his knees behind a short-legged table that was beautifully varnished, waited for the priest. On the table before him was a single sheet of paper, a ceramic cup filled with black ink, and a dry brush resting on a rectangular ceramic plate; and on the floor next to the table was a pile of neatly stacked rice paper. To his left there was the priest's table, which had the same items as what was on his table.

He looked through the old glass windows across the room and noticed that the branches of the autumn trees outside were swaying with the winds. And on the wall before him there was a shrine to an old, red Buddhist painting that detailed the story of a war waged by a thousand Buddhas against ten thousand demons. On the shelf below the painting there was a box of incense sticks, a ceramic cup filled with white ash, lit candles, and one plate of fruit.

The tearoom door slid open and the priest walked in and bowed to the shrine. He closed the door behind him, approached the shrine, bowed three times before it, lit three incense sticks, and placed them into the ceramic cup of ash. He bowed again, stepped back, and turned to Kieko. "Today is your first lesson on the written script of the old tongue of the Middle Kingdom. Our own Lemurian script is derived from this script." He slowly approached Kieko while running his fingers through his beard and staring at the wall behind him. "The Middle Kingdom is fading from the pages of its own history . . . This is a reminder that all things are born, rise, and fall into death. The Middle Kingdom is dying, but in another age it shall return. Lemuria will be no more then. Only a few of our many islands shall remain. And there will be no memory of us . . . in that time." Kieko listened slightly frightened by his master's words. The priest shook his head, focused his eyes on Kieko, and continued, "The script I am going to teach you is the most complex script on the Mother. It will take you decades to study, learn, and read. The script is composed solely of characters. There are over seventy-five thousand characters in the script of the old tongue of the Middle Kingdom. I know less than a fifth of them. I am still studying and learning more.

"It is the obligation of every Ki disciple to study and learn the script. It is a key. With it you can read from the many scrolls that are ages old within this temple—or from other temples. You can learn of poetry, history, science, and philosophy. Your mind can grow and fill with knowledge. You can read and speak new chants, scriptures, and ancient Ki teachings."

Kieko nodded.

The priest walked from one end of the tearoom to the other, "Our Lemurian script is composed of both characters and an alphabet. Our alphabet is a true innovation. It has allowed us to write words phonetically, and because of this anyone of us can sit and write our thoughts without having to memorize the thousands of characters of our language . . . of course, not too many of us in Ikishi take advantage of this. Written words are for those who live in the guarded towns and royal cities of Lemuria. Kadek is simply on the western fringes of royal Lemurian ambitions. We do not pay tribute, although we all lovingly revere our Queen.

"Let us begin," he walked to his table and sat on his knees. "We will begin with numbers. Zero is simply a circle. Begin your stroke from the bottom and end it at the bottom. Like this—

O

"This is a sacred symbol for the Ki. It is the void, the nothingness that pervades in all things. It is from this nothingness that all things come from and return to. Now you try."

Kieko lifted his brush and wetted it with ink. He pressed the brush down lightly on the paper and moved it carefully in a slow circular motion. But, before he finished, the priest slapped him against the back of his head.

"Where is your mind?"

Kieko, confused, searched for an answer.

The priest asked again, "Where is your mind?"

"It's here."

"Where?" the priest asked again.

"I don't know."

The priest slapped Kieko again against the back of his head. "Do not think when you write. In fact, never think. That is the point. When you write, write and that is it. Your mind was too full of thinking. Do not seek anything when you write. Just write. You were striving for perfection through thought in your stroke. Do not strive. Do not seek. Do not think. Simply write. Try again on a new piece of paper."

"Yes, Master Shinsei," Kieko placed a new sheet of paper on the table. He tried again. This time he drew the circle without hesitation.

"Good, that is better," the priest complimented. "The number one is simply a horizontal line. The brush stroke goes from left to right. As so—

一

"Now, you try."

"Yes, Master Shinsei." He placed another piece of paper on the table and drew the line.

"Good, Kieko, very good. The number two is this—

二

"Now, you try."

On another piece of paper Kieko drew the two lines and smiled. The priest slapped him against the back of his head again.

"Thoughts have entered your mind. You were thinking that this is easy, that you are good. Do not think. No thoughts. Simply write. And when you are done writing, simply *be*. Be without thought."

"Yes, Master Shinsei." He thought about what his master had just said.

The priest slapped him again, but this time on the top of his head, "You are thinking!"

Kieko's face turned red with anger.

"Now you are mad. Mad with thought and mad with emotion!" the priest shouted.

"What do you want me—"

The priest slapped him across the face.

Kieko shot his hand up to strike back at the priest, but he froze. Looking at the priest he saw that he was completely open to his strike, but that he was calm, even smiling with eyes as bright as daylight.

"Strike me, Kieko, and you will fall. You can see this. You know this. Let it go."

Kieko lowered his arm and relaxed his breathing while listening to his beating heart.

"There is no power in anger, young Kieko."

Kieko, feeling slightly hypnotized, looked down at the table and listened to his master's words.

"It is an illusion. It is an emotion tied to thought and thought is tied to mind. Mind too is an illusion. It is not real, and never has it ever been. When you realize this and see with conscious eyes you will know and understand of what I speak."

Kieko nodded.

"Let us continue. The number three."

三

Kieko carefully wetted his brush with more ink and drew the three lines on the same piece of paper that he had used before.

"Good," the priest complimented. "The number four consists of six brush strokes." He counted as he drew.

四

Kieko executed the strokes perfectly.

"The number five," he then counted as he drew each stroke.

五

Kieko rubbed his eyes with his forearm and drew; his Master Shinsei praised his effort.

"The number six has four strokes."

Kieko placed a fresh sheet of paper on the table and drew flawlessly.

"The number seven–"

七

Kieko drew.

"The number eight looks like the slopes of our sacred Mount Kadek."

Kieko drew and agreed.

"The number nine is only two strokes."

九

Kieko drew flawlessly.

"And the number ten."

十

Kieko drew the cross and put down his brush.

The priest placed a fresh sheet of paper on Kieko's table and drew all eleven characters while counting out the names of each one.

〇一二三四五六七八九十

When he finished he said, "From zero comes one, from one comes two, and from two comes the many. When you look up into the night's sky what do you see? Stars: thousands and thousands of stars. There is no character that we can write that can help us understand just how many stars there are in the night's sky. It is impossible for our mind to comprehend how many grains of sand there are on a beach. This is the limitation of the mind. The mind is finite and full of form. It is concerned with the past and the future. It sees and believes in what is not real."

Kieko gave a puzzled look.

"Is the past real, Kieko?"

Kieko thought about the question.

"You are thinking, already. You do not know or understand, and never will you know or understand if you think that your mind can comprehend or answer such a question. If you answer without answering then you understand. Then you know what is real and what is not. These characters on these pages are simply lines on paper. Our mind has given meaning to these lines by equating a symbol to a particular word. These symbols—these characters—simply point the way toward a mental understanding of what we find in our material and impermanent world. That is all. The true essence, the true nature of what we see or hear or touch can never be captured through song, books, words, or any science of the

West. How can a word or a belief capture that which is infinite and formless?"

"But, we have form, Master Shinsei," Kieko objected respectfully.

"We have form? We have form? Does this brush have form?"

"Yes, it does. That brush has the same form as this brush."

"I see. But, are they the same?"

"No, they are not, but they have the same form."

"And did these two brushes have the same form before they were made?"

"No, they did not exist before being made."

"So, they are formless." Kieko was fumbling in his mind for what to say. The priest continued, "And will these two brushes have the same form–as you call it–decades from now? Did you have form before you were conceived and will you have form years after your death? You are–just as I am–just as these brushes are–formless." He then looked at the ink on his table. "Water. What is the form of water? When you pour it into a cup what is its form. And if the cup falls and shatters what is the form of water then? Has its form changed? Is it still water? And when it turns into a gas and rises to the sky does it still hold form? Water, just as you are, just as everything is, is formless. It is beyond form, beyond words, beyond thought, beyond mind. It is infinite and boundless. It is formless.

"So, with that do not become attached to words, a belief, or a philosophy. Nothing that is written holds truth. It may point the way to truth, but beyond that it is nothing else."

"Then, what is real, Master Shinsei?"

"Ah, that is your koan," he smiled.

It was afternoon. Kieko, concentrating, was sitting on his knees in the tearoom before his short-legged table practicing the strokes of the new characters he had learned from the priest. He looked at his wrist as he wrote and observed how his hand moved with the brush; he realized that the movement was nearly the same as a sword technique he had seen the priest use during a dance at the last festival. *There is sword in writing*, he thought.

"There is sword in everything!" the priest exclaimed.

Kieko's heart jumped. He turned to face his master and saw his master's sword pointed straight at him.

"You are dead," the priest said. "How did you not notice my entry into this room? How did you not hear me draw my sword from its sheath? How did you not hear my footsteps toward you?"

Kieko was speechless.

"Because you were thinking!"

Kieko looked down in defeat.

"If you were present, truly present in your writing, then you would have heard every sound in this room, felt everything. But, no—you began to think—you began to wonder. You want to learn sword. And your attached mind began thinking of the future—of yourself in the future dancing with a sword. But, there is sword now! There is sword in writing, in cooking, breathing, in listening. There is sword in everything. A master of the sword does not need a sword. A master of the sword is present. He is aware of all things with no thought for the past or future.

"Come, Kieko, leave your brush and writing mind. Come with me to the garden."

"Yes, Master Shinsei."

Autumn leaves whirled in the air. The priest was sitting on his heels between rows of cabbages. He was wearing a heavy wool robe and a thick cotton cap over his head. He plucked a head of cabbage from the ground and passed it to Kieko who was about to drop it into a basket. "Wait," the priest called out. "Hold it for a moment. Take a look at it. What is it?"

"It's cabbage, Master Shinsei."

"Yes, and no. It is cabbage, but how is it different from the other cabbages we took from the ground?"

Kieko looked with discriminating eyes at the cabbage and said, "The shape is a bit different."

"Yes, it is. It is called michi in the old tongue of the Middle Kingdom. The texture of its leaves is between that of a cabbage and lettuce, and it does not cause digestive discomfort like cabbage. The leaves are milder, sweeter; but they are not good for the making of kimu ki. It is sown in the summer and harvested, as you can see, in the fall. You can now place it in the basket."

"Yes, Master Shinsei."

The two continued moving up the row of cabbages plucking one cabbage after the other and placing them into the basket.

When the basket was full Kieko picked it up, took it to the front door of the temple, and left it there. He then walked to a shed by the garden and took a basket from the top of a stack of baskets. When he returned to his master he saw that he was planting bulbs into a row of uplifted dirt that he had plowed earlier that day.

The priest stopped what he was doing, looked up, and gave Kieko a cotton bag full of bulbs. "Those are buck-choi bulbs. It is called white stem in our tongue. We will harvest it in the winter. We can use it in stir-fry dishes composed of chicken or shellfish. We can also use it in soup or steam it to be used as a side dish. You want to plant it only so deep," he inserted his index finger into the ground up to his second joint. Kieko nodded. "And you want to keep the bulbs about a hand apart. In about a week they will begin to emerge. Now, just watch." The priest sowed one bulb into the ground after the other. When he finished sowing one complete row he asked Kieko to sow the next.

Kieko sowed the row while the priest smoked from his long pipe. His hands began to shake from the cold as the skin above his knuckles cracked open releasing thin streams of blood. He cupped his hands together and blew warm air into them.

"Hurry up," the priest called out.

"Yes, yes," Kieko whispered bitterly to himself.

The priest heard the sourness in Kieko's words, but said nothing. He continued smoking from his pipe while listening to the winds blow through the trees that lined the far side of the garden. He looked up at the clear sky and smiled. All became still for between the sounds of the trees and the winds he heard the grand and vast silence that permeated all things.

Seven days passed. Kieko, raking the leaves in the garden, looked at the winter trees and listened to the wind. He remembered his Thinking Tree; it had been months since he had last seen him. He shook his head, scratched his leg, and continued raking the leaves as he ran through a list of plants and their medicinal properties in his head.

"Kieko," the priest called out.

Kieko saw his master walking toward him.

"Answer this. Your liver is full of shang. You have listened to your breath and find it full of metal. You have listened to the rhythm of your blood and it is full of water. Your color is red. What has caused this and what will cure it?"

Kieko answered, "My diet has too much meat, not enough soy beans, and too much black tea. And there is anxiety—"

"What is causing the anxiety?"

"Attachment to the past," Kieko said unsure of his answer.

"Correct, but wrong; that was a guess. Not good enough. If you do not know, do not answer."

"I'm tired, Master Shinsei," he replied feeling a rushing wave of anger overcome him when he heard the words, "not good enough," from the priest.

"What?"

"I'm tired of this," he said. "Nothing I do is correct. So what if I guessed."

The priest stood silent observing Kieko.

"Why are you looking at me like that?" he said feeling uncomfortable with how the priest was looking at him. "Stop looking at me, Master Shinsei."

The priest stared straight into Kieko.

"Please . . . stop it, Master Shinsei."

"You are resisting it."

"Resisting what?"

"What I am sending into you."

"I . . . I don't understand–"

"Be still! Quiet your mind."

"I . . . I won't . . ." he whispered feeling exhausted as he tried to hold onto his troubled feelings.

The priest shook his head, "I am tired too, Kieko. If you wish to act like a child then do so and leave these temple grounds."

"I'm–I'm sorry–"

"Enough!" the priest hollered. "Do not apologize to me. Do not! If you want to complain and think that all you do here is clean and cook and rake leaves then go, for you truly do not understand a thing of what I have been teaching you." Ashamed, Kieko looked down at the cold ground. "This is just the beginning, Kieko. If you can not handle what I ask of you–what is expected of you as a Ki disciple–then pack up your things and return to Ikishi." Kieko looked up at his master pleading with his eyes to not be sent back to the village. "Why do you look at me so? Why, Kieko? Is it not what you want? Do you not want to tell me to leave you alone?" he asked with his arms spread open. Kieko shook his head. "Then quiet your mind and never speak back to me with words of disrespect. I am your master! I am sheltering you, feeding you, and teaching you. But, if you do not want what is expected of you as a Ki in this temple then go–go!" Kieko stood still before the priest.

The priest calmed himself by taking a deep breath. "There is no comfort in what we are doing, Kieko. If you can not handle and pursue what you must in this temple then go." He looked long and hard into Kieko's eyes making him feel very uncomfortable again. "But, if you want to continue, then keep your words to yourself, accept what you are expected to do in this place–and finish out here with a clear mind. Otherwise go." He shook his head at Kieko. "It's getting late and I must prepare dinner," he finished and walked away.

Kieko watched the priest enter the temple. His mind began to fill with bitter thoughts: thoughts that the priest did not understand him; thoughts that the priest did not want to help him; thoughts that he did not need the priest; that he could leave, run away, and travel west. But, he saw these thoughts; he saw them passing his mind's eye; and he realized that he had to cut those thoughts if he wanted to continue on the path of the Ki. *Yes, that is what I want*, his heart confessed. So he listened, and his heart said to let it all go. He took a deep breath and slowly freed himself of his acrid thoughts.

When he felt clear and refreshed his body shivered as the frigid air carressed his skin, and he began raking the leaves again.

CHAPTER IV

It was the last month of the year. The priest and Kieko had just finished dinner. They both stood up from the kitchen table and took their bowls and cups to the sink. When Kieko finished washing his bowls and cup he placed them on the counter to dry, and began sweeping the floor. And by the time the priest had placed his bowls and cup on the counter and began wiping down the kitchen table, Kieko was already sweeping up the piles of dust and dirt he had collected around the kitchen floor and brushing them into a basket. When Kieko finished he put the broom away, picked up the basket filled with dirt and dust and the basket of food scraps within the sink, bowed to his master, and exited the kitchen.

After he had thrown the food scraps and dirt and dust away outside he returned to the kitchen and found his master sitting at the kitchen table with two cups of tea.

"Have a seat, Kieko. It is time to learn a bit about our Lemurian past."

"Yes, Master Shinsei," he sat down.

The priest's eyes narrowed on the candle's flame before him, "The tradition of the Ki warrior priest is really an Atlantean one. Originally the Lemurian faith had no Ki warriors, only Ki priests and priestesses." He looked at Kieko and gave a very small smile, "Although, the Ki combative arts were—and still are—a part of the Lemurian Ki practice they were never meant to be used in warfare. The Ki combative arts were simply the means by which Ki priests protected themselves against the bandits and thieves they came across during their journeys between temples." He took his tea and sipped it. Kieko sensed a slight hesitation within the priest. The priest continued, "It was in the dark days of the Age of the Fire

Rat that the Lemurian Ki combative arts were revealed to those who were not Ki disciples. The threat of an advancing Atlantean army provoked the kings and queens of old Lemuria to persuade their Ki priests and priestesses to train their armies. The High Ki priests eventually agreed and unveiled the Ki combative arts to the Eight Lemurian Royal Armies; they fought alongside them as well. But, soon after, dissident Lemurian soldiers, motivated by greed, taught the Ki combative arts to the Atlanteans. Thus began the Atlantean tradition of the Kai guardian.

"The High Ki priests, realizing that their teachings were now falling into the hands of the Atlanteans, ceased teaching their combative art to masses of Lemurian soldiers. And since then there has never been a Ki priest who has fought in a war. There are Ki warriors, yes, who serve lords and royalty. But, there are no Ki priests who serve and fight for the material gain of a lord or royal family."

"When was the Age of the Fire Rat, Master Shinsei?"

"Three thousand years ago."

"And the Wars of Kurai, Master Shinsei? I thought there was a Lemurian priest who fought in those wars?"

The priest's eyes widened, "No; that is not true. As I have just explained. No Ki priest has fought in a war since the Age of the Fire Rat."

Kieko thought for a moment, "Master Shinsei, what will the priests of Lemuria do then if Atlanteans try to attack these lands?"

"They will fight, but not in the name of a Lemurian king, queen, or lord. They will fight to protect the people they are bound to. Ikishi is my home, and I will protect the people here for as long as I live."

"So, Ki priests have fought, Master Shinsei."

"Yes, but since the Age of the Fire Rat they have never done so for a kingdom."

"But, Master Shinsei, I have heard the old men of our village speak of a Ki priest who fought for Kurai."

"Kieko," the priest said shaking his head frustrated, "as I have said, that is not true; those old men are promoting a ridiculous rumor, and nothing more. I assure you that there has never been a priest who has fought for any king since the age that I have spoken of."

"Have you seen warfare, Master Shinsei?"

"Yes . . . yes, I have."

"What have you seen?"

Disappointed, the priest looked at Kieko, "Why are you interested in such a thing? Do you think war is glorious? Do you believe there is victory in war?"

"Isn't there, Master Shinsei? If Ikishi was to be attacked, isn't it right that we fight? And if we win, isn't it a victory, a testament that we are strong?"

"And if we lose? What will become of Ikishi then? Men slaughtered; women raped; children sold as slaves; homes burned to the ground; the Kadek Temple destroyed. Is there glory then? Is there victory?" Kieko looked down in deep thought. "Would you have felt better if you had beaten Aiko in the tournament? And, if yes, then how long would it have lasted? Only a moment. After that you would have found that you are still angry, still sad, still displeased with yourself and with others; and you would continue searching, looking for things in your future to silence the regrets of your past."

"I don't regret losing to Aiko, Master Shinsei. I don't regret anything in my past."

"Oh, no?" he asked amused by Kieko's words. "Then why are you seeking to learn more about your father's past? Why do you often find yourself wishing that you had known him? And why do you wish that you were stronger and faster than Aiko in Teshi-do?"

"Those are wishes, Master Shinsei. They are not regrets."

"But, why wish for your past to have been different if you are content with it, not regretful of it?"

"I . . . I don't know," he said frustrated.

"Because you are not happy with your past, and because of that you wish for, and believe in, futures that you think will bring you happiness. Do you not see that any glory that you want to accomplish in your future will never bring you happiness, just more confusion and sadness?"

"I . . . I don't understand what you mean . . . Master Shinsei," he said shaking his head.

The priest took another sip of tea, "Let me tell you about a king from the desert lands west of the Middle Kingdom. It is an old tale, one that I learned from my own master when I was young. The story begins at an end for this king. He is lost in his sadness while walking under a desert moon between the mountains of a valley. He is walking, looking down at all the grains of sand between his toes. He then looks to the east and west knowing that all he sees is his, but it means nothing for he has lost his one true love. So he continues walking, falling deeper into his thoughts, traveling south seeking that which cannot be found.

"What does it mean that he is seeking 'that which cannot be found'?"

Kieko thought for a moment and answered shrugging his shoulders, "I don't know, Master Shinsei."

"The King has gained everything. All that he sees is his. But, yet, he is still not happy for he has lost his one true love. So he travels seeking her, but the tragedy is this: he will never find her. He will never find happiness. Because he believes it exists somewhere in his future. If you seek happiness in the future, in a distant place from where you are now, you will never find it because it does not exist. Now, I ask you; is the future real?"

"I believe it is real, Master Shinsei. Tomorrow will come."

"Yes, it will. But, where is it now? Can you touch it or describe it for me?"

"No, Master Shinsei," he said as if the answer was obvious.

"Then, is it real? Is time itself real?"

"Isn't it, Master Shinsei?" he asked before taking a sip of tea.

"Do birds know of time? Does a tree know it? Does Jomana pass her days counting the hours?"

"No, Master Shinsei."

"That is right. Birds, trees, and Jomana have no attachment to time. They do not care for the past and have no wants for the future. They are living in the present completely, totally. Have you ever met or seen a depressed bird, a sad tree, a hateful deer?"

"No, Master Shinsei."

"Of course not. If you are living totally in the present; hearing every sound; feeling every touch; seeing every moment, then you are being without any wish or want. You are not seeking any future or regretting any past because they are not real, they are illusions of your mind, a mind that binds itself to time."

"How can any of us live only in the present, Master Shinsei?" he asked irritated with the priest's reasoning. "We have goals set in the future to ensure our survival. If we do not sow in the spring, we have nothing to reap in the autumn, and nothing to eat in the winter."

"Of course, we, as humans, have the ability to think. We divide and organize time to live, enjoy, and survive. We create goals and accomplish them. But, we arrive only through the present. It is only in the present that we take each step to arrive at our destination."

Kieko thought about what the priest had said for a moment. "I think . . . I think I understand what you are trying to say."

"No, you do not. Do not think!" he shouted causing Kieko to jump in his seat. "Thinking is mind; it is only in no-mind that time does not exist. When you have freed yourself of mind, you have freed yourself of time."

"Are there other ways for the mind to achieve a state of no thought other than sitting meditation, Master Shinsei?"

"Have you learned nothing from me?"

Kieko shook his head and rubbed his eyes with his forearm. "I'm sorry, Master Shinsei. I know . . . I know . . . zazen is in everything we do. Every moment is a moment to live totally in the present. When I eat, I should eat only. When I drink, I should drink only–"

"That is correct, Kieko."

Kieko drank more of his tea.

"You are tired, Kieko. Be tired only, and go to sleep. You have much work to do tomorrow. You need your rest."

"Yes, Master Shinsei."

"Leave your cup. I will wash it for you."

"Thank you, Master Shinsei."

Kieko stood up, bowed, and left.

The priest poured himself another cup of tea and listened to the silence of the kitchen.

CHAPTER V

It was late in the night and Kieko was in the Great Hall of the Buddha cleaning the floor. Carefully he pushed a folded, filthy rag with his hands from one end of the hall to the other until the rag had collected with too much dust. He stood up, hearing his neck and back crack in several places, and walked to a bucket of water near the entrance of the hall to rinse the rag. He then heard something, and stopped to listen. The sound was not constant; it was soft and swift, and then it was loud and powerful. *It's coming from the dharma hall*, he realized. There was a hard bang that shook the floor like someone who had just jumped and landed on the ground. "That's it," he realized. *Master Shinsei is training.*

He walked toward the wall slowly, nearly creeping toward it, and passed the stacks of zabutons; he then touched the wall with his fingers and cautiously pressed his ear against it holding his breath. He could hear his master in the dharma hall moving, stomping, attacking, and defending. There was a shout. He backed away from the wall in fright. When he caught his breath he pressed his ear to the wall again hearing a swooshing sound. It was his master's sword. It was cutting rapidly through the air. In awe he listened wondering when he would begin studying Ki sword; he began to daydream of how Kira and the villagers would admire him when he was finally recognized as a great master of the sword. His master shouted again. He shook his head of his thoughts and stepped away from the wall. "What a silly fool I am," he whispered and turned around to begin cleaning the floor again.

CHAPTER VI

Kieko rose from his futon as he heard the distant, but annoying, percussive knocks of his master who was walking through the temple hitting his bekuru. He looked at the window and saw the faint light of the sun shining through and yawned before stretching out his arms. He threw his wool blanket to the side, shivered from the chilly air that had swooped all around his body, and descended the steps.

"Kieko!" his master yelled.

"Yes, Master Shinsei?"

"Come down, now!"

"Yes, Master Shinsei!" He rushed across his room, opened the door, put on his temple shoes, and descended the steps. When he reached the foot of the staircase he found his master standing before him fully dressed. He bowed and greeted, "Good morning, Master Shinsei."

"Every morning–from this point forth–we will meditate together in the Great Hall of the Buddha before breakfast."

"Yes, Master Shinsei."

"Put on your temple clothes. I will be waiting for you in the Great Hall."

"Yes, Master Shinsei." He ran up to his room, got dressed, and went to meet the priest.

He slid the door to the main hall open, bowed, and walked in seeing that his master was already seated on his zabuton before the golden statue of the Buddha. He grabbed a zabuton and sat next to his master.

The priest picked up his bekuru and bowed, as did Kieko, and reached into the fold of his top-gi, pulled out a scroll, and gave it to Kieko.

Kieko unrolled the scroll and found that it was the long chant of the *Buddha of a Thousand Eyes*. It was written in hiragan, the Lemurian alphabet system. He read what he could from the scroll and smiled with pride that he was now semi-literate. But, as he mouthed the words he realized that he understood none of what he was reading.

"Remember," the priest began, "the long chant, as are all the Ki chants, is in the old tongue of the Middle Kingdom. This is an advantage to you because as you read, learn, and speak this chant you will not become attached to the meaning of the words. What is important is the sound. Listen to the sound and rhythm of the chant, and nothing more. In this way you will clear your mind."

"Yes, Master Shinsei."

The priest began the long chant and Kieko followed as best as he could by reading and speaking, often stumbling over words and sounds, and, at times, getting lost and keeping silent until he found his place again.

After an hour the priest had finished repeating the chant several times leaving Kieko mentally exhausted.

The priest bowed, "It is now time for breakfast."

"Yes, Master Shinsei," he happily agreed.

Kieko ate his rice in silence, and when he finished he drank his soup.

"Tonight, at the midnight hour, you will meditate," the priest said as he placed his cup on the table. "You will do it every night after you have finished cleaning the temple."

"Yes, Master Shinsei."

"Remember, keep your mind here and now, and if thoughts appear observe them, if emotions appear observe them too, and let them go. Be ever present. Hear every thing in the Great Hall of the

Buddha. Feel it with your whole body. Focus only on now for there is nothing else."

"Yes, Master Shinsei."

"Focus on your breathing, Kieko. That is your meditation."

"Yes, Master Shinsei," he repeated.

The priest poured himself another cup of tea. Kieko continued eating as he thought about, and dreaded, all the chores he had to perform that day.

CHAPTER VII

Holding a sheathed sword Kieko ran across old farmer Toasu's fields feeling the tall, dry grasses pelt his knees. Abruptly, he dived, rolled on the ground, and sprang back up to his feet with the sword unsheathed and shining. He swung the sword before him, the sword sang, and struck another blade. He withdrew his sword and struck again with greater force against his enemy's blade, pushing his foe back with faster sword movements until his sword pierced flesh, and sank deep into his enemy's tight muscles. He had won.

Sitting in the zazen position he smiled and opened his eyes seeing the glimmering golden statue of the Buddha on the altar before him. He looked to his right, heard his neck crack, and rolled his shoulders hearing his back crack as well. His left leg felt numb. He patted it and thought about the sword fight he had won by replaying it in his mind. He then took a deep breath and looked up to the ceiling hoping to see the bats, but saw no sign of them. Tired, he yawned and stretched out his arms, cracked his fingers, and closed his eyes trying to focus on the silence again, but thoughts entered his mind. He thought of Kira and wondered what she was doing, and if she missed him. He wanted to kiss her. He wanted to touch her wet lips with his and embrace her, and feel her breasts tight against his chest. Warmth grew between his legs. Embarrassed, he opened his eyes, shook his head trying to rid his mind of all thoughts, and looked around the main hall to see if his master was watching him. There was no sign of the priest. Relieved, he exhaled and closed his eyes again, straightened his back, and placed his hands below his waist. Breathing deeply and listening to the quiet of the main hall he tried to clear his mind of all thoughts.

Time passed and soon thoughts entered his mind again, and he observed them. There were thoughts of Kira and Aiko, and images of himself fighting with a sword, but he eagerly returned to his thoughts of Kira, and did not let them go.

"Kieko!" the priest yelled.

His eyes shot open and his face turned red with embarrassment. "Yes, Master Shinsei," he said turning around seeing his master by the open doorway.

"Your mind is full of foolishness!"

"Yes . . . Master Shinsei."

"How are you to survive against an enemy blade if your mind is full of foolish thoughts?"

"I don't know, Master Shinsei," he said praying that he would not have to stand before the priest.

"A sword fight begins and ends in the blink of an eye. If one thought enters your mind, in that moment, you are defeated."

"Yes, Master Shinsei."

"Go to sleep. Your weak attempt at zazen has ended."

"Yes, Master Shinsei."

The priest slammed the sliding door closed.

He heaved a long sigh and realized that the warmth he had felt between his legs had ceased. He rubbed his eyes and yawned again from an exhaustive day of chopping wood, building an extension for the garden shed, cleaning the temple floors, and cooking. He stood up, bowed, and put away his zabuton; he then walked to the door, bowed, slid it open, closed it behind him, and walked to his room eager to fall asleep in his warm, welcoming futon.

The next morning, after breakfast, the priest and Kieko were standing outside in front of a pine tree. The priest explained, "We can gather Ki, harvesting it like a crop, into our bodies from all that is around us, but, it is divided into two parts, shin and shang, and you must beware of which part, and how much of it, you draw." Kieko nodded. "The shang side of the Ki is the aggressive side of the life force. It can be drawn during the day from the sky and mountains. At night, shin can be drawn from the earth: caves, and the like. But, drawing only shang or shin will create great unbalance within you. Only under the most extreme circumstances should you do this. What is correct and wise is to draw the Ki from that which harnesses both shin and shang. What I have been taught, and have found through practice, as the ideal source, are pine trees. Look at this tree, Kieko. What is it pointing to?"

"The sky, Master Shinsei."

"Yes, the sky. It is naturally drawing shang from the sky. And its roots? Where are they? What are they pointing to?"

"They are underneath and pointing toward the Mother."

"Yes, the Mother. A pine tree is naturally drawing shin from the Mother and shang from the Sky. Thus, during the day this pine tree is drawing in shin and shang and sending it out. We can tap this tree for its Ki. But, remember, the Ki within a tree is only balanced during the day for at night it is unbalanced." Kieko looked at his master expecting an explanation. The priest went on, "The roots of this tree draw shin during both the day and night, but its branches draw shang only during the day for it draws it from the sun and sky. At night there is no sun, there is only the moon and the darkness of the night, thus the sky becomes shin in the night. So, if a tree draws shin from the ground and shin from the night's sky it is unbalanced and an unhealthy source for a Ki disciple to draw upon."

"Master Shinsei?"

"Yes, Kieko."

"What really is the Ki?"

"The Ki is *the* force–the life force–it is within and between all things; without it nothing can exist. Like a river it flows from the Source. But, it is divided, as are all things in this realm, into light and dark elements. Thus, it is flawed, as we are. But, it points the way. It points back to the Source." Kieko looked at the priest and at the tree with extreme curiosity. "The Source is beyond the mind's understanding, Kieko. When you have achieved a true and constant state of no-mind then you will know it . . . you will know it because you *are* it."

"I . . . I am the Source, Master Shinsei?"

"If I answer that question with words then you will think and try to understand by being attached to the meaning of my words. But, my words, and your mind trying to make sense of my words, will lead you only into more thinking, thus leading you farther from the truth. That is why meditation is so important. Through meditation we can achieve a state of no-mind and thus connect with the Source.

"Why do our bodies need to sleep, Kieko?"

"I do not know, Master Shinsei," Kieko answered with shrugging shoulders knowing that the priest would answer his own question.

"When we sleep our minds are quieted so that we can connect fully to the Source, so that we are one with it." Touching his head with his finger, "The mind, Kieko, is simply a tool and nothing more. It is a tool that is to be picked up when needed and put down when done. The mind can only exist in the realm of time; it is of the world of form. The mind divides all things into past and future. It cannot exist in the present, and that is why Ki masters often describe the present as a state of no-mind. When we attach ourselves to mind, when we believe that we are our mind then madness sets in, we become insane, we suffer, we hate, we search for happiness in our relationships, in our work, in our past, and in our future. The mind is heavily attached to the future and to the past. It is afraid of the present because it cannot survive in the present. There is no-mind in the present. The mind works desperately to create thoughts that we believe are our own, but they are not. We are not our thoughts."

"Whose thoughts are they then, Master Shinsei?"

"They are the thoughts of the mind. But, you are not your mind."

"I am not my mind?" Kieko asked still trying to understand.

"You are not your thoughts, you are not your mind, you are not any of your possessions; you are not a great many things. Whose tree is this, Kieko?" he asked pointing to the pine tree. "Is it mine? If I own this land is the tree mine? And if I own this land then in a thousand years time, when I am long dead, who owns the tree? Is this tree real? Am I real? Are you? Nothing that you see or touch or taste or hear Kieko is real. Everything, all things around you, is impermanent and false."

"Then what is real, Master Shinsei?"

"Live in a state of no-mind and you will see what is real."

"Are you living in a state of no-mind, Master Shinsei?"

"Yes, I am. There are times when my thoughts return and I attach myself to them, but then I realize that I am not my thoughts, and I simply observe them until I have returned to a state of no-mind."

"Are you enlightened, Master Shinsei?"

"We are all enlightened, we are all one with the Source, but our mind keeps us from seeing what we are."

"Why, Master Shinsei?"

"Because the mind will die if it allows us to see what we truly are. The mind does not want to die. It will tell you any lie to stay alive. It is very selfish and fearful."

"But, we need the mind, Master Shinsei."

"It is a tool to be used and nothing more."

"Nothing more, Master Shinsei?"

"Yes, nothing more," he said with growing impatience. "Stick out your hand." Kieko stuck out his right hand. "Just relax," he advised as he placed his hands out so that Kieko's hand was between them. He then moved his hands slowly toward and away from Kieko's hand. Kieko began feeling a prickling sensation all over his hand and a strong wave of heat. "That is Ki, Kieko."

"It's so warm, Master Shinsei."

"Heat is life," he withdrew his hands. "Now, do as I do, move your hands toward and away from each other; do it slowly. You will gradually feel that they are repelling each other like two magnets."

Kieko first observed his master moving his hands slowly toward and away from each other. He then did as his master did and discovered that when his palms were very close to each other they were actually repelling each other. "Yes, I feel it, Master

Shinsei. I feel it. It's like there is a small ball between my palms when they are close to each other, pushing back against my hands."

"That is the Ki, Kieko."

"I have felt something like this before."

"Yes, you have," the priest answered with a serious tone. "Now . . . as you move your hands apart the sensation will lessen. But, over time, as you practice zazen, and what I am about to teach you, the sensation will strengthen, and you will feel it become greater and greater as your hands move farther and farther apart."

"Yes, Master Shinsei."

"Now, let us return to the tree. Stand next to me before the tree and keep your hands to your sides . . . relax . . . relax your shoulders; let them fall. Relax your muscles . . . let all the tension go. Now, point your palms toward the tree, point them at the center of the tree, and slowly move your hands toward and away from the tree . . . You will feel your hands grow warm. You will feel the same magnetic feeling as before, but between your hands and the tree . . . breathe in deeply. See the Ki flowing into you, filling you."

"Yes . . . Master Shinsei."

"Close your eyes and continue."

"Yes . . . Master Shinsei," he said again.

Kieko breathed in and out moving his hands toward and away from the tree. He could feel a thin stream of warm air flowing from the tree into his hands filling his body, healing it, strengthening it.

"Now open your eyes," the priest asked.

Kieko opened his eyes feeling like he had just woken up from a long afternoon nap. He rubbed his eyes with his forearm and shook his head; his eyes focused and he realized that it was nearly afternoon. "How long have I been taking in the Ki from this tree, Master Shinsei?"

"For just over an hour."

Kieko's jaw dropped, "I can't believe that . . . I . . . my body, my body feels tired, but it still feels like I have only been standing here for a few minutes."

"That is good, Kieko, it means that you are improving in your practice of zazen." Kieko smiled with pride. "Now," the priest began, "take a step away from the tree and shake your hands like this." The priest shook his hands and arms and began flicking his fingers. "Do as I do. We must rid ourselves of any excess Ki. If you do not expel this excess Ki from your hands and arms they will begin to swell."

"Yes, Master Shinsei," Kieko shook his hands and arms and flicked his fingers.

"Wipe your hands and arms down as if you were drying them with a cloth."

"Yes, Master Shinsei."

"Let me take a look at your palms." Kieko showed the palms of his hands to his master. "Yes, that is good. Look, can you see that your palms are full of these red spots?" Kieko nodded when he saw what his master was describing. "That is a very good sign. You have absorbed much Ki." Kieko smiled. "Now, let us return to the temple. I suggest that you go to your room and rest. Take a nap. When lunch is ready I will call for you."

"Yes, Master Shinsei."

They then made their way back to the temple enjoying the shine of the sun while watching a few birds fly in the winter sky.

CHAPTER VIII

It was another night in the kitchen. Kieko was tired and wanted to finish his dinner, clean the temple, meditate, and go to sleep.

"Pass me the rice wine."

"Yes, Master Shinsei," he passed a ceramic jug to the priest.

"You are cleaning the temple well."

Kieko looked up, "Thank you, Master Shinsei."

"You are doing well, and your cooking has improved. Your mother would be proud." He poured himself another cup of rice wine.

"Thank you, Master Shinsei."

"No need to thank me," he said shaking his head, "no need."

"Yes, Master Shinsei," he continued eating.

"You must begin building your hut in the traditional way. You must do so soon. You will live in it during the winter months." Kieko stopped eating and looked at his master. "And before spring arrives you must live on the Kadek Mountain," he paused to sip his tea, and continued, "for your meditation retreat."

"Yes, Master Shinsei," he smiled brightly; finally, in his master's eyes, he was improving as a Ki disciple. He continued eating.

"Why are you in such a rush to finish eating? Take your time and drink with me."

Kieko did not reply; he did not want to drink with his master; he wanted to finish his temple cleaning duties, meditate, and go to sleep.

The priest finished his rice wine and poured himself another cup. "Well, I think it best to tell you now, Kieko, that I will begin teaching you in the art of Ki sword tomorrow," he burped. "Excuse me," he apologized embarrassed.

Kieko's face beamed.

"Do not smile, Kieko. I am still watching you. You have impressed me in recent weeks with your temple cleaning, and I am happy to find you meditating every night, but I am still watching you. You still think and dream during your night meditations, and, although you have controlled yourself from doing so, I know that there are still moments when you want to lash out at me with harsh words. So be warned: if you fill with too much pride, anger, or violent thoughts—or speak back to me in any unacceptable way—I will stop teaching Ki sword to you. There is nothing funny or fun in learning Ki sword. The sword gives or takes life. I will stop teaching you if I find for even a moment that your mind is learning the art to take life. I will stop. Do you understand?"

"Yes, Master Shinsei," he nodded.

"Good then," he drank more wine and burped again. "Excuse me." Kieko shook his head at the priest for he did not like that he was getting drunk. "Why did you do that?" the priest asked.

"Do what, Master Shinsei?"

"Why did you shake your head?"

"I don't know, Master Shinsei."

"Yes, you do. Why did you shake your head?" he insisted.

"I . . . I think you are drinking too much, Master Shinsei."

"Yes, yes I am drinking. And, yes, I am drinking too much," he smiled. "I am enjoying this drink. That is the way, Kieko. When I drink, I drink. I drink fully, completely. Just as when I train—I train completely, fully. Just as when I clean, I clean completely. That is zazen. That is the way of the Ki."

"Yes, Master Shinsei," he said not too convinced as he finished his bowl of rice and stood up.

"What are you doing?" the priest asked.

"I'm going to wash my bowls and begin cleaning the kitchen."

"No, you will not. You will stay with me."

"But, Master Shinsei, it's late," he complained. "I would like to clean the temple so that I can go to sleep soon."

"No, you will stay with me and have a drink."

Kieko bowed his head, "Yes, Master Shinsei," and sat back down at the table.

The priest poured him a cup, "Drink Kieko, drink."

"Yes, Master Shinsei." He took his cup and sipped at the warm rice wine with cringing lips.

The priest laughed, "I see that you have yet to develop a taste for this wine." Kieko looked with displeasure at his master. "Don't give me that look," he laughed again.

"Yes, Master Shinsei."

"Soon it will be the winter festival in Ikishi. You will stay here and guard the temple while you begin working on your hut. Is there anything you would like for me to take to your mother?"

Kieko gave the question some thought. "I will bake something for her."

"Very wise, I say, very wise. She will be very proud that you can bake and cook. I will tell her all about the dishes you have been cooking. Yes, yes, this I say," his grin widened while his face turned red. "Drink, I say, drink!" he then gulped the wine from his cup.

"Yes, Master Shinsei," Kieko said as he sipped.

"I must tell you—I must tell you this. I told your father this many times." Kieko leaned forward listening with great intent. "I often admitted to you father—in a joking way, of how much I hated—no, that is too strong a word," he laughed out loud. "Of how much I disliked preparing for all the festivals: putting on the robes, carrying the appropriate scrolls, performing the rites and rituals, chanting, and so forth . . . it is all so silly. But, the villagers believe in such nonsense and they look to me to uphold such nonsense. They look to me," he said proud and pointing to himself. "They . . . they look to me," he frowned. "And when they come to me seeking wisdom, and I explain to them that wisdom is simply seeing what they already know within—and that they should not look to me for wisdom, but within themselves, do you know what they say, Kieko? Do you know what they say—or do rather?"

Kieko, nervous, uncomfortable, shook his head.

"They laugh! They laugh. They believe I am joking. They believe that they do not hold wisdom—that it is I who holds wisdom—they leave it to me to show them what I cannot. It is ridiculous that they believe I can show them what they already know. That is why I tell everyone—everyone who seeks wisdom—to meditate, to quiet their mind so that they can realize what they already know." The priest shook his head while looking down at his nearly empty cup. "I am growing tired, Kieko . . . I am growing tired. I am finding less and less strength to teach and care for my people. There is too much ignorance, fear, and hatred within so many of them. They are all too busy pointing fingers and blaming others for their woes, when it is really themselves who are the cause of all their suffering and pain. Such ridiculousness, such ridiculousness, I say."

Kieko did not say a word. He looked at his master saddened that he was not as strong as he had thought. But, as he sat and thought he realized that the priest was simply a man who was separated from his own people because so much purity and integrity was expected of him; and he could see that the priest felt alone and tired of keeping his thoughts to himself.

"You are thinking, Kieko, you are thinking."

Kieko looked at his master, "Yes, Master Shinsei."

"Yes, my friend. I am alone. I am a priest. And foolishly our people—some of them, not all—believe that they can behave as they want and leave the art of goodwill and peace of mind to me. They—some of them—feel that it is simply not their responsibility to improve themselves mentally, physically, spiritually. They leave it all to me . . . somehow believing that I will save them when their time comes, or when they fall and find fear all around them . . . yes, this I say . . . this I say . . .”

Kieko looked down at his cup. It was still full.

“I can see that you will not touch much more of your drink. I excuse you from the table. I excuse you.”

“Yes, Master Shinsei.” He stood up and gathered his bowls and cup, but stopped; he now did not want to leave, he wanted to stay with the priest and keep him company.

“Go, Kieko,” the priest said angrily. “Hurry and be gone. You must clean and meditate and go to sleep.”

“Yes, Master Shinsei.” He took his bowls and cup to the kitchen sink and washed them. When he was done he dried them and began cleaning the kitchen counters.

“Kieko!”

“Yes, Master Shinsei.”

“I will clean the kitchen! You are done here. Go and clean the rest of the temple.”

“Yes, Master Shinsei.” He bowed to his master and left the kitchen chamber relieved.

The priest sat silently listening to Kieko’s footsteps echo from the tunnel. He took a deep breath and sighed. He was exhausted and looked with lazy eyes into the flame of the candle that was on the kitchen table. And his eyes grew heavy, and he drifted into sleep.

His body jerked. His head shot up. He rubbed his eyes and looked around the kitchen noticing that the flame of the candlestick had burned a quarter of the wax. He breathed in deeply as he yawned and listened for only a moment to the silence of the night before stretching his arms and back. He then stood up and began cleaning the kitchen eager to finish so that he could train and go to sleep.

The moonlight shined through the window of Kieko’s room as the burning logs of wood in the fireplace crackled. Lying beneath the wool blankets of his futon he stared up at the ceiling wondering just how long it would be before he held a real Ki sword. He imagined himself training with the priest near his old Thinking Tree against a red sky and setting sun. Kira would be watching him. *Yes, so proud will she be of me,* he thought. He wondered what she was doing and how these past few months had been for her, and if she thought of him—missed him. He then realized that he was forgetting what it was like to be near her, to be touched by her. She was fading from him—he didn't like that—and he prayed that he would soon see her.

He turned to his side and looked at the dark wall feeling his thoughts fade before closing his eyes and falling asleep.

Chapter IX

After eating lunch in the kitchen chamber the priest and Kieko ascended the staircase to the antechamber that preceded the Great Hall of the Buddha. When they reached the antechamber the priest raised his lantern and began feeling one of the cobblestone walls with his fingers as Kieko watched unsure of what his master was doing.

"It has been some time since I have opened this chamber."

"Which chamber?"

"The weapons chamber."

"The weapons—can I help you?"

"No. Just give me a moment . . . there, I found it." He pressed his thumb into a groove between two stones and stepped back.

Large metallic gears began to turn behind the walls. The two took a few steps back. There was a hard thud. An outline of a door then appeared within the wall and retreated slowly as stone ground against stone. The priest held the lantern higher. Kieko could see, and hear, the door retreat further into darkness. The door stopped. The metallic gears stopped. "Come with me," the priest said as he walked into the dark pathway created by the door.

Kieko followed and felt a cool draft flowing past him. He could see old cobwebs flapping like sails along the walls. The priest walked around the door. He followed and found himself in a very dark and cold room.

"This is the weapons chamber," the priest raised the lantern again so that Kieko could see.

Kieko's mouth fell open. He saw hundreds of wooden swords stacked on tiered racks on every wall.

"These are the practice swords of all the Ki priests and priestesses that have ever resided in the Kadek Temple."

"How many swords are there, Master Shinsei?"

"Perhaps two thousand or more."

"And what is that, Master Shinsei?" Kieko asked pointing to what appeared to be another stone door behind one of the racks.

"That is a door to another weapons chamber. There are two other doors: one over there and there," he said pointing to the other walls.

Kieko looked and saw the other doors. "Are there real Ki swords behind those doors, Master Shinsei?"

"One day you will find out. For now let us pick out a wooden sword that you may practice with."

"Yes, Master Shinsei."

The priest looked carefully at each wooden sword. Kieko could see that the majority of the swords were heavily scarred and splintered. The priest lifted one sword off the rack, raised it, and swung it down with lightening speed causing Kieko's eyes to widen in awe.

"Yes, this, I believe, will do," he gave the weapon to Kieko.

Kieko took it and swung it up and down.

"How does it feel? Is it heavy?"

"Just a little, Master Shinsei."

"Good, it will strengthen your arm so that you will be able to handle a real sword when you are ready. Now, check the sword. Is it warped?"

Kieko looked down the shaft of the sword checking with what little light he had if the sword was curved or not. "It looks straight, Master Shinsei."

"Good, that is good. That is your sword. You must care for it as if it was a real sword. Treat it with complete respect. Be humbled by it for it is a weapon that can give or take life. It is a weapon, Kieko. Even with a wooden sword you can strike someone down, killing them. It is a dangerous weapon. It is very dangerous."

"Yes, Master Shinsei," Kieko said feeling the weight of his master's words.

"Come, let us go."

Kieko followed the priest back into the antechamber. The priest, with his fingers, felt one of the antechamber's walls again until he found a small crevice; he pressed his fingers into it. Heavy metallic gears began to move again. Kieko watched the stone door advanced until it stopped with a loud thud kicking up dust. He looked at the wall and could not see the outline of the door anymore.

After taking off his wooden sandals the priest slid the door to the main hall open, bowed, and walked in. Kieko took off his wooden sandals, bowed, closed the door behind him, and followed after the priest. When the priest reached the center of the main hall he faced the golden statue of the Buddha and said, "Stand next to me," to Kieko who swiftly stood by his right side. "Remember, stand a bit behind me. I am elder. You are junior. You must always stand behind me."

"Yes, Master Shinsei."

"With reverence, put your sword on the ground–by your right side–with the handle pointed toward the altar."

"Yes, Master Shinsei." He did as instructed.

"Let us warm up, but first we must chant. Do as I do."

The priest spread his legs open and lowered his upper body. "This is the horse stance. Over time you will be able to stretch your legs farther and farther apart keeping your upper body as low to the ground as possible."

"Yes, Master Shinsei," he spread his legs into the horse stance.

"That is good," the priest complimented, "your stance is good." He raised his hands up to the golden statue and shouted, "Ki!" before snapping his fists back to his waist.

Kieko followed his master's example feeling a little embarrassed after he shouted the word, Ki.

The priest raised his hands again to the Buddha and shouted, "Takana!" before snapping his fists back to his waist again. Kieko followed. The priest repeated the act–and Kieko followed– shouting one word at a time until he finished the chant: Ki-Takana-Do, Ki-Kami-Do, Ki-Atama-Do, Ki-Kokoro-Do. "Let us try again," he advised. "But, this time we do it together, as one."

"Yes, Master Shinsei."

Together the two raised their hands to the Buddha and shouted, "Ki-Takana-Do, Ki-Kami-Do, Ki-Atama-Do, Ki-Kokoro-Do!" snapping their hands back to their waists and up again with each word.

"Let us bow."

The two, together, then brought their legs together, held their clasped hands before their hearts, and bowed.

"Pick up your sword and give it to me–pick it up slowly, respectfully, with both hands."

"Yes, Master Shinsei," Kieko picked up the sword and gave it to the priest.

"Good," he took the sword with his left hand. "Now, give me three full bows. Bow and be humbled by the Ki knowledge I am about to reveal to you."

"Yes, Master Shinsei." He gave his master three full bows.

The priest bowed to Kieko when he had finished. He then held the wooden sword with the handle pointed up in front of his chest with his left hand, and aligned his right hand over the area where the sword guard would have been on a real sword. He extended the sword out and bowed, "That is how you begin." He shouted and took a step back with his left leg swiftly moving the sword to his left side holding it at an angle. He shouted again taking a step back with his right leg swinging the sword to his right side and stopped. "That is the most basic way we defend ourselves with a sheathed sword. You can see that this sword–with the way it is angled from top to bottom–protects my head, chest, and stomach. Only my legs are exposed." He retreated several more times allowing Kieko to observe the technique. "Now I will advance." He advanced, shouting, swinging the sword from one side to the other, and stopped. "Now, you try." He handed the sword to Kieko.

Kieko took the sword.

The priest pulled out a short wooden sword from within his robe. Kieko's eyes widened. "Do not be alarmed, Kieko, I will show you how this defensive technique works. Now, bow with the sword and defend your left side."

"Yes, Master Shinsei." He extended the sword out, bowed, and shouted taking a quick step back with his left foot, swinging the sword to his left side. He heard a bright clank sound. He looked at the handle of the sword and saw that the priest's sword had struck it.

"That is good, Kieko. Now you can see how this technique protects your head. Try again."

Kieko stepped back with his right leg blocking a strike to his chest.

"Now you see, Kieko. Again!"

Kieko shouted and retreated. Clank! He had blocked a strike to his head again.

"Good! Again!"

He retreated blocking another strike, then another and another.

"Now advance."

He advanced blocking one attack after the other to his head and chest. The priest stopped, "Good, Kieko, good. That is very good. Now practice this technique for an hour."

"Yes, Master Shinsei," he replied with pride.

"Do not think," he warned. "This is your meditation: retreat and advance and only that. Do not think. Do not let your mind wander. Is that understood?"

"Yes, Master Shinsei," he bowed.

The priest bowed. He then faced the Buddha and bowed again before walking away and exiting the main hall.

Kieko began practicing the Ki sword technique. He retreated and advanced, and retreated and advanced, imagining his opponent trying to strike his head and chest. He heard his thoughts: *She is forgetting me. Damn her. She should be here watching me.* He shook his head and continued going through the technique while observing his thoughts. Kira was on his mind, as was Aiko. He imagined himself fighting Aiko, and Kira cheering him on and running up to him after he had defeated him. That was what he wanted; he wanted to beat Aiko; he wanted to defeat him before Kira and all the villagers. He stopped remembering that if the priest found him thinking of using the sword to hurt others, or to take life, that he would cease teaching him. He shook his head again trying to clear his mind of all thoughts, bowed to the Buddha, and swung the sword to his side with an abrasive shout. He retreated and defended with the sword, and advanced warding off all thoughts.

An hour passed. The priest entered the main hall and bowed. Kieko stopped and bowed to his master. "Show me your technique."

"Yes, Master Shinsei."

The priest bolted at him. Kieko jumped back in fright and landed into a hard stance. The priest lashed out at him with his short wooden sword. Kieko retreated and blocked. The priest lashed out again. Kieko blocked. The priest attacked his head and chest. Kieko blocked and blocked. Then, in a thin moment, he thought of Aiko; the priest's sword passed his block and stopped hard against his forehead.

"You are dead," the priest declared.

Kieko, breathing heavily, dropped his shoulders and stood up straight disappointed with his performance.

"Thinking is the death of you. It is the death of all of us. Thinking is a product of the mind. The mind creates thinking. But, thinking blinds us from the present. It prevents us from seeing all that is here and now. Thinking fills us only with the past and the future. They are illusions! And when we believe in these illusions, when we attach ourselves to these illusions, we become insane; we worry about tomorrow or we are fearful of what we have done in the past. We fear, and allow these fears to control us, rob us, and destroy us.

"You are not your thoughts, Kieko, remember that. Do not attach yourself to your thoughts. If thoughts arise observe them, and let them pass. A true master of the sword is free of all thoughts. When he fights he fights completely. A master will always persist against his enemy because he has already destroyed his own ego, his own self. Thus he is unclouded; he is devoid of mind. He is pure. He becomes a mirror for his enemy, a reflection, and simply throws back what his enemy throws at him. It is the enemy who defeats himself . . . not the Ki master."

Kieko bowed his head thinking about what his master had just said.

"Do not think! You already know this. Deep in you heart you know of what I speak. Now, rest. Wash yourself and relax in the bath. Clear yourself of all your thoughts, and when you are ready go over what you have learned of the sword."

"Yes, Master Shinsei."

"Go, then."

"Yes, Master Shinsei," he bowed. He took his practice sword and walked to the door that led to the antechamber. At the door he stopped and bowed to the Buddha. He slid the door open, searched for a pair of wooden sandals with his feet, put a pair on, and slid the door closed behind him.

The priest looked at the Buddha, bowed, and whispered while nodding his head, "He is improving, yes. He is improving." He turned, walked across the main hall, and exited it.

Kieko scooped up some rice and ate it before drinking some tea; he and the priest were in the kitchen chamber having dinner. He drank some of his soup and when he placed his soup bowl back on the table he began to go over the new sword technique he had learned in his mind.

"You learn fast, Kieko, just like your father. Tomorrow, I will teach you how to draw the sword, how to block strikes to your legs, and how to attack. What I taught you today, and what I will teach you over the next few days, are the basic forms of Ki sword. They are the foundation of the art. Whenever you begin training you will go over these basic forms before practicing long forms. You will enjoy long forms; that I can see." He drank some tea. "And in the night you will meditate on these techniques and forms."

Kieko smiled; he couldn't wait for the next day to come so that he could train again in the art of Ki sword. He decided that in the night, when he knew his master was training in the dharma hall, that he too would train in Ki sword instead of meditate. Meditation made him drowsy. He would rather practice something that kept him awake, strong, and powerful.

"What are you thinking?" the priest asked with squinting, suspicious eyes.

"Nothing, Master Shinsei. I am done with my meal. I will begin cleaning the kitchen."

He looked straight into Kieko's eyes. "Clean . . . and after go up and meditate—and meditate only! I will retire to my room to chant and pray." He rose from his seat and took his bowls and cup to the sink to wash them; and when he had dried them and put them away he turned to Kieko and said, "Goodnight."

"Goodnight, Master Shinsei," he bowed.

The priest bowed back and left.

Kieko rushed around the kitchen cleaning it as fast as he could. When he was done he threw out the garbage and cleaned the floor in the main hall and in the dharma hall before running up to his room to put on a fresh top and bottom-gi. Dressed, he returned to the main hall, bowed, and approached the altar. He bowed again before the altar and lit three incense sticks before taking a few steps back while imagining that he had his sword in his hand. He stopped, held his imaginary sword before him, extended it out, and bowed. In the blink of an eye he shot his foot back and blocked his left side. He stepped back again and blocked his right side. He continued stepping back blocking the strikes of his fictitious enemies with speed. He then heard what sounded like a stomp and stopped knowing that it was his master training in the dharma hall. Nervous, he stood completely still until he was sure that his master had not heard what he was doing in the main hall and, quietly, slowly, continued training.

After working up a sweat he decided to go to sleep before his master finished training. He bowed to the altar and felt a faint soreness in his throat. "I hope I'm not getting sick," he whispered to himself. He walked to the entrance door of the hall while listening to the bats flying high above him and heard a splat on the floor. "Bat dung," he said. *I'll have to clean that up tomorrow.* When he reached the door he turned to face the altar, bowed, slid the door open and closed it behind him, and returned to his room.

CHAPTER X

It was cold outside; the air was dry and stiff. The trees had only a few leaves hanging from their branches. Kieko coughed as he walked. He then looked up past the trees and saw the Mountains of Shinohi in the distance noticing that their peaks were now completely covered in snow. He thought of Buko and wondered what had become of him. The priest was walking with his staff ahead of him leading him through the garden of the temple. He coughed again feeling that the soreness in his throat had worsened over the past two days, stopped, placed the shovel he was carrying against his leg, and rubbed his hands together to warm them.

"You are getting sick, Kieko," the priest said as he walked and smoked from his long pipe.

Kieko could smell the bitter scent of the smoke from the pipe and coughed again. The priest shook his head, stopped, and bowed before the tori gate. Kieko caught up to the priest and bowed to the tori gate as well. The two walked through the gate and continued down the path that led back to Ikishi.

As they walked Kieko observed his surroundings; he looked at the trees, the piles of dead leaves that had fallen over the past few weeks, and at the ground. Everything around him was dying. The wonderful colors of autumn: the oranges, the reds, the browns, and yellows, were no more. There were only the colors of winter now: greys, blacks, the metallic browns of the tree branches, the dried dirt hues of the hardened earth. He stepped on the dried leaves along the path and listened to the crunch sounds they made as he looked up to the cloudy sky. He exhaled and saw his frozen breath rise.

The priest turned off the path and walked toward the forest. Kieko followed and saw, high up in the trees, a pack of large crows shivering and standing on naked branches; one of the crows croaked, and then another and another. The collective cries of the crows grew louder as the priest and Kieko neared the forest. They then bolted and flew up into the sky crying out. The priest, and Kieko, stopped, and together they waited until the crows had gone.

The priest puffed on his pipe, "It is not good to see the black bird on such a day."

Kieko stood silent.

"Come, Kieko, come. We are nearly there."

"Yes, Master Shinsei."

The priest led Kieko to the edge of the forest and bowed. Kieko bowed after his master. The two entered the forest and walked carefully between the trees until they reached a clearing within the forest.

"Here, it is here that you will build your hut," the priest said as he walked across the clearing looking up at the trees as if he was searching for something. Kieko looked up trying to find what the priest was looking for, but saw nothing other than the tops of pine trees. The priest walked into the center of the clearing and looked in the direction of where the temple stood. "Kieko, come here." Kieko went to his master and stood by him. The priest pointed through the trees. Kieko looked and saw the temple in the distance. "I will be able to keep an eye on you as you work on your hut, and when you begin living in it as well."

"Yes, Master Shinsei."

"Find me four strong sticks that we can fix into the ground so that we can outline your thatched dwelling."

"Yes, Master Shinsei." He placed the shovel down, coughed again, and went into the forest searching for four strong sticks.

When he returned he found that the priest had finished smoking his pipe and that he was unraveling a ball of thin rope.

"Let me see the sticks you found," the priest asked. Kieko showed him the seven sticks he had collected. "Throw this one, and these two to the ground." Kieko threw the three sticks to the ground. "Those four will do. I placed four rocks on the ground: one over there, there, there, and here," he pointed. "Stab the sticks into the ground where those four rocks are."

"Yes, Master Shinsei." After he had plunged and twisted the first stick into the ground the priest began wrapping the thin rope around it. He jabbed and twisted the other three sticks into the ground and saw that the priest was following him and wrapping the rope around each stick leaving the outline of a rectangular.

The priest tied a knot, cut the string with a knife, stood up, and took a step back, "Dig into the rectangle as deep as the length of your leg."

Kieko looked at his master, coughed again, and cleared his throat.

"You are getting sick, Kieko," he shook his head at him again. "You are coming down with a fever–you see how the anger within you is affecting you."

Kieko kept silent, but he felt that he had improved in taming his anger.

"Regardless, you must stay out here and dig. The ground is hard. It will be difficult for you to dig. Use your strength. Use your arms and legs. Do not use your back. By the time you finish building this hut you will be strong and well-muscled."

Kieko picked up the shovel.

"Start on the north side of the rectangle."

"Yes, Master Shinsei," he stepped into the rectangle and approached the north side of it.

"I will return to the temple to prepare lunch. When it is ready I will come for you and check on your progress."

"Yes, Master Shinsei."

"Do not fool around; do your work, focus, and dig with a clear mind."

"Yes, Master Shinsei."

"Remember, I can see you from the temple," he turned and left.

Kieko spat into his hands, rubbed them together, and began digging.

The temperature dropped dramatically by afternoon causing Kieko to shiver and sneeze as he worked. He spat at the ground and cursed the gelid air before shoving the shovel into the earth again. Slamming his foot down on the shovel he put his weight on it and watched cracks form in the ground around the shovel. He jerked the shovel forward and back, and side to side, until he had freed a large piece of earth. He lifted the piece and threw it out of the hole. "Enough of this," he threw the shovel down and sat on the edge of the hole he was in. His arms were sore, as were his legs and back. He looked at his palms and saw that the blisters that had formed while he worked were getting bigger. Worried, he searched through the trees with his eyes and saw the temple; smoke was rising from one of its chimneystacks. His stomach grumbled. He rubbed his arms and prayed that the priest would arrive soon so that he could return to the warmth of the temple to rest and eat. Feeling a faint headache he massaged the back of his neck while looking at the hole hoping that it was deep enough for the priest. He coughed up some phlegm and spat at the ground again before picking up the shovel to start digging again.

An hour later the priest returned seeing that Kieko had dug out about a fifth of the rectangle, and that he was exhausted, hungry, and cold. "Good, Kieko. You have accomplished quite a bit. Come, I can see that you are tired, it is time to eat."

"Should I leave the shovel here, Master Shinsei," he asked.

"No, bring it back with you."

"Yes, Master Shinsei." He took the shovel and followed the priest back to the temple.

Inside the temple he went to his room to change out of his dirty clothes and to put on a thick pair of cotton pants, an old wool sweater, and a fresh pair of wool socks. He wanted to crawl onto his futon and sleep, but he had to eat. Still shivering he decided to take the blanket from his futon and wrap it around himself. "That's better," he walked to the door, slid it open, and slipped on his temple shoes.

The priest greeted him when he walked into the kitchen chamber and asked him to sit and drink the tea he had made for him. He sipped the hot tea savoring its taste and how it felt as it trickled down his throat. When he was done the priest poured him another cup and gave him a bowl of soup. They ate together in silence. As he ate he felt his headache grow stronger. He finished his soup and stood up to wash it, but he sat back down again for he felt very weak and lightheaded.

"Go to sleep, Kieko."

Kieko looked at his master, "I'm sorry, Master Shinsei."

"Sorry for what? Sorry because you are sick? Go to your futon and rest. You will have dinner with me tonight, and you will clean this kitchen and the temple floors, and you will meditate on the forms. Do you understand?"

"Yes, Master Shinsei."

"Clean your bowl and cup, and go up and rest."

"Yes, Master Shinsei," he stood up and took small steps to the sink. He washed his bowl and cup, and placed them on the granite counter to dry. "Will you wake me, Master Shinsei?" he asked bowing to his master.

"Yes, yes, now go."

Kieko left.

The late afternoon had come and gone, and in the evening the priest woke Kieko so that they could have dinner together.

After dinner Kieko did what was expected of him: he cleaned the kitchen, washed the temple floors, and meditated in the main hall. He felt worse than he did during the middle of the day as he crawled back onto his futon late at night coughing and shivering. He felt his forehead with his forearm; it was burning. Pulling his blankets tight around his body he stared at the moonlight that shined through his window and thought of his mother, and how she would care for him when he was sick. He prayed to the moon goddess that he would heal soon, and that his mother was safe and healthy.

In the middle of the night Kieko woke up coughing uncontrollably until he had hacked up a considerable amount of phlegm from the back of his throat. Sitting up he wanted to spit out what he had in his mouth, but he had nothing to spit into, and feeling utterly sick and feverish he had not the strength to descend from his lofted futon to fetch a cup or cloth. Deciding to use his sweat drenched shirt he took it off, spat into it, and collapsed feeling very warm. To cool himself he threw his blankets off his body and allowed the chilly air to caress him. He soon fell back to sleep and dreamed.

He was in the dark of the temple underground. Nearly unable to see he walked down a tunnel toward a faint flickering light from a cavern ahead of him. He heard a voice, but when he heard two voices he stopped. Frightened, he wanted to just stand still and not continue. But, when he recognized the voices he decided to take a few steps forward. The two voices began laughing in an evil delight; and there was a third voice; it was faint, but sweet. Then there was a slap—a hard hand against flesh—and the laughter continued. Anger began to pulse through him; he could feel it running through his veins moving into every part of his body. He neared the cavern and readied himself for what he felt he knew he was about to find. He walked into the cavern and saw two boys, about his age, with their backs to him standing over a woman. His hands became tight fists. One of the boys slapped the woman straight across the face while the other laughed. Kieko called out. The boys turned to him smiling. Kieko's eyes widened when he looked at their faces of grey rotting flesh spotted with bright red sores and saw that they had no eyes but deep empty eye sockets. The woman, naked, beaten, held out her hand and reached for him, but he could not see her face for it was covered by the shadows of the room.

"Come, come," one of the boys said giggling.

"Niko?" Kieko asked recognizing the voice.

"No!" the boy shouted and turned to kick the woman in the face. "But, she is your mother," he smiled.

Rage exploded throughout him and he launched himself at the two animated corpses, but an unseen force threw him back. Crashing against a wall of stone he fell to the ground and looked up in a daze not knowing what had happened. Then, from the shadows behind the woman, appeared the outline of a dark figure that was wearing a black, heavy wool cloak with a hood that concealed its face. The two boys silenced their laughter and bowed to the dark figure. The dark figure stepped over the woman and pointed back to her while looking at Kieko and said, "It is your mother, Akai?" Kieko tried to get up, but the shadowy figure pointed the palm of its other hand at him, and held him down with its black unseen magic. "What are you doing to—" he tried to shout, but the figure silenced him with one swipe of its hand through the still cool air. "She is mine, Akai," the dark figure declared. Kieko recognized the voice; it was that of Aiko's father. Fighting the force that held him down he squirmed and resisted but could not break free. "Do not waste your time, Akai," the figure called out as he stepped into the light; Kieko could see his black lips, and when he smiled he saw his gross, dark yellow teeth. "Her life will soon be at an end, and so will yours." The force that was holding him against the wall was then gone and he stood up to fight the three figures before him. But there was a horrible, deafening, moaning sound coming from all around him; and from the shadows of the cavern stepped out several more living corpses in varying stages of decay. Kieko bolted at the dark figure in a foolish attempt to save his mother, but he was thrown to the ground by the same force that had pinned him against the wall; and all at once the bodies that now filled the room attacked him. He kicked and screamed at the hundreds of hands that grabbed and pulled him, and tried to punch the mouths that bit his arms, feet, and legs. But, it was useless; he was being torn apart by the mob of the living dead.

Kieko shot up from his futon in a panic. Sitting up in a cold sweat he punched the air several times before realizing that he had just woken up from a nightmare. Out of breath he looked at the moonlight that was trickling in through the window and tried to relax by massaging the temples of his forehead. When he had caught his breath he sat still and remembered what had been done to his mother by Buko. His thoughts later drifted to Aiko and his father, and to Niko. He wanted to punch the wall and release his contempt for them, but, he did not, his headache was too strong and painful. Lying back down on his futon he tried to block out the pain, but could not, and so he looked up at the ceiling praying to fall asleep again to avoid feeling the throbbing of his mind.

CHAPTER XI

Three days passed before Kieko overcame his fever and gained the strength to become active again within the temple. He spent his first morning out of his futon cleaning the temple floors and practicing the forms while the priest watched and corrected his movements. In the afternoon he chanted and meditated with the priest, and when the sun had set into the horizon he sat at the kitchen table sipping tea as the priest cooked.

"There," the priest said as he placed a lid over a pot of stew, "now we just wait until it is done and ready to fill our stomachs." He sat down at the kitchen table and drank some tea. "Are you feeling better?"

"Yes, Master Shinsei, much better than the past few days."

"But, do you feel better now as opposed to this morning?"

"Yes, my strength is returning, Master Shinsei."

"Good. You must begin work again on your hut early tomorrow morning. I hope you can make up for the time you have lost before I leave for the winter festival."

"I will, Master Shinsei."

"Today is . . ." he calculated, "that means you only have three days."

"What do you mean, Master Shinsei? I thought the winter festival was four—or five days from now?"

"It is Kieko, but we need one day to clean as much of the temple as we can together, and do not forget that we need to make mochi."

"Oh, you are right, Master Shinsei," he said realizing that he had forgotten about the mochi they were to make the night before the winter festival.

The priest drank some more tea. "What did you realize during the three days that you were sick?"

Kieko gave a quizzical look at the priest, "I . . . I was sick, Master Shinsei. I didn't realize anything. I was just in my futon sleeping. When I was awake I mind-trained on the forms you taught me—"

"And you meditated on your futon."

"Yes, I did, Master Shinsei."

"So, what did you realize?"

Kieko shook his head not knowing what to say.

"So, you realized nothing."

"I–I realized that with the forms—"

"No!" the priest interrupted, "not the forms. I am not asking about forms. I am asking you what you realized in being sick."

"I was sick, Master Shinsei. I was sick . . . I . . . I remember you telling me—before—that I was getting sick because of my . . . my anger—"

"Yes, that is it. That is what I said. Those are *my* words. But, what have *you* realized from that?"

"Nothing, Master Shinsei," he said shaking his head again confused as to what the priest wanted to hear from him.

"That is obvious. You truly wasted three days. Did you not quiet your mind and observe your condition, observe your fever?"

"I did meditate," he said with growing impatience, "but on the forms."

"And when you were not meditating—when you were lying on your futon—what were you doing? Thinking? Thinking of Kira—of your mother—of Aiko? Were you thinking of painful things in your past—hurtful things that villagers had done to you, to your mother? Were you thinking of the tournament and the moment

Aiko broke your arm? Were you thinking of Niko—of Kono—of Buko?"

Kieko looked at the priest not wanting to answer his questions.

"You are too full of thinking, Kieko! You had three days to rest, heal, and quiet your mind, but instead you filled yourself with thoughts, with pain from your past, with anger! It is no wonder you were sick for three days. You should have healed in one day, not three. But, there is too much anger within you!"

"Yes, there is anger within me!" he barked back at the priest.

The priest fired out of his seat and slapped Kieko hard across the face. "Never speak to me in such a way! I am your master."

Kieko covered his stinging check with his hand afraid to look at the priest.

"What are you afraid of?" he asked. "You are here in this kitchen under my guidance. Your mind is racing with anxiety. It is creating fear within you. But, nothing is happening to you. And there you sit fearful of me—a priest."

Kieko looked up to his master.

"You have much to learn, Kieko. Much to learn," he sat back down across from him. "If you are not in a state of no-mind, you are in a state of mind. Mind is bound to time, and time is an illusion of the mind. If you are not watchful of your mind, if you believe you are your mind, then it is the mind that is controlling your actions, feelings, and emotions. Thus, in that way there is pain within you, pain that was created by your mind through its resistance—judgment—of the present. Mind cannot survive without time, and the present is devoid of time."

"I don't understand, Master Shinsei," he said shaking his head. "I don't understand. I know you keep telling me that I am not my mind, but I still don't understand how I can be without the mind? I think. My thoughts, my judgments, are my own, and my thoughts come from me—my mind."

"You are not your mind!" the priest shouted again waving his arms out in frustration. "You are what is when there is no-mind."

"Then . . . then there are two of me?" he questioned.

"No, there is only one."

"Then, what is my mind, if I am not my mind?"

"Your mind is an entity that lives within you. It is limited and finite and can only survive within the constructs of time. It is fearful of the present and preys on you to identify with it so that it can control you to ensure its own survival. In that way it creates pain within you, for it clouds you from seeing what you are."

"Seeing what I am? I . . . I have thoughts," he said realizing that he was thinking. He observed his thoughts for a moment and continued, "Of . . . of course, perhaps, there are moments when I do not think . . . but it's only a moment. We all need to think. I still don't understand how anyone can survive without the mind, Master Shinsei? We all need to think and make decisions—"

"As I have explained to you before, the mind is only a tool to use in this world. It is a tool—nothing more—it is not who you are. Pain is created when we believe we are our minds. Our minds think, judge, resist, anger, hate. It dwells on the negativity it creates through its resistance of the present, and its dissatisfactions with the past and future. This is exactly what I see in you, Kieko. You dwell on anger by thinking of what others have done to you, and what you will do to them. You become the pain by allowing it to enrapt you, and you lose yourself . . . you become unconscious, sick, a slave to your mind." The priest paused for a moment and continued, "The mind is dangerous, Kieko. It fears death. It will fight, even if it means to kill, maim, or torture, to ensure its survival. Those who are strongly identified with the mind create pain and suffering within and without. But, do not concern yourself with observing their actions and words, only focus on you by observing your thoughts and watching your feelings. If you become defensive ask yourself, 'What am I defending?' Are you defending your beliefs, your feelings, your wishes and desires? If you are fearful then ask yourself if you are attached? Do you fear losing those close to you? Do you fear losing your hatred and anger? Witness your thoughts and actions. Listen to the words you use when you speak. Be your own watcher so that you can cease to identify with the mind and find your true self again."

"And what is my true self, Master Shinsei?"

The priest was silent.

The pot of stew began boiling causing the lid over it to dance with the escaping steam. The priest stood up to attend to the pot. Kieko thought about what the priest had said. In a moment he realized that he was thinking about the priest's words, and slowly he felt himself drift back so that he could observe his thoughts. He listened and heard: *he is a stupid old fool . . . of course, I am my mind, I need the mind . . . the cold caused me to get sick, not anger . . . what rubbish he speaks . . .*

"Kieko."

He shook his head and looked at the priest in a daze.

"That is it. Just relax and observe your thoughts. Do not judge them. You will have moments when you feel that those thoughts are not your own. Those moments will grow with practice–with meditation–and you will be able to attain a true state of no-mind."

"Yes, Master Shinsei," he said nodding his head.

"It is time to eat. Just relax and enjoy your stew," he said as he placed a bowl of stew on the table.

"Thank you, Master Shinsei."

"You are very welcome," he smiled.

CHAPTER XII

It was the night before the winter festival, and the priest and Kieko were in the kitchen cooking. "Be careful," the priest said to Kieko, as he was about to pour water from a large steel pot into the kitchen sink. "Remember, each grain of rice is the soul of one of our villagers."

"Yes, Master Shinsei." He tipped the pot over allowing the cloudy white water to flow into the sink. And as he poured he thought for only a fraction of a second about the festival, and a grain of rice escaped from his steel pot. His eyes widened. The grain flowed to the drain and disappeared.

"One fell!" the priest exclaimed. "You fool."

Kieko quickly tipped the pot up.

"You are better than that, Kieko. You have impressed me these past couple of days with your skill in Ki sword. Now you disappoint me. Do you have no respect for the food that will fill you? Every grain is precious. Every grain gives life to each of our villagers. Nothing is to be wasted. Nothing. No respect do you have for our people."

Kieko wanted to speak up and say that the villagers had no respect for him, but he did not; he kept his head down.

"Keep pouring, and no thoughts beyond pouring," the priest commanded.

Kieko focused all of his attention to the pot and tipped it over allowing the cloudy water to flow into the sink again. When he was done he tipped the pot up and looked at the gooey mess of rice within it.

"Put the rice into one of the square wooden containers on the countertop."

"Yes, Master Shinsei." He angled the pot over the container and shook it trying to shake the rice free; the rice rolled and fell into the container.

"Flatten it out with that large wooden spoon."

"Yes, Master Shinsei." He took the spoon and patted the sticky rice down molding it into the shape of the container.

"Are you finished, yet?"

"Almost, Master Shinsei. The rice keeps sticking to the back of the spoon."

"Be quick." The priest checked the water in the large caldron that was sitting over the fireplace and saw that the water was beginning to boil and steam.

"I'm finished, Master Shinsei."

"Good, now place that lid–the one over there," he pointed, "over the container and bring the container over here."

"Yes, Master Shinsei." He did as asked.

The priest took the container and placed it over the cauldron. "This is not the most efficient way to steam the rice. As you can see a lot of steam is escaping from the sides. I will have to repair the other container that I have. It is a circular one–not a square one like the one we're using–that fits perfectly over this cauldron."

Kieko nodded.

"Have a seat, Kieko. It will take some time to steam the rice." Kieko sat down at the kitchen table. The priest prepared some tea.

When the tea was done the priest poured two cups and sat down with Kieko. The two sipped their tea and smiled. "Tomorrow, I leave for Ikishi." Again, Kieko nodded. "I expect you to train, to work on your hut, to clean the temple, and to eat. I will not be back until sometime after midnight. Do not fool around tomorrow. You have a lot to do."

"Yes, Master Shinsei."

"Is there anything you would like for me to tell your mother?"

"Just tell her that I love her and that I miss her very much."

"Is there anything you would like for me to tell Kira?"

"No, Master Shinsei."

"No?"

"No, Master Shinsei," he said again.

"I am sure that she would like to hear something from you. Are you sure that you want to begin the New Year by holding a simple hello from her?"

He did not reply.

"Well, I will give her some of the mochi we are making and tell her that they are from you."

He nodded.

"Tomorrow will be the first time that you will be celebrating the New Year by yourself."

He nodded again.

"You are quiet."

"Yes, Master Shinsei."

The priest could see that Kieko was sad that he was going to be alone and far from his mother, and from Kira, during the winter festival. "Well, you know what you must do tomorrow—clean the temple well, with a clear mind, before we enter the New Year."

"Yes, Master Shinsei."

They were quiet. The sound of the boiling water from the cauldron filled the air.

"Master Shinsei?"

"Yes, Kieko. How am I doing? How am I doing here?"

"You want to know. You want to know what I see of you. Well, why not tell me what you see of yourself and your progress here?"

Kieko thought for a moment. "I think . . . I think that I still . . . think too much," he began to blush. The priest laughed at the irony of his words. Kieko continued as he began to rub his hands nervously, "I . . . am not always focused on the task that I am asked to do . . . At times, I do not do what you ask of me."

"There, you see. You see and know what you are failing at. Those are your weaknesses, Kieko. And your anger? You still have a lot of anger. You must let go of your anger."

Kieko's body tensed.

"There, you see. There it is. Your anger."

"How am I to let it go, Master Shinsei?"

"How do you let go a hot coal?"

"By dropping it, Master Shinsei. But, it's not the same. It's not that easy to simply drop my anger or any other emotion that arises."

"Ah, because of thought, because of mind. Your mind keeps you in the past. It keeps you away from the present. If you cease all thoughts, if you defeat mind, then you are completely, and totally, in the present. And in the present you simply are without any attachments to feelings or thoughts."

"But . . . but, I still feel we need mind, Master Shinsei. We need thoughts to get things done."

"When you get those things done do you continue to need thinking, do you continue to need mind?"

Kieko was silent.

"When you cook you may need to think, you may need to remember an ingredient. But, after you remember that ingredient do you need to continue remembering it, do you need to continue to think? Your mind tells you that you do. Your mind fills you with thought as you cook. It tells you that you must clean your clothes after cooking, or clean a room, or it may remind you of why you were so angry by someone's words and why you need to continue to be angry. But, you are cooking, and only that, so why the need to think of things that have nothing to do with cooking? There is no need. It is a waste of energy to be caught up in the poisons of the mind. The present is all there is. So be fully aware of it. Live in it completely. From the present will all things be revealed to you, Kieko."

"Yes, Master Shinsei."

The priest shook his head. "Yes, yes to what? When you *do*, then you will know." He stood up and walked to the cauldron. He lifted the lid off the container and checked the steamed glutinous rice with a wooden spoon. "It will be ready soon." He sat back down at the table and poured Kieko another cup of tea. Kieko poured another cup for his master. The two, together, drank their tea. "Just drink and enjoy the tea, Kieko. Be completely aware of the cup in your hand, its weight, and its texture. Be fully aware of the tea itself. Be aware of this room and everything within it. Just be and breathe."

"Yes, Master Shinsei." He took a deep breath and drank the tea feeling the warm liquid slide down his throat into his stomach. He closed his eyes and listened. He could hear the beat of his heart, the boil of the cauldron water, and his master breathing.

"That is good, Kieko. Just relax and breathe. Put down the cup." Kieko placed the cup on the table. "Straighten your back." Kieko straightened his back. "Keep your eyes closed. Listen. Listen to all that is around you. Listen to my words. Listen to the space—the quiet—between my words. Listen to that space between all things that sound. Hear the nothing. Hear the void."

Kieko listened trying to hear that space between all things.

"Do not think! Just listen, Kieko."

Kieko listened. He heard the boiling water, bubbles rising from the bottom of the hot iron cauldron to the steaming surface, popping, ceasing to be. He listened carefully. He heard a thousand bubbles pop before he heard groups of bubbles pop. He quieted his mind and heard each and every bubble pop. And between the pops he could hear it, a faint silence. The silence between each pop grew until the popping sounds just became part of a distant background. Soon, there was only silence, and he became frightened. He heard a voice speak, *you fool.*

He opened his eyes. "What happened?"

"That was good, Kieko. That was good," the priest said nodding his head.

"What happened?" he asked again.

"You—for a very brief moment—were in the present."

"I was?"

"Yes, you were."

"But, but how do you know?"

"I heard what you heard."

"What did I hear?"

"You tell me, Kieko."

He thought for moment and explained, "I heard nothing—I mean, I first heard the bubbles of the boiling water in the cauldron popping . . . and then I heard them in groups, then each and every one, and then between the popping . . . I heard the quiet, the silence, and, and . . . that silence grew . . . and somehow I . . . I lost myself within that nothing . . . and then I heard a voice."

"That voice was your mind, Kieko."

"My mind?"

"Yes. What did it say?"

"It said that I was a fool."

"Typical," he puffed.

"What do you mean, Master Shinsei?"

"What have I told you about the mind, Kieko?"

"I am not my mind."

"Yes, but you do not really understand this. Nearly everyone believes that they are their thoughts, their wants, their desires, and their attachments. We are none of these things. We, in true form, are no-mind."

Kieko had heard this speech too many times now from the priest.

"Listen to me, Kieko. You are not listening. Your mind is interrupting you. It tells you not to listen to me for you have heard me speak of this before."

Kieko looked at the priest embarrassed, and in disbelief.

"Your mind–at times–is easy to read, Kieko."

"You heard my thoughts?"

"I can do many things; things that you cannot even fathom."

"How, Master Shinsei?"

"I have already told you how. Free yourself of all thoughts, free yourself of mind, and you will see."

"See what, Master Shinsei?"

The priest stood up, "The rice is ready."

Kieko looked at the priest confused.

"Get up, Kieko. Dust the countertop by the sink with rice flour."

"Yes, Master Shinsei." He picked up a metallic bowl filled with rice flour, went to the countertop, and began sprinkling the flour over it.

The priest lifted the wooden container off the cauldron and placed it in the sink. He then lifted the lid off the container releasing a strong gust of steam. "Get the mortar."

Kieko stopped dusting the countertop with flour and went to the corner where the stone mortar sat. He took off the white cloth that covered the mortar, folded it, and placed it on the kitchen table before using his strength to tip the heavy mortar onto its side so that he could roll it toward the sink.

"Wash the inside of the mortar with a wet cloth," the priest asked when Kieko had placed the mortar by the sink.

"Yes, Master Shinsei."

The priest washed his hands and waited.

When Kieko had done what was asked of him the priest dug his hands into the sticky steamed rice, gathered it all up into an oblong ball, picked it up, and threw it into the mortar. "Get the mallet," the priest ordered before washing his hands again.

"Yes, Master Shinsei." Kieko lifted the heavy wooden mallet off the wall and gave it to the priest.

"Have you done this before?"

"Yes, Master Shinsei, when I was a very young."

"Good. Wash your hands and get a bowl of water."

Kieko washed his hands, got a bowl of water, and placed it by the mortar between his legs.

"Are you ready?"

"Yes, Master Shinsei. I'm ready," he said squatting down.

The priest raised the heavy mallet over his head and slammed it into the mortar pounding the sticky rice. He raised the mallet again while Kieko shouted and reached into the mortar to turn the rice. The priest threw the mallet down and raised it again. Kieko shouted and reached in to knead the rice before wetting his hands with the water from the bowl. The priest picked up his pace. Kieko reached into the mortar every other time the priest threw the mallet into the mortar. Soon, all that was heard in the kitchen was the slam of the mallet into the mortar and Kieko's shouts. The two continued this rhythmic cycle until the rice had become smooth and dough like.

"Do you need a break, Master Shinsei?" Kieko asked.

"No," he lifted the hammer and slammed it into the mortar again. "I do not." Kieko reached into the mortar after the priest had lifted the hammer and knead the rice. The priest threw the mallet into the mortar one last time and said, "There, it is done." He lifted the mallet and placed it in the sink.

Kieko rolled the rice into an oblong ball, picked it up, and placed it on the countertop he had dusted with flour before putting the bowl of water he had used into the sink and rolling the stone mortar back to its corner.

The priest washed his hands, dried them, dusted them with flour, and began tearing small pieces from the mound of sticky rice. Kieko joined him. Together they tore off nearly one hundred sixty pieces before flattening the pieces with their hands. When they had finished the priest went to get a bowl of the sweet bean paste that he had prepared the night before from the chamber that had a cold-water stream flowing through it. While the priest was away Kieko ate pieces of the sticky rice and remembered how delicious were his mother's mochi cakes.

The priest returned with the bowl of sweet bean paste and placed it on the countertop. The two then scooped small chunks of the paste out of the bowl and placed them onto the flattened rice pieces before placing another flattened rice piece over them. They rolled their own two pieces into a ball and then placed the finished treat on the counter before getting started on another one.

When they finished they each had made thirty-eight mochi cakes. To celebrate they each ate two.

"Your mother will be pleased."

"I hope so."

"She will be. It is late, Kieko. I will go to my chamber to meditate. Clean the kitchen, the main hall, and the dharma hall. Leave the mochi cakes ready for me in a basket for tomorrow. I will wake up very early and leave for Ikishi. Remember, you have a lot to do tomorrow. You must train with a clear mind, clean this temple with a clear mind, and work on your hut with a clear mind. And at night, when we have passed into the New Year, you must meditate with no-mind."

"Yes, Master Shinsei."

"Good night."

"Good night, Master Shinsei."

The priest left and Kieko began cleaning.

CHAPTER XIII

Kieko woke up to the piercing sound of the bekuru as the priest hit it from a rapid to slow decrescendo. He rubbed his eyes and looked at the window; the faint, grey morning light was trickling in. Sitting up he wondered how his mother had liked the mochi cakes the priest and he had made. He then thought about the work he had done on the hut while the priest was away and smiled; he was proud that he had finished more than he had expected on the hut by working out in the cold, from just after dawn until dusk, resting only to eat a mid-day meal. He was happy as well to have had the temple to himself to practice all the basic forms, and the first five long forms, in the main hall at night without worrying if the priest was watching him or not.

"Kieko! It is time to rise! Go and cook the first meal of the year!" the priest shouted.

"Yes, Master Shinsei!" he shouted back with a hoarse voice. "I will be right down." He put on a wool sweater and rushed down the steps as the frigid air bit his face and hands. He was about to grab the towel that he had left to dry on his chair, but decided that it was too cold to take a bath. He went to the door, opened it, and put on his temple shoes before rushing down the steps. As he made his way to the main hall he could hear his master chanting in his chamber; he wondered how much more he had to learn of the long chant of the *Buddha of a Thousand Eyes* before he could chant it perfectly with his master. He slid the door to the main hall open, bowed, and closed it before running across the hall and down to the kitchen chamber to begin preparing breakfast.

His mind was full of Ki sword thoughts as he cooked, and as he thought he realized that there were vast and important elements of the art that his master would probably not reveal to him for years, perhaps decades. He also felt, and knew, that his master was watching him carefully, taking note of every thing he said or did to see if he truly understood what he had been taught. *He probably knows that I did not meditate last night while he was gone . . . that I was fooling around with my sword while practicing forms. And so what? He drinks—*

"Good morning, young Kieko, and good New Year to you," Master Shinsei greeted as he walked into the kitchen taking his bowl from the shelf.

"Good–good morning, Master Shinsei," Kieko said as he settled down after having been frightened by the priest's sudden appearance.

"I scared you again. Stop thinking," the priest said as he sat down at the kitchen table. Kieko served his master his food noticing that he was agitated. "Why are you not wearing your cap?" the priest barked.

"I forgot to put it on this morning, Master Shinsei."

"Forgot to put it on? You should have put it on last night and left it on."

"Yes, Master Shinsei."

"It is a very cold morning. I gave you that cap to keep your head warm. You better not get sick again. And do not forget. Today is the third day. Shave your head before you go to sleep."

"Yes, Master Shinsei," he turned away and rolled his eyes.

"What thoughts are filling your clouded mind?"

"I'm not thinking, Master Shinsei."

"Your mind is always filled with thoughts."

Kieko hesitated.

"Out with it."

"I was . . . I was . . ."

"Out with it!"

"I was just thinking of something you had said some weeks ago."

"When? When I was drunk? That is it, isn't it?"

"Yes," he looked down, "yes, Master Shinsei."

"When I am drunk, I am drunk, and only drunk. When I train, I train, and only train. When I meditate, I meditate, and only meditate. That is the way of the Ki: drunken mind, training mind, meditating mind. The Ki mind becomes what it is in each moment and lets it go when it is done. That is what you have to learn. Your mind has too many thoughts. Always are you dreaming of fighting when there is no fight. When you clean you are thinking of Ki sword, or of more fighting, or of your mother–or of Aiko. When you cook you are remembering events in your past, wishes and wants for the future. Too many minds do you have. There is only one true and clear mind. When your mind is clear all will be revealed to you."

"Yes, Master Shinsei."

"Why are you attached to something I said when I was drunk? What was said was said and it is done. Leave it in the past and focus only on what is before you."

"Yes, Master Shinsei."

"Sit down and eat."

"Yes, Master Shinsei," he sat down and began eating.

When the priest had finished his breakfast he stood up and said, "Clean the kitchen when you are done. I'll be waiting for you outside."

"Yes, Master Shinsei."

The priest cleaned and dried his bowl and placed it on the shelf. "I'll be waiting for you," he said again and left.

Kieko threw his fists into the air and cursed silently. The priest was not in the best of moods. "The lack of sleep," he reasoned. He then calmed himself and finished his rice.

After he had cleaned the kitchen he went to his room to get his cotton woven cap and to put on some durable clothes before going outside to work on his hut.

It was raining lightly outside and a fog was rolling in from the surrounding forest. Kieko stopped, after working on his hut for a few hours, to retie the long leather straps that held his black cotton pants to his forelegs. He finished tying the straps and stomped his foot; clumps of mud fell off his leather shoe. He checked the leather sash that was wrapped around his waist and saw that his skin was cracking at the knuckles. After rubbing his arms to warm them he re-rolled the sleeves of his coarse, cotton top-gi, coughed, spat on the ground, and looked at the Kadek Temple in the growing fog.

"Come now—we do not have all day," the priest complained.

Kieko spotted the dark spires of the temple, picked up his shovel, and began digging again into the frozen earth. The priest, wearing a thick wool shawl over his robe and garments, smoked from his long pipe and simply watched from the outer edge of the rectangular ditch that Kieko was digging in.

An hour passed. "Time for tea," the priest said deciding it was time for a break. "You may continue working if you wish while I prepare it."

"Yes, Master Shinsei."

The priest picked up his staff and headed back to the temple. Kieko continued working; he lifted the frozen dirt out of the ditch, threw it into a pile, and dug some more. He then felt something, and after he had rammed the shovel back into the ground again he stopped and stood up to look into the surrounding trees. *Something isn't right.* The fog was moving gently through the forest. He turned his head. His body tensed. *There's danger in those woods.* He sniffed the air like a dog. The wind hissed. A shadow moved in the trees. *Something is preying on me.* He could feel a strong hate being shot straight into his heart. *What is this threat?* He threw down his shovel leaving his hands at his sides.

An arrow flew through the trees. He tried to react but was not fast enough—the arrow had already stabbed itself into his abdomen. "Cursed demons!" he shouted before collapsing to his knees. He looked down, held the tail end of the arrow, and snapped it off. Dark, warm blood oozed down onto his leg. He tried to move; a sharp pain surged straight up to his head. "Bastard!" he exclaimed. He clenched his teeth, reached behind his back, gripped the pointed end of the broken arrow, and pulled it out. Screaming with horrific pain he punched the ground repeatedly. "Where are you devil!" he shouted before seeing a shadow deep in the forest move. He threw the arrow away; rage now flowed through his every vein. He picked up the shovel and ran toward the shadow howling. Another arrow was shot at him; he swatted it away with the shovel and ran faster at the shadow. The shadow nocked another arrow. He raised the shovel over his head, "You will die!" The shadow threw down its bow. He made his strike, but the shadow blocked it with a staff it had shot up from the ground with its foot. He rounded the shovel for another strike. The shadow twirled the staff and attacked. "Curses!" he cursed when the staff had slammed into his forearm. The shadow swung the staff up. He moved out of the path of the staff, crouched, and launched the shovel straight up into the shadow's jaw. The shadow flew back and crashed onto the ground. He ran up to the shadow and slammed his foot into the shadow's chest. "Who are you?" he demanded pointing the sharp end of the shovel at its masked face. "Take off the mask!" He slammed the shovel into the wooden mask. "Take it off or I'll smash the mask into your face!"

The shadow did nothing.

"Take it off!" he slammed his shovel again into the wooden mask.

The shadow, now shaking, brought its nervous hands to its face and took off the mask.

"Aiko!" he cried in disbelief. "You cursed–I will kill you!" He raised the shovel high above his head.

Aiko looked at Kieko horrified and shut his eyes waiting for his death. But . . . nothing happened. He opened his eyes and saw that the priest was holding Kieko's shovel back.

"Give it to me!" the priest demanded.

"No!" Kieko contested.

The priest tore the shovel out of Kieko's hands.

"No!" he shouted again. "No, no, no!" He collapsed to his knees grabbing his wound and mumbled, "you bastard," as pain returned and flooded his senses.

"Never have I seen such wickedness between two boys!" the priest shouted as he stood over them. "You can be tried by the Council for this!" He threw the shovel down. "I have had enough of this mongering between you two. Enough, I say! Kieko!"

"Yes-s, Master Shinsei?"

"Invite Aiko in for tea."

"What?" he questioned with hateful, confused eyes.

"Do as I say!" the priest barked back.

Kieko looked down and whispered with bitter lips, "Stupid old man—"

"Do not try me, boy!" the priest stabbed his fingers into Kieko's back. "Do not try me!"

Aiko snickered.

The priest backhanded Aiko hard across the face. Aiko tasted blood in his mouth. "Don't even look at me!" the priest hollered. "Your father sickens me, he sickens me! Your mother is dead. And what? Kieko's father is dead. My father is dead. Everyone has lost! Everyone! But you—you and your father think that you have suffered more than most; that you are above others because of your wealth. You are nothing, Aiko. Your father and you are less than nothing to me."

Aiko looked at the priest.

"The two of you," he shook his head, "what am I to do with the two of you? I am tired—I am tired of all of this." He paused, inhaled deeply, and finished, "Kieko—I will not say this again—invite Aiko in for tea."

"Yes . . . yes, Master . . . Shinsei," he said in complete defeat.

The priest turned and walked through the fog back to the temple.

Kieko tightened his fists. He wanted to slam his foot into Aiko's face breaking his nose and ramming its broken bits into his head. He wanted to finish him, *finish him*. He thought about what the priest had said to Aiko and took in a deep breath before exhaling heavily. He slowly stood up while holding his wound and spat on the ground, "Come with me, you filth," and limped back to the temple.

Aiko, feeling as if he had just run for half the day, wiped his face and exhaled a dark heavy breath. He then stood up and followed after Kieko keeping the distance between them great.

Kieko limped through the fog wishing that his master had not stopped him. *I could have finished him off.* For a moment he imagined what his life would have been like if his wish had come true. He thought of the true repercussions of such an act; he would have been banished for his crime, his mother, alone, would have no one to protect her. *She would be raped again.* He held his wound tighter. He passed through the temple's tori gate—Aiko followed—walked up to the stone water basin, picked up the wooden ladle that was resting on one of the basin's sides, and filled it with water. He drank. Aiko stopped and waited by the tori gate. He placed the ladle down and continued to the temple's main entrance door. Arriving at the door he slid it open, took off his shoes, and entered waiting for Aiko.

Aiko walked up the steps to the temple door.

"Take off your shoes."

Aiko approached the door pretending not to have heard what was asked of him.

"I said take off your shoes."

"I know!" he growled. "Go on in, Akai."

Kieko punched him in the face.

Aiko fell to the ground and looked up holding his mouth and cheek. Kieko was gone. He stood up, took off his shoes, walked in, slid the door closed behind him, and slid the next door open; it was the first time he had ever been inside the temple. "Follow me," he heard Kieko say from the next room. He followed while looking at all the scrolls that were hanging on the walls. Kieko slid another door open. He looked in and could not believe what he saw.

"This is the Great Hall of the Buddha," Kieko explained. "You must bow before entering it."

"I already know that—I live in a temple."

Kieko ignored him and continued into the main hall.

Aiko took a moment to marvel at the beauty of the golden Buddha statue. He bowed and cautiously walked into the main hall looking at the pillars of zabutons and the long calligraphy paintings that were hanging from the high ceiling amazed at how clean the hall was kept. He heard faint swooping sounds above and looked up to see bats flying high up through the air.

"I'm going to have to clean that up," Kieko said to himself realizing that he was tracking blood across the floor. He stopped in the middle of the hall and motioned for Aiko to bow with him. He bowed; Aiko did as well, which surprised him. He then led Aiko to the altar and whispered, "You must do as I do."

"I will not, Akai—"

"Be quiet. Master Shinsei is watching us."

Aiko looked around the hall trying to find the priest. Kieko held his hands together and kneeled. Aiko simply stood and watched as Kieko placed his hands and forehead on the floor and turned his palms up.

Kieko grimaced in pain for a moment before sitting on his knees again and standing back up; he gave two more full-bows. After the last bow he stood up cringing from a sharp pain that was now shooting up into his chest causing him to hold his wound tighter. He signaled to Aiko to do as he had done.

Aiko gave three full-bows fearful of what the priest might do to him if he did not. When he finished Kieko approached the altar, bowed, rang the shrine bell three times, and lit three incense sticks before placing them into a ceramic bowl filled with ash. He bowed again, took three steps back, and bowed one last time.

They exited the main hall and descended the spiral staircase into the temple underground. Aiko peered fearfully into each chamber that they passed as they walked down the tunnel that led to the kitchen chamber; he saw the flickering candlelights bring to life the faces of the statue gods and goddess that had been carved out of the bedrock. He was afraid of this place, but then he smelled the aroma of boiling soup.

"This is the kitchen," Kieko said.

"Really?" Aiko replied sarcastically.

"To hell with you."

"Kieko!" the priest shouted. "Kieko and Aiko. Both of you, quiet!"

The two cowered before the priest.

"Kieko, sit down over there and take off your shirt. After I am done with you I want you to go to the hall and wipe up all the blood you spilled."

"Yes, Master Shinsei," Kieko answered with bitter lips.

"Watch yourself," the priest warned.

"Yes, Master Shinsei," he said again before sitting down and taking off his shirt.

The priest finished cutting some carrots and threw them into a small cauldron of boiling water that was hanging over the fireplace. He then took a ceramic mug of hot tea and gave it to Kieko, "Drink from it." Kieko drank. He reached over and took a cloth and a jar of oil from the kitchen table. "This will hurt." He soaked the cloth into the jar and wiped it over Kieko's wound. Kieko hissed in pain. The priest, now seated, pressed his thumb into the wound. Kieko clenched his teeth and grabbed the arms of the chair he was sitting in trying to resist the pain. "There is nothing in there. You took the arrow clean out. Aiko, come over here and put some pressure on your brother's wound."

"He's not my brother."

The priest flew out of his seat and struck Aiko across the face with the back of his hand. Aiko fell to the ground and looked up at the priest's furious eyes. "Get up and help your brother!" the priest demanded.

Aiko gathered himself.

"Get up, now!"

Aiko stood up and dragged himself over to Kieko.

"Good. The two of you fools have a lot to learn." He shook his head whispering the word "fools" again.

"I heard what you said," Aiko spat out.

"Fools are what the two of you are!" the priest hollered stabbing his fingers into Aiko. "Don't you ever disrespect me. What in the name of Mount Kadek were you trying to do? I don't understand you. Trying to kill him? I can take you to the Council and have you banished for even thinking it, and there is nothing that you father would be able to do to prevent it. Now shut your mouth and put some pressure on your brother's wound."

"Yes," he nodded.

"I am Shinsei to you!"

"Yes . . . Shinsei."

Aiko took the cloth from the priest and pressed it against Kieko's wound. The priest took more cloth from the kitchen table and cut it into long strips. When he was done he went to the fireplace and pulled out a red-hot poker.

"What–what are you going to do with that, Master Shinsei?" Kieko asked in fear.

"I have to cauterize your wound."

Both Aiko's and Kieko's eyes bulged.

"It will be fast–it must be done to prevent infection." He pulled out his short wooden sword from within his robe and gave it to Kieko, "Bite down on this."

Kieko took the short sword and put it in his mouth.

"Let us be swift. Aiko, hold him down."

Aiko held Kieko down by the shoulders.

"Close your eyes," the priest advised.

Kieko closed his eyes; he could hear the hissing sound of the hot poker getting closer. The priest pressed the poker against Kieko's wound. Kieko screamed between his teeth and jerked and moved with incredible pain.

"Hold him down!" the priest shouted.

"I'm trying!" Aiko shouted back.

The priest whipped the poker back. Kieko collapsed in his seat; the wooden sword fell from his mouth; his burnt flesh filled the air.

"We must do the other side—Aiko, lift him and turn him around."

"What?"

"Lift him up and turn him around! Be quick, be quick!"

He lifted Kieko up from his seat and turned him so that his back was facing the priest.

"Hold him," the priest commanded just before he pressed the poker against the wound. Kieko shouted and cursed again spraying spit and drool. The priest finished. Aiko fell with Kieko's exhausted body to the floor. "Lift him up and place him over there," the priest pointed to the smooth groove in the bedrock that was covered with pillows.

Aiko lifted Kieko, dragged him to the spot, and laid him on the pillows noticing that his eyes were moving aimlessly in a half sleep. "Is he all right?"

"He will be fine. He is exhausted and needs to rest. We must dress his wound, Aiko. Lift him up so that I can roll this around his waist."

Aiko lifted him up again. The priest rolled several strips of cloth around his waist. When he was done he placed a blanket over Kieko and returned to the cutting board. Aiko sat still at the kitchen table and watched the priest in silence.

After making dinner the priest placed several bowls of food on the kitchen table and motioned for Aiko to begin eating. He approached Kieko and, standing beside him, raised his arms and moved his fingers as if he was trying to tickle the air. Aiko watched and wondered what the priest was doing. The priest then lowered his fingers and pointed them at Kieko as he exhaled a long heavy breath.

"It burns . . . it burns," Kieko whispered as he moved his head from side to side.

"What—what are you doing?" Aiko asked.

"Silence."

"What . . . is . . . that?" Kieko whispered.

"What you feel is the Ki. It will heal you."

"It burns."

"Heat is life."

Kieko moaned trying to resist the heat of the Ki.

The priest turned to Aiko, "Your training begins today. The two of you will train together."

"What!" Kieko exclaimed.

"Be quiet and rest!"

Kieko resisted, "I'm . . . I'm not going to–"

"Silence!" the priest thundered.

The two boys were both quiet.

"Aiko, go back to your home and get your things. Do not tell your father. I will deal with him tomorrow. When you return clean the dharma room floor. You will sleep with Kieko in his room until the two of you complete the hut within the forest."

"When should I go?" he asked relieved that he would be living under the priest's protection.

"Now."

"Yes, Shinsei." And as he was about to exit the kitchen he paused and asked, "Where is the dharma room?"

"I'll show you when you return. Now go."

"Yes, Shinsei," he said again.

"Come back here!" the priest commanded.

"What?"

"You will address me as Master Shinsei from this point forth. You must always give me three full-bows before leaving the temple grounds."

"Yes . . . yes, Master Shinsei." He gave three full-bows and left.

The priest continued transmitting Ki into Kieko who moved uncomfortably and said, "I . . . I had to . . . I had to answer your koan," he coughed, "to begin my . . . my training—and, and, and Aiko shoots to kill me with an arrow—and now he can begin training?"

"Aiko mirrors your anger. Through him you will see you. He will be a great teacher for you."

"I . . . I don't understand . . . Master—"

"Rest, Kieko. Rest." He shook his hands and wiped them down as if he was drying them with a cloth.

"What are you doing?"

"I am ridding myself of excess Ki."

"Yes, yes . . . that is right . . . that is right . . ."

"There, I am done. Now, rest. I will be just here eating."

"Yes . . .yes, Master Shinsei."

The priest sat down at the kitchen table, prayed, and began eating his hot vegetable and noodle soup. *He heals faster than his father*, he thought. "Must be his youth," he mumbled.

When he finished his meal he cleaned his bowls, made some tea, and sat down again to keep an eye on Kieko who was sleeping deeply.

An hour passed before Kieko woke up. "You . . . you are still here," he said with a tired voice when he saw the priest.

"Yes, of course I am here."

"That is good . . . that is good," he said feeling as if he was still dreaming.

The priest spoke: "You said to me once, Kieko, that you feared attachment. You have a great attachment to anger. What are you hiding behind your anger? Be honest—tell me about your Kira."

"She . . . she is not mine to . . . to talk about."

"In her heart she is yours."

He began shaking, "I . . . I like the way I feel when I'm with her . . . but . . . but, I can't tell her how . . . tell her how I feel.

Sometimes I want to . . . but I can't. She is . . . she is very kind to me. I care for her . . . but . . . but I can't tell her that. I hate myself for that. I . . . I don't understand why . . . why I can't speak to her . . . and I hate myself for that."

The priest smiled and said, "When you learn to leave your anger behind you will learn to speak from here," he pointed to his heart. "Until then you will continue to fill your mind with anger, like Aiko. Aiko is a mirror for you and you are a mirror for him. Learn from him and be compassionate. Remember, he has no mother."

"Yes . . . yes, Master Shinsei," he said and fell back asleep.

The priest turned and looked at the flame from the candle that was standing at the center of the table and became utterly absorbed by it. The world began to fade. He felt his mind clear, but then thoughts and memories of his past flooded his mind. He shook his head and wiped his eyes before standing up to begin sweeping the kitchen floor.

OF THE KI FORMS

Yes, we see that you are most interested in the Ki forms. You are no different from any boy or man, we should say. That was our joke, hee hee hee.

Why is it that men and boys share such a deep interest in the instruments and arts that bring destruction? Is it this masculine side that you speak of? We know all too well that that is the riddle, which plagues your mind. You have sought to discover what it means to be a man in this world. Well, we are very happy to say that you have already found the answer, and that you are doing well in bringing both yourselves together. By that we mean you have addressed and recognized that feminine aspect within you. Yes, that is the goal. That is the way. A man should not, so much, seek to be only a man; and a woman should not, so much, seek to be only a woman. You are human, and you should seek to be so by recognizing and accepting your duality. That is the true human organism. That is the true nature of the spirit. The spirit is neither masculine nor feminine, but both, living in unison, flowing into and out of each other.

There is power in the unmoving rock that sits in a stream, and there is power in the water that flows around the rock, slowly carving it away into nothing. A man must discover the feminine, and a woman must discover the masculine. That is the path of the true human being.

The Ki forms were a wonderful representation of this beautiful dance between the aggressive and passive forces that define us. That was why the Ki martial way was an art. The Ki martial arts were a dance between defensive and aggressive forces. We are not particularly attracted to this type of dance, but we can appreciate it. Actually we had fallen in love once with a Ki priest who performed his forms with such grace that it excited us when we gazed at him practice by the river. That was so long ago, yes. He was so beautiful and kind. We would give anything to relive those moments with him. Oops—attached are we becoming? No, we are not.

We must move on. Look at us. We are sorry to diddle dally into one of our own personal stories. It is better that we remain unattached to things in our past that will never come again. Of course, we should never say never, now shall we?

Well, yes, getting back to the Ki forms. You see the Ki forms are a perfect representation of the balance to be sought between the aggressive and passive forces of the material world. The movements are always moving into and out of balance to find balance. When the movements are reaching far into the yang they will then fall quickly into the yin. If an attack is made then a defense must balance it, and so on, you could say.

We do not want to speak more of this. How about trees and flowers? No, you say. Fine, so be it. The philosophy of the Lemurian Ki permeates the forms, from beginning to end. In the beginning, there is nothing, then there is one, and from one there is two, and from two the many; and back again to two, then to one, then to nothing. Like a musical composition there is silence before the piece is played, then the first note, then the many notes, then the last note, and then the silence again. It is simply like life. There is nothing, then there is life, then there is death, and then there is nothing. This is the cycle of all things in this world of the material.

The Ki forms trained the Ki disciple to maintain himself in the here and now. This is the way of your Zen masters, in your world, today. All that there is to have is before you only here and now. All that you were, and all that you had in the past, is no more. All that you will become and gain in the future is not here. All you have is here and now and nothing more. This is the truth that so many fail to see. Those who are not blind to this truth, you will find, are the most compassionate living beings. They are not afraid of death.

We believe these were the words of an old adversary of yours who once said, "It is when we avoid death that we refuse to live." No farther was he from the truth. Yes, you are correct, that old enemy was from the lands north of the White City.

But, do not think that finding this truth could only be gained through the Ki forms. No, please do not think that. We beg that you do not see it that way. Every moment, and everything that you do, is an opportunity to live in the here and now. As you would say in your words, and in your world, cooking is Zen, playing music is Zen, cleaning the toilet is Zen, making love is Zen. Every moment is Zen; a chance to be living in the now, and in the now only, with no desire or thought for the past or future. And that is all we will say about that.

CHAPTER XIV

Aiko woke up to the distant percussive knocks of the priest's bekuru. "What the hell is that?" he asked rubbing his eyes.

"It's time to get up," Kieko answered from his lofted futon.

"What time is it?"

"Time to get up—come on, we got to go," he rose from his futon, "aggh," he cringed from a sharp pain that had shot up to his chest.

Aiko, annoyed, shook his head at Kieko.

Kieko put his hand over his wound and crawled to the edge of his lofted futon to look down at Aiko who had slept the entire night on the hard wood floors. "Sleep well?"

"Considering that I didn't have a futon to sleep on, no."

"Poor, poor baby."

"To hell with you, Akai," he glared.

"Just get up."

"Akai bastard," he said under his breath as he stood up. "It's cold."

Kieko descended the steps and walked past Aiko who was stretching his arms and legs. "The gods, I'm tired of this," he muttered as he searched through a small stack of folded clothes. He found a pair of black pants, a brown top-gi, and threw them at Aiko, "There, put those on."

"Come down!" the priest shouted.

With haste they put on their pants.

"Come down, now!" the priest shouted again.

Kieko jumped to the door and slid it open.

"Get down here, immediately!"

Together they rushed down the steps and stood before the priest. Kieko then gave his master three full bows. Aiko did not.

"Bow to me."

Aiko carelessly gave one full bow to the priest.

"Do it again!"

He shrugged his shoulders and gave another full bow.

"Two more!" the priest shouted stabbing his fingers into Aiko's chest.

Aiko clenched his teeth and gave two full bows to the priest. Kieko shook his head; he knew that the day was already off to a horrible start.

"How does your wound feel?" the priest asked Kieko.

Kieko felt the bandages over the wound and applied a bit of pressure feeling a strong pain, "It hurts, but I feel fine, Master Shinsei."

"You feel fine–good." He turned away and said, "Come with me."

In silence they followed the priest to the main hall.

They each bowed after entering the hall and approached a stack of zabutons. The priest took three zabutons: one for himself and the other two he passed to Kieko and Aiko. He then walked to the center of the hall, placed his zabuton on the floor, and waited for his two disciples to take their places at his sides just behind him so that they could begin by giving thirty-three full-bows to the golden Buddha statue.

After finishing the bowing ritual Kieko sat down, as did Aiko. The priest bowed and approached the altar. He bowed again and lit three incense sticks before taking the bekuru and mallet from the altar. He bowed again, walked back to his zabuton, faced the altar, bowed, and sat down. Aiko rolled his eyes at the priest's constant bowing.

The priest bowed again and began knocking on the bekuru. Kieko bowed after his master; Aiko did not. "Bow!" the priest demanded of Aiko. Aiko bowed. The priest began the chant of the *Buddha of a Thousand Eyes*:

shin go-on shin-on

su-ri su-ri ma-ha-su-ri su-su-ri sa-pa-ha-ri

o-ban-na-ho an-u-shi-shin-jin-no

na-mo sa-man-da mo-ta-na

o-do-ro do-ro shi-mi sa-ba-ha

o-do-ro do-ro shi-mi sa-ba-ha

o-do-ro do-ro shi-mi sa-ba-ha

ke-gu-gu

me-shi shi-shi mi-mo-bo

be-chu ma-go na-jo-o

a-go mo-go do-su-shi

hon-ha yo-ra shin-shi-o

gab bo-cho shin-no

om a-ra-na a-ra-da

na-mo de-bi kon-se-om   won-a su-ki iru-shi-bu

na-mo de-bi kon-se-om   won-a ju-do shi-he-an

na-mo de-bi kon-se-om   won-a shi-do iru-chi-ju

na-mo de-bi kon-se-om   won-a so-do ban-yan-son

na-mo de-bi kon-se-om   won-a do-ko ban-rom-sai . . .

Kieko still did not know the chant in its entirety, but he followed its rhythmic pulse and knew when to bow with his master during the breaks within the chant. Aiko, tired and bored, did not try to anticipate when to bow.

. . . o-shi jun-riku-ri-do

o-shin ri-ho-no-ri

o-gun di-ro-hi-ro

om-a-ra no-ra-do

na-mo de-bi kon-se-om	*won-a su-ki iru-shi-bu*
na-mo de-bi kon-se-om	*won-a ju-do shi-he-an*
na-mo de-bi kon-se-om	*won-a shi-do iru-chi-ju*
na-mo de-bi kon-se-om	*won-a so-do ban-yan-son*
na-mo de-bi kon-se-om	*won-a do-ko ban-rom-sai.*

The priest and Kieko bowed slowly to the decrescendo of the bekuru. Aiko was relieved that the chant had finally ended. They all rose, bowed to the Buddha, and returned their zabutons.

"Now it is time to train," the priest declared. "Kieko, take Aiko to the weapons chamber and pick out a wooden sword for him. And do not forget to get yours."

"Yes, Master Shinsei."

Kieko led Aiko to the antechamber with a candle he took from the altar and began feeling one of the walls with his fingers.

"Are you trying to excite it?" Aiko joked.

Ignoring the comment he kept feeling, searching. He then found it. He pressed his fingers into a groove between two stones and stood back. Rusted iron gears began to sound and move. A door appeared within the wall and receded creating a pathway.

"How far back does it go?" Aiko asked not enjoying the sound of stone grinding against stone.

Kieko ignored the question.

"Fool," he whispered. He heard a heavy thud.

Kieko walked into the pathway. Aiko followed.

The air within the weapons chamber was dry and cool. Aiko rubbed his arms and looked with unbelieving eyes at the incredible number of wooden swords that were racked on every wall. "How many swords does he have?" he asked.

"These are not his swords."

"Whose are they then?"

"They are the practice swords of all the Ki priests and priestesses that have ever lived within the Kadek Temple."

"How many swords are there?"

"I don't know. There are more behind those locked doors."

"Real swords?"

"I believe so."

"Real blades—weapons—that had belong to Ki priests?"

"Yes . . . I think so."

"Why weren't they buried with their masters?"

"That has never been a Ki tradition," Kieko corrected. "Ki priests and priestesses have never been buried with their swords. That is only the tradition of the Atlantean Kai, and the armies of our Queen and her royal family."

"I thought Ki priests were buried with their swords."

"Why would you think that? A Ki priest would never take such an instrument to the afterlife." He looked at one of the racks, "Let me find you a sword—Master Shinsei is waiting." He held his candle higher and searched.

"All those swords are scarred and splintered," Aiko commented. "They're better off feeding a fire."

"Here we are—this should do nicely," Kieko said pleased with his find.

"Let me see," Aiko snatched the sword from Kieko's hand. "Kadek!" he exclaimed. "This sword just gave me a splinter!"

"Well, if you didn't just grab it out of my hand—"

"Shut up—you gave me this cursed sword to stick a splinter in me."

"Then you choose," he smirked pointing to the swords.

"Fine then."

Aiko took the candle from Kieko and looked at the racked swords. He found one, picked it up, and felt its weight and balance. Not satisfied he placed the sword back and kept looking. He found another that pleased his eye and swung it several times. "This one will do—and it has no splinters. It's as good as new."

"Good, let's go." He took the candle back and led the way out of the weapons chamber.

"What took so long!" the priest demanded when they returned.

"I'm sorry, Master Shinsei," Kieko apologized.

"Come here, now!"

They approached the priest.

"Kieko, stand by my side. We will do the first form together. Aiko, pay attention, this is what you are about to learn."

Kieko stepped up to his master's side and realized that he had forgotten to get his wooden sword from his room.

"Let us—Where is your sword?"

"In my room, Master Shinsei."

"The gods. Go up and get it!"

"Yes, Master Shinsei," he rushed out of the main hall.

Aiko snickered.

"Shut that mouth of yours before I cut it off!" the priest threatened.

Aiko was now beginning to realize that the priest was not the calm man he had grown to know as a child.

"Give thirty-three full-bows to the Buddha," the priest ordered.

Aiko's face tensed.

"Thirty-three full-bows!"

"Yes, Master Shinsei," he began bowing.

When he was done Kieko had returned with his wooden sword and ran up to stand beside the priest.

"Let us warm up."

"Yes, Master Shinsei."

Together they placed their swords on the floor, spread their legs, lowered their upper bodies, raised their hands to the Buddha, and shouted, "Ki!" before flinging their fists back to their waists. They raised their hands again and chanted in the old tongue, "Takana-Do-Ki-Kami-Do-Ki-Atama-Do-Ki-Kokoro-Do!" while moving their hands rapidly up and down between each word. When they finished they brought their legs together, held their clasped hands before their hearts, and bowed.

They picked up their swords, held them perpendicular to the floor and before their chests, and bowed. The priest shouted; swiftly they both took a step back—Kieko cringed after feeling a sharp pain shoot up his body from his wound—and swung their swords at an angle to their left sides to defend their heads and chests. With the second shout they stepped back again—Kieko ignored the pain he felt from his wound—swinging their block to their right sides. They continued retreating, and then they advanced using the same defensive sword technique. The priest accented his last shout and together they drew out their wooden swords from their imaginary scabbards and pointed the swords before them in a straight line—Kieko clenched his jaw tight trying to bite down on the pain. They then stepped back and defended by swinging their swords from one side to the other before advancing with the same technique.

The priest and Kieko went through all the basic forms while Aiko simply watched analyzing their techniques and stances. They finished, sheathed their swords, and bowed.

"True Form One!"

"Yes, Master Shinsei," Kieko replied with a firm, but pained voice.

The priest and Kieko extended their swords out before their bodies and bowed before stepping and leaning the upper part of their bodies to their right sides. They drew their swords out from their imaginary scabbards in a line that ran from their chests to the crown of their heads. Aiko could see that the technique was meant to block an immediate strike to the head. The priest and Kieko swung their swords before them beheading their fictional foes and defended their left sides. They then jumped and swung their swords down cutting the space below them. Aiko was impressed with how high Kieko could jump. They landed and guarded their right sides before lifting the hilt of their swords to the left side of their faces; Kieko's body, especially his arms, began to tense heavily from the pain. They whipped their swords out severing the necks of their imagined enemies before turning around to defend their right legs. They attacked, advanced, withdrew, and defended. When the last of their fictional foes had been slaughtered they sheathed their swords, held their swords before their chests, and bowed.

"That is True Form One," the priest said aloud to Aiko. "Kieko will teach it to you since I know that your father has already taught you the basic forms of Ki sword. I will return to my chamber to do my morning chant. You will respect, Kieko. He is elder than you in the Ki forms. You must bow to him before learning what he is to teach you."

Aiko looked at the priest with hardened eyes. The priest glared at him. He cowered, "Yes, Master Shinsei." He went before Kieko, and bowed.

"You must ask him to teach you," the priest explained.

Aiko took in a long, tired breath, and passively said, "Please, teach me."

"Good," he walked away and exited the main hall.

"Let's get this over with," Kieko said as he bit down on his lip trying to ignore the pain that continued to shoot up from his wound.

Aiko sneered.

Kieko began teaching the true form by explaining the purpose of the first few movements and sword techniques. Aiko, not interested, just looked around the hall. As a result, he asked Aiko to perform the techniques he had just taught him and discovered that he already knew most of what he was demonstrating. Feeling a bit like a fool he continued teaching the sequence of movements while Aiko stood and yawned. When he was done he asked Aiko to perform the true form in its entirety.

Aiko patted his mouth and easily went through the true form. "How was that?" he asked with a grin when he finished.

"Yes, that was good . . . good," he nodded trying to hide how impressed he was with how Aiko wielded his wooden sword. "We should practice the form together. I often have to practice with Master Shinsei side by side trying to mirror him exactly as if we were one."

"Can you handle that?" he asked referring to the pain Kieko was suffering from.

"Yes, yes I can handle it," he answered looking down trying not to show through his eyes and facial expressions just how much pain he really was experiencing.

"All right then."

They lined up next to each other and began almost simultaneously, and when they finished they performed the long form again and again.

The priest was watching them as they ran through the first true form from the shadows of the main hall. He ran his fingers through his beard as he analyzed their movements and saw that although they did not perform the form in perfect unison there was much power in their movements, and a vengeful pride between them. He could see Kieko moving through certain sequences within the form faster than Aiko or Aiko adding a strike or kick to show off his strength and agility. At times, he could see that Kieko was suffering severely from the pain shooting out from his wound, but he could also see that he was strong and able to take the pain. And when he had seen enough of the two he exited the main hall unnoticed by either Kieko or Aiko.

CHAPTER XV

The next morning, over breakfast, the priest explained to Kieko and Aiko that he was going to Ikishi for the day; he had also asked Kieko to teach Aiko how to clean the kitchen, the floors of the main hall and the dharma hall, the altars, and the bathroom; and that they meditate and practice the first true form together in the afternoon. When he finished eating he got up to clean his bowls and cup, said goodbye to his two disciples, and went up to his chamber to fetch his staff and to put on his heavy wool robe.

At the entrance door he put on his leather boots and slid the door open; the brisk air rushed in causing his body to shudder. He put on his old straw hat and looked at the garden, which was covered by a thin sheet of fresh snow, and at the tori gate and at the surrounding bare trees; he smiled at how the snow made everything so peaceful and serene. He walked down the path that divided the garden and stopped just before the tori gate to pull out his pipe. Taking a deep breath he closed his hand and concentrated on it with his eyes for only a moment before opening it to reveal a small flame. He inserted the tip of his index finger into the opening of his pipe, puffed on the pipe, and smoked from it before shaking his hand to extinguish the flame. A small, grey bird landed at the top of the tori gate. "Hello my friend," he greeted looking up at her. The bird chirped. "Shouldn't you be far south of here?" The bird looked at him curiously and flew away. "Perhaps you still have just a bit of time left," he cracked a smile and walked through the tori gate making his way toward Ikishi.

Not minding the cold he walked the entire morning looking at all the thin lines of snow that covered the branches of the trees while listening to his own footsteps. He saw a rabbit dart from one tree to another and the grey bird he had seen earlier fly from one tree branch to another. "Following me?" he asked the bird. The bird, standing on a high tree branch, looked at him and turned her head awkwardly. "Funny little thing you are." The bird flew up again searching for the next tree branch to land on. The priest smiled and continued walking between trees and over hills.

By early afternoon he was walking within the sharp valley that led to Ikishi and the sea and admired the distant rocky cliffs and the birds hovering above them. The path he was on then split in two and he chose the route leading to the House of Kono.

He followed the path through a small forest and up a hill. As he ascended he saw, in the distance, a thin line of smoke rising into the cloudy sky and knew that Kono was at home cooking his midday meal. When he reached the top of the hill he looked down and saw the temple that Kono called home; it was a prestigious, but small, temple built on stilts. Behind the temple he could see a barn and several of his prided cows huddled together within a large, fenced pasture. He walked down the hill toward a small tori gate. When he reached the gate he bowed, walked through it, and approached a small, stone water basin. He lifted a bamboo ladle from the basin, filled it with water, and drank from it. "Welcome, priest!" he heard someone shout. Not alarmed he put the ladle down and turned to see Kono standing on his porch with his arms crossed over his chest and his long sword tucked into the folds of his belt.

"What are you doing here?" Kono demanded.

"Where is your son?" the priest asked as he approached Kono.

"You should know, priest."

He saw Kono's hand tighten around the hilt of his sword. "Then you admit that you had sent him."

"You should leave, priest, before I strike you."

"I did not come here to fight you. I came here to tell you that Aiko is now under my guidance."

"To hell he will study with the Akai!" he drew out his sword. "Send him back to me."

"I will not. I will not have you beat and fill him with your hate."

"You send him to me or I will strike you—"

"Stand back!" Shinsei flew into the air and landed before Kono on his porch whipping his staff at his face, "You cursed disease!"

Kono—shocked by the priest's speed—took a step back.

"Your boy will stay with me or I will have you brought before the Council!"

Kono knocked the priest's staff from his face and swung his sword at him. The priest leaned back allowing the sword to swing past his chest before flinging the bottom end of his staff at Kono's face. Kono blocked the strike with his forearm, but the blow threw him back and down when he lost his balance causing him to drop his sword. Swiftly the priest stood over him pointing his staff straight at his face again, "You listen to me!" Kono looked up at the priest and saw that his face was now red with fury. "Your boy stays with me! He stays! And if you even attempt to approach the Kadek Temple I will strike you down and bring your crippled body before the Council to be tried for seeking vengeance upon Kieko through your own son!"

Kono looked at the floorboards while massaging his forearm; from the corner of his eye he could see that his sword was just within reach. "You lie, priest. You would do no such thing." He then snapped his leg at Shinsei—who jumped—and grabbed his sword. The priest landed and shot his staff down at Kono who blocked the strike with his sword and snapped his body up to his feet. The priest struck him across the face with his staff. Kono, after taking the hit, stepped back and then charged at the priest. The priest back flipped off the porch and landed on the ground. Kono dived at the priest. The priest jumped back. Kono landed and sprang at the priest again violently screaming and slashing. The priest blocked every strike with his staff. The air filled with the *cling, clang, cling* of sword against staff as Kono kept striking hoping to tear the staff to pieces. "What is the cursed thing made of?" he spat frustrated that he could not even stab a single mark into it. In that moment the priest swung low, caught Kono's legs, and tripped him, causing him to fall hard to the ground, and slammed his staff down smashing Kono's chest. Kono heaved an airless cough. He could not breathe. He panicked and writhed trying desperately to crawl away from the priest.

The priest watched Kono squirm away like a worm.

Kono coughed, grabbed his throat, and gasped for air.

"Crawl back to your hole, Kono. Be gone from my sight. Your boy stays with me until his training is complete."

"Curse . . . curse you, priest," he spat, "curse you."

"Hold your tongue!"

"Curse you—curse you . . . your days are numbered," he spat again, "mark my words."

The priest stared at him with threatening eyes not saying a word.

"Go, priest, go," he coughed violently, "go and train that Akai . . . go train that wicked filth for I know my son will defeat him when the time is right . . . he will defeat him . . . he will defeat him! He will defeat him!"

"Soon comes the day when your son will join with the Kai boy and defeat you."

"Lies! Lies, you speak, priest. Lies!"

"Lies they are not. Let this be a warning, Kono," he turned and walked away.

"Liar!" Kono screamed fidgeting on the ground. "You lie! My son will never betray me!"

The priest continued walking, but shouted back, "It is not he who has betrayed—coward."

"Curse you, priest! Curse you," he spat. "Then go back to my son. My son! And tell him that he is to wed Kira before spring!"

The priest stopped.

"That's right—that's right, you old fool. My son is to marry Kira. You tell my son that. And tell that filthy Akai—tell that Akai boy that I forbid him from even looking at her! Tell him that! Tell him!" he laughed.

"Goodbye, Kono," he walked through the tori gate and up the hill ignoring Kono's unending spiral of curses and words.

CHAPTER XVI

The priest looked at his two disciples as he stood before them in the main hall with bare feet on the cold floor. He approached them and heard a bat swoop high above him; it was night, an hour after dinner. "Stand in the opening position."

Kieko and Aiko extended their wooden swords out before their chests.

"The weapon," the priest began, "that you are holding vertical to the Mother covers all your vital parts: the head, the heart, the stomach, the groin. This is symbolic. The sword represents the unborn child that is one with both mind and body." He bowed; Kieko and Aiko bowed back. "When you bow you are lowering your head, you are, in essence, preparing for birth–Ka!"

Kieko and Aiko instantly, although not in unison, stepped forward blocking the left side of their bodies with their swords.

"This is birth–Ka!" he shouted again.

They drew out their swords from their imaginary scabbards and held their swords straight out before them.

"The child has opened his eyes–Ka!"

Kieko and Aiko squatted down holding their swords vertical to the ground.

"The tips of your swords point up to the heavens. The hilts of your swords point down to the Mother. Perfection. The roots and dreams of the child are one–Ka!"

Kieko and Aiko defended their right and then left sides.

"The child asks, 'Am I man or woman?' Ka!"

The two stood up and defended their right and left sides again.

"The child becomes an adult and sees that he is both man and woman, both the shin and the shang–Ka!"

They stepped forward and swung their swords down in two motions to defend both sides of their right legs.

"The adult has reached down to help a person in need–Ka!"

They raised their swords up to defend the crowns of their heads; Kieko performed the move faster than Aiko.

"Together!" the priest shouted before explaining: "The adult has lifted up this person in need–Ka!"

Aiko launched his sword into a neck attack faster than Kieko.

"Together!" the priest shouted again. "And sends him on the path–Ka!"

The priest continued explaining the meaning of each movement as Kieko and Aiko continued through the basic motions of Ki sword. Finally the two performed the last basic motion by moving their swords from a left defensive stance into a stab attack in which their swords were pointed in a straight line before them. "The last basic motion," the priest explained, "is Enlightenment. Ka!"

Kieko and Aiko brought their feet together, sheathed their swords in their imaginary scabbards, bowed, and stood before the priest.

The priest approached the boys, "You know the basic motions of the sword forms." He ran his fingers through his beard. "You have learned them well over these past few weeks. But, you have only seen them as attacks, strikes, slices to the neck, or blocks protecting your head, parries against an enemy sword. You have not seen these motions as the growing stages of the Ki disciple, the natural path of the Ki disciple: the path of birth, of growth, of understanding, compassion, Enlightenment. You only saw the sweeping neck attack as a strike of death when in fact it is you, the Ki monk, sending a child onto the path of Enlightenment. You have failed to see. You have failed to perform the basic motions of the sword forms with a clear and compassionate mind. Instead, the two of you have only competed against each other. The two of you have only furthered the polluting of your minds with the hate you have for one another." Kieko looked down. Aiko looked away from the priest and rolled his eyes. "Look here!" shouted the priest. Kieko and Aiko looked at the priest trying to hide the anger within their eyes. "Your mind and actions must be one. A true Ki master–a master of the sword–has a mind as clear as water flowing from a spring. He is devoid of useless thoughts and emotions, and is fully present in the here and now. He is compassionate. He is a mirror to all those around him, including his enemy. It is not the Ki master who defeats the enemy; it is the enemy who defeats himself through the Ki master.

"And here you two are. Living and working in this place. I see only frustration and growing resentment in your actions. Kieko, I see your lack of focus, your apathy for zazen–I know that you practice sword forms instead of meditating in the main hall at night!" Kieko looked down again in shame wondering how long the priest had known. "And you, Aiko; I see your hatred for Kieko in your sword movements; I see your anger, your sadness, your respect for your father in your steps." Aiko looked away from the priest again and ground his teeth; his entire body was hard and tense. "You both are far from becoming true Ki monks. You both are far from becoming true Ki warriors."

"You know nothing, priest," Aiko said under his breath.

"Come, Aiko," the priest invited. "Come and strike me down."

Aiko looked straight into the priest's eyes, "I would do so gladly, but you are a priest, a holy man."

"Come, Aiko. Come and strike me. I am not as holy as you think. I too have a dark side. Your mother was murdered by the Red race. And your father was not there to save her. It is your father's fault that she died!"

Aiko threw up his wooden sword and charged at the priest. The priest stood, but then moved with lightening speed. Then it was done. Within the blink of an eye the priest had grabbed the weapon out of Aiko's hand, threw him down to the ground, and stood over him with the tip of the wooden sword pointed straight at his right eye.

"You are defeated," the priest smiled.

"To hell with you, priest! I curse you into the mouth of the dragon."

"Silence!" the priest thundered with a voice that shook the walls.

Aiko went silent. Kieko looked with fear at the priest.

The priest threw the sword down at Aiko and stepped back. "Get up, you fool!"

Aiko did not move.

"Get up!" the priest boomed.

He got up to his feet.

"Pick up your practice sword."

He hesitated.

"Pick up your sword!"

He picked up his wooden sword.

"You will face Kieko."

Kieko gripped his sword.

"The two of you will fight. But, you will do only what I say. Is that understood?"

Both Kieko and Aiko nodded.

"Is that understood?" he shouted.

"Yes, Master Shinsei," they replied.

"Face each other."

They stood before each other.

"Bow and draw your swords."

Kieko bowed, as did Aiko; they both drew out and extended their swords while stepping forward with their right legs.

"Kieko, attack the head, leg, and chest."

Kieko tightened his grip; a bead of sweat rolled down his forehead.

"Kieko!"

"Yes–yes, Master Shinsei."

"Attack the head, leg, and chest!"

"Yes, Master Shinsei," he answered.

"Ka!" the priest shouted.

Kieko raised his sword and struck down aiming for Aiko's head, but Aiko shot his sword up and blocked the strike. He then dropped the tip of his sword and swung it at Aiko's leg, but Aiko stepped back and blocked the strike with ease. Angry, he tensed his arms and trusted his sword at Aiko's chest, but Aiko stepped back again and swung down at the sword.

"Stop!" the priest shouted. "And bow."

Kieko put his feet together and bowed. Aiko bowed after him and smiled mockingly.

"What are you smiling at?" Kieko barked.

Aiko kept smiling.

"What are you–"

"Quiet!" the priest roared.

Kieko looked down and kicked the floor.

"Aiko."

"Yes, Master Shinsei."

"Attack the chest, knee, and head."

"Yes, Master Shinsei."

"Bow."

The two bowed to each other.

"Ka!"

Aiko launched his sword at Kieko who stepped back and knocked his sword away. He then used the force that Kieko had thrown into his sword by allowing it to circle down at Kieko's knee. The priest, impressed, nodded to himself. Kieko, not fast enough to block the strike, jumped back. In that moment Aiko saw that Kieko had lost his balance and ran at Kieko, jumped high above him, and swung his sword down at his head. Kieko threw his sword up, blocked the strike, but fell down to the ground.

"Bow," the priest requested.

Aiko bowed with a wide grin. Kieko stood up, bowed, and kicked the ground twice.

"Kieko!" the priest shouted.

"Yes! Yes, Master Shinsei."

"You lower your tone with me."

"Yes, Master Shinsei."

"The chest, left arm, and head."

Kieko nodded, clenched his teeth, and gripped his sword.

"Bow."

The two bowed.

"Ka!"

Kieko lashed out with rapid steps screaming before swinging his sword at Aiko's upper body. Aiko jumped back allowing the sword to swing clean past him. Kieko's eyes widened; he realized that he had thrown too much energy into his swing. Thrusting his sword forward Aiko stabbed Kieko in the shoulder and then slashed him across the whole of his back.

"Bow," the priest commanded.

Aiko brought his sword before him and bowed. Kieko threw his sword to the ground and kicked it across the floor. Aiko smiled.

"Kieko!" the priest hollered. "How dare you disgrace your sword, and this hall, before the great Buddha!"

"He cheated!" Kieko yelled back.

"You speak like a child!"

"How can you let him train in this place?" he shouted pointing at Aiko. "How can you teach him here? You are supposed to help me! Me! Not him. He tried to kill me! And you reward him with taking him into this place so easily. I had to answer your damn koan! Your stupid, cursed koan! I don't understand you—"

"Shut your mouth!" the priest roared.

Kieko turned, kicked the air, and began walking away.

"You face me!"

Kieko continued walking.

"Kieko!"

"To the mouth of Mount Kadek with you!"

The priest flew into the air; his robes fluttered and sounded. Aiko looked in awe as the priest flipped in midair and landed striking Kieko down with his palms.

Kieko fell to the floor gasping for air, legs kicking, and pounding the ground with his fists as a powerful electrical surge that had been pumped into him by the priest slowly drained out of his body.

The priest stood over Kieko, "Never forget who I am. I am your master and you will do as I say."

Kieko began hitting his chest as his face turned red.

The priest looked at Aiko, "Take your brother to his room where he can rest."

"Yes, Master Shinsei."

The priest turned and left.

Kieko coughed out loud repeatedly and spat on the floor before being able to swallow some air. Aiko approached him. "Don't come near me!" he ordered Aiko.

"You heard the priest. I have to take you up to your room like a little baby."

"Shut—shut your mouth . . . Shut your mouth," he coughed.

"You see, Akai. You are useless at the art of Ki sword. Just give up. I belong here. Not you. This temple is Lemurian; it's not meant for your mixed racial kind."

"Shut your mouth, Aiko."

"Or what? What will you do to me from down there?"

Kieko coughed up blood and spat at Aiko's feet.

"You missed. Is that all you can do? Just give up," he began walking away, "Just give up. I belong here, not you, Akai. This place belongs to my kind. Not yours."

"Curse you, Aiko. To hell with you!"

He bowed to the Buddha and said before exiting the main hall, "No, it is you who is cursed, Akai."

CHAPTER XVII

The seventeenth true form was extremely difficult. He tried the form again. He bowed, shouted, and jumped forward unsheathing his sword cutting the air before him. He moved through the next four motions, but hesitated on the next strike. Realizing that he was practicing the form too fast he stopped, sheathed his sword, and began jumping in place to loosen up his muscles. *Let's try this again*, he thought. *And cut thinking, must cut thinking.* He bowed again, shouted, and slowly went through the first few movements until he had to whip the sword down in a motion that outlined the shape of a half circle. *That's what's hard.* He stopped again and practiced stepping forward while whipping the sword down. He cleared his mind and repeated the whipping motion feeling how the sword moved in his hand while also trying to relieve any tension in his forearm. Again and again he practiced with increasing speed until at last he could see how the whipping motion could cut an arrow shot at his legs in two. *That's it, that's it. Let's try this again from the beginning.* He sheathed his sword again, bowed, and went through the entire long form with no hesitations or doubts. Over and over again he practiced gradually quickening the pace until he finally felt confidant with the form. Satisfied he sheathed his sword and bowed.

Opening his eyes he looked and noticed that the fire in the fireplace was dying. He shivered from the creeping cold, rolled his head, and went over the seventeenth true form one more time in his mind as he sat in the zazen position. "Yes, I've got it," he said to himself as he fed the fire more wood. The fire grew stronger and he held his hands out before the fireplace to warm them. "Time," he yawned, "time to get ready to sleep." He began to undress himself, but he stopped when he heard footsteps coming up the staircase. "Kieko," he said bitterly. "The idiot was probably training in the hall instead of meditating." The door opened. Aiko turned his back to Kieko and continued undressing. Kieko, ignoring him, walked across the room and up the steps to his lofted futon.

"Still training?" Aiko asked as he began putting on his nightwear.

"Shut up," Kieko answered with an exhausted voice.

"You know it's not good to go to sleep in the clothes you've been sweating in."

"Yes, I know," he said as he began undressing. "I'm going to put on my night–"

"The priest knows that you're still training in the main hall when you should be meditating."

"I was meditating with you."

"Yes, but after I left you began training like you've been doing probably ever since you started learning Ki sword."

"So what?"

"So, the priest knows."

"Then why doesn't he come into the main hall and say something? Any way, what does it matter to you? All it means is that I'm putting more time into training Ki sword than you."

"You haven't learned a thing from the priest."

"I've been here longer than you so what do you know of what I've learned or not."

"You think that by just practicing Ki sword that you will become better at it? Why then? Why do I keep defeating you when Shinsei has us duel against each other?"

"That doesn't mean a thing. Your father has always taught you in Teshi-do and Ki sword. If my father was here teaching me then I'd be beating you at everything."

"That's a dream," he scoffed.

"You'll see. I saw how you were struggling with that whipping arrow block. I spent the night perfecting that technique and all of form seventeen. Tomorrow, when Master Shinsei asks us to go through that form, you'll see how simple it is for me and how difficult it will continue to be for you."

Aiko laughed as he shook his head, "Yes, we'll see then, Akai. We'll see."

Kieko finished putting on his nightwear and crawled onto his futon.

Aiko blew out the candles on the table and unrolled his futon on the floor.

Lying on his futon he waited. Kieko started to snore. "Finally," he said to himself. He sat up and listened making sure that Kieko was sleeping deeply. He then sat in the zazen position and began meditating on true form seventeen again with a smile.

Before dawn the priest called his two disciples down from their room and sent them straight to the main hall to begin cleaning the floor of all the bat droppings that had fallen during the night. When they finished he ordered them to get their practice swords from their room and to return to the main hall where they would go over the basic forms and the first seventeen long forms of Ki sword.

Standing before the priest Kieko and Aiko began going through the basic forms and the first sixteen long forms with only a few mistakes. It was then time for true form seventeen. Kieko glanced at Aiko with a sneer full of confidence and pride. Aiko simply smiled back. The priest asked them to bow. They bowed and when the priest shouted they began the seventeenth true form performing it in perfect unison until they went through the sequence of wiping motions where Kieko lost control and dropped his sword. Aiko continued and finished the form.

"What happened to you is typical of a student who does not mind-train," the priest said to Kieko.

Kieko gave the priest a hard look, "I can do it, Master Shinsei."

"Really? Then go ahead and show me the form."

Kieko took up his sword, bowed, and began the form. It was apparent to both the priest and Aiko that he was full of determination and forced concentration. He went through the sequence of wiping motions and nearly lost control of his sword again. The priest asked him to stop. Frustrated, he stopped and looked at the priest waiting to hear what he had to say.

"Why is it that Aiko performed the form so easily on his first try this morning and you are having so much difficulty with it?"

Kieko could only shake his head at the priest's words.

"Have you no answer?"

Kieko remained silent.

"Answer me!"

Aiko smirked at Kieko. Kieko responded by clenching his hands and teeth.

"Answer me," the priest demanded again.

"I . . . I don't know why, Master Shinsei."

"Because you do not meditate on the forms! The only way you will be able to master Ki sword is with a clear mind. Clear your mind and you will reflect back your enemy's strikes so that he defeats himself. Strength and determination have no place here—especially in Ki sword. Clarity, and your ability to react before thought, is what will make you a great Ki swordsman. Although Aiko is far from clearing his heart and mind of the pollution his father has filled him with he is progressing much faster than you in Ki sword because he meditates on the forms. No more foolish business with you. You still have learned nothing from me. Train in Ki sword one more time at night when you should be mind training and I will throw you out of this temple!"

Kieko looked down biting his lips.

"Do you understand?"

"Yes . . . yes, Master Shinsei."

Aiko giggled.

"Out with you!" the priest hollered at Aiko.

Aiko looked at the priest innocently.

"Put your sword away and go down and cook breakfast."

"Yes, Master Shinsei." He walked past the priest and stuck his tongue out at Kieko.

Kieko shook his head and silently cursed Aiko.

When Aiko had exited the hall the priest approached Kieko and said, "I am not your friend here. I am your master and I am here to teach you. If you continue doing what you are doing then you have proven false and are not worthy of further Ki teachings."

Kieko, looking down, kicked the floor.

"All I ask of you is to meditate on the forms, Kieko. If you can not do that for yourself then do it for your father. He is watching you."

Kieko looked up, "Yes, Master Shinsei."

"Come. Let us have breakfast so that you and Aiko can train more on the forms outside before working on the hut."

"Yes, Master Shinsei," he followed the priest out of the main hall and down to the kitchen chamber with his wooden sword.

Chapter XVIII

It was a cold and grey winter morning, and the priest, standing in the open plain within the forest where the hut was being built, could see the snow covered roof of the Kadek Temple, and the long, thick icicles that hung down from it as a thin line of smoke rose up from one of the temple's chimneystacks. He looked at the tori gate, admired its red-painted pillars that shot up from the snow-covered ground to its black-pitched roof, and closed his eyes. He heard the trickling water of a stream in the distance, opened his eyes, and saw his two disciples working on the thatched roof of their hut; they were working quickly, completely aware of each other's progress, while refusing to look at one another as they tied a wooden covering together over the opening at the peak of the angled roof.

The priest stepped forward and said, "Tonight will be your first night in this dwelling that you will now call home."

"But, it's not finished, Master Shinsei," Aiko complained. "We need two more days."

"You are finished," the priest contested.

"Are you blind?"

The priest flew up, landed before Aiko on the thatched roof, and slapped him across the head knocking his wool cap off. "I'm not going to repeat myself!"

"But, we'll freeze—"

Again the priest slapped Aiko across the head; Kieko let out a short burst of laughter. The priest slapped Kieko across the face, which caused him look away in shame. The priest jumped and landed on the snow, took out his long pipe, and lit it. "Finish your work," he said with his back to Kieko and Aiko as he puffed on his pipe and walked back to the temple.

"Wicked curses," Kieko whispered.

"That's right. We're going to freeze tonight. I can't believe this."

Kieko looked at the priest worried that he would be able to hear them, "Shut up so that we can finish this."

"Don't tell me to shut up."

"Do you want Master Shinsei to hear you?"

Aiko looked and saw that the priest had just walked out of the forest and was approaching the path back to the temple, "Don't tell me to shut up, Akai."

"Just get back to work so we can finish this damn thing."

"Don't tell me what to do."

"I'm not telling you what to do—I'm reminding you that we need to finish this so that we don't freeze to death tonight."

"If you say one more thing to me—Akai—I swear I'll finish what I started with you—"

"What? You mean shooting me with an arrow from the shadows of this forest like a coward instead of facing me without a mask like a man?"

"To hell with you," he spat.

"No, to hell with you. And shut up and go back to work!"

"You shut up!" Aiko jumped at Kieko and threw a punch at his face. Kieko blocked the punch, grabbed Aiko's wrist, and pulled him forward nearly throwing him off the roof, but Aiko regained his balance and pointed the palm of his left hand at Kieko. Kieko responded by spreading his arms out inviting Aiko to attack him.

Aiko attacked. Kieko deflected and punched, but Aiko had flipped his entire body up and away from Kieko's strike. Landing safely on the roof of the hut Aiko jumped and flew down hard at Kieko with his right knee aimed straight for his face. Kieko tried to swipe the knee strike away, but the force of Aiko's body threw him down the slope of the roof; and Aiko, having lost complete balance, crashed straight through the wooden covering of the hut that they had been working on.

Kieko fell hard to the ground, but stood up ready to fight and saw that Aiko had crashed through the roof of the hut. Relieved, he wiped the snow off his arms and legs.

"You cursed, Akai!"

Kieko took a step away from the hut.

Aiko jumped up through the hole he had fallen through and landed on the roof with his body bent forward. When he spotted Kieko he jumped down and launched a series of kicks and punches at him.

Kieko, overwhelmed, tried to deflect the strikes and kicks. He then saw that his wooden sword was close and ran to it. Aiko stopped and ran to grab his own sword.

Kieko kicked up his sword, grabbed it by the hilt, turned, and saw that Aiko was now also armed. The two paused recognizing the sudden escalation in their fight.

"I will cut you down, Akai!"

"Come and try you motherless freak!"

Aiko ran at Kieko screaming and jumped flipping himself over him as he slashed. Their wooden swords clashed; blood was drawn. Wounded in mid-flight Aiko fell staining the snow with his blood. Kieko now stood over him aiming his sword at his neck and said, "It's over."

"You are a curse, Akai!" he spat breathing heavily. "Your father was a curse and now you are a curse. You will lead us all to our deaths, so be over with it and kill me!"

"I'm—I'm Lemurian!" he protested still trying to catch his breath.

"You are Akai! You will always be Akai. Your people killed my mother and I swear to the gods that if not in this life—then in another—I will strike you down!"

"Why are you blaming me for your mother's death? I'm Lemurian regardless of what I look like."

"You are hated here!"

Kieko threw his sword up and shot it down with lightening speed. Aiko rolled. Kieko struck the ground, shouted, and hacked his sword at Aiko who continued rolling away until finally he struck him in the arm and began pounding his chest with uncontrolled rage. Then, within a moment, his eyes widened and he stopped. Aiko coughed up blood as he groaned and huddled up in pain. He had lost himself; lost himself within his anger. It was enough. Exhausted, he threw down his sword, spat at Aiko, and stumbled back to the hut. *How . . . how am I to live with him in that?*

He crawled through the small entrance of the hut, started a small fire, and sat before the flames holding his knees to his chest trying to keep warm as he stared lost in his spiraling thoughts.

Nearly an hour later he heard Aiko's footsteps and realized that he had nearly forgotten about him. The short door creaked open and Aiko stepped in. Keeping his back to Aiko he threw some dried leaves and twigs into the fire. Aiko, limping, approached the fire and collapsed; he spat out some blood, coughed, crawled to the wall of the hut, and sat against it. Kieko ignored him, but he began to shiver as he felt the back of his throat become sore; and as he stared into the flames he gave into his exhaustion and fell asleep.

Aching with pain Aiko checked his injuries and found that none of his bones had been broken, but he saw that bruises discolored his arms and chest. He thought of his father and of how much he hated him. Soon the cold grew stronger and he began to shiver. He wanted to move closer to the fire but was too weak and tired to do so. *I want to be gone from here*, he thought. *I want to be gone from here.*

The priest knocked on the hut's small door. It was morning. He puffed on his long pipe as he went over the fight in his mind; he had watched most of it from his temple. He was disappointed with both Kieko and Aiko. But, he knew that the fight was necessary, that they needed to release their anger on each other. "Kieko and Aiko wake up," he knocked again on the door. He heard nothing. He knocked again and heard someone limping toward the door.

Aiko opened the door and peered out from the darkness within, "Good morning, Master Shinsei."

"Are the two of you all right?"

"Yes, Master Shinsei. Kieko has been sleeping since yesterday afternoon. I think he might be sick."

"Yes, I was afraid of that. Let me in so that I can check."

"Yes, Master Shinsei," he backed away allowing the priest to pass into the cold, dirt-floored dwelling.

Once inside the priest straightened his back and looked up at the large hole in the thatched roof, "What happened?"

"I fell through."

"I see," the priest said shaking his head. "The two of you do not cease to humor me."

"And why is that?"

"Master Shinsei!"

"Yes, Master Shinsei."

"You two remind me of how my brother and I were when we were young."

"And why is that, Master Shinsei?"

"We used to fight each other. Several times we nearly killed each other. Our father would then punish us by beating us."

Aiko looked down and said nothing.

The priest approached Kieko's huddled body and could see that he was shivering and sweating. He raised his hand over Kieko's body and was silent for a moment before he said, "A strong fever is brewing within him. Aiko, come and help me carry him to the temple."

"I'm not in any condition to carry him, Master Shinsei. Didn't you see that I was limping? And my arms are too sore."

"Do not argue with me–you have the strength." The priest rocked Kieko with his hand trying to summon him. Kieko woke up and looked at the priest with exhausted eyes. "Kieko, we need to take you back to the temple. You need to get up." Kieko nodded.

The priest signaled to Aiko with his hand to help him and together they lifted Kieko up to his feet.

"Do you have him?" the priest asked Aiko.

"Yes, Master Shinsei."

Kieko coughed.

"Good." The priest went ahead and exited the hut.

Aiko limped forward supporting Kieko, and at the door, from the outside, the priest grabbed Kieko and pulled him through thus allowing Aiko to crawl out of the hut.

It was a dull grey, but warm morning. The snow was melting revealing rocks and the muddy earth. Aiko got up from his knees and could hear small streams of water flowing within the forest. He wrapped Kieko's arm around his neck and steadied himself trying to support Kieko's weight.

"Do you have him?" the priest asked again.

"Yes, Master Shinsei."

Kieko began coughing violently.

The priest raised Kieko's head and looked into his eyes. "How do you feel?"

"Terribly weak . . . Master Shinsei," he wheezed.

"Come, let us go," the priest said as he began to make his way back to the temple with his staff. Aiko followed, but he could not keep up with the priest for it was too difficult for his injured body to walk and support Kieko.

Black crows watched and observed the priest and his two disciples from the tops of several trees. One of the crows crooned causing Aiko to look up and see the black birds as he walked with Kieko on the path to the temple. He did not like the look of the crows; their movements seemed unnatural to him. He continued walking trying to ignore the birds, but he looked up again and saw that they were following him with their beady eyes. "What do they want?"

"What?" Kieko asked with a faint voice.

"Nothing," he answered. Suddenly all the crows flew up into the cloudy sky; he watched the crows fly west toward the Mountains of Shinohi until they had disappeared over the trees. He shook his head of all thoughts and saw that the priest had just bowed before the tori gate. He picked up the pace and soon they were before the tori gate where they bowed, proceeded through the gate, and approached the stone water basin. Taking the wooden ladle from the basin he dunked it into the cold water, took a sip from it, and passed it to Kieko who began coughing again as soon as he drank from it. "Are you all right?" he asked. Kieko did not answer. "Come on—let's go," he said annoyed, and together they approached the temple.

It was warm inside the temple; Kieko and Aiko were greatly relieved. After they had removed their shoes and put on their temple shoes they followed the priest through the main hall and down the staircase into the underground where, in the tunnel that led to the kitchen chamber, they could smell the spicy scent of boiling soup.

"Lay him down over there," the priest instructed Aiko when they entered the kitchen chamber.

Aiko limped toward the groove in the bedrock wall that was covered with pillows, lay Kieko down, and sighed. He limped toward the kitchen table and asked, "Master Shinsei, I have not eaten. May I help myself to your food?"

"Yes, go ahead," he answered as he cooked. "Thank you for assisting your brother."

He did not reply.

The priest turned and pointed his cutting knife at him, "Thank you for assisting your brother!"

"Yes, Master Shinsei," he said as he took his bowl from the shelf. He went to the kitchen counter and filled his bowl with rice and vegetable soup, sat down at the kitchen table, and began chugging down the soup.

"Slow down—you will choke if you continue like that," the priest warned.

"Yes, Master Shinsei." He placed the bowl down on the table, stood up, walked to the cupboard to fetch his spoon, returned to the table, and began eating again.

The priest approached Kieko and whispered, "Rest, you must rest."

Kieko closed his eyes, took a deep breath, and exhaled releasing some of the tension in his muscles.

"Listen to my voice, Kieko," he began. "Let every part of your body fall deep into the heart of the Mother. Allow all your thoughts to fall. You are surrounded and protected. Let your strength give way. Let go and fall deep into the heart of the Mother. Rest. Relax. Relax and let it all go." He could see that Kieko was falling into a deep, peaceful state. "Just fall. Let everything fall. Allow gravity to pull everything down. That is it. That is it. Now, take a deep breath."

Kieko tried, but his chest would not rise.

The priest could see that there was a darkness guarding his heart. "Take another deep breath."

Kieko drew the kitchen air into his lungs.

"Take it into your belly. Breathe it in and pull your belly down, not up."

Kieko drew in more air and pulled it into his stomach; his stomach rose. He tried again and sucked his stomach in.

"Good. Now let your chest rise and let the air in your belly flow into your lungs."

Kieko tried, but he had difficulty channeling the air into his chest.

"Let it all go. Exhale. Exhale all your thoughts, desires, and attachments."

A low-pitched note sang from Kieko's mouth. Aiko stopped eating and looked at Kieko.

"Good . . . good. Again; breathe the air into your belly and then into the whole of your lungs."

Kieko tried again, but the priest could see that his chest was still blocked; a shadow was pinning it down.

"Breathe in . . . and out . . . breathe in . . . and out. Let go . . . let it all go and fall deep into zazen."

Kieko continued breathing.

The priest held his hands out with palms facing up, closed his eyes, and inhaled absorbing Ki from his surroundings. Aiko sat still watching the priest. The priest then held his hands over Kieko and expelled Ki into him.

"What . . . what is that?" Kieko asked.

"It is Ki that you feel. It will heal you."

"It burns."

"Heat is life."

"Yes," Kieko said faintly as his head began to shake.

"Relax," the priest moved his hands over Kieko's chest and felt a dark pressing force. *It comes from his past. I will need much time with him to rid the darkness that has rooted itself so deep into his heart.* He moved his hands down to Kieko's knees and to his feet.

Kieko began sweating profusely. He moaned and said, "I have to pee."

"Can you hold it?"

"No—please let me pee."

"Just hold on a little longer."

His legs kicked and moved. His body became tense.

The priest was now finding it difficult to send Ki into Kieko. "Relax," he asked, "relax." But Kieko did not. The priest could no longer continue his efforts. "I will count to three and as I count each number your conscious self will slowly rise, and when I say three your eyes will open and I will help you to stand on your feet." Kieko nodded. "One . . . two . . . three."

Kieko opened his eyes and saw the light and shadows dancing on the cavern ceiling revealing and hiding its uneven grooves.

"Let me help you get up, young Kieko."

Kieko held out his hand, and the priest took it. He rose up to his feet feeling tired and faint, and for a moment he could not see. Blood returned to his eyes. He regained some of his strength and sight and saw Aiko staring at him. "What—what are you looking at?"

"Nothing," Aiko replied.

Kieko eased his feet into his temple shoes and slowly walked out of the kitchen chamber and down the tunnel that led to the bath chamber to use the toilet. After relieving himself he felt better, but his fever still lingered. He stood up and wiped his buttocks with a wet cloth. After, he pulled up his pants up, tied them, and walked back to the kitchen chamber.

"I will start cleaning the temple, Master Shinsei," Aiko said as he stood up.

"Thank you," the priest answered.

Kieko entered the kitchen chamber.

"Well, young Kieko, it is time for you to eat."

"Yes, Master Shinsei."

Aiko took his bowls and cup to the sink to clean them.

Kieko sat down at the kitchen table.

The priest placed a hot bowl of rice and vegetable soup and a cup of warm tea on the table for Kieko.

Kieko bowed his head to his food and began drinking his soup. The priest sat down, lit his long pipe, and began smoking from it. After a few moments Kieko placed his bowl down and took a sip of tea. He felt a pain in his chest and paused for a moment, and said, "You . . . you felt something . . . something within my heart, Master Shinsei."

"Yes, I did," he replied as he ran his fingers through his beard.

"What . . . what did you feel?"

"I believe you already know what is there bending your heart."

Kieko thought for a moment.

"Tell me what it is."

"I don't know. Please, tell me; tell me what you saw—what you felt."

"No, I will not. You know what is there. You are the one who must say what is there blackening your heart."

Kieko was silent.

The priest puffed on his pipe and continued, "We are all mirrors for one another, Kieko. So, tell me what you see in Kira."

"I don't want to talk about her."

"There, you see, you are putting down your heart."

Kieko's chest began to shiver.

"Why do you shake?"

"I don't know. I hate when this happens."

"Kieko, I want you to listen very carefully to what I am about to tell you."

"Yes . . . Master Shinsei. I'm listening," he said with a quivering voice.

"You have been asking yourself what the answer is to a very old koan."

"What . . . what koan?"

"You know, Kieko. Tell me the koan."

He thought for a moment, and said with hesitation, "What . . . what does it mean to be a man?"

"Yes, it is an ancient question that men have always asked themselves and sought an answer to. You have been seeking the answer, and the answer is there deep in your heart, not in your mind.

"As I have told you, Kieko, your mind is a tool. But, it is not you," he took another puff on his pipe. "Most believe that we are our thoughts, we are our minds. But, the mind is full of thinking. And thinking creates worry, stress, anger, and confusion. Observe your thoughts and you will see that they speak of memories or desires for things in the future. They tell you that you shouldn't have done this in your past or that you need some *one* or some *thing* to be happy in the future. So, you are never really in the present. You are not paying attention to what is around you each moment. But, the present is all you have. Regardless, you continue to think in the past or in the future living completely blind to the present. You are not your mind, Kieko. And at the same time you are not your heart, but your heart is a gateway to discovering who you truly are. Follow your heart, go deep within her, and you will see your true self–the answer to your koan."

Kieko was silent.

"You are thinking," the priest observed.

"Yes, Master Shinsei" he answered.

"And of what are you thinking about?"

"I'm trying to understand what you said, Master Shinsei."

"Your mind is trying to understand it. But, the understanding that you seek cannot be understood by the mind."

"Master Shinsei," he said annoyed, "how can I understand it without the mind?"

"With no-mind."

Kieko's brow curled for he was tired of that answer.

"It is the same as I have told you with Ki sword or any other task I have had you do in this temple. Perform all action with a clear mind, with no-mind. When you clean, you clean, and only clean. When you cook, you cook, and only cook. When you practice sword forms you practice, and only practice. You do not clean your bowl with a sword form mind just as you do not practice Ki sword with a gardening mind. When you do action you do that action and only that action. But, *you* do not. You have tiny moments when you are cleaning, or gardening, or cooking with a clear mind, but most times you are cooking and thinking of Ki sword forms, or you are practicing Ki sword forms and thinking about Kira, or about how you would like to beat Aiko, or of things in your past you wished you could have changed–"

"I don't want to change my past, Master Shinsei," Kieko interrupted.

"Oh, no?" the priest smiled. "If you could go back and change the past what would you do?"

"That's impossible, Master Shinsei."

"But, you think it is possible. Why then do you waste so much time wishing that you had known your father? Why do you wish that he was here to protect your mother and to guide you into manhood?"

"I never met him!" Kieko cried out. "He was a man, my father. He should be teaching me, not you or the old farmer. My father should be the one!"

"Your father you will never know, Kieko."

Kieko looked away from the priest.

"That is the truth. He is dead. You must let him go."

"He sees me," he contested. "I know he does. He is watching me. He is guiding me."

"Yes, Kieko, he is. He is guiding you so that you can find a way to let him go."

"No," he said shaking his head, "that is not true—that is not true." His eyes began to fill with tears. "I . . . I don't . . . have him. I don't have . . . a father." He began crying. "I . . . I don't have . . . a grandfather. I don't have . . . friends. All I have are women," he covered his face with his hands, "my mother and Kira. I have . . . I have no father . . . to show me how to be a man."

The priest put down his pipe, went around the kitchen table to sit by Kieko's side, and took him into his arms. Kieko held his master as if he was holding his own father for the first time and released a storm of tears. The priest patted and massaged Kieko's back.

When Kieko had calmed down the priest whispered into his ear, "You must let him go." Kieko pushed himself away from the priest. The priest continued, "You are a man, Kieko—and beyond that, spirit, light—but you do not even see it. If you fail to see who you truly are you will bend all that is good within you, and you will bring pain and suffering into this world; you will betray out of fear. You must meditate and begin to see that freedom is had when you are completely unattached to all that is in and around you. When you have discovered this you will find that you are, and forever will continue to be, a true light for many. You will see your past, your demons, your betrayal, your sins, and cast them all into the light. And you will embrace the light and awake as a god, a goddess, a savior, a saint, a muse, a great lover; a spirit devoid of gender, infinite in mind and thought, creating wonderful dreams."

"I don't understand, Master Shinsei."

"Words are primitive, Kieko. They are limited in scope and vision. They cannot convey experiences. You must understand what I speak through your own experience of it, and not by reading or listening about it. Books fail, stories fail, lessons and rules all fail."

"That I understand, Master Shinsei."

"Even if you do not, your answers will come, and with that I think it is best that you rest. I do not want to exhaust your mind, heart, and body. Leave your bowls and cup. I will clean them and put them away for you."

"Yes, Master Shinsei. Thank you for being my friend," he wiped his eyes.

"Thank you for being mine. You are brave. You have taught me much."

Kieko stood up and walked toward the kitchen exit deep in thought.

"Good night, Kieko."

"Good night, Master Shinsei," he whispered. He looked down feeling the pain in his chest beating down on his heart and walked out of the kitchen eager to sleep on his own futon.

CHAPTER XIX

It was night and the land was grey. The trees were devoid of leaves. The air was still. The stones and rocks were dry. The ocean did not move or sound; it was like a vast sheet of glass.

Kieko looked at the land and felt chills run up his back; the rhythmic thump of his heart drove dread into his mind. *Where am I? I do not recognize this place, although it is home?*

Lightening shot across the sky, but it did not sound.

"Can anyone hear me?" he said, but he did not hear his words. He spoke out again and heard nothing. *Am I deaf?* From the corner of his eye he saw a shadow move in the darkness beyond the surrounding trees. Frightened, he stepped back, looked carefully beyond the trees, and saw nothing. He stepped forward and saw the broken branches of a dread bush in the distance. He walked further into the forest. Darkness enclosed him. Unable to see he looked up hoping to find the light of the moon, but he did not for the high branches of the trees were too many.

There was a faint light in the distance. He walked toward it avoiding the broken branches and stones that littered the ground, and as he neared it he could see that it was a growing blue flame within a pit. He approached the flame and held out his hands, but, strangely, he felt no heat from it. He looked at it with deep curiosity before realizing that there was something–or someone–behind the flame.

"Who is . . . who is there?" he tried to say. The thing moved. *It's a beast.* Bright golden eyes appeared and stared at him. He could not move. The beast growled. He could see its white jagged teeth dripping with blood. Terror filled him. The beast moved. He could see that the dark robes that covered the beast's body cloaked its head. It moved again, but unlike a four-legged beast, instead it moved as if it was an upright creature bent over its prey.

It is feasting. I am disturbing it. His mouth watered. *I want to see it.* He stepped forward and saw the remains of a woman who had been shredded open by the claws of the beast. Her intestines had been ripped out. Her hair, long and thin, covered in blood, had been torn from her scalp and tossed violently all over her face and body. He looked at her with strange delight.

The beast stopped and looked up at Kieko before delving its mouth back into the woman's stomach to pull and tear out more flesh. The beast chewed on the meat ignoring Kieko as strips of flesh hung from its mouth.

He wanted to be like the beast. He wanted to destroy as it did.

"I am the shadow," the darkness said within him. *"It is my path that you must follow. Through me you will enslave all who are against you."*

"All who are against me," he repeated. *"And for what price?"*

"The price is only what you will lose if you do not follow the dark path."

"What will I lose?"

"You will lose all those you know."

"Who are you?"

"You do not know?"

"Reveal yourself to me."

The beast stood up towering over him.

Fighting the fear within him he said, *"Let . . . let me see your face."*

"No—but, I will reveal to you who I have slaughtered." The beast looked at its lifeless prey and brushed away the torn up hair that covered her mangled face.

He stopped breathing. "No!" his words sounded. "This can not be!"

"Why is it not so? Your mother was weak. You have no need for her. I came here to free you, to cut you from your chains. I am here to make you strong so that you can destroy the one who killed your father."

"What?"

"You do not believe me? Then it is time to reveal who I am."

The beast removed its hood. Kieko stepped back and fell to the ground trembling before the beast that bore his own bruised and twisted face.

"It is not over, Kieko. If you do not choose the path that I speak then this will be her fate." The beast moved back revealing the remains of another mangled but burnt body.

"Kira," he said out of breath. "No. This can not be—this can not be. I will not—I will not move. I will not follow this path. I will sit still!"

"You pathetic little boy, there is no middle ground. You must choose."

"No! I will not choose. Curse you. Curse you! I will not move. You may slay me. You may cut me down. I would rather die than choose!"

"I do not know why there is so much fuss over you," it groaned. "You are weak. You are foolish."

He shut his eyes and grabbed his head as he began rocking his body back and forth. All sound ceased again. He opened his eyes and saw that the beast was gone but that it had left for him the remains of his mother and Kira. He stood up and approached the corpses. Standing over his mother he looked down seeing the blood that had dried around her mouth and stared into her lifeless eyes. Her skull was crushed and her hair was drenched in blood; her cheeks were torn and ripped. He kneeled fighting back his tears and closed her eyes. *Now you may rest.*

He needed to bury her body. He looked for anything that would allow him to pry open the hardened ground and saw a shiny long device in the distance leaning against a tree. He stood up, ran to it, and discovered that it was a double-edge sword, which he picked up and jabbed into the ground. *This will do*, he thought before yanking the sword out of the ground and carrying it back to where his mother and Kira lay.

Kneeling before Kira he wept as he closed her eyes with his callused hand. Deciding to bury his mother first he slammed the sword into the ground and dug up earth. A long period of time passed before he had finally convinced himself that the grave he had crudely dug was deserving of his mother's body. He stopped and placed the sword on a large flat rock so that he could rest and drink out of thirst, but after looking in all directions he could see, and sense, that there was no water, or source of it, in sight. Realizing that he could not wash and clean his mother's face or body he took off his shirt and ripped it into long thin shreds so that he could wrap and cover her broken skull, ripped ears, and mangled jaw; he saved several shreds of cloth for Kira. He lifted his mother, carried her to her grave, and lay her down within it placing her hands over her stomach. There were no flowers to bury her with. He kneeled and said with words that did not sound: *Mother, thank you for all that you have given me. You brought me into this world with all your love and light. You fed me, bathed me, and raised me. You are the reason that I am, and I pray that I will not fail you as I carry on in this world without you. I will always carry you deep within my heart. Please guide me. I love you. Your son . . . Kieko.*

He wept for his mother and for the cruel world she had lived and died in. Taking a handful of dirt from the ground he dropped it into the grave and bowed. He began filling her grave with dirt until the whole of her body was gone from the world. There was no tombstone or marker. There was only a small mound.

He sat down exhausted; he had little strength to continue digging another grave. He decided to rest and sleep in the dark of the silent forest.

"Kieko, wake up and drink," the priest whispered as he shook Kieko's body. "You must wake." Kieko moaned; his eyelids fluttered. The priest shook him again. "It is time to wake."

Kieko opened his eyes. "How long . . . how long have I slept?"

"Two days."

"Two days?"

"Yes, two days."

Kieko tried to get up. The priest held him down. "Rest, Kieko, rest. Your fever was strong. It was very strong."

"I . . . I saw things."

"You were hallucinating. Your body filled with too much fire. You woke and panicked several times."

"I . . . I did?"

"Yes. And you suffered from terrible dreams. Do you remember your dreams, Kieko?"

"My dreams?"

"You kicked and moved and spoke for most of the night. You were suffering from a nightmare. Do you remember?"

"I," he thought a moment. "I don't remember, Master Shinsei."

"You must try to remember," the priest insisted. "You spoke out of not choosing something. Do you remember that? Do you remember refusing to do something?"

"Not choosing something?" he said under his breath. He thought and answered, "I'm sorry, Master Shinsei, but I don't remember."

"I see," he said disappointed. "Please, drink this." He handed a cup of tea to Kieko.

"What is it?"

"I did not ask you to ask me what it is. I asked you to drink it."

"Yes, Master Shinsei." He sniffed the tea. "This doesn't smell good, Master Shinsei."

"I did not ask you to smell it!"

"Should I drink it fast?"

"Just drink it!"

"Yes, Master Shinsei." He drank the tea in one gulp and gave a look of disgust to the priest.

"Good."

Kieko stuck out his tongue, "Yuck."

"You will drink that every night and every morning for the next three days."

"Yes, Master Shinsei." He looked at what he could see of his room from his lofted futon and listened. "Where's Aiko?"

"He is training in the main hall. Soon it will be time for the two of you to go off on your meditation retreat."

Kieko looked at the priest, "I am ready, Master Shinsei."

"You are ready?" the priest laughed. "You are ready?" he shook his head. He crawled back and began stepping down the steps from Kieko's lofted futon.

"Where are you going, Master Shinsei?"

"The fire is dying." He stepped onto the floor and walked up to the fireplace to throw in another log. Embers sparked and floated up the chimneystack. He looked into the fire watching it grow strong again and saw images from his past. He ran his fingers through his beard allowing the silence between him and Kieko to build. When he was ready he said: "When . . . when I lived in the Yama Te Temple, training as a novice under the guidance of my master, I remember wanting so much to be granted permission to leave on my retreat . . . that, my young friend, was long, long ago."

Kieko crawled to the edge of his lofted futon.

"You know me well, Kieko. I am happy that you are my disciple and . . . my friend." He looked down. "It has been a long time since I have had someone like you to speak with—about that which haunts me in the night." He began staring deep into the fire. "The dragons . . . Kieko . . . are stirring. A storm is coming. We must all face the shadow."

"What are you speaking of, Master Shinsei?" Kieko asked feeling a chill run down his spine as he peered down from his lofted futon.

"Do you believe that you can cross the oceans and lands of this world alone?"

Kieko looked at the priest not understanding what he meant.

"I have tried to live my life doing just that. I have tried to live alone–independent from all those around me–but, in the end . . . after so many decades I realize that I have only been trying to hide from the person I had once been. And I see now that I must face my past. You, Kieko, are leading me to that end."

"Master Shinsei, I don't understand what you are talking about," he said frightened.

"I have visions, Kieko, of things that were, that are, and that will be. I have visions of you and what you will do in the future. You are a dreamer, Kieko. You can heal many. You do not belong in this place; you do not belong to me; you do not belong to your mother; and you do not belong to Kira. There is something more that awaits you beyond the great sea."

"I . . . I remember my dream, Master Shinsei."

The priest looked up, "Tell me everything you can remember."

"I . . . I remember not being able to speak–or not being able to hear my own words as I spoke. And there was a creature–a creature of the night–and it . . . it . . . ."

"Tell me Kieko."

"It killed my mother . . . and . . . it killed Kira. I had to bury them, but I only had the strength to bury my mother."

The priest stared again into the fire going over Kieko's words before pulling out his long pipe and lighting it with the candle that was sitting on the table by the fireplace. He puffed on his pipe and ran his fingers through his beard again and said, "I see."

"Are they going to die?" he asked regretting the question.

"You said in your sleep that you did not want to choose something. Do you remember what you did not want to choose?"

Kieko thought for a moment, "I'm sorry, Master Shinsei, but I do not remember."

"This will be your koan. You must see what it is that you do not want to choose."

"Master Shinsei, what do you think it is that I do not want to choose?"

"Only you can answer that." He stared deeper into the fire. There was a long silence. Kieko waited. The priest spoke: "Did you know that I was born more than sixty years ago on an island once named Kurai."

Kieko's eyes widened.

"I was once named Kuro by my father . . . Kurai IV."

"Your father was Kurai IV?" he asked in disbelief. "The warlord who corrupted King Kanda?"

"Yes, he was my father. I was born in his castle—born into royalty and wealth." He paused and stared again long and hard into the fire. He continued: "My father's empire was won by the blood spilt from many men, women, and children . . ."

Kieko, shocked by what he was hearing, did not move.

"I . . . I loved my father. As a young boy I prayed for the day when I would be allowed to follow him into battle. I wanted to fight. I wanted to kill. My older brother always fought alongside my father. I was envious of him . . .

"In my youth I studied under many skilled artisans and philosophers. I trained in the art of war by the guidance of generals. I followed the faith of my people. And although I had it all, so to speak, I was unhappy . . . I never knew my mother. I grew up among men." He puffed on his pipe. The fire crackled. Kieko waited for his master to continue.

"I will never forget the first moment I saw her," he smiled. "She was the most beautiful woman I had ever seen. Her black hair . . . her eyes . . . I wanted so much to be with her—but she was a slave—a slave in my father's castle. I tried desperately to hate her—to convince myself that she was less than the spit of a dog, but I could not. I wanted her, so I saw her in secret . . .

"Her name was Emira. She had lost her entire family by the cutting blades of my father's army. She wanted nothing to do with me. She spat at me. It took so many months before she would even allow me near her. I tried to give her flowers, letters . . . she could not read," he grinned. "She wanted nothing to do with me, but somehow, through my persistence, she saw me not as the son of my father, but as someone different . . . someone different from him.

"We would meet at night and I would listen to her speak about her life and her people. I learned of how my father, and his ancestors, had destroyed in the name of greed for more land, wealth, and power. I learned of the evils of this world and how I was intimately a part of it. So the day came when I had to choose. I had to choose between my own father and her. And . . . I did not want to choose."

"What happened, Master Shinsei?"

"My father had finally corrupted King Kanda. The war campaigns to unite the northern islands of Lemuria had begun. I was fifteen, just old enough to fight with my father and brother. And I was called to fight. I did not know what to do. If I fought and conquered I would be killing off more of Emira's people, and if I chose not to fight my father would disown me, consider me weak, foolish, not worthy of his bloodline.

"I spoke to Emira about this. She was angry and demanded that I not fight. She wanted me to stand against my father, and to tell him that his war had only brought loss, pain, and suffering to too many. She asked me how I could love my father, a man responsible for the deaths of tens of thousands. She screamed and punched my chest begging me to choose her over my own father.

"I did not know what to do. I loved my father and I loved her. But, after I had left her, a great anger came over me. I hated what she had said about my father. I hated her words. I hated her.

"I rose to my father's call. And I killed . . ." his eyes narrowed on the flames as he remembered. "Years . . . years later I returned to my castle home with my father and brother. I saw Emira again . . . she was a ghost. She had gone mad and had been chained to a wall in the deep underground of the castle. My father had no interest in keeping servants that could not serve so he had her executed. I watched as they slew her. I remember her eyes . . . how they recognized me and looked deep into my heart," he wiped his eyes. "I . . . I could not live with myself after witnessing her death, so I ran away desperate to redeem myself of all the evil and betrayal I had brought into the world. I found my Ki master when I was nineteen. That was how I gained my new name and became a Ki priest."

Kieko stared at his master's back saddened by what he had heard.

"You and your father are the only two people I have ever told about all of this." He closed his eyes. "There is a whisper in the wind that my time will come soon." He opened his eyes and looked up to Kieko. "When it is time you must choose. You must listen to your heart and choose what it wills. If you do not, if you betray all that you are, then all will be lost."

Kieko was silent.

"When it is time you must choose, Kieko."

"Yes, Master Shinsei . . . I understand and . . . I will."

"You do not understand," he said. "You will understand when you do and know."

Kieko followed the smoke from the priest's long pipe with his eyes. "How . . . how will I know when it is time to choose, Master Shinsei?"

"You will know when it is time. You will know." The priest checked the knot of the belt that held his robe tight around his body, looked at Kieko, and left.

CHAPTER XX

Kieko spent each day and night, as he lay recovering on his futon, thinking about what the priest had said concerning his past. He wanted to learn more, to hear more stories, and to hopefully begin learning about his father's past, but the priest continued his care of him as if nothing had been said about his father, the warlord, or his love, Emira.

When he had fully recuperated from his fever he found that Aiko had learned two new long forms and that he could now meditate for two, sometimes, three hours straight. The competitive spirit within him had caught fire again and he trained harder and spent more time meditating at night. But, he was still unable to clear his mind as he meditated for he was still too strongly attached to mind-training on the sword forms.

The nights, the cold nights, were spent with Aiko in the hut they had built. They never said a word to each other. They simply sat around the burning hearth rubbing their hands and legs to keep warm until they fell asleep. Each morning they woke up yawning and shivering from the cold as they stretched out their stiff bodies before getting dressed and practicing their sword forms outside in the snow. Once they saw smoke rising from one of the temple's chimneystacks they would return to the temple to have breakfast with the priest and to clean the temple before practicing more sword forms and sitting meditation.

Then, on the first day of the second month of the year forty-four, they were sent off by the priest to Mount Kadek to begin their one hundred day retreat; they were armed with short swords, their wooden practice swords, and a bow and a quiver of arrows that the priest had only given to Aiko. They ate whatever they could hunt and capture in the forest and slept in caves, and they meditated every night, at the midnight hour as requested by the priest, seeking the Enlightenment that had been gained by so many Ki disciples before them. And although they had only each other to depend on for their survival, very little of the anger they had for each other had been quelled.

It was another day, and Mount Kadek was covered in snow. Kieko, sitting, hiding with Aiko behind a large smooth rock, looked up to the cloudy sky. He could see his breath in the cold air. His stomach grumbled. Aiko looked at Kieko holding his finger to his lips and crept up to peer over the rock.

"What do you see?" Kieko whispered.

Aiko did not answer; he held his finger to his lips again requesting silence before signaling to Kieko that he needed his bow. Kieko, with shivering hands, passed Aiko his bow and one arrow. Aiko took his weapon ignoring the bitter cold that bit at his hands and fingers and nocked his bow. He pulled the tight string back and aimed at the stomach of a doe. He inhaled, holding the cold air in his lungs until all was silent within him, and released.

The arrow hissed, flew, and struck the doe directly in the stomach causing her to jump in fright and searing pain. She kicked her hind legs wildly and tried to run, but could not. Instead, she stumbled to the ground feeling the arrow restrict the movements of her muscles. She cried for help. Another arrow struck her.

"Give me another, damn it!" Aiko demanded.

Kieko fumbled for another arrow.

Aiko, impatient, threw down his bow and leapt over the rock. With his short sword already drawn he ran to the doe, jumped over her, and sliced her neck open when he landed on his knees. The doe looked up at him. He looked into her eyes. Her body jerked; blood streamed onto the snow.

Kieko approached the doe and kneeled before her watching thin lines of vapor rise from her wounds into the cold air. Aiko cleaned his sword with a cloth and sheathed it. Kieko held his hands together, bowed, and said, "Thank you creature of the tree gods for your strength. We honor and admire you. Go into the light and be free of this place." He closed the doe's eyes and held his hand over her mouth, catching her last breaths, and inhaled the scent from his hand. Aiko placed his hand over the doe's mouth as well and performed the same rite.

"We will need a long, thick branch to tie her to," Kieko said.

"Yes, I know that," Aiko said annoyed. "You go and find one. I killed her."

Kieko shook his head at Aiko and stood up.

"Hurry up. It's getting late."

"Why don't we both go look for one?"

"I'm staying right here. I shot her. I deserve to rest."

Kieko walked away. When he was far enough from Aiko he quickened the pace of his search for a strong, long branch that would hold the weight of the doe. Most of the branches he came across were too thin or rotting. The day was growing darker. He began to worry that they would not be able to return to their cave dwelling before nightfall. He then saw the end of a thick branch sticking out above the snow. He ran to it, lifted it out of the snow, and saw that it had fallen to the ground no more than a few weeks ago. The branch was long enough and appeared strong enough. He hoisted it up onto his shoulder and walked back to Aiko.

"What took you so long?" Aiko asked when he saw Kieko approaching him.

"Let's just do this as fast as possible so that we can get back."

Aiko said nothing, stood up, and took the front end of the branch from Kieko. Together they laid the branch by the doe's hooves. Aiko took some rope from his leather bag and began tying the doe's front two hooves to the branch. Kieko tied the doe's back two hooves to the branch. "Hurry up!" Aiko shouted when he finished. Kieko finished tying the last knot. "I'm done."

"Good," Aiko said. "Let's get her up and out of here."

Aiko took the front end of the branch and Kieko took the back end. They counted to three and lifted the branch up and onto their shoulders, and together they marched back to their cave dwelling.

They arrived at the cave just before nightfall; they had been living within the cave for just under a week. They entered the cave, walked up to a charred fire pit, and placed the doe down beside it.

"You start the fire," Aiko requested.

"I started it last night!"

"Then do it again." He turned his back to Kieko.

"You do it!"

Aiko turned around. "You do it Akai or we fight."

Kieko threw down his leather bag. "Let's fight, you motherless curse!"

Aiko kicked his wooden sword up from the ground and ran at Kieko who instantly took a defensive stance. He leapt, swung his sword at Kieko's head, and missed. Kieko then ran for his own wooden sword that he had hidden behind a rock near the cold fire pit. Aiko inhaled deeply and closed his eyes calming himself. Kieko kicked his sword up and looked at Aiko; Aiko had just bowed and was going through the first few movements of the first long form. Kieko waited. Aiko finished the form, brought his sword before his heart, and bowed again before opening his eyes and stepping forward, "What are you waiting for, Akai?" Kieko ran screaming with his sword held high above his head. Aiko stood still. Kieko attacked. Aiko swung his sword up and blocked allowing the force from Kieko's strike to drive his sword down and up again so that he could naturally slice Kieko clean across his back. Kieko crashed into the ground.

"You're dead, Akai," Aiko said with a smile. "Start the fire before the wolves come."

Kieko tasted blood in his mouth; he had hit his chin on a rock. He spat out some of the blood and looked out beyond the cave. It was nearly dark, and just beyond the trees of the forest that surrounded the cave he saw shimmering eyes. He coughed and spat out more blood.

"Hurry it up!" Aiko shouted.

"To hell with you!"

"Should I strike you down for dead and be done with it?"

Kieko punched the ground.

"I've beaten you again, Akai. I've beaten you again. Now get up and warm this place. We need fire or the wolves will come."

"They're already here," he whispered to himself. He stood up and coughed again. He kicked his sword and walked with a small limp to the fire pit. Aiko began untying the doe's hooves from the branch. Kieko gathered dry branches into his arms from a pile that both Aiko and he had built during their stay in the cave. He carried the branches to the fire pit and dropped them into it. He then collected dry leaves and grasses and placed them into the fire pit as well. After, he took out a small piece of flint from a pouch on his belt and began his effort to start a fire.

Aiko cut the deer open and began pulling out its internal organs. A wolf howled. Both Aiko and Kieko stopped and looked out beyond the cave where they saw several wolves moving beyond the dark of the forest with their eyes reflecting the light of the moon. "Hurry it up!" Aiko exclaimed.

Kieko continued striking the flint against his knife seeing sparks each time. Then it happened; a spark, and then a thin line of smoke emerging from the dried grasses and leaves. He bent down and blew softly into the smoke causing it to grow until there was fire. "I got it."

Aiko looked at Kieko and then out beyond the cave keeping a close eye on the wolves.

Kieko sat back and watched the fire grow as it fed off the dried leaves and branches. Aiko returned to his work on the doe and said, "Come and help me with this." Kieko, hungry, crawled to the doe and kneeled before her. Together they stabbed their knives into the doe's chest and began skinning her, cutting off pieces of flesh, and sticking them onto the charred sticks that they had used the night before to cook rabbit.

That night they feasted while keeping a worrisome eye on the dark forest and the wolves within it. The wolves, with their eyes reflecting the firelight, moved impatiently through the trees as the scent of cooked deer's meat filled the air.

"Foolish wolves," Aiko said to himself shaking his head as he took another bite of meat from his stick.

"I just hope they don't get the sense to team up and charge in after us."

"As long as that fire burns, we don't have a damn thing to worry about."

Kieko threw his stick into the fire. "That's enough. I ate too much, too fast."

Aiko shook his head, "That's you."

"What do you mean?"

"Everything you do is too fast."

"What do you mean?" he asked again.

"Nothing."

"What do you mean?" he asked for the third time feeling very irritated.

"Shinsei is right—you should listen to him."

"Listen to him about what?"

"How did I beat you? I beat you again today," he laughed. "It's not even a challenge anymore. I know exactly how to control you, to anger you. It's becoming too easy now. Before—before Shinsei forced me to stay in that temple with you I thought you were a good fighter. Now I see that you're just full of anger—and it's easy now to defeat you—all because I began listening to Shinsei."

"What do you mean by that?"

"Shinsei is not fooling you when he tells you to meditate every night. One night, while you were training on sword forms, I realized that both you and I are fire—fire fighting against fire—and that to beat you I had to become water."

"What?" he asked not believing that he was hearing this from Aiko.

"Why do you think Shinsei gave you a box of incense and me a bow and a quiver of arrows for this retreat? I almost laughed when he did that."

"I don't need to hear this. I'm going to sleep." He turned to his side with his back to Aiko and pulled a wool blanket over his body.

Aiko shook his head at Kieko and finished the last remaining pieces of meat on his stick. He then stood up and massaged his eyes with his wrists; his fingers were covered with grease. After washing his hands in a pot with the snow he had melted he took off his leather jacket, wool sweater, and cotton top-gi.

Kieko sat up to drink some water and saw, as he had many times before in the temple, the many scars on Aiko's back. "What happened to your back?" he asked hoping to hurt Aiko by reminding him that his father was responsible for those scars.

Aiko faced Kieko. Kieko could see the burned flesh and scars that marked Aiko's chest and stomach. "These are my scars," he said proudly, "scars from fighting."

"And that burn?"

"A scar you fool."

"From fighting?" he asked sarcastically.

"Yes. And you, Akai? Do you have scars?"

Kieko stood up and rolled up the sleeves of his thick wool sweater to reveal the scars he had along his forearms.

"I've seen those before. They are nothing. They are from training–not from real fighting."

"So! The scars on your chest and back are not from fighting. They are from beatings–your father's beatings! They mark nothing more than his hate of you."

"Damn you, Akai!" he spat. Kieko looked down regretting what he had said. "Don't begin with me, Akai," he said aiming his finger at Kieko before putting on his cotton top-gi.

"I'm going to sleep."

"Good. Good, Akai. Go to sleep. I've had enough of you for one day."

Kieko ignored him by drinking some water and pulling his blanket over his body before lying back down on the ground.

Aiko, flustered, hit the cave wall with his fist. He repeated what Kieko had said in his mind and reacted by picking up a stone and throwing it at Kieko hitting him in the back.

"You bastard!" Kieko shot up and threw the ceramic cup he had drunk from at Aiko. Aiko smacked the cup away. Kieko charged at him. Aiko charged at Kieko. The two jumped at each other and fell to the ground rolling and wrestling. Aiko grabbed Kieko's hands and held him down as he pelted his knee repeatedly into Kieko's groin. Kieko spat at his eyes. Aiko punched him in the face; blood began streaming down Kieko's noise. Kieko spat again and clawed Aiko's face. Aiko punched him again. Kieko grabbed Aiko's forearm and bit hard into it. Aiko screamed; the sound echoed thoughout the cave scaring the wolves. Kieko tried to tear flesh with his teeth but Aiko slammed his forehead into Kieko's face knocking him unconscious. Relieved, Aiko collapsed to the ground and rolled onto his back cradling his arm.

Curse the gods, he thought. "Curse the gods," he said. He looked at his bloody forearm and saw that Kieko had bitten deep into it. "Wicked Akai," he punched the ground. "Curses!" He sat up. He looked again at his forearm and stood up so that he could walk to a pot of water that was sitting by the fire pit. He sat down and washed his wound before dressing it with several clean strips of cloth that he had pulled from his leather bag. When he was done he fed the fire more branches and sat before it with his legs crossed. The heat of the fire warmed his face, his chest, and his knees. He wanted to drink some tea, but decided not to prepare one. He looked at the cave walls and watched the firelight play along its curved and sharp edges. He straightened his back, took a deep breath, and placed his hands below his stomach. A burning branch cracked releasing glowing embers into the smoky air. His mind began to quiet.

He observed his thoughts. He missed the metallic hum of insects during the summer. The sounds of winter—winter nights—were of cold winds howling and bare tree branches creaking. He listened. There was the sound of wood burning and cracking. In his mind he heard his father ordering him to train harder under the priest. He felt his father's fists beat him; his body tensed. He wanted to leave Lemuria; he wanted to travel far away. Then, he saw Kira in his mind and wanted her to love him. "Damn her," he whispered remembering her love for Kieko. "Enough." He threw Kira out of his mind and tried to focus on his sword forms, but he saw the shadowy face of his mother and sadness consumed his heart. He missed her. The cave became colder, and the outside quieter. He felt completely alone. "Wicked devils," he whispered. He punched the ground again, which caused his forearm to surge with pain. He didn't care. He began punching the ground repeatedly and then stopped. He sat up straight again. *No more thoughts*, he thought. He placed his hands just above his groin and focused on his breathing while listening to the pockets of silence within the night. The silence grew. Thoughts still lingered within his mind, but when he became aware of them he ended them. Soon there was only the darkness of his mind and silence. He felt himself drifting within a void. The void was cold and dreadful. He heard a whisper far in the distance. Chills ran up his spine. His arms shivered. He sat still. He heard the whisper again. He was afraid. The whisper came closer and closer to him. He kept his eyes closed and became more nervous. He felt a cold breath upon his ear that whispered, "Darkness comes." He opened his eyes looking for the voice and saw nothing. Afraid, he desperately looked around again, but there was nothing, only the fire, Kieko unconscious on the floor, and the dark outside. He crawled to his bow and nocked it with an arrow and sat before the fire waiting.

The night carried on. His exhausted body weighed heavy on him and he soon fell asleep.

Chapter XXI

Aiko woke up from a nightmare. He could not remember what he had dreamt, but he knew that something was coming. Something deep within his heart urged him to go north immediately. *Go, go, you have to go. You have to go now.* Delirious he rubbed his eyes, stood up, and walked to the mouth of the cave. Cold winds brushed up against his body as his eyes tried to focus. He squatted down, took some fresh snow from the ground, and rubbed it over his eyes. His eyes focused. It was snowing lightly. The urge to go north was still there. He went back into the cave to put on his wool sweater, saw that Kieko was still sleeping, and walked out of the cave.

He ran north dodging branches and fallen trees while kicking up snow onto bushes and tree roots. When he saw a deer behind a tree bolt away from him he realized that he had forgotten to take his short sword and his bow and quiver of arrows. He stopped for a moment trying to decide if he should turn back or not, and decided to keep going.

Running through the forest he felt like a tiger pursuing its prey, but he felt foolish; he had no idea why he was running north. He slowed down to a walk and stopped bending over to hold his knees as he caught his breath while shaking his head. "This is stupid," he said to himself. "What the hell am I doing?" He decided to turn back, but he heard something. Holding his breath he listened. The sound was, and strangely was not, rhythmic. Looking to where the sound was coming from he saw a small clearing and a mountain cliff. A chill ran down his spine. Afraid of what he might find over that cliff he silently cursed himself for not bringing any weapons and walked toward the clearing.

The trees ended. There was only untouched snow before him. He crouched down and crawled to the edge. The sound grew louder; his heart thumped faster. He crept up to the edge, prayed, and looked over.

An unending line of Lemurian men, women, and children were marching toward the Ocean of Mu. He looked at the long caravan perplexed; he had never seen so many Lemurians in his life. *What can cause this?* he thought. *Something's strange.* He realized that there were significantly more women and children than men in the caravan and that they were all dirty and exhausted from days of unending travel. *Why are they going to the ocean—to Ikishi?* He panicked at the thought of them reaching his home and crawled back from the edge. "I have to go back. I have to tell Shinsei." Something then growled deeply from behind him.

He turned his head and saw a white, mountain tiger; her lips curled revealing long white fangs as she grumbled. His eyes widened. He cursed himself. He had no weapon and was at the edge of a cliff.

He stood up slowly. The tiger roared. Fear penetrated his heart causing him to shake. He then decided that if he was going to die he would do so fighting. "Come on!" he shouted at the tiger as he stood his ground. "Come on!" The mountain tiger ran and dove at him catching him with her claws, throwing him down, pinning him to the ground. Clawing at his chest she sliced it open spilling blood all over his body and the snow. He screamed. It was over. He could not compete with her towering strength. She clawed deeper into his chest and sliced his face, blinding him with blood, sending him into shock.

An arrow shot through the air and pierced the tiger's stomach. The tiger roared. She looked and saw the arrow sticking out of her. She roared again. A second arrow hissed through the air and delved into her neck. Unable to move her neck she cried out in torment as two more arrows were shot into her.

Kieko nocked another arrow onto Aiko's bow and approached the tiger taking aim at her heart. She growled at Kieko. He could see that she was now weak. She stepped off Aiko's body and stepped toward him. He released the arrow and struck her heart. She stumbled from left to right, and collapsed.

Blood, spilling from Aiko and the tiger, fanned out into the snow. Kieko went to Aiko and kneeld before him. "Aiko!" he called out. He shook him. No response. "Aiko!" He slapped him across the face. No response again. He took Aiko's wrist and checked his pulse; he was still alive. Relieved, he let out a sigh and took out the extra top-gi he had in his leather bag and cut it into long strips with his short sword. He applied pressure on Aiko's wounds and began bandaging them with the strips of cloth. As he worked he knew that trying to carry him in his battered condition was dangerous. He had to build a stretcher and drag him back to the Kadek Temple.

When he had finished bandaging as many of Aiko's wounds as he could he stood up and looked at the forest searching for strong, long branches. But, he heard a slightly rhythmic hum coming from over the cliff's edge. "What is that?" he asked himself. He had never heard such an unusual sound. He walked to the edge and saw the unending line of hundreds, if not thousands, of men, women, and children who were all marching toward the sea and noticed that there were far fewer men than women and children. He did not understand why so many Lemurians were traveling away from their own lands. Questions raced through his head. Feeling the urgency to return to his master he stepped away from the cliff and began working on Aiko's stretcher.

Just as the sun was setting Kieko collapsed to the ground exhausted after an entire day of dragging Aiko through the snowy terrains of the mountain forest. Massaging his temples with his cold hands he rolled his head and stretched his back before crawling to and sitting against a tree. All was quiet within the forest. He looked at Aiko who was still asleep and shook his head dreading another day of dragging him on the stretcher through the snow. "It's getting dark," he said to himself. "I'll need to set up camp soon." He crawled to Aiko and placed his hand over his forehead. "The fever is getting worse." He scratched his chin and thought for a moment. "We should be with Shinsei by tomorrow evening . . . I hope." He took a look at the stitch work he had done on Aiko's cheek and got to work on starting a fire.

By nightfall he had skinned a rabbit that he had shot in the morning with Aiko's bow and sat back before the campfire waiting for it to cook as his stomach grumbled. It began to snow. He looked up at the trees feeling a few snowflakes land on his face before fading into droplets and took another sip of tea. He moved closer to the fire to turn the stick that the rabbit had been impaled upon so that all sides of it cooked evenly, and when the air filled with the scent of cooked rabbit he said to himself, "It's time to eat—it's time to eat." He lifted the stick with the rabbit off the two branches he had stabbed into the ground at the opposing sides of the campfire and stuck it into the ground. He cut and ate a piece of meat realizing that it was burnt, but he did not care, the meat was delicious and satisfying. He cut off more pieces of meat and stuffed them into his mouth.

When he had finished chewing off the meat from nearly every bone he threw the bones into a pot that he had filled with snow, placed it next to the fire, and sat back and waited for the snow to melt, boil, and become a broth.

The broth began to boil and Kieko pulled the pot away from the campfire, filled his cup, waited, and took a sip to ensure that the broth was not too hot before taking it to Aiko. Holding Aiko's head up he pressed the cup to Aiko's lips and poured the broth into his mouth. Aiko coughed and spat the broth out; he opened his sick, exhausted eyes and saw that Kieko was trying to help him drink; and with what little strength he had he drank a third of the broth and fell back to sleep. Kieko drank the rest and got ready to sleep.

The next morning Kieko woke up and found that he was covered under a thin sheet of snow. He sat up, dusted the snow off his shoulders and chest, and yawned while stretching out his arms. He went to Aiko and dusted off the snow from his body before checking his temperature. "He's still burning," he whispered. "Need to make some tea." He stood up, collected as many dry branches as he could find, dropped them over the charred remains of the campfire, and got to work on starting another fire.

Soon a strong flame was burning and Kieko boiled some water to make tea while chewing on the last few strips of deer meat that Aiko had dried and salted during the first week of their retreat. When the tea was ready he drank a full cup and, as before, took a cup to Aiko, held it to his lips, and poured the tea into his mouth. Aiko began coughing. "Are you all right?" Kieko asked. Aiko fell back asleep. He checked his temperature again, "He's burning up—damn it." Frustrated, he looked around scratching his head repeating the words: "He needs the priest." He stopped and thought for a moment. "I'm still a half-day's walk from the temple." He stood up and began walking around the campsite. "What am I doing? What am I going to do?" He began scratching his head again. "He needs Ki."

He walked up to a pine tree and stood before it. Closing his eyes he pointed the palms of his hands toward the tree and breathed in deeply while slowly moving his hands back and forth. He felt a small magnetic pull between his hands and the tree and imagined the flow of Ki from the sky and the ground moving into the tree and out toward him. The magnetic pull between his hands and the tree grew stronger. Quieting his mind he listened to the faint gusts of wind and the movement of the tree branches above him. He felt a wave of warm air overcome him as he lost himself in his surroundings. He then became aware, and in that moment he awoke from his meditation feeling incredibly alert. With eyes wide open he stepped away from the tree feeling dizzy and bent down to hold his knees. His vision blurred and he went blind. He shook his head and rubbed his eyes with his hands. His vision returned, and carefully he walked back to Aiko and sat down before him.

Closing his eyes and taking a deep breath he held his hands over Aiko's body and imagined the Ki from within him flowing out of his palms and into Aiko. Aiko began moaning and moving. He continued imagining the Ki flowing from him into Aiko, but he heard something. It was far in the distance. He listened. The sound was growing; it was growing rapidly. He opened his eyes and looked up at the sky. The sound became a high-pitched scream. And then, in an instant, two metallic birds shot straight over him.

He ducked down in fright. "What—what was that?" The piercing sound diminished to nothing. "What was that?" he asked again looking in the direction that the two metallic birds had flown. He did not know what to do. "Shinsei—I need Shinsei," he panicked. He kicked snow into the campfire and began packing up their campsite as fast as he could. When he finished he lifted one end of Aiko's stretcher and began dragging it.

Morning turned to early afternoon. Kieko, exhausted, panting, stopped. Gently placing Aiko's stretcher on the snow covered ground he sat down and scanned the forest with his eyes. He saw a cliff beyond a few trees and listened hearing a faint buzz. He wiped his brow with his arm and remembered the long caravan of Lemurians. He stood up and approached the cliff. At the edge of the cliff he looked out and saw in the distance the line of Lemurians he had seen before pouring into a large circular campsite within the valley that led to the sea. They were pitching tents, building fires, and cooking over flames. He looked down the valley and was just able to see the sea and his village. "I'm close to the temple," he said relieved. He then wondered why the Lemurians had stopped a few hours short of Ikishi, and walked back to Aiko.

He saw Aiko moving his arms and ran up to him.

"Kieko," Aiko said softly.

"Are you okay?"

He coughed, "Where are we?"

"We're about half-a-days walk from the temple," he said kneeling before him.

"Where's Shinsei?"

"I don't know . . . but I think he's near. I can feel him now," he said surprised that he could now sense his master.

"Yes . . . it's strange," he gave Kieko a quizzical look. "I can feel him too," he coughed again. "Why doesn't he help us?"

"I think . . . I think that this is how it's supposed to be."

"That man's a fool. I was mauled by a tiger!" he began coughing violently. "Forget—forget the temple, let's go back to the village."

"I can't. I can't pull you that far. The temple is closer. We can get there before nightfall."

Aiko was silent. He was listening. "What's that?"

"What's what?"

"That—that noise!"

"Oh that! You're not going to believe it, but there are hundreds—maybe even thousands of people camping in the valley. They're headed for our village."

"I saw them."

"When?"

"Just before the tiger attacked me. Did you find her cubs?"

"What cubs?"

"The tiger's cubs!" he groaned shaking his head.

"What?"

"Are you stupid or what? The cubs!"

Kieko realized that the tiger had attacked Aiko because he was in close proximity to the den where she had hid her cubs. "No, I didn't find them. After what had happened to you I didn't even think about that."

"Well, by now I'm sure they're starving . . . perhaps dying."

"I saw something this morning . . . something in the air."

"What did you see?"

"I don't know. They weren't birds; they were far too big and fast—and loud."

"Was it a flying machine?" he asked sarcastically.

"I don't know?"

Aiko looked at Kieko with a stern face.

"All this is not right," Kieko said with urgency. "Something's wrong."

"Of course something's wrong! Why do you think so many people are marching to the sea?"

"I—I don't know." But then he knew.

"The Akais are attacking Lemuria!"

"We don't know that. There could have been a storm—or a fire that is driving them this way."

"Shut up, Kieko. You can feel it. You know what is coming."

Kieko was silent.

"We need to go back to the village."

"I already told you. I can't take you that far. We can reach the temple by nightfall. Shinsei can heal you and we can go back to the village together."

"Then let's go!" he commanded.

"Don't order me, Aiko."

"Don't order you. Don't order you! The Akais are coming to kill us, you red faced freak—"

"Shut your mouth! I'm in charge here! I am! You are tied to a stretcher. Your body is littered with ripped flesh—perhaps broken bones. I have cared for you and carried you. And I will take you to the priest! Don't you ever talk down to me again!"

Aiko was silent.

"I'm sick of you . . . I'm sick of you." He stood up, lifted the stretcher, and began dragging it.

After reaching the base of the mountain Aiko began coughing violently again. Kieko placed the stretcher down. "How are you feeling?

"If you," he cleared his throat. "If you can believe it I feel a bit better. The priest must be near," he joked.

"Do you think you can walk?"

"I think so. I don't think any of my bones are broken."

"You don't feel a fever or anything?"

"I'm still burning, but not as bad as this morning. Just get me out of this."

Kieko began cutting the rope that held Aiko down to the stretcher and helped him rise to his feet. "Are you sure you can walk?"

"Don't let go of me," he barked as he placed his arm around Kieko's shoulder for support. Kieko then stepped forward and Aiko limped.

"I think your ankle's sprained," Kieko said.

"Wicked curses!" Aiko shouted frustrated.

"What? Does it hurt?"

"No, I'm just angry I have to deal with this. Ugh—I'm going to walk, I'm going to walk," he tried to convince himself. "Just help me a bit. I'm not going to have you drag me the rest of the way to the priest."

"Are you sure?"

"What did I just say?"

Kieko did not answer.

Aiko shook his head. "Come on. Let's just go."

"Wait. Stand still." Kieko went to the stretcher and began taking it apart.

"What are you doing?"

"We'll be able to walk better through the snow with a staff."

Aiko knew that he was right. Kieko took the stretcher apart and gave one of the two tall branches he had to Aiko. Together they walked over the icy terrain, and after a few hours they recognized the forest they were traveling in and felt relieved that they were now near the Kadek Temple.

Master Shinsei waited by the tori gate of the temple for his two young disciples; he had felt their presence in the morning when he had woken up and knew that they would arrive before sunset.

And when he saw Kieko and Aiko he smiled, waved to them, and could see by how Aiko looked and by how he limped that he had sprained his right ankle, had cuts across his chest, and was ill from a fever. Kieko and Aiko waved and smiled back as a strong emotional wave of relief overcame them.

"It's good to see you again, Master Shinsei," Kieko greeted when they reached the priest.

"It's good to see you, Master Shinsei," Aiko greeted.

"I am happy to see you both, my young Ki Guardians," the priest replied.

"Then . . . then it is done, Master Shinsei," Aiko said.

"No, it is not done, but I fear that time is short and that you both must rise quickly into manhood."

"What do you mean, Master Shinsei?" Kieko asked concerned.

"Come. Let us speak within the temple where it is warm and where there is food to fill your stomachs."

"Yes, Master Shinsei," Kieko and Aiko said together.

The priest and the two disciples walked back to the temple that was now cloaked by the shadows cast by the setting sun feeling the unknown before them, their fear of it, and the realization that they could do nothing more than proceed into the darkness.

Chapter XXII

The kitchen chamber was the same; clean and orderly, but there was an unnerving stillness in the air that Kieko and Aiko felt and did not like. The priest was aware of this stillness, but he did not dwell on it. Instead, he went straight to work on Aiko by laying him down and going over his wounds before dressing them with new bandages. When he was done he gave Aiko a strong tea to make him drowsy and began preparing a bitter, salty soup. Kieko sat at the kitchen table listening to the boiling water, the crackling sparks of burning wood, and the priest cutting a carrot. Strangely he was not hungry, and neither was Aiko.

"Kieko, you will return to Ikishi and find out what is happening," the priest said with his back to his disciples.

Kieko looked at the rice wine bottle on the kitchen table and replied, "Master Shinsei, you have the respect of the Elders. They will tell you things that they will not to me. Let me stay—I can care for Aiko—so that you can go."

The priest stopped cutting. "That is true, but . . . do not question me Kieko, do as I ask."

"Yes, Master Shinsei," he bowed his head; he could feel a troubled sadness eating away at his master. Aiko looked at Kieko expressing through his eyes that he too felt something wearing down on their master.

"Time to eat," announced the priest.

"Shall I serve, Master Shinsei?" Kieko asked.

"Yes, please do."

Kieko went to the cupboard, took three bowls, and went to the kitchen counter where he saw one pot filled with vegetable soup and another filled with boiled fish. "Should I put the fish into the soup or keep them separate, Master Shinsei?"

"Place the fish into the soup."

Kieko prepared the bowls and placed them on the kitchen table.

"Sit, Kieko," the priest said seated after pouring two cups of tea.

"Yes, Master Shinsei," he looked at Aiko and saw that he had just fallen asleep.

"He'll be all right," the priest assured him.

Kieko sat down and bowed his head with the priest. He then drank his soup finding it to be very bitter, but his stomach had awakened with severe hunger and he tilted the bowl up to drink it as fast as he could.

"You will upset your stomach. Drink slowly. Drink with a spoon."

Kieko placed the bowl on the table and wiped his lips with his hand. "Yes, Master Shinsei."

The two continued eating.

The priest finished first and sat silently as he watched Kieko who was too hungry to mind his master's observations of him.

When all was done of their food the priest poured two cups of an old rice wine; Kieko frowned.

"What is wrong?" the priest asked.

"Nothing, Master Shinsei."

"You don't want to drink."

Kieko shook his head.

The priest took a sip from his cup. "You are worried."

"Yes, Master Shinsei, I am."

The priest, silent, ran his fingers through his beard. Kieko looked down and nervously rubbed his hands together.

"You saw something . . . you and Aiko both saw something."

Kieko nodded.

"What did you see?"

"We saw people," he said looking up to his master, "thousands of them marching toward Ikishi."

"Hmm," the priest hummed.

"Did you see them, Master Shinsei?"

"No."

"Something is going to happen to us," Kieko blurted.

The priest was silent.

"What's happening?"

The priest took another sip from his cup and held his hand to his lips.

"What will happen to Aiko?"

"He . . . he will be fine. You cared for him well in those woods."

"What is going to happen to us, Master Shinsei?" he asked feeling a dark weight pressing down on his chest.

"Be careful, Kieko."

He looked at the priest.

"The darkness is growing in you . . . as it is within me . . ."

"What . . . what do you mean, Master Shinsei? What—what is going to happen to us?"

"Quiet down . . . quiet down."

"You're scaring me, Master Shinsei. What's wrong with you?"

"Nothing is wrong with me . . . nothing is wrong . . ." he said with eyes that avoided Kieko. "What are you afraid of Kieko?"

"I . . . I don't like how you're acting. You don't seem yourself, Master Shinsei."

"The temple is as it was when both Aiko and you left it," he took out his long pipe and lit it. "But . . . something has changed," he puffed on the pipe; white smoke swirled from his lips. "Things that I had hoped to never see again are now coming and there is someone . . . who I have not felt since I was young," he took a long puff on the pipe, "is very, very near."

"I . . . I don't understand what you're saying, Master Shinsei."

"Of course you do not, but . . . you will, Kieko."

"Why are so many Lemurians walking to the sea, Master Shinsei? Have you seen . . . have you seen something like this before?"

"Yes, Kieko, I have . . . it is not a good sign."

"What does it mean?"

"It means that either a new Lemurian warlord has gained power west of here and is seizing land or that the Atlanteans have come . . . although of the two . . . I am afraid that it is the latter," he puffed on his pipe, "we do not have much time."

"The Atlanteans are coming," Kieko said to himself looking down at the table. "What should I do, Master Shinsei?"

"You will do what I asked you to do. You will go to Ikishi and gain news from the Elders, and you will come back and tell me what you have learned." Kieko tried to interrupt, but the priest hushed him and continued, "You will leave early tomorrow morning. Get ready for sleep. Do not worry tonight about your temple duties. I will clean the kitchen and watch over Aiko."

Kieko wanted to express his hesitation to the priest of returning to the village alone to seek word from the Elders, but he remained silent and stood up to bow to his master, "Good night, Master Shinsei."

"Good night, Kieko."

He exited the kitchen chamber and made his way to his room.

At dawn Master Shinsei entered Kieko's room and shouted, "Kieko, wake up!" Kieko bolted up from his futon ready to attack, but he heard the priest say, "Kieko, it is I, the priest," and calmed down. He rubbed his eyes, looked over the edge of his lofted futon, and saw the priest looking at him.

"There is a snow storm coming—you need to prepare for the journey back to the village immediately. Here," he pointed to the table by the fireplace, "I have these undergarments for you. They are clean and warm for this type of weather. Also, it is not necessary for you to keep your head shaved—allow it to grow out again."

"Yes, Master Shinsei," he said before walking down the steps from his lofted futon; and when he stood before the priest he gave him three full bows.

In the bathing chamber, in the underground of the temple, Kieko washed, soaped, and scrubbed his body with the warm water from the wooden buckets that his master had already prepared for him. When he was done he stepped into the hot spring bath and placed his head on a headrest made from cut bamboo stems. He was eager to see his mother and Kira again, but he did not like the circumstances under which he would see them. Although his mind kept him tense the warm waters softened his skin and healed his many scabs and wounds from the weeks he had spent in the wild. He looked at the scars that ran along his left arm and smiled with pride.

He stepped out of the bath, exited the bath chamber, and put on his new undergarments after drying himself.

Returning to his room he found garments of black, dark brown, and dark green laid out for him on the floor; he had never seen clothes such as these; they were made of leather, heavy cotton, and wool fabrics. He put on the dark brown, leather pants to see if they would fit, which they did, and fastened them tight around his knees and shins with thin leather straps. He then put on the black, cotton top-gi and a dark green, wool top-gi before tying a leather belt around his waist. Last was the black wool cloak, which had a large hood to cover his head and conceal his face.

"Do you like them?" the priest asked standing at the doorway.

"Yes, I do, Master Shinsei. Thank you so much. I don't understand why you have given these to me."

"Whether you like it or not, Kieko, you are a man now. You need new colors as a testament of this."

"Where did you get them?"

"They are mine, or rather, I should say, were mine. They were one of several attires that I took with me from my royal wardrobe. I will give Aiko new garments as well, but he needs to rest and sleep . . . he will need a few days to recover from his wounds. I altered his clothes just a bit—he is taller than I was—while you both were away on your retreat."

"Thank you, Master Shinsei."

"You are a good student, Kieko . . . even if you think too much," he smiled. "Come and eat some breakfast with me."

"Yes, Master Shinsei."

Warm soup, rice, and tea awaited Kieko. He ate and before he finished the priest said, "Be cautious, Kieko. Try to gather what you can from a distance, and if you think it is safe then proceed into the village and reveal yourself. Remember, it appears that the Atlanteans are attacking Lemurian lands and there are those in the village who will not look kindly upon your mixed blood."

"Yes, Master Shinsei."

"Everything will be fine. Just get back to me as soon as you can."

"Yes, Master Shinsei."

"Leave your bowls. I will clean them for you."

"Thank you, Master Shinsei."

Back in his room Kieko checked his futon and the area around it for anything he might have forgotten and needed, he then remembered his first night in the temple and how much he had missed his mother. He smiled when he realized that he had changed quite a bit since his arrival at the temple: *I wonder what will become of me in a year?*

"Thinking again?" the priest asked from the doorway.

"No, Master Shinsei," he said with slight hesitation. "I was just saying goodbye."

"Ah, yes . . . goodbye to who you were. Be sure to light three incense sticks at the main altar and to give three full bows at all the temple shrines before you leave."

"Yes, Master Shinsei," he said as he descended the steps from his lofted futon. "Is it all right if I ask you a question before I go?"

The priest thought for a moment, "Yes, go ahead."

"Do you really believe in all this ritual that we do everyday in the temple?"

"Yes, I do believe in what I practice in this temple . . . and that is why I feel as I now do," he looked down.

"What do you mean, Master Shinsei?"

"It is hard for me—a priest of the Ki—to say goodbye to all that I am . . . and all that this temple has given to me . . . I am . . . attached."

"Why? Why would you need to say goodbye, Master Shinsei?"

He looked up, "It is time to say goodbye, Kieko. It is time."

Kieko did not like the frailty that he now saw in his master, "What—what is wrong with you, Master Shinsei? You look weak—I need to see your strength. Especially now—especially now before I go."

The priest simply looked at Kieko.

"Master Shinsei," he said with anger creeping up behind his words, "I need to see you strong before I am to go. What's wrong with you? Ever since Aiko and I arrived I can see that you are different. What happened? What's happening to you—to those people I saw?"

"Something that cannot be avoided—"

"How can you speak like that? You are a priest—you must show another way!"

The priest struck Kieko hard across the face with his hand, "Never speak to me with disrespect! I am your Master! Leave my sight and return to me when you have news of the village."

Kieko wanted to curse his master.

"Do not even think it!" the priest shouted. "You have much to learn of the world, now leave my sight and return with news from the Elders."

Kieko grabbed his leather bag, past his master, and made his way down to the temple entrance door.

The priest stood in the old room regretting his words, and when he had heard the faint sound of Kieko slamming the entrance door closed he went down into the temple underground to light candles and incense sticks at all the shrines praying for Kieko to have a safe journey and return.

By afternoon the snowfall had increased and the temperature had dropped making it more and more difficult for Kieko to see far ahead as he walked with a staff. He charged through the accumulating snow determined to arrive at the village by nightfall, but the cold bit his cheeks and numbed his hands and feet while his mind tormented him with what had happened between him and his master. Frustrated with the heavy snow, strong winds, and his master's last words he launched his staff into a series of attacks against a frail, sick old tree until all that was left of it was a jagged stump of bark and pathetic wood.

"Who goes there?" a voice called out.

Kieko took a defensive stance and searched with his eyes through the heavy snowfall for the voice, but he could not see far into the forest that surrounded him. "I'm armed, don't come near!" he shouted ready to fight.

"Is that you, young Kieko?" asked the voice.

"Who are you?"

A figure appeared through the trees covered in heavy garments and approached Kieko with a walking staff. The figure's movements were familiar, "Is that you, old farmer Toasu?" Kieko called out relieved.

"Yes, yes, dear boy. What," he coughed, "what may I ask are you doing in this madness? You should be with the priest, should you not?"

Although he could not see his eyes or nose Kieko could see the old farmer smile beneath his wool hood. "Master Shinsei asked me to go to Ikishi and speak to the Elders—if it's safe for me to do so—about these people approaching our sea. Have you seen them?"

"Our sea?" the old man said sarcastically. "I do not recall the sea being ours? Was there something I missed while living my life alone these past years?"

"You do know what I mean, don't you, old farmer Toasu?"

"Yes, yes, boy, I am just having a bit of fun. It is not often that I have the opportunity to play tricks, or at least attempt to play tricks, on young folk like you."

Kieko looked at the farmer thinking that he was indeed losing his mind, "What about you, old farmer Toasu? What are you doing out in this weather?"

"What do you care? I am doing what crazy old hermits are expected to do. I am out in this madness appeasing my need for a walk, when all those who are sane hide within their huts." Looking up and revealing more of his wrinkled face he continued, "So tell me, about these people who march to the sea, for I have seen them too."

"Old farmer Toasu, I don't know much about them, that is why I have been sent by the priest to seek knowledge about them from the Elders."

"And what makes you, or the priest, think that the Elders know any more about them than you do, or even if they will speak to you?"

"They should answer me, shouldn't they? I go to them for Master Shinsei."

"That is the exactly why they will not speak to you. Elders do not speak to messengers. Master Shinsei should know better than to have sent you . . . I suspect that he is not himself."

"No, no, he is not."

"I sense anger in you, Kieko. Do not take your anger into the village. Do not make that mistake," he scratched his beard. "Of course, what do I know? I am simply an old fool."

"What should I do then, if I can't go to the village? I can't return to my master with no news from the Elders."

"I suspect you need some time to rest your mind and thoughts. If you wish you may return to my home for warmth, food, hot tea, and my answers."

"You know what is happening then?"

"I may know something . . . But most do not seek the council of an old hermit like me. So what do you say?"

Kieko took in a deep cold breath, exhaled, and said, "Yes, it feels right that I should go with you."

"Then come along, I wish not to freeze in this any longer."

"Yes, old farmer Toasu."

"Stay close to me. You can easily lose sight of your own hands in this snow."

"Yes, I'll stay close."

"What did you say? Speak up, I can't hear you in this!"

"I said that I would stay close!"

"That is better."

The old farmer began walking through the snow and Kieko followed right behind him.

After an hour had passed Kieko looked ahead hoping to see some sign of the old farmer's home, but all he saw was white. "How can you see anything in this, old farmer Toasu?"

"What gives you the impression that I can see? I only have one good eye, and an old one at that."

Just then Kieko saw a faint, dark image in the distance. He squinted and was able to make out that it was a roof, "I believe I see your home."

"Thank the gods, boy, because I had no idea where we were."

"Are you out of your mind?" Kieko asked shocked. "You could have gotten us lost!"

"How is that?"

"I was following your lead."

"I didn't ask you to follow my lead. I decided to continue my walk first before returning home, and you followed."

Kieko could not believe what he was hearing, "How could I have known you were continuing your walk when you didn't even tell me that! You asked me to stay close because we were returning to your home."

"I did? Well, in any matter, what of the matter? We have arrived, and I am cold and in need of a warm fire, food, and drink. So now then, follow my lead."

Kieko, frustrated, followed.

The winter winds blew hard and strong against them causing their teeth to chatter and hands to shake until finally they arrived at the old farmer's home.

Jomana barked at the old farmer and at Kieko when they entered; Kieko, too cold to pet her, went straight to the faintly burning fireplace and threw in some more logs before sitting down and taking off his boots. As he sat in a chair before the fire rubbing his hands together he saw that the objects that were on the shelves of the wall were still covered with old cobwebs; on the shelves there were crescent shaped daggers with ivory handles fitted with small jewels and inscriptions made in a tongue from a land far into the west; there were heavy necklaces strung with large metal spheres and bone beads; large golden earrings shaped like a woman's breast; thick silver bracelets covered with gems and marked by strange designs.

"You are still curious about those things?" the old farmer asked as he remembered his youth.

"I don't understand most of the things that are on those shelves."

"You know," he began as he sat down to pet Jomana, "that when I was about your age an outsider came to our village. His skin was dark, darker than any night . . . I feared him," he laughed, "many in our village feared him. At first we thought he was a devil that had come to bring death to us . . . but, although we did not understand his words, we understood that he wanted food and shelter. In fear we fed him and sheltered him. He wore beautiful bright clothing, and jewelry that shined like the stars—like sparkles of sunlight reflecting off the sea . . .

"I remember his eyes, his bright white eyes. His skin was so dark that in the night, around the village campfire, when he looked to his sides, all you could see of him was the white of his eyes. At times it appeared as if there was no face for those eyes; those eyes just seemed to hang in the darkness, like a ghost, or a bodiless creature of the night.

"One morning he left and that was the last we ever saw of him. Everyone gossiped about who he was or where he had come from. Some said that his skin was so dark because he had burned in the fires of hell and had somehow escaped to wander the lands of the world lost."

"Did you ever find out who he really was? I think he was a devil."

"Why do you say that?"

"Because he is a creature of the night, if his skin is black then he could've only been born in a dark land."

"You have much to learn of the world, Kieko." Jomana barked, the old farmer continued, "You will find that those who live in the light betray, and those who live in the shadows save."

"I don't understand what you mean, old farmer Toasu?"

"Nothing is ever as it seems. Although your eyes may see the light, your skin may feel its warmth, and your mind may understand it, if your heart is doubtful then there is a shadow—

always there is a shadow when there is doubt—and when there is doubt there is a trick being played against your senses. As you grow and experience this world you will learn to trust your instincts when your senses fail you. Do not be quick to believe in what you see. Only be quick to believe in you, and from that all else will come."

"So, if I am wrong, then who was this man?"

"I never found him, so I do not know his story, but I did find the land from where he came. My curiosity to discover who this man was, and to see all the worlds that he had seen before arriving to our village, drove me west. After the death of my parents I had nothing to keep me here, so I left and traveled the world for more years than I can possibly remember."

"What did you see beyond the western sea?" Kieko asked as he moved his chair closer to the farmer.

"It has been some time since I have had someone here in Lemuria to share my story with. Most are not interested to learn of the outside world. Most are content to be left to the comforts of the home that they have always known. It is safe for them, and any talk of what lives beyond their borders frightens them. But, you, Kieko, are different. I have kept my eye on you, and I can see that you are destined for things greater than any of us can imagine. You are brave and you have much to be proud of."

Kieko looked at his feet as his shoulders caved in to his center.

"Why do you frown?"

"I want to be like my father."

"Your father you say. You wish you could have known him. I wished I could have had my parents live a long and healthy life, but if they did not die when they did then I would have never traveled beyond the borders of Kadek, and I would not be here with you, right now, sharing what I am about to share of the outside world."

"So, what are you trying to say? Are you saying that it is a good thing that I never knew my father?"

"Did I say that? Do not speak to me in such a way. I have seen and known more than you can ever imagine. You will pay your respects for you are in my home!"

"I apologize, old farmer Toasu."

"If there is any greater truth, it is this. Everything happens for a reason. There is no such thing as chaos or random circumstance. The child born deaf, the man dying of a wasting disease, and the mother who loses her son to war, are all examples of the order and wonder that permeates the world. We choose the lives we are going lead before coming into the world. All that ails us, all that plagues us, all that strengthens us, and all that fills us with love, are all a part of a grand plan that we have designed for ourselves, with the aid of others, before we even come into this material land.

"I chose my parents because there was something that I wanted to learn from them, and they chose to die when they did to set me free into the world to become who I am now.

"You do not have to accept this, but you will find that the moment you choose to live your life with intention, as opposed to being the victim of uncontrollable circumstances, you will live and die in a light so bright that you will change this world in a very beautiful way." Seeing the exhaustion in Kieko's body the old farmer stood up and went to the kitchen to get an old ceramic mug. He put a spoonful of dried tealeaves into the cup and poured some hot water into it from an iron pot that was hanging over the fireplace. "Here you are," the old farmer said giving the cup to Kieko.

"Is it all right to drink the tea leaves?"

"Yes, drink them. They will heal your body from the cold."

Kieko sipped the hot tea and accidentally drank a tea leaf, "I don't like these leaves—they're slimy."

"Yes, yes, no one likes them, but you have to eat them anyway."

"Is that because I planned to be here and eat them or because I have no choice and you are going to force me to eat them?"

Old farmer Toasu stared at Kieko, but Kieko smiled, and together they laughed.

"I think it's late, should we prepare for sleep?" the old farmer asked.

"I would like to sleep, but I would like to hear some of your tales."

"So be it," he smiled. "Where shall I begin?"

"From the beginning," Kieko said with enthusiasm.

"Would you like a blanket before I get started?"

"Yes, that would be nice," he said sitting back in his chair.

"What? Do you expect me to get it for you? The wool blankets are in there," the old farmer said pointing to the trunk in the far corner of the room.

Kieko got up and walked to the trunk. The truck lid was heavy to lift, but inside he found several wool blankets that had been poorly folded. He chose the top blanket, wrapped himself in it, and returned to his chair.

Old farmer Toasu prepared his pipe. "Well, I do not suspect the night long enough to tell all of my tales, and I also suspect that you will fall asleep soon to the rhythm of my words."

"I feel fine," Kieko commented. "I will stay awake."

"We shall see," he ran his fingers through his bead. "Well, I left this village at seventeen. I left in the night not telling a soul as to where I was headed. I simply disappeared, which is funny now because after my return I discovered that many here explained my disappearance by suggesting, or believing, that the black man—or 'devil' as they called him—had come and taken me away. What rubbish, but that was how they made sense of my disappearance."

Smiling as he remembered his youth the old farmer continued, "I traveled west and crossed the Ikishi forest and the Shinohi Mountains. I found many Lemurian villages of varying dialects of our mother tongue. I ate foods prepared in ways that I had never seen before, and saw women that froze me with their beauty. But, this was only the beginning. I tell you, the women in the lands of the far west are far more exotic and voluptuous than our women here. There is nothing in this world like a gorgeous woman . . ."

"Did you find someone on your travels? Did you fall in love?"

"Yes, of course–I found many women," he smiled again. "Well, maybe it is safer to say that I was infatuated with many women and in love with only one. Women are beautiful. I don't understand their attraction to men really. If I was a woman I would love women," he chuckled.

"Tell me more about what you saw abroad."

"Well, women were a big part of what I saw abroad. Maybe it's foolish that I live here alone with my cats and dog, but in retrospect this is what I have chosen for myself, because when I had the chance to declare my love I ran away and abandoned all that I desired. Sad really, my life is, living in solitude holding onto a past that cannot be unmade."

"I didn't know you had cats," Kieko said as he looked around the room trying to find any sign of them.

"Yes, I have two, but they never reveal themselves to outsiders like you. Only to me do they share themselves. In any case maybe you can learn a thing or two from the mistakes of my life."

"Such as?"

"Do you not listen, boy?"

"You mean about women?"

"No–I mean about declaring love."

"Declaring love to a woman?"

"Declaring love to a woman, yes, but also declaring your love for your dreams. It is in my experience that unhappiness arises from believing that you do not deserve the love of others, or that you do not deserve what your heart desires. Many are too afraid of their first failure and simply fall into the safe light of an ordinary life.

"Why is it so difficult for us to see that there are extraordinary elements within us that need to be shaken and awoken? If you believe in yourself that is something that no one can ever take from you. If your foundation is your faith, that you are unbreakable, then the world is there to be had, and once you have crossed through that barrier the real trials begin."

"What do you mean? What comes after?"

"So many trials will come crashing down upon you. Once you have declared your strength know that demons and dark angels will have been awoken by your call, and they will take you to the gates of hell. They will whisper in your ear and try to steer you away from falling into the unknown dark of your faith. They will wave wealth and women in your eyes, and tempt you away from what you seek. They will rip and scar you. You will die a thousand times and grow stronger with each rebirth.

"And, yes, you may find yourself in love, but there is a difference between being in love and loving someone every morning you wake. Being in love is magical and seems infinite and flawless. This is how it begins, and we fall into the trap of the ideal and the fantastic, but when events occur that we did not plan we find ourselves willing to betray because we are too afraid to fight for it by facing our inner demons. It is okay to be afraid of a past that haunts you, but you must slay it before it controls and keeps you from loving those who are with you."

"Old farmer Toasu, I don't understand what you are trying to tell me?"

"Well, of course, you don't. You will only understand it when you have experienced what I speak. Nothing I can say will reveal to you what I have come to know as true. Although, let me simply say this. Everything we do, both good and bad, is in some strange way an act of love. There is only love. Judgment, hate, anger, and violence are not real and devoid of power. They are acts stemming from a person who does not love himself and expresses it so. If you are brave and wise enough to not be offended by the horrific actions of your enemies, and simply seek to understand why they do the things that they do, then you will be acting as a compassionate human being.

"Compassion arises from understanding, from intelligence, and fear arises from ignorance. If you seek to understand your enemies and display empathy to them then you will have done something glorious. If you do not demonize your enemies as an outside other, then you are on the path to peace, and in this way you have the power to end the cycles of violence that plague our Mother so."

Kieko's eyes began to weigh heavy.

Taking notice the old farmer decided to continue speaking and allow his young guest to fall asleep. "Much ugliness have I seen in this world. Much suffering and poverty there is in the lands of the West. Many wars have been and are being fought for conquest of land and territory. I have seen so many wonders: I have seen the great Orion pyramids; I have seen Sirian attack ships destroyed by Phoenix strong holds off the Pillar Gates to Og; and I have seen the Atlantean Royal Towers, and their Kai before their demise by the one named Maniok. And now . . . I see you falling asleep before me . . ."

The night was silent; there were no howling winds to cause the window shutters to flap against the cabin. The fireplace hissed as the old farmer threw in another log to feed the flames. Embers crackled as orange light moved and danced with shadows to animate Kieko's face; the darkness, unconquered by the firelight, nested within the round oval pockets of the boy's eyes.

Old farmer Toasu tried to see Kieko's face clearly in the growing dark of his home, but a cold shiver ran down his spine. The light and shadows altered Kieko's face and the old farmer backed away in fear for he saw the paradox in Kieko: a young man destined to do so much good if he chose to follow his heart, but capable of unimaginable destruction if he betrayed it. In that moment the old farmer saw himself within Kieko and realized that it was he who had betrayed his heart so many years ago. "I must not confuse this boy with myself," he whispered. "He has not chosen yet. I pray that he chooses wisely."

The old man, now unafraid, approached Kieko and molded the wool blanket warmly around him as Jomana licked his hands. Moving to the kitchen he poured himself a cup of wine, drank, and rested by leaning against the kitchen counter. Old and nearly forgotten thoughts drifted through him as the wrinkles in his forehead curled and slithered. In the silence he heard the faint voice of death call to him: *Your time is near.* "I know," he answered.

Placing the cup on the kitchen counter he looked at his rough hands. "Too long have I lived without love . . . and now it is done. Soon I shall be carried to the sea. My lessons have been learned, and if I may prove an example let it be known that a life without love is not a life at all." He then looked at Kieko, "I pray that he will not live a life of solitude as I have. I shall retire into the night."

Unwilling to fight his end the old man drank his last drink, moved into the room where Kieko slept, rested upon his old thinking chair, and stared into the fire until his light was no more.

PART III

CHAPTER I

The bitter cold of the morning caused Kieko to wake. The fire had died and the cabin creaked as it settled into the ground while the winds howled and blew against the windows. Rubbing his eyes he yawned and stretched his back hearing it crack in several places. Jomana went to his side and began pushing his leg with her nose. "What is it?" he asked her. She whimpered and continued pushing his leg as if there was something urgent that she wanted him to do. Too tired to understand what she wanted he went on stretching his neck and arms until he sat up and was startled by the old farmer who he saw staring at him. "I didn't know you were in here," he said to the old farmer as he bent forward to rub his feet. The farmer did not reply or move. Jomana barked at Kieko. Kieko looked again at the old man and saw his two cats licking his fingers. "Old farmer Toasu, are you all right?" he asked. Again there was no response and again Jomana pushed, but with greater force, against Kieko's leg. Kieko then felt a sharp pain cross his chest; he somehow knew that the old farmer had died during the night. He stood up and approached his old friend; the cats dashed away.

Crouching down before the old farmer Kieko looked into his eyes and saw that they were indeed lifeless. Jomana began to whimper. He waved his hand before the old man, and as expected there was no reaction. He then, with hesitation, touched the old farmer's hand feeling the unnatural cold of his body. Deeply saddened he bowed his head and closed the old man's eyes.

After a brief moment he stood up and stepped back realizing that he did not know what to do next. He knew a prayer was needed, but after that he did not know if he should leave the old farmer in his home with his cats and return to his master or if it was better to return to Ikishi with news of the old man's death.

Before making a decision he held his hands together before his heart again and said, "Thank you old friend for your words and your example." He paused and whispered as if confessing a secret, "I should have asked about my father last night . . . I didn't think to do so," he regretted. "I'm sorry. I'm being selfish, but please know that as a child, and now, I respected you and I will always respect you. You have traveled farther beyond our borders than any other in our village. I hope to see what you have seen, and to grow wiser by those sights and sounds. If you decide to linger awhile on the Mother please guide me as I go into the West. I love you, old farmer Toasu." Jomana barked in agreement.

He went to the window and looked out seeing that the snowstorm was over and decided that it was best for him to return to his village so that he could bring news of old farmer Toasu's death to the Elders. Before he began preparing for his journey he laid the old man's body down on a futon that he had unrolled on the floor and placed a thin cotton sheet over him. He went to the kitchen to search for food and after finding and wrapping up several slices of dried deer meat he filled a flask with cold tea and began repacking his bag.

Setting out into the morning cold with old farmer Toasu's staff Kieko plowed through the snow that covered the land with Jomana following behind him. The sun was bright and the winds blew just enough to sound a whisper through the trees while grains of snow fell from tree branches.

As he neared his village he thought of how he had changed since he had last seen the sea; he wondered if the Elders and villagers would accept him as a young Ki disciple or if they would continue to degrade him as a boy of mixed blood. But, as he thought of this, he noticed that a large part of him no longer sought the acceptance of his people for he somehow knew that he would soon travel to a place far from the islands of Lemuria.

It was afternoon, the day was growing dark, and ahead of him was a cliff that he knew would reveal an impressive view of both his village and the sea. Reaching the edge of the cliff he looked out and saw not the pleasant site he had hoped to see; instead he saw hundreds of dirty and heavily worn tents filling the valley that his village sat within. He saw iron pots steaming over campfires;

children running and playing in the snow; women he did not recognize talking and working on various chores like skinning dead rabbits and mending ripped clothing; and men–sad men–huddled together smoking from their pipes, talking, planning. The sight frightened him for he feared that his village too must pick up and leave as these people had done. But, to where would they go? He did not know. There was only the sea, unless they all decided to travel back and out of the valley to go north between the coast and the Mountains of Shinohi. He could not imagine himself traveling among so many to a place unknown to them all. If he was to leave he would do so alone, but he remembered his mother, and Kira, and felt ashamed that he had nearly forgotten about them. Jomana began to growl, and just as he was about to turn to see what she was growling at he heard a rough voice behind him: "Are you of the village?" He faced the voice with hands ready to fight and saw a large, strongly built, aged man who was dressed in old studded leather armor and wearing a dark, heavy, fur and wool cloak with a hood that concealed most of his face except for his dark grey beard, his chapped lips, and the finely crafted pipe he was smoking from.

"Afraid are you, boy?" asked the man as he stepped forward revealing the hilt of the long sword that hung from his belt.

"No, I am not afraid of you or anyone who seeks to harm me," he replied.

"What gives you the impression that I am here to harm you?"

"The feelings in my heart tell me so."

"Ha!" laughed the man, "your feelings will betray you, boy."

"No, I . . . I feel they have betrayed you."

The man approached Kieko, the scale mail beneath his armored sleeves sounded as he moved, and said, "You do not know of betrayal, but I can assure you that it will come."

"What do you want?" he said feeling very irritated as Jomana continued to growl with drool now dripping from her lips.

"I was sent here–by *those* down there," he smirked as he pointed down over the edge of the cliff, "to keep an eye-out."

"An 'eye-out' for what?" he asked wondering why he insolently referred to his people as "those down there."

"An eye-out for things like you."

"I am neither a thing nor a threat to 'those down there.' "

"Then who are you?" he demanded.

"I am Kieko, son of Nishiaka and Madonai of the Ikishi village."

"Yes, just as I suspected," he said as he puffed on his pipe. "The Elders informed me that the one they call *Shinsei* would send you to us."

"Then they are expecting me and you must take me to them—"

"No, it is not so, boy. They gave to me a message for you to pass back to your master."

"I don't understand?" he said shaking his head. "I bring news of the death of old farmer Toasu. It is right for me to speak to the Elders."

"No. I will inform them about the old man named Toasu. What you are to do is return to your master with the news that I have for you."

"What news? What news am I to bring to my master?"

"Tell him—this man, this priest who is called Shinsei—that the Elders are insulted that he has not made himself present during these past pressing days. Tell him that he is commanded by the Elders to appear within the Council Hut tomorrow night. How pathetic it is that he has sent them you—a messenger—a boy," he spat.

"Yes . . . I understand," he said looking down in defeat. "I will go back . . . I will go back to the temple."

"Yes, you will," the man smiled. "I look forward to meeting this Shinsei." He crossed his arms over his chest, puffed on his pipe, and waited for Kieko to leave.

"Come Jomana," he walked past the man with the old farmer's staff, entered the forest with Jomana at his heel, and began his journey back to his master's temple.

CHAPTER II

"You did not learn his name?" the priest, seated at the kitchen table, asked Kieko.

"No, Master Shinsei, he did not reveal his name to me, he only told me what I have already explained."

"Aiko—stop fiddling with those plates, come here and sit with us."

"Yes, Master Shinsei." Aiko left the plates he was cleaning in the kitchen sink, dried his hands, and sat down at the kitchen table; he eyed Kieko revealing his concern for their master who had not been his usual self since their return from their meditation retreat. "Something . . . is something troubling you, Master Shinsei?" he asked as he scratched the bandages that covered his forehead and left eye.

"Don't scratch!" the priest exclaimed. "You will undo your stitches."

"Yes, Master Shinsei," he nodded and continued. "I believe I speak for both Kieko and I, Master Shinsei." Kieko's eye widened. "We are both worried about you."

The priest fumbled with the empty cup in his hands. "Kieko already knows a bit of this," he stopped fidgeting with the cup and looked at his two disciples. "And time is short. So, there is no more running away for me." Aiko looked at Kieko wondering what the priest was talking about. "I can feel his presence; I can feel how close he is. It seems that he has finally caught up with me." Aiko leaned forward. "I have a brother, Aiko. He was a soldier when I knew him, and he fought to unite the northern islands of Lemuria."

"You speak of evil, Master Shinsei!" Aiko shouted nearly bolting out of his seat.

"Aiko! You must calm yourself. You must listen." Tense and nervous Aiko resisted his master's words. "Aiko, look at me. Look at me!" He looked at the priest. "You must listen for if you respect me as your master you must understand where I came from—who I was."

"Respect you? You have been lying to us—all of us—about who you are," he said standing.

"You know who I am, Aiko. In your heart you know who I am. But, this is my past. This is *my* past. It is who I was that I am speaking of—not what I am now."

"You have lied to us and fooled us!"

"I have never lied to you—Aiko—or to anyone!" the priest slammed his fist on the table causing his cup to fall to the ground and shatter. "I have simply not spoken of my past."

"And now that your brother is here you suddenly feel obligated to tell us that he—and probably you—were fighting for Kurai IV. What if he had never come? Would you have shared your secret to us?"

"In confidence I have revealed my past to others."

"Like Kieko. Why did you tell him? Why did you wait to tell me?"

"Because you were not ready to hear it."

"And now I am? Or is it because you have no more time to keep your secret?"

"It is because there is no time!" the priest rose from his seat.

"Your brother is a murderer!"

"Shut your mouth and listen to what I have to say!" the priest boomed nearly shaking the walls of the kitchen chamber with the volume of his voice. "Judge my brother as a killer, Aiko, but know that my brother and I were not soldiers of Kurai IV, we were his sons." Aiko, now unable to speak, looked at the priest in complete disbelief. "Did you not try to kill Kieko, Aiko? Was it not you who shot an arrow into his stomach?" Grinding his teeth Aiko said nothing. "Now you know what brought me here. Now you know what inspired me to become a priest. I am not perfect. I never said that I was. And like those who are old and regretful I have a past. And my past is here soon to face me. And regardless of the fact that my father was the warlord who corrupted King Kanda he was, and will always be, my father. Just like you, Aiko. You will always love your father regardless of how he treats you or others. I know of the many nights you had stayed up thinking of how to run and leave your father because for me it was the same. But, unlike you, I left him as he continued his conquest with my brother to expand their empire. And when my father was assassinated, and his army finally crushed, I knew not of what had become of my brother. But, now, after so many decades he is here, with us, in this dark hour."

"What does he want, Master Shinsei?" Kieko asked. "You think the man I met was your brother?"

"From the way you described his armor and the hilt of his sword I would say that if it was not him then this man killed and stole from my brother his precious armaments."

"I felt only darkness around him, Master Shinsei. I don't trust him."

"Of course you don't," blurted Aiko. "He is a murderer."

"Aiko!" the priest hollered. "I am done with your comments." Aiko kicked the leg of the table and looked away from the priest. The priest continued, "Kieko, I understand how you feel, but we must not judge so hastily."

"I did not judge, Master Shinsei, I felt this deep within me. Something is not right with that man."

"Be it so, I must face him."

"What will happen, Master Shinsei?" Aiko asked with bitter lips. "You have meditated in the time that Kieko was away. What have you seen of the future? Why are the Atlanteans attacking these lands? Why is your brother here?"

The priest thought for a moment trying to choose his words carefully, and answered, "Soon you both will see a very dark aspect of humanity at work . . . I wish we had more time—you both are far from finishing the next stage of your training. This coming war, that we will face, will only speed your maturity . . . although it will scar you in many ways. I only hope that the two of you, who make me so proud, can remain true and clear so that you can rise above those scars and heal them. You must remain clear in both mind and spirit." He took a deep breath, "It is now time to face the Elders and all their talk. Prepare for the journey back. Together we return to Ikishi."

"Yes, Master Shinsei," Kieko replied.

Aiko looked at the priest and said with resentment, "I'll be ready in an hour." He then left the kitchen chamber.

"Go and begin your preparations for the trip back to the village," the priest said to Kieko. "I will finish cleaning the kitchen chamber."

"Yes, Master Shinsei," he bowed to his master and left.

The priest listened to Kieko's footsteps until they faded trying to let go of the guilt he felt as a result of the argument he had had with Aiko. He silenced his thoughts and began his work by picking up the scattered fragments of his cup from the ground.

CHAPTER III

The harsh, howling winds of a fierce snowstorm swiftly covered the tracks of the priest as he hiked up a small hill with his staff; following behind him were Kieko and Aiko, and following behind them was Jomana. Holding his hood tightly over his head with his gloved hand the priest stopped and looked out, but through the dense storm of whiteness he could see nothing. He removed the scarf that he had been holding over his mouth, looked back to his two disciples, and called out, "The storm is getting worse and soon it will be night! We must hurry!" Kieko and Aiko could not hear what the priest had just said. "What?" Kieko shouted back noticing the many frozen bits of clustered snow that were clinging to his master's beard as it flailed with the unrelenting winds. "What did you say?" The priest repeated his words with a stronger more forceful tone, and when he saw that both Kieko and Aiko had understood him by nodding he continued up the small hill by leaning against the freezing winds that attacked the exposed skin of his face and neck.

Not too far from the priest and his two disciples was a boy not of the Ikishi village who was standing alone in the vast whiteness of the storm; the boy had snuck away from his mother to be more like his uncle who was out somewhere within the unseen wilderness scouting the land for intruders. With squinted eyes he tried to look deep into the storm hoping to see some sign of his uncle and luckily enough, there in the distance, he saw someone approaching. He was relieved, but when he discerned that what he saw did not move in the same manner as his uncle a pang of fear gripped him. Paralyzed by dread he tried to make out just who it was that was coming so that he could somehow prepare himself for a fight, and then he was able to see, in the storm that blurred nearly everything into white, a shadowy figure with a staff approaching with two following behind him—one of the two moved with a slight limp in his step—and following behind the three was a smaller shadow, which he believed was a wolf by how it moved. The stranger with the staff came closer, and just as he felt his knees about to give way he saw the two white flower insignias on the front of the heavy wool robe that the stranger was wearing and realized that the stranger a priest. Relieved, his shoulders collapsed and he let out a deep sigh. The priest waved to him. He waved back and saw that the two figures he had seen following behind the priest were actually two young men and that the smaller shadow was not a wolf, but a dog.

The priest approached the boy and smiled. The boy smiled back. "You are a brave little one," the priest greeted. The boy nodded. "Those two behind me are friends."

"Is t-t-that your dog?" the boy asked with chattering teeth.

"That is a good question, for you can say that he is now our dog. He belongs to all of us."

"The three of you?"

"Yes, the three of us."

"The three of you," the boy said to himself wondering how a dog could have three masters.

"Can you help me?" the priest asked.

The boy nodded.

"Can you point the way to the village?"

The boy nodded again and pointed to the thick snowy scene behind him.

"Thank you. I believe it is best that you follow my friends and I back to the village." The boy agreed without hesitation. "Have you a mother?"

The boy nodded.

"Have you a father?"

The boy bowed his head and remained silent.

"Take my hand and I will take you home," the priest said rubbing the boy's shoulder trying to comfort him. The boy took the priest's gloved hand. Kieko and Aiko walked up to the priest and the boy.

"Is he lost, Master Shinsei?" Aiko asked the priest.

"No," the priest answered. "But, we need to take him back to the village. I believe his mother is there."

Together they continued their hike; and when the storm grew weak and night approached they saw not too far ahead of them scores of worn and beaten tents resisting the winter winds. They could see old men, frail, weathered, and weak, huddled around campfires while groups of children ran between rows of tents or danced and played near the fires; the desperation so deep in the eyes of the old men haunted Kieko and Aiko. A few women saw the priest and his small band approaching, they called out to the others, and those who were near the edge of the camp turned to look at them, to judge them, to swiftly decide whether they posed a threat or not. The priest and his disciples, along with the boy and the dog, continued, and when they reached the edge of the camp they bowed their heads to all those who were staring at them, and entered the campsite. They walked between the tents passing men who gripped the hilts of their swords, and women who kept their children behind them.

The priest could hear the whispers of a dialect from far to the west. He looked with great attention at the exhausted women, the muddied but playful children, and the dispirited men he passed who in turn looked at him with strong glares of disapproval. Kieko and Aiko too did not feel kindness or warmth in the eyes of the people they passed. "I don't like this," Aiko confessed to Kieko.

"Why are they looking at us that way?" Kieko murmured not expecting an answer.

"They look at us as if they hate us."

"I can't wait until we find out what is going on."

The young boy who was holding the priest's hand shouted, "Okusen!" and ran off to a woman who the priest could only assume was his mother. The woman picked up the boy and stepped back looking at the priest with an untrusting, but thankful stare.

A few men approached the priest, his two disciples, and the dog, and stopped and stood before them as a means to prevent them from advancing. One of the men stepped forward with his thick arms crossed over his chest and asked in the high tongue, "Where did you find that boy?"

"We found him near a hill about an hour in that direction," the priest pointed.

"You are a priest?"

"Yes, I am. And they behind me are my Ki disciples—not the dog of course," he joked hoping to ease the anger he felt within the man.

"I don't find your words amusing, priest."

"What is it then that you want from us for we must pass and speak to the Ikishi Elders?"

"You are the priest of Ikishi?"

"Yes, I am."

"The one they call Shinsei?"

"Yes, that is me."

"Then you bring shame to this place. All here—and there in Ikishi have been waiting for you. But, you did not come."

"But, I stand before you now."

"Too late, priest."

"Too late for what?" the priest asked raising his voice. "We have no time for this nonsense. Let us pass!"

The man stood his ground and the men behind him took a step forward. The priest gripped his staff, "We do not mean to harm you. But, if we must, we will."

"Ha!" the man laughed.

"I am warning you."

The man threw his right arm at the priest, but the priest blocked the strike with his staff and punched the man's chest with an open palm sending him flying back. Kieko and Aiko looked at each other stunned by what the priest had done. "There is no more time to waste!" the priest shouted to the line of men before him. "Stand back and let us pass!" In fear the line of men parted in two leaving a path for the priest to pass through. The priest signaled to his two disciples to follow him, and together they continued through the large campsite. And as they walked they heard babies within tents crying hysterically for food and milk, and they saw women, both young and old, mourning the loss of their husbands, sons, or brothers by clinging to the garments or objects their dead had left behind while a few children, with faces that were dirtied by mud, played around the campfires. A few children, unafraid and curious, stopped and approached them, and when they had reached them they went straight to Jomana and began petting her fur. The priest and his two disciples watched the children shower Jomana with attention, but then the children began to ask questions about who they were, where they were going, and where they had traded to get the different articles of clothing that they were wearing. The priest answered their questions while Aiko, annoyed, brushed them aside like pests. Kieko, noticing that two of the children were missing a finger, looked with saddened eyes at the girls who pulled at his cloak begging for sweets or some food to fill their stomachs.

Impatient and cold Aiko looked ahead and saw the village Council Hut with its snow covered thatched roof that shot up in a sharp arc to the night sky from its oblong circular base, and at its peak there was a red flag; and at each side of the Council Hut there were red banners flapping from tall wooden poles. "There is a red flag at the Council Hut," Aiko announced.

The priest and Kieko looked and saw the large hut and a long line of men, both Ikishi villager and refugee, entering the hut. "Come, we must go," the priest said, and together they walked leaving the children behind. And as they neared the hut they began to hear the strong voices of hundreds of men speaking and shouting angrily from within it, which drove unease deep into both Kieko's and Aiko's hearts.

"Do not be afraid," the priest said sensing the fear within his two disciples. "I need your strength. Keep up—walk beside me."

Kieko and Aiko looked at each other realizing that the priest intended to take them with him into the Council Hut. They followed the priest to the large, ash filled cauldron that stood before the two rows of fire staves that illuminated a short path to the entrance of the hut, and did as he did by removing their hoods, leaning over the cauldron, cupping their hands, and wafting the rising scented smoke over their heads. All the men who stood briefly around the cauldron performed the same rite as the cold winds blew the rising smoke into spiraling swirls. The priest placed his hood over his head again, as did Kieko and Aiko, and bent down to Jomana asking her to stay and wait for them. He then joined the line of moving men and walked into the darkness of the hut; Kieko and Aiko exchanged looks of uncertainty and followed after the priest.

Inside there was no order to the angry yells and debates of the hundreds of men within the large, dimly lit hut. Several tall, muscular men pushed and shoved past Kieko and Aiko, which caused Kieko to feel small and insignificant, and for Aiko to feel livid at having been disrespected.

"Come with me," the priest called to his two disciples.

"Yes, Master Shinsei," Kieko answered with trepidation.

"Yes, Master Shinsei," Aiko answered with a bold and strong voice.

The priest, staying close to the pockets of dark within the large hut, moved through the crowd unnoticed until he reached the center of the hut. The shouting and bickering of men soon turned into slithering whispers. The priest called his two disciples to his side and together they stood before the seven Elders who were seated on their wooden thrones. Two guards, armed with spears, approached the priest and his two disciples. "Stop!" Elder Subo shouted to the guards. "They are friends. They are friends." The two guards looked at the Chief Elder and then to three hooded figures before them and backed away. The priest, keeping his back to the crowd, removed his hood and approached the Elders to bow, apologize, and embrace each of them. Kieko, nervous, looked at Aiko, who ignored him, and waited for the priest and the Elders to finish greeting each other.

"Reveal who you are!" someone shouted causing several seated men to rise from the ground and shout the same demand.

The priest turned and walked into the light of a nearby fire stave revealing his face to the crowd, "I am Shinsei, the priest of Ikishi."

A refugee stood up and hollered, "Where have you been?"

"You will speak with respect to the priest," Elder Subo warned the refugee.

The priest looked at Elder Subo telling him kindly with his eyes that he did not need his help. He then faced the refugee and explained, "I have been in my temple, waiting for the return of my two apprentices who stand here beside me."

Rakima, seated beside Kono and Tsuwata, craned his neck so that he could see the two young men who stood by the priest.

"Command them to remove their hoods!" demanded the refugee. Other men shouted in agreement.

The priest nodded to his two disciples and together Kieko and Aiko removed their hoods.

"They are pathetic, little boys!" a man yelled sparking the crowd into a roar of anger.

Kieko heard one man argue: "They don't even carry long swords!" while Aiko, who was scanning the crowd for his father, heard: "They are not men! They should not be here!"

"Silence!" the priest hollered back. "This chaos of the mouth will solve nothing, and *this* is your darkest hour! I suggest you all restrain yourselves. Restrain yourselves!" The crowd quieted. "There is not much time—"

"That is why we are upset!" a man hidden within the crowd spat. "We have all been waiting for you!"

"Enough!" the priest answered silencing the crowd before they could begin voicing their harsh opinions again. "I am here, now! And there is not much time."

"So you know what drove us east!" another refugee yelled.

The priest eyed the crowd searching for the voice. "Yes, I know what has driven so many of you here." Kieko and Aiko looked at each other confused and irritated as to why the priest had not explained to them what he knew, and was now about to express. "I have seen it in my dreams, in my visions at night—this force that is driven by a greed that cannot be quenched; a greed for wealth, a greed for power. Some of you have been waiting fearfully of the day when they would come again and take from us what is not theirs. For those *new* to us here that day has come, and for those of us born of this land . . . that day is coming—"

"Atlantis!" a refugee shouted driving fear into the hearts of all the men present. "You cannot fight them—they have machines that no man has ever seen before. They have metal beasts, dragons that shake the earth and turn dark the sky." Raki-ka, seated beside the standing refugee who spoke, looked at his two friends, Hirotake and Watanoro, uneasily. "They destroyed my village in the blink of an eye. Their fires burned my son and wife until all that was left of them was ash and . . . and charred bone," his voice quivered. "They . . . they will kill us all! They will kill us all!" he shouted again.

"How can they do this?" Tsuwata bellowed with his deep, commanding voice. "How can they destroy us?"

"They will hunt us down," another refugee answered. "They will kill us!"

"Your people were at least spared the horror that I will forever carry in the memories of my mind," an old, bearded man said to the refugee who was standing next to Raki-ka. "I am the only male survivor of my village. At least your village was destroyed by their fires—your people died a speedy death," he coughed. "My people were slaughtered not by machines, but by the hands of these, these Akai soldiers. They came through and killed the men first. They killed them so that they could rape their wives. Then—then they hunted down and killed the oldest children so that they . . . so that they could rape their . . . their mothers. They shot old men and raped old women. They killed fathers . . . and—and raped their daughters," tears began to drip down his cheeks. "And this is not the worst of it!" His old, wrinkled hands began to shake, "For fun . . . for fun they spared a few men—and forced boys to copulate with their own mothers—and their own grandmothers. They forced our priest to . . . to . . . to fornicate with a priestess from another village. They killed children by beheading them! The river . . . it was thick and red—red with blood. They dumped the bodies into the river. People began drowning themselves. They began killing themselves— they would have rather died by their own hands than by the hands of these wretched Akai!" he spat on the ground. "They are demons—devils. They are not human. If this is our last hour . . . then—then I will not perish without tasting the blood of the Akai!"

The crowd of men called out in agreement pumping their fists into the air. The priest looked down knowing that there was nothing he could do to prevent the terror that awaited his people. He debated in his mind whether or not he should speak of the dark premonitions he had had during the past few nights with all those before him, and as the yells and shouts grew louder and filled the hut with more furious and frustrated anger he could no longer bear the burden of his thoughts. "If you were to ask me to see the light," the priest began, "I have already seen it! And this, I'm afraid, is our last hour." The crowd of men silenced each other after the priest's last words. "And if you choose to fight I will fight alongside you . . . and face death with you as we stand together . . . die together." There was only silence. The Elders, Kieko, Aiko, and the crowd of men now realized that the priest had foreseen their future, and their imminent deaths. The priest continued, "The Atlanteans will come in three days time. For those that survive you will be enslaved and forced to serve the Atlanteans. They will be your masters and your memory of this place, your land, will be erased through the searing pain brought on to you by the power of lightening pulsing through your every living vein. This is what I see. You may choose to fight, but in so doing you will leave our women and children helpless. The Atlanteans will try to keep our children alive so that they can enslave them—turn them to become that which they are not. And as for the women . . . the majority of our women will be tortured, raped . . . killed, or sold into slavery and prostitution to service the soldiers of the vast Atlantean Empire. When upon the field of battle we find defeat inevitable . . . then it is up to you as fathers, husbands, and sons to take the lives of your wives . . . your mothers . . . your . . . your children."

All the men sat in silence pondering the priest's bleak words for none of them had even considered the possibility that they would need to kill their own women and children to save them from the horrors of prolonged torture, rape, and enslavement.

"What in the name of Mount Shinohi are we going to fight with?" a bald refugee shouted as he shot up from his seat.

"We are not an army," another refugee dressed in ripped and dirtied clothing began, "we are farmers. All we have are farm tools and our family swords."

"We have three days to organize our defenses!" the priest boomed. "We must focus on what we *can* do. Those with military experience must step forward."

Several men who were in their fifties, sixties, and seventies moved and shoved past the crowd to approach the priest and the Elders. Kieko and Aiko, along with most of the men within the hut, shook their heads at the handful of old, now fragile, men who had stepped forward.

"Who else among you has led men to war?" the priest asked straining to see through the dim light. "There must be more than just these brave men before me."

A large bearded man who kept his face hidden beneath the hood of his dark, heavy, fur and wool cloak stepped forward with long powerful strides into the fading light of a fire stave revealing the old, heavy, studded leather armor that protected his chest and legs. Kieko recognized the dark man. "I have led men to war," bellowed the man. "I led the armies of Kurai to unite the northern islands of Lemuria."

"He is a man of darkness!" shrieked a very old refugee causing the entire crowd to raise their arms and weapons into the air shouting their hate and spitting at the dark hooded man who had willingly served a long despised Lemurian warlord.

The priest could not see his brother's eyes, but he felt his heated stare and looked into the darkness that hid his brother's face with strong, peaceful eyes.

The hooded man turned his back on the priest to face the crowd and shouted, "You all have every right to hate me! You have every right!" Elder Sobu-Ta stood up commanding the crowd to quiet down. The hooded man stood silent until the crowd had finally lowered their voices. He continued, "Until this moment I had lived in secret hiding my name." He took off his hood exposing his heavily scarred face, and the eye patch that covered his left eye, to the crowd, "My name is Shimura."

"Shimura!" a man yelled. "Shimura, son of Kurai IV! You should be executed!" The crowd shouted out in agreement.

"You may choose!" Shimura yelled over the hateful crowd. "You may choose to execute me, but I will do you no good dead when death for all of *you* is just three days away!" Many within the crowd quieted down after Shimura's last words curious to hear more of what he had to say. "I led a dark army to more victories than any of you can ever hope to boast more than forty years ago!"

"That is the difference between you and us!" shouted an old, white bearded man from the crowd. "We would never brag about the raping and pillaging of Lemurians!"

Shimura ignored the comment and continued, "I have lived in regret and solitude ever since!"

"Good!" another man shouted. "That is what you deserve!"

"You may choose to execute me for my crimes, or you may give me the opportunity to redeem myself by organizing and leading you against an Atlantean army." Many more within the crowd quieted down. "If you want to execute me go ahead, I have been dead for over forty years. All of you will die in three days time. You can choose to die fighting, or you can choose to be slaughtered by the Akai!"

The crowd began arguing and debating, as did the Elders over Shimura's proposition. The priest stood by his two anxious disciples waiting patiently for a resolution. But when he could see no end to their bickering and curses he decided to leave and made his way toward the exit with his two disciples following behind him.

"Shinsei, where are you going?" Elder Subo asked as he stood up from his throne.

The priest turned and replied, "You all have very little time!" He stepped forward and spoke directly to the crowd, "And I will not waste mine listening to all of you argue with confused anger! Be men and organize your efforts. Leave your pride and egos outside. And when you have chosen what will be done, I will return," he then made his way out of the hut with his two disciples.

"You are just going to leave your brother like that?" Aiko asked the priest when they had exited the Council Hut.

"Yes," he answered annoyed by the question. "I will speak to him when the time is right. He is too full of scorn now for me to approach him." Jomana barked and ran up to the priest wagging her tail. He bent down to greet her letting her lick his hands.

"You just ignored him," Aiko remarked to his master as he scratched the bandage over his left eye.

"I did not," he said looking up to Aiko as he continued petting Jomana. "I looked into his hood and greeted his eyes with my love of him as my elder brother—"

"I want to see my mother," Kieko interrupted.

"And I want to see my father," Aiko blurted.

"Master Shinsei," Kieko pleaded, "I want to see my mother if we are going to die. We—we should leave this place—"

"You will do no such thing!" the priest commanded as he stood up pointing his fingers at Kieko. "I am your master. You will obey my words. The Atlanteans are advancing and will soon surround us. They know exactly where each and everyone of us are—they know that we intend to fight them. They can see us from beyond the heavens," he pointed up to the night sky. "They are toying with us like a game played between a cat and its prey. There is no escape. You must understand that. There is no escaping them," he grabbed Kieko's arms. "If you decide to leave they will follow and destroy you and your mother!"

"Then I am going to leave tonight!" Kieko shouted back at his master. "I don't care what visions of the future you have."

"You will do no such thing, Kieko! You will do no such thing," he shouted as he shook him by the arms. "You and Aiko will stand together behind our defending army and protect our women and children. Do you understand?"

"You mean you expect Aiko and me to kill our women and children?" he barked back with glaring eyes. The priest became silent. "You said that the Atlanteans will defeat us—they will defeat us. There is no hope now because you just destroyed it!" The priest let go of Kieko realizing that what he had said was true. "I'm not going to stay here and serve you by killing my own mother," he declared as he began shaking with uncontrollable emotion. "Or . . . or our women—or children before we are . . . before we are defeated." He turned and began walking away from the priest and Aiko.

"Kieko!" Aiko called out. "What are you doing?" Kieko entered the circular plain that he and Aiko had once fought in and continued walking. "What are you doing?" Aiko called out again as Jomana began barking. "You coward! You little coward! How dare you leave us—abandon us!" Kieko stopped right at the outer edge of the circular plain. The priest, Aiko, and Jomana, now silent, looked at Kieko waiting. Kieko stepped forward watching his foot cross the white chalked boundary and, without hesitation, continued his march toward the huts that were ahead of him passing women and children who he did not recognize.

"Kieko!" the priest shouted—Jomana began barking again—as a sudden flurry of snow began swirling with the winds through the air. "Come back here! Kieko!" The priest stopped—as did the dog—and, disappointed with both Kieko and himself, allowed the dark of his mind to speak against him for not confronting his only brother, and for telling his people that there was no hope in their fight against the Atlanteans. The fury of the men who had still found no agreeable solution within the Council Hut echoed louder into the night. Women and children, who now surrounded nearly half of the circular plain, stared at the priest trying to understand what had happened between him and Kieko, and why there was now so much arguing within the Council Hut.

A woman not of the village whose hair was tightly bundled and kept beneath a red cotton cap caught the priest's eye; she was standing behind several women. As she rubbed her hands together to warm them he could see that they were rough and scarred by the thorns of bushes; a sign that she had worked fields picking exotic berries, roses, and cotton. The posture of her body echoed years of sadness, pain, regret, and suffering. The priest looked into her eyes causing her to look away. In that small moment he felt her anguish for he now knew that she had been raped many, many years ago leaving her most precious feminine part diseased.

The woman backed away trying to hide from the priest. She felt him within her, trying to understand her. She felt the urge to let out and cry for she somehow heard his voice speak that she was indeed beautiful. But, a woman was not what she felt like for *they* had taken that from her, stealing it, feeding it to wild boars.

Regardless of all the pain that she had endured, and how bitter she felt for that which was no longer a precious part of her body, the priest found himself staring at where she had once stood wanting to hold her, to care for her. He then understood that she reminded him of Emira. She reappeared again within the crowd of women and children, and as she pressed her fingers against her cracked lips the priest remembered what it had been like to be in love.

The priest decided to let Kieko go and leave him be with his mother knowing that the brief bond that had held his two disciples together, and to him, had been broken.

"Do you really expect us to kill our women and children?" Aiko asked breaking the priest's thoughts.

The priest was silent; he began to doubt whether it was right of him to share with his people what he had seen of their future. But, his visions had been clear: if the strength of his band held true they would survive the coming menace. He shook his head. He now felt that his dark vision was of a vague, unknown future; and he had been wrong before in his interpretations of things to come. "Am I false?" the priest whispered.

"What did you say?" Aiko asked.

The priest began to doubt himself.

"Are you all right, Master Shinsei?"

The priest decided that he had been wrong in wanting to keep Kieko from going back to his mother, and said, "You have my permission, Aiko. You may go to your father."

Aiko saw the light in his master's eyes fade; ashamed and disappointed he wanted nothing more to do with the old man. He remembered his father. His father was determined, confidant, and unbending, regardless of his abusive nature toward him, and if their last hour was soon to be upon them then he would rather be by his father's side fighting than with a priest who had lost his way and light. And with that he abandoned his master leaving him with the dog.

Chapter IV

Madonai was standing outside watching children play around a communal campfire that had been built by the refugees who were camped all around her thatched home. She smiled at the children, pulled her faded red shawl tightly around her body, and went through old memories of her son until a child ran past her kicking dirt up onto the muddied snow from a heavily tracked upon path. She did not like how dirty the snow had become all around her home; she hoped that another snowstorm would come and cover the village again with a fresh sheet of snow.

Kieko stopped along the heavily tracked upon path when he saw his mother. It had been too many months since he had last seen her and for that he felt a sudden sadness pain his heart. A flurry of snow began to blow around her and he stood watching and memorizing how she held herself and how she smiled at the children as they played. She then approached the campfire and fed it a few broken branches to keep the children warm. He could see, and somehow feel, that she wanted to reach out and hold the children, and feed them a warm meal.

The temperature dropped and became abrasively cold and metallic. Kieko shook his head ridding himself of his thoughts. The children began to run around his mother and she turned to watch them, and she saw him. Her eyes filled with joy and disbelief, but she closed her eyes wanting to be sure that the young man she had seen was not some figment of her imagination. And when she opened her eyes and saw her son smiling at her she called out to him with open arms. Kieko went to his mother who hurried to him with adoring eyes, but as he walked from the light of the moon toward the light of the campfire she became afraid of the darkness she could feel within him as the firelight slithered between the shadows of his hardened face. The shadows claimed and covered his eyes causing her to remember the horrid dream she had had of her son for he now looked as he did in that dream: dark, and aged by years of a war that had destroyed his heart.

Kieko stopped and embraced his mother feeling an overwhelming wave of heat overcome him as she squeezed her love into him while whispering of how much she had missed him. A child laughed and he looked and saw that the children were now running around them. He tried to push his mother away so that he could see her face and speak to her, but she did not let go, she only held him tighter. The night winds blew and the air became colder. Finally she weakened her grip allowing her son to lean away from her. "You have grown," she said looking up at him.

"Perhaps . . . perhaps, I have," he said noticing that he was taller than his mother.

"It's cold. We should get back into our home."

"Yes . . . yes we should," he replied as she led him by the hand to their thatched dwelling.

Inside their home Madonai went straight to work at brewing some tea for her son who went to sit in the old chair that his father had built. Kieko looked around his home and saw that nothing had changed. He then watched as his mother prepared his tea and could see that she had more grey hairs than when he had last seen her, and that she now appeared older and fragile. He did not like seeing her like this.

"What would you like to eat?" she asked him.

"Uh," he thought for a moment, "I'm not really hungry."

"You have to eat," she looked at him and smiled. "It is a blessing to have you back home."

Kieko sat in silence feeling a little like a stranger in his own home.

"What's wrong, my little monkey?" she asked.

He shook his head and muttered, "Nothing, mom. Nothing."

"You have to eat so I will cook some soup," she said trying to sound cheerful but with obvious concern in her eyes.

He leaned forward in the chair wanting to ask his mother how the past few months had been for her, but he did not want to remind her, or himself, that she had been alone, and so he remained silent and simply watched as she worked.

"Here you are," she said handing him a cup of tea.

"Thank you, mom."

She smiled and returned to working on her soup.

He drank his tea, and when he finished he leaned forward again and asked, "Did Ruka and Kira take care of you while I was gone?"

Madonai stopped cutting the carrots on the cutting board and answered, "Yes . . . they have been very kind to me while you were away but . . ."

"But . . . but what?" Kieko asked with a furrowed brow.

"Things . . . things have changed . . . everything changed when Kira–"

"When Kira what?" he asked almost demanding an immediate answer.

"I . . . I don't know if you know what has happened."

"Did something happen to her? Is she all right?"

"Yes, yes she is all right."

"Then what are you talking about?"

"Kira . . . Kira is engaged, Kieko."

Kieko's face dropped and he slid back into his chair with eyes filled with disbelief. "When . . . when did this . . . when did this happen?"

Madonai rushed to her son, kneeled before him, and held his knees trying to comfort him.

Again he asked, "When . . . when did this happen?"

"A few months ago. Around the time Aiko began training with you."

"You knew he was training with me?"

"Yes, everyone knew. Kono announced it to everyone when—"

"Did he announce it with Shinsei?" he interrupted as he began to curl his right hand into a fist.

"No, no he did it alone. Shinsei has only come back to Ikishi for the festivals."

"Did Shinsei know about the engagement?"

"I—I don't know," she said shaking her head. "He—he didn't tell you?"

"Of course he didn't tell me!" he barked at his mother. "Do you think if he told me that I would be reacting like this?"

"I'm sorry—I'm sorry," she apologized to her son desperately not wanting to fight with him.

"But . . . but Shinsei must have known about the engagement. Don't you need his blessing before announcing an engagement?"

"Yes, you do, but Shinsei was not with him when he announced the engagement."

"With who?"

"With Kono," she answered as if the person she was speaking of was obvious.

"With Kono?" he asked himself. "What do you mean with Kono?"

Madonai's eyes widened; she did not want to say to whom Kira was to marry.

"Who in the name of Mount Kadek is she going to marry?" Kieko demanded.

"With," she hesitated, "with Aiko."

Kieko gave a look of complete disbelief to his mother, "With Aiko—with Aiko? What!"

"Yes . . . yes," she said nodding her head. "Kono announced to all of us that Aiko was to train with Shinsei, and that after his training he was going to marry Kira."

"Who else was with him when he announced this?"

"Tsuwata and Rakima."

"And Kira? Her mother?"

"No, they were not there."

"Have you spoken to them? How does Ruka feel about this?"

"They did not have much choice, Kieko. They did not. You have to understand that."

"I don't understand it! I don't understand it at all. I don't understand why I am the last to know about this. I feel like a fool—an idiot. I have spent months with that priest, and with Aiko, and they had said nothing to me. They said nothing!" he stood up.

"Kieko," she begged trying to calm her son down. "Kieko, please."

"I feel like a total fool. To hell with them! Curse that stupid priest!" he howled kicking the dirt floor. "Wicked beasts and demons. I curse them all!"

"Kieko, please—"

"Mom, we have to go. We have to leave tonight."

"What are you talking about? Why?"

"We have to go," he ordered her. He went to the area around her futon and began gathering any of the clothing he could find into a pile.

"What are you doing?"

"We have to go!" he shouted to his mother. "I told you. What else do you need?" he continued piling her clothing up on her futon. "Where is your old satchel?"

She went by the door and lifted a faded, dark blue satchel off a wooden peg from one of the wooden poles that supported the thatched roof. "It is right here," she said taking the satchel to her son.

Kieko grabbed the satchel from his mother and began stuffing it with her clothing. "Do you need anything else?"

"Kieko, please, stop," she begged her son. "You're frightening me."

"Mom," he pleaded. "There is no time. We have to go."

"No!" she shouted with the strength she had gathered to confront her son. "You tell me what is going on. You tell me!"

Kieko stopped what he was doing and looked down at the dirt floor.

Madonai kneeled and placed her arm around her son, "Kieko, please, please tell me what is wrong." Kieko ground his teeth and clenched his fists. She could see that her son was thinking about too many things at once. "Kieko . . . please talk to me." Kieko remained silent. "Kieko, I don't know what has happened to you. You spoke of Shinsei, your master, with such disrespect, with anger. What happened between you two?"

"Nothing," he muttered.

"Where is he?"

"He's probably with Aiko or whoever. I don't care where he is."

"Kieko, please . . . please, what happened between you and him?"

"I . . . I left him at the Council Hut . . . he said some things . . . he said some things there that he shouldn't have. He said we are all going to die."

Madonai's eyes filled with anxiety, "Why . . . why did he say that?"

"He said that because he had a vision of what was to become of us–of all of us here in this village and all those that have come these past few days seeking refuge."

"So," she hesitated, "so it is true. The Atlanteans are coming."

"Of course it's true," Kieko remarked agitated. "Have you heard nothing of what all these people–these refugees," he said having difficulty pronouncing the word, "have said about what drove them here?"

"Yes, I know, I know. I guess . . . I guess I was hoping–I guess there was some part of me that was hoping that it was not true."

"It's true. They are coming. My father's people are coming here to finish us. So, we must go."

"Just us?" she asked.

"Yes, just us?"

"And Kira?" she asked with faint words.

"I said just us!" he snapped. He stood up and swung the satchel full of his mother's clothing over his head and across his chest. "Come. We leave now."

"What about your things here? You don't want your things?"

"What things? I never had much, mom. I have everything I need," he said revealing the hilt of the short sword that was tucked into the fold of his belt. "The rest should be left here and burned."

Madonai looked away from her son hurt by his words for he now rejected the thatched dwelling he had once called home and wished it to be destroyed.

"Come, let the hearth fires burn. No one from Ikishi should know that we have left," he said putting on his cloak.

Madonai put on her old wool shawl and wrapped a hide of bear fur around her body. Kieko then exited the hut, and Madonai followed.

CHAPTER V

High up on a mountain cliff that overlooked both the valley and the sea, Kieko looked out and saw hundreds of campfires sparkling in and around Ikishi, and a circular void that he deduced to be the open plain beside the Council Hut. He noticed a faint line moving between where the campfires dwindled to a few and where the darkness of the valley began. He squinted trying to see just what it was that was moving in the dark; and he soon realized that the faint line was a long line of men that were digging what he assumed to be a trench. "They are preparing for battle," he said to himself as he enjoyed the silence of being so far from his village. He then saw something dark and large moving fast down the line of working men. "A horse," he realized; it was the first time he had ever seen such an animal. "It has to be," he whispered to himself as he remembered the details of the war stories he had overheard from the elder men of his village when he was young. Behind him he could hear his mother struggling to climb up. He looked down to where she was and saw that she was nearly to where he stood. "Are you all right?" he asked her.

"Yes," she wheezed as she ascended the rocky terrain of the Kadek Mountain. "Yes . . . I'm all right. But, I need to rest soon."

"We will," he replied as he reached for her hand and pulled her up.

She collapsed on the cliff, rolled onto her back, and tried to calm her labored breath as she looked up at the clear winter sky that was filled with as many stars as there were trees upon the mountainside. "It's . . . it's beautiful," she said to her son.

"Did you see Ikishi?" he asked her.

She sat up and looked out seeing the incredible number of campfires that flickered in the valley below her.

"Can you see the horse?" he asked pointing to where the horse and its rider had finally stopped.

"Where?" she strained her eyes. "Oh yes–yes I see," she said with an uncomfortable shake of the head. "It belongs to one of the men that had come with the refugees."

"How do you know?"

"I saw this man, with his horse, yesterday evening by the Council Hut. He was speaking with Elder Sobu-Ta and Jime-Ro. Many men were admiring his horse, but I did not dare go near it. There was cruelty in its movements . . . and malice in its eyes."

Kieko's brow furrowed as he went over his mother's words in silence.

"It's so beautiful."

Kieko looked at his mother and realized that she was speaking of the view.

"Can we . . . can we rest here a bit?"

"Yes, of course," he replied as he looked out at the scene before them. "Beyond that line of men working–digging–there are no more campfires. The House of Kono is in that darkness . . . as is the old farmer's home," he said with sorrow.

"Kono is in Ikishi," she remarked.

Kieko looked at his mother, "What do you mean?"

"Tsuwata gave him, or gave back to him, the hut that is next to his home. The Elders requested that he live in Ikishi since no protection can be provided to any of those who are living far from the village."

"When did this happen?"

"Two days ago."

A gust of wind blew causing them to quiver. "We should, we should keep moving," he advised with chattering teeth. Madonai agreed. He helped his mother get up to her feet, and together they continued their hike up through the mountain forest.

When an hour had passed they found themselves deep within a dark forest of very tall pine trees. Kieko looked up hoping to see the night sky from beyond the treetops but instead he noticed that the crooked branches of the trees were pointing down at him as if blaming him for all their woes.

"I don't like this," Madonai remarked.

"Why? What's wrong?" Kieko asked her.

"I have a strange feeling. I don't think we should be here. I think we shouldn't have left."

"Don't worry," he said trying to comfort her. "We'll set up camp soon and we can rest–sleep–and by tomorrow morning you'll feel fine."

"Do you know where we are going?"

"I have an idea. After we passed Devil's Mouth we have been traveling up along the coast away from Ikishi."

"I'm tired and cold, Kieko. I need to rest, please. I can't take much more of this."

"Yes, all right. I'm sorry . . ." he paused and looked around at his surroundings. "I think that this is a good place to spend the night."

"Good, good," she smiled and sat down with a sigh of relief. "I'm . . . I'm still thinking about that view we saw of Ikishi. It looked so beautiful, don't you think?"

"Yes, yes it was," he replied still looking around at their surroundings.

"I'm so happy that I got to see Ikishi with so many lights. It looks," she thought, "as if . . . as if the stars had been thrown down upon the Mother."

"Yes, Mom. It did look nice," he commented as he searched the ground for a good place to build a fire.

"I think . . . I think I can die happy now," she laughed to herself, "after seeing such a wonderful sight in the night. It's always comforting to know that there are so many of us out there. I don't feel so alone."

"What do you mean?"

"There are so many of us in the dark calling out to one another with light. I like knowing that there is someone not too far away, whom I can see at night."

"Did you feel alone while I was away with Shinsei?" he asked with a look of mixed guilt and concern.

"You should call him Master Shinsei."

"For now I will not."

"He makes mistakes just like the rest of us. You shouldn't be so angry at him."

"I'm not," he said annoyed.

"He's the only person who has ever come close to being your father."

"He's not my father! I don't have a father."

Madonai knew that she had stung a deep scar within her son, and she also knew that it was better to give him some space than to try to pry into how and why he felt as he did. "We should get some rest," she said as she leaned against a tree to rest her eyes.

"I'll get a fire started." He began searching for dry branches.

Soon a campfire was burning and Kieko poked and stabbed the flames with a stick pretending it was necessary for him to do so, but in truth he did not want to sit by his mother and comfort her by holding her; he did not want to play the part of a father who cradled a frightened child. Keeping his back to her he continued poking the fire until his mother fell asleep, and when she began snoring he listened enjoying the sound before deciding to go to sleep as well. He pulled his cloak tighter around his body and faced his mother as he lay upon the soft snow. Small puffs of cloudy air left his mother's lips and floated up before fading into nothing. He looked at her and prayed that these small breaths would carry her dreams far up so that they could be answered, and with that final wish he fell asleep.

CHAPTER VI

Kieko's eyes shot open as he gasped for air, sat up, and grabbed the hilt of his short sword before looking into the darkness beyond the trees that surrounded him. He strained his eyes, but he could see nothing within the darkness. His teeth began to chatter from the cold night air, and his left hand began to shake from the unease he felt in his belief that he was being watched. He got up on one knee.

"What is it?" Madonai asked as she awoke rubbing her eyes with her hands.

"Shhh," he hushed.

Madonai's eyes focused, and with what remained of the camp firelight she could see the tension in her son's body. Fear then gripped her; she asked again, "What is it?"

Agitated, Kieko looked at his mother and whispered, "Someone . . . something is here," he corrected. "Something is watching us."

"Who?" Madonai asked with chattering teeth.

"Shhh," he hissed with his finger held to his lips.

BOOM!!! A blinding explosion of lights struck like thunderbolts through the trees blasting and shredding them apart. Kieko jumped and dodged the bolts of light, threw his sword at the source of what was burning a path clean through the trees, and heard a distant clang. The firing ceased, but another round of thundering lights shot through the trees, and at him. It was then that he saw from the corner of his eye the silhouette of his mother's body flying back through the trees. Crying out in horror he ran toward the source of what had shot her, dived to the ground, grabbed a rock, rolled back up to his feet, and threw the rock before tripping on the root of a tree, and crashing to the ground. He heard a sharp clank sound, looked up, and saw a hovering metallic object spinning out of control as it shot jagged beams of light in all directions before slamming straight into a steep mountain wall. The machine reacted and fired repeatedly into and up the mountain shooting off large chunks of rock that rained down upon it, damaging it, until at last a boulder fell and crushed it.

Darkness claimed the forest again, and all was strangely silent. When Kieko's eyes adjusted to the darkness, he could see that the moonlight was reflecting off the scores of metallic pieces that had been flung from the machine as sparks ignited and smoke spiraled up from beneath the boulder and rocks that had crushed it. Anxious to see his mother, he stood up feeling a sharp pain in his leg, and limped toward her feeling the weight of his heart grow heavy with remorse. When he reached her, he saw that both she and the snow around her were covered in blood. Perturbed, he collapsed to his knees and saw a blast burn the size of his fist that had blackened, and burned clean through, her stomach. Her arm then jerked and twitched. Frightened, he fell back. She spat out blood and coughed. Scrambling back to her, he pulled her into his arms and rocked her body unable to believe that his mother had been murdered in such a way. She looked at him and tried to speak, but all that he could hear was the sound of blood gurgling in her throat; and then her eyes became lifeless, and her body became limp. He squeezed her body as if trying to meld her skin into his, and pounded the ground with his fist until at last the rage within his heart could remain silent no more; and he screamed a horrific cry as his body trembled and shook.

And as the night passed his voice became faint, and he fell to the blood stained snow in a stupor of bewilderment, rage, shock, and horror, until at last he subsided into a deep state of exhaustion and sleep.

CHAPTER VII

Hearing the howl of the wolves, the priest admired the moon as he sat near the edge of a cliff that overlooked the midnight sea. He had been thinking about Kieko, who had run away with his mother to escape the fate that he had seen. And as he thought of what had happened between him and his young disciple, doubt began to fill his heart, for he still questioned if it was right of him to have voiced his dark vision to the Elders, and to the men who had gathered in the Council Hut. *Perhaps Kieko was right*, he thought. *As a priest I am to provide comfort and hope to my people, but I have only declared our future death . . . and thus robbed them of hope.* He remembered the look on Kieko's face when he had revealed to him, and his mother, that Nishiaka was truly dead. He had known of how much Kieko idealized his father and awaited his return, but the truth was what they had wanted of him from his journey into the spirit world.

However, his words that had declared the ultimate end of Ikishi by the approaching Atlantean army was a different matter entirely for it had not yet happened; Nishiaka's death was written, but the fate of Ikishi was not. Nonetheless, the priest believed that what he had seen would come to be, and he had felt it right to speak his truth to his people. Yet, as a priest, he had failed them for his words had stolen from them their frail hope. And into this very night he knew they worked preparing for battle with what little light remained within their hearts for they believed his words, and they would face the coming darkness like an army that had lost the will to fight.

"You look like a ghost," Shimura said to his brother as he approached him with his heavy boots that crushed and kicked at the icy snow. The priest looked down at his worn hands. "Why did you choose this place?" Shimura asked. "I find it odd that as your people work into the night you choose to be here, away from them, for this place on the fringes of your village overlooking that godless sea."

"You see that tree over there?" the priest said pointing to the tree that stood near the edge of the cliff. "That tree reminds me of a friend that I fear I have lost."

"Don't speak to me of tree spirits, young brother."

"I forgot, you were never one for matters concerning the metaphysical."

"And why should I be? Do you forget that this is the material world that we are trapped in? There is no promise of anything beyond death. Death is a darkness that will come to us all."

"And it is brought on by the oppressive blades of people like you."

"How dare you!" Shimura shouted disturbing the quiet of the night with his right fist that shook at the air. "You are as guilty as I am in bringing death to the innocent. You cannot hide from the crimes that you have committed in your youth, under the orders of our father. You can not pretend that your devotion to your faith can absolve you–redeem you of that in your past which haunts you."

"Why have you come to me?"

"I have come to remind you of who you are."

"So, brother," he paused for a moment. "Now you have me. Tell me who I am."

"You are a betrayer of hope."

The priest felt his heart descend further into an abyss of guilt as all that he had desired to be, slipped from him. He had betrayed himself. In that moment he was nothing: he was neither his word nor his actions. He was not a man.

"Before your people," Shimura laughed, "you stole any hope that they could fight and win against this darkness that is coming. I know that one of your disciples has left you, and that the one called Kono has reclaimed his son who now limps and sees with only one eye. You are not a priest, brother. You betrayed your precious Emira, your father, and me. I can never forgive you. I have traveled for years, decades alone wondering where my kin, my brother could be, and why he was not by my side. Are you ashamed of the legacy of our family? Our dark legacy?" he asked with words that weighed heavy. "You cannot run from the blood that runs through your veins, Kuro. Did you believed that living a celibate life could keep our dark line from continuing? Perhaps you thought that a child born from you would have to pay for your sins—our sins, but you forgot that a child of your blood—our blood—could have risen above that which haunts our family, and move into the light. But, no—you failed to face the darkness that runs through the blood of our family. And now our line is done. You and I are all that is left. No son of ours will carry our name, and we, as a family, will disappear when all the works and conquests of Kurai, our father, is turned to dust."

Shinsei looked away from his brother trying to hide from his judging eyes as he foolishly wished to turn into a bird and fly to the end of the dark ocean. The ocean waves crashed up against the rocky mountain cliffs leaving the fizzing sound of the waters as they retreated. Crows then flew across the night sky, and the old priest followed them with envious eyes. His wrinkled skin felt heavy; a pressing reminder of his age. And as he sat there on the cliff before the vast unending ocean he began to feel small and insignificant, lost. He was now in a dangerous state for he knew that he could be easily swayed like a sick tree no longer able to stand against the winds. "You should leave me, Shimura. I am not sound of mind to speak."

"So you run."

"I am not running," he said weakly. "I am not sound in mind, body, and spirit. I will spend my night here with all the sounds of the world before me and seek the Light. Leave me and know that I am sorry that I had left you. I have always loved you as my brother. We will speak again before all is done between us."

"You are a fool!" Shimura barked. "I have waited decades to speak my mind to you, and now you choose to ignore me. We will not speak again. We are done as kin. I will see you on the battlefield and enjoy seeing your end." He turned his back on his brother and walked toward the shadows of the forest with his sword clanging against his armor.

Tears welled in Shinsei's eyes for he knew that he had lost his brother. He looked up to the moon seeking forgiveness, and then down to the open sea before collapsing to the ground feeling a forgotten hurt pain his heart. He gazed up at the stars feeling the pain spread and took a deep breath. The cold air rushed down into his lungs and as he exhaled, feeling the air stream over his heart, he closed his eyes and reached for the cause of the pain.

In his mind's eye he saw several flashing images of his father and brother scolding and beating him when he was very young. This was when it had begun for he had taken in their anger and buried it deep into his heart. With this realization his heart rejoiced and asked him to see and understand that both his father and brother knew not how to mourn the loss of Erura, his mother, who had died soon after his birth. It was with this loss, this grief, that they had poisoned his young heart with their harsh words.

Now able to see what had happened to him when he was a child the priest forgave his father and brother and let out a long, heavy breath to unburden his heart; his entire body shook. When his body stopped shaking he wiped his eyes and felt a light sensation in his chest. He rubbed his chest for a moment trying to understand the lightness he felt there, and decided to sit up to meditate on his past to discover what other pains he had unknowingly buried into his body as a young boy.

The night carried on, and the priest sat still and silent as he focused and saw, deep within his neck, chest, arms, and legs, small demonic creatures and sharp symbolic objects. Slowly, and carefully, he addressed each ailment and expelled it from his body as if it was as easy as dropping stones from a basket that he no longer wanted to carry.

The night sky became grey, until a ray of the dawn light broke through the winter clouds and shined upon the priest's closed eyes. The priest felt the sun on his face, smiled, rose to his feet, and declared, "It is done, for now I am whole again."

CHAPTER VIII

"Get up!" Kono shouted kicking his son in the stomach. Aiko heaved an airless cough and curled his body in toward his stomach. "Get up I said!" he shouted again as he stood before his son fully dressed.

"Yes—yes, father," Aiko coughed as he moved to stand up.

"There is no time to sleep. We only have today and tomorrow to finish preparations for our war against the Akai." Aiko looked at his father apathetically. Kono—not noticing how his son had looked at him—continued, "I heard that the Akai boy ran away last night with his mother—the cowards." He spat on the ground of the bare thatched hut they had slept in. "That boy is weak. I hope his people find him and kill him off."

"You shouldn't say that," Aiko said speaking up to his father.

"Who are you to tell me what I should or should not say? What did that damn priest teach you? I am your father!" he backhanded Aiko hard across the face causing him to fall to the ground. "Never—for as long as I am alive—will you speak to me like that!"

Shaking nervously, Aiko did not want to look up at his father.

"Look at you!" Kono howled as he pointed his finger at his son. "You are as pathetic as a helpless girl. How dare you—you are my son damn it! You do not cry before we prepare for war. You do not shake. You shame me, Aiko. You shame me! I knew it. I knew it was wrong to have allowed you to train with that Akai. The priest is a fool. He knows nothing of the ancient ways of the Ki. He has betrayed us, and left me with a son who can not see or stand his ground—"

"I can hold my ground," Aiko interrupted.

"What did you say?"

"You heard me," Aiko said as he stood up again staring straight into his father's eyes. "You want to fight me? I'm ready for you! I am trained in the way of the Ki, and I will break you if you try to harm me anymore!"

Kono threw his fist with all the hate he had ever held for the Akai, but Aiko dodged the strike. Surprised that his fist had not made contact with his son he launched several more punches. Aiko leaned away from his father's fists and then, by pure instinct, swept his foot at his father's leg causing him to trip and fall to the cold dirt ground; his eyes widened at what he had done to his father, and he cracked a proud smile. Kono rolled onto his back and kicked up his legs in a motion that sprung the rest of his body up to his feet. "Curse you!" he growled before exploding out at his son in an uncontrolled rage. Again, Aiko simply leaned or moved away from the next combination of his father's strikes and kicks and said with a grin, "I am too fast for you."

"Fight me!" Kono shouted with slight exhaustion in his breath.

"I will not."

"Fight me!" he begged.

"I will not."

"You stupid, little idiot boy! You stupid, cursed boy. You are no son. You are no son to me." Aiko looked at his father with sad disappointment. "Go away from me!" he spat. "Go and leave me. Go to that priest, or to that filthy Akai, and leave me! You are not my son. You are not mine. You are weak and foolish. You do not deserve a girl like Kira. She is too good for filth like you!"

"Father," he called out trying to stop him from saying anything more.

"You are worthless. She deserves a man—a true man—not some weak filth like you," he began to laugh.

Aiko went to the short door of the hut and opened it.

"Where are you going?" he demanded of his son

He looked back at his father and said, "I am leaving you."

Kono ran and threw a brutal punch to the side of his son's face before grabbing him by the head, throwing him down to the ground, and kicking him in the face, chest, and stomach; Jomana could be heard barking desperately outside. Aiko tried to block his father's kicks, but could not. A quick kick to his nose released a flood of blood. "Father, please," he begged. "Please stop!"

Kono began to foam at the mouth as he kicked repeatedly at his son while cursing and almost laughing at him. The laughter triggered the repressed rage within Aiko to ignite and he exploded from the ground with a fury of kicks until he was able to grab his father's right leg, yank him down to the ground, and sink his teeth into the flesh and bone of the leg.

Kono screamed a horrid cry and tried to shake off his son's deepening bite by slamming his fist on his son's head. Tasting a torrent of blood Aiko let go of his father's leg and rolled away from him. Kono scurried away from his son. At opposite ends of the hut they looked at each other; Jomana continued barking and whimpering outside. Aiko, nearly panting, wiped the blood from his mouth, spat on the ground, stood up, and went to the door again feeling a sharp, and intense, pain shooting up from his recovering ankle.

"Where . . . where are you going?" Kono asked his son.

Aiko stopped, "I am done with you! I am done."

"I am your father! Do not forget. Do not forget that you are my son."

"I will not—I will not allow you to treat me as you do. This is not how a father should treat his son."

"What do you know about being a father?" he joked. "Go then. Go! Go and never come back to me. I am done with you. I am done. Go and be with that priest, or with that Akai."

"That 'Akai' saved my life."

"That Akai did no such thing! You should have killed him!"

Aiko opened the door allowing the morning sun to shine into the dark of the hut.

"How dare you leave me," Kono contested. "I am your father!"

Crouched on his knees, and between the light of the outside and the dark of the hut, Aiko paused and said, "Master Shinsei is my father and my teacher. He helped me heal the scars that you had cut into me."

"I am your father!" Kono cried out with tears that began to well in his eyes.

Feeling good and right with what he was about to do he looked at his father one final time and entered into the light of the morning sun where Jomana had been waiting anxiously for him.

CHAPTER IX

Kieko spent the entire morning kneeling before the stiff, pale body of his mother that was resting on a crude altar built from the branches he had gathered at dawn. He stared at the snow that he had placed over the singed hole in her stomach, and at the blood that stained her clothing, and tried to imagine that it was spring and that she was lying on a bed of daisies with three roses held between her clasped hands: one rose for her, one for him, and the other for his long deceased father. But the cruel reality of the morbid scene before him could no longer be avoided by his wishful imaginings. His mind whispered, and the anger that was still buried deep within his heart began to rise. He ground his teeth and pounded the earth with his fists allowing the menacing voices of his mind to gain more of him with each hardened strike. The searing frustration, and guilt he felt in not being able to find anything more decent to adorn his mother's body, filled his lungs and boiled up to the surface of his skin as he repeatedly pounded the earth until at last a haunting and prolonged scream escaped from his bitter lips filling the frigid air with misery and despair.

Soon there was quiet again in the forest. Exhausted, tired, frustrated, and disheartened Kieko hunched his body forward, rested his forehead and arms on the cold snow, and took a deep breath. Clarity of thought returned to him and he decided to voice his last prayer, to give his final bow, and to get on with what he knew he had to do according to his Ki faith. He sat up, picked up the torch he had stuck into the ground, looked up to the sky, and said, "Father, please welcome and care for her." He looked down to his mother and whispered, "I love you, mom. I love you. Forgive me . . . I failed to protect you." He bowed his head, lit the altar with the torch, and watched the fire grow and burn the branches and his mother's clothes. Soon the fire consumed the whole of his mother's body filling the air with the stench of burning flesh, which caused him to stand up and take several steps back to avoid the smoke and burning embers that began to swirl up toward the sky. He watched her hair burn and shrivel away into nothing, and saw her flesh turn black and begin to bubble, melt, and stream down to the ground exposing her muscles and organs that began to hiss and sizzle. Unable to look more at what he could no longer recognize as his mother, he turned away and decided to go and look at what remained of the machine that had killed her.

Standing before the pile of rocks and the boulder that had destroyed the machine he decided to get on his knees and look carefully at the metallic pieces that were scattered all around him. He took one metallic part, or burnt wire, after the other into his hand and went over ever detail trying to understand any aspect of what he held. But he did not understand anything, and the more time he spent trying to put pieces of the machine together the more aggravated he became until he saw from the corner of his eye a metallic sheet, no bigger than his hand, reflecting a beam of sunlight. He crawled over on his knees to the metallic sheet, picked it up, turned it over, and saw a symbol that had been pressed into it. He studied the symbol and realized that it was a six-sided star, but that it was composed of two interlaced, three-dimensional pyramids—one pyramid faced up, and the other faced down—with four crystal shards located at the top, bottom, left, and right of the star, and four thinner crystal shards located between the larger crystal shards. Deciding not to waste more time he stood up with the metallic sheet, walked over to his mother's satchel, wrapped the sheet in a leather rag he had pulled out of the satchel, and placed it into the fold of his top-gi. He then swung the strap of the satchel over his head and across his chest, and returned to the altar where what remained of his mother continued to burn. He coughed and gagged as the wind carried the foul scent of his mother's burning body toward him, and pulled a tattered wool scarf out of the satchel to cover his nose and mouth before sitting on his heels to wait for the fire to fade and die.

A thin line of smoke rose from what was now only a pile of ash and charred flesh and bones. He stood up, walked to the burnt pile, and looked at what had once been his mother seeing that her left hand and forearm, and the lower half of her right leg, had not completely caught fire. Gagging again he turned away and vomited before falling to his knees and vomiting more. When he stopped heaving he wiped his mouth and rested. Knowing that he could not bury his mother's remaining body parts in the frozen earth he decided to empty the satchel of all its contents, place her remains in it, and to search for a place where he could bury her parts. After emptying the satchel he went to the burnt pile and brushed with his hand all he could of the ash and burnt bones into it, but when it was time for him to pick up her partly burnt left hand and forearm he began to hack uncontrollably until he began vomiting again. When he finished he screamed out in hatred and began pounding the ground repeatedly with his fist as he had done earlier that morning. He began to fatigue and wanted to cry, but did not. Instead, he punched the ground one last time and quickly picked up his mother's left hand and forearm and threw them into the satchel. He then picked up the lower half of his mother's right leg and threw it into the satchel as well. Relieved that he had finished sweeping and placing his mother's remains into the satchel he let out a sigh and placed the strap of the satchel on his shoulder and stood up. He looked in the direction that his mother and he and come from to escape Ikishi, shook his head with disbelief, and began his journey back down the mountain.

In the evening, as the light of the sun began to fade, he saw up ahead, before the sharp drop of a sea cliff, the massive opening of a large cave and realized that he had reached Devil's Mouth. He approached the cave and stopped before its gaping dark entrance and remembered his younger days of when he had wanted to explore its depths as a test of his own courage. He took a step toward the cave and placed the satchel on the stone littered ground. He then turned to face the sea cliff, approached it, and looked down seeing far below the strong ocean waves crashing hard against the exposed rock of the mountain. "That is where she belongs," he said to himself. "She belongs to the sea." He went back to pick up the satchel, approached the cliff again, and began swinging the satchel until he let it go sending it out and down toward the icy ocean waves. He watched as the satchel sank into the sea while the bitter ocean winds blew hard against him. Shivering, he rubbed his hands together, blew into them, and continued down the snowy path that led to his village.

An hour passed, and the sun was just about to dip into the horizon, when he saw a clearing and another cliff ahead. He walked to the clearing and up to the edge of the cliff and saw his village far down below him illuminated by hundreds of campfires and fire staves.

At that same moment a child not of Ikishi looked up at the Kadek Mountain and saw the silhouette of a man standing on the edge of a cliff, and saw a shadow that was growing around him as if consuming him.

Kieko could see hundreds of villagers and refugees moving hurriedly from one place to the other as a long line of men and women dug deep into a trench that stretched the length of Ikishi and curved downward toward the sea. He then noticed a group of children who had stopped playing around a campfire to look up at him. Uncomfortable, he stepped back and clenched his teeth as he realized that it was just yesterday when he had seen his mother watching children play around the campfire near her thatched home. *Curse them*, he thought with a tight fist not knowing exactly why he was cursing children. He shook his head and continued his trek down the mountain. And as he walked down the rocky path he thought about what he would say or do once he had returned to his village, but then, suddenly, he felt the earth move beneath his feet. *This mountain no longer sleeps*, he thought as he stopped and looked back trying to see the peak of the mountain, but he could not, the trees were too tall and blocked his view. He waited and listened, but the ground was now still, and so he continued for another hour until he passed the line of trees that marked the end of the mountain. And there before him was the outer boundary of his village where he found hundreds of tents flapping and battling the cold ocean winds, and the waste and leavings of the refugees who were simply too many for the land. Moving silently, and avoiding the lights of the campfires, he weaved between the tents until he arrived at one curved end of the trench that ran parallel to an icy stream. He looked up the length of the trench and saw in the distance fire staves that had been stuck into the ground to light the work of hundreds of people who were digging into the trench to expand it. He crossed the stream, ran, and jumped to the other side of the trench where the thatched huts were and followed the trench up to get a better look at the people who were digging into the early night.

Close enough now to see a few of the faces of the workers who were digging, he hid within the shadow of a large hut and watched. He could see Watanoro slamming his shovel into the frozen ground, and then pounding it down with his foot trying to free earth; and Raki-ka, tired and cold, trying to warm his cupped hands by blowing into them. Kesake appeared bringing a tray filled with steaming cups of tea from his tavern to those who were working in the trench; happily he served them, and those who took a cup thanked him with a smile and a respectful bow of the head. Raki-ka sipped and drank from the cup he had taken, and when he finished he returned the cup to Kesake and picked up his shovel before saying a few words to someone that Kieko could not see. There was laughter, sweet laughter. Kieko recognized it. Raki-ka leaned forward and Kieko saw Kira laughing with a smile.

"He hasn't changed," Kieko whispered not approving of what Raki-ka had said to make Kira laugh. The laughter and the smiles between Raki-ka and Kira soon faded, and together they looked down into the trench and began digging again. He felt a touch of anger rise within him toward Kira for having agreed to wed Aiko, but as he watched her, seeing her in dirtied and muddied clothing, digging into the earth with dry hands that looked as if they were about to crack and bleed, he began to remember how she had been with him, how she had reached out to him, before he left to be with the priest in his temple. He felt guilty for how he had pushed her away when she had tried to get close to him.

Kira stopped digging and began coughing violently.

Kieko rose from where he hid ready to run to her, ready to help her, but when he saw Raki-ka stop to care and comfort her he sat on his heels and waited.

"Are you all right?" Raki-ka asked Kira.

"Yes, thank you. I'm fine."

"This is a man's work. You and the other women shouldn't be doing this."

Kira looked Raki-ka in the eye, "Keep—" she coughed, "your idiot comments to yourself."

"I didn't mean it like that," he apologized.

"Yes, you did," Watanoro joked.

"You're not helping," Raki-ka said to Watanoro.

"I'm not trying to," Watanoro replied as he continued digging.

"That is not what I meant," Raki-ka said turning to Kira.

Kira ignored his words and slammed her shovel into the earth.

"I know you're strong—"

"Look," she interrupted, "I'm cold and tired." She paused and tried to calm herself. "I . . . I know you mean well. I just want to finish this and go home and sleep. So, please, let's just dig."

Raki-ka looked at her surprised by how strong she appeared and started digging again without saying a word.

Kesake returned, but this time with no tray filled with cups of hot tea. "I just received word from the Elders that we must stop digging," he said to those in the trench. "We need to extinguish the fire staves and as many of our campfires as we can. We don't want the Atlanteans to see what we are doing if they are watching us."

"I don't think any of what we are doing here is going to make a difference," Raki-ka said aloud. No one responded to his comment; people simply put down their shovels and began climbing out of the trench tired and relieved to go to their tents, or huts, and rest.

Rakima moved past several people who were about to climb out of the trench and approached his daughter, "Where is your mother?"

She looked down and explained, "She stopped working in the trench an hour before sunset. She went home to prepare dinner."

"Fine then," he then thought for a moment. "Go home. I have some things to do."

"Yes, father."

Rakima turned, gave an unpleasant look to Raki-ka just as he climbed out of the trench, and walked away.

Kira felt something familiar, but she brushed the feeling off as if it had been an ant that was crawling up her arm. Raki-ka sat on his knees and offered his hand to Kira. She grabbed his hand and with his assistance climbed out of the trench. When she had dusted off some snow and dirt from her dress she saw the silhouette of a person move from the corner of her eye, looked, and saw what she thought was a face, a familiar face, within the shadow of a large hut.

"I can walk you home, Kira."

"Leave her alone," Watanoro said half-joking to Raki-ka.

"I'm fine, Raki-ka. I'll go home by myself."

"Well, don't tell your father that I wasn't looking after you today," he smiled.

"Don't worry. I won't."

"Goodnight then," he said as he began walking away with Watanoro.

"Goodnight," she smiled.

When most of those she had been working with in the trench had gone she walked toward the hut where she thought she had seen someone and saw a movement within the shadow of the hut. "Who's there?" she called out. "Reveal yourself or I'll scream for help."

Kieko crawled back looking for a way to escape.

"Reveal yourself or—or I'll scream. I swear it! I'll scream."

Kieko stopped.

"Reveal yourself!"

Not wanting Kira to attract any more attention with her voice he stood up allowing the light of the moon to shine upon him.

Kira nearly did not recognize Kieko when she saw him dressed as he was with stains of dried blood on his clothes, but when she was sure it was Kieko she ran and embraced him. "I was afraid that I would never see you again," she said with joyous relief. "They told me that you had run away—that you had left with your mother."

Kieko pushed her away and looked at her, "My mother is dead."

"What?"

"She was murdered. There was something in the night that attacked us. It killed her."

"I'm . . . I'm so sorry, Kieko. I'm so sorry."

"I don't understand what killed her," he said looking at her with blank eyes. "I don't understand this thing that killed her. It was a machine of some kind."

"Kieko, you need to rest. You are not yourself. Please—please come with me."

"No, I will not."

"Kieko," she said looking into his eyes. "What's wrong with you?"

"What happened?" he demanded. "What happened to you?"

"What do you mean?"

"You know what I mean. Don't play ignorant with me!"

"Kieko!" she barked back. "What do you mean? I haven't seen you since you left to be with Shinsei. I haven't heard a word from you! Not a word," she declared feeling her own anger toward him grow. "And here you are, after you had run away with your mother, without even having said goodbye to me?"

Kieko looked at Kira never having seen her look at him with such disappointment and annoyance.

"How dare you! How dare you," she slapped him across the face. "Even now—regardless that you ran away without saying goodbye—I ran to you and hugged you, and you just stood there—like a stone, like a cold stone! You are heartless, Kieko. You are a heartless little man." Kieko could see the waves of strong emotions washing over her, nearly driving her to both fury and tears. "You had no right to have done what you did," she proclaimed by hitting his chest. "You had no right. I watched over your mother. I cared for her while you were away. And never did you send a word with Shinsei to me—only to your mother, only to your mother! I was alone here, Kieko! Alone!" Kieko grabbed her arms and tried to hush her. "Don't hush me!" she shouted as she threw his hands from her arms. "Don't touch me. Don't touch me," she repeated as he tried to hold her arms again. "You weren't here—Kieko! You weren't here. And all the time you were away studying or learning how to fight—or whatever it was you were doing up there—I was alone here with my father, and my uncles, watching them plan my future with a man, and his son, who I have no respect for. And where were you to help me? You were nowhere! And after all these months of you not making any effort to at least send a message to me, I finally agreed to marry Aiko—I finally agreed because I felt that you had forgotten about me! That you didn't care about me."

"Kira—" he tried to say.

"Don't, Kieko. Don't. I . . . I still can't," her voice began to crack, "I still can't believe you left without even seeing me. How am I supposed to feel?" she began to cry. "When . . . when it seems that we are all doomed . . . doomed to be killed—massacred?"

Kieko grabbed her arms again and pulled her toward him as she let out a stream of tears and coughed while her chest heaved uncontrollably. "I'm sorry," he whispered as he held her. "I'm sorry. Please, I'm sorry. I'm so sorry, Kira."

"Why?" she asked through her tears. "Why . . . why did you not want to see me?"

"I . . . I didn't want to get . . . to get too close to you."

"Why?" she cried. "You don't like . . . you don't like," she paused having difficulty trying to say the last word, "me?"

"No, Kira, no," he shook his head. "I didn't want you to suffer—like my mother. I didn't want you to be treated as she was treated."

"What are you talking about?" she asked not believing him.

"If we came together–and everyone knew–you would have been treated differently–badly–for being with me, for being with someone of mixed blood–of mixed, Atlantean blood."

"What are you talking about? How can you believe that?"

"Look at what happened to my mother," he said with some force. "She was violated. Why? And her mother–my grandmother–abandoned her–us–before she married my father. You know how the villagers see me. You know how they had looked down on my mother. Do you think I wanted you to go through all of that?"

"Why didn't you tell me this before? Why didn't we talk about all of this?"

"Because talking about it would have solved nothing. The only choice we would have had would have been to keep a distance between us–"

"And for me to marry, Aiko," she interrupted. "Because that is what is safe for me–to be with a man, and his son, who propels our fear, our hatred for the Red race."

Kieko was silent.

"We could have run away too, Kieko. We could have left this place."

"Kira, I know you. You wouldn't have left your mother and your father."

"You don't know that," she contested. "You don't know that, and you didn't have the right to believe that I wouldn't have done that. We could have married in secret," she said with a small smile. "Raki-ka has joked to me these past days that he would do just that with a woman he has fallen for. We could have done that and left to find a new home far from here."

"You would have left your family?" he asked her with a degree of skepticism.

"Yes, my mother has my father. They have each other."

"And my mother? We would have left her here?"

"She lived her life, Kieko. She chose your father, and lost her own family because of it, because that was what she wanted.

She wanted to live her life—even if it meant to later lose her husband. That was what she wanted."

Kieko thought for a moment.

"I know I would have left Ikishi for you, Kieko. But, would you have done the same for me?"

Kieko was silent again.

Kira, disappointed, looked away from Kieko. "So it is you who is still unsure of what you want."

"I . . ." he said unable to say anything more.

"You should let me go," she pushed herself away from him.

"I . . . I'm sorry, Kira."

"Me too," she said with a saddened heart.

"I . . . I want to say more."

"Shhh," she tried to hush him not wanting to hear more of what he had to say.

"I want to say more, Kira. But, now is not the time."

"When then?" she asked. "We are out of time, Kieko. There is no more time left."

"I know that. I know. But for now I think we should rest. I should rest. I have been through a lot with the death of my mother. I don't think I can think straight. I need to mourn. I need to rest."

"Where will you go?"

"To my home," he said as if the answer was obvious.

"A family of refugees moved into your home after word had spread that you had run away with your mother."

"How many people know that I left?"

"Many," she said. "Kono's temple home is empty. He has been staying here in the village for the past few days."

"Yes . . . I know."

"The coward. He was probably afraid of being attacked during the night since his home is more or less on the outskirts of the village."

"Perhaps, I should stay there."

"I only said that as a joke," she smiled. "You can stay with us."

"What about your father?"

"He will be busy planning with the Elders and the others. Come home and rest, if my father comes just pretend to be asleep. He will allow you to sleep in our home for a night after he learns of what had happened."

"To my mother you mean."

"Yes," she said weakly, "to Madonai."

The two walked to Rakima's home and entered it finding it empty, but busy with boiling pots of water and soup, and burning wood in the hearth.

"Would you like something to eat?" she asked Kieko.

"Yes, that would be nice. I haven't eaten all day."

"Neither have I. My mother and I, as for most of the people, had to work out in the cold digging or making weapons or traps. You can rest over there," she said pointing to a side of the hut that had a pile of pillows and warm blankets.

Kieko went to the pile of pillows and sat down. Kira poured two bowls of soup and served one to Kieko. Together they drank their soup in silence.

"That was very good," he complimented when he finished drinking the soup.

"You can thank my mother."

"Where is she?"

"I don't know. But, she didn't leave too long ago. She will be back soon. She would never leave soup boiling for too long without her supervision."

"Then I should get to sleep before she gets back. I will thank her for the soup in the morning."

"Fine then," she said and took Kieko's bowl. "You have everything you need right there." She stood up and walked toward the cauldron of boiling soup.

"Kira," Kieko called out.

She turned and looked at him.

"I'm sorry."

She cracked a smile and said, "You don't have to be sorry for anything. I'm just happy you're here . . . with me."

Kieko smiled to her and got ready for sleep.

Frigid winter winds blew into the hut when Ruka entered it. She saw her daughter and said as she unrolled the scarf around her neck, "You're home, good. I have some soup for you." She heard a noise. "What is that?" she asked her daughter.

Kira pointed to where Kieko snored beneath a few layers of wool blankets.

"He's back!" she exclaimed. "What's he doing here? Where's his mother?"

Kira approached her mother and whispered, "She . . . she is dead."

"What?" she said in disbelief as she shook her head. "What happened?" Kira explained what Kieko had told her. "Oh my," Ruka said with her hand held over her mouth. "I don't believe it . . . I don't believe it," she said shaking her head again as tears began to well in her eyes. "This can not be," she collapsed to the ground; Kira sat and comforted her mother. "Now he has no one . . . no one. He has lost his entire family."

"He has us," Kira said.

"Come here," she said to her daughter pulling her into her arms. "I c-c-can't believe it . . . I was wi-with Madonai, talking to her, laugh . . . laughing with her, just a day—just a day or so ago." She began to cry, "It's . . . it's my fault. I . . . I should have . . . I should have had her stay with us."

"It's not your fault," Kira assured her mother. "It's not your fault."

Ruka began to sob, "This . . . this is n-not fair. She . . . she d-d-didn't deserve to die. She was . . . she was a g-g-good woman."

"Mom, please," Kira said as she weeped with her mother. "Please . . . please tell me that we . . . we will b-be fine."

"Yes, yes we will," she heaved with determination in her voice. "We have to—we have to pull ourselves together." She began wiping the tears from her eyes with her forearm. "Come . . . Kira, we have to pull ourselves together. For his sake." Kira slowly calmed herself.

When Ruka had regained her composure she stood up and walked to Kieko to take a better look at him. "Where did he get those clothes?"

"I don't know," Kira answered.

"There is blood on them," she noted. "I saw Aiko today. He was wearing something similar to this."

Not wanting to talk about Aiko she said of Kieko, "He was exhausted."

"Like the rest of us," Ruka remarked.

"As soon as he fell on the floor and pulled the blanket over himself he fell asleep."

"Well, we should do the same. Let's eat and get ready for sleep."

"I already ate."

"You did?"

"Yes, with Kieko we had some of your soup. He liked it very much."

Kieko let out a loud snore. Ruka looked at her daughter and together they giggled. Ruka then said, "Between the snores of your father and Kieko I'm not sure we'll be able to get much sleep."

Rakima entered the hut allowing a flurry of snow to blow in, "Why are you two laughing?"

"It's snowing outside?" Ruka asked her husband. Kira turned away from her father and went to sit down by the hearth.

"Yes, it just started to snow. Why were you two laughing?" He heard Kieko snore and looked down at him. "What in the name of Kadek is he doing here?"

"Shhh," Ruka hushed. "Don't wake him."

"What is he doing here?" he looked with stern eyes at the back of his daughter's head.

Ruka quickly explained to her husband what she had learned from her daughter concerning Madonai's death and asked if it was all right if Kieko spent the night in their home. Kira turned to see what her father's answer would be. Rakima thought for a moment feeling very uncomfortable that he had Kieko sleeping in his home and said, "Kira, for you I can see that you wouldn't mind to have him stay here. You expect me to say that it is all right that he stays here. How you expect that of me after months of you not acknowledging me when have I come home—my home—is a mystery to me. I see no reason why we should keep him here."

Kira stood up, "You know why I have been as I have been with you in our home."

"Kira, I had very little choice—"

"You mean you chose what was easy by listening to what Tsuwata wanted. You chose him over me—me, your daughter—your only child," she said trying not to shout. Lowering her voice she continued, "I expect you to allow him to sleep here because that is what good people do. I don't care what your brother will think. Kieko needs a place to rest. He needs us. He needs you to treat him as he deserves."

"He doesn't deserve much, Kira. He left the priest and ran away from Ikishi like a coward with his mother."

"Do you blame him?" she asked. "No one here has treated him or his mother as human. They have all treated them like dogs. Why? Because of Nishiaka? Because of where he came from? Why is it their fault that the Atlanteans have done what they have done to us? It is not their fault. They are people—simple people and nothing more."

"Kira, Kieko is not simple. Everyone here saw that he could conjure Ki. They fear what that means."

Kieko began to wake from the tense words he heard between Rakima and Kira. Rakima looked at his daughter and stepped out of the hut not wanting to be seen by Kieko or to speak with him.

"Is everything all right?" he asked Ruka and Kira as he rubbed his eyes.

"Yes, Kieko, everything is all right," Ruka assured him. "You were having a dream. Go back to sleep."

Kieko looked with unfocused eyes at both Ruka and Kira and relaxed. "I . . . I thought I heard your father."

"It was just a dream, Kieko. Go back to sleep," Ruka advised.

Kira went to blow out a few candles to darken the hut so that Kieko could fall asleep again.

Kieko dropped his head on the pillow and closed his eyes. Within moments he began to snore again.

Ruka wrapped a wool blanket around her body and said to her daughter, "Stay here. Let me speak to your father." She exited her home to speak to her husband.

Outside Rakima was smoking from his long pipe, but when he saw his wife he looked at her and said, "It is not right that that boy is in our home."

"Rakima," she began, "now is not the time to talk about what is right or what is best. Kieko lost his mother last night. He is tired and has no one. Let him rest." Rakima turned away. Ruka grabbed his arm and said, "Let him rest just for tonight."

"Fine then," he agreed. "But, I will not stay here. If that is what you want then you can have it, but I will not spend the night here."

"Rakima—" she now pleaded.

"No, I have things to do—things to prepare for tomorrow."

"Rakima, I expect you to sleep by my side—especially now, especially when I need you through all of this."

"You want that boy to stay there. You have it." He then walked away.

"Don't you walk away from me, Rakima! I am your wife."

He waved his hand at her as if he was trying to swat something away and walked in the direction of the Council Hut.

"Rakima!" she shouted. "Rakima, come back."

Rakima continued walking and puffing on his pipe. Ruka, emotionally hurt and feeling completely unwanted, turned and entered her home.

"He will not sleep here will he," Kira asked her mother.

"No, he will not."

Kira embraced her mother, "Mom, it's all right. Everything is all right. He just has a lot on his mind."

Ruka held her daughter tightly and began to cry. "I'm tired," she wept, "I'm . . . I'm tired of him. I'm . . . I'm tired of him always thinking . . . thinking," she stuttered, "more in what other's want than—than—than in what we need. And now . . . now with all this uncertainty I need him. I need him," she cried more, "I need him by my side. And—and he left. He left me."

"Mom, everything will be all right," she tried to comfort her mother. "Everything will be fine. Let's just have some soup—I could have a little more—and we'll go to sleep. We'll go to sleep, together, holding each other."

"Yes . . ." she said softly. "That would be . . . that would be nice."

They heard Kieko snore again, looked at each other, and smiled. They served each other a bowl of soup, ate silently together, and went to sleep holding each other, comforting one another, beneath several layers of warm, wool blankets.

CHAPTER X

It was night, and the deep interior of the Ikishi forest was very dark. Raki-ka squinted and could just see the flowing robe of the priest near the front of the long line of men who were walking quietly, but swiftly, to the Kadek Temple. With hurried steps he advanced past a few more men, but he tripped on a snow-covered tree root.

"What are you doing?" Rakima questioned when he grabbed Raki-ka's arm.

Raki-ka, frightened, looked directly up at Rakima's eye patch and nervously shook his head.

"Answer him!" Tsuwata barked as he pulled the nocked arrow on his bowstring closer toward his body.

Raki-ka noticed Niko who was smirking and standing beside his father with his bow and nocked arrow. "I–I–" he tried to answer.

"I–I–what?" Niko said with a dark, demeaning laugh.

"Quiet," Rakima ordered his nephew. "We must keep moving."

Together they moved and quickened their steps so that their pace was the same as that of the long line of men.

"What were you trying to do?" Tsuwata demanded from Raki-ka.

"I was–I was trying . . . trying–"

"Trying to move up in the line?" Tsuwata finished.

Raki-ka nodded.

"And why would you want to do that?" Rakima asked with growing impatience.

"I–I need to ask the–the," his teeth chattered from the cold, "the priest something."

"It will have to wait," Rakima interjected. "Go back to where you were."

Raki-ka bowed his head seeing Niko continue to smirk at him from the corner of his eye, took a few steps to his left, and stopped so that the line of men behind him could pass.

"I told you," Watanoro began when he and Hirotake had caught up to Raki-ka.

"Please, don't remind me," Raki-ka replied annoyed.

"There was no possible way for you to walk up all that way to the priest. Especially with Tsuwata somewhere up there."

"Well, I tried."

"What is it that is so urgent that you ask the priest?"

"Yes, what is so urgent?" Hirotake asked.

"It's nothing," Raki-ka answered.

"I don't believe you," Watanoro remarked.

"I don't either," Hirotake agreed.

"What does it matter–I can't ask the priest anyway so forget it–"

"Quiet," interrupted a refugee who was walking ahead of them.

Raki-ka glared at the refugee.

"We're sorry," Hirotake apologized; Watanoro then elbowed him in the arm. "Why'd you do that?"

The refugee shook his head at the three of them and faced forward.

Raki-ka and Watanoro began making both cruel and funny faces at the back of the refugee.

"Stop it," Hirotake whispered.

The refugee looked back to Raki-ka and Watanoro, but they had already turned their heads to look at the trees they were passing. He then shook his head at the three of them again, faced forward, and continued walking.

"How much further is it?" Hirotake asked his two friends.

"We should be walking . . . more or less parallel to the path that leads to the temple," Watanoro answered. "So we—"

"No we're not," Raki-ka interrupted. "If that was true we would have arrived to the temple by now."

"You don't know what you're talking about," Watanoro retorted.

"Why? Do you always walk to the temple through the forest?"

"Quiet!" the refugee ahead of them nearly shouted with glaring eyes causing other men who were walking further ahead to look back with strong looks of disapproval.

Hirotake's body cowered as his face turned red with embarrassment.

"All right," Raki-ka said to the refugee. "We'll be quiet."

The brow of the refugee furrowed as he gave a hard stern look to both Raki-ka and Watanoro.

"We'll be quiet," Watanoro agreed.

The refugee gave a disbelieving look at the three of them and continued walking.

"Cursed dog," Watanoro said under his breath.

"Shhh, please," Hirotake urged Watanoro fearful of another confrontation with the refugee.

"What does it matter if we're heard? If the army of the Akai wanted us dead they would have killed us by now," Watanoro reasoned.

"You don't know that," Raki-ka expressed.

"Look at us—there are about a hundred of us marching in the dark through a forest—there are fish in the sea that can hear us."

"I thought fish don't have ears," Hirotake commented.

"Right, that's the point!" Watanoro exclaimed.

"But, they do have ears," Raki-ka disputed.

"Damn the gods," the refugee barked. "Shut your damn mouths!"

More men stopped and turned to show their intolerance for Raki-ka's and Watanoro's noisy behavior.

"We're sorry," Watanoro apologized.

"That is not good enough," the refugee replied. "Your idiot mouths are putting us all at risk." Many men who were both ahead and behind Raki-ka and Watanoro nodded and muttered in agreement.

"Look, we're sorry," Raki-ka began. "We apologize. We're just a little unnerved by everything—"

"So am I. So is everyone. But, we all have the intellect to keep our mouths shut. So shut your mouth so that we don't attract any attacks." Again many men nodded and muttered their contempt. "No more words," the refugee turned and began walking again.

Both Raki-ka and Watanoro felt completely embarrassed and began walking with their heads slightly bowed.

After an hour had passed Hirotake pulled at Raki-ka's sleeve and whispered, "How much farther?"

"We'll get there when we get there," Raki-ka answered with irritation.

Not satisfied with the answer, but too afraid to press Raki-ka further, he murmured, "Yes . . . we'll get there when we get there."

"What do you mean, 'we'll get there when we get there'?" Watanoro asked. "If 'we'll get there when we get there' then why in the name of Mount Kurohi did you ask when we'll we get there in the first place?"

"No—no," Hirotake answered as he shook his head nervously from side to side, "you misunderstood me—"

"Be quiet," Raki-ka interrupted. "I think we're there. The line is stopping."

Hirotake and Watanoro looked ahead and were able to see a group of men gather at the front of the line right at the edge of the forest, where beyond it, there were a clearing and the Kadek Temple.

"I can just see the temple through those trees," Watanoro explained as he pointed.

"Yes, I can see it," Raki-ka said.

Hirotake squinted, "Yes—me too."

"There's something happening at the front of the line," Watanoro reported. Hirotake and Raki-ka began moving their heads from side to side trying to get a better view of the front of the line. "I see . . . I see the priest and . . . and the blacksmith moving out and into the clearing."

"They'd better be armed," Raki-ka said.

"I can't see," Hirotake complained.

"I see two other men . . . I can't tell who they are but . . . but they too are moving out into the clearing with . . . with bows—"

"They're scouting the land," Hirotake realized.

A few moments passed and the three of them waited and listened with great unease for any unusual sounds.

"There are three . . ." Raki-ka paused and squinted, "three men—and they just ran into the clearing."

"This is ridiculous," Watanoro said as he shook his head. "We should all just walk out into the clearing and to the temple and stop this nonsense."

"We'd all be out in the open if we did that," Hirotake replied.

"I am telling you that if the Atlanteans wanted us dead we would be dead right now. But, we're not. So there is no threat. We should just get on with it and all walk to the temple—"

"Quiet—you three or we'll gag you," someone said from behind them.

Watanoro ground his teeth and kept his head down not wanting to look back and face the scorn of those behind him. Hirotake and Raki-ka bowed their heads as well and remained silent as the line slowly moved up toward the edge of the forest.

When they reached the forest boundary they saw Sekihi and Niko keeping guard between two large trees by holding the nocked arrows of their long bows tight against their chest as they looked and aimed into the trees that were at the sides and far end of the clearing.

"You three, get ready," Sekihi said to three refugees who were at the front of the line. The three refugees walked up to the very edge of the forest and looked ahead seeing the path of kicked up snow that led to the temple's tori gate where Tsuwata and Rakima kept guard. "Go—go now," Sekihi ordered. The three refugees ran across the clearing toward, and then through, the tori gate. The blacksmith ordered the next group of men to run out into the clearing and then another. "Move up and get ready," Sekihi said to Hirotake, Raki-ka, and Watanoro. The three of them moved up, but Hirotake began to shake with fear and nervousness.

"Don't worry," Watanoro said trying to comfort his friend. "If the Atlanteans wanted us dead we would have been dead already."

"Unless they're playing with us, or waiting for us all to collect in the temple before sending a hail of burning arrows down onto it," Raki-ka reasoned.

"Go you fools—go," Sekihi commanded.

The three of them ran out toward the tori gate where they saw Tsuwata and Rakima aiming the nocked arrows of their long bows into the dark of the trees that surrounded the clearing. Feeling their hearts race within their chests they ran through the tori gate and across the snow covered garden seeing the granite steps of the temple ahead, and an open entrance door. One after the other they jumped up the steps and leapt into the darkness beyond the door.

"We . . . we did it," Watanoro wheezed as he tried to catch his breath.

"There is no time for proper temple etiquette," the priest declared as he emerged from the shadows of the antechamber to look out and see if the next group of men was coming.

"Mount Kurohi," Watanoro nearly exclaimed. "You scared . . . you scared the living spirit out of me."

"I apologize," the priest said with urgency as he tightened his grip on his staff. "Do not take off your shoes—go ahead into the temple."

Raki-ka looked at the priest, "Shinsei—there is something I need to ask you—"

"Another group is coming," the priest interrupted. "Go—go into the temple. You can ask me your question when we return to Ikishi."

"Yes, Shinsei," Raki-ka said disappointed.

Hirotake walked into the next antechamber with Watanoro and Raki-ka following behind him and turned to his left where he walked into the reception hall which was dimly lit by a few burning candles.

"Where is everyone?" Watanoro asked, as he looked at the calligraphy paintings that were hanging on the walls.

"I don't know," Raki-ka answered as he looked with wonder from one painting to the other.

"You three," someone whispered. "Over here." The three of them looked to their right and saw a golden glow emanating from another hall. "We're all in here." Raki-ka approached the hall. "You must bow." Raki-ka bowed, as did Hirotake and Watanoro, and one after the other they entered the main hall.

Their eyes widened, and their jaws dropped, when they saw, at the opposite end of the hall, the massive golden statue of a Buddha sitting on a large altar that was covered with hundreds of lit candles and offerings of cabbages, radishes, and carrots on silver plates and silver bowls filled with rice wine.

"It's beautiful," Hirotake said in awe.

"Yes . . . yes it is," Raki-ka agreed.

"We must remain quiet," a refugee who approached them whispered with his finger held to his lips. "The priest said that we must stay here and wait in complete silence."

The three of them nodded in agreement as they noticed all the groups of men who were standing silently in the shadows of the main hall. Watanoro looked at his two friends and motioned with his hand that he wanted to go to the altar. Hirotake and Raki-ka nodded, and together they walked down the center of the hall toward the golden statue of the Buddha seeing the neatly stacked columns of zabutons and the long vertical calligraphy paintings that were hanging from the old wooden walls to their left and right. They stopped before the golden statue and looked with great interest at the other items that were on the altar: a shrine bell, three finely carved boxes of incense, a ceramic bowl filled with white ash, a bekuru, and a wooden mallet. The three of them heard a faint splat on the floor and looked down seeing something small, lumpy, and wet.

"What is that?" Hirotake asked in disgust.

Watanoro looked up and saw two bats fly across the high ceiling, "Bat droppings."

"There are bats?" Hirotake asked with fear.

Annoyed by the question Watanoro answered, "Yes—and there are Akai out there hesitating to attack us so don't waste your thoughts on bats—"

There was a sudden noise and movement from the entrance of the main hall and everyone turned their attention toward it, but they were all relieved to find that it was just the priest who had entered with Sekihi, Tsuwata, Rakima, and Niko following right behind him. The priest hurried across the main hall with his staff as men stepped back to part a path for him. When he reached the altar he bowed, took a lit bronze lamp from it, went to the door at the far left side of the altar, faced and bowed to the golden statue of the Buddha again, slid the door open, and walked in; Sekihi, Tsuwata, Rakima, and Niko followed the priest into the darkness beyond the door. A flickering light was then seen emanating from beyond the door; several groups of men began to gather before the door and the altar.

"Do you see anything?" Watanoro asked Raki-ka as they tried to push through the crowd that had gathered before the door.

"No—I can't see a thing. There are too many people and not enough light."

"Quiet you two," a refugee said from behind them.

"Yes, be quiet," a villager hushed.

The sound of large, metallic gears beginning to turn could be heard emanating from within the walls, which caused several of the men who were standing before the door to push back against the crowd. Then there was a hard thud and the uncomfortable sound of stone grinding slowly against stone until finally the metallic gears stopped. Patiently the crowd waited, and as the moments passed several men began to whisper voicing their speculations, fears, and doubts.

"Form a line," Rakima ordered as he stepped out from the door. "We will pass out the weapons from the temple's armory and pile them at the rear of the main hall. You, you, and you," he pointed to the three men standing directly in front of him, "and you two, and you five come with me." He stepped back into the faintly lit chamber and the men he had pointed to followed him; those who remained in the main hall promptly formed a line from the door to the rear of the main hall. Long, thin, heavy objects wrapped in dusty deer hides emerged from the door and were passed from one set of hands to the other until they were carefully placed on the floor at the rear of the main hall.

"What are these?" Hirotake asked as he passed one of the wrapped objects to Raki-ka.

"These are probably the old, curve-bladed spears of the Ki priests who had lived here," Watanoro answered.

Soon sheathed, long and short swords were being passed down the line, and then long bows and quivers full of old arrows were passed until at last there were more weapons piled on the floor than what the men, who had come to the temple, could possibly carry.

"That is enough," Rakima said as he walked into the main hall with his nephew, Niko, following behind him. The sound of large metallic gears beginning to turn, and stone grinding against stone, was heard again causing several men to cringe until there was a hard thud, and the metallic gears slowed to a complete stop.

Sekihi and Tsuwata emerged from the door, and the flickering light beyond the door was then no more. The priest stepped out from the darkness and walked toward the pile of weapons with his staff and with two swords that were wrapped in black suede cradled in his left arm. Men followed after the priest, and when he stopped before the pile they gathered around sensing his discomfort in having so many Ki weapons on the floor of the main hall before the statue of the Buddha.

"It may appear that there are too many weapons for us to carry back to the village," the priest began, "but it must be done. The lives of our people depend on it. Sekihi, Tsuwata, Rakima, and Niko will go out first, secure their positions, and provide cover as we retreat from the temple in groups of three to the forest and make our return to Ikishi. I will see you all at the Council Hut. Now—let us move with haste."

Sekihi, Tsuwata, Rakima, and Niko bent down and each took two quivers full of arrows by their straps from the pile and threw them over their heads so that the straps ran across their chests, and exited the main hall with the priest following behind them.

The crowd of men began picking up quivers, long bows, sheathed long and short swords, and the curve-bladed spears that were wrapped in dusty, deer hides from the pile. Many men slid the sheathed swords that they had taken through the folds of their belts while others tied them together with rope and strapped them across their backs before taking a quiver of arrows and a long bow, or a curve-bladed spear, as their weapon of choice if attacked during the journey home. And when the majority of the men had securely fastened these weapons to their backs or belts and were able to maneuver with their bows or curve-bladed spears they exited the main hall in groups of two or three.

"Are you ready?" Watanoro asked Hirotake who was having difficulty trying to throw another quiver of arrows over his head.

"Yes—nearly ready," he answered.

"Just place the strap over your shoulder—you have too many quivers already on your back," Raki-ka advised with growing impatience.

"But, if I have it hanging from my shoulder I won't be able to nock my bow quickly—" Hirotake tried to explain.

"It doesn't matter—you can just grab an arrow from the twenty odd quivers you already have strapped to your back," Raki-ka rolled his eyes as he shook his head. "Come—let's go before we are the last to leave."

Together the three of them made their way to exit the main hall as a few remaining men took what was left from the pile of dwindling weapons.

In the reception hall they discovered a line of men slowly progressing toward the entrance of the temple and went to stand at the end of it. As they waited they looked, as they had before, at the calligraphy paintings that decorated the hall, admiring their simplicity and beauty, while also wishing that they had the ability to both read and write, and draw with such grace.

The line moved and they entered the next room; an antechamber with a cold breeze that was causing the three calligraphy paintings that were hanging on one of the wooden walls to flap against it. They looked ahead into the dark of the next antechamber and were able to see the snow covered garden beyond the open entrance door and, in the distance, Tsuwata and Rakima at the base of the tori gate with their nocked arrows pulled tight against their chests.

"Go," the priest ordered from the dark of the next antechamber.

Three men ran out and down the granite steps and across the garden as fast as they could with the heavy weapons they were carrying moving and rattling against their bodies.

"Looks as if one of them is going to fall and spill all those swords on the ground," Watanoro joked.

Hirotake and Raki-ka did not reply; they simply watched praying that nothing would go wrong.

The priest sent out another group of men and then another. "You three—come here," he said to Hirotake, Watanoro, Raki-ka. The three of them walked into the dark of the antechamber where the priest was standing. "Be careful with that spear," he advised Watanoro before looking back out with attentive eyes into the forest beyond the tori gate.

"You don't really believe that there's something out there?" Watanoro asked the priest.

The priest's brow furrowed. "Yes . . ." he answered as he looked out with even greater concentration and concern into the dark beyond the trees. "There is something . . . but it waits."

Hirotake, Watanoro, and Raki-ka's eyes widened. "What— what do you mean?" Watanoro asked.

"Get ready," the priest said.

"Wait—what do you mean there's 'something'?" Watanoro asked the priest. "I'm not going out there until you answer me."

The priest turned to Watanoro, "There is something that has been watching us since we arrived to the temple—and it is watching us now. But, it is not armed—or at least it does not intend to harm us."

"And how do you know that?" Raki-ka interjected.

"Because if it had wanted to harm us it would have done so by now," the priest explained. "Now get ready. I will not be too far behind you three. If something does happen I will protect you. You have my word."

Hirotake began shaking his head out of fear and resistance to running out into the cold open air.

"Hirotake—look at me," the priest said with profound strength behind his words, "nothing will happen to us tonight. Your wife is waiting for you. Do not fail her. Now go—you three—go."

Raki-ka pushed Hirotake out the door and Watanoro followed. They ran down the granite steps and across the temple garden as the weapons they carried clanged against each other and their bodies.

"Come on, Hiro, we have to make it to the trees," Raki-ka urged Hirotake as he pulled him by the arm to keep up with him.

"I'm . . . I'm running . . . as fast . . . as fast as I can," he panted.

Watanoro passed them and ran through the tori gate.

"Keep running you fools," Tsuwata said when Hirotake and Raki-ka passed him and his brother Rakima at the tori gate.

"I can see Sekihi and Niko," Raki-ka said to Hirotake. "We're almost there."

Hirotake slipped and the weight of the weapons he was carrying threw him forward causing him to crash down to the ground spilling arrows out in all directions. Watanoro stopped, ran back, and grabbed Hirotake by the arm while Raki-ka was already dragging Hirotake by his other arm.

"Wait," Hirotake pleaded as he was being dragged. "My bow—I need my bow."

"It's broken," Raki-ka growled. "Now get up and run."

"I need my bow," Hirotake insisted.

"Forget the damn bow," Watanoro protested. "Get up and run, you stupid fool."

Watanoro and Raki-ka lifted Hirotake to his feet and together they ran to the edge of the forest where Sekihi and Niko were waiting for them to arrive.

"You brainless monkeys," Sekihi sputtered to Hirotake, Watanoro, and Raki-ka when they finally reached the edge of the forest.

"I'm sorry," Hirotake apologized to the blacksmith.

"Just try not to fall again and spill more arrows on the ground," Sekihi said as he shook his head.

"That's right," Niko spat, "don't fall and waste more arrows."

"Shut your mouth, you little bastard," Watanoro snarled as he approached Niko with a tight fist.

Niko stepped back and aimed the arrow on his long bow at Watanoro's chest.

"Are you going to shoot me?" Watanoro asked trying to provoke Niko. "Go ahead and do it."

Sekihi stepped in between them and placed his hand over the arrow on Niko's bowstring. "We don't have time for this, damn it. There is another group coming. Watanoro—just go. Raki-ka—"

Raki-ka placed his hands on Watanoro's shoulders and led him away while Hirotake motioned to Niko to look the other way. Sekihi took Niko and led him back to the edge of the forest again so that they could provide cover for the next group of men who were running toward them from the temple.

When the last group of men had entered the forest the priest took his staff, and the two swords that were wrapped in black suede, and stepped out from the dark of the antechamber into the moonlight. He took a deep breath of the frigid night air, gave a deep solemn bow to the temple, and slid the entrance door closed for what he knew would be the last time. He descended the granite steps, walked hurriedly across the garden seeing the snowcapped Mountains of Shinohi far in the distance, and joined with Tsuwata and Rakima at the tori gate so that they could return to the forest together. When they reached the edge of the forest the blacksmith greeted them with a bow before going ahead to catch up with the long line of men who were making the trek back to Ikishi. Tsuwata followed after the blacksmith with his son, Niko, and the priest and Rakima then followed after them.

"Do you still feel this . . . this entity watching us?" Rakima asked the priest as he pulled his nocked arrow closer to his chest while looking carefully into the darkness beyond the trees ahead of them.

"No," the priest answered, "but, I still feel as if we are being watched—not by this entity . . . but by something else—something high above," he pointed up.

Rakima looked up at the dark canopy of the forest seeing nothing unusual other than the reflecting eyes of an owl. "Your words do not encourage me."

"Yes, I know," the priest acknowledged with sorrow, "my words of late have provided little assurance to our people."

Rakima looked at the priest and was not encouraged by the doubt within him. Disappointed, he looked ahead and tried to focus on the trail they were following.

"You are upset by me," the priest said to Rakima.

Rakima clenched his teeth not wanting to answer and continued walking, and together they walked in silence listening to the footsteps of those before them while keeping their eyes attentive to the darkness around them.

After a half hour had passed Rakima began to slow his walk so that there was more distance between him and his older brother. The priest noticed this but said nothing and kept pace with Rakima. "I am finding it hard to admire you," Rakima said to the priest with his deep, rough voice.

"Good," the priest praised. "You are throwing out what you have been thinking."

"Do not commend me," he bit back. "You are failing our people. They are looking to you as an example. If they see doubt in you—a holy man—a man not of despair—fall into despair then they will lose the will to fight."

"Do you speak for them or for you?" the priest asked. Rakima's eyes twitched. "And there is the answer."

"What does it matter?" he asked. "Many here feel as I do about you."

"And what is it that they feel about me?"

"They are disappointed. They seek an example in you in how they should be—especially now—especially at this time when we face what we face."

"And what is it that we face?"

"Do not play games—" he stifled his words before raising his voice.

"But answer me that, Rakima. What is it that we face?"

"Isn't it obvious? We face death. The death of our people, of our way of life–the death of our culture."

"Is that what upsets you? Or is it your own death that upsets you?"

"Why are we talking about me? Why don't you speak and criticize yourself?"

"You are right," he recognized by nodding his head. "I will speak about me. I had fallen. I had fallen into self-doubt. But, I am rising to confront a past that has pursued me, found me–one that I had so foolishly believed that I could escape from. And I will face it before my death. I will face it with all of my strength just as I know you will when the time comes."

"I will do what is required of me. I will fight and lead these people to victory."

"And if there is no victory?"

"Do not even try to tempt me with that possibility," he growled at the priest. "There will be victory. We will win. You have no right to even try to steal that hope from me."

"What will come is what will come, and we will perform as we must when that time comes. But, we must do so free of heart– unattached and with no expectations."

"That is the philosophy of the Ki. I speak of reality."

"So do I."

"You do not. The reality of our situation is that a great army comes to destroy us. I know that we can defeat them. I will have that–I will protect my people, my family, our way of life."

"And tonight. When you arrive home. What will you do?"

"I will not go home . . . I will work into the morning preparing for our stand against the Akai."

"So, tonight your family will not have you."

Rakima stopped and looked at the back of his brother afraid that he might hear what he was about to say. "The boy," he whispered, "sleeps in my home."

"Kieko."

"Yes, it was the wish of my wife and daughter. I do not support their wish and so . . . I will not go home."

"So you speak of protecting your family, but you will not be with them tonight. But you are here in the dark of night following after Tsuwata and his wishes."

"Do not speak to me of the decisions I have made with my family," Rakima objected. "What gives you that right?"

"Nothing gives me that right, but I know that your long held guilt in not having followed the wishes of your own wife and daughter is what drives you to gain victory in this coming battle, for if we win you will gain the time to finally do what is good and what is right—to stand by your wife and daughter and put down the wishes of your elder brother and kin."

"If that is how you feel about me then let me tell you this, priest. Your guilt in not having had the courage to face the demons in your past is what is driving you to accept and give into our defeat and your death." The priest was silent. "There—you see. We are one and the same. Perhaps for that we deserve death. But, if I am to die I will do so fighting. So I will see you on the battlefield, old friend." He then walked ahead leaving the priest behind.

The priest saw the truth in Rakima's words, but he did not let these words affect him for he quieted his mind and listened to the sound of the cold winds blow over the trees and the sound of the long line of men who were making the journey back to Ikishi. In the background of his mind he could feel sadness and distress trying to rise into the fullness of his consciousness; he could hear the words of his mind repeat: *You are a betrayer of hope. You are not worthy of the Ki. You are not what you seek to be.* He wanted to push down and banish those words, and the negative feelings surrounding them, but he did not. Instead, he closed his eyes, acknowledged the words, and allowed them to be within his mind. And as he took a deep breath, filling himself with all that was of that moment, the words began to fade until at last they were no more. The priest opened his eyes and walked clear of mind and clear of heart seeing that Rakima was not too far ahead.

All was silent when the priest, along with all the men that were traveling ahead of him, reached the outer edges of the Ikishi village. The long line of men quietly greeted the scouts they came across, and quietly did they pass between the tents and fading campfires of the refugees and the unlit thatched homes of the Ikishi villagers until at last they reached the open plain before the Council Hut. Tired and exhausted, and in groups of two or three they entered the Council Hut, which was lit by a few fires staves, to drop the weapons they had carried into a pile behind the wooden thrones of the Elders. Relieved of the burden of carrying such heavy weapons they then sat, or stood, and waited for the priest.

The priest entered the Council Hut, and as he walked toward the center of the hut he saw Rakima standing with his thick arms crossed over his chest between his elder brother, Tsuwata, and his nephew, Niko. When he reached the center of the hut he stopped and saw the messy pile of weapons behind the wooden thrones of the Elders. "I know that you are all tired and wish to rush to your families and homes to rest before the light of dawn calls us all back to this Council Hut, but there is one last thing I am to ask of you." Groans and muttered complaints were heard from many of the men. "I need for you all to separate and stack the weapons into five piles: one for the spears, the long swords, the short swords, the long bows, and the quivers. Once you have done that you may all leave."

Sekihi, Tsuwata, and Rakima took the initiative to organize the men into groups that were to separate the weapons accordingly and stack them neatly. In less than a quarter of an hour the task was done and the men made their way to return to their homes.

Hirotake and Watanoro pushed and shoved to get through the many men who were now gathered before the exit of the hut since they were both desperate to rest and sleep before early morning. Raki-ka was behind his two friends, but he was not as anxious as they were to return home. Instead, he tried to move further and further back.

"Raki-ka," Watanoro called out as he tried to look back and see where his friend was within the crowd. "Where are you?" Raki-ka did not answer. "I see you. What are you doing?"

Raki-ka looked at Watanoro and mouthed the word, *the priest*, with wide eyes. Watanoro understood and shook his head at his friend before someone from behind him lightly pushed him forward. Raki-ka then turned and went against the crowd until at last he was free from it. He saw the priest and Sekihi checking the piles of weapons behind thrones and went to them.

"Shinsei," he said respectfully. "There was . . . there is something that I need to ask of you."

The priest turned to Raki-ka, "Yes, what is it that you would like to ask me?"

"I . . ." he looked from the corner of his eye at the blacksmith who was counting the number of short swords in the pile, "I would like to speak with you privately . . . if you don't mind."

"Yes, of course." The priest led Raki-ka away and asked, "Well, what is it?"

"I . . . I know you must be very tired . . . but there is something . . . a favor that I would like to ask of you."

"Yes, what is it?"

"I would like for you to . . . to . . . to marry Koko-maki and I."

"Does she know about this?" the priest asked in a joking manner.

"Yes, of course. Yes, she does."

"I'm sure she does. I only said that to tease you," the priest smiled. Embarrassed, Raki-ka held his head down unsure of what to say next. "I can assume then that neither her father nor her grandfather knows about this."

"No, they do not," he whispered afraid that the blacksmith might somehow overhear their words.

"Marriage is not something to be taken lightly, and neither is it something to be rushed into."

"Well," he interrupted. "Under these circumstances . . . it is something that I must rush into."

"And why is that?"

"Because if I am to die . . . I want to do so in the arms of . . . my wife."

"So, you see her now as your wife then?"

"Yes, yes I do. I see her as my wife. And I see myself as her husband. She has cared for me . . . she has loved me."

"And have you done these wonderful things for her?"

He hesitated for a moment, "I . . . I am not proud of how I have lived my life, Shinsei. I am not proud of what I have done to other women."

"Then how do you know that this sudden desire for marriage, in the face of death, is not a repetition of your drive to not be alone, to not die alone?" He was silent as he went over the priest's words. "You are a good man, Raki-ka. All that I am asking of you is if your request—your request for marriage—is sincere."

"Yes, Shinsei, it is. It is sincere," he answered looking straight into the priest's eyes.

"Yes, I can see it is," the priest smiled again as he saw the last remaining men exit the hut. "Well, how should we go about with this . . . this secret marriage?"

"She is waiting, Shinsei. She is waiting for us at the top of Mount Kurohi."

"She is already there? Has she been waiting there all night?"

"No, no. I told her that when she saw us returning to Ikishi to begin ascending the mountain and to wait for us at the top by the cliff where the lone tree stands."

"I see . . . well, there are some things that I will need. Go ahead and I will meet you at the top."

"Thank you, Shinsei," he said with a voice filled with happiness. "Thank you so much."

"Go then, go. We do not have much time before the sun begins to rise."

Raki-ka gave a deep and earnest bow to the priest before running across the Council Hut to exit it.

A strong gust of cold sea winds blew against the priest as he climbed up a thin rocky path that meandered up a steep exposed surface of mountain rock. And as his robes fluttered around him he reached for the root of a dead, wind-beaten tree, grabbed it, and pulled himself further up the side of Mount Kurohi while feeling stones and pebbles trickle down from beneath his feet. Far down below the priest was the village, which was illuminated by moonlight, and eerily still and silent. To the south was the vast shimmering calm of the winter sea, and the priest paused to admire it and the wan moon while rubbing his fingers over the knot of the strap that held the two swords that were wrapped in black suede to his back. He looked up the sharp slope of the mountain and saw, not too far away, the silhouette of a large grouping of leafless shrubs with twisted stems and knew that he was now very close to reaching the irregular terrain of the Great Forest of Ikishi. He continued his hike and climb up the rock-strewn path focusing only on each step until at last he reached the tall pine trees that marked the beginning of the forest. He swiped his hand at the dirt and earth that had muddied his robe during his climb, took a moment to catch his breath, and entered the dark of the great forest before him.

Tree branches moved and creaked as the sea winds blew over the forest, and the priest listened hearing the faint sound of the trees whisper of wicked things to come. Not wanting to listen more to what he already knew he quickened his steps through the forest and searched the ground with narrowed eyes. He neared the southern edge of the forest where silvery beams of moonlight passed through the tops of the trees and saw what he had been searching for; an ancient and hollowed tree sprawled on the snow-covered ground illuminated by a ray of pale cool light in a small, almost circular, plain. Pleased that he had found the tree he smiled and approached the middle of it where there was a hole of significant size, and when he was just within reach of the fallen tree he stopped before it and bowed. He lifted the two swords off his back, held them in his hands, fell to one knee, and looked at one of them allowing a sudden rush of long ago memories to fill him. "Yes, my old friend," he whispered. "It is time for your sword to meet the hand of your son . . . he is young still yes, but . . . he is a

Kai. May the strength of your blade protect him. And may he wield it well." He then slid the swords carefully through the opening in the ancient tree, placed them on a bed of rotting leaves, and covered them with damp leaves, twigs, and pieces of bark. After that he stood up, wiped the snow from his leg and knee, bowed to the tree again, and walked to the southern edge of the forest where beyond it he could see a snow-covered plain, and at the end of it the tree that his old friend Nishiaka was so fond of meditating beneath.

He walked out from the darkness of the forest into the moonlight and began to cross the plain while looking at the clouds as they drifted slowly across the ashen face of the moon and the star-filled sky. And as he walked toward the tree that stood at the end of the plain he saw the silhouette of a hooded woman appear from behind it. Knowing that it was Koko-maki he waved to her and then saw the silhouette of Raki-ka appear next to her. He hurried his pace, and when he reached them they greeted him with a bow, which he returned. Koko-maki stepped out of the shadow of the tree into the moonlight and the priest could see that she was covered from head to toe by her hooded, crimson robe. As for Raki-ka the priest saw that beneath his tattered, dark brown cloak he was appropriately dressed in a short, wide-sleeved, black cotton robe; a black top-gi that folded over a thin, white top-gi, which were both tucked into his baggy, dark grey trousers that fell down to his white socked and rope sandaled feet; and tied around his waist was a thick, black cotton belt with a wooden fan tucked into it.

"How are you both?" the priest asked.

"Nervous," Raki-ka answered with chattering teeth as his body shook from the cold.

The priest smiled. "And you Koko-maki?"

"I'm excited and . . . and nervous as well, Shinsei."

"Well, we should begin, should we not?" the priest asked. Both Raki-ka and Koko-maki nodded to the priest. "I have here a small bottle of rice wine and three cups."

"Thank you, Shinsei," Raki-ka uttered. "I wasn't sure if we needed to bring the wine or not."

"He forgot," Koko-maki interrupted with a hint of disappointment.

"It is my responsibility as a priest to bring the wine, so it is done," the priest explained as he took out from within the folds of his garments a small ceramic bottle with a cork lid and three flat cups escalating in size, and gave them to Raki-ka. "Place the cups, one over the other, at the base of the tree with the rice wine."

"Yes, Shinsei," he replied.

"Shinsei, I have the offering to the kami of this tree. Should I place it with the wine?" Koko-maki asked.

"No, you must give it to me," the priest replied.

She pulled out from within her robe a small bundle of twigs that had been tied together with white silk straps and gave it to the priest who then placed it on the ground by his feet.

"You may take your cloak off, Raki-ka," the priest suggested. Nervously, Raki-ka took off his cloak, folded it, and placed it on the ground by his feet. "May we begin?"

"Yes, Shinsei," Raki-ka said as he straightened his back.

"Yes, Shinsei," Koko-maki nodded with a bright smile.

"Please face each other before the kami of this brave tree." Both of them faced each other. The priest raised his hands up into the air and proclaimed in the old tongue: "We call on you, Great Spirit, who is one with the kami of this tree that is of both earth and sky, to witness and protect the union between man and woman so that what had divided into two may again become one, and from one return to the void that proceeded all things. Before me stand two who are filled with the trappings of *self*. Cleanse them, purify them, fill them with the awe of what is when the illusion of self is gone; a spirit undivided, a soul connected to all." The priest placed his hands above the heads of the young couple. "May the Ki fill you with each breath." Raki-ka and Koko-maki began taking deep breaths. "Breathe as one so that when one inhales the other exhales, and when one exhales the other inhales." Raki-ka began to inhale as Koko-maki exhaled a long breath. "Feel the air and the space between the two of you, and feel the air and the space between you both and the tree. Now close your eyes and allow the flow of Ki to consume you until at last all that is you is forgotten." Together Raki-ka and Koko-maki closed their eyes and relaxed, and as they breathed they could feel a flow of warm tingling air slowly swirl down and around their bodies. "You both are being cleansed of that which is not you so that you may wake and see each other as you truly are: two souls, pure in heart and spirit, seeking togetherness by allowing the space that lies between you to be, for no tree can grow when in the shadow of another. Now open your eyes." Raki-ka and Koko-maki opened their eyes simultaneously and looked deep into each other's eyes. "Find the silence within you that is without thought, and see with unclouded eyes the Light. Breathe in and fill with love, and share that love with each other for from this moment forth you are forever entwined to face times of joy, and moments of shadow, as one until death." Koko-maki began to sway slightly from side to side. "Are you all right?" the priest asked.

She lightly shook her head as if waking from a dream and refocused her eyes, "Yes . . . I'm . . . I'm all right."

"I feel . . . dizzy, Shinsei," Raki-ka said with concerned eyes.

"It is the Ki," the priest explained. "Do not resist it. Breathe deeply and let it be so that its effects may pass." Both Koko-maki and Raki-ka nodded to the priest. "It is time to drink. Raki-ka, when you are ready, please take the cups and give me the wine."

"Yes, Shinsei," he took a moment to regain his sense of balance and then bowed to the tree before carefully picking up the bottle of rice wine and the three cups.

"Thank you," the priest said when he took the bottle from Raki-ka. "Hold the cups out before you with both hands." Raki-ka did as asked while the priest removed the cork lid from the bottle. "Look into each other's eyes, and be still." There was a light breeze, and the priest, and the young couple, observed the peace and silence of the night. The priest stepped forward and began to pour the wine into the top cup, allowing it to overflow so that the wine could cascade down into the second and third cup. When he finished pouring he looked directly at Raki-ka and said in the old tongue: "You may speak what you feel in your heart." Raki-ka's forehead wrinkled with worry. "Do not think," the priest advised. "Simply speak that which is in your heart."

Raki-ka hesitated and then said, "Before this tree–this ancient tree of sky and earth I . . . I look into you with my heart and see all that . . ." he stopped as he felt a sudden wave of emotion overcome him, and he shook his head as if trying to rid his mind of some thought. He looked deep into the eyes of the woman who would soon become his wife and began: "I . . . I know that I had hurt you–that you felt abandoned by me, used by me and . . . and I am not proud of that . . . and I am not proud of who I was or of what I had done in my past. But, I am here standing before you not as what I was, but as what I am now in this moment."

The priest placed his hand on Raki-ka's shoulder and said again, "Speak from your heart."

Raki-ka looked at the priest and then to his wife, "I am now you. Through you I have found peace. In you I have found that which I had been searching for all my life . . . a love for myself, a love for all others, and a true and faithful love for you. I am not perfect and nor do I seek to be, but in you I have found perfection. Perhaps these are not the words that you wish to hear. But, I speak from my heart. You have saved me; you have found me and guided me when I was lost. Never in my life have I felt as I do when I am with you–so free in your presence. In you I have found that which I seek and strive to be. You are beautiful and serene. You are my angel. As I walk, you are there, and when I am still, you are there for where you go I will go, and where you stay I will stay throughout all the coming seasons of life. And when the eternal night comes, when death has taken you, I will die and there will we be buried."

Koko-maki smiled at her husband with gentle eyes. Raki-ka smiled back to his wife feeling vulnerable in what he had said.

"You may drink, Raki-ka," the priest instructed.

Raki-ka lifted the first cup of wine to his lips, took three sips, and passed it to his wife who also took three sips before passing it to the priest. Raki-ka and Koko-maki repeated the drinking rite with the second and third cup, and when the priest took the final cup from Koko-maki he bowed to both the tree and the couple and drank from the three cups.

"Three sets of three sips equates to nine," the priest said aloud in the old tongue. "Thus is sealed your union in the eyes of the Great Spirit. Raki-ka, you may remove your wife's hood."

Raki-ka stepped toward his wife, bowed to her, and carefully removed her hood to find her long black hair, which was decorated with three flower-shaped hairpins, done up in a wavy, elegant fashion that revealed the sensuality of her long neck. Her entire face and neck was powered white, and her lips were bright red from a cream that she had applied to them. Her eyebrows were thick and dark, and her eyelids were thinly outlined by black eye shadow. The priest then helped Koko-maki remove her crimson robe. And there in the full light of the moon she stood before her husband dressed in a thick, white glowing gown that folded over a silk, white top-gi; embroidered in white into the gown were depictions of cranes, exotic flowers, and ocean waves; and tucked into the white sash that was tied around her waist was a white wooden fan. She wore white socks and stood on wooden, platform sandals. Raki-ka stood in awe of his wife and displayed it with wide, unbelieving eyes and a dropped jaw. Naturally Koko-maki was pleased to see that her enhanced, physical beauty astounded her husband. The priest picked up the small bundle of twigs from the ground and said to the young couple, "You both must take this offering, a symbol of that which you have left behind to become one, and place it at the foot of this tree so that it may be swallowed by the earth and be forgotten." Together Raki-ka and Koko-maki took the bundle of twigs from the priest and placed it on the ground before the old tree. "Now stand before each other and join as one through a kiss so that this ceremony is sealed and ended."

And before the vastness of the winter sea and sky Raki-ka took his wife into his arms and kissed her as what remained of the night faded into the first light of a new day.

CHAPTER XI

"Wake up–it's morning–time to go," Rakima growled as he stood over Kieko with his broad shoulders casting a shadow over him. Kieko stirred for a moment, but he did not wake. "Get up," he repeated with light kicks to Kieko's stomach. Kieko's eyes shot open and he bolted up reaching for where the hilt of his short sword had once been.

"Reaching for a weapon that is not there?" Rakima asked.

"What? What's happening?" Kieko asked in fear as he looked up with squinting eyes trying to see the face of the familiar voice in the dark of the hut.

"Easy now–it's just me."

"Rakima," Kieko said with apprehension before rubbing his eyes. "What? Where am I?"

"You don't remember?"

Kieko spun his head to look at his surroundings. "Yes, yes . . . I am in your home," he answered in the high tongue ready to stand before him. "I'm sorry for having slept–"

"Save your words. Get up, we have to go."

"And where exactly do you have to go?" Ruka asked as she and Kira rose from their futons with waking eyes.

"There is a meeting. All men must go."

"With all the digging we have been doing I think it right that women be allowed to attend as well."

Rakima turned to his wife, "The boy and I have to go."

"Fine then, go," she barked feeling both sad and disappointed that her husband had not first come to her in the morning and apologize for not spending the night in their home.

"Come on," he ordered Kieko, "there is much to do today."

Kieko stood up, threw on his wool cloak, and followed behind Rakima to the short door, but then he stopped, looked back at Ruka, and complimented her on her soup and thanked her for allowing him to sleep in their home.

"No need to thank me, Kieko. It is good to see you again—"

"Come, Kieko," Rakima interrupted. He then exited the hut allowing, for only a moment, the grey morning light to break in before closing the short door.

Kieko bowed his head to Ruka and looked at Kira. "Good morning, Kira," he said with a soft voice.

"Good morning, Kieko," she replied.

"Thank you . . . thank you for bringing me here, and thank you for everything you said to me last night. I'm sorry for how I was."

"I'm sorry too and you should go," she said with coldness in her voice as she looked at the door. "My father is waiting."

Kieko looked to the floor, bowed his head again, and exited the hut.

Kieko stepped out into the brisk air and heard several barks; it was Jomana, and she ran up to him with her tail wagging feverishly. He bent down to pet her as she bounced around him but saw from the corner of his eye his master standing with his staff and Aiko standing beside him.

"I told them last night about what had happened to your mother," Rakima explained. "I am sorry."

"As are we," the priest said.

Kieko stood up and looked at his master and Aiko unable to speak for he did not know if it was right of him to have abandoned them when he did or if he should allow the anger he still held toward the priest to persist.

"There is no need to feel guilty," the priest said reading Kieko's thoughts. "And there is no reason to feel angry. What is done is done. What matters now is what we do together from this point forth."

Aiko nodded in agreement with the priest. Jomana barked at Kieko and began dancing around him again. "She missed you," Aiko said.

Feeling the pain of his mother's death weaken him he bent down again and tried to pet Jomana's rapidly moving body. "It's good to see you," he whispered to her to which she happily barked back.

"We don't have time," Rakima reminded them.

"There is time, Rakima," the priest assured him. "Do not worry just yet."

"No, there is no time. If you want to stand here and talk then do so. But, do so without me. I have brought the boy out to you and so you have him. I go to the Elders to plan and prepare," and with those words he left.

Kieko and Aiko were silent as they watched Rakima walk in the direction of the Council Hut.

"So impatient is he," the priest said under his breath.

"What . . . what do we do now?" Kieko asked.

"We go together to the Council Hut," the priest answered.

"All of us?"

"Yes, all of us," Aiko repeated.

"There is a meeting," the priest explained. "Perhaps it is the last one. We go in together, and we leave together. We do what is asked of us, and we face what comes tomorrow."

"What . . . what of the others?" Kieko asked them. "Many will . . . many will see me as less than I was for leaving–for running away."

"Does it matter what they think of you?" the priest asked. "You, and many here, did not think much of me after I had said what I said—and it ate at me—breaking me down. But, I did what I did because that was what I believed was right in that moment—at that time. I said the truth, my truth, and you did what you did feeling that it was right. That is all that matters. Now, let us go together and hear what needs to be said by the Elders and the others and do what needs to be done today so that we can face what we need to face tomorrow."

"Yes . . . Master Shinsei," Kieko agreed.

"Good then," the priest said pleased that he had regained his last disciple.

There were hundreds of men gathered before the Council Hut who were slowing filing into its entrance after performing brief rites at the cauldron. The priest, with his staff, led his two students with Jomana following at the rear to the cauldron where they soon found the unpleasant stares of many men who did not approve of them; and farther up along the southern side of the Council Hut they could see Shimura's black and fierce horse moving restlessly toward and away from those who tried to near him. The priest ignored the gazes of the crowd while Kieko and Aiko repeatedly glanced at the horse while also trying to keep their heads down to avoid the uncomfortable stares of those around them.

At the cauldron they wafted the rising incense smoke over their heads, prayed, and then went to the end of the line where the priest pointed to the ground and asked Jomana to sit and wait. She barked and sat with her tail wagging, which swept away the snow on the ground around her. The line advanced, and as they neared the entrance they could see that to the sides of it were two men sitting on short wooden chairs before their own small wooden tables writing continuously with brushes and ink on small wooden tablets.

"What are they doing, Master Shinsei?" Aiko asked.

"They are writing down the names of each man who enters the hut," the priest explained.

"Why are they doing that, Master Shinsei?" Kieko asked.

"Tasks will be assigned by lottery."

Soon enough the three of them gave their names to the two scribes and together they entered the dark and noisy hut.

Inside they found an intimidating number of men seated or standing in all directions talking and arguing. They walked through the crowd trying not to draw any attention, but a few men recognized them and stopped to stare at them with heated eyes while others shook their heads and lowered their voices to a murmur. The priest ignored their foul whispers–but Kieko and Aiko could not–and when he had finally found a suitable patch of open ground he led his disciples to it and together they sat down.

When all the men from the outside had finally gathered into the hut the Elders took their seats on their thrones and called for silence and for Shimura to step forward. The crowd of standing and seated men grew silent and Shimura appeared from within a group of men who had been huddled around him. With heavy steps he approached the Elders, bowed to them, and took his seat on a crude, old chair that was set away from the fire staves that gave light to the Elders. Whispers and talk against Shimura began to fill the hut causing Chief Elder Subo to stand up and order that all men be completely silent. Hushes were heard in all directions and within moments the crowd became soundless again. Elder Subo sat down and Shimura rose from his seat, went to stand before the Elders, bowed to them, and faced the crowd. "According to your *priest* the Atlantean army will arrive tomorrow to fight us," he began with a bold, hardened voice. "There is only today to finish what we have planned for them–and you all know what you must do. That leaves us with what we will do tomorrow. The strategy is simple. At dawn Sekihi, with Elder Tobu-Jo, and Rakima, with Elder Muraka, will each take two platoons of our best archers up into the mountains; the blacksmith to Mount Kurohi; and Rakima to Mount Kadek. There they will wait.

"The path to Ikishi is a corridor between these two mountains. The Atlantean army must come to us through this corridor. From behind the trench line will our army stand in three companies; I will command the center company with the priest and the Chief Elder; Kono, with both Elder Rinton and Rinton-no, will command the company that will stand to my left; and Tsuwata, with the aid of Elder Haru, will command the company that will stand to my right. You will all be lightly armed with bows and arrows, long swords and short swords. Since you will not be weighed down by heavy armor you will be mobile enough to exploit opportunities as they arise on the battlefield."

"This is foolishness!" an old voice shouted from the crowd. "I have seen the armies of the Atlanteans and they will strike us down before even coming within a stones throw of us. What use is mobility if we will never even come within reach of a single Atlantean?" Many men called out in agreement.

"Silence!" Shimura roared. "I have been chosen to lead you! I am the only one who has faced and fought in war–learned and improved by it, and commanded against odds much greater than what we will face tomorrow. How dare you question and challenge me!" he spat. "I am your leader in what we face tomorrow. I will not have doubt fill your minds in what we must accomplish. Follow the orders of your commanders and we will win. You are to fight– not doubt or think in the heat of battle. Trust in me and we will succeed. Do not, and we will fail!" He looked at the crowd with red intense eyes and saw no one who would now challenge him. "Good," he declared, "be still and listen for your very lives depend upon each word that I speak.

"When the weapons of the Atlantean army are within range they will begin to fire upon us. We will stand our ground and fire back with our arrows, which will most likely be completely out of range from striking them. I will then give the signal for my company to move forward into the trench while Kono's and Tsuwata's companies fall back giving the enemy the appearance that they are retreating–abandoning–our army. Seeing this the enemy will advance, and when they are within range of Sekihi's and Rakima's archers I will give the signal, and they will begin to fire a hail of arrows upon them, striking them down while our three companies and those platoons under the command of Elder Sobu-Ta and Elder Jime-Ro–who will be hiding in the huts and tents of the village to give the impression that it has been deserted–advance and send more arrows upon them, breaking them down until they either scatter or charge in after us. When that happens we will all charge in and meet them in battle, face to face and blade to blade."

"They have machines that can fly, Master Shinsei," Kieko whispered to the priest.

"Yes, I know," the priest answered. "And Shimura knows as well. But, that is the plan he has devised. Any comment or suggestion to remind him will serve very little for he will not–as he said–'be challenged.' He would rather ignore the fact that the Atlanteans can attack from the sky than face it. And many will pay with their lives as a consequence."

"We can't let that happen, Master Shinsei," Aiko pleaded.

"I know, but under these circumstances there is very little that we can do."

"So we let this suicidal insanity occur?"

"Aiko, look at me," the priest said. "We cannot change what is occurring here. There is fear driving every individual in this place. The crowd has surrendered their right to make decisions to Shimura and the Elders. If they really wanted to face the problem of what will come tomorrow they would rise and speak, but as you can see no one rises to speak–"

"That is why we must, Master Shinsei," Aiko interrupted.

"That is the very truth, but it is not up to us to save them. They each must be responsible for their own decisions; they each must face themselves to save themselves. But, they will not and I will not waste my energy in trying to guide them when they do not want to see. They will see and understand the error of their ways when what they have tried to avoid finds them and flings its ugliness upon them. Then they will see, and then they will change and become more of who they truly are." The priest paused allowing Aiko to contemplate his words. "If you want to stand and speak up then do it–I will not keep you from doing so. But, if you do, you will do so alone."

Aiko did not like a single word of what the priest had said to him, but in his heart he knew that the priest was correct in his reasoning. Shimura began to speak louder to the crowd and he turned his attention to him along with the priest and Kieko.

"I must finally address the issue concerning our women and children!" Shimura's words rang out. "If our women and children fall into Atlantean hands they will not be put to death, but they will be turned. The Atlanteans will mind-manipulate your children to become soldiers, slaves, and whores to them. The same will happen to your women. Your women will be forced to bring pleasure—sexual pleasure—to the soldiers of the Atlantean armies. We must then—if it is seen that we are to fall tomorrow—execute our women and children before any Atlantean can ever place a hand upon them." The crowd made not a single sound as the grave weight of Shimura's words reverberated through their hearts and minds. "I must ask for volunteers—those who will stay behind with the women and children and be responsible to bring freedom—by death—to them if we are to fail in battle." No one spoke or raised an arm. And Shimura waited, but still there was no one who would even consider volunteering for such a horrendous and unthinkable task. "So be it!" he shouted out in frustration. "You leave the Elders and I no other choice. We will do a lottery." He called forth with a wave of his hand one of the two scribes who had written the names of every man who had entered the Council Hut. The scribe approached him and held out to him a black leather bag. Shimura grabbed the bag, dug his arm deep into it, pulled out a small wooden tablet, and read the name that was written on it aloud, "Shinrin!" There was movement in the crowd, but no one stood. "Shinrin!" he called out again. "If you do not come forward to stand behind me then those who know you—friend or kin—will take your place!" Movement in the crowd increased as individuals turned their heads searching for any sign of the one whose name was Shinrin. Finally someone stood up. "Come forth now!" Shimura demanded. The man who had stood up weaved through the crowd and went to stand behind Shimura. "There is no time to waste! When I call your name stand and come forth." He reached into the leather bag again, pulled out the next tablet, and shouted the name, "Yamano!" A short man stood up from the crowd and walked forward. Shimura went on to read aloud several more names, but when he pulled out a tablet with a name he recognized he smiled with pleasure and yelled, "Kieko!"

Kieko's head shot up when he heard his name called as an immediate feeling of dread overcame him. He looked with wide concerned eyes at the priest seeking protection, but the priest motioned for him to stand. "You must stand," the priest said to him. "But, do not fear for all things occur as they should." Shimura shouted his name again and with enormous hesitation he stood up.

"Come forth now!" Shimura barked.

Kieko was unable to step forward. "I . . . I can not," he said with a faint, fearful voice. "I can not do . . . what you want me to do."

"What–what did he say?" Shimura asked the men who were standing behind him.

With sudden confidence rising into his heart he repeated, "I can not do what you want me to do."

"I will not be challenged!" Shimura spat as he stepped forward with his fist waving in the air. "Damn the gods! Step forward and stand behind me!"

"I–I can not." Angered voices from the crowd replied with demands that he step forward and take his place behind Shimura.

"You have no choice in this matter!" Shimura roared. "You–as everyone else here–must do as I say!"

"I can not spend my last moments alive killing my own people!" Kieko hollered back with a rapidly beating heart. "My mother is dead–"

"Silence!" Shimura interjected as the foul whispering words of the crowd began to rise.

"Some machine–an Atlantean machine–killed her," Kieko continued.

"Guards!" Shimura bellowed. "Take him!"

"If I am to die let me die fighting the Atlanteans!" Kieko pleaded.

"Take him!" Shimura repeated to three guards who were approaching Kieko.

The priest stood up to stand beside Kieko and shouted, "There is no need for this!"

"Stay out of this, priest!" Shimura shouted ready to confront his brother if he tried to defy him.

"There is no need for the guards," the priest declared. "He will go and stand behind you for I command him to do so."

Kieko looked at the priest feeling utterly betrayed, but the priest grabbed his shoulder and whispered into his ear in the old tongue, "Give in and do as told, my young Kieko. Your path does not end but will continue so do not resist it for it is important that you reach the West." Kieko did not understand all that the priest had said to him in the old language, but the peace and depth in his master's voice caused him to feel that it was right for him to go forward and stand behind Shimura.

"Silence!" Shimura demanded again of the crowd when he saw Kieko finally approaching him. "Anyone else who speaks up against me will be thrown into the prison chamber at the edge of this village!"

The crowd became silent, the three guards returned to their positions, and Kieko took his place behind Shimura.

Shimura reached again into the leather bag he was holding, pulled out another tablet, and called out the name, "Ueno!" A refugee stood up and took his place behind Shimura. Shimura called out several more names: "Shi–shitaka . . . Nabe-no . . . Sakurai . . . Takuan . . . Yamata . . . Kogaku . . . Ippen . . . Hotto . . . Aiko!"

Hearing Aiko's name Kieko felt relieved that he would now not be alone in the execution of a task he knew he could not accomplish. He looked for Aiko in the crowd and saw him stand up, weave through the sea of seated men, approach him, and take his place beside him.

Shimura continued reading more names: "Koshi . . . Tai–Taitetsu . . . Yamamoto . . . Koshi . . . Raki-ka . . . Hojo . . .Satoshi . . . Hirotake . . . Kato . . . Maru." When he had finished reading the names of a few more men he turned to face the group he had amassed and ordered those who did not possess family swords to come forward; several men, including Kieko, Aiko, Raki-ka, and Hirotake, stepped forward. He gave a signal with his left hand, which caused Sekihi and several guards to go and pick up as many long and short swords as they could carry from the piles of weapons that were behind the thrones of the Elders, and to place them on the ground before him. He then instructed the small group of men who did not have family swords to form a line and for the first man in the line to step forward. Sekihi passed a long and short sword to Shimura who then passed both swords to the first man in the line, and in this manner were the swords given to each man, but when it was Kieko's turn to receive his two swords the priest appeared with his staff from behind Sekihi and moved in to stand between Kieko and his own brother.

"I will arm my apprentices," the priest said with great calm.

Shimura clenched his teeth and stared with flaring red eyes at the priest.

"I will take them, arm them, and return them to you," the priest explained.

"Why?" Shimura asked with a deep hate. "Are these swords not good enough for *this* boy of mixed blood?"

Kieko fists tightened.

"No," the priest answered. "These swords are fine, but it is my obligation as a priest to arm my own students."

"Fine then. I have no time for this. Go and return them to me when you are done."

"Thank you." The priest motioned for Kieko and Aiko to come with him, and together they walked to the exit of the Council Hut.

Outside the priest stopped and inhaled the cold morning air smelling the scent of the incense sticks that still burned from within the cauldron. Pensive he ran his fingers through his beard and said to his two disciples, "Come—there is not much time." A bark was heard, and at the end of the circular plain they saw Jomana kicking up snow as she sprinted toward them. They walked to and through the circular plain as Jomana jumped around them with her wagging tail and at the end of it, at the very spot where Aiko had snapped in two Kieko's left arm, the priest stopped and turned to face his two students. "Aiko," the priest began with a solemn voice, "both your sword and Kieko's sword are hidden up Mount Kurohi within the Great Forest of Ikishi. I will take Kieko to help me retrieve the swords for there are things—private things—that I must tell him."

"Are these secrets, Master Shinsei?" Aiko asked upset. "You don't trust me?"

"What I am to tell Kieko is not for me to tell you. If Kieko desires to tell you what I have said after he has heard my words then so be it."

Kieko's eyes widened as his eagerness quickened the pace of his heart for he knew that the priest was going to speak to him of his father's past.

"What am I to do then, Master Shinsei? I can't just wait here out in the open. Shimura—my father—the others will know that you have gone somewhere without me."

The priest looked at the grey clouds that were rolling south toward the village and thought for a moment. "We will leave Ikishi by taking the path that leads to the Kadek Temple," he began. "Once out of the sight of the village and the camps of the refugees we will part and you will wait until we have returned from Mount Kurohi. Reunited we will return to Ikishi and you both will go back to Shimura to be trained under the command of one of his men for tomorrow."

Aiko's upper lip curled with displeasure, but he nodded to the priest and said with a sigh, "Fine . . . Master Shinsei."

The priest went ahead and walked with his staff in the direction of the Kadek Temple and Kieko, Aiko, and Jomana followed as snow began to fall.

From the path that led to the Kadek Temple the priest veered east and led his two disciples toward the Ikishi forest. Upon entering the forest he asked Aiko to stay with Jomana and wait for him and Kieko to return. Aiko unhappily agreed. The priest then led Kieko through the forest and when they reached the base of Mount Kurohi they ascended it, as they had always done, by carefully hiking, and at times climbing, up its thin rocky path while the snowfall and strength of the sea winds increased.

When they reached the tall pine trees that marked the beginning of the Great Forest of Ikishi they both looked down and saw that they could no longer see the village through the heavy snow and low clouds. After swiping the dirt, earth, and snow from their clothes and catching their breaths they entered the dark of the great forest before them and traveled through it hearing the winds blowing relentlessly over the trees. The priest led Kieko to the southern edge of the forest until at last they saw illuminated by a pale cool light an ancient and hollowed tree that was sprawled on the snow-covered ground within a small circular plain. They approached the tree mystified by how the snow swirled down toward it, and when they were just within reach of it they both stopped and bowed.

"I have never seen such a tree," Kieko whispered.

"When I was here last night the tree appeared beautiful in the light of the moon, but it did not look as it does to you now," the priest whispered back.

"What is this then? Some kind of magic?"

And with those words the light that illuminated the tree faded making the tree appear ordinary and terribly old.

"Kneel," the priest instructed as he went to sit on the tree.

Kieko was surprised to see his master going to sit on what he considered to be a sacred tree, but as asked he got down on his knees and sat on his heels.

"I must be getting very old to tire so fast," the priest said with a sigh. "I thought I was stronger than this, but my body does not seem to agree." He looked down at Kieko and smiled. "Well, I assume you know why I have brought you here?"

"To tell me of my father," Kieko replied.

The priest nodded and looked for a moment at his staff. "Yes, before I am to arm you I must tell you what you have sought so long to know. In my eyes you are a young man, Kieko, and you deserve to hear what I have to say.

"I found your father nearly twenty years ago two days west of our village. I found him in a cave barely alive. He was suffering from a severe infection that had left him dehydrated and nearly unconscious. I built a stretcher–like you had done for Aiko during your meditation retreat–and brought him back to the Kadek Temple where I nursed him back to health. It was during this time that your father and I became close friends. And it was during this time that he confided his past in me.

"Your father was the last Atlantean High Kai Guardian of the Clan Order of Drakul. His name was Arkan, and he was a guardian of a High Kai Priestess named Neva Yun Ra. Your father fell in love with Neva Yun Ra—as she did with him—but the love between a Kai Guardian and a Kai Priestess was forbidden in Atlantis. They kept their affair secret, but then Neva Yun Ra became pregnant and soon after she began to lose herself as she tore her mind apart between the man she loved and the Clan Order she had chosen to serve until death.

"Coincidentally this all occurred during the darkest hour for the Atlantean people. A twisted power named Maniok destroyed the political strength of the Atlantean Royal Family. He corrupted and held firmly within the palm of his cruel hand politicians, bureaucrats, corporate nobles, the military elite, Ideo-clans, and even several Kai-Minor priestesses to legitimize his corporate and political ascent. Those in power who were not turned by him were ultimately killed in a violent take over that placed him—this Maniok—as the political, military, and corporate head of the island continents of Atlantis.

"Your father was the only Kai guardian who survived and he sought refuge here in Lemuria, but in so doing he was also trying to escape his past. He wanted to forget where he had come from and what had happened to his people, his High Kai Priestess, and to him. And so living here in Ikishi he found peace again, and in your mother he found love again.

"When you were born he was so proud and so full of life and love. But, when a year had passed after your birth we began to hear news that the new Empire of Atlantis had begun to wage war on the fragmented territories of the old Middle Kingdom and the desert sovereignties west of it. Horror stories came to us month after month about the horrendous crimes committed by Atlantean soldiers in the lands that they conquered. With all of that a dark cloud began to hover over your father. His guilt grew, as did the resentment against your father from the villagers. Men from the surrounding villages were recruited to fight as rebels against the Atlanteans. Aiko's father was one of them, as was Rakima and several sons of the Elders. As for your father he chose to stay and care for you.

"When Aiko's mother went missing word was sent out to Kono, and he returned. With a search party formed he went out and found the body of his murdered wife. A council meeting was held leaving your father to take the indirect blame for the Atlantean crime. But, the anger that was placed against your father was not what drove him away from our village. He left because he knew that if he did not rise and face the darkness in his past and cut off the head of the one responsible for feeding the narcissistic wickedness of his people, then the world you would come to know would be an unjust, cruel, and defiled one. He realized that it was his responsibility to return to Atlantis and face Maniok and destroy the evil that had poisoned his mother country. And so he left . . . and failed in what he had set out to do for Maniok killed him.

"By blood that leaves you, Kieko, as the last of the Atlantean High Kai Guardians. The power of the Kai is strong in your veins. You will survive the battle tomorrow. You must remember to continue your meditations and align your heart with peace. You are in a fragile state; hate can easily overcome and rule your mind and poison your heart. If you lose sight of the Light and allow fear and hate to rule you then you will be forever lost to the shadow—caught in an endless cycle of pain and suffering that you will willingly spread to others. This will be hell, Kieko; this will be your hell.

"I am warning you, do not lose sight of the Light. You will see and experience that which all men call evil, but through those experiences you must always keep your heart and mind clear. You must focus on the Light and ascend above all the negativity and pain that strives to bring you down. Do not lose hope; never lose hope for justice is served to all men. We reap what we sow for it is the order of things. You must always be patient and hopeful. If you engage in the cycle of vengeance that knows no end you will lose— you will have betrayed yourself and the spirit of your father and mother. I have faith in you, Kieko; I know that you will do what is right in your heart."

"Yes . . . yes, Master Shinsei," Kieko replied feeling the weight of his master's words. "I will not . . . I will not fail you."

The priest placed his staff on the ground, leaned his body forward, reached into the hole in the tree, and pulled out the two swords that were wrapped in black suede that he had hidden the previous night. He laid the wrapped swords down on his lap, untied several leather knots, slid out one of two sheathed swords, unsheathed it, and held it out before him with one hand. "This was your father's sword."

Kieko looked in awe at the glorious double-edged sword that appeared to glow as it reflected off all light.

"It is a Kai sword and it will protect you," the priest explained. "And now it is your sword." He pointed the hilt of the sword to Kieko and handed it to him.

Kieko reached for the sword and wrapped his fingers around its hilt while noticing the strange fluid script on the cross-guard and pommel. He tightened his grip hoping to feel or sense some essence of his father within the faded leather of the hilt's grip. And when the full weight of the sword pressed down upon the strength of his arm he saw as a flash in his mind's eye a brilliant white light and the quick sensation of the sharp sting of freezing seawaters surrounding the whole of his body. He shook his head as if waking from some vivid dream and refocused his eyes on the sword.

"You had a vision," the priest said.

"Yes," Kieko answered still unsure of what he had seen or felt.

"There are memories, past memories, in the metal and leather of that sword. The sword is—just as a rock or tree is—alive. It has its own will and can guide you when you fight in a state of no-mind." As the priest spoke Kieko's eyes ran up and down the shaft of the blade memorizing every smooth metallic detail of the finely crafted sword. "You may sense the history of the sword through touch, but do not dwell in the memories that it will reveal to you for memories are of the past and you—as everything else in the world—must live and fight in the now."

"Yes, Master Shinsei."

"Sheath your sword and carry it for we must return to Aiko and present to him the sword of his grandfather who was a pupil of the Ki priest before me," the priest said as he handed a metal scabbard to Kieko.

"Yes, Master Shinsei," he took the scabbard and sheathed his sword.

The priest took up his staff, stood up with the sword that would soon be Aiko's, and commanded Kieko to rise to his feet.

Kieko rose to his feet with his sword.

"You have been a good friend to me," the priest said as he looked deep into Kieko's eyes. "Thank you for all that you have taught me as both a friend and as a student."

"You have been a good friend to me," Kieko said as he felt a strong, overwhelming sadness rise up into his heart. "You have been . . . a great teacher, my best friend, and . . . and a father."

Not wanting to speak more the priest pulled Kieko into his arms and hugged him as he felt his own sadness rise into his aged and tired heart.

Black crows that stood on the naked branches of a dying tree looked down at the old priest and his young apprentice. Disapproving of their actions they flapped their wings and cackled as they skipped and moved until the largest bird of the pack flew up, causing all the rest to follow, and headed west toward a distant growing darkness in the dark horizon sky.

"Come, Kieko, come," the priest said with urgency as he wiped his eyes and looked up to where the crows had been before taking flight. "This place is no longer safe."

"What is it, Master Shinsei?" Kieko expressed with great concern.

"It is not long now before they come," the priest explained. "We must hurry back to Aiko, return to the village, and help with all that needs to be finished for tomorrow."

"Yes, Master Shinsei."

The priest rushed ahead, and with Kieko following behind him they crossed through the Great Forest of Ikishi and made their way back down Mount Kurohi.

CHAPTER XII

The first light of the morning sun reflected off the pristine blade of the unsheathed Kai sword and onto Kieko's face causing him to wake. Letting out a strong exhaustive yawn he moved and rubbed his eyes before stretching out his arms and legs on the hardened ground. Smelling the faint scent of burnt wood he sat up and looked at what remained of the campfire he had built the night before seeing a faint line of smoke rise from it. He looked at his sword, which he had carelessly left leaning against a log so that he could admire it before nodding off after a tiring day of war preparations and training, and took it. Feeling incredibly foolish he sheathed the sword and prayed with whispered, pleading words to the dragon god of his ancestors for forgiveness for having disrespected the sword that had once belonged to his father.

He had spent most of the night sitting outside within a grouping of tents and thatched homes, and among women and children, staring into the flames of the campfire as he held the cold steel of his Kai sword while thinking endlessly about what his master had revealed to him about his father. And as he thought and wondered into the growing dark of the night the sad realization that he was the last of his father's ancient Kai line depressed him until he fell into a deep state of sleep.

He stared at his sword, as the faint light of the rising sun shined upon him, and doubted whether or not he could wield the double-edged weapon with any degree of accuracy since the shape, length, and weight of it were different to the single-edged practice sword he had been trained and meant to use as a Ki disciple. This doubt was then furthered by a memory of the old farmer who had once expressed to him that Ki swords were far stronger, and thus superior, to Kai swords. He went on to recall how Ki swords had been tested, centuries-ago, on criminals who were tied to oak logs and cut in two; and if the sword, in one effortless stroke, cut clean through the flesh and bone of the criminal's body, it was deemed a strong and worthy sword. This horrific practice of Ki swords being graded by their ability to cut in two a living man caused Kieko to again appreciate the Kai sword he was holding for he hoped, and desperately wanted to believe, that his father's sword had never been used in such a wicked act.

More ancient Lemurian practices, histories, and stories began to fill his mind until at last he gravitated toward an old tale that the priest had related to him a year or two after his mother and he had learned that his father was no longer living. The story concerned the Sakura twins, who were, in their time, deemed the greatest of all Ki swordsmiths. Their names were Kokoro and Hone.

Kokoro followed in the footsteps of his father, a swordsmith priest, and studied diligently in the old Ki faith, but Hone, his brother, was a maverick who rebelled against the holy legacy of his family by running away to become an apprentice under Ka-Nami, an old and mysterious swordsman who had settled into retired life by crafting dark swords and daggers.

The years passed, and as they did Hone, faithful and diligent to his study of the dark arts, slowly discovered many of Ka-Nami's secrets through his nightly sessions of heavy drinking in the kitchen of his shop. The old swordsman had been a mercenary for most of his life, selling his deadly skills to divided island-nations, dark lords, wealthy nobles, corrupt bureaucrats, and even cheated wives and husbands. He never knew love beyond what he took from the prostitutes he so proudly boasted about when he was drunk. His heart was as cold as a winter mountain stone, and this, he explained to Hone, was how a man of his work had to be to survive and succeed. Soon Hone grew into manhood and learned all of his master's skills in both the dark art of combat and sword craft.

The old swordsman soon perished and left all his possessions to his apprentice, Hone, as if he was his own son. Hone spent the next few years living like a hermit within the dark of his blacksmith shop melding metal ores with bright liquid flames in search of the strongest metal alloy. Rarely venturing out into the light of the world he began to speak to his twisted self of his obsession to become the greatest of all swordsmiths.

One bright morning Hone emerged from his shop at the surprise of many townsmen who had not seen him in the light of the sun for many years. His face and skin were as pale as white snow leaving him to have not the look of a man, but that of a ghost. With a long sword wrapped in quilted rabbit skin he approached the town square and faced one of its many tall maple trees. He unwrapped the quilted skin and pulled out the sword as a crowd gathered behind him. Raising his unpolished black sword he threw it down and cut straight through the trunk of the tree. Everyone gasped both in awe of the incredible power of his sword and in complete disbelief of his act of sacrilege in cutting down one of the sacred trees of the town.

Smiling with delight Hone went back to his old reclusive ways by returning to his blacksmith shop and locking himself within it. Many in the town feared that Hone had somehow become a great sorcerer, and for that he was never fined or tried for destroying the tree in the town square. All men, women, and children stayed clear of Hone's shop, but in the night dark men whose faces were hidden by the hood of their black cloaks began to appear in the town and were seen entering through the door of Hone's store. Rumors spread that the dark outsiders had come to buy the dark swords of Hone, and soon a conspiracy to burn Hone's shop before any more of his swords be sold to the outsiders was devised by the townsmen and nobles.

The night was silent and the moon full when the last of Hone's patrons had exited his shop. A town noble fired a burning arrow into the air giving the signal to scores of townsmen who charged forward with burning torches toward the shop. They threw their torches up onto the thatched roof of the shop setting it on fire. But, as the shop burned and was soon consumed by the flames no screams were heard from within it, which caused the horde of men to doubt as to whether or not Hone had even been in the shop. They hushed at each other to quiet their talk and yells so that they could listen, and within the winds that danced and swirled with the fires that rose up into the night sky they heard a faint, eerie laugh.

The next morning the townsmen searched the burnt wood and ash of the property that had belonged to Hone, but they could find not one of his skeletal remains. As a result the townspeople feared that Hone had somehow discovered their plan and escaped from his shop before their failed attempt to end his life and craft.

The years passed and the people of the town gradually forgot their once obsessive fear that Hone could one-day return to seek vengeance upon them. But then, on a dark winter night, a sharp masculine scream was heard. The following morning the townspeople discovered that a noble had been murdered on his futon by a sword that had cut him clean in two from head to bottom. Rumors spread that Hone had returned to seek his revenge, but as the days, and months, and years passed no more unexplained deaths came to the people of the town.

"Thirteen swords . . . thirteen long swords were believed to have been crafted and sold by Hone to men allied to the dark leagues," Kieko whispered to himself as he stared with cold eyes at the Kai sword in his hands. "Only six of these swords have been found and destroyed, the remaining seven are still scattered and hidden somewhere deep within the islands of Lemuria. It is said that anyone who wields a Hone blade will be forever tainted by its malice for the blood of the dark blacksmith had been cast into its metal thus giving it its avid need to cut and tear flesh." He stopped reciting what he could remember of the tale for he realized that he had never asked the priest to hear the story of Kokoro and the swords he had forged under the guidance of his father; swords he assumed were crafted and dedicated to peace and harmony, which would naturally stand in opposition to the dark blades of Hone.

He placed his sword on the ground, stood up, and looked at the sun as he yawned, stretched out his arms and legs, and rubbed his eyes again. He looked around seeing the cluttered, huddled groupings of women and children who were still sleeping on the ground beneath tattered, wool blankets and focused on their faces. He could see within the folds and curls of their wrinkled brows and closed eyes the anxiety, nervousness, and unease that were plaguing their dreams. A mother gripped her child tightly. Envious of this unconscious, protective, instinctive act he began to long for his mother as images of her death filled his mind. And from those horrific images he remembered what was to be required of him if the armies of Atlantis were to win in their battle against his people. Now unable to bear the sight of the women and children around him he picked up his sword and took cautious steps to escape them without waking any one of them.

People began to emerge from their tents and thatched homes, but Kieko paid little attention to them, he kept walking until he saw not too far ahead of him a group of ragged old men he did not recognize seated around a campfire. He approached them seeing that they were shivering as they held their hands out before the flames and that they were not speaking to each other. Finding these silent men to be more depressing than the sight of the women and children he had seen asleep he continued in the direction of the Council Hut where he knew he would find his master and Aiko.

Entering into the circular plain of his village that was now filled with the activity of armed men who were either seated before campfires drinking and eating, sharpening weapons, or moving from one place to another he heard the familiar call of his master. He looked and saw that the priest was enjoying a bowl of rice soup with Aiko while Jomana sat patiently before them waiting for some scrap of food. He went to them, bowed to his master, and sat down before a campfire.

"How are the women and children? Had fun keeping guard?" Aiko asked.

"They are fine—as far as I can tell. All of those who had to sleep outside were still asleep when I left."

"Have some soup," the priest said as he handed Kieko a bowl; Jomana followed the bowl with her eyes and let out a small whimper.

"Thank you, Master Shinsei."

"Elders Muraka and Tobu-jo, and Sekihi and Rakima have already left for the mountains with their archers," Aiko began. "Scouts were sent out late last night. We will need to wake the women and children and get them fed before we make our way up to—"

"Eat your food," the priest interrupted. "Now is not the time to talk of such things. Now is the time to eat."

"Yes, Master Shinsei."

Together they ate their food as the water in a pot that hung over the campfire from a tripod made from wooden sticks continued to boil.

When they had finished eating the priest put down his bowl and said, "Keep your swords close and do not draw them out unless absolutely necessary. I trust in you both to watch over each other, to protect each other, and to do what is right. I am proud of you both as young Ki disciples." He then took his staff, stood up, and continued: "Now the time has come for our paths to depart," he looked down to Jomana. "The old farmer's dog will go with you. Now go and wake the women and children and make sure that they eat. I will send for the other men to join you. Once everyone is gathered and ready begin the journey to Devil's Mouth—you must reach it by late morning."

"Not the most appropriate name for a cave, Master Shinsei," Aiko remarked.

"Yes, not exactly the most appropriate name," agreed the priest who appreciated Aiko's attempt to make the three of them laugh. "Now go—it is not long now before the Atlanteans will be upon us."

"Then . . . then this is good-bye, Master Shinsei," Kieko said as he stood up with Aiko while trying to restrain the sadness that began to overwhelm his heart.

"Yes, Kieko, this is good-bye," the priest answered with an endearing smile; he took his two disciples into his arms and embraced them as Jomana nervously moved around them. Kieko gripped the folds of his master's robe holding him tightly, pressing into him the sadness that had overcome his heart, and then, unable to hold back the tears that had welled in his eyes, he let go and began to cry. Aiko became stiff and uncomfortable as Kieko wept for he was finding it difficult to resist the pain and sadness that was growing within his chest. The priest tried to ease Aiko of his emotions by rubbing his back, but Aiko resisted by stepping back and giving three full bows instead. Kieko clenched his teeth to keep himself from sobbing, and shamefully he looked down to the ground, took a step back from his master, and wiped the tears from his eyes as Jomana whimpered and barked. "It is all right to cry, Kieko," the priest tried to reassure him. Kieko looked into his master's eyes, and as Aiko had done, gave three full bows to his master. "Now go," the priest urged his two disciples. "Go and do what you must do." The priest gave a deep bow to his two students, gently patted Jomana's head, turned, and walked away. Kieko and Aiko looked at each other and then to the priest as he walked waiting for him to turn back and wave a final goodbye, but he did not turn and wave back, he simply continued walking through the crowded circular plain until he was lost to their eyes.

"So . . . that's it," Aiko said as he continued to stare ahead.

"Yes," Kieko agreed; Jomana continued to whimper and bark. "But . . . do you think . . . do you think—when this is all done . . . that we will see him again?"

Aiko turned his head and looked deep into Kieko's eyes, "I . . . I don't think so." He took a step forward and said, "Come, we should go to where the women and children are being kept under guard."

When they arrived to the site they found that many of the men who had been assigned to escort the women and children up to Devil's Mouth were already there and that they were busily moving about either waking up those who were still asleep or serving those who were awake with warm bowls of soup and cups of tea. Kieko and Aiko sprang into action by going into one tent or thatched home after the other, but they were only able to find a few more quiescent women and children to wake. And as they woke one woman or child after the other Kieko found the undertaking more and more difficult for he could see in the eyes of the women he woke their lingering dreams; dreams and wishes that would fade when their eyes focused on his face recognizing who he was and why he had come for them.

After all the women and children had eaten their light morning meal Kieko and Aiko, along with the other men, began to organize them into groups, which they then ordered into a line that was three, four, or five people across; Hirotake and Raki-ka hastily placed Tomoko into the group at the front of the line. When the long caravan was ready Kieko, Aiko, and Jomana followed behind a handful of armed men to the head of the line, and once there they began to lead the drab caravan southwest through the village toward a path that began at the forested base of Mount Kadek.

"How long have we been traveling?" Hirotake asked Raki-ka as they ascended the inclining, snow-covered mountain path before them.

Raki-ka looked up to the dark overcast sky and said, "It seems . . . it seems that the sun has reached its apex–it must be midday."

"How can you tell?" Aiko asked.

"Look–there," he pointed up past the far-reaching heights of the tall pine trees that lined the path before them.

Aiko looked to where Raki-ka was pointing and saw a very faint glow through the grey clouds.

"That is the sun . . . and as you can see by its position, it's midday."

"Then we've been hiking up this mountain for quite some time," Kieko commented.

"Yes . . . quite some time," Raki-ka agreed.

"Further up there is a ledge where we can get a good view of the valley and the village," Kieko explained. "If the Atlanteans are coming we should be able to see them making their way down the valley toward the village."

"How much further to the cave?" Hirotake asked.

"We're not that far now. After the ledge it's perhaps less than the time it took us this morning to reach the base of Mount Kadek from the village," Kieko answered.

"And how would you know?" Raki-ka questioned. "Explore Devil's Mouth as a child when you shouldn't have been doing so?"

"No," Kieko answered. "I was here not too long ago."

Aiko grabbed Raki-ka's arm and shook his head signaling to him to not ask Kieko any further questions.

Raki-ka looked at Aiko and nodded back to him.

"I remember my mother telling me about the cave," Hirotake began. "She used to tell me so many horrible stories about it . . . that there were creatures living within it . . . things that would come for me if I even dared go near it. And here I am . . . a grown man–"

"You're not that grown," Raki-ka joked.

Hirotake shook his head at his friend and continued, "And here I am going toward it for the first time in my life . . . leading women and children to it. Those stories were old stories; stories that were created to sow fear into the hearts of all Ikishi children so that none of them would be foolish enough to seek it and get lost in its darkness. And here we are leading children to it . . . leading children to it."

"That's enough, Hiro," Raki-ka interrupted.

"When I was young my father sent me to that cave," Aiko said with soft words. "He wanted me to be stronger than the other children. He wanted me to prove to him that I was not afraid . . . and so I went seeking the scabbard of a short sword he had hidden within the cave. But . . . I was not brave enough. I was shaking with fear with each step I took into the darkness of that cave, and the further I went into it the stronger the sound . . . the stronger the sound . . ."

"What sound?" Hirotake asked.

"I don't know . . . and I didn't travel far enough into the cave to discover what was the cause of it."

"What did it sound like?" Raki-ka inquired.

"It sounded like a shimmering whisper . . . if that makes sense to you."

"Yes, yes it does make sense. There are supposed to be springs, maybe even underground lagoons, in the deep of the cave. One of my great uncles told me that when I was just a child . . . I remember."

"Springs in the cave of a volcanic mountain–they must be hot, poisonous, perhaps undrinkable," Hirotake theorized.

"Or cold water, Hiro," Raki-ka returned. "It could be run off water from the melting snow."

"That's true," Aiko remarked.

"There—there is the ledge," Kieko almost exclaimed.

Quickly, the four of them, along with Jomana and several of the other armed men at the head of the caravan, hiked up the path until at last they reached the ledge. With racing, nervous hearts they looked up the valley and saw in the distance what they had feared to see: lines of tanks and other undescribable metallic machines trampling down trees as if they were blades of grass followed by a vast army of soldiers that were marching through the newly created open plains of the valley floor. Jomana revealed her fangs and began to growl.

"There are too many," one of the men panicked. "There is no chance for us."

"Silence—you idiot!" Raki-ka ordered. "Hiro—and you three—go back and lead the women and children away from this ledge. Take them straight to the cave. And say nothing of what you have seen. We don't need a panic from them or from any of the other men. Do you understand?" Hirotake and the three men nodded back. "Good—now go!"

"I can't believe how many there are," Kieko said with disbelief as he looked at the sight that began to terrify him.

"The damn priest was right," Raki-ka whispered to himself as he thought of Watanoro who was hiding, along with the other men who had been assigned to Elder Sobu-Ta's platoon, within one of the tents or huts of the village.

"What are we going to do?" one of the other men asked.

"We are going to protect the women and children. If we're lucky we will not be discovered within the cave. We'll go as deep as we can within it and stay there until we can decide what to do next."

"Those are not our orders," a refugee contested. "You know what we must do if we are discovered—if the Akai do come for us."

Raki-ka became silent for a moment and answered back, "Well, let's just hope for our sakes that we're not discovered."

"This is ridiculous. Look at that army. It is inevitable. They will destroy that village just as they had done to mine and come for us. They will rape the women and children before they slaughter them—and they will kill us!"

"Quiet you!" Raki-ka shouted causing many of the men, women, and children who were moving up the mountain at a distance from them to look at him.

"I will not," the refugee spat back as Jomana snarled at him. "You are not the leader; you are less than a commoner—a peasant for all I know; and I will not take orders from someone weak like you."

Raki-ka grabbed the hilt of his sword.

"Stop!" Aiko shouted as he signaled to Jomana to come and sit by his side. "You're drawing too much attention from the others—we don't know what's going to happen so let's stop wasting time and only ask ourselves what we're going to do right now."

Raki-ka looked at Aiko, "He's right."

"Right—right, right is not the point," the refugee disputed.

"Then what do you suggest we do?" Raki-ka asked. "Should we begin chopping heads off now? If that is what you want, then go ahead. I'll follow you."

"What is going on, Maru?" a hefty refugee called out as he approached the men who were standing near the ledge.

"Nothing, Kogaku," the refugee replied. "Nothing, but you must see what we have seen. Come, look, and see, and make a decision—"

"A decision to do what?" Raki-ka asked Maru. "You want him to give the order to begin killing our women and children?"

"Shut up," Kogaku ordered. "Both of you shut your mouths. Everyone can see your tense behavior from down there, but luckily they can't hear you." He then stepped up onto the ledge and looked down seeing the Ikishi village far down below and the three companies that were being commanded by Shimura, Kono, and Tsuwata marching toward the trenches.

"Look up the valley, Kogaku," Maru urged him.

Kogaku looked up the valley and saw with disbelieving eyes the ferocious size of the Atlantean army in the distance making their destructive way toward the sea. "The gods," he said with a faint voice. "There are so many of them?"

"Do you see those moving beasts—iron beasts?" Maru asked as he pointed at them.

"Yes . . . I see them . . . I've seen them before . . . they used them when they attacked and destroyed my village."

"Then you know what will become of the Ikishi army against that force. The priest was right—it is inevitable that they will destroy us. We must begin executing the women and children. I would rather have them die by the blades of their own people than be raped or killed by the Akai!"

"We can save them," Raki-ka said with both urgency and a faint trace of hope. "We can save them—"

"He is afraid!" Maru interjected. "He wants to save his own neck. Look!" he demanded of Kogaku, "You can see with your own eyes that there is no chance for us. Look at them. Most of the men down there are armed with farming tools—they look pathetic and unthreatening. The only way for us is to do what we were appointed here to do."

"Are you so thirsty for blood that you would condemn our own women and children to death before we even try to hide them—save them?" Raki-ka asked Maru as his body began to shake with anger.

"Yes," he answered. "If I can spare them the horrors of what was done to my wife, my son, before my very eyes, then yes—yes, I would condemn them to an immediate and painless death."

"Damn it—be quiet!" Kogaku ordered. "In the name of the gods let me think." He took another step toward the ledge, looked out again, and scratched his beard with extreme agitation and nervousness. "Bring me a messenger," he ordered as he continued to look out into the valley, but those who stood behind him took no action. "I said I need a messenger!"

"Why?" Maru questioned.

"No more words from you—I've made my decision. Now bring me a messenger." Again no one did anything.

"We have no messengers," Raki-ka explained. "You will have to choose someone to be a messenger."

"Fine then—you there!" An Ikishi villager pointed to himself. "Yes, you. You are to run back to Ikishi and inform Shimura and the priest of what we have seen."

"What good will that do beside sending him to his death?" Maru asked.

"The blacksmith and Rakima are high up in the mountains with their archers," Raki-ka began. "They see what we see. It is their responsibility to inform Shimura of the Akai army not ours. They also have their scouts."

"Yes . . . yes, you are right," Kogaku agreed.

"There is Shimura," Kieko called out as he saw Shimura galloping on his black warhorse down the frontline of his company. Kogaku and the others looked down and saw Shimura riding his horse. Kieko searched for his master in the organized crowd of men far down below, but he could not find him. Instead, from the corner of his eye, he caught the movements of a man who was running from the Ikishi forest toward the frontline of Shimura's company.

"There—" Raki-ka pointed, "you see. There is one of their scouts. He is bringing news of the size and advancement of the Atlantean army to Shimura."

"You don't know that," Kogaku disagreed.

"Then what do you suggest that scout is doing?" Raki-ka retorted. "Bringing news of some change in the wind? It is up to Shimura, the priest, and the others to decide and command. There is nothing else for us to do but to do what was asked of us and take the women and children to the cave."

"Why? So that we can simply wait for our inevitable deaths," Maru retorted. "They will find us—and they will kill us off—us, the men—with cruel efficiency, and then they will take our women and children and enslave them, turn them to serve the Akai. And that I will not have!" Several angered men yelled out in agreement with Maru as they either pumped their long swords into the air or slammed their fists against their chests.

"The gods—be quiet!" Kogaku commanded. "I will not have a mutiny. I am commander—Maru," he spat. "If you are so eager to kill our own people then you will be the first to be executed by me. I will hear no more from you or anyone else. We are to protect our people—not slaughter them. We will hide the women and children in the cave and build up a defense. If the Akai discover us then we will fight back . . . and if our defense fails then we will do what we must to protect our women and children from falling into the hands of the Red race. Is that understood?" A few men nodded. "Is that understood?" he shouted. All the men, including Kieko and Aiko, nodded and spoke out in agreement with Kogaku. "Fine then. Let us go and continue leading the line to the cave." He then walked down toward the moving line of women and children.

"But shouldn't one of us stay to watch the battle unfold?" Raki-ka asked Kogaku. "If by some miracle we win then it would be good if one of us brought some news of it to us in the cave."

Kogaku stopped and turned back to look at Raki-ka, "Yes . . . you are right. You—the young one."

"Me?" Aiko asked.

"Yes, you will stay and bring word to me of what will become of Shimura and his army—"

"He has been having difficulty hiking up the mountain," Raki-ka interrupted. "I believe his ankle or leg is less than good."

"Is this true?" Kogaku demanded to know of Aiko.

Aiko shook his head and said, "No—no this is not true—"

"You lie," Kogaku interjected. "You there—next to him. Can you run?"

"Yes . . . yes," Kieko answered.

"Then you will stay and be my scout."

"Alone?"

"Yes, alone." He gave his back to Kieko and the other men and went down again toward the moving line women and children. Raki-ka followed, as did Hirotake and the rest of the men leaving Maru and Aiko as the last to descend from the ledge.

"Will you be all right?" Aiko asked Kieko.

"Yes," he said nodding his head nervously. "I'll be fine. Just . . . just–"

"Come on you–" Maru barked at Aiko. "It's time to follow after that fool."

"Watch over her," Kieko said at last to Aiko.

"I will," Aiko replied with a small smile appearing from the corner of his mouth, which was then accompanied by a bark of assurance from Jomana. "I will." He turned and followed after Maru with the dog leaving Kieko alone on the ledge.

CHAPTER XIII

Exhausted the scout ran up to Shimura, who was sitting high up on his warhorse, and panted, "I . . . I don't know . . . I don't know what to say . . ."

"What do you mean?" Shimura shouted as he looked down with impatient eyes.

"Yes, what do you mean?" Elder Subo asked as he stepped toward the scout.

"I've . . . I've never seen what I saw—"

"What did you see?" the priest interrupted as he went to stand beside Shimura and his horse.

"There are thousands of soldiers—foot soldiers . . . but their faces—their faces are metal! And . . . and there are giant machines that crush the land . . . and I saw several giant iron birds that were flying—hovering low to the ground."

"How much time?" Shimura demanded.

"Soon . . . soon," was all that the scout had the strength to say.

The land began to shake and move as a thunderous boom sounded into the air causing Shimura's horse to neigh with unease and to nearly jump up onto its hind legs. But, Shimura kicked the spurs of his heels deep into his horse and shouted out curses in the old tongue to retake control of his animal. The horse snorted and calmed itself slightly, but its right front leg began to scrape at the ground. The organized lines of armed men that were behind Shimura could see the fear and agitation in his horse, and as a result they too began to fill with a fear that spread throughout the company as men whispered from one to the other of the wickedness that was coming with each shake and movement of the ground. A loud screeching sound then consumed the sky until the source of the sound flew straight over Ikishi toward the sea to then diminish into a faint hiss. With astonished eyes every man of the Ikishi army was looking up toward the winter clouds, or back toward the ocean, unable to understand what they could only describe as three, giant metallic birds that had flown with such speed that many of them could not believe it.

"Do not waver!" Shimura demanded of his men as he saw the disbelief and dread in their eyes.

"Face forward and hold your positions!" the priest hollered.

Disgusted by the fear he saw in his army Shimura turned his horse so that he could face the open field before him with his own sense of determination and hatred. And there in the far distance he could see trees being felled and the growing sound of machines crushing all in their path as hundreds of Atlantean troops advanced. And then, without warning, large horrific explosions erupted along the sides of the Kadek and Kurohi Mountains causing Kono and Tsuwata, the Elders, and nearly all the men of Shimura's army to dive to the ground. The explosions grew fiercer, larger, and more violent as the trees that had for so many centuries covered the grand slopes of the mountains were torn and blown apart by the fiery havoc, to then tumble and crash down onto other trees. Enormous bursting balls of fire were seen rising up toward the cloudy sky as another wave of explosions blew up more trees and large pieces of rock from the mountains.

"Those are our men!" the scout shouted to Shimura, Elder Subo, and the priest as he pointed toward the explosions on Mount Kurohi. Shimura and the men that stood in the first few lines of his company, and the priest and Elder Subo, looked toward where the scout was pointing, and there in the blazing hell that now defined Mount Kurohi could they see burning men being launched by the explosions into the smoky air to fall straight down to their rocky deaths. "They are killing them!" the scout frantically continued. "They discovered them—the archers. We are going to be killed— trapped!" Shimura and his army then saw scores of burning arrows being shot high into the darkening sky from the exploding cliffs of

Mount Kadek, which soon descended into the valley. "It's Rakima and his archers!" someone from Shimura's company cheered. "Get those bastards!" another soldier shouted causing an immediate roar of praise and war cries from hundreds of others. A second wave of arrows was shot up into the sky from what remained of Rakima's platoons on Mount Kadek. But, in the distance, rising above the tall pine trees of the valley, were three, large, hovering metallic aircrafts that glided up toward the exploding fires of Mount Kadek to discharge a storm of rapid plasma-fire directly into the flames causing hellish explosions that released large burning fragments of rock to tumble down the mountainside.

"We must draw them in!" Shimura barked; the priest shot his eyes to his brother not believing that he was going to go ahead with his war strategy. "Signal the retreat!" As ordered his runner took up a black banner that was hanging from the top of a pole, raised it up, and waved it before the frontline; accordingly Kono's and Tsuwata's runners took up their black banners and began waving them before the frontlines of their appropriate companies. Kono's and Tsuwata's companies began their retreat back to the village, which appeared deserted, while Shimura motioned to his company to run forward into the long trench before them.

"With haste!" the priest shouted to the lines of men that ran past him. "Run—run into the trench—into the trench!" The piercing sound of hundreds of trees being felled grew stronger.

"They're advancing!" Elder Subo warned Shimura from the trench.

"Let them come!" Shimura returned as he looked with stern eyes deep into the forest beyond the plain ahead of him. He then looked back toward the large number of remaining men that were running past him and pouring rapidly into the trench and barked, "Faster damn it! Faster—" but a series of thunderous pops silenced his commands; and from behind his company a chaotic array of explosions rocked and blew up the ground sending a vast amount of earth into the air to hail down upon them. "Signal the archers!" he ordered to his runner as he tried to control his panicked warhorse that had jumped up onto its hind legs. From within the trench the runner spat out bits of dirt from his mouth and began tying a red banner to the pole that had the black banner hanging from it. "You fool!" Shimura barked. "Signal the damn archers now!" The runner tied the last knot, lifted the red banner up high, and waved it with frenzy. The last few lines of men from Shimura's company ran and jumped into the trench while those who saw the raised red banner from within the trench began to nock their long bows and aim for the sky. A second succession of deafening, popping discharges were heard, and again from behind the trench was the land battered and ripped apart by blasts and fiery explosions that launched more earth into the air. Shimura kicked the spurs of his boots hard into the sides of his horse, rode down a slope of earth into the trench, and spat out, "Fire!" A black cloud of arrows was released to fly up toward the threat that was advancing within the forest toward them, followed by a second and unexpected wave of arrows that was discharged by both Kono's and Tsuwata's companies, and from the other men who had been hiding within the huts and tents of the abandoned village.

"What are they doing?" the priest questioned as he looked at both Kono's and Tsuwata's scattered companies nocking their long bows out in the open, beaten plain between the trench and the village. "Retreat!" he hollered at them. "In the name of all the gods—retreat!" He looked back at the men in the trench and saw that his brother had ridden away along the narrow path of the trench. "Scout—come here," he commanded. The scout that had explained what he had seen of the advancing Atlantean army to Shimura stepped forward. "Run to Kono and tell him to follow orders and retreat back—" but his words were cut short by the calls of many men within the trench who were repeating Shimura's order to fire their arrows.

A second black cloud of arrows was shot up toward the dark, winter sky from the trench. But their effect, if any, on the Atlantean force would not be discerned for just as the arrows were about to make their descent another and greater number of earsplitting popping booms were heard causing nearly all of Shimura's men within the trench to dive down, cover their heads, and wait. And in less than a breath, explosions of an intensity never seen or felt before tore apart the already pummeled plain between the trench and the village causing the ground beneath every man's feet to tremble and shake. The bombardment continued unrelentingly until burnt and bloodied legs, arms, and torsos began to hail down upon the men within the trench. The barrage of hellish explosions then ceased, and those who were still alive within the trench got up from the dirt and earth that had covered them and began to shout at each other for the penetrating sound of exploding bombs and shellfire had deafened their ears to nearly all sounds.

The scout rose from the ground wiping and throwing off as much dirt as he could from his hair and face and stood up seeing that nothing now remained of Kono's and Tsuwata's company except for a few men–two of whom he could barely recognize as Shitsu who was southwest of the trench, and Tonono who was southeast–in the distance trashing about in agony on the smoky destroyed plain. And beyond the plain there was only fire for all the huts and tents of the village were now burning and collapsing to the ground. Something fairly large then rolled up against his feet and he looked down and saw the severed, disfigured head of Tsuwata's son, Niko. Revolted and horrified he kicked the head away and doubled up to vomit on the ground. When he was done he wiped his lips and felt a faint, rhythmic thump beneath his feet, and reached for his long sword. But, down the long stretch of the trench he saw Shimura on his black, ferocious warhorse cantering toward him. The priest got up from the ground–as did the Chief Elder, the runner, and many other men who were still in shock from what they had just experienced–and went to stand beside the scout. Soon Shimura arrived before them and ordered his runner to signal their attack. Filled with fear the runner looked at Shimura in complete incredulity, but again Shimura shouted the order.

"You are mad!" the priest exclaimed to his brother. "You will send them all to their deaths!"

"This–this . . . this can not be Shimura," Elder Subo urged as he coughed in disgust after recognizing that the severed head before him belonged to Tsuwata's only son. "You . . . you can not do this."

"We will fight these bastards!" Shimura hollered back. He turned his horse so that he could look back at the line of remaining men that were slowly rising from the trench and shouted, "You will stand and fight! If you are true Lemurian men you will climb that trench wall, run, and take down those Akai bastards!" Most men could not hear or understand what Shimura was shouting at them, but it was clear to all of them that he wanted them to fight to the very end. Shimura turned his horse back again and ordered his runner with an authority that could not be refused to signal the attack. Slowly the runner raised the red banner again and waved it in the air. "Kill those bastards!" Shimura roared with heated red eyes before riding his horse up the slope of earth exposing himself completely to the enemy. He galloped along the side of the trench trying to inspire his men to fight as he called out to them, and he turned his horse back, galloped again at full speed, jumped clean over the trench while shouting out the command to attack, and galloped across the plain toward the Ikishi forest. The vast majority of Shimura's men shouted out their war cries, climbed out from the trench, and ran after him toward the forest unsheathing their swords and waving them high in the air. Twelve, large, black iron combat tanks broke through the Ikishi trees, sped across the plain, and opened fire blowing holes clean through the irregular line of running Lemurian men. Shimura turned his horse the other way around and began galloping back toward his men, which confused his men for they did not know whether to continue running toward the advancing iron beasts or to turn back and retreat. Shimura called out his war cry as his horse dashed toward the now erratic line of running men that were being blown apart by the heavy plasma-fire of the Atlantean tanks and sneered before pulling out his black long sword from his sheath and raising it high up for all his men to see. He raced toward his scout—who was running desperately toward him—and with one swift motion he swung his sword down as he passed him splitting his head in two.

"Traitor!" a refugee who had witnessed Shimura's crime screamed, but before he could call out another warning he too was cut in two by Shimura's black sword.

Kesake stopped in disbelief when he saw Shimura's blatant acts of betrayal and threw down his sword and took up his long bow, but before he could nock an arrow and aim for Shimura's diseased heart he was struck down by a red beam of light that tore clean through his chest. And as he lay limp on the ground that trembled beneath his partially severed body he looked up toward the dark grey winter sky and saw the light of his wife as he remembered his only son.

Shimura continued charging, hacking, and cutting down several more men until he saw Elder Subo running like a coward toward the burning remains of his village. He grinned with satisfaction and kicked his heels hard into his horse for he wanted to charge in after the Chief Elder and cut him down, but a single beam of plasma-fire tore clean through the Elder's chest and ended him.

The ground shook violently as both tanks and several large hovering metallic aircrafts poured their ammunition down with incredible accuracy onto what remained of the scattering Lemurian line of men who were cut down and slaughtered by the plasma-fire, and the shrapnel of bombs, that ripped them apart into grotesque pieces of exploding flesh.

Shimura slowed his black horse so that he could turn back and cut down more men, but when he saw scores of broken men still painfully alive crawling on the dirt and blood covered snow he halted his horse and began to move back. The scent of death had reached his nostrils, and he took a deep breath of it and smiled as his eyes burned red with glee from the sight of fire and ash that now scorched the land before him, but then a frown marked his face when he felt a strange electrical static in the smoky winds that came and swirled around him. The wind patterns then began to change. The grey sky grew unnaturally dark not by the charred fumes of acidic gases and flames that spiraled and rose up toward it, but by some other mysterious force. Seeing an unusually strong radiance of light suddenly emanate from behind him he turned his horse around, held his hand out before his face, and saw with squinted eyes the silhouette of his brother who was standing behind the trench and encased in a luminous and expanding sphere of bright, white light that was filled with sporadic flashes of lightening. He felt the atmosphere around him fill with the tingling sensation of electrical charges, which caused his horse to neigh, snort, and move with agitated motions before the growing sphere of light. Unable to understand what he was witnessing he began to stare into the light becoming mesmerized by it while his horse continued to move restlessly back and forth as if trying to wake him from a dream.

The priest's voice boomed in the old tongue the song of an ancient Ki chant as his robe, long garments, beard, and hair flew about his body with the storm winds that had gathered within and without the swelling sphere of light. Orbs of white electrical light began to form before his forehead and with the sharp forward motion of his staff the orbs were shot out toward the Atlantean machines that were taking aim at the sphere of light. The orbs sped across the plain leaving a trail of faint sparks and tore straight into several Atlantean tanks and hovering aircrafts causing them to almost simultaneously erupt into exploding balls of fire that hurled black hellish clouds of burning smoke up toward the darkened sky.

Shimura shook his head and woke from his gaze of the sphere of light as the machines of the Atlanteans exploded and burned. More orbs were shot clean across the plain to destroy more of the metallic beasts that the Atlantean army was now desperately trying to send forth. He shot his head toward the bursting tanks and burning trees of the Ikishi forest and then back toward his brother and saw, as an image in his mind, the priest with a body full of strain and tension, but with a face and closed eyes that were as peaceful and serene as that of a sleeping child.

Explosions, rapid blasts of plasma-fire, and projectiles radiated out with greater intensity from the remaining machines of the Atlanteans, but as Shimura observed they all seemed to have absolutely no effect on the sphere of light for the plasma-fire was absorbed by it, and the projectiles that had been launched were slowed by some unseen means to a stop, and held in mid-air before the nearly transparent wall of the sphere. Hundreds of Atlantean infantry began to emerge from the Ikishi forest and took fire upon the sphere of light after taking defensive positions behind felled trees and burning tanks, and from the craters that now dotted the plain before the forest.

Now caught within the heat and chaos of the escalating crossfire Shimura struggled to control his horse that kicked and moved wildly as nearby explosions rained dirt and frozen pieces of snow upon them. And then—in one swift, sudden motion—his horse jumped up onto its hind legs, causing him to fall down to the ground, and ran east across the plain toward the trees at the base of Mount Kurohi. Abandoned by his horse he looked at the sphere of light, gripped his bloodied sword, stood up, and saw the light of the sphere become more brilliant. Again mesmerized by what he saw he began to stare deep into the light as cold and violent winter winds blew all around him, and at all that was behind him. A long vast string of images and sounds from his past fled past his sight within the light and he saw and felt all the torment, hurt, and pain he had caused to others by following the vicious ways of his father. The deep, repressed shame he had always felt in what he had done now boiled up to the surface of his mind and skin, and he fell to his knees ashamed by the betrayals—to both his people and himself—that had defined the whole of his life. The skin of his exposed hands and face turned red as pus accumulated and broke through sores, warts, and pimples that had formed within the blinking of his eyes. He cried out in pain as he felt his heart pound rapidly within him. He now knew that he was done. He cried and shouted out viciously as the shadow within him tried to claim him. Judgment filled his heart for he could not forgive his own wrongdoings, and although he could hear the sweetness of his brother's words call out to him—begging him to step forth toward the light—he turned his eyes away and gave in to the hellish, ghastly demons that now rose from the depths of the shadow that appeared to all sides of him. But, before death took him, and led him to the shadowy world that exists between this world and the next, he looked one last time into the eyes of his brother and saw his love and forgiveness as the grand light of the sphere radiated out and consumed him, burning him, until his own light was no more.

CHAPTER XIV

Horrified by the sight before him Kieko fell to his knees and watched as the towering walls of Mount Kadek and Kurohi were ravaged by the unrelenting blasts and explosions that caused the very ground beneath him to tremble and shake. He then witnessed the resistance put up by the crude Ikishi army as the arrows they had shot up into the blackening, ash-filled sky were swallowed whole by the advancing Atlantean force, which responded by hailing down upon them a barrage of bombs, leaving only those who were within the long trench as survivors. Next, he watched as Shimura rode his black steed out of the trench to then jump over it so that he could gallop across the beaten plain leading those who had climbed the trench wall to charge in after him with their swords raised high. Then, the unexpected–the hideous happened. Shimura had turned on his own army by galloping back toward his broken line of running men to cut down his scout. Disbelief, confusion, and angered tears welled in Kieko's eyes as he watched Shimura cut down more of his own men. He could not understand what he was doing. This could not be. And as he looked on seeing that there was nearly nothing left of the scattered army of poor fishermen and farmers the afternoon grey of distant winter clouds turned abruptly black by the sudden and swift strength of twirling, howling, smoked filled winds. A startling and luminous sphere of light appeared before the trench. Kieko squinted and held his left hand out before him so that he could just recognize within the brilliant light his master who had raised his arms to cause the sphere that encased him to expand and fill with dazzling flashes of lightening.

The boom of his master's voice could be heard within the howl of the growling storm winds before fiery orbs were launched from the sphere destroying several of the iron mechanical beasts that were now firing and advancing toward it. The sphere of light swelled, became instantly more brilliant, and began drawing in the clouds and the sea winds making them swirl around it like some kind of horrid typhoon. Atlantean foot soldiers were easily dragged across the broken earth and sucked into the twisting globe of radiant light and storm winds. Atlantean tanks and hovering aircrafts were next to be pulled into the priest's storm and destroyed by it. And then, without sound or warning, the blinding light of the sphere turned black, and all that could be seen was the rough outline of the Ikishi valley trapped in the expanding darkness of a colossal twisting storm that pulled all into its core. And as Kieko held himself tightly to the thick root of a tree he looked down into the valley and was able to see, through the harsh winds, a faint light within the sphere that instantly grew—within the span of his own heartbeat—to encase the entire sphere, which he could now see had grown in height and size to reach clear over the peak of Mount Kurohi. And then it happened; the sphere erupted into an astounding explosion of cascading storm winds, light, and shock waves that threw Kieko back over a great distance.

Lying on the snow-covered ground in pain he shook his head, wiped his eyes with his forearm, and sat up while trying to understand just what had happened to him. Feeling a throbbing pain from both the base of his skull and neck he touched the back of his head and felt a thick, warm liquid drip over and coat his fingers. He jerked his hand forward and saw his own blood running down his fingertips. He looked behind him and saw that when he had been thrown back by the exploded sphere of light his head had slammed hard against a sharp rock that was now covered with his blood. He instinctively reached for his short sword, which he had again forgotten was not there, to cut some cloth to stop the bleeding, but he looked ahead through the broken trees and saw a fading beam of light that extended up toward the heavens and beyond. The light soon became pale, and simply disappeared.

Rays of sunlight broke through the grey clouds that were rolling toward the sea and Kieko, captivated by what he saw, stood up and walked back to the rocky ledge seeing plumes of black smoke rising up from within the valley. When he reached the ledge he looked down and saw that where his master had once stood there was now an enormous crater of scorched earth. He noticed that nearly all the remaining trees of the valley and slopes of the mountains had been snapped and thrown back pointing away from the crater; and as for the huts and tents of his village, they were simply gone. Crippled tanks, aircrafts, and other mechanical beasts that had collided into trees or crashed deep into the earth were scattered around the perimeter of the crater whereas hundreds of dead foot soldiers littered the valley in all directions.

A strong gust of wind blew over the ledge, and within its howl Kieko heard his master's voice calling out to him, telling him: *It is not over.* A chill ran down his spine as he felt an unnatural danger approaching. He drew out his father's sword and saw gigantic machines that were each shaped like an armored man rising from the sea and advancing toward the shore. He stepped away from the ledge, turned, and ran with great haste to Devil's Mouth.

"I see him!" Raki-ka yelled when he spotted Kieko running toward the cave.

"Where?" Kogaku asked with great urgency. "Where is he?"

"There—I see him," Aiko said relieved as he pointed toward where Kieko was running. "There's blood on him—on his neck!"

"Yes, I see him," Kogaku uttered while keeping his eyes on the dark plumes of smoke that were rising in the distance. "He has a lot to explain."

At that moment a loud screeching sound—similar to the one they had heard before—consumed the sky causing them all to look up and duck down when they saw three monstrous, metallic birds fly directly over them before veering east, and then north, toward Mount Kurohi; the horrific sound quickly faded into a faint hiss.

"What in the name of the gods was that?" Raki-ka shouted trying to understand what he had just seen.

"Three of their cursed flying beasts," Kogaku answered. "There is nothing that can stop them. They decimated my village within the blink of an eye." He faced Raki-ka, Aiko, and a few other armed men who had come out of the cave and continued, "We don't have much time now. If they spotted us their machines will be upon this sea cliff very soon."

"Kieko!" Aiko called out.

Kieko ran into the small, rocky clearing before the cave, stopped before Kogaku, sheathed his sword, and tried to catch his breath as Jomana moved anxiously at his feet.

"What happened?" Kogaku asked him. "What news do you have for us?"

"They . . . the Atlanteans—they're coming," Kieko panted.

"And the Ikishi army?"

"Gone—all gone, but the priest . . . the priest was able to destroy many of their machines . . . and—and most of their soldiers."

"Rakima—Kono—Shimura?"

"Elder Sobu-Ta, Watanoro?" Raki-ka added.

Kieko shook his head, "They're gone . . . all of them, but—but something happened . . . Shimura—he . . . he was cutting down our own people."

"What?" Raki-ka asked in disbelief.

"What do you mean he was 'cutting down' our people?" Kogaku questioned him.

"He . . . he rode out to meet the Atlanteans—leading our remaining men—but . . . but, he then turned back and cut down his scout, and then a few more men—"

"That doesn't make any sense!" Raki-ka exclaimed.

"He betrayed us," Kogaku realized. "That bastard betrayed us. He was in league with the Akai. He planned all along to trap us in that valley."

"But why?" Raki-ka asked. "Why would he do that?"

"I don't know—and it doesn't matter. It's done. Shimura betrayed us."

"Then the Akai know about the cave," Aiko expressed. "They know!"

Kieko's eyes widened for he had not realized that truth; Jomana looked toward the sea and began to snarl exposing her fangs and teeth. He walked toward the cliff leaving the others to debate on what could be done next, and when he reached it he looked down and saw crawling swiftly up the cliff wall seven black, spider-shaped metallic machines and two grey, hovering aircrafts. "THEY'RE HERE!" he hollered as he looked back toward the cave pulling out his sword. In that moment the two aircrafts flew up and hovered before the mouth of the cave shooting out columns of hot air causing Kieko's clothes—and the clothes and hair of the men before the cave—to flap violently against their bodies. Kieko looked back at the hovering metallic beasts and saw through the dark tinted glass of what he had thought were large black eyes a masked humanoid who was looking straight at him.

"RUN!" Kogaku shouted. "Run into the cave!" He took aim and threw—with all his strength—his long sword straight at the dark tinted glass of the aircraft that was to Kieko's right. The sword twirled rapidly through the air, struck, and broke clean through the glass killing the pilot inside. A short, red beam of light was fired at Kogaku from the other aircraft burning a hole clean through his chest, and for a moment he stood in place devoid of life until his knees buckled and he collapsed to the ground.

A brilliant series of lights then shined upon Kieko and the other men, nearly blinding them, from the aircraft that had shot and killed Kogaku. Kieko broke out from his shocked state and sprinted toward the cave with Jomana unable to see Raki-ka, Aiko, and two other men ahead of him who were also running toward the cave. "Run you fools—run!" he shouted to three stunned and frightened men he had just passed who were still standing and staring into the bright lights. But it was too late. Rapid plasma-fire shot at them, and just as he entered the cave the exploded and burning limbs and torsos of the three men he had warned flew at him and the dog, nearly hitting them, and landing everywhere before them. He continued running as fast as he could while hearing a thunderous metallic shrieking sound swell behind him until there was a massive explosion that threw him to the ground. Deaf, he looked up into the darkness of the cave and shook his head seeing a refugee boy not too far from him crying frantically from his hiding place behind a rock wall. He shouted at the boy to run further into the cave. The boy saw him, stepped out, and collapsed to the ground. Brilliant lights filled the cave again and Kieko, disoriented, stood up hoping to reach the boy. Plasma-fire rained into the cave and Kieko took his sword, ran to the boy, grabbed him by the arm, and dragged him with him, but then something wet and thick splashed up onto his face. He looked down and saw that the head of the boy had been blown clean off his little body. Disgusted—horrified he let go of the boy's body realizing that fragments of the boy's skull and brain now covered, and were falling off from, his arms, chest, and face. In complete shock he fell to his knees, dropped his sword, and looked back into the blinding light seeing the distant silhouettes of five or more spider-like machines moving rapidly toward him. Sound was returning to his hears. He could now faintly hear Jomana barking at him and the rapid plasma-fire of the spider machines that were advancing toward him. "Get up," he told himself. "GET UP!" he ordered himself. And then from behind he felt someone lifting him up from beneath his arms. He tried to grab his sword. "It's me!" Aiko shouted at him. Relieved—surprised—he grabbed his sword and stood up. "RUN DAMN IT!" Aiko shouted.

They both ran with the dog further and further into the cave as blasts and small explosions hailed dirt and stones upon them as the spider-droids gained on them. "We're almost there," Aiko shouted back at Kieko. Kieko continued running and soon saw that the tunnel they were running in turned sharply to their left. He veered left and Aiko, unexpectedly, grabbed him and threw him down to the ground. "Stay down," Aiko ordered. Kieko looked further into the tunnel and saw twenty to twenty-five armed men hiding behind walls of jagged rock with arrows nocked and ready to be fired from their long bows. The sound of many mechanical legs moving toward them was growing louder. "They stopped firing," Kieko said of the spider-droids. "Not for too much longer," Aiko replied. One, two, then all seven of the spider-droids appeared and took aim.

"Fire!" someone shouted.

Arrows were released. Rapid plasma-fire filled the tunnel again with explosions and flashes of lights. The spider-droids— organized in three lines of two, three, and two—began advancing toward the men who were now trying to nock and fire more arrows at them. Aiko reacted by running up—from behind the third line— and with Jomana right behind him—to the spider-droid closest to him and began hacking at one of its legs with his sword. The spider-droid stopped, turned, and kicked him with one of its six thin legs throwing him hard against a ragged rock wall, and then stomped on Jomana piercing and crushing her body. Dread and anger consumed Kieko as he stared at Jomana's ruined body. And with an uncontrollable rage that pulsed through every one of his veins he stood up; "YOU CURSED AKAI BASTARDS!" he shouted and spat as he charged in with his sword, and within a moment—when he was upon the spider-droid that had murdered the dog—he swung down at one of its legs believing he could cut it down. Surprisingly—miraculously—his sword cut clean through the steel leg as the last remaining men ran foolishly toward the machines with their long swords. The spider-droid faltered. He wasted no time; he went for another leg and sliced through it. Amazed by his father's sword he attacked and cut off another two legs; the droid collapsed to the ground, but still continued firing. This act inspired the few remaining men who were having absolutely no success in cutting down even one of the spider-machines to call out to Kieko in celebration of his deed. Kieko looked to them, but saw two of them blown apart. He went for another spider-droid and weaved through its legs cutting them down until it too crashed to the ground.

Two of the five remaining spider-machines were now firing upon Kieko. He dodged and dived away from the volley of their plasma-fire and went for the machine closest to him. He dived and rolled beneath it and cut off a leg. He stood up to his feet, swung, and cut off another and then another leg, and like the two before it the machine collapsed. But, just as he eyed his next prey a spider-droid came from behind and kicked him across the width of the tunnel with one of its metallic legs. He hit the ground, tumbled violently, and smacked hard against a rock wall. Dizzy, he looked up and saw the spider-droid coming for him. He panicked and searched the ground with his hands for his sword, but could not find it. He then tried to scramble away, but it was too late, the droid was upon him taking aim on his rapidly beating heart. Bracing himself for the shot that would end him he closed his eyes. But, he heard the droid turn. His eyes shot open and he saw that Aiko had just jumped onto one of the legs of the spider-droid, and then up onto its body with his Kai sword. The spider-droid moved freneticaly trying to throw Aiko off its body, but Aiko raised the sword and slammed it straight into its body. Sparks and flames erupted up from where the sword had punctured the droid making it difficult for Aiko to yank the sword free. The droid stopped to face a jagged rock wall and charged toward it intent on smashing Aiko. With agile skill and speed Aiko freed the sword from the body, jumped down, and rolled on the ground. BOOM!!! The droid had crashed into the sharp rock wall, and the tunnel filled with black plumes of smoke that were rising up from its destroyed and burning mechanical body.

Another spider-droid began firing at Aiko as he ran over the rough terrain of the tunnel toward Kieko. Kieko looked at Aiko and to the other two spider-droids seeing that behind them there were more men–led by Raki-ka–coming in to fight the remaining three machines. He got up to his feet, but he did not know what he could do for he was no longer armed. He looked back to Aiko and saw him stop, turn, and throw his father's sword straight at the many cluttered black eyes of the spider-droid that was pursuing him. The sword spun across the tunnel and slammed straight into it, blinding it. Aiko then ran toward Kieko while the droid he had just blinded fired aimlessly in all directions.

"I need my sword," Kieko told Aiko when he reached him.

"When this is over you are going to tell me where the priest got you that sword," Aiko panted.

Together they waited until the blinded droid had crashed into a wall and ceased firing; and they ran out toward the wrecked droid as the remaining two spider-droids fired upon Raki-ka and his reinforcements illuminating the tunnel with the brilliant flashes of their rapid shots. They reached the droid and climbed on top of it as sparks and small flames erupted from its ruined body, and when they arrived to the sword Kieko grabbed its hilt and began pulling and yanking it trying desperately to free it.

"Something's coming," Aiko said with urgency as he looked back hearing the irregular metallic sounds of more droids scurrying toward them. "Hurry up–move!" He placed his hands over Kieko's tight grip and began pulling on the sword with all his strength. "Pull–damn it!" Together they leaned back and pulled on the sword until at last the sword gave way and slid out from the droid's broken body. "Got it!" Kieko exclaimed, but he lost his balance and fell back, tumbling down, taking Aiko with him.

"Retreat!" Raki-ka called out.

Kieko and Aiko stood up and looked to where Raki-ka and his remaining men were fighting seeing them retreat from the two spider-droids that were firing unrelentingly upon them.

"We have to cut them down!" Aiko hollered over the sound of the intense rapid plasma-fire.

"I'll do it!" Kieko shouted back. "Stay behind me!"

Kieko sprinted, leading Aiko, toward one of the spider-droids and when he was just behind it he raised his sword and began hacking and slicing one leg after the other until the droid lost its balance and smashed into the ground. "Go!" Kieko ordered Aiko. "I'll catch up with you!" He ran for the last droid—that had just turned to aim at him—dived, rolled on the ground, jumped up right before it, and brought down his sword cutting its front, left leg clean off. Now moving beneath its body he cut off another leg and ran out from its rear before the droid slammed its body down on the ground in an attempt to crush him.

Artillery droids—each moving on four pointed legs—appeared from around the sharp turn in the tunnel and began firing their heavy, rotating plasma guns into the narrowing tunnel the men had retreated into. Kieko sliced and hacked two more legs off the faltering spider-droid and ran for the tunnel dodging the rapid plasma-fire that was blasting the ground just behind his fast-moving feet.

The artillery droids stopped firing and advanced into the dark of the tunnel moving faster and faster on their sharp mechanical legs.

Kieko sprinted and soon caught up to Aiko, and together they ran trying to catch up to the others who were now far ahead of them, but behind them they could hear the artillery droids catching up to them and firing several shots past them. "They'll soon be upon us!" Aiko shouted fearing that it was not long now before they were to be eliminated by the machines. "Keep close to the walls," Kieko advised. The machines were now just behind them, but, strangely, they did not fire upon them, instead they ran past them firing upon the men ahead. "Keep running!" Aiko hollered confused as to why the machines were dashing past them. "They're killing the men—we have to destroy them!" The swift-moving artillery droids were now ahead of them running farther and farther away until all that Kieko and Aiko could see and hear of them were the thunderous flashes of their heavy and rapid plasma-fire.

Soon more artillery droids could be heard chasing behind them in the distance. Kieko and Aiko continued moving betweens bouts of running and sprinting, but behind them the rushing sound of the fast-moving legs of the machines swelled until they reached them—and strangely rushed past them—to eventually disappear into the darkness of the tunnel ahead.

"Why—why don't—why don't they fire on us? Kill us?" Aiko panted as he ran.

"I . . . I don't know?" Kieko answered not able to understand why the machines had permitted them to live.

"I . . . I can't see them anymore."

"Just follow the sound."

"If . . . if we keep running in the dark like this . . . we risk running into a wall . . . or . . . or falling into something—breaking our . . . our legs—"

"There!" Kieko interrupted as he pointed ahead in the dark of the tunnel. "There—there is a light."

The two gathered their remaining strength and ran toward the light and the growing sound of rapid plasma-fire and horrific screams.

The light ahead grew thicker and brighter as they neared it, but they both tripped and fell to the ground cutting up the their hands, arms, and knees on the coarse stones that littered the uneven floor. Kieko picked up his sword and stood up trying to resist the pain that was shooting up from his injured leg. Aiko crawled forward, stopped, and looked back trying to see just what it was that he and Kieko had tripped over, and as his eyes adjusted again to the darkness he began to see the outline of a body that had been twisted into an unnatural position on the ground.

"Cursed gods!" Kieko exclaimed. "What—who is that?"

Aiko crawled toward the body and turned it over to find that it was headless.

Kieko looked all around him searching for the head, but instead he found scattered all around him the murdered corpses of several Lemurian men, a few women, and one child.

"Their heads?" Aiko said with a frantic voice. "Where are their heads?"

Kieko looked again with discriminating eyes at the bodies and realized that the women and the child had all been beheaded.

"They're killing them," Aiko said in disbelief, "the women . . . the children."

"Maru–Maru started this," Kieko said with urgency as he thought of Kira and her mother. "These cuts are clean–they were done with a sword–a Ki sword!"

"No! That can't be. The machines did this." He then saw by Kieko's feet the head of someone he recognized. "There," he pointed, "by your feet."

Kieko looked down and saw the severed head of Raki-ka. A horrifying, feminine scream could then be heard between the gaps of rapid plasma-fire from up ahead.

"Come on!" Kieko ordered Aiko, and without waiting for Aiko to stand he ran off toward the light. Aiko stood up, but when he placed some weight on his right leg he felt a sharp pain shoot up from his injured ankle again. "Damn it!" he cursed, but he ignored the pain and ran with a slight limp after Kieko.

Kieko could hear the screams and cries of women and children echo from a large cavern ahead that was lit by the floodlights of the artillery droids that were firing at the few remaining Lemurian men. His rage fueled his exhausted legs to move faster, and then he saw what he thought he would never see, the sight of terrified men raising their swords up and slashing down to behead women and children. He ran straight into the cavern and sighted a man who had just grabbed a woman by her long hair, threw her down to the ground, and was now raising his sword up to behead her. He hollered to the man to grab his attention–the man looked up–their eyes locked and he threw his sword. The sword spun through the air and pierced straight through the man's skull. The man's body collapsed and the woman fell back to the ground horrified by both what Kieko had done and the massacre of men, women, and children that was occurring all around them. The woman scrambled away from Kieko, stood up, and ran toward a large crevice at the far end of the cavern. Kieko ran toward the woman but stopped when he reached the man he had just killed to collect his father's sword.

"Kieko!" Aiko shouted.

Kieko turned and saw Aiko running toward him and an artillery droid chasing and firing from directly behind him. He took the other sword from the dead man's hand and ran toward Aiko. The artillery droid aimed its rapid plasma-fire at Kieko, but it was too late. Kieko had already launched himself toward the droid by jumping far up into the air and coming down upon it by slamming his sword clean through it, slicing it in two. He then landed on the ground and the two halves of the droid collapsed into each other. In awe Aiko stared at Kieko unable to understand just how he had done what he had done. Kieko turned to face Aiko, went up to him, and gave him the sword he had taken from the man he had killed. Together they looked around the cavern and saw a few remaining men running after and slaughtering as many women and children as they could while the artillery droids fired only upon these few remaining men. The sight, mixed with the hideous screams of children who had lost their mothers in the madness, was intolerable.

Unable to understand the continuing butchery Kieko and Aiko looked on in complete horror unsure of what they could do next. But Kieko saw from out of the corner of his eye Kira being pursued by an executioner who he quickly recognized as Maru. He broke out and ran toward her shouting out her name. She turned and saw him but tripped and fell to the ground beside the cavern wall. "NOOO!!!" Kieko screamed as he watched Maru reach Kira and pull her up by her hair. He ran and cut through two men who had tried to stop him—a third man came up from behind him, but he was shot in the back by Aiko who had taken up a bow and a quiver of arrows from a beheaded Hirotake—he called out his wrath to Maru, raised his sword, and when Maru looked up he threw down his sword cutting off—at an angle—the top half of his head.

Kira collapsed to the ground and Kieko continued hacking and cutting down Maru's still erect body before kicking what remained down. Covered in blood Kieko looked at Kira and pulled her up into his arms, holding her, pressing her into him with all his remaining strength.

"Where is your mother?" he asked her as he saw three men at the other end of the cavern being hunted down and killed by the artillery droids while other droids captured and tranquilized small groups of women and children who were running out of the large crevice he had seen before.

"They already killed her," she said as she let out and cried into his body. He held her for as long as he could with one eye closed—enjoying the familiarity of her warmth and scent—while his other eye watched as the droids began to swarm before the large crevice. Small tanks began rolling into the cavern just when Aiko had reached them.

"What's happening?" Kira asked as she looked out into the cavern seeing the tanks parking and dropping their rear planks near the center of the cavern. Her question was then answered as they saw the artillery droids begin to collect and carry the bodies of the women and children they had anesthetized toward the tanks. Several plasma shots were then fired at them by two artillery droids that had sighted them.

"This way!" Aiko yelled as he ran ahead leading them toward a narrow and dark tunnel he had seen.

Kieko grabbed Kira's hand and together they ran, but suddenly from ahead and behind them small hovering surveillance droids appeared firing thin repeating beams of plasma-fire at them.

"We're almost there!" Aiko shouted as a trail of plasma-fire fired at his feet and then up behind him blowing shards of stone and rock off the cavern wall until two shots struck his right forearm and wrist. Cursing out violently in pain as the plasma burned deep into his arm he dropped his bow, sprinted, and nearly dived into the long narrow dark of the tunnel.

The surveillance droids increased the intensity of their shots at Kieko and Kira exploding off more shards of rock from the ground just behind their quick-moving feet and from the cavern wall that they were running alongside of, causing them both to cover their heads with their hands and arms.

Seeing the opening into the tunnel just ahead Kieko pulled Kira up ahead of him by the arm and pushed her into the narrow tunnel. Kira collided straight into the tunnel wall and fell to the ground scraping up her arms and legs, but Kieko and Aiko swiftly brought her up to her feet and began dragging her until she was able to run with them as they moved deeper and deeper into the dark passage. Aiko then took the lead.

Five surveillance droids pursued them into the tunnel and fired at them illuminating the tunnel for fractions of a second with their plasma-fire.

"Keep running!" Kieko shouted. "They're not too far behind me!"

"Oh the gods—oh the gods," Kira repeated with dread as she ran behind Aiko gripping his belt.

"I—I can't see where we're going!" Aiko shouted back as he ran deeper into the darkness hearing the sound of fast-moving waters up ahead. More shots were fired at Kieko, each just missing him. "They're going to get me—run faster!" he shouted as he ran through the darkness with his hands outstretched before him to prevent himself from running accidentally into Kira or a wall. Another shot was fired, and then another and another, which allowed Aiko to see for just an instant the cold mist that they were now running through and what he thought was a cliff not too far ahead.

"Why are you slowing down?" Kieko hollered as more plasma-fire was shot at him.

"There might be—there's a cliff up ahead!" Aiko answered as he heard the sound of rapids echoing up from some watery abyss beyond the cliff.

An intense series of plasma-fire shot past them, illuminating the passage ahead, which allowed Aiko to see the cliff again and the endless chasm beyond it.

"Oh the gods—oh the gods," Kira continued repeating as she looked wide-eyed into the darkness knowing that they were soon to be upon the cliff and their end.

A barrage of plasma-fire came at them blowing apart the tunnel walls to Kieko's sides and the ground just behind him. Desperately trying to avoid the shots and the hail of debris Kieko pushed hard against Kira until three shots struck him in the leg, back, and foot. Dropping his sword and crying out in searing pain he stumbled forward onto Kira who tripped onto Aiko, who then fell forward slithering down a slope toward the edge of the cliff.

"AIKO–NO!" Kira screamed as she threw herself at him trying to grab his leg, but it was too late, he slid fast out of her reach toward the edge and then he was gone hollering as he fell to the rapids of freezing waters that was to consume him.

"AIKO–KIRA!" Kieko screamed as he saw Kira also beginning to slither down the slope.

"Ki–Ki–Kieko help me!" Kira called back as she felt herself sliding down toward the edge.

"Don't move!" Kieko ordered as all five artillery droids were now hovering above him about to take their final shots. Knowing that he had absolutely no other option he dived forward hoping to grab Kira's arm so that they could fall to their deaths together, but the artillery droids opened fire upon them, and as he slid toward her he saw her lose her grip and slide toward the edge, and then over the cliff, falling into the darkness beyond it. "KIRA!" he cried as he slid rapidly toward where she had been before falling over the edge straight down toward the underground stream of cold rushing waters.

Crashing into the icy rapids Kieko let out an inaudible yell as a strong current pulled him deep into his watery grave crushing more of the air out of his lungs. Trying desperately to fight off the painfully deadening—numbing—effects of the frigid current he kicked his legs and moved his body seeking air, and then he felt his whole body being pushed up by the current until at last he broke through the surface gasping for air while thrashing about to keep his head above the rapids. Unable to see within the darkness he called out Kira's name with a shivering voice, but their was no strength or volume to his words for the artic waters had virtually frozen his body–making the whole of him as stiff and as still as a broken tree moving within a fast-moving, meandering stream–nearly robbing him of all life. He was soon thrown up against a smooth protruding rock at a turn in the stream and he grabbed it, wrapping his frozen arms around it, pressing his body hard against it. But, he could feel his body beginning to slip and give way for he could no longer feel or manipulate his own hands and fingers. Desperate to hear some sign of Kira's voice before being taken again by the waters he tried to call out her name over the roar of the rapids, but, "Ki-ki-Kira," was all he could muster with his faint, hoarse, and shivering voice. Several beams of light then illuminated the tunneling scene of rushing waters before him. His eyes widened with hope and he looked back seeking the source of the lights and realized that three surveillance droids had sighted him and were hovering toward him. He let go of the rock and accepted his end, and as he flowed with the rapids with little strength to fight he traveled deep into the earth until at last he was swallowed and taken into the dark of his cold, watery doom.

CHAPTER XV

Kieko woke up to pain, and all that he could hear in the darkness was the constant crashing of cold waters. Feeling the spray of the rapids upon his face he carefully brought himself together and felt his surroundings finding that the stone barrier above him was too low to allow him to stand; he realized that he was in some sort of groove within the bedrock, and that he had been flung into it by the fast moving stream that was flowing beside him. He called out hoping to hear some word from either Aiko or Kira, or from both, and then waited and listened. There was nothing to be heard other than the almost rhythmic sound of the crashing waters. He called out again, and then again, but as before there was nothing that could be heard other than the sound of the rapids. He contemplated his situation and decided that he had no other choice but to continue down with the rapids to await whatever he may find at the end of it. He lowered himself into the frigid waters until the strength of the current took him. He was pulled under the waters, and there within the freezing, watery darkness he could feel the pace and movements of the current quicken and become more violent until at last he was thrown out into the air to then fall toward whatever death may lie below.

He crashed into a pool of water and was driven deeper into it be the beating storm that hailed down upon him from the waterfall above. Instead of fighting his way back to the surface he allowed his body to flow with the undercurrent that he was in until he could feel himself beginning to drift up toward the surface. Swimming up, breaking through the surface, and gasping for air he looked about and saw that the darkness was still too thick, and with not knowing where he could swim to in the waters that were gradually becoming calm he allowed his body to float and drift until he came upon a sandy shore. Crawling on the shore and feeling the wet sands creep between his fingers he felt the pain and exhaustion of his body catch up to him telling him to rest. Dragging himself a bit more up the shore he then collapsed to the ground and turned his body over so that he could look up into the darkness. And as he stared into the emptiness listening to the beat of his own heart and the pulse of his blood coursing through his veins he thought in both Shinsei and Kira and gave thanks to all the gods that he was indeed still alive.

The earth shook to the distant sound of explosions causing Kieko to wake from his brief sleep as he felt dust and pebbles fall upon his face. He sat up, the ground beneath him trembled for a moment, and again he could feel more dust, pebbles, and stones fall upon him. There was a loud blast and a large barrage of stones and large fragments of rock fell from above. He covered his head and tried to crawl back to the pool of water he had fallen into, but three beams of light shot into the surrounding darkness and illuminated what he could see was an enormous cavern. The ground ceased to shake leaving only dust to continue to fall from the high rock ceiling. He waited until his eyes had adjusted to the light and then stood up and limped toward where the three beams of light made contact with the ground. And as he limped he shielded his eyes and tried to look up into the light in the hope of seeing some scene of the winter world beyond, but the openings in the rock ceiling were too small, and too far up, for his wish to be granted. Another series of explosions shook the cavern and he lost his balance and fell to the floor. The trembling earth soon stopped again, and he looked up and saw with unbelieving eyes the altar to an ancient and abandoned temple that had been carved from out of the bedrock; behind the altar sat a gigantic, but very tarnished, golden Buddha statue that was covered in layers of sand, dust, grime, and cobwebs. And to the sides of the Buddha was a line of statues of various demons and Buddha incarnations that stretched out along the cavern walls nearly reaching him. In awe he looked and admired the statues and the Buddha seeing that some of the statues were faceless or limbless, which he assumed was caused by centuries of neglect and earth movements. Standing up again he walked toward the altar and the large sitting Buddha feeling great honor in being the first, after so many centuries, to see such a glorious sight.

He walked up a series of steps and there upon the large and intricately carved stone altar was a white, sheathed Ki sword. He kneeled before the altar, bowed his head, and prayed for the lives of all his people who had met their end. He soon felt the deep seeded pain within his heart rise up to his throat and fill him like a storm with anger, hatred, sadness, and remorse, which twisted and turned within him until at last he could hold it no longer. And with clenched fists he cried out in horror as he remembered every detail of what had happened to his mother, the priest, Kira, Aiko, and his people. He crouched forward and pounded his fist at the stone floor until his knuckles bled and splashed blood up onto his wrist and forearm. Tired, angry, alone, and heartbroken he sat up and stood before the altar, took the Ki sword with two hands, and unsheathed it. Marveling at the sword's discolored but single-edged perfection he stepped away from the altar and bowed, and with renewed strength he decided to begin looking for a way to escape from the cavern temple and search for both Kira and Aiko for he knew in his heart that they were still alive.

The hours passed, and soon daylight turned to night, and he found no way out of the cavern. Hungry, tired, and cold he sat huddled against a cavern wall trying to convince himself that everything had been nothing more tham a nightmare. And with those thoughts he willed himself to sleep with the small, false hope that when he would wake he would find himself cradled within his mother's arms.

Three days had passed, and weakened by both infection and hunger he lay on the floor of the old temple feeling death begin to caress him. And there in the twilight before the night he gladly welcomed his end, but just as the beams of light grew thin, the cave walls erupted into fire; and the last thing he remembered was the cold touch of thin, metallic fingers pricking his pale dry skin.

OF KIEKO'S THINKING TREE

Oh dear—it is quite late. No more of this talk. You are tired and we seek to rest as well. We are sorry that we must end this story here, but tomorrow is another day, so be patient for many things will be revealed to you in the nights ahead. But, before we say goodnight, we think it wise to tell you of Kieko's Thinking Tree.

Yes, Kieko's wonderful Thinking Tree. Long have we admired him and brave was he. What a glorious creature he was and one whose dream was granted by the angels he praised. In the aftermath of the battle that stole the Ikishi village from the islands of Lemuria the land shook in a violent quake. The Kadek Mountain had awoken spitting molten rocks into the air as great rivers of lava rushed down its slopes poisoning the land before spilling into the sea. The earth and the trees burned merging their fires with the great plumes of black smoke that rose from the mouth of Kadek up toward the darkened winter sky. The day had become night and when the earth trembled once more the sea cliffs of Mount Kurohi weakened and crumbled to the sea.

Kieko's Thinking Tree fell into the Ocean of Mu uniting earth, wood, and water as metal and fire burned. And as the cold ocean waves slammed against the cliff walls the tree drifted and floated farther and farther away seeing that the Forest of Ikishi, and all within the valley, was now completely ablaze; the sky and shimmering surface of the sea had become the same fiery image. The tree then began to sink into the cold depths of the ocean allowing the darkness of death to take him for he had fulfilled his dream to become one with the never-ending sea. And with that let us end with a tone of hope for in the darkness there is the light . . . yes, light for this is only the beginning of Kieko's dark legacy. Good night.

WORDS AND TERMS

A

The Age of Virgo – The last Age of the reign of the *Atlantean Oracle Kings and Queens*.

> See also: *the last days of the Age of Virgo*.

Akai – A derogatory term for the *Red race* (*the Blood race*) used by Lemurians.

Amilius the Wise: The most ancient and revered prophet of *Atlantis* who reigned during *the Golden Age*; founder of *the Law of One*.

Angels of the Seven Stars – Refer to the list of defined words and terms in *Book V: Time* of the *Dark Legacy* books.

Aqua-Krotrak – A heavy artillery transport submersible.

The Ara Mountains – Also referred to as the *Moutains of Ara*. It is a chain of mountains surrounding *Atlas*.

The Arakara Mountains – Also referred to as the *Mountains of Arakara*. It is a chain of mountains on the island continent of *Og*.

> Of Note: It was where *Skaton-ka* (refer to the list of characters in *The End of the Kai* of the *Dark Legacy* books) went on his three hundred day retreat and gained the *Enlightenment*.

Aryan – The island continent of *Atlantis* between *Poseidia* and *Og*.

> See also: *the Second Great Quake of Ara*.

The Atlantean Empire – The territories, regions, colonies, and kingdoms under the supreme rule of *Atlantis*.

The Atlantean Ocean – One of the five great bodies of salt water on planet Earth. It is located in the *West*.

The Atlantean Oracle King, Queen – The sacred and traditional ruler of the *Atlantean Empire*. Only one Oracle King or Queen can be elected to rule *Atlantis* at any one time.

Of Note: The Oracle King has the power to oversee the *High Kai Guardian Elder*, the *Kai guardians*, and the *Kai priestesses*. The Oracle Queen only has the power to oversee the *Kai priestesses*.

See also: *The High Kai Guardian Elder*.

The Atlantean Royal Families – There are seven platonic Royal Families: Drakul, Libra, Virgo, Leo, Cancer, Gemini, and Taurus. Each Royal Family is composed of a *High Kai Guardian*, a *High Kai Priestess* and the *Kai Order* bound to them. Each family governs (with the aid of regional governments) one or more regions of the *Atlantean Empire*.

See also: *Kai Order*.

The Atlantean Royal Throne – The royal seat of the *Atlantean Oracle King, Queen*.

The Atlantean Royal Towers – The eight royal towers of the *Atlantean Empire* that are the official residences of the *Atlantean Oracle King, Queen*, and the seven *Atlantean Royal Families*.

Atlantis – The most powerful civilization in the *West*.

Atlas – The largest *city-galaxy* of *Atlantis*, and the capital of the *Atlantean Empire*. It is located on the island continent of *Poseidia*.

B

Bekuru – A wooden percussive instrument used by *Ki* disciples during chants.

The Blood race – Also referred to as the *Red race*. A term used to describe the human populations of *Atlantis*.

Bottom-gi – Traditional *Lemurian* pants made from a cotton canvas.

See also: *gi, top-gi*.

Buddha – 1. The ancient *Lemurian* mystic who founded the *Ki faith*. 2. A term giving to anyone who has achieved *Enlightenment*.

C

The Children of Belial – Any and all disciples who oppose the *Kai*.

> See also: *The Children of the Law of One.*

The Children of the Law of One – Any and all disciples of the *Kai*.

> See also: *the Law of One.*

Chief Elder – In *Lemuria*, an *Elder* who is chosen by the landowning men of a village to lead the *Elders* for life.

City-galaxy – A city with a population of more than twenty-five million people.

Clan Order(s) – Refer to *Kai Order(s)*.

The Clan of Uminote – Also referred to as the *Lemurian Royal Family*. They reigned over the extensive island regions of *Lemuria* for over five centuries.

Corporate noble – An individual of significant wealth and political power possessing hereditary rank in a corporate conglomerate.

Council – In *Lemuria*, it is an assembly of the *Elders*, and the priest(s), of a village who are responsible for final decisions, judgments, and law making.

Council Hut – A large hut typically placed in the center of a *Lemurian* village where the priest(s), *Elders*, and village men convene to discuss and make decisions on important village matters.

Cutting ceremony – The *Lemurian* formal act performed on a young boy in which his head is shaved to mark his passage into manhood.

CybOr-technology – Referring to any technology that synthesizes a living organism with mechanical or electronic devices.

Cyborg – A cybernetic organism.

D

Dharma hall – The hall within a *Lemurian* temple used by a *Ki priest* for meditations, training, and teachings.

Domek – A citizen in *Atlantis* who has authority, power, or control over others.

E

The East – The portion of the world influenced or ruled by the *Lemurian Kingdom*.

The East Sea – A sea located between the *Middle Kingdom* and the *Shinobi region* of the *Kadek Island*.

Elder(s) – One or all of the seven oldest men of a *Lemurian* village who compose its high council.

The Enlightenment – The blessed state achieved by a *Kai* or *Ki* disciple who transcends all attachments and desires.

Erima – A small village located to the north of the *Ikishi village*, in the region of *Kadek*, on the *Kadek Island*.

> Of Note: It is the village that Kania (refer to the list of characters in *Book I: Trinity* of the *Dark Legacy* books) was born and raised in.

The Etheric races of Lemuria – Refer to the list of defined words and terms in *Book V: Time* of the *Dark Legacy* books.

F

Fornax-Serpens – Also referred to as *Seeker Killers* or *S.K.'s*. In *the last days of the Age of Virgo* they were the machines built by the Atlantean military at the request of the Atlantean government to patrol the *Ideo* sewer systems to prevent the flow of *Ideo ghosts* from illegally entering into and out of the citizen sectors of *Atlas*.

G

Gi – A traditional *Lemurian* jacket and/or pants made from a cotton canvas.

> See also: *bottom-gi, top-gi.*

The Girus Temple – A *Kai* temple of *Atlantis* located on the island continent of *Og.*

> Of Note: It was the temple where *Skaton-ka* (refer to the list of characters in *The End of the Kai* of the *Dark Legacy* books) was raised and trained.

The Golden Age – The spiritual apex of *Atlantis* under the enlightened reign of *Amilius the Wise.*

The Great Forest of Ikishi – It is the most sacred forest in the region of *Kadek*, on the *Kadek Island.*

The Great Hall of the Buddha – The largest hall, within a *Lemurian* temple, that enshrines the altar dedicated to the *Buddha.*

The Great Spirit – It is the principal deity in the *Lemurian Ki faith* who is responsible for the cyclic creation and destruction of all life.

Guardians of the Kai – A general term used to refer to both the *High Kai Guardians* and the *Kai-Minor guardians.*

H

Hakunus – A *Lemurian* ceremony celebrated every season that marks the passage of a girl, or girls, into womanhood.

The High Kai Chancellor – The position held only by the *High Kai Guardian Elder* who serves the *Oracle King, Queen* as secretary and chief confidant.

The High Kai Council – A council composed of the *Oracle King, Queen*, the *High Kai Guardian Elder*, the *High Kai Guardians*, and the *High Kai Priestesses*. Upon the death of the *Oracle King, Queen* they are vested with the power to appoint a new *Oracle King, Queen* to the *Atlantean Royal Throne.*

The High Kai Elder – Refer to the *High Kai Guardian Elder.*

The High Kai Guardians — There are seven High Kai Guardians, and each is bound to a *High Kai Priestess*. They each lead and protect, with their *High Kai Priestess*, the *Kai Order* to which they are bound.

See also: *The Atlantean Royal Families*.

The High Kai Guardian Elder — Also referred to as the High Kai Guardian Elder of the Order of Light; the Kai Elder King of the Order of the Kai Guardian guild; the *High Kai Elder*; and the *Kai Elder King*. He serves the *Oracle King, Queen* (who he is bound to) as *High Kai Chancellor*. He also serves the *High Kai Council* (who he is a member of) as its sole protector.

Of Note: If the High Kai Guardian Elder is in service to an *Oracle Queen* he is first in command of all *Kai guardians*. If the High Kai Guardian Elder is in service to an *Oracle King* he is second-in-command of all *Kai guardians*.

The High Kai Priestesses — There are seven High Kai Priestesses, and each is bound to a *High Kai Guardian*. They each lead and protect, with their *High Kai Guardian*, the *Kai Order* to which they are bound.

See also: *The Atlantean Royal Families*.

The high tongue — The formal speech of any of the dialects of the *Lemurian* language.

Hiragan — A *Lemurian* alphabet writing system.

I

Ida — Refer to *The Sea of Ida*.

Ideo-clan(s) — A secret, criminal organization(s) based within the *Ideo sector*.

Ideo ghosts — The non-Atlantean citizens of the *Ideo sector*.

The Ideo sector — The economically decaying, industrial sector of *Atlas* where all non-Atlantean citizens in *Atlas* must reside.

Ikishi village — A fishing village composed of several hundred *Lemurians* in the region of *Kadek*, on the *Kadek Island*.

Island of Kadek — Also referred to as *Kadek Island*. It is one of the furthest western islands of the *Lemurian Kingdom*.

Island of Kurai – Also referred to as the *Kurai Island*. It is an island located in the northern region of the *Lemurian Kingdom*.

K

Kadek Island – Also referred to as the *Island of Kadek*. It is one of the furthest western islands of the *Lemurian Kingdom*.

Kadek region – The eastern half of the *Kadek Island*.

> See also: *Shinohi region*.

Kadek Mountain – Also referred to as *Mount Kadek*. The largest volcanic mountain located in the *Kadek region*, on the *Kadek Island*.

The Kadek Temple – The sacred temple of the *Kadek region*, on the *Kadek Island*, where the village priest of *Ikishi* resides.

Kai – 1. The *life force*: the vital force of nature and of all living things. 2. The religious faith and practices of the *Atlantean Oracle King*, *Queen* and the *Atlantean Royal Families*. 3. Any and all laymen disciples of the religious faith and practices of the *Atlantean Oracle King*, *Queen* and the *Atlantean Royal Families*.

> Of Note: The word was derived from the *Lemurian* term *Ki*.

> See also: *the Law of One*.

The Kai Elder King – Refer to the *High Kai Guardian Elder*.

Kai guardian – A general term used to refer to either a *High Kai Guardian* or a *Kai-Minor guardian*, or both.

Kai line(s) – Referring to one or all eight of the ancestral lines of the *Kai Orders* that a *Kai guardian* or a *Kai priestess* is derived from or adopted into.

The Kai-Minor guardians – There are a total of forty-nine Kai-Minor guardians. They are divided into one of the seven *Kai Orders*, and thus there are seven Kai-Minor guardians for each *Kai Order*. They are each bound to a *Kai-Minor priestess*.

The Kai-Minor priestesses – There are a total of forty-nine Kai-Minor priestesses. They are divided into one of the seven *Kai Orders*, and thus there are seven Kai-Minor priestesses for each *Kai Order*. They are each bound to a *Kai-Minor guardian*.

Kai Order(s) – Also referred to as Order, or *Clan Order*. There are eight Kai Orders: Light, Drakul, Libra, Virgo, Leo, Cancer, Gemini, and Taurus.

> Of Note: The Kai Orders of Drakul, Libra, Virgo, Leo, Cancer, Gemini, and Taurus are composed of both *High Kai* and *Kai-Minor* guardians and *High Kai* and *Kai-Minor* priestesses. The *Order of Light* is simply composed of the *Oracle King*, *Queen* and the *High Kai Guardian Elder*.

> See also: *The Atlantean Royal Families*.

Kai priestess – A general term used to refer to either a *High Kai Priestess* or a *Kai-Minor priestess*, or both.

Kai-Ra – Energy shield that only a *Kai priestess* can create while in an intense meditative state.

Kai Royal Highness – Refer to the *Atlantean Oracle Queen*.

Kami – The *Lemurian* term for spirit.

The Kami of Shinohi – The spirit of the *Mountains of Shinohi*.

Kata – A short or long series of offensive and defensive combative movements.

Ki – 1. The *life force*: the vital force of nature and of all living things. 2. The religious faith and practices of the *Lemurian Royal Family*. 3. Any and all laymen disciples of the religious faith and practices of the *Lemurian Royal Family* and the *Lemurian Ki priests*.

> Of Note: The word inspired the *Atlantean* term *Kai*.

The Ki faith – Also referred to as the *Lemurian Ki faith*. It is the beliefs and religious practices of the *Lemurian* culture.

Ki priest, priestess – A *Lemurian* man or woman who has the authority to perform and administer the rites of the *Ki faith*.

Ki sword – The *Lemurian* art of swordsmanship.

Ki warrior – A soldier knowledgeable in *Ki sword* who serves *Lemurian* lords and royalty.

Kimu Ki – A traditional *Lemurian* fermented dish made of vegetables with a variety of herbs and spices.

The Kingdom of Lemuria – Also referred to as the *Lemurian Kingdom*. It is the extensive island territories under the rule of *Lemuria*.

Koan – A paradoxical statement or story used by *Ki priests* to puzzle the meditating minds of their *Ki* disciples as a means for them to achieve spiritual awakening.

Kragita-droid – A colossal, heavy artillery droid.

Kurai Island – Also referred to as the *Island of Kurai*. It is an island located in the northern region of the *Lemurian Kingdom*.

Kurohi Mountain – Also referred to as *Mount Kurohi*. It is a volcanic mountain located east of *Mount Kadek*.

L

The last days of the Age of Virgo – The last decades of the *Age of Virgo*.

The Law of One – The holy doctrine of the *Kai* faith established by *Amilius the Wise* during the *Golden Age* of *Atlantis*.

Lemuria – The most influential civilization in the *East*.

Lemurian Ki faith – Also referred to as the *Ki faith*. It is the beliefs and religious practices of the Lemurian culture.

The Lemurian Kingdom – Also referred to as the *Kingdom of Lemuria*. It is the extensive island regions under the rule of *Lemuria*.

The Lemurian Royal Family – The long ruling *Clan of Uminote*. They reigned over the extensive island regions of *Lemuria* for over five centuries.

The life force – The vital force of nature and of all living things. It is divided into two opposing, yet, coexisting parts: *shin*, and *shang*.

See also: *Kai, Ki.*

M

Maldek – Refer to the list of defined words and terms in *Book V: Time* of the *Dark Legacy* books.

The Middle Kingdom – The fragmented and fading kingdom located west of the *East Sea*.

Mochi – A sticky rice cake typically made in winter in *Lemuria*.

Mother – The planet Earth.

Mount Eve – The hollowed mountain enclosing the *Atlantean Royal Towers*.

Mount Kadek – Also referred to as the *Kadek Mountain*. The largest volcanic mountain located in the *Kadek region*, on the *Kadek Island*.

Mount Kai – Mountain on the island continent of *Poseidia* that *the Wise* considered to be the birthplace of the *Red race*.

> Of Note: The *Atlantean Royal Throne* was cut and made from this mountain.

Mount Kurohi – Also referred to as the *Kurohi Mountain*. It is a volcanic mountain located east of *Mount Kadek*.

The Mountains of Ara – Also referred to as the *Ara Mountains*. It is a chain of mountains surrounding *Atlas*.

The Mountains of Arakara – Also referred to as the *Arakara Mountains*. It is a chain of mountains on the island continent of *Og*.

> Of Note: It was where *Skaton-ka* (refer to the list of characters in *The End of the Kai* of the *Dark Legacy* books) went on his three hundred day retreat and gained the *Enlightenment*.

The Mountains of Shinohi – Also referred to as the *Shinohi Mountains*. It is a chain of mountains running from north to south that divides the *Kadek Island* into two regions: the western *Shinohi region*, and the eastern *Kadek region*.

Musca-technology – Referring to the science and technology of constructing electronic circuits and devices from atomic and subatomic particles.

N

No-mind – A present state of being that is devoid of all thoughts and attachments.

O

The Ocean of Mu – One of the five great bodies of salt water on planet Earth. It is located in the *East*.

Og – The eastern-most island continent of the three island continents of *Atlantis*.

> See also: *the Second Great Quake of Ara.*

Okusan – A respectful term used by *Lemurians* for married and/or widowed men.

Okusen – A respectful term used by *Lemurians* for married and/or widowed women.

The old tongue – The ancient language of *Lemuria*.

Ophiuchus – The most powerful of the *Ideo-clans* in the Age of Virgo.

The Oracle King, Queen – Refer to *the Atlantean Oracle King, Queen.*

The Order of the Kai Guardian guild – The fellowship to which all Kai guardians belong to, which is led by the *High Kai Guardian Elder.*

The Order of the Kai Priestess guild – The fellowsip to which all Kai priestesses belong to, which is led by the *Atlantean Oracle King, Queen.*

The Order of Light – The fellowship composed of only the *Oracle King, Queen* and the *High Kai Guardian Elder.*

P

Plasma-fire – The discharge of highly ionized gas from a fast-action firearm.

Pleiadia – Refer to the list of defined words and terms in *Book V: Time* of the *Dark Legacy* books.

Pleiadians – Refer to the list of defined words and terms in *Book V: Time* of the *Dark Legacy* books.

Poli-ki-clan(s) – A radical right-wing political group(s) of *Atlantis*.

Poseidia – The western-most island continent of the three island continents of *Atlantis*.

     See also: *the Second Great Quake of Ara.*

Potion-magics – Any of the illegal substances in *Atlantis* that caused addiction, habituation, or drastic changes in consciousness.

R

The Red race – Also referred to as the *Blood race*. A term used to describe the human populations of *Atlantis*.

S

The Sea of Ida – Sea in the *Atlantean Ocean* that *Atlas* faces.

The Second Great Quake of Ara – The horrific series of earthquakes that swallowed two of the once five island continents of *Atlantis*.

Seeker Killers – Also referred to as *S.K.'s*. Refer to *Fornax Serpens*.

The Seven Stars of Pleiadia – Refer to the list of defined words and terms in *Book V: Time* of the *Dark Legacy* books.

The Sirian Creator – Refer to the list of defined words and terms in *Book V: Time* of the *Dark Legacy* books.

Sirians – Refer to the list of defined words and terms in *Book V: Time* of the *Dark Legacy* books.

Shang – It is the aggressive aspect of the *life force* that can be characterized as heat, motion, and outward centrifugal force.

     See also: *Kai, Ki, life force.*

Shi sticks – A pair of sticks used in *Lemuria* as an eating instrument for lifting food to the mouth.

Shin – It is the passive aspect of the *life force* that can be characterized as cold, stillness, and inward centripetal force.

     See also: *Kai, Ki, life force.*

The Shinohi Mountains – Also referred to as the *Mountains of Shinohi*. It is a chain of mountains running from north to south that divides the *Kadek Island* into two regions: the western *Shinohi region*, and the eastern *Kadek region*.

Shinohi region – The western half of the *Kadek Island*.

    See also: *Kadek region.*

S.K.'s – Also referred to as *Seeker Killers*. Refer to *Fornax Serpens*.

Sky-towers – The tall buildings and towers of the cities of *Atlantis* defined as having more than 150 floors or levels.

The Source – The *life force* is derived from it. It is the ultimate nothingness. Ancient Lemurian philosophers described it as the void and boundless state, which prevailed before the world was created, and from which the universe was formed.

    See also: *life force.*

Speed tribe(s) – A gang(s) of adolescents within the *Ideo sector* who are often hired by or in league with one or more *Ideo-clans*.

Spheres of Ra – Compact orbs of highly volatile ionized gas that a *Kai priestess* can create instantaneously while in an intense meditative state.

The Sun race – Also referred to as the *Yellow race*. A term used to describe the human populations of *Lemuria*.

T

Teshi-do – A popular combative sport in *Lemuria*.

Teshi-do Ko-Tenso – The title given to an adolescent *Lemurian* male who successfully defeats all of his opponents in the seasonal *Teshi-do* tournament.

Top-gi – A traditional *Lemurian* fold over jacket made from a cotton canvas.

    See also: *bottom-gi, gi.*

Tori gate – A gate placed before a *Lemurian* temple or natural formation that has been deemed sacred.

The Tower of Light – The *Atlantean Royal Tower* where resides the *Atlantean Oracle King, Queen* and the *High Kai Guardian Elder*.

Y

The Yama Te Temple – A temple near the southern coast of the *Lemurian* Island of Kurai.

The Yellow race – Also referred to as the *Sun race*. A term used to describe the human populations of *Lemuria*.

W

The West – The portion of the world influenced or ruled by the *Atlantean Empire*.

The Winged Creator – Refer to the list of defined words and terms in *Book V: Time* of the *Dark Legacy* books.

The Wise – Refer to *Amilius the Wise*.

Z

Zabuton – A pillow a *Ki* disciple sits on during *zazen*.

Zazen – Meditation as practiced by *Ki priests* and disciples.